"Who are you, in truth,
Raven Barrancourt?"

There was no reply, the upturned face exquisitely lovely in the filtered moonlight. Charles uttered a hoarse groan and slipped his arms about the tiny waist, drawing the unresisting Raven against his broad chest. Raven tried to jerk away when she felt his hot lips come down in a bruising kiss upon her own, but the strong arms that encircled her made escape impossible.

Charles, drinking in the heady perfume of her hair and the softness of her lips beneath his, could feel the heat begin to rise again in his loins, spreading like fire through his veins. Plundering the as yet unresponsive sweetness of her lips, his hand guiding her slender body closer to his, he willed her with the sheer power of his desire to yield and Raven, the heat of Charles' passion enveloping her, felt a curious languor spread through her, a melting of resolve that made her tremble.

"Raven," Charles whispered hoarsely, the balmy night air of India heightening his senses, "I mean to have you, my wild, tempestuous Raven."

Also by Ellen Tanner Marsh

REAP THE SAVAGE WIND

Wrap Me in Splendor

Ellen Tanner Marsh

BERKLEY BOOKS, NEW YORK

WRAP ME IN SPLENDOR

A Berkley Book/published by arrangement with
the author

PRINTING HISTORY
Berkley trade paperback edition/September 1983

Book design by Barbara N. Cohen.

ISBN: 0-425-06181-7

A BERKLEY BOOK ® TM 757,375
The name "BERKLEY" and the stylized "B" with design
are trademarks belonging to Berkley Publishing Corporation.
PRINTED IN THE UNITED STATES OF AMERICA

To Mutti and Vati,
with love

To Hilari,
with gratitude

Wrap Me in Splendor

Chapter One

The great house of North Head had been built facing the sea. The grand casement windows that lined the herringbone-patterned brick walls opened to the waters that surged on relentless tides against the granite cliffs and pebble beaches far below. Weathered to a warm, rosy hue by countless storms and sun-washed summer days, the corniced walls were stalwart and comforting, the manor house's architectural beauty belying the unyielding strength of its Cornish foundations. To the west lay Land's End, the tip of England itself, yet North Head dominated the countryside with its fertile farmlands and desolate heaths so that one could well believe that nothing more existed of civilization beyond its rambling walls.

North Head, with its beautifully landscaped parks and tall, latticed windows that permitted the sun to pour in while diminishing the fury of the winter storms, hung majestically at the edge of the world, rising strong and unmovable from the sea, its twin towers of warm, golden stone like sentinels that guarded both the main block of the house and the stately wings that flanked it. From the top of the towers one could look west beyond Land's End to the white-capped waters of the Atlantic and east toward the fishing village of St. Ives, where Cornwall unfolded itself in a stark but achingly beautiful panorama of undulating heaths and terraced meadows.

For over two hundred years North Head had been the home of the Barrancourts, a powerful and respected family in the ancient duchy, and as proud, stoic and unyielding as Cornwall itself. Neither storm, famine, civil war, nor insurrection had daunted their spirits, and it was said among the local folk that every Barrancourt was born with a few drops of fairy blood.

How else could North Head have survived its savage past and prospered so well without a bit of magic? Laughter and love, betrayal and bloodshed—the strong, embracing walls had echoed with every facet of human nature, its inhabitants invariably embodied with an unquenchable thirst for life and all that it offered.

On this, a surprisingly cool, overcast June morning in 1848, the towers were obscured in rolling mist, the rosy bricks damp with moisture, North Head seeming to cling brooding and remote, like some great, predatory bird to its position high on the cliffs. Far down the slope, where the grass was wet, the earth fragrant and damp, a solitary horse and rider came galloping across the heath. The horse, a long-legged, heavily coupled bay stallion, was flecked with foam, his breath clouding, iron-shod hoofs drumming on the turf. With only the slightest shifting in weight, his rider turned him away from the drive that wended its way through the landscaped gardens toward the whitewashed stables.

"I know you're not tired yet, old boy," the slim young woman on his broad back whispered into his ear. "You can still catch the wind if you try." As she spoke she leaned low in the saddle, and the stallion, responding to her movements, took off across the turf, mud flying from beneath his hoofs, the landscape passing in a blur.

Raven Barrancourt, the blood throbbing in her veins, loosened the plaited reins from her slender fingers to give Cinnabar his head. The big stallion moved rhythmically beneath her, infecting her with his desire to run, and she lifted her small oval face so that the cool summer wind fanned the mist against her soft cheeks. Her sloping eyes, of an astonishing tawny gold, glowed with excitement, and her soft rosy lips were parted as she laughed in sheer delight at being so free.

At the top of a small rise she reined the reluctant stallion in, letting him stamp impatiently and snort while she turned to look down at North Head, which clung to its promontory of massive granite cliffs. The sullen, heaving sea dashed across the strip of sandy beach far below, the tide high, sending showers of icy salt spray upward into the sky. From where she sat Raven had the impression that North Head was about to be engulfed by the fiercely pounding waves, but that, she knew, was only an illusion. North Head stood safe and guarded upon the cliffs, the east and west wings stretching away from the main block that faced the length of the sea, the inner parks and courtyards, protected from the buffeting winds, planted with flowers, shrubs, and ancient trees that lent an aura of delicate beauty to the harshness of the shoreline beyond. It was a sight of awe-inspiring grandeur, the magnificent house as strong and stalwart as the granite cliffs themselves, the shrubs and gloriously blooming summer flowers that dotted the southern exposure of lovingly tended parkland a haven of beauty in a harsh and uncompromising land.

This was Raven's favorite view of her home, and she never went riding without pausing there first to drink in the comforting, strengthening sight before heading onward to Land's End. She turned the quivering Cinnabar and urged him to a smooth canter, her gloved hands tightening on the reins to inform him that she did not care to gallop again. The big stallion submitted obediently to her commands, but his pricked ears and flaring nostrils showed his desire to continue their previous mad pace. Raven petted his sleek neck affectionately, her tawny eyes dancing. She had raised him from a foal and with her father's help had trained him herself. She smiled now, recalling the countless spills she had taken while rearing the big animal through his difficult years as an uncontrollable colt, and how his stubbornness had at times reduced her to tears. Yet she had been patient and persistent and as stubborn as Cinnabar himself and had schooled herself a very pleasing mount indeed, as her father was always fond of saying in his simple way of praising her. Yet Raven knew that he had been very proud of her and had even talked of mating Cinnabar next year when he was old enough; but those plans had come to naught with her father's untimely death.

A spasm of pain entered the tawny eyes, and Raven's rosy lips tightened, determined not to spoil the beauty of this ride after so many relentless days of rain with memories still too raw and painful at times to bear. The big stallion, sensing her changing mood, increased his stride from a canter to a flowing gallop, and Raven did not bother to slow him down. Instead she pulled her small plumed hat low onto her smooth brow so as not to lose it, and allowed him to have his head.

On the narrow, winding cart trail that led from Land's End to Penzance, a small gig crested the hill ahead of them, and Raven, sailing with Cinnabar over a low stone wall that divided the field from the roadway, slowed to a trot to see who it was.

She groaned inwardly as she recognized the erect, soberly attired figure of the Reverend Parminster, his skinny, ill-fed mare plodding listlessly before the squeaking vehicle. Aware that he had probably seen her, Raven drew to a halt and waited quietly for the cart to draw near.

"Good morning, Reverend," she said politely as the minister approached, Cinnabar tossing his head and snorting at the sight of the rickety contraption.

The Reverend Parminster glanced up into the flushed face of the beautiful young girl seated on the stamping, high-spirited mount, his thick lips pursed with utter disapproval. "You're not wearing black, Miss Barrancourt," he observed in a nasal tone that reminded Raven of his dull, uninspired Sunday sermons.

She glanced down at the trim green velvet habit she wore. "I—"

"The Devil always lies in wait to claim the souls of those who do not follow the path of the Lord," Reverend Parminster intoned, his long, thin face exuding self-righteousness. "Be forwarned, Miss Barrancourt. It is frowned upon when you do not observe the proper period of mourning."

"By whom?" Raven countered, knowing the Reverend Matthew Parminster far too well either to be intimidated by him as the townsfolk were or to feel the need to be polite merely because he was a man of the cloth. "By God or you?"

A flush spread across the minister's sallow cheeks. "I will overlook your tart tongue, my child, because I know that grief guides your every movement, your every word and thought." He looked at her kindly from his perch in the gig, his thin shoulders still ramrod stiff. "Bless you, my child. I intend to see that you follow the righteous path now that your father is gone."

"Did you think him a bad influence on me?" Raven demanded sharply, knowing full well that he did. Everyone in this part of Cornwall knew that James Barrancourt had permitted his only daughter to rove wild on the land, but Raven knew also that few people, if any, thought bad of the Barrancourts and that their own tenants as well as the villagers and the fisherfolk of St. Ives had respected and even worshiped her father, who had been kind, honest, and always willing to help them when they asked.

"I will have to labor hard to save your soul from eternal damnation, poor, wayward Raven," the minister vowed, his eyes lingering with an obviously lustful glint on her slender, velvet-clad form and tiny waist.

"Will you be pressing your suit again, Reverend?" Raven asked sweetly, her tawny eyes spewing liquid fire. "Do you think you have more of a chance of succeeding now that my father is dead? Well, don't believe that I'll welcome you after he called you a vile and evil scoundrel and the last man on earth who would have me as a wife!"

She whirled the nervous stallion unexpectedly, causing him to rear, and had the satisfaction of seeing the fear in the long, thin-featured face before vanishing in a whirlwind of mud and flying turf over the next rise. Raven shivered, thinking how odious the man could be and wishing he hadn't made her so unaccountably angry. She wondered with a small frown of anxiety how vulnerable to the minister's attentions she would be now that her father was gone. How happy and safe she had always been with him here, and how lonely and afraid she had felt at times since he had left her!

Now the pleasure of the ride was gone, and Raven, after taking Cinnabar down to one of the sheltered coves below the cliffs to allow him to splash through the icy sea water, turned back toward home. The big stallion, lowering his head and prancing impatiently, was reluctant to do her bidding and took the bit between his teeth as the towers of North Head came into view through the misty morning air.

"Easy, my sweet, easy," Raven whispered, leaning forward in the saddle and urging the stallion with her voice to turn up the winding drive that, flanked by an avenue of towering cedars, led to the shingle-roof stables. Snorting and tossing his head, Cinnabar pranced into the stable yard where a grizzled groom in boots and a leather apron emerged from the barn to take his reins.

"Had a good workout, did ye, Miss Raven?" he asked with a toothy grin.

"Aye, Sam," Raven replied, sliding her small, booted foot from the stirrup iron and dismounting gracefully. She was tall and sinuously slender. Her dark green velvet habit was fashionably cut, and the tiny jacket trimmed with gold braid fit snugly to her narrow waist and flared over her curving hips. Her dark, glossy hair, as black as jet, was plaited into a chignon and held with delicate netting against her long, graceful neck.

The wayward curls that had worked themselves loose during the whirlwind ride were tucked in a haphazard fashion beneath the small plumed hat she wore on her head. Her eyes were large and sloping in her perfect oval face, their golden depths still smoldering with the intensity of her anger at the unpleasant Reverend Parminster.

"He's wild as ever," Sam remarked with a shake of his grizzled head as the big stallion, relieved of his mistress's weight, leaped eagerly forward. The groom's firm hand on the bridle kept him from breaking free. Snorting, the whites of his eyes showing, he pawed the ground, his iron shoes ringing against the cobblestones.

"Poor Cinnabar," Raven murmured, stroking his sleek, muscular neck with one gloved hand. "Maybe I'll ride him again this afternoon."

"Nay, Miss Raven, ye'll not be havin' the time," Sam informed her apologetically. "Mr. Haggart's clerk was out here while you were gone. Said the old man'd be by to see you around two."

"I wonder what for," Raven mused. A frown marred the smoothness of her brow.

"He wouldn't say, miss."

Raven shrugged her delicate shoulders and smiled at the old groom, her tawny eyes kind. "No matter, Sam. Have one of the lads run him later on. That should work off some of his energy."

Sam puffed out his round, reddened cheeks as he loosened the girth and slipped the saddle from Cinnabar's broad back. "If the wild gallops ye take him on don't do the trick, Miss Raven, I don't see as another run will, even if I do convince one of the lads to get up on him."

Raven's response was a low, musical laugh, and she turned and started across the courtyard toward the house, her velvet skirts swirling about her as she moved, her bone-handled riding quirt held in one small gloved hand. Slipping soundlessly through the service entrance, she hurried up the winding staircase to the west wing, where her bedchamber was located, unmindful of the stern faces of her ancestors that peered down at her as she passed through the Long Gallery. All of them were Barrancourts, fierce, proud, and dark with good Celtic blood burning in their veins. Most of them had been warriors, tribesmen, and later knights and trusted lords of the English kings. In their stern profiles were locked the history of Cornwall and the future destiny of their heirs, including Raven, whose dark, awesome beauty was as much a part of that inheritance as her proud, indomitable spirit.

Raven's bedchamber opened to the sea, the tall casement windows revealing a magnificent view of water and sky, although today it was difficult to tell where one ended and the other began, as the horizon was so obscured by a thick blanket of rolling mist. Moisture dripped from the eaves above, and rooks cawed raucously as they circled through the wind-swept sky. It was a scene that Raven knew by heart, though the same sullen sea could be transformed into glittering aquamarine when the golden rays of the sun warmed both surf and beach with its light. How many sunny days had she seen from this window, Raven wondered, drawing near, her small hand holding back the damask drapes. How many tempest-tossed nights and cold, wintry days?

Not nearly enough, she thought to herself, a soft, loving smile curving her lips as she turned her golden eyes westward to Land's End. An entire lifetime would not be sufficient to gain her fill of the savage beauty of Cornwall, and she was content to do little else today than stand here by the window and dream. A small sigh escaped her, and the delicate shoulders slumped. If only that were possible, but the amount of work that awaited her downstairs was far too demanding to ignore. Raven sighed again as she reluctantly turned away from the window and began to pull off her riding boots.

When she appeared downstairs, she was dressed in a full-skirted gown of dark ruby velvet, the flounced lace at the scooped neckline revealing the long, slender column of her throat and the rounded swell of her breasts. Her narrow waist was emphasized by the tight-fitting bodice, whose smooth material fell gracefully over curving hips. Her glossy blue-black hair was unbound, swept back from her small face and secured with a pair of exquisite mother-of-pearl combs. The vibrant curls tumbled below her hips and swayed provocatively as she walked, although Raven, musing silently to herself, was unaware of how beautiful she appeared. She frowned slightly. There were debts to be settled before the end of the month and wages to be paid out the day after tomorrow. Which should she tackle first? she wondered. Would she have enough time to complete the ledgers before Mr. Haggart arrived later that afternoon?

The tiny frown disappeared from Raven's smooth brow, and her eyes brightened. Why couldn't she call upon Mr. Haggart to spend a little time answering some of her questions concerning them? Perhaps if she were to show him the ledgers, he might explain why she always came out a wee bit short every month no matter how prudently she juggled the expenditures. If the truth be told, she had been too ashamed of her lack of business acumen to go to him sooner; yet if he were here, surely he wouldn't hesitate to help her just a little!

Feeling cheered by the prospect, Raven headed for the study, but, passing the double doors that led to the Great Hall and finding them open, she paused there for a moment and stepped inside. The salty tang of the sea mingled here with the pleasant scent of beeswax: apparently the enormous refectory table had just received a good coat of polish from the energetic downstairs maids. A huge brass bowl stood in the center of the table, filled with summer wildflowers, daisies, baby's-breath, violets, bluebells, and lady's-slippers mingling with dark green foliage clipped from the ancient yews in the park outside.

The flagstone floor, quarried in Cornwall itself, gleamed with a soft patina, worn over the years by the countless hunting balls, wedding feasts, and banquets it had endured. Though the stately room was enormous and the raftered ceiling high above lent an aura of immense grandeur, Raven had always loved the informally cozy feeling that surrounded her whenever she stepped inside. Ancient weapons, some used by her ancestors in times of war and civil unrest, hung from walls that were softened by the warm, rich colors of tapestries. A cavernous fireplace, half again the height of a man, took up one entire corner beneath the minstrel's gallery. The polished rose-colored marble that surrounded it had been imported over a century ago from Italy.

Raven wandered slowly about the enormous hall, her soft kid slippers making no sound, her velvet gown whispering as she moved, and she thought of all the music and laughter that had echoed to the vaulted ceiling in the past. Barrancourts had, for over two hundred years, celebrated the feasts of life within these thick stone walls, and she herself had participated in some of the harvest balls and rousing levees her father had held. Though she wouldn't have made her formal debut until this coming winter, he had insisted that she act as his hostess, and all of the guests had been charmed by the beautiful, smiling young girl who stood at her father's side and curtsied so prettily upon receiving them.

They had begun making plans for her coming-out ball shortly before her father's death. Remembering this, Raven's golden eyes took on a sad, wistful look. He had promised her it would be the affair of the season and that her gown would be more beautiful than the gossamer wings of angels. He had even begun teaching her the intricate steps of the dance traditional in opening every formal occasion at North Head. It was a lively dance similar to the volte that had originated in France and been so popular in England in Queen Elizabeth's time, but also added the more stately steps of the Italian pavan. None of the Barrancourt ancestors had claimed credit for introducing the dance into the household, and the archives gave no indication of its origin either, but it had become such a firm tradition among North Head's inhabitants that generation upon generation of Barrancourt sons and daughters had been taught by their elders to perform it.

Could she remember the lively, intricate steps and the lilting melody that accompanied it? Humming to herself, Raven began to tap her small, slippered foot on the polished stone floor, and as the rhythm and melody began to come back to her, she lifted her heavy skirts, revealing slim, shapely ankles, and whirled gracefully about the empty floor as though dancing with an imaginary partner. To her delight the steps came naturally, and she pirouetted around and around, her ruby skirts billowing about her, slender arms in the air, her long black hair swaying sinuously below her curving hips. She could almost hear her father's voice correcting her for an incorrectly pointed toe or praising her for a particularly graceful step, and the light that leaped to her eyes was warm and rich with memory.

"Ahem!"

Raven came to an abrupt halt at this self-conscious announcement of arrival, and her soft cheeks flamed with color when she saw the liveried footman standing in the doorway. Though he was doing his best to look suitably grave, she detected a look of admiration and enjoyment on his kindly face, and she was forced to laugh at herself for behaving so foolishly.

"I'm sorry, Timms. I was wondering if I could still remember the steps."

"Apparently you can, Miss Raven," the footman replied, permitting himself the liberty of laughing with her. "And very well, I might add."

"Were you looking for me?" Raven asked innocently, smoothing back the wayward curls from her face and straightening the folds of her dusky velvet gown.

"No, miss, I was coming in to close the doors. Molly must have left them open when she finished cleaning."

"It's rather sad, actually," Raven said wistfully as she stepped out into the richly carpeted corridor while he swung the gilded doors shut. "I really don't know if we'll ever use the Great Hall again."

"Oh, you mustn't say that, Miss Raven!" Timms protested. Having spent most of his life at North Head, he remembered well how singularly wonderful the Barrancourt balls had always been.

Raven shrugged, but her face was filled with sadness. "As a young, unmarried woman I certainly can't hold any feasts or parties of my own, and I wouldn't want to without Father anyway." She sighed and gave him a soft, unhappy smile. "I imagine I'd better get to work."

Timms watched the slender form vanish down the long corridor and frowned to himself, sharing his young mistress's sadness at the loss of the master. But Miss Raven was uncommonly beautiful, he told himself encouragingly, and it would not be long before she found a gentleman worthy of her. Then the Great Hall would echo again with the laughter of guests and the music of the orchestra.

Raven's mood grew bleak, and she sighed disconsolately as she opened the study door and saw the assortment of documents and buckram-bound ledgers piled upon the huge oak desk that had been her father's. Sometimes the amount of paperwork was so staggering that she wanted to scream and throw the lot into the fire. How could she have suspected, growing up wild and carefree on North Head's barren heaths, that so much work was involved in running the enormous estate? After all, her father had handled everything—the management of the household, the tilling of the countless acres of rich farmland, the tenant rent, the livestock, the wages, the servants.... Though Raven had accompanied him many times to the fields during planting and harvest, and had even learned to cull and select the breeding stock, she had never disturbed her father while he worked alone in his study on the books, and had therefore been forced to take over those responsibilities without an inkling of where to start.

Yet things were certainly easier now than they had been three months ago when she'd first inherited the workload, Raven decided, seating herself in the big leather chair, her velvet skirts swirling about her. Though the crops were doing poorly this year with the cold, rainy growing season they'd been having, there'd be enough to pay the hands and take care of most of North Head's expenses. Finally, the enormous file that she had painstakingly plowed through, a little each day, was updated in an order that she could understand.

With a wistful sadness Raven opened the ledger nearest her elbow and saw the rows upon rows of figures jotted down in her father's bold, neat hand. She could well remember how frightened and desolate she had felt sitting down for the first time behind the big, gleaming desk, grieving for the loss of him and terribly afraid that she would not be able to keep North Head going. Apparently none of the neighbors had thought she could do so either; they called to pay their condolences only to leave shaking their heads among themselves. Raven had heard the whispers, the doubts that a slender lass of barely eighteen could shoulder the burden of running North Head's vast holdings herself. Still, they had all been kind and had offered to help; but Raven, too proud to accept their charity, had taken over the responsiblility alone.

"And you've done well, lass," she said to herself, tracing down the column of figures with one tapering finger. "I think." She giggled, the soft cheeks dimpling. She thought she must be getting addled to be talking to herself like that. Growing serious, she pushed a strand of dark black hair from her small face, dipped the pen in the inkwell, and began to write. For several hours she worked undisturbed, her smooth brow wrinkled with concentration. The ormulu clock ticked in the stillness, and the faraway pounding of the breakers and the mournful cry of the gulls were so familiar a part of the background of sounds that they went unnoticed.

"Why, just look at you, Miss Raven! Don't you even bother to eat anymore?"

Raven, startled from her work, looked up quickly as the study door opened and a small, primly attired woman entered, hands propped sternly on ample hips. Her straw-colored hair was knotted into a bun at the nape of her neck, and unruly wisps of it clung to her broad forehead. Though her face was lined with age and careworn, her eyes and her step were lively. Hannah Daniels always claimed that looking after a charge as difficult and energetic as Raven Barrancourt had helped keep her young.

Raven's eyes flew automatically to the clock above the cavernous tile fireplace, and widened when she saw that it was half past one. Immediately her stomach chimed in to proclaim the lateness of the hour, growling is so unladylike a fashion that Raven was forced to laugh, the clear, sweet sound bringing an answering smile to Hannah Daniels's lips, for she had not heard Raven laugh like that very often in the past few months.

"So you find it amusing, do you," she went on, feigning disapproval, "that Mr. Haggart be due here in half an hour and you've not even breakfasted yet?"

"I took Cinnabar out so early," Raven explained, hurriedly stacking the folders. "There's time for a quick meal before he comes, isn't there?"

"Quick meal?" the former governess echoed with a derisive shake of her head. "I'll hear of no such thing. It's a proper luncheon you'll be having, Miss Raven, and Parris has already laid it out for you."

"Don't worry, Danny," Raven soothed, rising from the big leather chair to smooth the folds of her velvet gown. "I'm fair starving."

Luncheon was spread out for her on the small occasional table in the pleasant Conservatory which had always been one of Raven's favorite rooms. Located in North Head's east wing, its large bay windows opened to the south, offering an uninterrupted view of the rolling meadows that stretched toward the wilds of the Cornish heath. Though trees were scarce in this desolate corner of England, the Barrancourts had, over the generations, planted enough of them to create a copse of towering cedars, chestnuts, and beeches that added a pleasant woodland vista to the southern exposure of North Head's rambling park. In autumn they provided a glorious contrast of scarlet and gold to the gray pall of hovering November mist, and in the summer the spreading branches were crowned with emerald leaves, the chestnuts bearing feathery catkins which would soon yield their nutty fruit.

A warm blaze crackled in the hearth to ward off the unusual

chill, and the scent of freesias and hothouse tulips, the bulbs forced by Raven herself, perfumed the air. Once the Conservatory had contained many lush green plants, flowering tuberoses and exotic orchids, which had been her father's favorites, but Raven had found them too difficult to maintain after his death, already overworked with managing the estate, and had placed them in the care of Parris, who, though Raven would sooner have bitten off her tongue than tell him, had more talent for preparing a good shoulder roast or leg of lamb than tending hothouse flowers. Still, the few specimens that had survived the old man's dubious care were blooming and colorful, and Raven sighed contentedly as she slipped into the delicate damask-upholstered chair before the small table overlooking the park. Parris had meticulously set out the delectable dishes on a white linen cloth. The chafing dishes were steaming, and Raven's slim nose twitched hungrily in response to the enticing smells. Serving herself a helping of each, she became aware of Danny watching her surreptitiously from the padded window seat across the room.

"Now what am I doing wrong?" Raven asked, her eyes wide with innocence.

Danny shook her head as she surveyed with compressed lips the mountain of food on Raven's china plate. "How many times have I told you that a lady eats daintily, and then only a little at a time?"

Raven dimpled, her golden eyes glowing mischievously. "I vow you are the most exasperating creature, Danny! Nine times out of ten you berate me for not eating enough. Besides," she added reasonably, attacking a slab of steaming roast Angus beef, "there's no one here to succumb to an attack of the vapors because of the amount I'm eating."

"And fortunately no one can overhear that tart tongue of yours either," the old woman added severely, speaking with the familiarity only long years of acquaintance could bring. She had been summoned to North Head by James Barrancourt himself after the untimely death of his wife.

When Raven was barely a year old, her mother had delivered into the world a sickly boy child who had lived scarcely an hour while the effort of bearing him had taken her own life as well. Though quick to rebuke and fancying herself a stern disciplinarian, Danny was soft-hearted and easily swayed, a fact the young Raven had quickly capitalized on and used to her advantage quite often during her schooling years.

"My goodness," Danny went on, ignoring Raven's rebellious glare, "when I think of what the locals believe you to be, so demure, sweet, and shy... bah! You're an irrepressible, temperamental little firebrand, and I wonder how I've managed to come this far with the few gray hairs I have."

Raven laughed at this, accustomed to Danny's despairing criticism. "Well, no matter what our good neighbors thought of me before, I warrant they're convinced now that I'm rather fey." The tawny eyes hardened perceptively, and the slim jaw jutted. "But I'm not giving up North Head, Danny, no matter what lengths I have to go to to keep it. Father may be gone, but the Barrancourts will never leave Land's End."

"Now, now, no one says you have to go," Danny said quickly, rising and coming forward to pat Raven's shoulder reassuringly. "Everything's going well, and by planting time next spring you'll have the books balanced."

"I hope so." Raven's beautiful face was stark, the depths of her golden eyes filled with determination.

"Excuse me, Miss Raven." It was Parris standing stiffly in the doorway, chin held high above a starched collar and perfectly tied cravat, his voice sonorous and polite. "Mr. Richard Haggart has arrived. I've shown him to the Yellow Salon."

"Please tell him I'll join him directly," Raven replied, hastily shoving two more bites of roast beef into her mouth and following that with a buttered piece of pumpernickel bread. To Danny's horror the entire mouthful was washed down with a healthy swallow of claret, and Raven gave her an apologetic grin as she wiped her lips on her napkin and rose to her feet.

"I'll have better manners tonight at dinner," she promised. "I don't have time right now to observe them."

Danny was permitted no response, for Raven was already out the door. A swish of ruby skirts and her glossy black curls were the last her former governess saw of her.

The Yellow Salon was decorated with a visitor's comfort in mind. Numerous plushly upholstered armchairs and settees were set about the pleasant room, and the saffron silk drapes were drawn back to allow daylight to pour in on the gold-flocked wallpaper and delicate scrollwork. An Aubusson carpet covered the hand-waxed parquet floor, and the brass wall sconces gleamed with polish. It was a warm, friendly room, the oak and mahogany furnishings softening the brightness of the yellow silk fabrics, and Mr. Haggart, wearing a black worsted wool suit and perched stiffly in a roomy wing-backed armchair, looked extremely somber by comparison.

When Raven entered the room, her dark ruby gown gave him the impression of a slender, budding tulip in a field of daffodils. Jumping to his feet, he bowed deeply. He was an uncommonly short man who was forced to look up to gaze into Raven's face, though his eyes lingered despite themselves on the enticing roundness of her breasts and the narrow waist, then moved admiringly to the mother-of-pearl combs that held her glossy black hair.

"Good afternoon, Mr. Haggart," Raven said politely when it became obvious that the little man was going to do nothing but stand there and stare at her.

"Ah, yes, yes, good afternoon, Miss Barrancourt." He flushed self-consciously and reluctantly tore his gaze away from her. "Forgive me for staring, b-but I was unprepared for seeing you in such a . . . such a bright color." He gestured weakly at the wine-colored gown, his flush growing deeper. His thin cheeks were soon suffused with red, reminding Raven of the Reverend Parminster's unkind comments earlier that day.

"Ah . . . if you're wondering why I'm no longer wearing black although my father is barely three months dead," Raven said a trifle sharply, indicating with a gesture of her small hand that he should be seated. "My father was never one to embrace the theory that social convention should be adhered to simply because we're told it must be so. He did not observe the standard year of mourning when my mother died years ago, yet I know that he grieved her loss until the day he himself died. I grieve for him, too, yet in here," she added softly, touching her heart, "and I don't need to display my devotion for him by wearing black." The soft lips curved into a wistful smile. "He always hated me in that color, you see."

"I quite understand," Mr. Haggart said, though it was obvious to Raven that he didn't. Clearing his throat nervously, he opened the leather case he had brought with him and shuffled through the numerous documents it contained as he perched again in the armchair that faced the sofa onto which Raven now lowered herself somewhat distrustfully. She wondered why her father's solicitor had chosen to come to see her so unexpectedly. After all, the matters of the will and the estate had been settled the day after the funeral.

"I've come to you in a legal capacity to discuss financial matters, Miss Barrancourt," Mr. Haggart said as though reading her mind. This time the small, close-set eyes traveled without pausing from the slender neckline to the oval face while Raven forced herself to sit quietly, her hands folded calmly in her lap although inwardly her heart was beating with a sense of impending danger.

"I had thought the finances were settled after the funeral, sir," she said, her eyes meeting his squarely.

The solicitor nodded and cleared his throat again, and Raven began to feel uneasy, for obviously he was distressed about something. She bit her lower lip with her small white teeth and willed herself to remain calm while steeling herself inwardly for the worst. What could it be? she asked herself anxiously. Were there unpaid debts he had overlooked before? Had she neglected to pay a creditor? Could a bill be overdue somewhere? Damnit, she breathed to herself, speak!

"Miss Barrancourt, I should have brought the matter up with you the afternoon we met in my office in Truro, but under the circumstances..."

"What circumstances, Mr. Haggart?" Raven asked sharply as the solicitor broke off and began to tug at his high collar as though it was suddenly irritating him.

"Why, your loss, of course. The shock of losing your father, your last living relation, in so violent a manner!"

"Accidents on horseback are not uncommon," Raven replied steadily, her pain-darkened cat's eyes focused on a cheerful landscape painting above Mr. Haggart's balding head. "My father was a fast and reckless rider, his mount an untried colt—"

"A shame the horse had to be put down," Mr. Haggart added with a shake of his head. "Finest animal ever bred in Cornwall. Why, the first time I saw your father put him over the fences, I thought to myself—" He caught himself with an effort and gave the beautiful young girl sitting quietly before him an apologetic smile. "I'm sorry, Miss Barrancourt, it must be painful for you to be reminded of all this."

Raven shrugged and smiled thinly, but the sorrow in her eyes was obvious to her visitor, and his nervousness increased, hating himself for being the one to bring her such ominous tidings. Though he had known James Barrancourt for many years, Richard Haggart had never met his daughter until the day of the funeral. There were few people in Truro, or in all of Cornwall for that matter, who hadn't heard of her rare beauty, but Haggart had been taken aback by it when he saw her for the first time in the fog-enshrouded churchyard. Raven had been dressed in black bombazine, a delicate veil obscuring her features, but the pallor of her skin and the feverish glow in her sloping eyes had lent her uncommon beauty a fragility that was breathtaking. Her sorrow had somehow enhanced her incredible loveliness, her features perfect, her cheeks soft and alluringly hollow, her nose small and aquiline, the sloping jawline that was visible beneath the netting so slender, the bone structure so delicate, that he had wondered how something so dainty and feminine could survive the harsh reality of Cornish life.

Yet Raven Barrancourt possessed an underlying core of strength, Richard Haggart decided now as she sat quietly before him, the tawny eyes boldly meeting his, the small chin imperiously lifted. There was a stubborn set to the slender jaw, and as the solicitor's gaze met hers, she tossed her head, causing the blue-black curls to gleam vibrantly and the mother-of-pearl combs to catch the light and sparkle as though she had studded her hair with diamonds.

"Mr. Haggart?"

The soft voice startled him. "Eh?"

"About these financial matters—"

"Oh, yes, yes, of course." Embarrassed, he shuffled a second time through the stack of papers; then, seeing the trepidation in her eyes, decided the kindest thing he could do for her was to speak the truth immediately. "We decided to wait a few months before coming to you, Miss Barrancourt, so that you could have time to recover a bit from your . . . from your sad loss. I—"

"We?" Raven asked fearfully.

"My client and I."

She wanted to ask who, but she had learned a great deal of self-control in the past few months and bit back the question that burned on the tip of her tongue, warning herself to be patient. She sensed uneasily that what the solicitor had to say was very grave indeed and might possibly affect the rest of her life. Dear God, she prayed silently, don't let anything be wrong with my rightful claim to North Head!

"To be frank, Miss Barrancourt, the problem is a debt owed my client and—"

"Oh, thank God!" Raven whispered, unable to help herself, relief transforming her expression into one of incredible loveliness. Indeed, her happiness seemed to radiate entirely from within. "I had thought—"

Mr. Haggart's voice was surprisingly hard, although he could not bring himself to look at her. "The debt is sizable, Miss Barrancourt. I don't believe you realize how very much so."

Raven swallowed hard, suddenly frightened by his tone. "H-how large, sir?"

"A mere figure is impossible to quote, Miss Barrancourt. Your father borrowed heavily during the past few years, invested in a number of items—experiments in which, I'm afraid, he incurred heavy losses." He held up the thick stack of documents before Raven's stricken eyes. "I have all of it written here."

"I don't understand," Raven whispered, feeling as though she had stepped into some awful nightmare. How large was a debt that one couldn't even add up? How was one to pay back such a staggering amount?

"For example . . ." Mr. Haggart leafed through his papers and, setting a pair of spectacles on the end of his thin nose, continued, "Two years ago your father borrowed nearly eight thousand pounds to invest in the new steamship *Henry Moran*. I don't believe you'll remember that the ship sank in the Channel that following winter?"

Raven shook her head numbly.

"Your father lost his entire share, as did the other investors. Not a serious loss under normal circumstances, yet there was another ship the following year that sprang a leak in the Atlantic and went down, and a heavy investment in a copper mine that produced no ore, and, earlier this year, the purchase of several experimental steam-generated pumps that proved useless, I'm afraid."

Raven's eyes were filled with disbelief. "I never knew," she murmured weakly. "My father never told me he was so heavily in debt."

"And why should he distress you?" Mr. Haggart asked kindly, and Raven hated the pity she saw in his eyes.

She sat quietly for a moment, staring down at her hands, wondering why she should feel so calm, so curiously numb, when her entire world had just crumbled about her. Here she had been disillusioning herself all along into believing she was doing well managing the estate, thinking that the unbalanced books were merely a result of her own ineptitude. Judas, how could she have been so stupid?

"What does this person . . . your client expect of me, Mr. Haggart?" she asked after a moment, her voice sounding thin to her own ears.

"Actually, he has a particular proposal he wishes to make to you, one that I believe will settle your debts in a manner that won't be distressing to you."

Raven's heart leaped, the expression in her delicate face growing hopeful. "Who—who is he?"

Mr. Haggart smiled without humor. "I'm not at liberty to say, but he requested that I ask for an audience with you tomorrow morning at ten o'clock, if that isn't too early."

Raven frowned, not caring at all for his secretive manner but as she knew she had little choice other than to agree, she lifted her chin and nodded bravely.

Mr. Haggart appeared greatly relieved. "Excellent! I'll inform him immediately." Rising to his feet, he smiled at her kindly. "Courage, Miss Barrancourt; all is not lost. You've no reason to fear losing your home."

"May I see those papers before you go?" Raven asked.

The solicitor was startled by her request but placed them willingly enough into her outstretched hand. "Certainly. Keep them overnight if you like and turn them over to your visitor tomorrow."

Raven rose also, clutching the documents to her breast, although they felt as though they were burning her flesh. As she tugged at the bell pull, she managed a weak smile of her own. "Thank you for coming, sir. Parris will show you out."

She waited until she was alone before collapsing onto the sofa to bury her face in her hands, the papers falling unnoticed to the floor at her feet. What was to happen to her now, at the mercy of an unknown man from whom her father had, unbeknownst to her, borrowed such a great deal of money, only to lose it all? Was everything that she had struggled to retain these past three months to slip from her grasp? Mr. Haggart had assured her that the debts could be settled without too much loss on her part, yet how could he be so sure?

"Miss Raven, Parris told me the solicitor's gone, and I—my lord, child, what be the matter with you?" Danny asked, stopping short in the doorway as she caught sight of Raven sitting forlornly on the sofa, her face pale, her golden eyes clouded with despair. "What is it?" she asked worriedly.

Raven smiled up at her tremulously, determined not to worry the old woman unnecessarily. "Nothing at all, Danny. Mr. Haggart brought some rather startling news. I'll explain everything tomorrow, after my ten-o'clock visitor has gone."

"Ten-o'clock visitor? Who can that be? Miss Raven, you're acting very strangely. What's amiss?"

Raven shook her dark head reassuringly and bent down to scoop up the fallen papers scattered across the carpet. "I'll be in the study if you need me," she added, and headed casually for the door, feeling Danny's anxious eyes upon her. Once safely inside her father's former haven, she closed the door firmly behind her and sank into the big leather chair, her expression stark. Oh, God, how she dreaded the morrow!

It proved to be a long, painful afternoon for Raven, who had somehow lost interest in the tasks that awaited her. The usually pleasant hours she spent on the moors with John Speedwell, the farm steward, became an endless session of chores. She worked numbly at the taciturn steward's side, with no real interest in the evaluation of the spring calves or the measurement of the winnowing rye in the fields. John, sensing his young mistress's distraction, kindly offered to finish the work on his own, and Raven agreed without much protest.

She ate little for dinner, despite Parris's polite protestations, and spent the remainder of the evening thumbing listlessly through the pages of a book she had taken down from the library shelf in the vain hope that it would divert her mind from her troubles. When the big clock in its cherrywood case struck ten, Raven gave up at last, tossing the book aside and smiling a vague good-night to the yawning footman who was waiting patiently to extinguish the candles and close up the lower floors for the night. In her bedroom she found the bedclothes turned back and a lantern glowing softly on the inlaid table standing nearby. The damask drapes had been drawn over the leaded casement windows, and the cozy room was a welcoming retreat from Raven's worldly cares. Yet she could not quite forget what tomorrow would bring, so certain she was that everything at North Head which she held dear would soon be taken away from her forever.

I'll never let that happen! Raven vowed firmly to herself, drawing to the window and peering restlessly out into the darkness. The dull booming of the breakers came to her from far below, the foaming whitecaps easily discernible wherever the pounding waves broke against the cliffs. She turned the latch and opened the window wide, letting the salty night air fan her hot cheeks. The wild scent invaded her senses and filled her with an unaccountable urge to immerse herself totally in the night and the freedom of darkness. As though it were urging her on, the tangy breeze brought with it from the stables the sound of an impatient whinny, and Raven recognized Cinnabar's call at once.

Turning away from the window, she pulled off her soft kid slippers and quickly changed into the emerald riding habit she had worn earlier that day, convinced that what she needed to rid herself of the depression that had dogged her since Mr. Haggart's visit was a good hard gallop along the cliffs. Never mind that it was nearly midnight! All the better to give her the privacy that she so craved from probing eyes.

Raven's eyes glowed with anticipation when she entered the darkened stables, and she laughed softly as Cinnabar nickered eagerly from his box stall at the far end. She stroked his velvet nose and allowed him to nip playfully at the tiny brass buttons that were sewn to the gold braiding on her bodice.

"Were you calling me, my laddie?" she whispered, taking his halter and leading him into the aisle. "Well, then, let's be off!"

The big stallion stood patiently as she slipped the heavy saddle onto his back, his ears flicking in response to her gentle voice and practiced hands. His iron-shod hoofs rang on the hard stone floor when Raven led him to the block, but she knew that Sam, who slept in the garret above, would think nothing of the activity below if by chance he did awaken, for he was well accustomed to her moonlight rides by now. She glanced up at the shuttered window as she slipped her small foot into the stirrup iron, smiling to herself when she saw that all remained dark. Doubtless Sam was so used to her nighttime sojourns that he didn't even wake up at all anymore.

A cool wind was blowing as the big stallion started off across the hard turf that led away from North Head in the direction of the cliffs. With the coming of the night, the heavy layer of clouds had finally dispersed, and the stars twinkled brightly, a crescent moon shedding its faint light upon the moors and the restless sea. Raven kept Cinnabar at a steady trot until they were on familiar ground, then gave him his head, unafraid as the big animal plunged off into the darkness, knowing that his footing would be sure. He snorted in enjoyment and lowered his noble head, his thick tail curved in a graceful arc that streamed like a banner behind him. Raven, her heavy velvet skirts billowing in the wind, leaned low over his crested neck, the blood coursing through her veins like warm, heady wine.

She did not know how long or how far they galloped, the wind roaring in her ears, Cinnabar moving rhythmically beneath her. She forced him to a walk at last, aware that he had already been ridden hard once that day and that it would also be a long way back to his stall. She paused on a small rise to get her bearings, searching through the darkness for a landmark, recognizing at last the outline of the cliffs below her, the rugged outcroppings and the sandy coves as familiar to her as the lines on the palm of her hand. North Head lay some two or three miles directly to the east, and if she turned Cinnabar south across the heath, they would end up eventually on the narrow cart trail that would take them back to the manor drive.

Still reluctant to turn back, Raven sat quietly for a moment on Cinnabar's broad back, savoring the feel of the salty spindrift in her face, her head tilted back, the jaunty plume of her hat caressing her soft cheek. Somewhere on the moors behind her a nightbird called, and far down the slope toward the distant fishing villages a dog barked, and Cinnabar, his ears pricked, snorted and pawed with his forefoot on the rocky ground.

"Oh, all right, we'll turn around," Raven said with a low laugh, patting his sleek neck affectionately. Lifting the reins, she cast one final glance at the foaming jetties below, but then her heart stopped suddenly, for out on the water, unnervingly close to shore, came a brief but unmistakable flash of light. Immediately thereafter came a response in the form of a long, slow arc of light that appeared on the face of the cliff not far from where Cinnabar stood, before vanishing abruptly into the darkness.

Raven knew immediately what the signals meant, having lived on the Cornish coast all of her life, and having practically been weaned on tales of pirates and smugglers. Yet whereas the stories of her ancestors' exploits had been colorful and filled with romance, Raven knew well enough that real smugglers were hard, unsavory men, criminals and drunkards who would not hesitate to kill to protect themselves and their contraband goods. Her first instinct was to wheel the nervous Cinnabar and flee, but as the signal was repeated and the long arcing response came again from the cliffs, her slim jaw tightened and her eyes began to blaze. Why, that was North Head property being used to unload the goods. The answering signal had come from one of the coves along where she had exercised Cinnabar that very afternoon!

How dare they! Raven thought to herself, angered to the point where her fear abruptly vanished. It would be useless, she knew, to ride to St. Ives and arouse Hamish Kilgannen, the excise man, for by that time the smugglers, their contraband unloaded, would be long gone. Yet what could she do? She couldn't let them overrun North Head beaches, especially not while engaged in criminal acts. Perhaps she could come close enough to recognize some of the faces, to point them out to Kilgannen later; surely the word of a Barrancourt wouldn't be discredited!

Her heart hammering in her breast, Raven guided the obedient stallion silently along the grass-covered crest of the cliffs, the darkness surrounding her like a cloak. On the beach below, all was silent save for the booming of the breakers, and though she strained her eyes, she could catch no glimpse at all of the ship that she knew lay just off the rocky shore. If she hadn't seen the signal light, she wouldn't have known at all that a smuggling operation was going on this very moment on Barrancourt land. Her golden eyes narrowed. Heathen swine, she'd indict every last one of them!

She was close enough by now that she could detect movement below, on the beach lit with a ghostly light. Several longboats had been pulled through the foreshore waves, the gunnels sinking beneath the weight of the stacked shipment of barrels, and Raven's lips compressed as she watched the black shadows wade out to unload them. Rum was the obvious cargo, doubtless brought in from the Caribbean, and anger swept her anew. For over forty years no one had smuggled anything onto Barrancourt land, and Raven could well remember how proud her father had been of the time, effort, and money he had spent in helping Cornwall stamp out the illegal practice with the wholehearted support of the village folk who, even though their own fathers and grandfathers had often participated in unloading contraband from ships, had prospered under the fair and honest Barrancourt rule.

"Well, we'll just have to see who's strayed from the righteous path this time!" Raven whispered to herself as she dismounted and looped the reins loosely around the cantle of the saddle. Cinnabar, trained to recognize this as a signal that he was not to stray too far, lowered his head and contentedly began to crop the blades of grass that grew sparsely on the rocky ground while Raven wound her way cautiously toward the edge of the cliff, where she would have an uninterrupted view of the beach below.

The moon was rising, its pale light defining the men who moved in a silent stream to and from the heavy-laden boats. Raven counted nearly a dozen, but she could not recognize any of them. The woolen caps pulled low over their eyes obscured their features. She gathered her skirts tightly in one hand and moved slowly along the face of the cliff, descending in the direction of the beach, careful to keep herself concealed behind the clumps of gorse and the piles of rocks that littered the ground before her. At last she came to a halt behind an outcropping of jagged boulders separating the sandy beach from the grass-covered slopes. There she cowered down, her heart beating wildly, her breast heaving as she tried to catch her breath. Eyes narrowed in concentration, she strained to recognize an obscured face or a muted voice, determined to bring much more than vague accusations and hesitant guesses to Hamish Kilgannen in the morning.

Engrossed in her observation, the blood pounding as loudly as the sea in her ears, Raven did not hear the stealthy footsteps behind her until a dislodged pebble bounced off the boulder near her face, and she whirled quickly about. A scream rose in her throat, only to end there as a big hand clamped itself firmly over her mouth. For a second she was paralyzed with fear, unable to move as her captor, a mere shadow in the faint moonlight, jerked her upright; but then she reacted, biting down as hard as she could with her small white teeth into the hand that covered her lips.

A muffled curse and a moment's loosening of the imprisoning hold were all Raven needed to prompt her escape. Ducking beneath the restraining arm, she darted nimbly between the legs of her unseen captor and took off at a run. Yet she was hampered by her skirts as they caught on twigs and branches, and when she stumbled over them and went down, scraping her palms on the rocky ground, she could hear him following close behind her. Another scream rose in her throat, but she bit it back, aware that she stood a better chance of escaping if she didn't draw anyone else's attention to her presence. If only she could reach the top of the cliff and whistle for Cinnabar, she would be free of the man who was coming up so quickly behind her.

Unfortunately, Raven stumbled again near the grassy edge of the slope, and this time the brief delay gave her pursuer the extra second's advantage he needed. With one quick lunge he threw himself on top of her, and Raven felt herself being jerked to her feet and imprisoned by a pair of burly arms possessing a great deal of strength. Struggling to free herself, she twisted back and forth, refusing to give in, until a harsh voice close to her ear snarled ominously,

"Be still or I'll slit yer throat from ear to ear!"

"You wouldn't dare!" Raven cried absurdly, so shocked by this vulgar threat of violence that she felt only outrage.

"Why, in God's name, its a wench!" her captor bellowed in amazement.

"Mr. Mudge, what the devil is going on here?"

Raven's captor was unable to hold back his quick intake of breath at the sound of the curt question coming from the darkness behind him. Turning her head, Raven could make out another shadow moving swiftly toward them through the blackness, this one more frighteningly large, and she grew still with fear.

"I caught me a spy, cap'n," Mr. Mudge said in an oddly humble tone quite unlike the snarl with which he had addressed Raven only seconds before.

"A spy, Mr. Mudge?" The deep voice hardened as the speaker came to a halt directly before them. Raven tilted back her head fearfully and found herself looking up at a tall, broad-shouldered man, the moonlight illuminating the rugged, angular contours of his handsome face. He was clean-shaven, his jaw square, his chin deeply clefted, and his chestnut hair, whipped by the wind, lay in an unruly fashion across a high, noble forehead. In the dim light his eyes glittered above an aristocratic, aquiline nose, their color impossible to determine, but as their steely depths met Raven's frightened gaze, she shivered, terror coursing through her.

This man, whom the cowering Mr. Mudge had addressed as captain, was regarding her with a glint of cruel mockery in his eyes, and Raven had the fleeting impression of how a hapless fieldmouse felt when it faced the iron talons and cold, predatory eyes of an eagle. He was standing before her with his powerful arms crossed before his massive chest, the whiteness of his muslin shirt standing out in sharp contrast to the darkness of the night. Open at the throat, the shirt revealed a dark matting of curling hair across his smooth chest, the fabric hugging his muscular torso and tapering down to lean hips and hard thighs encased in worn calfskin breeches.

"A spy, Mr. Mudge?" the captain repeated, his deep voice sending another shiver down Raven's spine. "You've caught yourself a child, a helpless girl."

"I am not a child!" Raven retorted angrily.

"Aye, she ain't, cap'n!" Mudge protested hurriedly. "Bit the hell out of me when I grabbed her, she did, and took off like some wild hare through the brush."

"Go on back to the others," the captain commanded coldly. "I'll deal with her."

"Aye, aye, sir!" Mr. Mudge's voice was filled with relief as he promptly released Raven and vanished into the darkness.

No sooner did she feel the hold on her loosen than Raven tried to leap away, but the tall sea captain moved forward with lightning speed and wrapped his ironlike fingers about her arm, jerking her back so that she fell against him, her firm breasts, encased in the tight velvet bodice, pressed against his hard chest.

"Indeed, you're not a girl after all," the glittering-eyed captain said, his deep voice filled with insolence.

"Let me go at once, you . . . you monster!" Raven commanded.

"So that you can run home and rouse the villagers?" he asked with a harsh laugh. "No, my fine lass, you'll stay right here until we're finished with our work."

"You're a criminal, a despicable cad, and I'll see you hanging from the gibbet!" Raven swore, trying to sound brave while in truth she was trembling with fright. Pressed against the smuggler captain's hard chest, his muscular arm encircling her as he attempted to subdue her, she was aware of his tremendous strength, and all the tales she had ever heard of cutthroats and murderers came back to her with sickening intensity. In addition, her hip was pressed against one of his hard thighs, and Raven could clearly feel the outline of a knife that was tucked into his belt, a knife she felt certain he wouldn't hesitate to use.

"Haughty little creature, aren't you?" he was asking with amusement.

Raven tried to pull away as his big hand took hold of her chin, but he laughed and deliberately tightened his hold, tilting back her head so that the moonlight fell full on her upturned face. She heard him inhale sharply, although she couldn't see his features at all, obscured as they were by the darkness and the plume of her hat, which dangled in her eyes.

"Far too comely to be a village lass," he said at last, his voice low. "Don't you know it's foolish to be out here on the cliffs so late at night?"

Raven's anger at this remark gave her the courage to retort boldly, "Indeed, I imagine it is, being as I've stumbled upon riffraff the likes of you!"

The long fingers tightened about her wrist so that she cried out in pain, and the clipped English accent was ominous as he leaned down to say harshly in her ear, "Hold your tongue, my lass, before I cut it out and feed it to the sharks."

"You c-can't scare me!" Raven whispered, her chin still clasped in his strong fingers.

"I c-can't?" he mocked, the glittering eyes focused on her upturned face, and Raven, catching sight of the rugged features in the dim light, was more unnerved by his aggressive masculinity than by the menacing warning in his tone.

"N-no." She willed her teeth to stop chattering. "I'm not afraid of you, and when I tell Hamish Kilgannen about you, he'll—"

"Kilgannen? That fop?" His laugh was derisive.

Raven's heart twisted in her breast. Who was this man? How could he know Hamish Kilgannen? He couldn't be from Cornwall, his accent was all wrong, and besides, she knew most of the sea captains who sailed the Channel and the Atlantic hereabouts, and this tall, mocking smuggler was certainly not one of them! Raven's sloping eyes were wide, the moonlight transforming their tawny depths to burnished gold, and the broad-shouldered man who held her captive stared down at her in silence for a moment, feeling the firmness of her rounded breasts against his chest and the wild pulse beating beneath his big thumb.

"You'll not be telling Kilgannen a thing," he said confidently.

"Oh yes, I will!" Raven vowed, her voice quavering despite her best efforts to speak calmly.

The smuggler captain's white teeth flashed in the darkness as he smiled. "Oh no, you won't, my lass. You see, I know your kind far too well, and I know how to deal with you, too." As he spoke he pulled her toward him abruptly so that she was pressed against the length of his hard, muscular body. To her horror, one of his strong hands slid around her small waist to press intimately against the small of her back, forcing her more closely against him, while the other, which still cupped her small chin, lifted her face so that she was unable to turn her head as his mouth came down on hers.

The touch of a man's lips upon her own was nothing Raven had ever experienced before, and she could scarcely credit their searing heat, a sensation she found terrifying. She felt as though she were drowning, suffocated by the onslaught of sensations that all but overwhelmed her. In panic she twisted her face away from his and glared fiercely into his glittering eyes.

"How dare you!" she breathed.

"Quite easily," he taunted, although his deep voice sounded oddly breathless to her. "Surely you didn't expect me to remain impervious to your charms?"

Before Raven could reply, he had lowered his head a second time, his lips devouring hers. Pushing ineffectually against his hard chest, Raven became aware of the ridge of muscles beneath her hands and the heat of his powerful body, a heat that threatened to engulf her completely.

"Don't!" she pleaded against his lips, but he ignored her, tilting her head back against the cradle of his muscular arm, his kiss growing deeper, more intense.

"Please!" Raven implored in a whisper, frightened by the passions smoldering within this man.

"Be still," he replied, his breath hot against her cheek, his voice little more than a guttural growl. "Your words mean nothing to me. Your body tells me all I want to know."

"Y-you must be mad!" Raven moaned.

"Am I?" Tilting back his head, he looked deeply into her eyes. "Are you quite certain of that?"

Raven gasped as his hand slid beneath the neckline of her gown, his big thumb stroking her naked breast, the nipple rising taut in response.

"You see? Your body hungers for a man's," he told her, and before Raven could utter a frightened denial he had pulled her against him again, his mouth closing over hers with bruising force. Raven was stunned by the carnal passion she could feel building within him, yet she was helpless to break free. She moaned low in her throat as her body, responding to some primal urge she could not understand, began to tremble with something that seemed much stronger and far more overpowering than mere aversion. Stronger than the fearful pounding of her heart, she could feel the burning of her blood in her veins, the throbbing in her temples, seeming to become one with the beating of his heart against her heaving breasts. While his sure hands roved her body, Raven felt herself beginning to quiver in response, as though she were no longer in control of herself. She struggled to resist, but these strange, never-before-experienced emotions washed over her with renewed force, sending a shiver of longing through her.

The tall sea captain somehow sensed this change, although Raven continued to resist him, pushing against his hard chest with her balled fists while his lips continued to devour hers. His big hands cupped her small buttocks as he half-lifted her off the rocky ground, his bold manhood pressing into her soft flesh. A moment later he had unlaced her bodice, his warm hand boldly caressing the rounded fullness of one perfect breast, and Raven shivered again as the nipple rose taut beneath his touch.

"Don't—" she murmured, but it was a breathless whisper that lacked conviction.

Her captor laughed at this ambivalent command, his strong fingers continuing to stroke the smooth ivory flesh, leaving trails of fire that matched the heat burning through his own loins. Lowering his dark head, he let his tongue travel over the rosebud peaks. When he felt the young girl shiver in response, he laughed again, triumphantly, his breath warm against her satin skin.

"Did I not tell you your body hungers for the touch of a man?" he demanded arrogantly, straightening to look deep into the wide golden eyes, but he forgot his taunting question as soon as his gaze fastened itself to Raven's parted lips, her breath coming in quick gasps that, with every intake, forced the heavy, rounded breasts more firmly into his cupped hands.

Groaning raggedly, he took her unyielding form into his arms, laying Raven back against the dense cushion of gorse and sea grass. With fingers that were wont to tremble slightly, he drew the unlaced gown back from her shoulders, revealing the curving expanse of delicate collarbone and the shadowed hollow between her breasts, which lay tantalizingly exposed to him. Because she had ridden out under the protective cover of darkness, Raven had not bothered to don her corset or confining stays, and the ivory flesh that lay ripely bared to him beckoned with irresistible allure.

Raven could see his angular jaw tighten in the pale starlight. Heavy-lidded eyes raked her with a smoldering fire that took her breath away. Standing over her with long, booted legs spread apart, he seemed the embodiment of ultimate masculinity, his collar wide open so that she could see the sheen of sweat on the rigid expanse of his wide chest.

Their eyes met, and his full lips twitched with a smile of satanic satisfaction when he saw the wide-eyed innocence tempered by a banking passion he knew his roving hands and lips had aroused within her. With bold, unhurried movements he stripped off his shirt, tossing it aside, and Raven caught her breath when she saw the play of muscle and sinew that rippled beneath the sun-bronzed surface. Then he was unfastening his calfskin breeches, dropping them away from his lean hips and flanks. His hard, flat belly was covered with a fine layer of hair that tapered down to a firmly erect manhood made bold with the anticipation of savoring the sweetness of her woman's flesh.

Dropping to his knees beside her, he pulled Raven up to meet him, his arms encircling her so that they knelt as one, her bare breasts brushing his hard chest, his manhood searing her with its insinuating heat. With lips that devoured, he kissed her, the smell and taste of him filling her senses. Raven shivered, but not with fear. Her slender arms entwined themselves about his powerful neck, her fingers sliding into the wind-blown curls as her tongue met his in bold response to his seeking need.

One big hand was wrapped about the back of her head, and his palm cradled her slender neck as he crushed her to him in a fierce embrace that left Raven dizzy with longing. Knowing that he could wait no longer and that he would go mad if he did not possess her now, the muscular sea captain laid her gently back, every fiber within him screaming for consummation. Never in his life had he held a more fragile, slender, yet vibrantly alive woman in his arms whose very flesh seemed molded for his seeking hands and fiery lips. The need to possess her consumed him and drove him to the breaking point. For a timeless moment he gazed deeply into her eyes, the wide, questioning look within their amber depths filling him with the uncontrollable need to hold her slender body to his burning one and slake his desperate thirst within her.

Raven uttered a whimper as he bent over her, reaching out his hand to lift away the cumbersome skirts that still covered her, but she herself did not know if it was out of fear or because of her own growing need. She felt as though she had become a stranger to herself and that she could no longer control her will or her body. Both seemed inclined to follow this one man's passionate guidance, despite where she knew he intended to take her.

As she made an involuntary movement to stay his hand, he reached out quickly and seized her wrist with a firm but gentle grip. "No," he whispered hoarsely, "don't fear me, lass. I swear to God I will not hurt you."

Her tawny eyes seemed enormous to him in the faint starlight, the delicate cheeks stained a wild, wanton rose, and he willed himself with his entire awesome strength to hold to his word. Gently he pushed her restraining hands out of the way, but even as he moved to disrobe her completely he froze, warned by a finely honed sixth sense that someone was approaching.

"Captain! The tide be turnin'!"

The shout from below was faint but unmistakable above the dull booming of the foreshore waves. With a savage oath the tall, broad-shouldered man lifted his head, his strong hands poised only inches above her quivering, half-naked body. Raven, acting on instincts that were born entirely out of shock, jerked herself away from him, then, with arms outstretched, threw herself against his bare chest as hard as she could, palms striking him directly in the hard, rigid expanse of muscle. Thrown off balance, he staggered backward, and Raven, teeth clenched with determination, struggled to her feet and flung herself at him a second time so that he lost his balance and went sliding down the steep slope, landing with an ignoble thump upon his rear.

"And you claim that you can deal with my kind!" Raven called down with sarcastic contempt, her breathless voice carrying through the night air so that the men on the beach jerked their heads around. Biting her lips, she fought back the scalding tears of shame, aware that her body was still throbbing with need despite the anger that was beginning to course through her, despite the agonized realization of what she had nearly allowed a total stranger to do. "Quite apparently you've never had much to do with women of genteel breeding," she continued, her voice catching in a painful sob on the mocking words, "f-for you certainly couldn't handle me!"

Pulling her gown up over her shoulders, she lifted her rumpled skirts and dashed up the slope, her eyes like a cat's in the darkness, so that she was able to elude the man who lunged after her. Breath coming in gasps, she reached the top of the cliffs and whistled piercingly for Cinnabar, who trotted immediately to her side. Hauling herself onto his broad back, Raven kicked him savagely, and the big beast sprang away with a snort, spraying sand into the grimly set visage of the sea captain, who had reached the top of the slope directly behind them.

By the time the safe, familiar walls of the manor house came into view, Raven's racing heartbeat had slowed, and her breathing was nearly normal as she trotted the blowing Cinnabar up the drive to the darkened stables. Inwardly she was in a turmoil; guilt, anger, and helpless frustration warred with the shameful remembrance of the handsome smuggler captain's disturbingly passionate kisses. She felt she hated herself almost as much as she did him, fully aware that some secret womanly part of her had enjoyed his fiery, artful seduction. She felt confused by the conflicting emotions within her and enraged by the fact that her own body had betrayed her in such a strange, disquieting way.

How could she have allowed him to kiss her, to fondle her breasts, to press himself so intimately against her thighs? But for the timely intervention of his men, she would have let a loathsome smuggler remove her gown and make love to her. What was wrong with her? Raven wondered frantically. Did the Reverend Parminster's claim that she was not a virtuous woman have the ring of truth in it after all? It couldn't be, Raven moaned to herself, dismounting and unbuckling the saddle girth in the darkness of the stable aisle. She had merely succumbed to the attentions of an experienced, lustful rogue, and, being innocent herself, couldn't be blamed for falling prey to his love-making skills.

"I'll go straight to St. Ives tomorrow," Raven vowed, latching the loose box door behind the big stallion and stepping out into the darkness. But her resolve faded as she crept back into the silent house and tiptoed up the stairs to her bedroom. No telling what that conscienceless adventurer would tell Hamish Kilgannen upon being questioned about their encounter! Doubtless he had a crafty, silvered tongue and would shame her in the eyes of her neighbors and friends, provided of course, that he and his band of criminals were caught. Raven's tawny eyes hardened, knowing his ship would be long gone by morning, with not a single clue left behind to identify it.

It would be useless to go to Mr. Kilgannen, Raven realized reluctantly, and useless, too, to torment herself about what had happened. Better to forget the entire unpleasant encounter and consider herself lucky for having escaped without more damage to her person. Right now she needed sleep more than anything, to have her wits about her when her ten-o'clock visitor arrived. Better not to think about what had happened to her ever again.

Yet Raven found it difficult to put the episode out of her mind as she lay down in her bed and pulled the soft blankets over her body. Her lips were bruised and painful to the touch, and she could not forget the feel of the demanding, passionate mouth covering hers or the insistent arms about her. Damn you to hell, whoever you may be! Raven cursed silently to herself. Someday, she promised, we'll meet again, my arrogant friend, and then, by God, you'll pay for humiliating me like that!

Chapter Two

At precisely nine-thirty the following morning Raven was seated behind her father's enormous desk, Mr. Haggart's papers spread out neatly before her. Sunlight streamed through the mullioned windows behind her, warming her slender shoulders, but Raven, preoccupied with other matters, didn't notice. She had dressed with care that morning in anticipation of her meeting, and her gleaming black hair was plaited and pinned to her head in a fashion that brought new maturity to her delicate features, emphasizing the hollow shadows beneath her cheeks and giving her, she hoped, a sophisticated look that would mask her young years. Her gown of soft gray muslin was of a simple cut, the collar lined with a ruching of delicate ecru lace, the trim bodice fastened with tiny pearl buttons. Although she was dreading the forthcoming interview, part of her could not help lingering on the night before. Memories of the disturbing encounter with the handsome sea captain invaded her thoughts far more than she liked and refused to fade no matter how often she pushed them from her mind.

"Will you be wanting tea when your visitor comes?" Danny inquired anxiously from the doorway, startling Raven, who hadn't heard her come in.

"That would be grand, Danny," Raven replied with a heartiness she was far from feeling, her soft smile reassuring nonetheless. She leaned back in the comfortable chair and peered up at the old woman with an anxious expression. "Do I look businesslike enough, do you think?"

This time it was Danny who smiled reassuringly as she looked down into the beautiful face, the shining black curls swept softly from Raven's smooth brow. The pleading, childlike expression was touching in contrast to the sophisticated hair style and prim, no-nonsense gown. "You look quite the role of Miss Raven Barrancourt, administrator of North Head estate," she assured her young mistress firmly. "Your visitor, whoever he may be, should be impressed."

Raven dimpled despite herself, her golden eyes glowing with some of her old spirit. "Oh, go on, Danny, you've a greased tongue not worth listening to."

The silver-haired governess looked relieved, not offended, to hear this, but wagged her finger warningly nonetheless. "Now, don't be too sassy with him, Miss Raven. Remember, you've got to be tactful. Your father always said one could attract more flies with sugar than with vinegar."

"Flies are easy to kill," Raven replied, growing serious, "but this one, I'm afraid, will require more skill to vanquish than the wielding of a folded newspaper."

"Miss Raven!" It was Parris hovering in the doorway behind Danny, towering over the small woman as he peered in at his mistress, who was trying her best to look commanding in the enormous leather chair that all but swallowed her up.

"What is it, Parris?" Raven asked worriedly, never having known the proper old butler to speak so excitedly.

"A carriage just pulled up in the drive, Miss Raven. It belongs to Squire Blackburn."

The rosy color drained from Raven's soft cheeks. "Squire Blackburn?" she repeated disbelievingly.

Parris nodded his graying head. "Indeed! I saw him myself from the window."

Raven chewed her lower lip nervously, then looked up at the two faithful servants, her eyes glowing with determination. "Danny, if you'll excuse me, please, I'll handle him alone. Parris, will you show him in?"

The relief was obvious in both kind old faces, Raven's arched eyebrows and set jaw a perfect imitation of her father's, had she but known it. Parris bowed politely and withdrew while Danny gave her defiantly scowling mistress a brief encouraging smile before following him out.

"Master Blackburn's in for a regular roasting if Miss Raven puts the Barrancourt hard-headedness to him the way she seems ready to," she remarked to the butler, who was fastidiously adjusting his cuffs and cravat.

Parris allowed himself the luxury of one brief grin. "I certainly wouldn't care to be in his shoes if that happens."

"Unless North Head belongs to him already," Danny added, suddenly anxious. "Is it possible, do you think?"

Parris's features settled into the stony, unreadable countenance for which he was best known. "I'm afraid Miss Raven owes him quite a bit of money."

"Surely not more than North Head be worth!" Danny persisted, twisting her hands together fearfully, her round face filled with despair.

"Miss Raven didn't elaborate when she explained the situation to me," Parris went on darkly, "but it might very well be, Hannah." A bold knock against the iron-braced front door brought an answering scowl of disapproval to the old man's face. "I vow that stuffy gentleman intends to force our brass knocker right through the wood."

Raven, hearing the dull boom echo through the hall, felt her heart twist within her breast. Not counting the Barrancourts, Squire Blackburn was the wealthiest landowner in all of west Cornwall, although Blackburn Hall was nowhere near as grand as North Head. It was said that the squire loved his money so well that he preferred to keep all of it in gold and silver coins rather than spend any on improving his residence. Doubtless it was true, Raven thought mournfully to herself, for how else could her father have borrowed so much from him if he didn't possess a lot of ready money, while the Barrancourt fortune was mostly tied up in land and other capital expenditures? Her father had always called North Head a working farm, though he had always laughed when he said it, but Raven knew that he had been ambitious and hard-working, never content to play the role of retiring gentleman farmer. Most of his investments had paid off handsomely, yet how could he have known in advance that those he had borrowed heavily from Squire Blackburn to invest in would prove so disastrous?

"Squire Blackburn to see Miss Raven Barrancourt," came Parris's stentorian tones from the doorway, and Raven, startled from her reverie, looked up quickly as her visitor strode inside. She knew him slightly, for he had come to North Head several times in the past, the last visit having been a month or two before her father's tragic accident. She had even poured tea for him back then, her father smiling paternally as she performed the duty of hostess with graceful, fluid movements, though she hadn't cared too much for the way the fat little squire kept staring at her breasts, whose rounded fullness was easily visible in the sprigged muslin gown she had been wearing. Afterward her father had dismissed her with a curt wave of his band, having business matters to discuss with the squire, but his warm smile, intended privately for her, had told her that she had done very well.

Now Raven knew exactly what sort of business had transpired within the richly paneled walls of this study, and her smile was forced and tinged with sadness as she rose to her feet to greet the squire, resplendent in dark blue superfine, his vest straining over his ample belly. Her tawny eyes were welcoming, but her expression was extremely wary.

"Kind of you to receive me so early in the morning, Miss Barrancourt," he said, accepting Raven's reluctantly offered hand and planting his moist lips upon her soft skin. His puffy eyes moved upward to her breasts and the creamy expanse of flesh visible above the frilly neckline of her gray gown. "You're looking well considering the shock you so recently received." He shook his head sadly. The wisps of oiled hair that covered his balding head exuded the odor of nauseatingly sweet pomade. "Terrible tragedy, your father's death."

"It was the will of God," Raven replied stiffly, retreating behind the big desk, where she felt safer.

The bushy eyebrows rose in surprise. "A realist, are you, Miss Barrancourt, or a fatalist?"

"Neither, I imagine, sir. My father always made it a point to ride high-strung, untried young horses, and I believe it was an act of God that took him from me this time and not some other."

"You Barrancourts have always been uncontrollably wild," Squire Blackburn stated, giving Raven an intimate wink as he lowered himself, uninvited, into the armchair that faced the big desk. "It must be that Celtic blood of yours."

Raven sat down distrustfully, her slim back ramrod-stiff, facing him as might a soldier squaring off against the enemy in battle, for indeed she felt that she would fight to the death if need be to keep North Head out of the squire's grasping hands. She knew him for what he was; the tales from the local folk were too numerous to be ignored: how tightfisted he was with the servants, how he beat them for any disobedience, real or imagined, how poachers on his lands were turned over immediately to the magistrates even if they had committed the offense because they were poor and starving. Oh, God, she prayed silently, let there be some simple way to settle my debts with this objectionable little man!

Raven became aware of the fact that Squire Blackburn was watching her covetously from beneath heavy lids, his eyes traveling slowly from the top of her glossy black head, down the long, arching column of her neck, to the bodice where her full breasts strained against the soft gray material of her gown. She forced herself to suffer his rude appraisal, her hands clenched into small fists in her lap, though the expression on her beautiful face was beguilingly innocent, her dimpled smile sweet.

"I imagine Haggart went over the paperwork with you yesterday," he began unexpectedly, making her jump, jabbing at the folders before her with a stubby index finger.

"Yes, he did," Raven replied, caught off guard.

The protruding eyes watched her keenly. "Then you must realize that your father owed me a great deal of money when he died, Miss Barrancourt. I could have laid claim to North Head before the estate was settled, but"—he spread his plump hands appealingly—"I couldn't be so unchivalrous to you in your time of grief."

"How very kind of you," Raven murmured, swallowing hard. "Squire, you said you planned to l-lay claim on North Head?"

"Of course. It's a perfectly legal move on my part. You see, were you to turn over to me your land, your livestock, your house furnishings, your mother's jewelry, the few oils hanging in the gallery that are worthy of note, the debt would, by and large, be repaid."

"But not North Head itself," Raven said.

Squire Blackburn squinted at her uncomprehendingly. "Eh?"

"If I deeded everything to you that you just named, the debt would be settled," Raven said.

"It would, yes."

"And North Head, the house itself, would still be mine."

"In effect."

"Then consider it done, sir!"

Squire Blackburn looked at her in bewilderment. Raven's cheeks were flushed, her eyes glowing like liquid gold. She was leaning forward in her chair, her breasts rising and falling, her breathing rapid, but the squire was, for once, oblivious to her beauty. "What are you saying, girl?" he sputtered in confusion. "You intend to turn it all over to me?"

Raven nodded eagerly.

"You must be mad!" the squire cried, striking his fist on the desk top for emphasis, his cheeks suffused with color. "All you'd have left is an empty house!"

"But it would still be mine," Raven countered proudly, her chin lifted, the golden eyes meeting his squarely.

"And you'd be a pauper! My God, girl, are you so stupid you don't realize you'd have no way of earning income, no land to farm, no tenants, no servants to keep the house from crumbling over your head?"

Raven blanched, not having thought of those things at all. Her elation died quickly, leaving a despairing numbness in its stead. Lowering her eyes, she fought back the tears that threatened to fall and said nothing.

"Now, now, Miss Barrancourt, I didn't intend to speak so roughly with you," the squire told her kindly. "I just wanted to make sure that you understand that your problems can't be settled quite so easily. When I told you you'd have to give me everything, I was merely trying to make a point about where we really stand in relation to your possessions, the house included."

He paused, his protruding little eyes roving the gleaming walnut paneling and the plush Oriental carpet covering the polished floor, then moving up to the shelves lined with buckram- and leather-bound books, their titles stamped in gold, many of them rare and extremely valuable. "I can well understand your reluctance to give up this house. Its charm has affected me also, and I've always thought of it as an extension of the sea itself. The way the windows open to the water and the sun, the high ceilings that give you such an open, airy feeling when you step inside. Truly a welcoming house, Miss Barrancourt, despite the fact that it sits so precariously here on these cliffs."

Raven studied his florid features sharply, her eyes filled with surprise and suspicion, never having thought of Squire Blackburn as the sort of man who would appreciate something like that about North Head, or would even have noticed, for that matter. Everything he had said about the manor was true, however, though the glint in his bovine eyes as he spoke had been more of avarice than of wonder. How could she explain to him that she loved every exposed wooden beam in the Great Hall, every beautiful hand-painted tile covering the big fireplaces, every towering tree that shaded the grassy glades and budding flowers? That she wouldn't give any of it up even if it meant condemning herself to a life of utter penury?

"No, Miss Barrancourt," Squire Blackburn went on, taking her silence for agreement, "North Head is far too grand, too magnificent to allow it to fall into neglect. I could take your lands, your stock, your belongings from you and cancel our debt, but your poverty and the demise of this wonderful estate would be on my conscience forever."

How odd, Raven thought bitterly to herself; it's said you don't even have a conscience, squire. Why, then, this stirring of compassion toward me now? What's in it for you?

"Therefore, the deal Mr. Haggart mentioned to you yesterday," he went on complacently, leaning back in his chair and lacing his blunt fingers over his rounded belly, beaming officiously at her, his confidence setting Raven's teeth on edge. "I plan to make you an offer, Miss Barrancourt, that will guarantee North Head to remain in your possession, every facet intact, for the remainder of your life."

Raven felt herself growing dizzy with hope, but struggled not to let her elation show, knowing enough of Squire Blackburn's true character not to trust him. Danny had sniffed disparagingly after the squire's last visit, saying the man hadn't a compassionate bone in his overweight body, and Danny's judgments of other people were not to be dismissed lightly. So Raven waited wordlessly, sitting straight and proud behind the polished oak desk, doing her best to look calm and collected, though inwardly she was greatly afraid.

Squire Blackburn cleared his throat, and his gaze slid away unexpectedly from the golden eyes that were watching him steadily. His fingers drummed a maddening tattoo on his belly; then he sat up suddenly and said boldly, "You'd keep all of this, Miss Barrancourt, if you agreed to become my wife."

Raven, who had been expecting anything but this, found it nearly impossible to keep the shock from her face. She gasped, her soft lips parted, her eyes wide, and clutched at the desk top with her slender fingers, wondering if she were going to faint. Wed Squire Blackburn? Why, the man was almost sixty, ugly, fat, unkind, with two horse-faced daughters named Cleone and Agatha or something utterly unattractive like that who were nearly as old as she was! Marry the man? He must be mad!

"Naturally the three of us would come here to live," Squire Blackburn went on jovially, oblivious to Raven's extreme pallor and unnatural silence. The puffy eyes gleamed with greed. "I've always fancied living in North Head manor myself, and I know Aggie and Cleone will be simply overjoyed to learn they're to have a new mother." He cackled gleefully. "I'm convinced our good Reverend Parminster would be delighted to officiate at the nuptials. He's always taken a special interest in you, hasn't he, my dear?" he added with ill-concealed contempt.

"And... and if I don't accept your offer?" Raven asked, ignoring his question, her voice barely audible.

Squire Blackburn shrugged. "It's really quite simple. North Head will be mine and you'll be without a home or a penny to your name." He spread his hands appealingly. "Be reasonable, Miss Barrancourt. My proposal would prove beneficial to both of us. Oh, I'm aware that now you've no feelings toward me in regards of the love that should exist between a man and his wife, but"—the protruding eyes fastened themselves to her breasts, and he ran a tongue across his thick lips—"I'm confident that will come in time."

Raven swallowed hard to overcome her nausea and despair. What Squire Blackburn was suggesting was thoroughly odious to her. She would rather die than marry him, even if it meant giving up North Head! Her eyes filled with tears. She could never give up North Head, never, so what was she to do? How could she find the money to pay the squire back, or even gain enough time in which to search for it before he pressured her either into marrying him or leaving her home? Despairingly she turned her trim back on the portly gentleman seated before her, trying to find an answer and drawing strength from the scenery that met her anxious eyes beyond the leaded windows.

The weather had finally cleared during the night, and the late-morning sun was spiraling slowly into a cloudless, azure sky. The sea beneath it was a deep indigo blue, and the gold of full summer touched the reeds that grew along the face of the cliffs beyond the small stretch of lovingly tended lawn that separated North Head from the barren cliffs. A single sea gull wheeled overhead, then dived with a rush of wings into the water, breaking the surface and returning to the heavens with a gleaming silver fish in its sharp beak. A fishing boat, lured by the return of warmer weather, had set its course from St. Ives toward the treacherous waters near Land's End, the sails freshening as they caught the brisk wind that sent it racing past the welcoming brick walls of North Head, which, for centuries, had greeted the fishing fleet as the boats returned, one by one, from a hard day's catch.

Raven tried hard to swallow the lump in her throat at the sight that met her eyes, every nuance as dear to her as her life itself. How could she give this up, her very existence? Worse still, how could she sacrifice her happiness by agreeing to marry a man whom she not only didn't love but who so thoroughly repelled her? As she sat pondering in anguish the sun-drenched, rugged beauty beyond the study windows, a noisy bottlefly that had somehow made its way indoors flew against the mullioned pane and buzzed fruitlessly in an effort to get out. Raven was suddenly reminded of what Danny had said earlier about attracting flies with sugar, and she bit down hard on her lower lip to keep from yelping in joy as the solution to her problem all but overwhelmed her.

"Miss Barrancourt?" the squire asked impatiently.

Raven turned around, her eyes wide and innocent. "Forgive me for seeming to ignore you, sir. I was considering your proposal."

The squire's moist lips were parted, and he leaned forward in his chair, eyeing her eagerly. "Yes?"

"I think," Raven replied, rising to her feet and moving gracefully around the desk toward him, "that I have no other means of repaying the debt my father owed you." She hoped her voice sounded sweet and guileless and revealed none of her revulsion. The art of deceit did not come easy, and she was not sure if the provocative swaying of her hips as she came to stand before him was so obvious as to be transparent. Yet she persisted, smiling down at him shyly, her tone suitably demure. "Under the circumstances, however, you must agree that it would be improper of me to accept your kind offer until the year of mourning has ended."

Squire Blackburn could scarcely believe his good fortune. "Yes, yes, of course," he intoned, rising quickly to his feet and gazing avidly into Raven's pale face. "Then I take it this means you'll become my wife?"

"If you will grant me a year's deferment on the loan," Raven replied with as saucy a smile as she could muster, dimpling impishly, though the expression in her eyes was strained and anxious.

Squire Blackburn contained himself admirably. "Why, yes, yes, of course, Miss Barrancourt... Raven, I quite understand!" Seizing her hand in his, he brought it to his lips, and Raven gritted her teeth, willing herself not to snatch it away.

"And the announcement," she added sweetly, "it should wait until then, too, don't you think? You wouldn't want people to say I'd been pressured into accepting your kind offer while under the influence of grief?"

Squire Blackburn's normally cautious and suspicious mind might have caused him to doubt his good fortune and look more sharply into Raven's motives for agreeing so quickly, but he was rather befuddled at the moment by her nearness, overwhelmed by the sweet, perfumed scent of her body and the close proximity of her firm, high breasts, almost level with his eyes as he raised his head after bowing low over her small hand. The golden eyes were looking boldly into his, and he thought he saw a provocative invitation in the wry little smile that twisted her soft lips.

"Naturally not," he assured her quickly. "I wouldn't want anything to mar the good name of my future wife, especially malicious gossip."

"Then it's agreed?" Raven asked innocently, her heart hammering so wildly that she felt dizzy. "In one year, if the debt hasn't been repaid, I'll become your wife?"

"It's what I wish more than anything, Miss Barr—Raven, my dear," the squire quavered huskily.

It was all Raven could do to continue smiling as he kissed her hand again and promised to call on her soon. When Parris appeared in response to her summons she was smiling still, but the faithful old servant was quick to notice the unusual pallor of her skin and the weakness of her voice.

"Yes, Miss Raven?" he asked, sounding anxious despite his best efforts to disguise his feelings.

"Show Squire Blackburn out, please," she said thinly, forgetting entirely that she should have offered her new intended refreshments, but the squire did not appear to have noticed the oversight either. With one last, longing look at the slender form Raven revealed for him in her soft gray gown, he put on his hat and allowed the silent Parris to lead him to the door. As soon as he was gone, Raven collapsed in the plush armchair he had recently vacated and vented her mingled joy, despair, and relief in a flood of tears so stormy that when Parris and a doubly anxious Danny rushed to her side, both of them were certain that North Head was doomed.

"No, no, that isn't it!" Raven assured them, smiling tremulously through her tears as she fumbled about for a handkerchief. "Actually, I've been granted a year's grace!"

Parris and Danny exchanged blank looks, and Raven was forced to laugh weakly at their bewilderment. "Squire Blackburn has agreed to make no demand for the money Father owed him until next June," Raven explained, drying her eyes and shaking her head disbelievingly. "I can't believe he was so easy to persuade!"

"Nor can I," Danny remarked acidly, not at all convinced.

"But how did you manage it, miss?" Parris asked wonderingly, though it was not his usual habit to interfere in Barrancourt affairs. Instantly he flushed, deeply ashamed of himself. "I'm sorry, miss, it's no concern of mine," he stammered miserably, turning away, but Raven's low laugh made him pause in the doorway.

"Naturally you've a right to know, Parris. You've been living at North Head even longer than I have, and your father and grandfather before you." She rose to her feet and smiled warmly at the two beloved faces regarding her intently. "You see, if I don't have the money when next June comes, I'm to become the squire's wife."

Danny's wail of despair drowned out Parris's shocked exclamations, but Raven refused to allow them to say anything more. Imperiously she held up her hand for silence and continued primly, "That, of course, will never happen, because I fully intend to have the money long before then."

"Where in Heaven's name will you get such a sum?" Danny demanded, unappeased, wringing her hands and fighting back her tears at the thought of her beautiful young Raven wed to the odious squire.

Raven shrugged with the optimism born of profound relief. "I don't know yet. One of Father's banks, I imagine. Surely they'll agree to extend credit if I explain the circumstances! And if not, there's Great-Uncle Hadrian living in London, who supposedly has more money than Croesus himself!"

"You've never even met your great-uncle Hadrian!" Danny cried, "and he never got on well with your father at all! Neither of them exchanged so much as a single letter these past fifteen years!"

"I don't care," Raven replied with a toss of her head. "He's a Barrancourt, isn't he, and he couldn't be so cruel as to ignore a member of his own family who truly needs him!" She stood with her arms akimbo, searching first one doubtful face, then the other, her delicate features filled with annoyance. "Honestly, I would have expected you to be happy about this! I've managed to keep the wolf from our door for at least another year, and both of you look as though I'm ready to take my marriage vows tomorrow!"

Parris shuddered as though this thought were too horrible to contemplate. "Shall I bring you a beverage, miss? Some tea perhaps?" he asked, certain that everything would be well at North Head as long as that proper custom was observed.

"Yes, please," Raven replied. "Oh, and bring some of those strawberry tarts, Parris. I'm fair starving!"

"Oh, Miss Raven, surely you didn't really agree to marry that horrible man!" Danny cried as soon as the two of them were alone in the comfortable study.

"I've no intention of doing so," Raven replied with a scowl. "How mad do you think I am? I'll have the money by then, that I swear."

Danny knew it was useless to argue when her young mistress chose to use such a stubborn tone of voice, but her misgivings continued to show in her set expression.

"After luncheon, Danny, I intend to drive to St. Ives and then to Truro," Raven added speculatively, her eyes focused on the sunlit ocean that lay placid and blue beyond the window panes. "I expect we'll have to spend the night there. Will you come with me?"

"And do you think I'd let you travel alone?" the old governess asked, shocked.

Raven's soft lips twitched at the sight of Danny's fierce expression. "Of course not." Her own determination grew. "Now, what do you think I should wear when I go see the bankers? Something not too frivolous, I imagine. Perhaps black would be the most appropriate since my rather unconventional ways aren't well known in Truro." Her small face was suddenly bleak. Oh, Papa, she thought to herself, forgive me for making a mockery of this mourning period for you! "Yes," she added in a soft whisper, "black would be best."

Truro was a thriving town sprawled along the banks of the winding Truro River. The houses and shops that greeted Raven and Danny as their carriage rolled down the busy streets later that afternoon were clean and well kept, the outlying cottages colorful and quaint. Street vendors hawked their wares, and in the noisy market square bull calves and fine dairy milkers were being auctioned while rough-clothed farmhands with powerful forearms and florid faces wrestled in a roped-off ring to the shouts and encouragement of boisterous onlookers.

Women carrying enormous baskets, with children clutching at their skirts of colorful homespun, pushed their way past richly attired merchants and shopkeepers who were standing beneath the awnings of their stores to enjoy the warm summer sunshine. Raven, who had been to Truro several times in the past, would have enjoyed the colorful sights and sounds of the market square and the busy streets, but she could not forget why they were here, and her eyes glowed almost feverishly as she sat quietly at Danny's side in the narrow confines of their carriage.

Their visit to St. Ives had been brief and disappointingly fruitless, the tiny fishing village being the residence of Sir Joshua Derwentwater, an old acquaintance of Raven's father who, upon retiring from active duty in his Truro bank, had built himself a small but charming home in a quiet cove by the shore. He had been cordial, greeting Raven fondly, but had been unable to lend the assistance she so desperately sought. A loan of such a large amount, he informed her, could not be made by a bank so limited in capital as Derwentwater and Trowbridge's in Truro.

Undaunted, Raven had thanked him politely and had set out for Truro anyway, for her father had done business not only with Sir Joshua's bank but several others, and she was determined to ask at all of them. Surely someone would be willing to take into account the well-respected Barrancourt name and lend her the amount she needed!

"Here we are, Danny," she remarked, returning from her reverie when the well-sprung vehicle jerked to a halt before an ornate building of warm, honey-colored stone, its name and the date of its construction carved in bold Roman letters above the brass-plated doors. Raven, leaving Danny inside the carriage to wait for her, stepped down onto the street and retied the ribbons of her bonnet beneath her small chin. The black gauze that obscured the upper half of her oval face did not conceal the glitter of her eyes as she swallowed hard and squared her slender shoulders before passing through the thick wooden doors.

The interior of the bank was cool and dark, the polished wood and the patterned tile floor as austere as the provincial furnishings. After addressing a uniformed guard, Raven was solicitously escorted into a back office that resembled the elegant study of a learned gentleman, with books overflowing the crowded shelves and a highly polished desk standing in the corner beneath the tall, curtained window. A gentleman in somber attire with graying muttonchop whiskers rose at the sight of the slim young woman dressed in mourning black. He reached out his hand so that Raven was forced to move across the room to lay her own small gloved one in it.

"My dear Miss Barrancourt," the gentleman said with a firm handshake, his moist eyes warm as they regarded her, "what a pleasure to see you here."

As soon as he spoke, Raven recognized the clipped, educated tone of Henry Metcalfe, who had been present at her father's funeral three months ago. That she could remember him, having met him only once and then when her mind was overshadowed with grief, was surprising to her, but she smiled back at him warmly and replied that she was delighted to see him again.

"I hope you've been doing well," Mr. Metcalfe went on kindly, pulling up a chair before his desk and seating Raven comfortably before sitting down himself. "The past few months couldn't have been easy for you."

"I've been doing my best," Raven assured him with a thin smile, removing her gloves and untying her bonnet, laying them down on the chair beside her. Smoothing back her shining black hair, she looked steadily at him, wondering how best to begin.

"A terrible tragedy," the elderly gentleman was saying with

a sad shake of his head, shuffling the papers about on his desk. "At least you can derive some comfort in knowing that your father did not suffer."

"His neck was snapped instantly when the horse rolled on top of him," Raven explained with lowered eyes.

"Terrible, terrible. You're looking rather peaked, Miss Barrancourt. Would you care for a cup of tea?"

"That's very kind of you, but thank you, no," Raven replied quickly, desperate to come to the point but afraid to seem pushy by broaching the matter first. Apparently Henry Metcalfe could sense her urgency, for he leaned back comfortably in his padded leather chair and regarded her in a fatherly fashion.

"How may we be of assistance to you, Miss Barrancourt?"

"I-I need a loan," Raven stammered, her face filled with desperation although she forced her voice to remain calm and low, certain that one thing all bankers abhorred in general was being confronted by a hysterical female asking for money. Twisting her hands together in her lap, she held her breath while Mr. Metcalfe pursed his lips and stared hard at a spot on the wainscoted wall beyond her slender shoulders.

"I can well imagine that running the estate is extremely difficult for you, Miss Barrancourt. Are you alone responsible for everything?" the gray eyes were kind as they regarded her, and Raven felt some of her trepidation begin to fade.

"Not really. There is... well, John Speedwell, my father's steward, has been a tremendous help since my father died. He manages the farms, the stock, and the acreage. I suppose you could say I take care of the administrative end, the bills and the books, that sort of thing."

"Most commendable of you, Miss Barrancourt," Henry Metcalfe said approvingly, his eyes lingering on her youthful face and slim, black-clad form, finding it hard to believe that such a slip of a girl could run an estate the size of North Head efficiently even with a steward's help. "Now, then." He leaned forward in his chair, the leather creaking, and steepled his long fingers together before him. "How much money did you have in mind, Miss Barrancourt, and how is it to be used?"

Raven swallowed hard, a wave of heat overwhelming her. "I-I—"

"Miss Barrancourt, aren't you well?" Raven heard him ask,

and forced herself to smile reassuringly, cursing herself for her sudden attack of cowardice. How could she present a capable, controlled image stammering like this?

"I'm fine, thank you," she said weakly and cleared her throat before speaking again. This time her voice was firm and steady, her eyes on level with his. "I'm afraid the sum is rather high, sir."

The muttonchop whiskers twitched as Mr. Metcalfe forced down a smile. "No loan we make is ever insignificant, Miss Barrancourt! Now then, how much?"

"I'm afraid I—it's over fifty thousand pounds."

"Preposterous!" Henry Metcalfe exploded.

"I beg your pardon?" Raven asked.

"I'm sorry, Miss Barrancourt. It's out of the question. Totally impossible."

"But—"

"Precisely how did you plan to pay back a loan like that? Why, the interest alone—"

"But you don't understand, sir!" Raven interrupted, her voice trembling despite her best efforts. "North Head is in danger of being forfeited, and I must have the money to repay my father's debts."

"I was aware that your father had made some poor investments recently," Henry Metcalfe said sympathetically, "though I wasn't personally involved. Derwentwater handled most of the negotiations along with that fellow Haggart from Tradby's. Seems the money was borrowed from a private source, wasn't it?"

"Yes, it was," Raven continued desperately, her soft cheeks flushed above the high ruffled collar of her black satin gown. "And the gentleman in question is expecting payment. Please, Mr. Metcalfe, if you don't give me the loan I'll lose North Head!" Her voice rang with passion, and though her vision misted she fought back her tears and sat regarding him anxiously, her small hands clasped as though for support around the hard wooden arms of her chair.

Henry Metcalfe's gaze slid away from her pleading eyes, and he shifted restlessly in his chair. For a moment there was silence within the elegant, dimly lit room, and the sounds of the street outside seemed unnaturally loud as they penetrated the thick stone walls. "Our bank would be happy to lend you a lesser sum, Miss Barrancourt, based on the excellent standing of the Barrancourt name within our institution. Say up to twenty thousand pounds with payments not—"

"That isn't enough!" Raven cried. To quiet her rising hysteria she bit down hard on her lower lip, and the pain brought her to her senses. "I need almost three times that amount," she finished quietly.

Henry Metcalfe spread his hands appealingly. "I'm sorry, Miss Barrancourt, it's impossible. Our creditors, the stockholders of the company, would never agree, especially since, I'm sorry to say, your age and inexperience are significant factors in assuring that the loan will be repaid."

"I'd pay back every penny," Raven replied through gritted teeth, her eyes glowing with determination.

The banker's expression was kind. "Raven, let me speak plainly. I knew your father well enough to see quite a bit of him in you, and I for one wouldn't doubt for a moment your ability to maintain North Head, even though you are a woman and of a very tender age. But I'm not the one who would make that decision. That is the responsibility of the Board. Quite frankly, personal opinions and long-standing friendships aside, they would all consider you a bad risk."

"Then I'll not get the money from you?" Raven asked, knowing she wouldn't.

He shook his gray head sorrowfully. "I'm afraid not."

Raven's lower lip began to tremble, and she bit down hard upon it again, welcoming the pain that kept the tears away. Oh God, if only she could make him see how desperate her plight was! A vision of Squire Blackburn's fleshy, insipid face floated before her, and she could almost see the avarice in his bleary eyes as they fastened themselves hungrily to her breasts, could almost feel his pudgy hands touching her intimately, as a man surely must when he makes love to his wife. Judas, no! The thought of sharing a bed with the fat, oily little man filled her with revulsion.

Raven glanced up into Henry Metcalfe's set, unyielding expression, hoping to find some sort of indication there that he was weakening. Her own beautiful features were outwardly composed, but inwardly she longed to scream at him, to shake him until he agreed to lend her the money she needed, or to throw herself at his feet and beg like some pitiful pauper. Yet she could not. Barrancourts did not grovel, and in the face of utter defeat her father would have expected her to behave graciously.

"You've been more than kind, sir," Raven said politely, rising stiffly to her feet and attempting to give him a steady smile. "Thank you."

"I'm sorry," he said simply, and she hated to see the pity and helplessness in the kindly gray eyes.

"I understand." She took a deep, shaky breath. "Good day, Mr. Metcalfe."

"Miss Barrancourt?"

Raven turned at the door, her satin skirts rustling. "Yes?"

"If there's anything I can do for you, in a personal or professional capacity, will you let me know?"

Despite her best efforts, tears gathered in her eyes as she inclined her head and tied the small plumed bonnet beneath her chin. "I will. Thank you." She fought the tears back as she hurried across the carpeted floor of the main room of the bank, ignoring the curious looks of the other patrons, and allowed the coachman to help her into the waiting vehicle, where an anxious Danny made room for her on the worn leather seat.

"Where to, Miss Raven?" the coachman asked politely, thrusting his head inside the door.

"North Head, Edwards, if you please," Raven instructed tearfully. "We'll not be staying the night in Truro."

The coachman touched his cap politely and latched the door firmly behind him. With a crack of the whip the coach lurched off down the street, the horses responding smoothly to his experienced hands. Minutes later they were swaying through the countryside, the outlying houses and cottages of Truro already behind them, the sun-drenched moors and lonely heaths ahead. Danny, casting a furtive glance at her, saw that Raven was staring unseeingly out the window, her delicate profile achingly defenseless.

Poor little lassie, Danny thought to herself. Opening her reticule, she rummaged about for a handkerchief, certain that her young mistress would burst into tears at any moment.

"Danny, we'll simply have to go to London!"

The determined little voice so startled the former governess that the reticule slipped, unnoticed, to the carriage floor. "What?"

Raven's golden eyes were glowing as she turned eagerly to face the astonished woman. "None of the banks will help me, so I have no recourse but to turn to the family. Great-Uncle Hadrian will lend me the amount I need or—"

"Or heaven help him!" Danny groaned, recognizing the fierce, determined look in Raven's eyes.

"If Great-Uncle Hadrian refuses to help me," Raven said softly, her slender jaw tightening, "then heaven help us all!"

Chapter Three

Dating back to the early eighteenth century, the residential architecture of Knightsbridge, south of Hyde Park in the city of London, rivaled in elegance those townhouses and rambling estates of fashionable Mayfair. On a quiet, winding street not far from Kensington Road stood the graceful home of Sir Hadrian Barrancourt, former director of Booth's, the enormous tea and silk emporium which, with backing from private citizens and the British East India Company, had held for many years a monopoly on the London market. The house was constructed of earth-colored brick, the mansard roof flanked by imposing corner towers and massive chimneys. Rows of shuttered sash windows opened to the pleasant garden, the comfortably crumbling brick wall that separated it from the street overgrown with lush green ivy.

It was midafternoon on a humid, overcast day when the Barrancourt coach rumbled to a halt near the curb. Edwards climbed down off his box to lower the steps and solicitously help his young mistress to the ground. Raven, stepping onto the sidewalk, paused for a moment with her skirts held in one hand, staring up at the imposing house and wondering if her great-uncle would be home to receive her. She felt both cross and anxious. She was exhausted from the long, bone-jarring journey and wished she had the time to bathe and rest before undergoing the interview with the great-uncle she had never met. So much depended on making a favorable impression, and for a moment Raven's courage failed her as the enormity of her responsibility overwhelmed her.

"Miss Raven, aren't you well?" Edwards asked kindly, noticing her pale cheeks and pensive expression.

"I'm fine," she assured him, giving him a weak smile.

"Are you sure you don't want Mrs. Daniels or myself to go in with you?"

Raven shook her head firmly. "I don't want to make Great-Uncle Hadrian feel as though his chambers are being invaded." Her soft cheeks dimpled, and the tawny eyes grew less apprehensive. "Into the lion's den, then," she said, half to herself. Squaring her delicate shoulders, she opened the wrought-iron gate and stepped into the garden, her head held high. Lifting her ruffled, sherry-colored satin skirts, she ascended the wide, flat steps and knocked boldly on the polished oak door. When it was opened several moments later, creaking on its heavy bracings as it swung inward, the immaculately attired major-domo who appeared on the threshold was permitted no time to step aside before Raven swept in, a swish of satin skirts and the faint, tantalizing fragrance of some sweet perfume accompanying her.

"I am Raven Barrancourt," she announced with an imperiously arched eyebrow. "Will you please inform Sir Hadrian that his grandniece is here from Cornwall to see him?"

"I beg your pardon?" the major-domo asked, blinking in astonishment at the sight of the beautiful, raven-haired girl who stood proudly before him in the elegant satin gown that matched the color of her eyes. A daintily woven shawl was draped over her slender shoulders, her glossy black hair gently brushing against it, and as the major-domo regarded her curiously she smiled at him, revealing the two dimples in her soft, rosy cheeks.

"I am Raven Barrancourt, Sir Hadrian's grandniece," she repeated, hoping she sounded suitably forceful, unaware that she had already conquered the major-domo with one simple, unaffected smile.

"I'm afraid Sir Hadrian isn't receiving visitors at present," the liveried individual informed her apologetically. "He hasn't been well of late."

The golden eyes hardened. "But I must see him! You don't understand. I—"

"I'm sorry, Miss Barrancourt, not today," the major-domo informed her politely but firmly, deliberately avoiding the pleading expression, knowing full well that his resolve would crumble if he glanced even briefly into the lovely oval face. "Perhaps tomorrow, if Sir Hadrian is feeling stronger."

Raven's soft lips trembled and her small jaw jutted. "I will not leave until I have seen him."

"I'm afraid—"

"Who the devil is it, Jeffords?" came a querulous voice from the interior of the stately house.

Raven turned her head quickly, her eyes falling on a gilded door that stood partially ajar farther down the mirrored hallway. Moving quickly, she slipped around the unsuspecting major-domo and reached the doorway just as the startled Jeffords reacted and sprang in front of her, attempting to block her way. Raven, equally determined to succeed, lifted her satin skirts and came down hard on the poor man's instep with the heel of her small traveling shoe. The astonished Jeffords let out a bellow of pain, and Raven, though she was extremely sorry for what she had done, took advantage of his momentary distraction to push her way inside.

Slamming the door shut behind her, she whirled about quickly to find herself in a pleasant drawing room of lush gold and red velvet, the flocked wallpaper of glorious red cupids, the length of the ceiling trimmed with gold-leaf molding. On a plush velvet sofa before an enormous marble fireplace reclined a wizened old man, his frail body covered by a thick throw rug despite the heat of the summer afternoon. Wispy gray hair clung sparsely to his head, but his silver beard was full and luxurious. Sunken cheekbones, lined with age, were set beneath a pair of glittering eyes that, to Raven's surprise, were the color of amber and as thickly lashed as her own. The old man had pulled himself upright at her whirlwind entrance, his white beard cascading over a silk shawl that covered his thin chest, and when her startled eyes met his, Raven's head thrown back, her expression proud and defiant yet oddly sheepish, a knowing smile curved the thin lips. Opening his mouth to speak, he was interrupted by a furious pounding on the door as the major-domo tried to force his way in, having recovered from the pain in his throbbing foot.

"Slide the bolt, girl, quickly!"

Raven obeyed without hesitation.

"Sir Hadrian! Sir Hadrian, are you all right?" came the frantic query from without, the latch rattling ineffectively.

"My major-domo is of a nervous sort," Sir Hadrian explained, winking at Raven conspiratorially. "Glad to have a few minutes' peace from the stuffy, overprotective fellow. Go away, Jeffords!" he added, raising his voice.

"But, sir, the young woman—"

"Won't eat me alive, though I vow she came bursting in here like a battle-starved Amazon!" Again the lively eyes twinkled at her, and Raven couldn't help smiling back at him. "Be of a good sort, Jeffords, and bring us some refreshment."

"Very good, sir," Jeffords replied with affronted dignity, the rattling on the latch ceasing instantly.

"You may unlock the door now, child," Sir Hadrian added with a wave of his thin, gnarled hand. "There's a good girl. Now come closer where I can look at you."

Raven obeyed, coming to a halt before the sofa, where a surprisingly strong hand wrapped itself about her wrist and pulled her down beside him. "My eyes ain't what they used to be," he explained, regarding her intently as she seated herself with rustling satin skirts on the sofa, "though they've not failed me yet, I vow, for I can see you're quite a beauty. James's girl, ain't you?"

"Yes sir."

"Raven he named you, didn't he? I remember thinking at the time how odd the name was, but looking at you now, I see it's suitable."

"Because my hair is so dark," Raven said helpfully.

Sir Hadrian cackled. "Aye, and you're a fey creature, too. Mysterious and dark, and not above breaking into an old man's house just to see him. Odd that you're beating down my doors now, when I'm dying, and your father never took the trouble of bringing you to London before."

"Oh, are you dying, sir?" Raven cried in dismay, finding it difficult to believe that he could possibly be as ill as the proper Jeffords had claimed, for he seemed to be possessed of a great deal of spirit, and the thin, blue-veined hand that still clasped her wrist was strong and did not tremble.

"Would it suit you if I were?" Sir Hadrian asked slyly.

The tawny eyes met the light amber ones and held for a moment before Raven shook her head. "No sir, it would sadden me a great deal."

"La, and I believe you mean that," Sir Hadrian said, sounding somewhat surprised and secretly very delighted. Raven Barrancourt was an exceptional beauty, he thought to himself, and he'd seen enough beautiful women in his day to be a good judge of 'em. Moreover there was spirit in her cat's eyes that he liked, and a tongue in her head that showed she had brains, something he'd always appreciated in a beautiful woman. Pity he and his nephew had never gotten on; he'd have liked to have known this enchanting creature better.

"I imagine you came here for a reason," he continued after a moment, releasing his hold on Raven's slender wrist and making himself more comfortable on the sofa, his frail body aching, though he hid his pain with stubborn Barrancourt pride.

"I did," Raven admitted, "but I see that you aren't well. Perhaps I'll come back later when—"

"After you've gone to so much trouble to get in here? No, m'girl, you'll not be leaving now. What did you do to Jeffords, eh? Haven't heard him bellow like that since dear Mrs. Jeffords, De'il rest her soul, thought he was frolickin' with the neighbor's little parlormaid and took a fireplace poker to his backside." He laughed aloud at the memory. "And there ain't a more honest soul than poor old Jeffords, either! Always wondered why he took on the old horse." He peered at Raven closely with a mischievous, gnomelike smile, his beard twitching. "Do I shock you, m'girl? No, I can see I don't though I imagine I could if I set my mind to it. Hee hee, you're not a bad one, Raven. I'm only sorry you never came to see me before today."

"I am, too," Raven replied truthfully.

"Now, then," Sir Hadrian said, sobering abruptly, "I take it you came here for a reason. Your father's been dead what...? Three months, now, and you've been running North Head by yourself. Magnificent estate, ain't it? Never forgave your great-grandmother for birthing Thomas first. Would have liked to have called it my own, though I left when I was nineteen and only been back once or twice since."

"Father told me you didn't get on with my grandfather at all," Raven said.

Sir Hadrian shrugged his thin shoulders. "I was young, headstrong, and had too much cursed Barrancourt pride. Since I couldn't inherit North Head, I simply went away. Vowed I'd never go back and that Thomas was welcome to all of it. So I made my fortune on my own, and even though I soon grew wealthy enough to build an estate twice as large as North Head, I knew it wouldn't be the same."

"But why didn't you come back after your brother died and Father inherited?" Raven asked, puzzled. "You were born there, and I know you must have spent a happy childhood there." A soft light of memory began to glow in her eyes. "How could you not?"

Sir Hadrian chuckled and patted her hand. "I can see you love it well, m'dear. I did, too, but your father and I didn't get along any better than I did with the rest of the Barrancourts. We banged heads like bantam cockerels, we did. Too much alike, I guess, and your father as stubborn as the rest." He chuckled reminiscently. "I remember coming for your christening. 'Twas the last time I was there, actually, and with your poor mother gone, I told James he'd have a rough time of it with no son to inherit, your little brother dead barely a month, and he looked me right in the eye—same color they were as yours, not yellow like mine—and said he had no need for a son because you were as good as any lad in stripling pants."

The amber-colored eyes narrowed shrewdly and regarded Raven searchingly. "And now you've come into your own, lass, and you've been running one of the finest estates and fertile farms Cornwall has ever seen. What," he asked abruptly, "is it you want from me?"

"Money, Great-Uncle Hadrian," Raven replied promptly, knowing she must deal with him directly, although her voice trembled a little as she spoke.

"Ah. How much?"

Quietly and matter-of-factly Raven explained the situation while Sir Hadrian listened, an attentive expression on his lined, bearded face. He asked no questions, although he nodded to himself from time to time, and when Raven finished speaking she leaned back in the plush armchair where she had seated herself in order to begin her discourse, and waited in an agony of impatience, though her delicate features were outwardly calm.

"I think—" Sir Hadrian began after a long moment, only to be interrupted by the entrance of Jeffords bearing a silver tea service and a covered basket from which emanated the tantalizing smell of freshly baked crumpets and muffins.

"Your tea, sir," the major-domo said stiffly, setting down a wafer-thin china cup on the occasional table before his employer.

"Oh, come, don't behave so miffed! Raven did what she had to do, and I'm certain she's very sorry."

"Indeed I am," Raven said sincerely.

"There, you see?" The amber eyes twinkled in a lively manner. "Nothing but remorse and compunction in that lovely little face. How can you bear a grudge against so delightful a Barrancourt?"

"Begging your pardon, sir," Jeffords added in a less bellicose fashion, "my aversion lies totally in the fact that she is a Barrancourt."

Sir Hadrian laughed and slapped his thigh, and Raven could see that the old man and the white-haired servant were obviously well acquainted. Indeed, their bickering reminded her very much of herself and Danny. Danny! "Oh, I've forgotten all about the poor dear!" she cried.

"Eh? What's that?"

Raven flushed, embarrassed by her outburst. "I'm sorry, I was thinking of my companion. I left her outside in the coach, and I imagine she's very worried about me by now."

Sir Hadrian signaled to the hovering major-domo, who dutifully left the room to bring Danny inside, then peered at Raven with raised brows. "Not Hannah Daniels, your old governess?" he queried.

Raven nodded, startled. "Do you know her?"

"Indeed I do. Had several tiffs with the old nanny goat when I came down to Cornwall for your christening. Is she still as difficult and meddlesome as she was then?"

Raven couldn't help smiling. She found that she liked her great-uncle very much. "Danny thinks she's rigid and domineering, yet she's very tame beneath that blustering facade."

"And I warrant, young Raven, that you manipulate her well enough."

"Oh, I do try," Raven confessed.

Sir Hadrian laughed and lifted his teacup. "Will you pour, m'dear? Must confess this is the first time I've ever had the pleasure of having a hostess serve me in my own home. Such a lovely one, too. Ah." He cocked his grizzled head to one side. "That must be Mrs. Daniels's voice I hear in the hallway. Raven, we'll discuss your finances later. First you must rest, and then we'll talk the matter over after dinner, if you're not too tired. If you are, it can always wait until breakfast."

"We can't impose on you like that!" Raven protested. "Really, Great-Uncle, I had no intention—"

He silenced her with an abrupt wave of his hand. "I know you didn't, m'girl, but you're family and you'll stay here with me. Hannah, too, bless her tart tongue!"

"But your health—" Raven said, continuing to look doubtful.

"And do I seem to be dying?" he asked with the proper amount of outrage.

"I can't really tell, sir. Father always said that Barrancourts age marvelously well."

"And wise he was," Sir Hadrian agreed with a laugh, delighted at the prospect of spending a few days in the company of this charming, young girl. How dull his retiring bachelor's existence suddenly seemed to him! "And as for your problem, child, don't worry your pretty head unnecessarily. I'll find a way of helping you."

"Oh, if you could," Raven breathed, her eyes misting with gratitude. "I-I can't tell you what that would mean to me!"

"Ha! You needn't!" Sir Hadrian replied, sipping his tea and looking smug. "I'm a Barrancourt myself, remember?"

Conversation flourished during tea, Sir Hadrian regaling both Raven and Danny with tales of his rigorous youthful years in London. Though his body was frail, his mind was sharp and his wits keen, and Raven found herself laughing as she hadn't done since her father died. Jeffords, apparently delighted by his master's animation, treated her with utmost deference and was quite willing to forget the fact that she had so cruelly abused him in trying to get in. After tea Sir Hadrian confessed that he was weary and excused himself to rest, while a smiling young maid with red curls and a floppy mob cap led Danny and Raven to their rooms.

Raven was surprised to find hers of a pleasing feminine decor, the draperies of pale rose, the canopy bed covered with a tester of the same color and amply fringed with fine spidery lace. A window seat of striped salmon damask offered a cozy place to relax and look out of the dormer window onto the quiet street below, pink and red geraniums blooming in the window boxes.

"I'll have a bath set up in just a moment," the curly-headed maid promised as she followed Raven inside. "Sir Hadrian said your trunks were to be brought up, too."

"Oh, that's kind of him," Raven exclaimed, "but we didn't bring very much." Moving to the window, she looked out into the overcast afternoon. The stately trees lining the cobbled street wore lush green mantles, their spreading branches soaring to the sky, and colorful flowers bloomed along the basket-weave brick walk that led through the neat little garden below. The faint but unmistakable din of traffic, rumbling coaches, hoof-beats on stone, the neigh of horses, and the shouts of pedestrians came to her dimly from the busy thoroughfares beyond the quiet neighborhood, and Raven, recalling how skillfully Edwards had maneuvered the cumbersome coach through that same traffic only a short hour ago, shook her head disbelievingly.

London was an awesome city that could have engulfed the entire town of Truro thrice over, perhaps more, and Raven, accustomed to the sleepy hamlets and quaint villages through which they had traveled for the past five days, wending their way along ancient post roads, had been unable to believe her eyes at the bustle of London Town itself. Bone-weary from the long, sleepless nights she had spent in uncomfortable, unfamiliar beds, Raven hadn't paid much attention to the crush of coaches, horses, and sedan chairs, and had given the elegant residences, the imposing businesses, and famous landmarks barely a glance. But under the circumstances, how could she be blamed, for—

"Here you are, miss."

Raven, startled from her thoughts, turned away from the window to find two burly footmen carrying in a brass hip bath, a third following close on their heels with the few battered valises and bandboxes she had packed. She smiled gratefully at all three of them, unaware that they blushed and shuffled their feet in response, staring at her admiringly until the redheaded maid, carrying in an armful of plush Turkish towels, shooed them out with annoyed exclamations.

"Good-for-nothing creatures!" she remarked contemptuously. "Always standing about doing nothing unless you make it a point to tell them to! The water's heating, miss. Shall I lay out your things in the meantime?"

"Oh yes, please," Raven replied gratefully.

When the hip bath had been filled with lavender-scented water, she allowed the garrulous Betsy to help her undress, then slipped with a contented sigh into the steaming tub. How wonderful it felt after the bucket-and-sponge washings she had had to make do with during the journey from Cornwall! Stretching a long, tapering leg out of the water, Raven scrubbed it clean, then washed the other, humming to herself as she did, scarcely daring to hope that her visit with Great-Uncle Hadrian was going to turn out as well as he had intimated it would. For the first time since Richard Haggart's visit to North Head, Raven felt confident and happy, certain now that she would never lose her beloved home.

"And God help him who tries to take if from me!" Raven whispered to herself, thinking how cramped and stifling Knightsbridge was to her in contrast to the endless, fog-enshrouded moors of home. No, London was not the life for her, Raven decided, stepping from the tub and wrapping her slender body in one of the soft towels that had been laid out for her. Better to be deciding what crops to plant that year or which bull calf to keep for breeding than to worry about which gown to wear to tea!

"Ah, Raven, you're naught but a rustic," she said aloud as she brushed her hair before the dressing table mirror, the blue-black masses springing to life beneath her hands. "And mad to boot to be talking to yourself this way!" She giggled, unable to contain her happiness, and studied her tall, graceful image in the looking glass, her hollow cheeks flushed, her changeable, sparkling eyes the color of sherry wine.

Rustic she may be, but at the moment looking self-assured and in command, not so frightened and uncertain as she had been the day she stood forlornly in the Truro graveyard, her happy, sheltered world seeming to have been laid to rest as well. Oh, she was still apprehensive at times, especially after Squire Blackburn had made that totally objectionable offer, but she found now that, having forced herself to do what she never thought she had the courage to do, she had succeeded in keeping North Head in Barrancourt hands.

At dinner that evening Sir Hadrian presided over the enormous table with the aplomb of a prince, looking well rested and alert, a congenial, entertaining host who kept his visitors plied with wine so that the evening was a festive one indeed. Raven, her cares forgotten, laughed at his jokes, her tawny eyes sparkling, and even Danny forgot her station and her own taciturn nature, and responded with smiles and girlish giggles to Sir Hadrian's witicisms.

"Oh, bless me, sir, I've never heard such a tale!" she choked at the conclusion of Sir Hadrian's colorful narrative concerning the adventures of an unscrupulous monk and a clever little ladybird. "Shocking, I must add, but amusing all the same!" She dabbed at her eyes with her lace handkerchief and added more disapprovingly, "but Miss Raven shouldn't be—"

"Oh, stuff and nonsense!" Sir Hadrian retorted, giving his grandniece a knowing wink across the richly spread board. "If your father raised you as I think he did, there's little you've not heard before." He wagged a finger at her. "There, don't be blushing so, m'girl. Just like fainting, that is, a female affectation of utter hypocrisy I can't abide!"

Seeing Raven's answering scowl, he added with a laugh, "But you've no pretentious bone in your body, I can see, so don't take offense at an old man's ramblings. Ah, here's Jeffords with dessert. What'll it be, m'dear, some lemon ice or a piece o' that butter cream torte?"

"The cake looks tempting," Raven confessed, covetously eyeing the rich torte with its sprinkling of walnuts and cherries.

"Jeffords, a slab for my grandniece," Sir Hadrian commanded instantly. "And what can I tempt you with, Mrs. Daniels?"

Danny held up her plump hands in mock panic. "Nothing, sir! I be fit to bursting already!"

Sir Hadrian studied her ample form with its covering of demure burgundy bombazine, his amber eyes twinkling. "Utter nonsense!"

Danny's lips curved into a smile. "You're ever so kind, Sir Hadrian, but I've eaten far too much and I'm tired, too. Will you excuse me?"

"Most assuredly! Jeffords, have Betsy show Mrs. Daniels to her room."

Both Sir Hadrian and Raven wished the former governess good night and waited in silence until they were alone, Raven toying with her cake, the hand that held her silver fork trembling slightly.

"Are you nervous, child?"

Sir Hadrian's quiet, unexpected question made her jump, and she looked up at him quickly. "I imagine I am, Great-Uncle."

"What about?" he asked, although he already knew.

The delicate features were oddly defenseless. "It's what you're going to say. Something seems to have been on your mind throughout dinner, though you were ever so charming. I-I couldn't help thinking that it has something to do with my problem."

Sir Hadrian grew serious, sipping his wine and studying his beautiful grandniece across the linen-covered table. "And so it does," he admitted. "After my nap this afternoon I spent some time going over my finances to see how best to help you. Obviously you must realize that I don't have fifty thousand pounds sitting in my vault waiting for you to claim it."

Raven nodded her dark, glossy head, her eyes filled with an odd mixture of dread and anticipation. In the same trim gray gown she had worn for Squire Blackburn's visit, the tiny pearl buttons shimmering in the soft candlelight, she looked breathtakingly beautiful yet defenselessly young, her oval face pale but for the soft rosy shadows of her hollow cheekbones.

Sir Hadrian leaned back in his chair, studying her assiduously, unconsciously stroking his long silver beard. "Fortunately I know of a gentleman who has enough available capital to supply you with the sum you need plus a little extra to cover the additional interest."

"I don't understand," Raven said somewhat unsteadily, the piece of scrumptious butter cream torte all but forgotten. "Are you saying I must seek out the money from someone else?"

"Let me explain the situation to you, Raven," her great-uncle replied. Gesturing at her plate, he added with mock severity, "And finish that cake, will you? You're thin as a rail, and you'll be insulting Jeffords if you don't. It's his own mother's recipe, and she was a saint of a woman."

Raven began to eat dutifully, though she scarcely tasted the rich cream and the sweet marmalade filling. Her eyes rested solemnly on her great-uncle's lined, bearded face while her heart beat a nervous tattoo within her breast.

"You know quite well that I never married," Sir Hadrian began, "though I must confess that I had enough ambitious mamas and their eager daughters chasing after me. Booth's was my one great love, you could say. I devoted my entire life to the business, and when the British East India Company finally bought out my share, I must confess I made out rather well."

Raven listened patiently, knowing that he was leading up to a specific point no matter how far from the subject of her loan he appeared to be. She took another bite of the torte, realizing all at once that it was quite delicious.

"That was ten years ago when I retired at last. I'm seventy-two now, so you can imagine that I'd had enough of the fast-paced whirl of making fortunes and losing them, outguessing the market, trying to decide when to buy and sell. It's a young man's world, Raven, and there's a new breed of trader on the frontier today that I can't even begin to keep up with even after all my years of dealing in Far East commodities." He shook himself free of obviously troubling thoughts and smiled at her encouragingly. "No matter. That's the past and it's buried now. Where was I? Oh, of course. I was saying I'd never married. Well, at the risk of shocking you, m'girl, I'll tell you that though I never had a wife, I didn't live the most pious of lives or make myself scarce with the ladies. There was a particularly fine woman—" He coughed and cleared his throat, suddenly unable to meet the solemn eyes across the board from him.

"Are you saying that you kept a mistress, sir?" Raven asked directly, her sweet voice clear and without censure.

"Why, yes, I am," the elderly gentleman replied with a trace of surprise. Then he collected himself and grinned at her so that Raven had an inkling of what a charming, handsome man he must have been in his youth. "I had several, actually, but this one was special. A fine woman, Raven, beautiful and loyal, with quite a bit of spirit. You remind me of her in a way, though you're as different in looks as day and night. Like you, she was tough and determined, a mistress of her own destiny." His voice grew warm with the memory.

Raven said encouragingly, "I imagine you loved her very much."

"Enough to give the son we had together a name," Sir Hadrian replied quietly. "My own."

Raven's delicate brows arched upward. "A Barrancourt?" she whispered, truly shocked.

Sir Hadrian nodded firmly. "Now, don't go condemning me for that, m'girl! We've enough pirates and smugglers in our history to make us less than companionable with the angels! Impossible, ain't it, for an old Cornish family not to be involved with ruffians like that?"

"I imagine so," Raven admitted doubtfully, the mention of

smugglers making her think for the first time in a great while of the handsome, unscrupulous smuggler captain who had kissed her so passionately on the dark, wind-swept beach. She scowled and forced the memory away, telling herself sternly that she mustn't think of that night again and that she certainly had no right at all to judge her great-uncle. Her dismay at learning of the existence of a Barrancourt born on the wrong side of the blanket bordered on snobbery, an inexcusable trait she had always disliked immensely in others. "I'm sorry, Great-Uncle," she said contritely. "Obviously you loved your son very much or you wouldn't have done him that honor."

Sir Hadrian's eyes twinkled beneath the bushy brows. "Quite right, child. Phillip grew into an admirable youth, intelligent, well behaved, dependable. My only reservations lay in his distinctive tendency toward bitterness at not being accepted by our illustrious *haut monde,* and his lack of ambition. No desire to make a name for himself, no interests other than fast horses and the gaming tables. I bought him a commission in the army, but that wasn't quite the answer, so when I retired and came into more money than I had use for, I set Phillip up in business."

"How generous of you!" Raven exclaimed sincerely, wondering why her father had never made mention of his cousin to her, ill-gotten as he may have been, for her father had been an extremely tolerant man and would assuredly have invited him to North Head had he known.

"Your father knew nothing about him," Sir Hadrian continued as though reading her mind, shrugging his thin shoulders flippantly. "As I've told you before, Raven, we didn't correspond much."

"It's Phillip who'll lend me the money I need, isn't it?" Raven asked.

"He's the one, child," Sir Hadrian agreed with a sly grin. His eyes twinkled. "And it won't be a loan but a gift from one Barrancourt to another."

Raven's smooth brow wrinkled. "But surely such a sum—surely he feels no loyalty to North Head as you do!" Inwardly her heart was hammering with disbelief.

"It's still my money," Sir Hadrian pointed out with a shrewd smile. "So long as I'm alive, I'll be keeping the reins in my hands where Phillip is concerned. I must say the responsibility of running his own business has matured him admirably, but one can never be too cautious when one's entire fortune is involved."

"And does he live here in London?" Raven asked eagerly, wondering when she would meet him.

"Indeed not." Sir Hadrian finished the rest of his wine and wiped his lips with a linen napkin. "Sent him to India some five-odd years ago after his tour of duty in the army was over. Started himself a fine private warehousing operation that supplies the East India Company with indigo, silks, and tea. Has enough money, I assure you, to give you the amount you need." He winked at her conspiratorially. "We'll call it a loan with no terms of repayment. After all"—his tone grew serious—"North Head is the Barrancourts' ancestral home, and no matter how long it's been since I've seen it, I'll not have some vile little squire with visions of grandeur setting up court there. Blackburn, you say?" He scowled. "I think I remember the family. All fat, overindulgent despots with the brains of guinea hens. I'd rather be dead than see them at North Head!"

"But how do we deal with your son when he's in India?" Raven asked faintly, scarcely listening, still recovering from the shock.

"Eh? Oh, how do I propose to get the money out? No problem, child. I'll send an official request and—"

"But a sum that size, surely you can't trust it to a mere courier!" Raven protested, her dismay growing, realizing that her problem was far more complex than she had originally suspected. "Isn't there anyone you trust well enough to go for you?" she asked anxiously.

Sir Hadrian laughed. "I trust no one but myself, m'dear, and I'm far too old!" He peered at her slyly. "If my proposal distresses you so much, why don't you go yourself?"

Raven stared at him, aghast. "To India?"

"Now, now, don't look as though I'm sending you to the moon! India isn't the dark, primitive continent you probably envision. More Englishmen over there than there are here, and it's become quite the fashionable place to travel to, you know. Families up and moving there by the hundreds, clerks, merchants, men of the cloth. I hear it's all the rage for newlywed couples as well. The journey ain't stressful, either. Read the other day where an American tea clipper made the run over in less than two hundred days! It'd do you good, too, I'm thinking," he added, warming to the idea, "to take a look at the rest of the world, shut away as you are at Land's End, and I can't think of anyone I trust more than you to bring that sum back to England." The thick whiskers twitched with amusement at Raven's lost expression. "It'll be good pounds sterling, girl. Quite worth the trip."

Raven's tawny eyes glowed in her pale face. "I couldn't possibly go, Great-Uncle Hadrian! India is so far away! Why, I'd be gone far too long, and North Head can't—"

"You told me you had a year before the loan is due," Sir Hadrian reminded her shrewdly, "and as for North Head, do you suppose your steward—Speedwell was his name, I think—would take orders from a crusty old man like me?"

Raven stared at him disbelievingly. "You'd run North Head in my absence?" she whispered.

"And why not?" Sir Hadrian demanded crisply. "I may be old, but my mind's in tune, and I must admit I've been rather bored since I sold out Booth's." He chuckled. "Always wanted to know what it felt like to run that impressive old manor and all that arable acreage!"

"You can't be serious!" Raven protested, convinced he was joking with her.

He gave her a sharp glance that reminded her very much of her father when he prepared to reprimand her for something she had done. "I'm making the offer, child. If you go to India, I'll make sure you've the proper papers with you so that Phillip won't hesitate to make the payment, and in exchange I'll manage North Head in your absence."

"I-I don't know what to say," Raven said haltingly after a long moment of silence, staring down at her empty plate. "I'm only just eighteen, Great-Uncle! Surely you don't believe I could travel to India alone to retrieve such a fortune!"

He startled her by giving vent to a great burst of laughter, his thin chest heaving, his eyes watering with mirth. "You, a helpless young orphan? Never, my girl! You had the courage to face Squire Blackburn and to come to me, a total stranger, in order to save North Head from falling out of family hands. Though you may be frightened of undertaking such a journey, you should keep in mind that I won't let you go without adequate protection. Furthermore, Raven, you're a Barrancourt, and they say we're all odd creatures. I wouldn't be surprised if King Arthur himself didn't bequeath North Head to a Barrancourt who sat at his Round Table. Surely you won't let a journey to India daunt you into accepting Squire Blackburn's marriage offer and simply throw away the hard won battles and the honor of our ancestors."

Her head bowed, Raven was silent, too bewildered to reply.

"Go for me, Raven," came her great-uncle's serious voice. "I've wasted my youth and my health, and now it's too late for me, but you, you're young and strong and you've more courage than you'll ever know. When you come back, you can tell me everything you've seen while we're sitting before the fire in the Great Hall at North Head and Squire Blackburn fumes impotently outside the stone walls!"

Raven's head snapped up abruptly, her eyes glowing, sharing his smile with an eager one of her own. "All right, then, I shall! Tell me what to do, where to go, and I swear I'll be back before the summer's done!"

Sir Hadrian beamed at her. "I'll make inquiries tomorrow, Raven. In the meantime you should go to bed. Try to get some rest, though I imagine it'll be difficult. Whatever you do," he added as she rose to her feet, her gray skirts swirling about her, "don't change your mind."

Raven's head was thrown back and her eyes blazed with determination. "Oh no, sir, I won't!"

There was a light shining beneath Danny's door, and Raven, hurrying across the landing in the direction of her own room, paused and knocked boldly, her heart hammering in her breast. When the door was opened and a sleepy Danny in nightrail and lace-edged cap appeared, Raven could tell instantly from the startled expression on the round, kindly face that some of the tremendous excitement within her must be revealed in her eyes.

"What is it, child?" Danny asked anxiously.

"Oh, Danny!" Raven cried, throwing her arms about the astonished woman, "Great-Uncle Hadrian is going to give us the money to pay back Squire Blackburn!"

The old governess, reeling beneath the news and her young mistress's affectionate embrace, tottered backward and sat down heavily on the coverlet of her bed. "I can't believe it!" she murmured weakly.

Raven was forced to laugh at her bewildered expression and

the wispy, sand-colored hair sticking out in riotous disarray from beneath the ruffled nightcap. "It's true, Danny! And he expects no repayment!"

Suspicion clouded the kindly face. "None?"

Raven was hard put to keep still, hopping from one small, slippered foot to the other, her hands clasped behind her back like a child's, her expression radiant. "Well, actually he's asked if he may manage North Head for approximately a year, just to alleviate his ennui and discover for a time what it's like to be the master of it."

"I don't understand!" Danny said, looking lost and confused amid the downy bedclothes that covered the wide expanse of her bed.

"Seeing as I won't be there, he's agreed to look after it while I'm gone," Raven explained with a mischievous grin. "You see, we've got to collect the money ourselves from his bas—I mean his son Phillip, who controls Sir Hadrian's entire fortune now."

Danny knew her young mistress far too well to be thoroughly taken in by the sparkling eyes and glowing expression. Tiny frown lines appeared on her brow, and her eyes narrowed suspiciously. "And just where be we going, Miss Raven?" she asked, dreading the answer.

"To India!" Raven cried. "Oh, Danny, isn't it grand?"

Danny's hands flew to her white batiste-covered breast, and a groan escaped her tightly compressed lips. "God in heaven, have mercy on us!" she whispered faintly.

"Indeed," Raven laughed, gripped with excitement and a sense of adventure that could only have come from the colorful pirates, smugglers, and roving knights whose Barrancourt blood flowed in her veins. Her tawny eyes danced. "Tomorrow we've got to hurry back home, Danny. There's not much time to lose if we're to make it back before the squire's reprieve expires."

Danny groaned again and shook her head despairingly. "God have mercy on us all," she whispered unsteadily.

Chapter Four

Amid the forest of spars, masts, and furled sails that crowded the harbor of London Town, the *India Cloud* bobbed serenely at her moorings, thick ropes holding her fast, the enormous anchor chain stretched taut beneath the black water of the Thames. She was an East Indiaman, sleek and weathered by long years on the high seas, and next to the countless tiny sloops and trim brigs, she appeared stately, even awesome. Her holds had recently discharged a fortune of precious tea, and indigo used to dye the uniforms of many a proud navy man, and countless yards of colorful silks that were in such demand by the fashionably attired aristocrats and the wealthy merchants who, in ever-increasing numbers, strove to attain the ranks of their blue-blooded betters by fortune alone.

The *India Cloud* was ready to sail, prepared to embark on another run for the far-off Orient, sailors scrambling about on the wide decks in response to the barked orders of the boatswain and the captain, both of them impatient to heave off with the tide. Raven Barrancourt, her eyes sparkling like cut topaz, stood near the railing, the hot breeze whipping the shining black strands of her hair across her smooth brow despite the fact that she had taken great pains to pin it carefully beneath her trim russet bonnet. She wore a gown of matching satin, the bodice braided with gold, the full skirts shot with matching gold threads. The people on the crowded wharves below seemed minute to her. The shouts, oaths, and heart-rending sobs as loved ones were separated from one another rose in a muted din, only to be drowned by the raucous shrieks of wheeling gulls and the piercing groan of metal on metal as the seamen began to haul in the anchor, leaning hard against the great capstan and singing lustily some ancient chanty that set Raven's blood stirring.

"Clear the decks, clear the decks for the sailors!" came the clipped order, and Raven pressed herself against the rail as crewmen scrambled up into the rigging once the enormous anchor was secured. Mooring lines were cast, and the big yards were turned, the canvas lowered with cracking thunder into place. The decks canted slowly as the *India Cloud* leaned leeward, sliding downstream and gathering momentum as it caught the current and the wind began to fill its sails. Raven, standing against the rail with the rest of the passengers, turned her eyes back to the crowded skyline of London. Oblivious to the brownish haze which hovered perpetually over the city, she saw only the beautiful outlines of stately St. Paul's Cathedral, the grim silhouette of the Tower, and Tower Bridge. The excitement that had gripped her since she'd first stepped aboard with Danny was tempered by a feeling of melancholia, or perhaps a pang of homesickness, she couldn't tell which.

Actually there was nothing in London Raven would miss. Great-Uncle Hadrian, having accompanied her back to Cornwall over a fortnight ago, was well sequestered in his new domain, looking stronger and healthier than he had when she'd first met him in Knightsbridge. The devoted Jeffords had informed her gratefully at their departure, *sotto voce* so that Sir Hadrian wouldn't hear, that she had given the old man back his will to live and that their tenure at North Head would doubtless be the happiest of his own life. Raven had smiled in response, knowing full well that all Barrancourts sooner or later returned to the place of their birth, whether to die or to live quietly for the rest of their days, taking strength from the hard but life-giving land that was part of her beloved Cornwall.

Great-Uncle Hadrian, Raven decided, gazing at the crowded buildings sliding past her line of vision, had merely allowed London, with its choked, teeming streets, countless faceless people, and bloodletting business practices, to sap him of his youthful strength. She herself had been pleased to see the bloom return to his lined, leathery cheeks, even in the few short days before her departure. How hectic that time had been and how relieved she had felt when she'd managed to slip away without the encounter with Squire Blackburn she had been dreading! Raven smothered a giggle with her gloved hand, picturing the lively meeting between Sir Hadrian and the squire that was to come. Sir Hadrian had promised her that he would tell the squire nothing of their scheming against him but that he would come up with some suitable reason for her absence. Raven suspected that the imaginative old man would regale the squire with surprising excuses indeed.

"Miss Barrancourt?"

Raven turned to find herself gazing up at the boatswain's mate, a burly sailor with sunburned skin and powerful forearms. "The cap'n asked me to be sure ye found yer cabin comfortable, miss."

"Indeed I have," Raven replied, unaware of the honor bestowed upon her as the grandniece of Sir Hadrian Barrancourt: she was the possessor of a private cabin, the most luxurious on the ship, the captain's own quarters notwithstanding. Captain Winters had known Sir Hadrian for many years and had personally promised at the old man's request to look after Raven and her traveling companion, Hannah Daniels, until they were safely delivered to Bombay, where Phillip Barrancourt made his residence.

"It's very kind of Captain Winters to take an interest in me when he's so terribly busy," Raven added, smiling warmly into the rugged face.

The mate's weatherbeaten cheeks quickly grew red, and he stared down at the polished deck below his feet, finding the young woman before him undeniably beautiful. "Aye, miss," he mumbled self-consciously. "Cap'n says if there's anything else ye be needin' to speak to him or Mr. Towers, the bosun."

"Thank you," Raven said with another smile, grateful for this offer of assistance. As the mate hurried off, she turned again to the railing, where, beyond the dark waters of the Thames, London was slipping away beyond the stern. Soon they would be in the Channel, then ocean-bound, with England astern and Africa off the sweeping bow. Raven's heartbeat accelerated, and a feeling of excitement gripped her. What would happen between now and her return from India? she wondered to herself. Still, come what may, North Head would always be hers, and she derived great comfort in the knowledge that even in her absence it would be inhabited by a Barrancourt.

With the harbor finally cleared and the wind-swept water of the Channel before them, Raven crossed the deck toward the aft companionway. Her gait was unsteady, unaccustomed as she was to the unnatural canting of the ship. She noticed with secret amusement that the rest of the passengers were also having difficulty in moving about, even more so than she herself, and tried to look suitably sympathetic when an overweight matron in puce bombazine tripped over a neatly coiled rope and fell heavily against her rail-thin husband, who walked at her side. Raven had noticed the woman earlier when they had first boarded—not only her brilliant attire, of which there seemed to be endless yards and yards, but also her bombastic voice, which had been impossible to avoid hearing as she ordered her somehow pitiable, weary-looking husband about.

The *India Cloud* had taken on only eight passengers this voyage, including Raven and Danny, for it was a private merchant ship under license to the British East India Company and was not by nature considered a passenger vessel. For this reason the berths were few, and Raven could not realize that she had already garnered the envy and dislike of that redoubtable matron, Mrs. Murrow, for being the individual who had usurped the spacious cabin which the overbearing older woman rightfully considered hers. As yet Raven remained blissfully unaware of the tiresome censure that would soon be directed toward her, and averted her face to hide her smile as Mrs. Murrow, recovering from her near-fall, vented her spleen in a bellicose manner against a hapless sailor who had been unfortunate enough to be standing nearby when she stumbled over the rope.

Raven hastily vanished down the companionway amid a swirl of russet-colored skirts to find Danny in the process of arranging their belongings in the drawers and cupboards of the teak highboy that was standing between their berths. Raven had been astonished to learn that passengers were expected to supply their own furniture, and had been grateful to Sir Hadrian for having seen to the purchase of two surprisingly roomy, comfortable beds and ample storage space for their clothing and toiletries. Her gratitude had increased even more when she had seen the rickety furnishings of the other passengers being brought aboard in nets and by muscular sailors through the entry port. The cots being carried below had been constructed of uncomfortable iron frames and thin, palletlike mattresses, the chest of drawers scratched and greatly battered—surely uncomfortable accommodations for a five-month voyage!

Only the Murrows, who indicated their wealth not so much by exhibiting genteel breeding as by flaunting their material possessions, had brought with them beds, cupboards, and various other accessories that matched Raven's in comfort and appearance. Watching from the narrow doorway as Danny placed a clean woven damask coverlet over each of their beds, Raven was forced to smile, her soft lips curving, revealing the bewitching dimples in her smooth cheeks.

"Oh, Danny, it looks almost like home now!"

The governess shot her a look of profound annoyance and would have snorted had the gesture not offended her proper sensibilities. "Home, Miss Raven? I daresay we could fit four of these stuffy cabins in North Head's larder alone!"

Raven laughed. "I can see you find our maiden voyage as exciting as I do! Best improve your disposition or it'll be difficult to deal with you for five straight months."

Danny rolled her eyes despairingly as her gnarled hands busily smoothed the soft damask material. "Lord, don't remind me of how long this trip will take or I'll be begging Captain Winters to let me off at the first port of call!"

"Even if it's darkest Borneo?" Raven asked mischievously.

"Miss Raven!" Danny said tartly, hands propped on her well-padded hips, "it would please me proper, it would, if you worked your energies out on someone else, not me! I've things to do and—"

"Oh, very well," Raven acquiesced with a grin, seeing that she was only getting in Danny's way. She returned to the deck to enjoy the bright sunshine and what she knew would be the last glimpse of England she would have in nearly a year. The thought brought an unexpected chill, and Raven prayed that she would find Phillip Barrancourt quickly and return home without incident before her year of reprieve was over.

When twilight fell the *India Cloud* was well out in the Channel, its spiraling masts bearing the weight of its taut, billowing sails, the beams creaking as it rolled through the waves, the sun sinking over a graying sea. The watch was changed with the clanging of the brass bell, and Raven, summoned by the taciturn cabin servant, accompanied Danny to the main deck, where the great cabin that normally housed the crew had been divided by the addition of a makeshift wall to supply the passengers with a saloon. It proved to be a long yet narrow, low-ceilinged room with lanterns swinging from the exposed beams and a rough, pockmarked table with squat-legged benches placed at the far end. The half-dozen fellow passengers were already assembled and were engaged, under Mrs. Murrow's vocal directions, in introducing themselves to one another.

Raven had dressed simply in a velvet gown of dusky rose, its sleeves frilled although it was otherwise devoid of extravagance. Her black hair gleamed in the swaying lantern light, and her eyes, as wide and observant as a cat's, gleamed with anticipation. In the shadowy light within the saloon her features were angular and sharply defined, the hollows beneath the smooth cheekbones accenting the perfection of her face. She came to a halt at the perimeter of the group, unwilling to interrupt Mrs. Murrow's monologue, but when her tawny eyes met those of Mrs. Murrow's husband, he came hurrying toward her eagerly, his hand outstretched.

"Ah, Mother, look here's the last of our little crew!" Taking Raven's arm, he led her forward, beaming up into her face, a small man with pale, watery eyes and a limp grasp, though his delight in seeing her seemed genuine. "You must be Raven Barrancourt," he went on, ignoring the fact that he had interrupted his wife's speech, "for everyone else has already been accounted for. I'm Edgar Murrow from Folkestone and—"

"I'm Sophie Murrow," his wife finished, pushing her way between her husband and Raven, her enormous bulk effectively separating the two. Raven looked in bewilderment into the catty eyes, wondering what she had done to deserve this unpleasant woman's enmity, for surely she was being stared at with immense dislike!

"How do you do, Mrs. Murrow," she said politely enough. "I'm Raven Barrancourt, and this is my travel companion, Hannah Daniels." She gestured toward Danny as she spoke, regarding the hostile, overweight woman with a warm smile. Mrs. Murrow, however, appeared even less impressed with the short, wispy-haired Danny, barely acknowledging the introduction with a nod of her elegantly coiffed head.

Raven chafed at the snub, perfectly aware that Mrs. Murrow considered Danny, as a simple lady's companion, totally beneath her notice, and opened her mouth to make a tart remark when Mr. Murrow, showing remarkable courage for such a beleaguered, long-suffering husband, spoke up again.

"May I introduce you to the others, Miss Barrancourt?"

Raven's smile was genuine; she felt sorry for the thin, nervous little man. How well she knew Mrs. Murrow's kind: overbearing, loud-mouthed, pretentious, a veritable Squire Blackburn in bombazine skirts!

"This is Mr. Theodore Stanridge of Portsmouth."

The elderly, whiskered gentleman bowed stiffly over Raven's hand and muttered a few unintelligible words of greeting before retreating into the shadows, where he gave himself up to the pleasures of reading the well-thumbed leather book he carried with him—a habit that Raven would soon discover filled almost his entire waking life for the duration of the voyage. Raven thought him a vague yet nice enough gentleman, fastidiously attired, yet certainly no one with whom she could spend much time throughout the long weeks to come. Thus, dismissing him, she looked with interest at the young couple who came hesitantly forward to be acknowledged by Edgar Murrow. They were newly married, the young groom flushing and stammering, unable to meet Raven's eyes as they were introduced, his bride a timorous creature with mousy brown hair and nondescript gray eyes. Her name was Letitia, she whispered shyly, shaking hands politely with Raven, hers as cold as ice, adding that she was delighted to find someone near her own age aboard before her courage failed her and she scurried protectively back to her husband's side.

"And I am Nathaniel Rogers, Miss Barrancourt," said a man emerging from the shadows where Raven had been unable to see him. Taking her hand in his, he bowed gallantly. "I saw you come aboard earlier today and could scarcely believe my good fortune." His eyes lingered on Raven's upturned face, his thin, rather plain features and insipid manner setting Raven's teeth on edge. He was dressed the part of a toff, his shoes silver-buckled, a pearl in his cravat, his powder-blue coat flaring over his hips. In the drab, dimly lit interior of the roughly paneled saloon, where only Sophie Murrow matched him in elegance of attire, he seemed overdressed and out of place, and Raven's nose wrinkled at the strong scent of rosewater pomade that wafted from his slickly brushed hair.

"Surely you'll consent to sit beside me at dinner?" he asked in a pleading tone, leering down at Raven's neckline where the dusky rose bodice was scooped to reveal the creamy smoothness of her throat. Without waiting for her answer, he led her to the table, pushing his way past the disappointed Edgar Murrow, whose wife beckoned imperiously for him to join her.

"I'm afraid the food won't amount to much," Nathaniel Rogers added, seating Raven solicitously at the end of the bench, "and I'm afraid it'll grow progressively worse as the journey continues and we're forced to turn to the last of the stores."

"You sound as though you know a lot about ocean voyages, Mr. Rogers," young Letitia Carmichael remarked with round eyes.

"This is my third visit to India," he explained, unable to keep the pride from his voice, preening like a peacock, his chest puffing. "Have you been there before, Miss Barrancourt?"

"I've never left England," Raven admitted, making room for Danny on the uncomfortable bench.

"What a pity for you," Mrs. Murrow declared authoritatively, "but then, you're young, with time ahead of you to travel."

"We've never been away from home, either," Edgar Murrow confessed. "Mother came into a bit of money when her father passed on last year, and we—"

"Of course, we were never badly off before that," Sophie Murrow interrupted sharply, "but Father insisted in his will that we spend some time seeing the rest of the world, and naturally we couldn't ignore his last dying request, could we?"

"Of course not!" Letty Carmichael agreed. "How fortunate of you to find that opportunity, Mrs. Murrow, though it's sad that you had to do so at the expense of losing your father!"

"Oh, he'd been ill for quite some time," the overweight woman replied practically, quelling her husband to silence with a sharp glance when he opened his mouth to speak. "And since traveling to the Orient was all the rage with our friends, Edgar and I decided to see for ourselves what all the fuss was about."

"You'll be quite impressed, I assure you," Nathaniel Rogers claimed. "The Indian subcontinent boasts a most diverse culture and geography. It's unlike anything I've ever seen, and I remember my first visit when I . . ."

The narrative which followed was long and rather dull, centering mainly on the exploits of Mr. Rogers himself, and had little, if anything, to do with the descriptions of India that Raven sought. She was curious about the vast continent of Asia, yet promptly decided to remain ignorant if asking about it meant that she had to listen to Mr. Rogers's boasting. Sipping the surprisingly good barley soup set out before her by the unenthusiastic cabin servant, Charlie Copper, she allowed her pensive gaze to travel from one unfamiliar face to another.

The Carmichaels, she thought to herself, were kind, simple, honest and, doubtless, agonizingly dull. Mrs. Murrow was definitely to be avoided at all costs, and, mainly for his own protection rather than Raven's own, Edgar Murrow ought to be ignored as much as possible lest his overbearing wife begin to accuse him of neglecting her. Theodore Stanridge, who hadn't said a word throughout the meal or even shown any interest in his fellow passengers, seemed far too vague and unaware of his surroundings to provide suitable companionship. And as for Nathaniel Rogers... Raven's soft lips tightened as he leaned toward her to whisper something secretive concerning his first trip to India in her ear, pressing his thigh far too intimately against hers and forcing her to move deliberately closer to Danny. As for Nathaniel Rogers, it would be wisest to avoid him altogether.

"Lord, how that young jackanapes can go on!" Danny complained when she and Raven were finally alone in their cabin, the tedious dinner behind them. "I vow if he gives you another of those winking, grinning stares, I'll take my parasol to his head! Oh dear," she added with a frown, "I can't remember if I brought it with me!" She made a hasty search for the desired article but failed to locate it in the numerous drawers she had filled earlier that day.

"Perhaps you left it in London," Raven suggested, busily unpinning her hair and allowing the heavy black mass to fall to her narrow waist. Though she was too excited to sleep and longed to go topside for one last look at the nighttime sky, she was afraid of running into Mr. Rogers, who had made his interest in her all too plain throughout the meal. Her eyes hardened, and she decided grimly that, Danny's parasol notwithstanding, she'd find some way to convey to him her lack of enthusiasm concerning his attentions, for she had no intention of hiding away in her cabin the entire journey!

"I tell you, Miss Raven," Danny added, busily turning back the bedclothes on her bunk, "I can think of plenty of other people I'd rather spend five months in close quarters with!"

"So can I!" Raven agreed heartily. "Let's hope that by the

time we make landfall the two of us aren't completely mad!"

In that respect neither Raven nor Danny had cause for additional concern, for the *India Cloud*, making excellent time, ran afoul of the weather some two weeks later south of the Canary Islands. Day after day the iron-gray skies opened up to dump torrential rains upon the heaving sea, the water whitecapped and dangerous, the waves dashing over the East Indiaman's bow, only to hiss away again in the scuppers. The portholes were shuttered and deadbolted, the decks ordered cleared by Captain Winters of all save the watches, and Raven saw next to nothing of her fellow passengers throughout the long, tedious journey as the buffeted ship plunged down Africa's western coastline.

Along with the *India Cloud*'s entry into the Indian Ocean came the monsoons, southwesterly winds that roared down upon the hapless ship, filling the taut sails fit to bursting, every beam and plank straining with the onslaught of the elements. The perpetual howling and creaking, the dull roar of the rain on the decks, and the explosive snapping of the canvas sails offered no peace to those passengers who were forced to take to their beds, the agonized victims of seasickness. Of the *India Cloud*'s eight passengers, only Raven and Edgar Murrow remained unafflicted, and during the long afternoons when Raven was not tending to Danny in their cabin or Mr. Murrow occupied with his suffering wife, the two of them met in the dimly lit, airless saloon to spend the time in what relief each other's company could offer.

Raven discovered that Mr. Murrow was an intelligent, learned man quite given to garrulousness when not in the presence of his formidable wife. Unlike her, he was not in the least given to putting on airs, and made no effort to appear as anything other than what he was: a simple, low-born, yet pleasant merchant from Folkestone whose wife's inheritance had endowed him with the means to travel, a dream he had been able to fulfill only after convincing his aspiring wife that no one but true members of the London ton ever traveled to Asia.

"I expect we'll be gone well over two years," he told Raven in his quietly enthusiastic voice as they met one storm-tossed afternoon in the empty saloon. The wind howled without and the *India Cloud* pitched and bucked like a wild horse through the waves, yet neither of them was aware of the movement, both having adapted to the sea almost from the very start.

"Mother intends to spend most of her time visiting the British cantonments in India, to make the proper contacts, you know," Edgar Murrow explained, shrugging his thin shoulders, his watery eyes focused on a lantern that swayed from the main beam overhead. "I've heard it said that if you stay at the military compounds you'll never set foot once in the real India, so like home the army's made everything. I ask you, Miss Barrancourt, in that case why bother leaving England to begin with?"

Raven, busy with the needlepoint sampler she had discovered in the bottom of the teak tallboy, smiled up at him warmly, her soft cheeks dimpling. "Then where do you intend to go?"

The timorous man's expression grew dreamy. "Everywhere! Persia, Nepal, Brunei, even Hong Kong. I hear a large British colony has been established there over the past few years."

"I imagine you'll see quite a bit of Asia," Raven said, secretly convinced that Mrs. Murrow would never agree to such an expedition, especially since it would mean more sea travel, which seemed to disagree with her violently. Raven felt slightly ashamed of the satisfaction she derived from knowing that both Mrs. Murrow and the obsequious Nathaniel Rogers were indisposed with seasickness, having enjoyed the journey particularly well since the two of them had been forced to take to their cabins. Of the other passengers only Stephen Carmichael had made several appearances at mealtime, looking wan and spent, but had withdrawn immediately thereafter to be with his wife, whose condition was poor.

Raven had offered to lend what assistance she could, but Letitia had been ashamed of her illness and the inconvenience she felt she was putting Raven through, and both Stephen and Raven eventually agreed that Letty would be far more comfortable without her there. Danny, grimly enduring her own bouts of illness, preferred also to be left alone, and Raven reluctantly abided by her wishes, though she didn't care at all for how thin the old governess had grown and how the shadows stood out beneath her eyes, her skin pale, her hands cold to the touch.

"Will we be seeing you after we disembark in Bombay?" Edgar Murrow asked, his timid question bringing Raven from her thoughts with a start.

"I don't see why not, if you intend to stay in Bombay for any length of time. My cousin resides there, you see, and I'm sure he'd be delighted to have you visit us."

"That would please Mother greatly, I'm sure," Mr. Murrow replied with a warm smile, for though his wife might envy Raven Barrancourt her spacious cabin, beautiful gowns, and breathtaking, youthful beauty, she couldn't deny that the Barrancourt name was a fine one and that it would do them little harm to be associated with it. He himself was reluctant to part with Raven when the time came, her warmth and sharp wit, her pride, and, above all, her moving beauty having endeared her to him immeasurably. Oh, how he admired her and looked forward to these quiet hours in the deserted saloon, an indifferent Charlie Copper bringing them their meals of hard tack, dried fruits, cold tea, and hard, crusty bread before vanishing again.

Raven, unaware of the admiring gaze that rested on her glossy head, was struggling to finish the sampler, needlework never having been one of her fortes. Yet the stitches were even and neat, and Danny, in a lucid moment, had cast an incredulous eye upon it, grumbling that only an endless voyage to India had succeeded in teaching Raven the art that Danny had tried so hard to get her to master in the airy nursery at North Head.

"You always fidgeted too much to get the stitches straight," she remarked when Raven had first shown her the project. "Never could understand what you had against sewing."

"It was because you always tried to make me do it when the weather was so beautiful," Raven explained, her slender arms akimbo as she stared down fondly at the wan woman reclining in the bed before her, "and I preferred riding with Father. Now, on the other hand," she added with a mischievous smile lurking in her eyes, "nothing else occupies my time other than acute boredom, so why not at least keep my fingers from growing idle?"

"Oh, go on with you," Danny replied with a weak smile. "When you finish we'll send it to your great-uncle so that he can see how productive you've been during the voyage."

Raven had laughed at this, yet now, as she finished the last few squares, she saw that it had turned out admirably enough and resolved to send it home after all, if only to prove, contrary to popular belief, that she did possess a few of the finer feminine attributes.

"Excuse me, Mr. Murrow."

Raven looked up to see Charlie Copper standing in the doorway dressed from head to toe in heavy rain gear, his eyes glowing in the shadowy darkness of his face. A pool of water was collecting around his booted feet, and raindrops dripped steadily from the wide brim of his oilskin hat. "Mrs. Murrow be callin' for ye, sir."

Edgar Murrow sighed and rose reluctantly to his feet. "Poor thing must be feeling ill again," he remarked as Charlie muttered something unintelligible beneath his breath. "Will you excuse me, Miss Barrancourt?"

"I may as well go with you and see how Danny's doing," Raven said with an answering smile.

"Best cross the decks carefully, Miss Barrancourt," Charlie Copper said to her when they exited into the narrow corridor and paused before the thick wooden door that led into the open air. "They're awash, they are, and proper slick. Wind's gusting wild."

Raven responded to the dour little man's grim warning with a reassured squaring of her shoulders. "Don't worry about me! I had no problem getting here earlier, so I think I can make it back all right. Besides," she added practically, "I don't mind getting wet."

Charlie Copper's response to her gentle teasing was a muttered comment Raven couldn't catch, and she exchanged a look of amusement with Edgar Murrow as the cabin servant struggled to throw open the outer door. Even from where she stood Raven could feel the wind slashing across the soaking decks and feel the icy rain splatter her gown. Instinctively she retreated a step in the narrow corridor, seeing that the storm had increased in force considerably during the last half-hour.

"Perhaps we better wait in the saloon a little longer," Mr. Murrow remarked nervously, squinting outside through the curtain of rain and howling wind. Roiling clouds obscured the sky, which was nearly as dark as night, savagely rent with searing bolts of jagged light.

"Yer wife be needin' ye right badly," the steward growled.

"Why don't you give me your arm," Raven suggested, "and Mr. Copper can take the other? That way the three of us will be able to anchor ourselves against the wind."

The timid gentleman brightened. "An excellent idea. If you'll be so kind as to assist us, Mr. Copper?" he added to Charlie, who was looking decidedly annoyed.

Grumbling in the affirmative, the cabin servant stepped out onto the deck and reached back to offer Raven his oilskin-covered arm. At that very moment a jagged bolt of lightning tore across the leaden sky, blinding them as it ripped from the heavens and struck deeply into the soaring tip of the battered merchantman's mainmast. Thunder exploded close on its heels, a deafening vibration that rocked the ship to its very core and drowned out the telltale sound of splintering wood as the top section of the mast, weighed down with soaking canvas, toppled and crashed into the forecastle.

Raven, half-blinded, her ears ringing, had no idea what had happened. She knew only that the planking under her feet suddenly lurched and groaned beneath some powerful blow and that Charlie Copper, whose arm she had taken in a firm grip, was suddenly gone, snatched away by some terrifying unseen force.

"Dear God in heaven!" she heard Edgar Murrow cry behind her, and jerked about to find him gazing past her shoulder, his eyes wide with horror, a sickening greenish cast to his thin cheeks.

"What is it?" Raven cried, infected by his fear, running forward to peer out of the companionway.

"Didn't you see?" Edgar Murrow's voice was shaking. "My God, lightning struck the mast and part of it came down. I think Mr. Copper's pinned under it!"

Her eyesight restored, Raven frantically searched the deck until she saw the slick oilskin coat of the little steward buried beneath a tangle of rigging and spars. She gasped, seeing that the force of the blow had swept him half over the side of the ship, where he hung with a death grip to a part of the gunnel damaged by the fallen mast.

"We've got to help him!" she cried, turning back to Mr. Murrow.

The thin, ashen gentleman appeared close to utter panic. "The wind will sweep us overboard if we go out!"

"But there's no one else on this side of the ship!" Raven protested. "Help me, please, I can't move him alone!"

Edgar Murrow's lips moved soundlessly as he retreated against the rough walls of the corridor. "I-I can't, Miss Raven," he murmured weakly. "I'm just a simple m-merchant from Folkestone, not a hero. I can't!"

Raven saw that it was useless to argue. Sweat was pouring down the grayish cheeks, and his hands trembled as though with palsy. Knowing there was little time to waste, that Charlie Copper could lose his grip at any moment, she dashed outside, the wind tearing her breath away. In less than a second she was soaked to the skin, her carefully arranged hair blowing behind her, the pins torn loose, hail pelleting her bare face and arms and stinging painfully.

"For God's sake, help me!"

Charlie Copper's voice was almost carried away by the wind, but Raven could hear the mortal dread within it. "C-Can't swim, Miss Barrancourt! Please!"

"I'm coming!" Raven called to him above the roaring of the wind, but even as she fought her way through the debris that littered the deck, a towering wave slammed against the side of the floundering vessel. Raven could hear Charlie's agonized scream as he was thrown against the unyielding wood, but his hold was tenacious, and she prayed that his strength would last.

"Charlie, give me your hand!" she cried when she reached him at last, dropping on her knees in the foaming icy water that churned in the scuppers.

"I can't let go! I'll fall!" Charlie screamed back, his eyes bulging with terror as he looked up at her anxious face hovering several feet above him. "Pull me up!" he commanded, every word punctuated with a wheezing gasp. "For the love of God, lass, pull me up!"

Raven leaned down, the shattered railing forming an opening that gave her a sickening view of the roiling sea below. Icy waves dashed against Charlie's inert form, sucking greedily at his dangling legs, and she could see the tremors that racked his arms and knew that his strength was almost gone. Seizing his wrists in her hands, Raven leaned back, pulling with all her might, but she scarcely succeeded in moving him at all. Above the howling wind and driving rain she heard his low moan of anguish, as though he knew her help was futile. She tried again, teeth clenched with determination, only to meet with continued failure.

Propping her slim booted feet on either side of the gaping hole, Raven wrapped her fingers so tightly about the steward's wrists that they began to tingle as the blood fled from them. Sodden skirts nearly touching the rain-soaked deck, she threw all of her weight into her legs and heaved, eyes shut, small teeth bared with the strain. For what seemed like an endless moment nothing happened, but then she felt something give, and Charlie's body began to inch slowly toward the opening.

An anguished groan rose in Raven's throat when she felt her strength give out in one swift, unexpected rush. Her fingers abruptly tore free from Charlie's wrists and she fell back with a painful thump, but when she scrambled upright she saw that her efforts had been sufficient for the little steward to curl his hands around part of the fallen beam. With Raven's grip under his armpits he was able to haul himself up, and both of them collapsed on the deck, utterly spent.

For a moment Raven lay still, the rain lashing her inert form, then she lifted her head to find Charlie's white face several inches from hers. "Are you all right?" she asked, her voice cracked from the strain and barely audible above the roaring of the wind and waves.

Charlie's chest heaved as he gasped for breath, but he managed to give her a shaky grin, the first she had ever seen on his dour, unfriendly face. "First time in my life I'm gonna thank the Lord for bein' small, miss! Ye saved my life!"

Raven returned his smile, but a wave of nausea overwhelmed her unexpectedly and she turned away, certain that she was going to be sick. Breathing deeply, she fought the urge and managed to control it even while she heard Charlie, the shock beginning to wear off, retching behind her. By then she was on her feet, staggering toward the companionway, where a shaken Edgar Murrow came forward anxiously to greet her.

"Is he hurt?"

"I don't think so," Raven replied unsteadily. Wavering, she allowed the relieved merchant to steady her with a hand beneath her elbow and, closing her eyes, she leaned on him for a moment. "We'll have to help him to his quarters and see that he gets dry clothes and a warm blanket."

"I'll take care of that, Miss Raven," Edgar Murrow said with a surprising amount of purpose in his voice. Opening her eyes,

Raven found him staring up into her face with an admiring expression. "It's the least I can do, after all, since you saved his life! I saw the whole thing," he added with rising excitement. "You should be commended for what you did!"

"It was nothing," Raven answered tiredly, wanting nothing more than to return to her cabin and go to sleep.

"Nothing?" Edgar Murrow repeated contemptuously. "It was magnificent! You go on now, Miss Raven, and I'll see that Mr. Copper gets medical attention." His face glowed. "Wait until the captain hears about this! And Mother! How delighted she'll be to hear what a heroine you are!"

Privately Raven thought to herself that Sophie Murrow would never appreciate the feat since it would inevitably force her to share the limelight with a younger woman. At the moment, however, Raven didn't care at all what anyone else might think. She was exhausted and wanted to go to sleep. While Edgar Murrow helped the weak but otherwise unhurt steward back to the crew's quarters, Raven made her way on wobbling legs down to her cabin, where she found Danny fast asleep, the small dose of laudanum she had given the older woman still working its effects upon her.

With a groan Raven collapsed amid sodden skirts on the rough blanket and closed her eyes, only to find sleep a thousand miles away. Over and over in her mind she replayed the harrowing minutes on deck, shivering with delayed horror now that the numbness which had encased her protectively during the entire episode was beginning to wear off. But she was young and strong, her youthful body resilient, and even as the storm continued to rage outside, Raven could eventually feel a welcome drowsiness overtake her.

A faint smile touched her soft lips as she drifted off to sleep, her last waking thought being how proud her father would have been of her today. In repose her oval face was serene and beautiful, the face of a young woman much changed by the day's events, and if anyone who knew her well could have seen her now, the difference would have been startlingly obvious. Raven was no longer the lonely, terrified girl who had sobbed quietly at her father's graveside or the bitter young woman who had let an unfeeling banker ride roughshod over her pleas for help. In testing her mettle today she had found a reserve of strength she hadn't known she possessed, and the strong, spirited temperament, which Hadrian Barrancourt had told his doubting niece was so integral a part of her, had become a facet of her character of which Raven was now finally aware.

Chapter Five

"Miss Raven! Miss Raven, wake up!"

The tawny eyes opened, and Raven regarded Danny with a sleepy yawn before turning over and snuggling deeper beneath the blanket, shutting out the sight of the round, excited face before her. "Go away, Danny, I'm tired."

"All right, then, sleep if you will, missy, but don't say I didn't tell you when we finally got to India!"

Raven leaped from the bed in one graceful bound, her black hair streaming behind her as she dashed over to the porthole. "India? We're here, Danny?"

The older woman nodded with a smug smile, satisfied at her young mistress's reaction. "Indeed we are. The lookout sighted land while Mrs. Carmichael and I were breakfasting." Her tone grew haughty. "Some of us prefer to spend our time doing useful things, not sleeping our lives away in our cabins!"

With the passing of the monsoons, Danny's health had improved, and she prided herself on the excellent sailor she had come to be ever since the *India Cloud* had entered the more placid Arabian Sea.

"That's not the tale I'll tell when Great-Uncle Hadrian asks how the voyage went," Raven replied with a toss of her glossy head, struggling to shed her confining night clothes so that she could go topside to see for herself whether Danny's claim was true. "Weren't you the one who spent the entire time before our stopover in Port Elizabeth flat on her back?"

"Don't remind me, child!" Danny begged, rolling her eyes at the memory. "I've half a mind not to return to England if it means getting aboard another of these bucking mules!"

"Do you have any idea how long before we dock?" Raven

asked eagerly, allowing Danny to lace her corset, the tops of her full, creamy breasts revealed above the lace-edged material.

"Hours, I'm sure," Danny replied. "Hold still, child, you're squirming so, I can't do a thing for you!"

Raven quieted obediently although her heart was racing. Landfall at last! No more endless days of glaring sun and oppressive rain, no more idle evenings and tasteless meals listening to Nathaniel Rogers, unfortunately quite recovered from his bout of sea-sickness, boasting of his numerous assets while Mrs. Sophie Murrow did her best to interrupt him at every turn and so claim everyone's attention for herself.

"Oh, Danny, do you think Cousin Phillip will meet us at the dock?" Raven asked excitedly, quickly plaiting her dark hair and pinning it in a becoming fashion to her head.

"I imagine so, if your great-uncle's letter arrived before we did," the elderly governess replied practically.

When Raven stepped out onto the deck she was instantly aware of the subtle changes about her. The sailors who had spent the voyage engaged in routine tasks were now moving about with a new sense of purpose, some of them bursting into lusty sea chanteys as they worked, their eagerness to be ashore obvious in their grins and bawdy jokes. Raven hurried to the rail, her eyes straining across the bobbing, sun-flecked waves to the horizon, where she could detect a thin gray line that may or may not have been land.

"There she lies at last, Miss Barrancourt," Nathaniel Rogers said in his familiarly pompous tone of voice as he took his place at her side. "The Indian subcontinent and our final port of call."

For once Raven found she could tolerate his presence, although he was standing far too close, his elbow grazing hers as she leaned against the rail, his eyes fastened hungrily to the square-cut neckline of her muslin gown. She tilted her chin, deliberately allowing him to feast on her delicate profile, too happy at the thought of the journey's end to care how rudely he was ogling her. In a few short hours she would bid farewell to him forever, and the thought was enough to make her smile up at him kindly.

"How anxious I am to see Bombay," she remarked, her tawny eyes glowing with anticipation.

"I hope your cousin will permit me the liberty of calling on you there," he replied huskily, laying his thin, lace-ruffled hand over her slender one where it rested on the rail.

"That would be kind of you," Raven said, moving away in a deliberate attempt to discourage him. He followed her eagerly, nearly running into her as she halted abruptly several feet away.

"Miss Barrancourt, surely you must realize that I—"

"Oh, look, what a strangely feathered bird!" Raven exclaimed, overriding what she felt certain would be an unwanted, embarrassing disclosure of his true feelings for her. "It's not a sea gull, is it?"

"I haven't any idea," Nathaniel answered glumly, giving the wheeling creature scarcely a glance. "Miss Barrancourt, I—"

"And there's a native fishing boat!" Raven added, pointing to a small black dot that bobbed about a mile astern, the distance too great for either of them to tell whether it really was or not. At any rate it was sufficient evidence for Raven to add, "Surely that means we can't be far away from the harbor, Mr. Rogers! If you'll excuse me, I better help Danny pack our possessions." Without giving him the chance to reply, she hurried below, relieved to have escaped him so easily. Honestly, he could be deuced annoying at times!

By late afternoon Bombay was in sight, a great city thrusting into the sea on a narrow finger of land. Raven, standing at the rail with the rest of the passengers, watched in silence as the *India Cloud*, its mainsails furled, slid quietly through the placid water that lapped against its sleek hull, the leadsman's crying of the fathoms the only voice that could be heard. Gulls wheeled and dived overhead, and the air was crisp and cool, India's winter season having begun nearly a month ago.

Above the crowded, multisided buildings that made up the eleven-mile-long waterfront of Bombay rose the lush green slopes of Malabar Hill with majestic blue mountains rising in the distance behind them. The East Indiaman was too far away for Raven to distinguish much of the city, but she felt excitement course through her, a sense of adventure as the exotic aura of the Far East surrounded her. In the harbor ahead of them lay what appeared to be an entire fleet of merchantmen, most of them flying the Union Jack, all bobbing serenely at their moorings while fishing boats, dugout canoes, and other native craft scuttled to and fro, dwarfed by these giants of the British Empire.

"Do you see the island there, Miss Barrancourt?"

Raven looked northward in the direction Nathaniel Rogers was pointing and nodded her head as she spotted the rocky outcrop rising from the dark water.

"That's Gharapuri, and it consists almost entirely of temples, resembling caves, that have been carved out of the rocks. I've never seen them myself, but they say the Hindu carvings are breathtaking works of art. You must insist that your cousin take you there."

"Oh, indeed!" Raven agreed, her eyes sparkling. Turning back to the city, her delicate cheeks flushed with excitement, she pointed to the dark green slope that had caught her attention earlier. "And that hill there, Mr. Rogers," she asked, grateful for once for his presence. "What is it?"

"That's Malabar Hill," he replied, his eyes gleaming as he looked down into her oval face, "but I seriously doubt that you want to go there."

Raven's smooth brow furrowed. "Why not?"

"Well, you can't see them through the mango groves, but the Towers of Silence stand there."

"The Towers of Silence?" Raven repeated. "They sound terribly intriguing."

"Oh no," the fastidiously attired gentleman assured her. "The Towers of Silence are where the Parsees, a religious people who follow the teachings of the prophet Zoroaster, bring their dead to be picked clean by the vultures before the bones are dumped down a dry well." Seeing Raven's slender shoulders shudder, he smiled grimly. "Only one example of the unpleasantries India can exhibit, Miss Barrancourt. You will find unbelievable beauty here, but also death, disease, poverty as you've never imagined—"

He broke off and, before the unsuspecting Raven could react, he had seized her hands in his, bringing them to his thin chest and looking deeply into her wide golden eyes. "Oh, my dear Miss Barrancourt, I cannot bear the thought of you traveling alone through this harsh country! If only you knew of the dangers you're exposing yourself to!"

Doubtless none would be as annoying as this, Raven decided, taken completely by surprise and trying her best to extricate herself politely from his amorous grasp. "Mr. Rogers, I would appreciate—"

"Raven, my dear, dear Raven," he murmured wildly, looking down into her exquisitely lovely face, her soft cheeks flushed, her eyes beginning to blaze, his own sallow features transformed with the intensity of his emotions. "I can't bear the thought of our separation. I simply must speak to you now or be damned as a man. Haven't I made my feelings for you obvious enough?"

"All too often," Raven replied through clenched teeth, beginning to struggle in earnest. They were standing in the shadows of a bulkhead where they could not be easily seen, and Raven suspected him of having deliberately entrapped her here where none of the other passengers or a passing sailor could come to her aid. "Mr. Rogers, I insist that you let me go at once!"

"Surely you must understand how I feel," he murmured, refusing to let her go. "In just a few short hours we must bid farewell. I simply can't bear to let you go!" As he spoke he bent his head, and Raven jerked back so that his hot, dry lips landed partly on her cheek. Undaunted, he pulled her closer so that his mouth covered hers, his thin arms wrapping themselves about her small waist.

It was the second time in her life that Raven had been kissed by a man, and even as revulsion and outrage overwhelmed her, she could not help thinking of that first kiss from the handsome sea captain who had aroused feelings within her that were the absolute opposite of what she felt now. There could be little doubt that Nathaniel Rogers desired her, but Raven, struggling frantically to free herself from his grasp, felt none of the tumultuous longing or odd, stirring warmth that had been her body's response to the passion of the tall smuggling rogue on the wind-swept beach of Cornwall so many months ago.

Seeing that she could not twist free of the sinuous arms that imprisoned her, Raven resorted in her panic to kicking at him, although her skirts impeded her movements so that she could not successfully deliver a painful enough blow to deter him. Mr. Rogers, apparently oblivious to her frantic attempts to free herself, pulled her even closer, opening his mouth wider so that his tongue snaked from between his lips. Raven, never one to overlook an opportunity, seized the advantage and bit down hard upon it.

Nathaniel Rogers yelped in pain, jerking away from her and clamping his hand over his mouth, staring at her accusingly while fumbling in his waistcoat pocket for a handkerchief. "You vicious little vixen!" he cried, his words slurred as he dabbed at his mouth and examined in horror the crimson stain on the white silk cloth. "My God, look at me, I'm bleeding!"

"You'll be hurting worse if you touch me again!" Raven retorted, standing before him with arms akimbo, her golden eyes spewing fire. "And I promise you that if you so much as speak to me even once before we disembark, I'll go directly to Captain Winters and make a complaint against you!" With a haughty toss of her head, Raven whirled and vanished below, stalking into the cabin, where she found Danny busily packing the last of their belongings, humming to herself as she did, obviously pleased that the journey was at an end.

"There you are, Miss Raven," she exclaimed, oblivious to her young mistress's flushed cheeks and fiery eyes. "Just a few more drawers to empty and we'll be finished."

"I can't wait to get off this ship," Raven snapped, hiding the anger in her voice with an effort.

"Amen!" Danny agreed innocently.

Rotten, lecherous adventurer, Raven thought to herself. Thank God he'd not had the courage to press his attentions on her before this! No telling how she might have reacted to the endless torment of such a slobbering fool! Men! How she hated them! Did they think so little of women that they could fall upon the ones that pleased them without so much as an inkling of invitation? She was angrier now at the handsome smuggler sea captain than she had been on the night their encounter had taken place, certain that he had been greatly amused by her wanton reaction to his kisses. Doubtless he'd gone back aboard his ship and regaled his men with a long, detailed narrative of his near-seduction of some simple village lass!

Raven was forced to smile at her vehemence, telling herself it would be better to put the episode completely out of mind, and deliberately busied herself helping Danny fold and pack away the remainder of their clothing, glad to find something to keep her occupied. She hoped that Nathaniel Rogers would take her advice and avoid her until the time came to disembark. She didn't know what she'd do to discourage him were he to make similar advances again.

By the time their cabin was empty of all save the few pieces of furniture Sir Hadrian had purchased for them, the trunks standing outside the door in the narrow corridor, the *India Cloud* had been made fast at the enormous dock. Amid the burst of activity that followed, Raven had only a little time to bid farewell to her fellow passengers and spent the last few minutes while the gangplank was being lowered and the entry port opened in looking down at the long, uneven length of dock and the multitude of ships berthed there. A forest of bare rigging and masts rose into the cloudless sky. The breeze was warm as it fanned her small face, bringing with it a thousand new and exotic smells.

The piers were lined with enormous warehouses, every available inch of planking taken over to the storage of barrels and crates, and the human throng that moved up and down the uneven boards was forced to fight for room. Raven saw mostly Occidentals in proper European dress, merchants carrying enormous portfolios stuffed with bills of lading, shoving their way forward in the hopes of being first to meet with the purser and claim their consignments.

Fashionably attired women wearing white gloves and carrying frilly parasols paraded in promenade back and forth, greeting the newest English arrivals that were being disgorged from two battered passenger ships further down the quay. Among them moved dark-skinned natives, the men wearing white dhotis and turbans or the traditional long jackets and loose-fitting trousers. In contrast, the Indian women were resplendent in brightly colored saris and richly embroidered cholis, the purples, greens, oranges, and yellows dazzling to behold. Though their heads were covered, Raven could see that they had rubbed oil into their hair to give it a glossy sheen, and armbands, bracelets, and rings dangled from their wrists and fingers. Mr. Murrow had told her that most Indian women kept their entire wealth in the form of jewelry which they displayed for others to see, as the more they donned, the more respect would be paid them by the rest of the citizenry. Oh, how impatient Raven was to go ashore for a closer look at all these strange and wonderful things!

Finally the *India Cloud*'s passengers were allowed to disembark, and Raven watched with a feeling of profound relief as Nathaniel Rogers vanished with his trunks and other belongings down the wooden walkway that led to the streets. Captain Winters had asked her to remain aboard until it could be discovered whether or not her cousin was here to meet her, and she paced impatiently from one end of the rail to the other, her sloping eyes filled with excitement, eager to see all of the intriguing sights Bombay had to offer. Danny, not seeming to share her young mistress's enthusiasm, inspected their luggage time and again as it was carried up on deck, fretfully certain that something would be left behind.

"Miss Barrancourt?"

Raven, who had been leaning against the rail watching as a trim little sloop cleverly maneuvered its way between the massive tea clippers and merchantmen to the docks, turned around quickly at the sound of the unfamiliar voice. The gentleman who had addressed her was tall and slightly overweight, his polished coat buttons straining over his ample middle. At first Raven thought he might be her cousin, then decided he couldn't be, for he was nearly sixty, his whiskers and hair snow-white, deep laugh lines etched about his merry eyes. No, she thought at once, there was no Barrancourt blood in him at all.

"You are Miss Raven Barrancourt?" he asked politely.

"Yes sir, I am."

"Captain Winters sent me over. My name is John Trentham, and I am Phillip Barrancourt's business associate."

Raven's heart leaped. At last she'd found a link to her mysterious cousin. "How kind of you to meet me here, Mr. Trentham," she said sincerely. "I assume my cousin is indisposed?"

John Trentham laughed, his belly shaking. "I imagine you could say so, yes. He's not in Bombay, Miss Barrancourt, he's in Lahore, in the hills at his summer home."

Raven's tawny eyes filled with worry. "He isn't here?" she echoed faintly.

Seeing that he had dismayed her, John Trentham quickly assured her there was nothing to be concerned about. "He's usually back this time of year, but he's been detained for another month or so. That's why I met you here today. I've been receiving all his mail in his absence, and naturally I saw the one Sir Hadrian sent announcing your arrival. I intend to make arrangements for you to join him in Lahore, and until I can book passage for you, I insist you stay with my wife and myself in Bombay."

Raven's knees grew weak as relief coursed through her. Though she was bitterly disappointed to learn that Phillip was still so far away, she was grateful to John Trentham for making himself responsible for her. "You're very kind, sir," she murmured, unable to adequately express her thanks.

Sensing her embarrassment, he patted her slender gloved hand where it rested on the rail. "There, there, think nothing of it, Miss Barrancourt. I'm deuced fond of Phillip, and I intend to do what I can for you since you've come all this way alone." He regarded her curiously for a moment, and Raven wondered if he had guessed why she had come, for Sir Hadrian had not elucidated at all in the introductory letter John Trentham had received. The details had been penned in another letter, one that Raven carried on her person and which would be delivered to Phillip Barrancourt by her hand alone.

"My carriage is parked behind the warehouses," John Trentham continued. "I'll have the coolie bring your trunks down."

"I'd like to say farewell to Captain Winters," Raven added, gesturing to the tall, familiar figure standing near the helm in deep conversation with the first mate and the purser.

Mr. Trentham agreed and waited patiently until she had rejoined him before summoning his Indian servant to carry down the numerous pieces of baggage. Danny, instantly taken in by his charming manner when they were introduced, accepted with surprising acquiescence the information that another voyage by ship lay ahead of them.

"So long as it won't take another five months!" she said, her elbow firmly taken by John Trentham as he led both of them off the ship and toward his carriage.

"Believe me, Mrs. Daniels, this one will be a great deal shorter!" he assured her with a laugh.

"Do you have any idea why Cousin Phillip was detained in Lahore?" Raven asked curiously as Mr. Trentham helped her into the well-sprung vehicle, their trunks strapped to the roof.

"I really couldn't say," he replied with a shrug of his pudgy shoulders. "Business matters, I imagine. He's a very busy man, your cousin Phillip, with quite a few warehouses to run up in the Punjab."

"And you believe you'll be able to procure us a cabin aboard a ship traveling north?" Raven asked worriedly, scanning the tangled masts and sails that rose from the ships crowded along the numerous docks.

"Rest assured that I'll find you one sailing with tomorrow's tide," he told her with a smile. "Soon's I take you to the house, I'll be back to investigate."

Raven was greatly relieved to hear this, and once the carriage moved off into the crowded thoroughfare she forgot her misgivings, fascinated by the countless colorful bullock carts, palanquins, rickshaws, and pedestrians that thronged amid the traffic by the thousands. The natives were dressed the same as those she had seen earlier on the docks, and each of them seemed to speak in a different tongue as they hailed one another from across the streets or paused to converse on a busy corner.

The great Hindu temples that Raven had expected to see in profusion were actually few in number, but the numerous gardens and small parks with their blooming trees and exotic flowers gave the city an aura unlike anything she had ever experienced in England. The buildings were fantastic, their proportions immense, the odd configuration of towers and arching windows made even more outlandish by the Gothic architecture, familiarly British, that mingled with them on the wide, well-kept streets. Palms towered along the thoroughfares, and stately cypress, mangoes, and other trees Raven did not recognize added a lush panorama to a city that she could see was for the wealthy alone.

Nathaniel Rogers had spoken of incredible poverty and disease, of slums and filth, but Raven could see nothing of the sort in the well-dressed crowds that moved up and down the walks past the elegant, spiraling buildings. She began to wonder if he had been exaggerating merely to press home his point, then reminded herself that there would be plenty of time to see the real India before they departed for England again, and based on what she saw she would draw her own conclusions.

John Trentham resided in an enormous, rambling bungalow of impressive architecture high on a slope above the island city, the back portion of the house lined with tall windows that opened up on a magnificent view of colorful rooftops and temple spires, feathery palm clusters and the harbor itself with the azure sea sweeping southward behind it. Raven was led to a bedroom that offered the same breathtaking view, and she was so enchanted by the sight that she scarcely took any notice of her other surroundings. By the time her luggage had been brought in, however, she had looked her fill, and turned curiously to take in the enormous bedroom with its simple yet pleasant furnishings.

When Raven spotted the adjoining bath with its magnificent brass tub, she grew weak with longing. Oh, to soak for just a moment in a real hip bath after the long months of having to make due with a tin pitcher full of tepid water and a rough sponge! As though in answer to her silent wishes, the gilded door flew open and two coolies hurried in carrying kettles of heated well water, which they dumped into the tub after adding perfumed salts.

While Raven bathed, reveling in this long-forsaken luxury, another pair of servants unpacked the few possessions she had set aside for use that evening, whispering together and exclaiming enviously over the delicate embroidery and lace ruchings of her gowns. Raven noticed that both young girls were extremely eager to please and that they unfolded, pressed, and hung away her clothing faster and more skillfully than even old Lucy Mariner, her upstairs maid back home in Cornwall, who had been a lady's maid for well over fifty years. She wondered with a pang, as the giggling girls helped her slip into the freshly pressed ivory muslin, what Lucy and all the other faithful servants at North Head were doing in her absence. Hopefully Sir Hadrian wasn't the domineering old curmudgeon he'd promised he'd be in dealing with them, Raven thought with a worried frown, then laughed at herself for fretting about something she was powerless to change, being half a world away, especially when she was also extremely confident of her great-uncle's ability.

As one of the servant girls deftly brushed and plaited her dark hair, marveling in halting English at its length and glossy brilliance, the door to the bedroom opened and a middle-aged woman with a kindly expression peeped inside.

"Hello, you must be dear Phillip's cousin."

Raven rose to her feet, while the Indian girls withdrew to a respectful distance. "I am. Mrs. Trentham?"

"Yes, dear. I'm sorry we weren't here to meet you, but I was out calling and John wasn't exactly sure when the *India Cloud* was due in." As she spoke, Mrs. Trentham came inside and took both Raven's hands in hers. She was plump like her husband, her black eyes twinkling merrily, her gown of beautiful, gold-edged silk, her wrists covered with jeweled armbands that jangled whenever she moved. "My, what a lovely thing you are!" she sighed, looking into Raven's delicate oval face without a trace of rancor. "Oh, what I couldn't accomplish if Thia had only half your beauty!"

"Thia?" Raven asked politely.

"My daughter, Corinthia. She's about your age. She's in her

room changing and should be joining us for tea at any moment. Are you ready to come down?"

Raven nodded, and Mrs. Trentham regarded her slender, muslin-clad form with another longing sigh. "I vow you never have to spend much time before the glass with those looks of yours, my dear! Come along, then. Mrs. Daniels is already in the parlor." She turned in the doorway and gave the two hovering girls the clipped command to hurry before exiting down the long, richly carpeted corridor.

Raven found Danny seated on a sofa in the parlor, the bric-a-brac and Queen Anne furnishings suitably British, and only the flowering bougainvillea climbing up the whitewashed trellis outside the window proved they were taking tea in India and not in some fashionable Mayfair townhouse. Danny was looking much more relaxed now that she was on solid ground for a change, the pallor that had dogged her throughout the long, turbulent voyage having been replaced by a rosy bloom of well-being in her round cheeks. Pleased that she was being treated not as a lady's companion but as a respected visitor in her own right, she perched regally on the edge of the sofa, her pale turquoise skirts spread about her on the plush cushions.

"Oh, Miss Raven, isn't it grand to be off the ship for a time?" she asked blissfully as Raven entered the pleasant parlor directly behind Mrs. Trentham.

"Don't get too accustomed to being ashore," Raven warned with a twinkle in her golden eyes. "We may be boarding another one tomorrow."

"Oh, the journey to the Punjab takes no time at all," Mrs. Trentham assured them brightly, seating herself in a wing-backed armchair and ringing a tiny brass bell that stood on the table near her elbow. Almost immediately a young serving girl in a gossamer sari appeared in the doorway bearing a silver tea service and a platter of scones, crumpets, and iced cakes similar to those which Raven had always enjoyed back home in England.

Pouring skillfully, Mrs. Trentham waited until the serving girl had disappeared before continuing brightly, "You'll like the Punjab, Miss Barrancourt, though naturally it's more primitive than Bombay. More Indians, you know, and they can certainly be—" She broke off as the parlor door opened a second time. "Ah, Thia, darling, here you are, just in time for tea!"

Corinthia Trentham was exceedingly plain, her carefully

tonged hair lank and dull brown in color, her figure already tending toward the pudginess that plagued her parents, though she had wisely dressed herself in a gown of retiring blue that tended to minimize her figure. Her smile was warm and welcoming, however, and she proved, while as garrulous as her mother, to be in possession of commendable intelligence and even a modicum of wit.

"What a shame you'll be staying for only one night!" she exclaimed, helping herself to several lemon-iced cakes at once. "There's so much to see in Bombay, and so many people to introduce you to!"

"I was hoping there'd be time to see a few of the sights this afternoon," Raven suggested hesitantly, not wishing to appear too forward.

"Why, of course," Mrs. Trentham agreed. "Bombay is India at its best. More British than any other city, if you don't include Calcutta, but at least here we have none of those horrible nawabs—those are Indian rulers, you see—thinking they can control the land as they see fit, as though we English didn't exist!" She sniffed disparagingly. "My goodness, it's gotten so I positively hate spending the summers in the hills, though the heat here is intolerable, what with the natives always there. They're forever holding silly processions and festivals, and take to the streets by the thousands, with elephants and bullocks, mind you, and the noise!" She rolled her eyes for emphasis. "Unbelievable!"

Privately Raven thought the idea of Indian festivals in the streets rather intriguing, but because Mrs. Trentham seemed to abhor them a great deal, she held her tongue and nodded politely.

"What did you want to see?" Corinthia asked.

"Oh, everything!" Raven exclaimed eagerly. "The Elephanta Caves, the temples, the Gateway of India, Malabar Hill... whatever you think would be of interest."

Mrs. Trentham exchanged an arch look with her daughter, then set her teacup down in the china saucer and regarded her lovely young guest with a condescending shake of her head. "My dear Miss Barrancourt, no one, simply no one of importance takes tours of that nature! Why, only the commoners come to gawk at such things. It's—it's downright inappropriate!"

Raven opened her mouth to protest when Danny's elbow

connected discreetly but painfully with her ribs. "I see," she replied, biting her lips in vexation, dismayed that the Trenthams considered the act of sightseeing beneath their dignity. "What, then," she asked sweetly, her tawny eyes gleaming, "is there to see in Bombay that would be considered acceptable?"

Mrs. Trentham pursed her lips thoughtfully. "I really don't know."

"What about the bazaar, Mama?" Thia suggested.

Mrs. Trentham beamed. "Oh, how lovely! You'll never be able to claim you've been immersed in Indian culture until you've been to a bazaar, Miss Barrancourt!"

Raven brightened. "It sounds interesting enough!"

"I'll have the carriage brought round," Mrs. Trentham added, tinkling her little brass bell, considering the matter settled.

"Would you think ill of me if I took a nap instead?" Danny asked hesitantly. "I'm not much for shopping, and I'd like to sleep in a real bed for a change."

"I quite understand," Mrs. Trentham assured her firmly. "I've always hated sea travel myself. Doubtless you'd find the bazaar tiring, Mrs. Daniels. It's rather crowded."

When the carriage arrived and the three of them were comfortably settled inside, the Indian driver took them down the steep hills toward the Arabian Sea, the elegant houses and bungalows along the winding streets stacked almost on top of one another and seeming to crop right out of the rocky slopes themselves. Mrs. Trentham chatted incessantly as they traveled, and Corinthia listening avidly, while Raven nodded her head and made polite replies, although she would have preferred to spend her time viewing the ever-changing scenery. The carriage was a wide-seated landau, the open roof affording an excellent view and Raven, the ribbons on her wide-brimmed bonnet floating behind her in the breeze, was unable to contain her excitement. All of the elegant, whitewashed houses were flung like jewels along the hillside, the gardens large and well tended, and everywhere she looked there were exotic shrubs and flowering trees the likes of which she had never seen before.

The carriage halted all too soon near the Colaba Market where the overpowering smell of fish wafted to them on the cool breeze, and Mrs. Trentham wrinkled her nose distastefully. "Are you certain you want to get out, Miss Barrancourt, instead of making a proper promenade?"

Raven nodded firmly, refusing to be daunted this time. The sight of sacred cows meandering through the square, the turbaned Indians walking unconcernedly around them as they bartered for wares, and the brass and silks and woven baskets displayed in the stalls had kindled her excitement, and she would not be deterred from taking a closer look. Mrs. Trentham and Corinthia obliged her without ill will, Corinthia immediately drawn to an awning beneath which a bowing, grinning merchant had spread a dazzling collection of hand-dyed cotton fabric.

"Ooh, Mama, wouldn't the yellow one make a wonderful walking gown for me?" she squealed as Raven and Mrs. Trentham descended from the carriage to join her.

"I think it would make you look too pale," her mother replied truthfully after studying her plain-featured daughter with a critical eye.

Raven paid them scant attention as she turned and looked eagerly about her. A small herd of goats baaed plaintively nearby, their glassy-eyed stares fixed on their owner, who paraded them up and down the length of their worn ropes to show them off. Beside him a coconut hawker announced his wares in a singsong dialect Raven didn't recognize, while spectators, buyers, and sellers jostled each other for room along the narrow alleyways between the rickety stalls. The air was filled with the din of countless Indian tongues, the lowing of the zebu, the shouts of children as they scampered over the rugs spread upon the hard ground, and the growling of pariah dogs as they scavanged amid the ever-present offal. Added to this confusion was a myriad of smells: coconuts, mangoes, the heady scent of incense being burned in several of the stalls, the delectable odor of curried dishes being prepared on braziers farther down the street, mingling with the unmistakable stench of poverty that wafted almost imperceptibly to them whenever the wind shifted.

Leaving Mrs. Trentham and Corinthia to haggle over the price of the saffron cotton, which Corinthia had insisted on buying despite her mother's objections, Raven wandered to a stall on the other side of the unpaved alley where a dazzling collection of silver and lapis lazuli jewelry was displayed by a smiling young Indian in a clean dhoti and turban. Raven returned his smile but was unable to buy anything, for she had no Indian currency at all, and furthermore, when she complimented the young jeweler on his talents, he rejoindered with a long discourse in some tongue that was totally incomprehensible to her. She smiled again, her soft cheeks dimpling, and wandered farther to inspect a selection of woven rush baskets, some of them large enough to contain a man.

Unaware that she had strayed from her hostess's line of vision, Raven continued slowly up the street, eyes sparkling with excitement, letting herself be carried along by the throng of natives who moved up and down the bazaar in a seemingly aimless fashion. At the far end of the square the rows of stalls eventually thinned, and Raven was ready to turn back when the thin strains of some oddly cadenced music came to her from one of the last booths. She moved closer, drawn by the sound, to discover that it came from a reed instrument something like a flute, the nasal tones almost hypnotic in their intensity.

She came to a halt at the end of a woven rush mat upon which the cross-legged musician sat, his eyes focused on a basket placed before him. Raven bent closer, filled with curiosity to see what the gathered spectators found so intriguing, and caught her breath as the basket lid began to tremble. A small scream escaped her lips when, without warning, a king cobra, its hood spread, lunged into view from the interior of the basket.

Horrified and repelled, Raven jerked back and, in doing so, barreled directly into the broad form of an obviously drunken sailor who was reeling down the alley behind her. Off balance as he was, the added impact of Raven's slender form sent him staggering backward into a produce stand across the way, and sailor, hapless girl, and a display of pungent onions collapsed to the ground. The ensuing confusion as Raven attempted to struggle back to her feet amid the hampering confinement of yards of ivory muslin skirts was nothing compared with the excitement of the spectators who gleefully made off with as many scattered onions as they could carry.

The unfortunate farmer whose wares had been stolen from beneath his very nose added to the chaos by running back and forth, gesticulating wildly and shouting in a Koli dialect in an unsuccessful effort to prevent further thievery. Seeing that the situation was hopeless, he turned and vented his outrage upon Raven and the big sailor, who had staggered to his feet at last, and now gripped Raven's arm with a huge ham-sized hand as though she were his only means of support. Raven found herself confronted by a giant of a man, his bearded face split with a huge grin, his breath reeking of alcohol. She tried to shake herself free, only to discover that his hold on her arm tightened even more as he gradually became aware of the prize he had captured. Raven's delicate cheeks were flushed and her eyes glittered like fire opals. She had lost her hat, and her thick braid had come loose, so that her hair tumbled down her slender back to her curving hips. Her soft red lips were parted. Her breasts heaved. The sailor, bedazzled by her beauty, grinned more widely, his black eyes gleaming beneath bushy brows.

"Kristos! Providence has provided me well!" he shouted gleefully in a thickly slurred Russian accent, shaking Raven slightly in his joy so that she thought her head would snap clear off her slender neck.

"Let me go, you brute!" she cried, struggling to no avail to free herself.

The big Russian looked instantly wounded. "You do not care for Dmitri Zergeyev's company, my little princess?" he asked sorrowfully.

Raven's furious reply was drowned out by an outpouring of unsavory oaths from the angry farmer, who had pushed his way between them, unmindful of the fact that his own eyes were barely on level with the big Russian's thick chest. Raven, watching him jump up and down as he ranted and raved, thought the man must have taken total leave of his senses. Not having seen the theft of his onions, she had no idea why he was so angry, yet knew only that she had to get away from both him and this drunken giant, not to mention the curious onlookers who had gathered in a semicircle around the collapsed produce stand to watch the ensuing argument. It was not faring well for either antagonist, the elderly farmer interrupting Zergeyev's incomprehensible Urdu with outbursts of equally unintelligible Koli. Raven, in the meantime, was squirming this way and that, but was unable to break free, her wrist beginning to ache beneath the unrelenting pressure of the Russian's big fingers.

"Dmitri! What the devil is going on here?"

The cool but authoritative English voice brought instant silence from both the Russian and the Indian farmer, and Raven turned quickly to see what nature of person had managed to end such a heated argument with one abrupt question.

The man who stood arrogantly before her was as tall as the drunken Russian but lean and hard in build, his broad shoulders and powerful forearms ridged with muscles that bulged beneath the muslin shirt he wore, which was opened at the throat to reveal a sun-bronzed chest covered with a thick mass of fine golden hair. Lean, tapering hips and muscular thighs were encased in worn, tight-fitting calfskin breeches, the ends tucked into polished leather sea boots. Thick chestnut hair, bleached gold by long years in the tropical sun, was worn carelessly long at the nape of his powerful neck and curled in a devil-may-care fashion over a high, aristocratic brow. His features were rugged and weatherbeaten, the retroussé nose set above full, finely chiseled lips and a strong, clefted chin.

Raven lifted her head, looking fully into his ruggedly handsome face, and as her tawny eyes met his she saw with astonishment that they were of a clear emerald green, the glittering depths fastened upon her. An unaccountable shiver went through her when their glances met and held, and she covered her confusion with anger, glaring at him boldly and saying in an icy tone, "Sir, if this... this barbarian belongs to you, would you please ask him to unhand me?"

"That depends," came the unfriendly reply, the deep voice hardening, "on whether or not you are innocent of whatever crime seems to have been committed here."

"None other than that this drunken savage fell on top of that stand there, dragging me with him!" Raven gave the Russian a disdainful glance as he stood with his big hand about her arm, blinking uneasily at the tall gentleman who stood arrogantly before them.

The Englishman laughed at this, throwing back his head, his white teeth flashing in his bronzed face, and it was then that Raven recognized him, the insolent tone of voice, the mockery that was obvious in his laughter carrying her back across the thousands of miles to the dark, deserted stretch of North Head beach where, while his crew unloaded smuggled kegs of rum, their ruthless captain had attempted to ensure his freedom by seducing her, albeit unsuccessfully.

Color rose high in Raven's soft, hollow cheeks, and her tawny eyes began to flash. "You!" she breathed, twisting out of the grasp of the big Russian, who let her go without protest. She came to a halt before the broad-shouldered Englishman, glaring up into his handsome, impassive face, her eyes searing him with her outrage. "I should have sent the grenadiers after you!"

The Englishman was not visibly shaken by her threat. With arms crossed before his powerful chest, booted legs planted arrogantly apart, he stared down at her with mockingly arched brows, a faint smile curving his full lips.

In her anger Raven was unaware of how breathtakingly beautiful she appeared. With only a hint of lace adorning the three-quarters-length sleeves and scooped neckline of her muslin gown, its simple cut enhanced her extraordinary innocence. She was bareheaded, having been unable as of yet to recover her bonnet, and her jet-black hair was pulled gracefully back from an oval face of delicate proportions. Hers were the features of true English aristocracy, the smooth, long column of her throat lending just the proper amount of shadowy depths to her slender jawline and hollow cheekbones. Her skin was golden and flawless, her nose perfectly formed and small, and yet it was her eyes that demanded and held her admirer's complete attention. At the moment they were filled with tumultuous emotions, the tawny depths transformed into golden pools of outrage. Their sloping corners and the angry flush in her cheeks gave emphasis to the flawlessly sculpted perfection of her face.

As the Englishman's gaze traveled insolently down the length of her, her rounded breasts rising and falling beneath the trim bodice of her muslin gown, her entire body seemed to quiver with agitated response. It was almost as though she were unconsciously beckoning him to hold her and slide his hands about the gentle curves of her tiny waist and explore the softness of her flesh as he had during their first, impassioned encounter. But the golden eyes were not filled with passion this time, only with anger and disdain, and her comment mystified him as much as the dislike which radiated from their fiery depths.

"Surely the behavior of my officer, albeit embarrassing enough, I'll grant, is no reason to call out the British army," he said with a mocking grin. "Dmitri will pay for the stand and any damage he may have caused your attire," he added, his sea-green eyes insolently roving her slender, muslin-clad form, "but surely your damaged pride can be sufficiently repaired by a sincere apology and no intervention by armed guards?"

Aware that he did not recognize her, Raven compressed her lips tightly to keep from uttering the truth, though she dearly longed to shock the tall, cocksure sea captain with her disclosure. No, she would handle this differently, she decided, by finding out who he was and then seeing to it that he was packed off to gaol, his drunken henchman included!

Taking her silence for agreement, the tall sea captain turned to his companion. "You will apologize to the lady, Dmitri," he said curtly, though Raven caught the glint of laughter in his sea-green eyes.

"That won't be necessary," Raven said coldly. "I'm not so vain that I can't tolerate a bit of humiliation without making a big to-do over it."

"You're most generous, mistress," the tall sea captain mocked, and Raven was hard put not to make a scalding retort, aware that he was deliberately goading her to anger.

Just you wait, she thought angrily to herself, her tawny eyes meeting his with cool disdain; you'll be swinging from the gallows soon enough, my robin goodfellow, and we'll see how cocky you'll be then with the rope tightening about your neck!

"It was an unfortunate accident, little princess," the big Russian hiccupped, beaming down with reddened eyes into her anger-flushed face, oblivious to the tension between her and his captain. "Are you certain you'd not care to come back to my ship with me?"

"I'd rather keep company with swine," Raven retorted, glaring up at him.

Zergeyev laughed uproariously, the sound rumbling in his enormous chest. "Ah, my little one, I've never had such a charming refusal!"

"And I've never had a more contemptible request made of me in my entire life!" Raven vowed, venting her anger not only on the drunken Russian but on his captain, who stood watching her in silence, his glittering green eyes heavy-lidded, a thoughtful expression on his handsome face as though something about her was troubling him.

Raven, in her anger, did not notice. Ignoring the confused Indian farmer and the few remaining onlookers who hovered nearby, she added disdainfully, "I was warned of the riffraff that frequented bazaars like these, but I must admit I never expected to encounter anything this contemptible!"

Her insult escaped Dmitri entirely, entranced as he was by Raven's breathtaking beauty. "What do you make of such a woman, eh, tovarich?" He glanced inquiringly at his captain, who was regarding Raven's flushed face with a mixture of impatience and annoyance and something else that Dmitri, in his alcoholic haze, could not quite recognize. He sighed heavily and shrugged his massive shoulders. "I have been refused before," he said to no one in particular, belching thoughtfully.

Raven, deciding that she had had more than enough of the unsavory pair, began to search about for her lost hat. She found it lying on the ground before the ruined onion stand and hurriedly dusted it off before setting it on her head and tying the ribbons beneath her chin.

"I believe you lost this as well."

She whirled about to find the green-eyed Englishman holding out a small leather walking shoe which Raven only now realized she had lost. Soft lips tightly compressed, she ignored the mocking laughter in the ruggedly handsome face and took the shoe from his big hand, only to jerk back when their fingers happened to touch, conscious of a curious tingling that shot through her entire body. Furious with herself, she lifted her flounced muslin skirts, beyond caring that in doing so she revealed her slender ankles and a portion of tapering calf to him as she slipped the walking shoe back onto her foot. With a curt nod she vanished into the crowd, her trim back straight, slender shoulders thrown back, and the last that both men saw of her was the flouncing of her billowing muslin skirts and the fluttering ribands of her bonnet.

"Ah me," Zergeyev sighed in the ensuing emptiness, the din of the bazaar fading unnoticed into the background, "now there is a goddess ripe for the taking."

"You've been in the desert too long, Dmitri," his companion replied briefly, his green eyes following the glossy dark head of the young woman as she threaded her way past the crowded canopies and disappeared behind a huge mountain of woven rush baskets piled at the opposite end of the square. "That one is as cold as the fires of hell."

Zergeyev grinned and rubbed his ham-sized hands together. "Even better! Melting her resolve, turning her unwilling protests into murmurs of passion, now there's a sport far more rewarding than taming stallions!" He cocked his dark head to one side, his reddened eyes searching the Englishman's impassive face. "You do not agree, eh? Very bad, my friend, to feel nothing after gazing into the face of Venus herself. It shows your age."

The Englishman shrugged his wide shoulders indifferently. "I'll admit she was a remarkable beauty, Dmitri, but I'd forgotten how cold and unfeeling English women can be. I'd not care to try to break through that icy exterior."

"Ah, but there's a woman of fire and passion beneath," Dmitri assured him, smacking his lips for effect. "Did you not see the flames in those enormous cat's eyes? I thought I saw a spark there when she looked up at you for the first time." He laughed suddenly, seeing the disinterested expression on his companion's handsome face. "I know what it is, tovarich! For the first time you have been confronted by a woman who hasn't fallen at your feet at a mere glance into your compelling devil's eyes!" Laughter doubled him over, and he slapped his massive thigh, delighted by the impossible. "Oh, it's too grand to be true! I should have made that wager with Pankopp years ago when he boasted that you would never meet a woman impervious to your charms!"

The Englishman waited patiently for the big Russian's bout of drunken laughter to end, then remarked with an indulgent smile, "Believe what you will, Dmitri, but yon mysterious beauty holds no interest for me whatsoever." He paused, his expression thoughtful. "And yet there was something about her that made me think I've seen her before."

"Only in your wildest dreams," Zergeyev laughed.

"Pay the old man for his onions, Dmitri, and hold your tongue," came the curt reply, and Zergeyev, recognizing the warning tone, obeyed without protest.

Meanwhile Raven, having rejoined her hostess at the same booth where she had initially left her, was quiet as they returned to the carriage and drove back to the Trenthams' pleasant bungalow. She brooded silently, ignoring Corinthia's eager description of her plans for the new yellow cotton material, annoyance with the big drunken Russian and the haughty Englishman all but choking her. Oh, how she had hated the arrogance in those heavy-lidded, thickly lashed green eyes that had sparkled with insolence and mockery as he watched her put on her shoe, the eyes of a man who knew no authority other than his own.

Granted he was more handsome than any man she had ever seen, his appearance almost aggressively masculine, but Raven refused to dwell on his dark good looks, angry at herself for thinking about them and especially annoyed that he had caused such an odd reaction within her when their hands had touched. Why, he was naught but a conscienceless, unscrupulous adventurer, and she intended to see that he paid for his dishonest ways!

Upon returning to the rambling bungalow, Raven was disappointed to learn that John Trentham was still away at the harbor, and she fretted restlessly in her room as she awaited his return. She cursed herself now for having been too stupid to inquire after the tall sea captain's name, but how could she have been expected to think clearly with all that had happened? No matter, the harbormaster would doubtless know which English ship had a hulking Russian officer by the name of Dmitri Zergeyev!

By the time Mr. Trentham returned, the evening meal had already been laid, and Raven, summoned from her room by the sound of the gong, was surprised to find the heavy board groaning with a great number of traditional British dishes. As the meal progressed, she began to see why all three Trenthams were so plump, for the variety and amount of food they consumed was amazing in comparison to her own and Danny's modest intake. There were kidney and mincemeat pies, fowl in curried sauces, stewed tomatoes and kippers and loaves of bread sprinkled with fragrant dill. The blend of Indian and English tastes made for an interesting meal, but Raven was far too preoccupied with her afternoon at the bazaar to enjoy her dinner.

"Mr. Trentham," she said after a suitable pause in the conversation, smiling at him across the table with wide, innocent eyes, "do you happen to know of a ship in Bombay Harbor with an officer aboard by the name of Dmitri Zergeyev?"

"Sounds Russian to me," Mr. Trentham remarked, his brow wrinkling as he searched his memory.

"Russian?" his wife echoed. "I certainly hope there aren't any in Bombay!" She turned and eyed her young guest with a fearful expression. "You didn't speak to him, did you, dear? It's said they're planning to invade the Indian subcontinent through Afghanistan," she added in a fearful whisper.

"Nonsense, m'dear!" her husband assured her with a laugh. "They've been predicting a Russian invasion since we first arrived in India. Ain't no way those drunken fools can conquer the subcontinent! Too many kingdoms and native tribes all wanting different things, ready to fight on a hundred different sides. They'd never stand a chance, the lot of 'em."

Raven, unwilling to listen to a long account of the state of political affairs in India, repeated her question politely but firmly, and John Trentham pursed his lips thoughtfully for a moment before shaking his head.

"I'm afraid I can't place the name. Is it important to you that we find him? When we return to the harbor tomorrow, I'll be glad to make inquiries."

Feeling his curious eyes upon her, Raven realized she couldn't pursue the subject further without making some sort of disclosure, and she shrugged. "Oh, it wasn't all that important. I met him at the bazaar today, and I was curious about his presence here, being as he is a Russian and I've never met one before. Corinthia," she added slyly, "what have you decided to do with that beautiful material you bought in the market today?"

With the conversation safely steered to a different topic, Raven listened and nodded her head politely at Corinthia's eager reply while inwardly she plotted. Mr. Trentham had told them earlier that he had booked passage to Lahore aboard the *Orient Star*, an English clipper sailing with the morrow's tide. Perhaps once they were in the carriage on the way to the harbor, she could speak to him honestly, tell him of her suspicions concerning the enormous Russian and the arrogant Englishman, omitting, of course, the brief encounter on the deserted beach back home, and hope that he would be able to initiate an investigation.

"If you'll excuse me, I'm off to bed," Danny said, rousing Raven from her thoughts a short time later. Looking up quickly, she was surprised to see that the servants had cleared away the dishes and that Mr. Trentham had finally emptied the bottle of claret at his elbow.

"I'm tired, too," she added truthfully. "Would you mind very much if I turned in early?"

"Of course not," Mrs. Trentham replied promptly, tinkling the little brass bell that never seemed to leave her possession. "I'll have your beds turned down right away. You've an early start of it tomorrow, don't you, John?"

"Indeed we do," her husband replied. "You'll have to be up at six, Miss Barrancourt."

Raven, accustomed to rising early at North Head, nodded to

show that she could be ready by then, while Mrs. Trentham shook her head vehemently.

"Heavens, six o'clock? We'd better say good-bye right now, Raven, dear, because I certainly won't be up at that hour!"

Raven dutifully kissed the offered rouged cheek while Mrs. Trentham patted her hand in a maternal fashion. "I'm certain we'll see each other on your return trip through Bombay. Please give my regards to your dear cousin."

"I will," Raven promised and, with a yawning Danny behind her, withdrew to her bedroom to find the bedclothes turned back and her nightrail neatly laid out for her. Hugging the weary Danny good-night, she undressed with the aid of a smiling Indian ayah and slipped between the covers. Closing her eyes, Raven wondered how she could possibly fall asleep when she was so eager to see the English smuggler arrested and to embark upon the upcoming voyage tomorrow, but she had scarcely dozed off, or so it seemed, before she was being shaken awake by Danny, who informed her sleepily that it was time to leave.

A misty haze hovered over the gardens as the Trentham carriage rolled down the steep hills toward the harbor, where the rising sun illuminated the tall masts of the ships lying motionless at anchor. The wide streets were already alive with activity, turbaned Indians mingling with the flow of traffic while beggars slept or bathed on the street corners and Hindu holy men chanted morning prayers on their woven rush mats. Raven was oblivious to the sights and sounds that surrounded their Western equipage, fidgeting nervously as she tried to think of some way of bringing up the subject of smugglers without alarming Danny, who sat quietly beside her, a woven shawl wrapped about her shoulders to ward off the early-morning chill.

Raven herself had dressed with care, and since the morning was cool she had donned a frilly gown of soft peach satin, the square-cut bodice trimmed with flounced rosettes, the skirts wide over the hoops, emphasizing her narrow waist. Her hair was plaited and pinned in twin loops that fell to her shoulders, and a tiny plumed hat was perched at a jaunty angle on the top of her head. Her eyes were dark and brooding, and she chewed her lower lip, her impatience evident in the restless energy in her slender young body. How best to begin? she wondered. Did she know John Trentham well enough to simply come out and tell him that she knew of a smuggling ship anchored here in Bombay? Would he dismiss her suspicions as nonsense or agree that the matter should be looked into?

"There she is, ladies," came the pudgy gentleman's admiring voice moments later, interrupting Raven from her somber musing. "One of the finest clipper ships that ever sailed the seven seas. Captain-owned, she is, and I hear she's the fastest afloat. The East India Company'd like to see her privately licensed, but as yet her captain hasn't been too willing."

"Do you mean the *Orient Star?*" Raven asked, unable to distinguish one ship from another as the carriage bowled toward the rows of warehouses behind which the entire fleet of merchantmen lay motionless at anchor.

"She's the last one at the far dock," Mr. Trentham said, turning in his seat to gesture at a rake-masted clipper moored slightly apart from the rest. Its hull planking gleamed in the gathering sunlight, and a gracefully carved figurehead of a woman in billowing skirts was visible at the beakhead. "Pity, actually," he said, shaking his head sorrowfully. "She'd make a fine addition to our fleet."

At the moment Raven was not at all interested in learning about the British East India Company's policies concerning privately owned ships, nor did the sight of the magnificent clipper stir her with awe as it normally would have. In just a few minutes they would be aboard, their luggage stowed, Mr. Trentham heading back to his carriage, and the chance to catch the band of rum smugglers would be gone forever.

"Mr. Trentham—"

"Ah, here we are, Miss Barrancourt," he interrupted jovially as the carriage jerked to a halt and the Indian driver hurried down from the box to open the door for them. "I've time to take you aboard and personally introduce you to the captain, but then I must be off. I've neglected my business far too long, I fear, so I hope you'll forgive me for abandoning you like this."

Without giving Raven time to reply, he took her firmly by the elbow and ushered both of them up the gangplank to the main deck. "You there, fellow," he said, addressing a sailor hurrying past, "where is the captain?"

"At the helm, sir," the sailor replied before disappearing down the companionway.

Raven noticed as they crossed the wide deck that there were

fewer crewmen visible than had been aboard the *India Cloud,* but that all of them went about their tasks in an orderly fashion, with none of the chaos that had marked the departures of the battered old East Indiaman. The thick ropes were neatly coiled, the belaying pins stacked in rows along the cabin walls and bulkheads, the decks gleaming with soapstone polish. It was obviously a well-cared-for ship, she realized, even with her scant knowledge of sailing ships, but still her thoughts continued to turn back to ways in which she might get Mr. Trentham off alone where she could discuss her problem with him privately so that Danny wouldn't become involved.

She was silent as Mr. Trentham led her to the aft deck and paused before a group of men who were clustered about the big, brass-plated wheel. When Mr. Trentham cleared his throat, all four of them turned simultaneously, the three officers staring admiringly at Raven, who looked like a flower in her ruffled peach satin gown. But Raven was oblivious to the minor sensation she caused. Her gaze had been caught and held by the eyes of the tallest of the men, who leaned languorously against the wheel, his long, booted legs crossed casually before him. Her mouth went dry and her heart began to pound, for there could be no mistaking the rugged, aristocratic features or the glinting mockery in the green eyes, as dark and clear as tourmaline. Raven's hollow cheeks flamed beneath the haughty amusement in his gaze, her own eyes faltering and sliding away at last in confusion, anger, and disbelief.

"Captain, I'd like you to meet Miss Raven Barrancourt of Cornwall," John Trentham said pleasantly, unaware of the charge in the air between the two of them.

The tall, long-legged Englishman bowed his head in a deliberately mocking salute. "Welcome aboard the *Orient Star,* Miss Barrancourt. I'm Charles St. Germain, your captain, and you'll be answerable to me alone for the next few weeks."

Raven choked down her anger, enraged by his insolence, knowing he was deliberately taking advantage of what was, to her, an intolerable situation. "I can't possibly travel aboard this ship!" she stated emphatically, speaking to John Trentham but continuing to stare back boldly into the laughing green eyes, her chin tilted, her golden eyes glowing.

"But my dear Miss Barrancourt, whyever not?" Mr. Trentham asked in confusion, unable to understand what had come over his young houseguest, who was glaring with what could easily have been hatred into Captain St. Germain's rugged face, her slender shoulders squared, reminding him of a general preparing to lead his troops to the charge. "I assure you that Captain St. Germain is quite prepared to see you safely delivered to the Punjab and that the *Orient Star* is as seaworthy as they come. Besides," he added practically, "there won't be another ship heading that way for another two months at least."

With no single outward change in expression on her lovely face did Raven reveal how shaken she was to hear this. Not only would a two-month wait in Bombay be intolerably dull, but she couldn't afford to squander that much time before the loan to Squire Blackburn became due. Yet what was she to do? she wondered frantically. She couldn't place herself or Danny into the hands of a ruthless smuggling captain, despite John Trentham's assurances that he was trustworthy!

"You may rest assured, Miss Barrancourt, that you and your companion will be treated with the same deference accorded any other passengers," Captain St. Germain added, his deep voice polite, though Raven did not miss the amusement in his tone. His gaze was challenging as it met hers, and she knew that he suspected her aversion to him stemmed from their unpleasant encounter in the bazaar yesterday afternoon.

Her soft lips tightened. So he thought her a coward, did he, a missish young socialite so affronted by her run-in with a drunken Russian that she would sooner give up her berths aboard his ship than face him during the voyage? Zergeyev? Where was he, anyway?

"Miss Raven, what be it?" Danny's question was quietly uttered, but Raven could hear the worry in it. Poor, dear Danny, she mustn't ever discover that Charles St. Germain and his crew were contraband runners! Yet which would be worse? Raven could have groaned aloud as the enormity of her dilemma dawned upon her. She couldn't allow this pirate ship to set sail with two defenseless women like herself and Danny aboard, and yet she couldn't risk losing two months of her precious time!

"Miss Raven?" Danny repeated, peering anxiously into the pale oval face, her faded eyes filled with concern.

Raven stared back into the mocking green eyes, which still held their silent challenge, visible only to her, the sun-streaked, curly head tilted at a cocky angle, a cynical smile quivering on the full, sensual lips, and her own rebellious nature flared. Let Charles St. Germain think what he pleased, she'd sail aboard his heathen ship, find undisputable evidence to prove what he was, and when they docked in Lahore she'd see him arrested and hanged for the criminal he truly was!

"Naught's amiss, Danny," she said, the tawny eyes hardening as she gazed insolently back into the handsome sea captain's face. "I had momentary qualms concerning the reliability of this ship and its commander."

The silent group of officers who had been gathered about listening murmured among themselves at her words, and Raven could tell by their disapproving expressions that her comment had not been welcome. Only Captain St. Germain continued to look amused,and she turned away with a deliberately haughty toss of her glossy head, the plume in her hat bobbing. Let these barbarians think of her as they liked, she intended to see that every single one of them ended up in prison!

With the weighing of the anchor and the singing of the great canvas sails into place, the *Orient Star* slipped from its moorings less than a half-hour later to begin her journey northward toward the Indus River. The crew, under the direction of Captain St. Germain himself, leaped to their stations with the ease of long years of practice, the mighty clipper's smooth departure from the Bombay docks an exercise in skill and experience that all watching sailors aboard the other ships deeply admired and envied. As the massive rudder turned slowly and the *Orient Star* began to drift with the tide, the sails were unfurled and the wind, blowing steadily from the southwest, quickly filled them. Gathering momentum, the big ship slid majestically past the docks, heeling slightly into the breezes, its beams and rigging creaking rhythmically. High amid the polished yards the crew-men grinned to one another, white teeth flashing in sun-bronzed faces, and congratulated themselves on work well done.

In her cabin amidships Raven Barrancourt had noticed the smoothness with which the *Orient Star* had cast its moorings and sailed out into the harbor, but she was too angry to give it much thought. Shortly before departure Captain St. Germain had ordered her below, claiming she would only be in the way if she remained topside, and Raven was furious at this offhanded banishment. In addition she greatly regretted her decision to sail with the *Orient Star* and its crew of smugglers, but it was rather too late to change her mind now, she decided, a rueful smile twisting her soft lips as she moved to the brass-plated porthole and peered outside.

Bombay was sliding away on the starboard stern, the green slopes of Malabar Hill still visible amid the spires and rooftops, and Raven felt a moment of trepidation deep within her breast. She was alone now, with only Danny to share the voyage ahead, and Raven swore to herself that she would never let the old woman discover the truth about Captain St. Germain and his crew, for if anyone must be protected from such a frightening reality it was dear, timid Danny. Raven's golden eyes darkened with determination. No need to be frightened, she reminded herself. Meeting Phillip Barrancourt in Lahore was the most important thing, after all, and as for finding the evidence she needed to implicate Charles St. Germain and his men, well, doubtless there would be enough time for that in the weeks to come!

Determined not to go back up on deck until she had regained control of her temper, Raven spent more time than usual unpacking her luggage, the heavy trunks having been carried below shortly before departure by a powerfully muscled sailor. She and Danny had each been accorded a private cabin, and Raven had to admit that the richly paneled walls and brass appointments, and especially the clean blankets covering the spacious bunk, far outdid the *India Cloud* in luxury. If one kind thing could be said about Charles St. Germain, it would be that he had certainly outfitted his ship with comfort and appeal in mind.

Raven's tawny eyes narrowed. The *Orient Star* was richly appointed, yes, but doubtless paid for with the spoils of ill-gotten gain! How many casks of smuggled rum had provided the burnished cypress paneling and the inlaid teak chest of drawers? John Trentham had told her earlier that the *Orient Star* was not normally a passenger ship and that Captain St. Germain had agreed to take them only after the portly gentleman had also offered him a high commission for transporting English goods into the interior, with Raven and Danny as part of the cargo. Though Raven was grateful to Mr. Trentham for his efforts in procuring their passage, she wished now that they had waited the two months for the next ship to sail, in which time Cousin

Phillip might even conceivably have returned to Bombay himself.

"Oh, speculate all you will, you silly goose," she said aloud, folding her lacy undergarments into the bottom of the hand-pegged chest of drawers. "Short of jumping overboard and swimming back to Bombay, you've no way of getting off!"

By the time she was finished unpacking, Raven's anger had largely abated. Finding Danny still in the process of situating herself in the cabin across the narrow corridor, she left the old woman to her task and returned to the upper deck, eager to watch the coastline of India slide past. The sun was pouring down through azure skies on a placid deep-green sea, and Raven wandered across the planking to the starboard rail, where the ruggedly arid vista of the Western Ghats was visible across the shimmering water.

"Keep her just so, Mr. Lytton, steady nor' by nor'east."

The order was not a loud command, only a calm statement, yet the deep voice that uttered it rang with authority, and Raven looked over one slender shoulder, the plume of her hat brushing against her soft cheek, to see Captain St. Germain standing at the helm with a short, sinewy man whose eyes were fastened to the binnacle. Though both men stood high above her on the quarterdeck, the wind had carried the words back to her, and Raven could not help feeling resentment surge through her at the sight of Charles St. Germain standing casually at Mr. Lytton's side.

The bosun's slight stature made the towering sea captain seem larger than ever, the fine chambray shirt he wore stretched taut over his muscular shoulders and chest. In the bright sunshine his thick chestnut hair was streaked with gold, and the profile turned toward Raven was uncompromisingly stern. Even from here she could see the deep emerald color of his eyes, heavily lashed and narrowed in concentration, and she bridled again, remembering the amusement in those glittering depths yesterday at the bazaar when he had openly laughed at her. Memories of the bazaar brought Dmitri Zergeyev to mind, and Raven wondered where he was hiding himself. Not that she especially cared to see the hulking Russian any time soon, but he hadn't been visible even during the casting-off preparations earlier that morning. Perhaps he wasn't even aboard; if so, that would please her greatly, for it would mean that she would have only Charles St. Germain to contend with during the voyage. Glancing up at his handsome profile, she decided with a dismal scowl that he would be protagonist enough for her.

An embarrassed clearing of the throat caused Raven to turn around quickly, breaking free of her dire musings to find herself confronted by a pleasant-featured young man who, upon finding himself the recipient of a questioning look from the sloping golden eyes, immediately flushed to the roots of his copper-red hair. Raven deliberately forced down the smile that rose to her lips at his obvious shyness, unwilling to let him think that she was laughing at him, but said nothing, waiting for him to take the initiative.

"Are...are you enjoying the voyage thus far, Miss Barrancourt?" he asked when the silence between them grew obvious, his lightly freckled cheeks still pink.

"In truth I've not been aboard long enough yet to form an unfavorable opinion," Raven lied with a glib smile.

Her bantering reply heartened him, and he moved a little closer, taking care not to come into contact with the soft peach skirts that rustled in the breeze. "I'm...er...very pleased to hear it. You see, we've never had such a...ah...such a lovely passenger aboard." He flushed again, but when he saw that Raven was not offended by his forwardness he continued, "I'm Jason Quintrell, the supercargo."

Raven's smooth brow wrinkled. "What exactly is that?"

He looked confused for a moment, then his expression cleared. "Oh, you mean a supercargo? Why, I'm in charge of whatever the *Orient Star* is carrying. I purchase the goods and sell them and act as agent representing the ship when it comes time to deal with the merchants."

Raven's golden eyes darkened. "All goods, Mr. Quintrell? Whether they're legally acquired or not?"

The youthful features remained blandly innocent. "I'm afraid I don't understand your meaning, Miss Barrancourt."

Looking into the guileless blue eyes, Raven was forced to believe him. Still, she found it difficult to accept the fact that the supercargo of a smuggling ship could possibly remain ignorant of the fact that his holds were filled with contraband goods. "Have you served under Captain St. Germain very long?"

she inquired, changing the subject, her tawny eyes sliding past the eager young officer to the tall figure on the deck above.

Young Jason Quintrell's chest filled with pride. "Almost a year now, Miss Barrancourt, and it's fortunate I am to have found a berth aboard the *Orient Star*. Captain St. Germain accepts only the best, you see, and I'm grateful that he agreed to take a chance on me."

Doubtless because you're so easily duped, Raven thought rather ungenerously, although her delicate face was filled with polite admiration. Actually she couldn't help liking the supercargo, who seemed an unpretentious, friendly sort, and found herself wondering again if he could be truly ignorant of the truth concerning St. Germain and his ship or if he was just a consummate actor.

"Mr. Quintrell!"

Raven saw the young man stiffen at the harsh tone and looked up quickly to see Charles St. Germain descending from the quarterdeck, his rugged countenance stern and forbidding.

"You're on watch, Mr. Quintrell, and I imagine the tally sheets are needed below."

"Aye, aye, captain, sir!" Jason responded, snapping smartly to attention before hurrying off without giving Raven another glance.

"Miss Barrancourt."

The tawny eyes met the emerald ones with defiance. "Yes, captain?"

"My men have duties they must perform, the neglect of which could jeopardize the safety of this ship. I expect you not to interfere with them during the voyage and lure them from their posts for intimate conversations."

Raven felt the heat rise to her cheeks. The arrogance in the deep voice and the implications in the harsh words brought her dangerously close to losing her temper. It angered her, too, that she was forced to tilt back her head in order to look into that handsome face. "Believe me, captain," she said coldly, "I have no intention of luring any of your men into intimate tête-à-têtes." Her tone indicated that she considered all of them far too odious for such a thing, and had the pleasure of seeing the emerald eyes darken, which she interpreted as a sign of pique.

Before she could feel smug, however, Captain St. Germain

took a step toward her, and although there was nothing threatening in his movement, Raven was unnerved by the aggressive masculinity and the sheer power that exuded from his body. Her eyes were on level with his bronzed throat, and she could see a vein beating strongly there before she quickly lifted her eyes to his forbidding visage and saw the full lips curve into a cruel smile when he saw the trepidation in their golden depths.

"I told you at our first meeting you would be answerable to me, Miss Barrancourt, and I wasn't putting on airs for your benefit. Our encounter at the market yesterday proved to me that you're spoiled and ill-tempered, and I've no intention of seeing my men dance attendance on you throughout the voyage. If you prove to be a disruptive influence, I'll have you confined to your cabin."

"Why, you insufferable lout, how dare you speak to me like that!" Raven flared without thinking, her hollow cheeks stained a rosy color, the tawny eyes sparkling with the angry fire his arrogant words had ignited. "No one has ever dared—"

"I can see they haven't," he interrupted, his deep voice effectively drowning her out, "and it's high time someone did. Be forewarned, Miss Barrancourt, I'm not an innocent young swain who can be duped by a simper and provocatively swaying hips."

Without giving her time to reply, he turned and strolled casually across the deck to confer with another of his crew, leaving Raven so choked with rage that she could do nothing but grapple with the urge to bash in his handsome head with one of the belaying pins that were stored conveniently in a rack along the railing nearby. Judas, why hadn't she given in to her original instincts and refused to board the *Orient Star?* Why hadn't she told John Trentham the truth while she'd still had the chance? Not only was Charles St. Germain a devious pirate and smuggler, he was also the haughtiest, rudest most insufferably proud man she had ever had the misfortune of encountering. Just you wait, you long-legged fiend, she thought to herself, glaring at the broad-shouldered object of her outrage, her rounded bosom heaving. I'll see you hanging from the tallest temple spire in India before this journey is over!

Chapter Six

"The Indus, Miss Barrancourt, is known in ancient Indian history as 'King River.' It flows almost two thousand miles across the Indian subcontinent from its origin beyond the Himalayas in Tibet before emptying into the Arabian Sea. You'll see quite a number of ships before we dock in Kasur. It's a major trade route between the coast and the Indian interior."

The speaker was Geoffrey Lytton, the bosun, a weather-beaten, age-hardened Welshman whose pale gray eyes were veiled and mysterious and whose knowledge of the seas and the stars was exhaustive.

"Everything looks so terribly flat," Raven replied, her gaze sweeping over the rugged landscape stretching beyond the wide, winding river as the pale, late-afternoon sun spiraled downward toward arid grasslands interspersed with copses of ancient trees. Beneath their spreading branches stood numerous thatch-roof huts with thin, bedraggled cattle, sheep, and goats grazing nearby. Now and then an occasional traveler could be seen guiding his bullock cart down the dusty road that wound its way along the riverbank, sari-clad women and noisy children following alongside.

"You'll see the mountains soon enough," the Oxford-educated Welshman told her, grinning at her disappointed expression. "As for the Himalayas, once you've seen them I believe you'll find yourself changed forever."

"Can they really be that spectacular?" Raven asked dubiously.

Geoffrey Lytton's faded gray eyes twinkled. "Just remember my words when you see them for the first time."

Raven promised she would, and they stood together at the rail in contented silence, the slender, beautiful young woman in the powder-blue frock, the breeze stirring her glossy black hair, and the short, stooped Welshman with his pale, intelligent eyes. They made an unlikely pair, and to the tall, chestnut-haired captain looking down on them from the deck above, there was an unmistakable intimacy between them as they leaned side by side, engaged in earnest conversation. Raven was not unaware of the brooding eyes resting pensively upon her, having become recipient of that heavy-lidded gaze every time she came on deck. Because Captain St. Germain had forbidden her to talk with any of his crew, Raven had deliberately made it a point to converse with them whenever she found the opportunity, and had discovered, much to her surprise, that most of them were well educated, polite, and extremely eager to answer her numerous questions.

Even Dmitri Zergeyev, who had made his appearance on the second day out, quite recovered from his crushing hangover, had shown himself to be well mannered and helpful. After his initial exclamations of delight at finding his "little princess" aboard, his bray of joy echoing over the entire main deck, he had proved a gallant and chivalrous attendant whose dogged determination to ingratiate himself in Raven's eyes had made it extremely difficult for her to dislike him. In truth she soon found that she had to deliberately remind herself that the crew members of the *Orient Star* were smugglers, desperate men willing to kill for the sake of profit, yet in the light of their gallantry and pleasantness to both herself and Danny, she found it difficult at times to remember.

Only Charles St. Germain continued to maintain that image in Raven's eyes, his sardonic cruelty and aloofness a distinct reminder of his pirate's nature. Raven hadn't spoken to him at all since their departure from Bombay over a week ago, and whenever they chanced to pass each other on the polished deck, Raven would turn away with a haughty toss of her head. She had half-expected him to reprimand her again for interfering with the work of his crew, but he had said nothing, although she could feel that unnervingly intense gaze upon her from time to time. Raven was still convinced that she would be able to find the evidence she needed to support her convictions about him, but although she had questioned some of his officers in what she'd hoped was an innocent enough manner, the men who served under him, she soon discovered, held their captain in highest regard, some of them even to the point of worshiping him. Raven quickly tired of hearing their unending praise and no longer made references to him, intending to find out for herself what she could concerning the cargo that filled the *Orient Star*'s holds, particularly the barrels of rum that had been unloaded on North Head's beach so many months ago.

"Miss Barrancourt?"

Both Raven and Geoffrey Lytton turned to find Ewan Fletcher, the cabin steward, standing before them. "Cap'n asks to see you on the quarterdeck, Miss Barrancourt."

Raven refused to glance up at the upper deck, knowing full well that Charles St. Germain would be looking down at her, his lips twisted with cynical amusement. Doubtless he intended to reprimand her after all for talking with his boatswain. "Thank you, Mr. Fletcher," Raven said with a sweet smile that revealed none of the annoyance she felt within.

"That Miss Raven's a gift from heaven," the steward remarked admiringly in his thick Irish brogue, watching the slender, muslin-clad young girl ascend to the quarterdeck, her ruffled skirts billowing in the stiff breeze. "Can't say as I've ever met anythin' so sweet. Ain't one for puttin' on airs, either, even though she's got a right to, bein' as bonnie as she is."

Geoffrey grinned at the normally dour Irishman. "Dmitri told me that she cursed him roundly when he knocked her over at the Colaba Market bazaar the day before we set sail."

"And she had every right to," the grizzled steward replied defensively, having taken a great liking to the beautiful passenger, whose needs he tended as devotedly as his captain's despite the fact that he was normally inclined to abhor having a woman aboard. "You know what an idiot Zergeyev can be when he's had too much to drink."

To Raven's chagrin, Dmitri had informed everyone of their eventful meeting in Bombay, embellishing the tale with colorful lies, which, she was relieved to learn, no one believed. The general consensus among the men was that Raven had handled herself admirably indeed in the face of the big Russian's drunken foolishness, and their admiration for her had increased a thousandfold.

Even if Raven had been present to overhear Ewan Fletcher's compliments, she would scarcely have acknowledged them, for at the moment she was concentrating on gathering her wits about her for what would be, she felt sure, a tiresome verbal exchange with Captain St. Germain. Charles could see the determined set to her slender jaw as she approached, the tawny eyes boldly seeking his, and it amused him that she was squaring off against him like an opponent in a duel, viewing him as an enemy to be defied and bullied as best she knew how. The humorous smile that had set his sensual lips twitching became dour as he wondered why an obviously well-bred, wealthy young woman like Raven Barrancourt should take such pains to engage in a battle of wits with the captain of a clipper ship.

Oh, warlike she was, for Charles had been the recipient of numerous icy stares ever since the *Orient Star* had sailed away from Bombay. Yet in contrast he had observed Raven Barrancourt's effusively charming behavior with his men. His men, in turn, had astonished and annoyed Charles with their foolish responses to her dimpled smiles, behaving more like besotted schoolboys in love for the first time than the experienced sailing men they were. Even Fletcher, his taciturn steward, who generally tended to condemn all women as useless pieces of baggage, and Dmitri, who tended to chase after every piece of flounced skirt he could find with the intent only of conquering and discarding, had all but literally thrown themselves at Raven Barrancourt's dainty feet.

What havoc this glossy-haired, mysterious beauty had wreaked upon his orderly ship, Charles thought irritably to himself, fully aware of the numerous pairs of eyes watching Raven's willowy, blue-clad form crossing the quarterdeck toward him. Thank God they'd be putting her off in Kasur! Any longer and he'd have naught but a useless crew of grinning, lovesick imbeciles on his hands. And yet one couldn't really blame Raven Barrancourt for her unconscious appeal to the masculine gender, for even Charles had to admit that her fragile beauty and fiery eyes were breathtaking to behold and that she never used her ravishing looks in a pretentious manner.

Or did she? he wondered as she came to a halt before him, tilting her small chin as though in deliberate attempt to give him an uninterrupted view of her beautiful features. Her remarkable eyes were cold, however, the dark brows that arched above them lowered in a scowl, and Charles could tangibly feel the dislike that radiated from her, wondering with a flash of renewed irritation why their harmless encounter in Bombay had given her cause to feel so resentful toward him. From the admiring comments of his men, Zergeyev included, and from the light-hearted, animated exchanges he had observed between Raven Barrancourt and his officers every day upon the main deck of his ship, Charles had recently begun to feel that his initial belief that she was vain and churlish had been mistaken. Yet did not her continued antagonism toward him prove that she could not rise above the petty anger he had instilled in her by laughing at her that day in the bazaar when she had lost her bonnet, her shoe, and her temper all in one unfortunate mishap?

"You asked to see me, captain?" the sweet, lilting voice was cold, which annoyed Charles considerably.

"I did, Miss Barrancourt."

"Pray forgive me for usurping the services of your bosun long enough to obtain a lesson in geography," Raven put in before he could continue, her tawny eyes challenging. "Being as I have never been to India before, perhaps you may be generous enough this once to forgive me my natural curiosity." Her disdainful tone indicated that she believed him thoroughly incapable thereof.

Captain St. Germain's emerald eyes glittered. "I was not at all concerned about your conversation with Mr. Lytton, Miss Barrancourt. I had intended instead to invite you and Mrs. Daniels to dine in my quarters this evening. It is customary aboard my ship, once I feel my passengers have adjusted well enough to their new surroundings."

Raven bit down hard on her lower lip, and Charles felt a moment of satisfaction as he saw the rosy color spread across her soft cheeks. "Would it be too presumptuous of me to set the time at seven o'clock, seeing as it's nearly five now?"

"Naturally not. You're more than kind, captain, and I thank you on Danny's behalf as well." Raven's voice was steady, and only the becoming blush on her delicate face gave evidence of her discomfiture.

"I'll expect you at seven, then," he replied, equally polite, the green eyes filled with mocking laughter.

Raven, realizing she had been dismissed, withdrew thankfully, feeling the intensity of those devil's eyes on her back as she descended the ladder and moved in a deliberately unconcerned fashion across the main deck before vanishing below. Once in the privacy of her cabin, however, she stamped her small foot in anger and roundly cursed the paneled ceiling.

"Ooh, that despicable man, I vow he invited me only because he wanted me to make an ass of myself about Mr. Lytton! Customary event, indeed!"

She stamped her foot again, realizing how foolish her haughty outburst had made her appear. "I should have refused," she muttered irritably, then admitted to herself within the next breath that she was actually looking forward to the event. Evenings aboard the *Orient Star* were admittedly rather dull, and her restlessness had been increasing of late, which Raven interpreted as a sign of the lack of activity offered by life aboard the close confines of a sailing ship. How long had it been, she wondered, drawing to the porthole and peering at the rugged vista of the Sulaiman Mountains rolling slowly past, since she had last galloped Cinnabar across the heaths of her beloved Cornwall, the icy wind at her back?

Over six months ago, Raven speculated, a look of longing on her beautiful oval face. A spasm of homesickness overwhelmed her, and she gazed at the arid, rocky mountains beyond the sweeping river, imagining that they were the fertile green hills of Cornwall, and that the many-spired Hindu temple half-concealed by cypress trees near the muddy riverbank was in truth the rosy-colored northern wing of North Head. But even Raven's vivid imagination could not replace the brown water and silt islands with the pounding Atlantic, or the inflated-skin Indian crafts with the tidy fishing boats of St. Ives. She was forced to laugh at her foolishness and, her anger forgotten, turned to the cubicle that served as a clothespress and began to rummage through its overflowing contents for something appropriate to wear.

It would be nice, too, she thought wistfully, if she could bathe instead of washing herself with the sponge and bar of rough lye soap standing in the porcelain bowl on the washstand beneath the porthole. Bathing was a luxury she dearly missed, and her skin, accustomed to being pampered with the finest hand-milled soaps from Scotland, chafed whenever she scrubbed herself, teeth chattering, with the lye. But Raven, whose impetuous nature had brought her much heartache in the past, had learned since her father's death that it was useless to wish for what one could not have, and she forced the image of a steaming, lavender-scented hip bath from her mind, ordering herself with stern discipline to select something suitable to wear before she lost track of the time and missed the captain's dinner altogether.

Shortly before her departure for India, Great-Uncle Hadrian had presented an astonished Raven with over a dozen new gowns, the patterns being the latest editions from France, the materials of heavy, cool-weather silks, satins, and velvets, telling her with a wink that he refused to send his grandniece off on a tour of the Far East without the proper attire. Raven, who had taken little interest in her wardrobe since her father's death, had been delighted by the delicate embroidery and flounced petticoats and the shimmering array of colors.

Several of these new gowns she rejected now because they required the use of cumbersome stays and hoop. Raven giggled to herself as she thought of negotiating the narrow corridor in a hoop skirt, becoming trapped by her gowns and requiring the assistance of the powerful Dmitri to set her free. The laughter died on her lips as she imagined the mockery she'd see in Charles St. Germain's emerald green eyes if such a humiliating thing were to happen to her. Honestly, the man had a way of provoking her merely with one of those heavy-lidded, arrogant looks, and even the mere image of his handsome face was enough to send resentment surging through her heart.

Raven had never forgotten the impassioned kisses and caresses Charles St. Germain had given her that night on the darkened beach, and it annoyed her considerably that whenever she saw him she was unable to force away those memories, a curious tingling shooting through her body as though it had happened only last night instead of months ago. Why he should have made her feel this way, when certainly she disliked him far more than the repulsive Nathaniel Rogers, whose kiss had left her feeling nothing but angry, was a mystery to her and one that Raven was reluctant to have explained. Instead she would hastily remind herself of how he had found amusement at her expense the day the drunken lout Zergeyev had dragged her down atop a display of reeking onions, and was grateful that anger washed away the unwanted memories every time.

"Damn him, anyway," Raven told herself, determined not to dwell on a topic as abhorrent to her as the captain of the *Orient Star*. In a rush of impatience she pulled out a gown at random and held it up to her body for inspection. It was an evening gown of watered burgundy silk that shimmered mysteriously in the soft lantern light. When she slipped it on, Raven found that the scooped collar had been cut unusually wide, revealing her creamy throat and shoulders, the sleeves edged with delicate rose lace. The full skirts were separated in panels and gathered in the front, held back by matching silk rosettes that revealed the frilly petticoats underneath. After some deliberation Raven deftly swept her hair from her face and knotted it at the nape of her long neck, securing the heavy black mass with the treasured mother-of-pearl combs she had brought with her from England. To her disappointment she could see little of herself in the small mirror that hung above her bunk, and wondered what she looked like in a gown she could remember only from two hasty fittings before the seamstresses had whisked the shimmering material away for alterations, time being of the essence as the *India Cloud* was due to sail in less than a week.

Hearing the ship's bell chime six times on the deck above, Raven left her cabin and knocked on Danny's door. She found the elderly woman busily readying herself for the grand occasion. Danny did not compliment her young mistress on her breathtaking appearance as she deftly secured the hooks and stays Raven had been unable to reach by herself, but Raven was familiar enough with the contented silence to know that Danny was extremely pleased.

"Oh, Miss Raven, isn't it wonderful? An invitation to dine with the captain, himself!"

Raven shot the former governess a sharp glance, well aware that Danny thought well of the swaggering sea captain—something that had surprised her, for Danny was not easily taken in by feigned gallant manners and a ruthlessly handsome face. If only Danny knew the truth about him, Raven thought to herself, but she would rather have bitten off her tongue than admit her suspicions to the elderly woman.

"If you don't come now you'll be late," she chided as Danny fell into an agony of indecision over which shawl to wear.

"Go on, Miss Raven, I'll be there in a minute," came the distracted reply, and Raven withdrew, an indulgent smile dimpling her soft cheeks.

Captain St. Germain's quarters lay at the far end of the short corridor, and Raven, certain that she and Danny would be the last to arrive, knocked boldly on the thick wooden door.

"Come in," came the deep voice she recognized, and she

obediently stepped inside, her silk skirts swirling about her. "I must say I admire promptness in a female, Miss Barrancourt."

Raven looked about the spacious cabin in confusion, hearing Charles St. Germain's deep voice but not seeing anyone at all. The table beneath the stern windows was set, and lanterns glowed softly from the beams, but the sea chairs surrounding it were empty. The sound of footsteps made her whirl about to see Captain St. Germain step from behind a brightly lacquered Japanese screen covered with beautiful hand-painted silk dragons.

"I had thought your species incapable of anything but fashionable tardiness," he added, but Raven, unprepared for the sight of him, scarcely heard his taunting words. Captain St. Germain was dressed in a coat of Prussian blue, with lapels of silk, that flared over his lean hips and hugged his broad shoulders. His tight-fitting trousers were of a matching shade, and a sapphire glittered in his snow-white stock. His chestnut hair, usually whipped in an unruly fashion by the wind, lay neatly combed over his wide forehead and curled below his fine Holland collar. Towering over her, he might have been a titled lord putting in an appearance at some touted London function, but for the vital masculinity that flowed from him, his bronzed face and sun-streaked hair, his robust, restless energy proving him a man of the elements and not the product of stifling, overindulgent city life.

Raven could scarcely believe the change in him and was unaware that he was studying her with the same silent disbelief, his emerald eyes narrowed so that only a sliver of green could be seen. The curved neckline of her silk gown revealed the creamy expanse of rounded breasts and slender shoulders, and the new Parisian cut emphasized the sinuous curves of her hips and tiny waist. Again Charles was made aware of her unconscious sensuality. Her body seeming to beckon him, to taunt him, and he turned away abruptly, his tone harsh, and gestured offhandedly at the empty table.

"As you can see, you're the first to arrive."

"But it's after seven," Raven said, deliberately looking away from the imposing figure before her, angry at the odd reaction that went through her as he reached up casually to adjust his cravat, the foaming lace at his wrist drawing back to reveal a strong, sun-browned hand. For some reason the sight of it reminded her of the exciting touch of his hand upon her breast, the strong fingers caressing her naked flesh, and she bit down hard on her lower lip, hating herself for her reaction.

"Surely you've attended enough social affairs in your life to remember that you should always arrive late," Captain St. Germain said, his emerald eyes taunting her.

"I wouldn't know," Raven snapped with unaccountable intensity, her eyes hardening. "My father always extolled the virtues of being on time, and since I've not made my debut yet, captain, I'm afraid I haven't learned the subtle art you seem to find so important."

Charles's brow shot up in mock surprise, while inwardly he was startled by Raven's disclosure of how young she really was. Though there was a touchingly youthful innocence to her delicate features, she had the grace and bearing of a woman of greater years, a maturity enhanced by the classic beauty of her oval face, the glossy black hair swept back from her high cheeks and smooth forehead, her full, womanly breasts straining against the shimmering silk bodice of her gown.

His reply to Raven's tart comment, whatever it may have been, was never made, for he was interrupted at that point by a soft musical sound that floated through the elegant cabin, filling it with an ethereal beauty unlike any Raven had ever heard. At first she thought it might be some delicate musical instrument, then realized that the notes were far too pure, the melody too fragile to be made by man. She looked up questioningly into Charles St. Germain's handsome face, eyes for once lacking their usual hostility, their golden depths alive with delight.

"What is it?" she whispered.

By way of reply Charles moved to the stern windows and drew back the polished wooden shutter to reveal a gilded cage containing a small, darkly feathered bird. Raven moved closer until she was standing at his side, staring in wonder at the creature from whose throat had come the achingly beautiful melody. In the lantern light its feathers gleamed, the color as dark and glossy as Raven's hair, cocking its head to one side as it looked down into her face quite unafraid.

"What is it?" Raven repeated curiously.

"A black nightingale, and I'm surprised he sang for you,"

Captain St. Germain explained. "Normally the sound of a stranger's voice inhibits him."

"I never realized they were so dark," Raven said wonderingly.

"They're not. It's the only one of its kind, I imagine."

"How did you manage to catch him?" Raven asked softly, still entranced by the sad, melodious sound she had heard.

"He had a broken wing and took refuge on my ship during a storm off the African coast last year. I imagine he was on some migratory route and the monsoon blew him into the rigging." Charles's voice was unaccountably gruff, for he had leaned down to hear Raven's question and, in doing so, had caught the wild, sweet scent of her dark, gleaming hair. Raven, suddenly aware of his nearness, her slim shoulder almost touching his muscular arm, jerked away, her eyes beginning to flash.

"You should let him go free now that he's well," she said accusingly.

"If I do, the *Orient Star* will be hounded with ill luck," Charles replied casually, latching the shutter and blocking out the gilded cage from Raven's sight.

She gave him a mocking glance much like his own. "I didn't realize you were of a superstitious sort, captain. I'd always considered that an indication of a lack of intelligence."

His answering smile was mocking also, but dangerous, the glint in the emerald eyes an unmistakable warning. "Don't let my crew hear you say that, Miss Barrancourt. They may all be educated, rational thinkers, but they're men of the sea and believers in tradition. If they choose to claim that the *Orient Star*'s luck will never run out so long as that nightingale sings in my quarters, then who are you to question them?"

Raven was saved from a defensive reply by a bold knock on the cabin door and the entrance of Dmitri Zergeyev, intimidatingly enormous as usual, but groomed in a manner that rivaled his captain in finery. His long hair and thick beard were neatly combed, his dark serge suit sporting polished brass buttons, and when he bowed over Raven's hand, his black eyes gleaming with unconcealed admiration, there was the swagger of a toff in his movements.

"Kristos, little princess, are you trying to blind an old sailor with your beauty?" he demanded, permitting himself the liberty of allowing his gaze to rove over Raven's silk-clad form, lingering for a wistful moment on her small waist and gently rounded bosom.

Raven dimpled, giving him the full effect of the sweet smile which the watching Charles had as of yet been unable to elicit from her. His emerald eyes narrowed in response, a warning sign that his first mate was quick to notice, sensitive as always to his captain's moods. Thinking perhaps that he had overstepped his bounds, he straightened quickly and released Raven's slender hand, but was unable to resist requesting that he be permitted to escort her to the table. Raven agreed willingly, resting her dainty fingers lightly on his big arm as he led her the few feet across the cabin floor to the table beneath the shuttered windows. A white linen cloth had been spread across the polished top, long, fluted wineglasses placed before each chair, the settings arranged with obvious care.

"A glass of Madeira, little one?" Dmitri asked as he seated Raven with a great show of solicitousness.

"Perhaps Miss Barrancourt would prefer canary," suggested the captain, and Raven, glancing up quickly into the rugged visage, wondered why he sounded so harsh.

"Oh, Madeira would be fine," she assured the Russian with another smile, her tawny eyes meeting his, missing the grim tightening of Charles's lean jaw.

The arrival of Geoffrey Lytton and Jason Quintrell, both as resplendently attired as their captain and senior officer, broke the tension that had settled over the darkened cabin. Raven was greatly relieved that she had chosen to wear such an opulent gown, for the gentlemen had obviously gone to great pains to look their best, and as her gaze moved from one smartly attired officer to another, she found it extremely difficult to believe that these men were smugglers, desperate fugitives from law and justice. Only Captain St. Germain, as usual, did not dispel that likelihood, his restless, menacing energy as he seated himself beside her reminding Raven that he was not a man to bow his head to any law unless it suited him and that he molded men, events, and even fate to his own purposes, however devious.

With Danny's arrival a few minutes later the table was complete, and after the gentlemen had risen to welcome her, the elderly woman blushing at their compliments as she seated herself with rustling bombazine skirts, Ewan Fletcher entered bearing the first course of a meal he had spent hours planning and preparing. Catching sight of Raven, her glossy hair pulled smoothly back from her oval face, the mother-of-pearl combs glinting in the lamplight to give the illusion that her hair was studded with diamonds, he came to an abrupt halt in the center of the spacious cabin, the admiration obvious in his widened eyes.

"The soup, please, Mr. Fletcher."

Charles St. Germain's deep voice held a note of irritation, and the Irishman hastily complied, though he could scarcely keep his gaze from straying back to the young woman in the shimmering burgundy gown, the smooth column of her throat and the whiteness of her shoulders and breasts holding irresistible allure. Raven was not aware of the glances sent her way, not only by Ewan Fletcher but also by the other officers, but Charles was, and his temper began to rise. Never had he known his men to exhibit such an infatuated display of woman-worshiping, especially toward a self-centered, tart-tongued wench like Raven Barrancourt. Arrogant little chit, were they truly deceived by those guileless golden eyes, the dimpled smile, or did they simply choose to overlook the fact that she was deliberately playing the innocent, enjoying the obvious sway she had over them? Charles St. Germain said nothing at all as they finished their bowls of delicious barley soup and began on the fried oysters and curried rice cakes. The heavy-lidded emerald eyes were secretive, giving no outward indication of his thoughts as he absently twirled the fragile stem of his wineglass in his long fingers.

"Do you know, Miss Barrancourt, you've never told us why you're traveling so far into the Indian interior," Geoffrey Lytton remarked, giving her an interested glance. Sitting as he was between the enormous Zergeyev and the captain, his lack of stature was made more obvious than ever, but he had dressed the part of a true London dandy, and that, along with his lively, intelligent gray eyes, commanded the attention that might otherwise have gone to his diminutive size.

"I've urgent business to conduct with my cousin, who resides in Lahore," Raven explained, reluctant to go into details, but at the friendly coaxing of both the bosun and the admiring supercargo, their open interest inviting confidence, the entire unhappy tale spilled out without further urging. She told them briefly of her father's tragic death, her golden eyes dry, and only

Charles heard the brittle quality in her soft voice, but her confession of the odious squire's intentions brought murmurs of indignation from Geoffrey and Jason and a bellow of outrage from Dmitri Zergeyev.

"*Metyeryebets!* I'll wring that fellow's neck like a rooster's!" he vowed, his cheeks pink above his bushy black beard, huge hands closing into awesome fists as though he were already holding the squire's fat neck between them.

Raven was forced to laugh at his indignation, the clear sound ringing sweetly above the tinkling of silverware on china. "I'm very flattered, sir, but thankfully my problems will be solved once I have the money safely in my possession. I don't believe choking him will be necessary."

Dmitri looked disappointed to hear this. "I understand what it means to lose your home, little princess," he told her, his black eyes filled with momentary sadness. "Once I had a house as grand as this North Head you describe, but I was young and hot-headed and thought a foolish cause worth more than the land of my ancestors."

"Dmitri fought in the Decembrist Uprising," Geoffrey Lytton explained, much to Raven's surprise, who knew from her history lessons that the ill-timed revolt had been instigated nearly a quarter of a century ago by discontented noblemen following the death of Alexander I.

Seeing her questioning look and correctly interpreting its cause, Zergeyev laughed, his massive chest shaking so much that Raven felt certain the shiny brass buttons would come popping off. "Indeed, little princess, your humble Dmitri was once a Cossack prince with a great many hectares of fertile Russian soil to his name."

Raven could easily imagine the hot-tempered Zergeyev in the role of Cossack prince, recalling that this particular tribe of Slavic peoples were fierce and unafraid, legendary horsemen and mercenary soldiers who bowed their heads to no one. She suddenly found herself looking at him differently, seeing not the hard-drinking, skirt-chasing sailor she had come to know, but a proud nobleman, a deposed prince who had lost everything for a cause he believed in. Was that why he had eventually thrown in his lot with Charles St. Germain? Because the two of them were of an undisputably kindred spirit? Her tawny eyes met the dark, bushy-browed ones, and something of her thoughts communicated to the big Russian, he lifted his glass and winked at her, their understanding mutual.

"Fear not the loss of your North Head, little princess, for if ever you need help in getting it back, Dmitri Zergeyev will pick up his sword for you."

The gallant words, which normally would have made her laugh, brought a rush of warmth into Raven's heart, for she saw that he meant them sincerely, and for the first time since her father died she began to feel that she had finally found someone she could rely on. Why she should be thinking such absurd thoughts she didn't know, unless it had something to do with the amount of Madeira she had consumed, but she felt herself warming to the big, likable Russian as never before. Apparently some of her feelings were obvious in her delicate oval face, for Charles St. Germain, glancing at her briefly, set down his glass, and remarked in a deliberately insulting drawl, "Why don't you kiss the hem of the lady's skirts, Dmitri, to seal the bargain, or ask for a frilly garter to wear as a baldric?"

There was a moment of tense silence, Zergeyev's face flushing a ruddy color, Charles's devil's eyes glinting with challenge, while Jason Quintrell grew pale and Danny began to fidget nervously with the lace at her sleeve.

"If Mr. Zergeyev is offering to become my champion," Raven remarked clearly into the silence, "then I'm honored to accept." Her smile was genuine, the golden eyes filled with a warmth that quickly dispelled the anger rising within Dmitri's heart, an anger born mainly of confusion, for he was unable to understand, for the first time in his long acquaintance with Charles St. Germain, the reasons behind the English sea captain's harshness. The strained moment shattered by the beauty of Raven's smile, he beamed at her, his black eyes twinkling, as tractable again as a faithful hound.

"Dmitri Zergeyev never makes promises he doesn't intend to keep, little one, and you must call me Dmitri now, seeing as I am sworn to defend your honor and your life." A charming grin split his bearded face. "If that doesn't suit you, I wouldn't mind if you called me 'darling.'"

Even the stoic Geoffrey Lytton joined in the laughter, the tension dispelled once and for all, while Captain St. Germain's lips twisted in a sardonic smile, his thoughts his own. Talk flowed as freely as wine, and the courses carried in by a grinning

Ewan Fletcher were comparable to any elegant dinner menu at a fashionable English soirée. Even Danny forgot her station, coming to life at the chivalrous coaxing of Dmitri Zergeyev and Geoffrey Lytton, while Jason Quintrell wore his heart on his sleeve, his bright blue eyes never leaving Raven's beautiful face as she laughed and chatted and felt happier than she had in quite some time.

A contented silence fell over the assembled group as dessert was served, the preserved fruit pies and sweetmeats so delicious that Raven could not resist helping herself to several. She was doubly thankful now that she had not chosen to wear a gown that required the use of confining stays, certain that she would have burst them long before this.

"There's something I've always been meanin' to ask you, captain," Danny remarked, her round cheeks flushed with wine, her normal reticence forgotten during the long evening of camaraderie.

"I'm happy to oblige, Mrs. Daniels," Charles told her politely.

The faded brown eyes were wide and innocent. "I'm afraid I'm being terribly nosy, but what be your reason for traveling to the Punjab? Surely the goods Mr. Trentham requested you to carry aren't the real reason for your voyage."

Raven was immediately aware of the brief look exchanged between Dmitri Zergeyev and Charles St. Germain, a look that sent a tingle of apprehensive excitement down her spine, although she was unable to interpret the charged emotion behind it. Oddly enough, it was Jason Quintrell who answered Danny's question, explaining obligingly that the *Orient Star*, though it was not licensed to carry goods for the East India Company, had agreed to make a special run for them in view of the fact that the merchantman that had been scheduled to pick up the silks, indigo, and teas from the interior had run afoul of the weather off the Bay of Bengal and had foundered.

"But surely there are enough ships in the East India Company to take her place," Raven pointed out, unable to help believing the supercargo's explanation, while wondering inwardly what Captain St. Germain's real intention was. Her heart leaped into her throat. Could it be that he was licensed by the company to run opium, smuggling the illicit drug to the West and returning with payment in pure silver bullion? Great-Uncle Hadrian had talked at length of the ugly reality of the opium trade, in which the East India Company was actively engaged, and Raven's tawny eyes were filled with new fears as she glanced at Captain St. Germain's stern, expressionless profile. It was difficult to believe that he was an opium trader, sitting there in his silken finery, expensive French lace foaming from his cuffs, his classic features those of a gentleman despite their unyielding harshness. Impossible to believe, actually, if she hadn't seen him with her own eyes, witnessed the unloading of the contraband barrels of rum. Unconsciously her eyes traveled down to the strong, sunbrowned hand resting on the linen tablecloth, remembering the feel of it cupping her small bottom that night in Cornwall months ago, his manhood pressing against her body, demanding a fulfillment that Raven, suddenly a stranger to her own self, had almost been willing to give.

"—unfortunate lack of ships in the area," Jason Quintrell was saying, and Raven forced herself to concentrate on his words while remaining acutely conscious of the few inches that separated her from Charles St. Germain's broad form. "Trade is so fierce between the company and private merchants that any delay, however small, can mean huge losses for investors."

"I see," Raven said, pretending to be vastly interested while mulling over the possibility of finding herself aboard an opium ship. What nonsense, she told herself sharply. Her reasoning was dulled by the excellent Madeira, her imagination running wild, fueled by a mere look exchanged between the captain of the *Orient Star* and his first mate, a look that probably held no significance whatsoever. Yet she continued to feel uneasy, and when the small party broke up a half-hour later, she was greatly relieved. Rising to her feet, her burgundy skirts rustling, she swayed a little and glanced up quickly to find the emerald eyes watching her intently, the sensual lips twitching with amusement.

"Perhaps you require an escort back to your cabin, Miss Barrancourt?" Captain St. Germain inquired helpfully, his voice so low that only Raven could hear it.

The flush on the delicate cheeks deepened, yet the golden eyes were filled with derision. "Thank you, no, captain. If I require anyone's assistance this evening, it will be someone of my own choosing."

She had the satisfaction of seeing the full lips compress into a thin line, too befuddled by the wine to feel afraid of the menacing anger her glib reply had evoked. Deliberately turning her dainty shoulder on him and missing the even grimmer tightening of his lean jaw in response, she graciously thanked the beaming officers for their company and vanished with a yawning Danny down the narrow, darkened corridor. Feeling not at all sleepy herself, Raven wished the former governess good night and climbed the narrow flight of steps to the upper deck. As she emerged topside, the cool night air fanned her hot face, a welcoming relief from the warm, close quarters of Captain St. Germain's cabin. A crescent moon was rising above the dark, uneven mountain peaks that sprawled, ridge after ridge, down to the banks of the Indus, playing in shimmering silver upon the slow-moving surface. The mud flats were pearl-gray in the half-light. Here and there along the riverbank the lights of villages twinkled through the trees, while the white onion domes of an occasional temple reflected the moon with eerie radiance. Dogs barked in the darkness and bullfrogs croaked in the reeds. The night and its sounds were alien to Raven, who was accustomed to the sousing of the wind and the dull, distant booming of the breakers.

Overhead a halyard pulley slapped rhythmically against the yard, and the stiff canvas crackled in response to the freshening wind. Raven, feeling slightly chilled in the cool night air, wandered across the deserted deck toward the leeward rail. As she rounded the aft corner of the main cabin, a tall form stepped out of the shadows into her path. Raven, unable to draw back in time, barreled directly into the hard, unyielding chest of Charles St. Germain himself. She jerked away quickly, the movement accompanied by a sharp rending sound as the flounced hem of her silk skirts caught beneath his heavy sea boots and tore free. Raven gasped in dismay and stared accusingly into the handsome face, the light from a lantern hanging from the cabin wall nearby reflecting the topaz depths of her golden eyes.

"My apologies, Miss Barrancourt," the captain of the *Orient Star* remarked in his most maddening drawl. "It would appear that our chance meetings never fail to involve damage to your habiliment."

Raven bit back a furious reply, granting that he was not entirely at fault for the mishap. In the alternating light and darkness made by the swaying lantern, his handsome face took on an intimidating harshness, his features angular, the aquiline nose more prominent, the gleam in his emerald eyes giving him a hawkish appearance. He had removed his tailored coat and towered above her in his shirtsleeves, the wind tugging at his chestnut hair. His full lips twitched as he saw her angry expression.

"What? No scathing retort from the touchy Raven?" he asked mockingly. "Or have you decided to continue playing the role of genteel young lady you so skillfully adopted at dinner? Ah, but I almost forgot," he added ruthlessly, "your parting comment to me should have proved that fancy clothes do not necessarily the lady make."

"What could you possibly know about women of genteel upbringing?" Raven demanded tartly, her words unconsciously echoing the derisive comment she had made to him that windy night on North Head's beach concerning his lack of familiarity with true ladies of quality.

Charles's rugged countenance went rigid and his green eyes narrowed as he stared down into the upturned oval face, the dim light illuminating her rose-stained cheeks and wild tigress's eyes. The wind stirred the raven tendrils that fell softly across her temples, and her lips were parted, her full breasts rising and falling beneath the shimmering watered silk of her gown. A disbelieving oath burst from him, the elusive stirring of memory which had to do with Raven Barrancourt's odd familiarity falling into place with explosive force at last.

Suddenly he was back on that forbidding stretch of rock-strewn beach, the Atlantic pounding in the background, the young girl whose unfortunately sharp eyes had detected their presence trembling like a frightened bird in his arms. How often in the days and weeks thereafter had he pondered over his unaccountably wild reaction to her beauty, as breathtaking and unearthly as a nymph's. He could well remember even now the softness of her lips beneath his, her breasts straining against his hand, his loins on fire, the blood throbbing in his veins.

"In God's name, woman, why didn't you tell anyone before the *Orient Star* left Bombay?" he demanded sharply.

Raven's delicate cheeks drained of color and her eyes widened and Charles could clearly see the dawning understanding in her face. But she recovered herself with admirable ease, squaring her shoulders and tossing her elegant head, her stance bold.

"Surely you must agree that I would have made a fool of myself, captain. Without evidence, who would have believed me?"

"And yet you agreed to sail with us—knowing what we are." The green eyes taunted her.

"My purpose for being in India is far more important than my reservations concerning the propriety of your ship and crew."

"Ah, yes, obtaining the money to save your beloved North Head. I must admit it's an impressive edifice. I wonder what Dmitri and the others would say if they knew we were discussing the same piece of property over dinner upon which we unloaded a shipment of contraband rum?" His green eyes glittered. "Had I known that night I had accosted the daughter of James Edward Barrancourt—"

"Did you know my father?" Raven asked disbelievingly, ignoring the heavy sarcasm in his tone. Her eyes were wide and filled with unconscious appeal, her voice trembling slightly.

"I've heard of him," was the curt reply. Charles's handsome profile now turned toward her, for he suddenly found himself unable to continue gazing down into her pleading face.

"And you knew Hamish Kilgannen," Raven remembered in bewilderment, "and yet you couldn't be from Cornwall."

"Indeed not." The deep, mocking voice indicated that he was thankful that he wasn't. "Before we made the run, I became acquainted with your local excise man."

Raven's dark eyes were wide with accusation. "And you smuggled contraband onto my land, captain, an unforgivable trespass I intend to see you punished for."

Much to her annoyance Charles threw back his head and laughed, the clear, amused sound ringing over the deserted deck. "Now I see why you agreed to sail with us! How clever of you to seek the damning evidence aboard the criminal vessel itself." The amusement vanished abruptly from his voice. "It was a charitable run, Miss Barrancourt, a shipment of rum to the taverns in the district that were being unfairly taxed by a greedy individual who holds a monopoly over the proprietors, forcing them to pay unlawful duties on their liquor. Being that the *Orient Star* had just made a legal run from the Caribbean and came out eighty barrels over, I agreed to the suggestion of our Channel pilot, Hubert Mudge, whom I'm sure you'll remember, to unload the excess in Cornwall."

"You call that a charitable act?" Raven demanded, unable to believe the audacity of this man.

"Certainly, when you consider how poor the tavern proprietors are becoming, all of them with hungry babes to feed. You'll be interested to know," he added with a devilish grin, "that their unfeeling supplier's name is Josiah Blackburn."

Raven's sharp intake of breath seemed to satisfy him, and the mockery in the green eyes vanished, Charles's gaze roving deliberately over her silk-clad body, lingering on the soft, shadowed hollow above the lacy décolletage of her burgundy gown. "I've surprised you, haven't I?" he asked silkily. "Touché, for I must confess that I'd never have recognized the passionate young woman who responded so willingly to my kisses as the proud, irascible Miss Raven Barrancourt of Cornwall."

"I'm afraid you've been deluding yourself, captain," Raven said a trifle tremulously, "if you thought I enjoyed your attentions that night."

Undaunted, the green eyes came closer. "Who are you, in truth, Raven Barrancourt? The aloof, unfeeling Englishwoman you prefer to show me now, or the Faerie Queen Dmitri feels certain you are?"

There was no reply. The upturned face was exquisitely lovely in the filtered moonlight, and Charles uttered a hoarse groan and slipped his arms about the tiny waist, drawing the unresisting Raven against his broad chest and cuppping her small buttocks so that the rustling silk skirts with their hopelessly torn hem were crushed against his lean, muscular thighs. Raven tried to jerk away when she felt his hot lips come down in a bruising kiss upon her own, but the strong arms that encircled her made escape impossible.

Charles, drinking in the heady perfume of her hair and the softness of her lips beneath his, could feel the heat begin to rise again in his loins, spreading like fire through his veins. It was an overpowering reaction that left him determined to fulfill his masculine need, a need Raven Barrancourt had aroused within him as no other woman before. Plundering the as yet unresponsive sweetness of her lips, his hand guided her slender body closer to his hard one. He willed her, with the sheer power of his desire, to yield, and Raven, the heat of Charles's passion enveloping her, felt a curious languor spread through her, a melting of resolve that made her tremble. With every passing moment she found herself growing weaker and more malleable. The sure, steady hands that roved her body so confidently caused the weakness to spread to her limbs until her trembling knees no longer held her and she found herself supported by the muscular arms alone, her body arched against his burning one where his hardness seared the soft flesh of her thighs.

"Raven," Charles whispered hoarsely, the balmy Indian night air heightening his senses. "I mean to have you, my wild, tempestuous Raven."

Cupping her small chin in his big hand, he drew back, gazing down into her lovely face, her remarkable tawny eyes redolent with awakening passion, her soft lips trembling in anticipation of another kiss. His loins tightened with longing, Raven's quicksilver response having left him breathless, aware that she, too, felt the irresistible urging of their bodies for each other. Lowering his head, he sought to drink again of the sweetness of her waiting lips when behind them on the stern deck, the ship's bell rang insistently, the eight reverberating chimes signaling the beginning of the midnight watch. Startled by the sound, Raven broke free of Charles's embrace, her eyes glittering, the sudden anger within their fiery depths reminding him of the sloping-eyed cats he had seen in the Grand Palace in Bangkok with their hostile, unpredictable temperaments.

"You are quite the accomplished femme fatale, my dear," he told her in his infuriating drawl, angry at himself for the fire that still throbbed in his veins and for the fact that she actually had the power to wound him with the hatred spewing from her topaz eyes. "Did you hope to gain from me evidence of my smuggling endeavors with passionate kisses where haughty indifference had failed? I must admit your first instructor in the lessons of lovemaking was quite an accomplished fellow, or am I mistaken? Have there been many others?"

The unexpected blow across his lean cheek cracked like thunder in the darkness, Raven's brittle voice, thick with breathless tears, cutting deeply. "Damn you to hell, Charles St. Germain! I vow I won't rest until I see you swinging from the gallows!"

In the dim moonlight he saw her flee across deck, her trim back straight, the burgundy silk skirts billowing behind her, glossy black hair disheveled from his caresses. Rage boiled up within him, and his big hand closed about the railing, steadying him as he fought for control. Inconceivable that he could allow something like this to happen to him, a man who was accustomed from youth to having women at his beck and call. Aye, damn the wench! Obviously she had intended all along to use her well-tutored body to her advantage, plaguing him with her aloofness, flirting outrageously with his men whenever she knew he was watching, knowing that at any time she could rekindle the flame she had ignited in his loins that night on the windswept beach of Cornwall.

Charles's handsome face was stark, the emerald eyes glittering with barely controlled rage as he cursed harshly beneath his breath. By all that was holy, and in spite of her deception, he wanted Raven Barrancourt still, and wanted her badly. A cruel smile curved the sensual lips, and his powerful hand loosened its death grip on the railing. Raven could not know that she had pitted herself against an unconquerable foe, that aboard the *Orient Star* he was master of all that surrounded him, and that she was helpless to prevent him from taking what she had so foolishly tricked him into believing she had offered. Aye, he would have her before the journey was done, and take her so completely that there would be nothing left for any man ever again once he was finished.

"Is something amiss, captain?"

Charles turned slowly and looked down into the anxious face of Peter Hagen, one of his junior officers, who, although he was accustomed to seeing his captain wandering restlessly about the darkened decks at odd hours of the night, had been lured to the leeward rail by what he had thought had been the sound of an argument. Seeing that the captain was alone, he had hurried over nevertheless, disturbed by the rigid stance of the towering form. Now, as he peered up into the ruthless face and saw the unnerving expression there, he retreated a hasty step, sensing danger.

Charles smiled grimly at the younger man's fear. "Everything's in order, Mr. Hagen. Carry on." Adjusting his rumpled cravat, he turned and walked away.

"Aye, aye, sir," young Peter replied dutifully, his eyes filled with confusion. What in God's name had gotten into the captain? he wondered, returning thoughtfully to the quarterdeck. Never in his eight years of service beneath Charles St. Germain had he ever seen him look quite so angry!

Alone in her quarters, Raven undressed in total darkness, shaking with anger and humiliation and not caring at all that she ripped out several of the painstakingly stitched hooks and eyes while shrugging out of the magnificent silk gown. What did it matter, she wondered furiously, since it was ruined anyway, the hem hopelessly torn? With a rustle of petticoats the beautiful burgundy gown went flying into a crumpled heap in the corner while Raven threw herself face down on her bunk and buried her hot face in the rough pillows. Never in her life had she felt so angry. She wished that she had had a pistol handy to put a hole right through Charles St. Germain's wide chest. How dare he, how dare he insinuate, nay, openly accuse her of having had numerous lovers in the past?

Damn his eyes! Her body and lips were bruised from his impassioned kisses and caresses, and Raven fumed silently as she shook with helpless rage. Never had a man made her feel like this, making her aware of her woman's body as never before and frightening her with the intensity of her response to him. Yet in the next moment he had spurned her, made scornful, cutting remarks that still left her quaking with impotent rage. Tears prickled Raven's eyes, and she pressed her slim nose into the clean-smelling softness of her bedclothes, trying to thrust away the masculine scent of Charles St. Germain that invaded her senses. She was frightened of her reaction to his kisses, frightened of the fact that such a ruthless man could affect her so deeply that she could no longer claim control over her own will. In just a short while, she knew, the *Orient Star* would be docking in Kasur and both she and Danny would be disembarking for the brief overland trip to Lahore. Please, God, spare me until then, Raven prayed, and wasn't even sure if she was begging for protection from the unwanted yet frighteningly irresistible attentions of Captain St. Germain, or from the awakening desires of her own body and mind. She no longer cared whether or not she found the damning evidence she needed to indict him, for she would be happiest now if she escaped this voyage unscathed and never laid eyes on the devilishly handsome sea captain again.

Clad only in a lace-edged corset and soft chemise, her slender body bruised from Charles St. Germain's roving hands, Raven drifted off into an exhausted sleep, a prisoner, still, of her tormented thoughts and unfulfilled longing.

Ewan Fletcher whistled a cheerful tune as he negotiated the narrow passageway belowdecks leading from his well-ordered galley to the officers' quarters. A golden sun was rising in an apricot sky, the westerly breezes from the plains bringing the promise of a cool, clear morning. On his tray sat the covered contents of Captain St. Germain's breakfast, the freshly baked corn bread giving off a heavenly odor, the coffee hot and black. His steady tread slowed as he passed by the narrow door belonging to Raven's cabin, for he did not want to disturb her at so early an hour.

Aye, and she could have charmed the gold from the King of the Leprechauns himself last night, Miss Raven could have, Ewan thought admiringly, a vision of the shimmering silk gown and the wine-brightened golden eyes passing tantalizingly before him. Even in the short time he'd known her, the dour steward had to confess, he was thoroughly smitten. Well, and who wouldn't be once they'd looked into that beautiful face and seen that dimpled smile? She had a way, Miss Raven did, of making a man feel good about himself when she asked a question and listened attentively to his answer, her beautiful eyes resting intently on his face. Sweet and unassuming, but certainly no priggish, high-flown miss who wouldn't give those beneath her the time of day.

"Mr. Fletcher?"

Ewan turned quickly at the sound of the soft voice. Raven's oval face was peeking from behind her cabin door. She looked tired, the normally rosy cheeks drained of color, dark smudges beneath her eyes, but her smile was as warming as ever.

"Top o' the mornin', mistress," the steward greeted her with a grin. "A wee bit early for bein' about, isn't it?"

"I couldn't sleep anymore," Raven confessed in a whisper so as not to awaken Danny, who slept directly across the corridor. She glanced longingly at the steaming pot of coffee as she spoke, and Ewan, following her gaze, winked at her conspiratorially.

"I'll bring you a big pot of your own, and some of my special biscuits, soon's I bring the captain his breakfast and heat his bath water."

The expression on Raven's features was touchingly eager. "Bath water? Captain St. Germain has a bath aboard?" she demanded incredulously.

Ewan Fletcher was familiar enough with the workings of the female heart to know the reason for the longing in her soft voice. "Aye, that he does. A fine brass tub sittin' behind the silk screen in his cabin. Does a lot of bathin'," Ewan added, shrugging, never having cared too much for the task himself. For a veteran sailor he had a fanatic aversion to water, had never learned to swim, and could not understand Captain St. Germain's preference for cleanliness. A weekly scrubbing from a tin ewer and a bit of soap was enough to satisfy his own self that his personal habits weren't lacking.

"Do you think—" Raven began, then broke off abruptly, her face falling, knowing that after what had passed between herself and the captain of the *Orient Star* last night he would never allow her the use of his coveted tub. She wished now, if only for the sake of a bath, she hadn't lost her temper and slapped him, but even as she found herself regretting her actions, a rebellious flame leaped in her heart. No, she was glad she had done it, and her hand ached to do so again when she remembered what he had said to her in his infuriating drawl.

"There, there, we'll be seein' no fine weather with that thundercloud of a face, Miss Raven," Ewan Fletcher chided, seeing the stormy scowl creep across her delicate features. "I'll tell you what," he added, lowering his voice, "seein' as you've your woman's heart set on takin' a bath and seein' as there's no sense in askin' the cap'n to let you use it, we'll have to arrange for a way of doin' so without his knowin' about it."

Raven's tawny eyes widened. "Do you think we can?" she whispered.

The steward's resolve hardened at the sight of the gratitude and hope shining in the comely face. "I don't see why not. The cap'n always takes the afternoon watch, from twelve to four, and if I heat the water for you and you lock the door, I don't see how anyone could have any objections."

Raven, examining the idea backward and forward, couldn't either, and she found her weariness vanishing in anticipation of the luxury of soaking for an hour or two in steaming hot water. Thus it began that, every afternoon precisely at one o'clock in the days following the making of their secret pact, she would knock quietly on the door of Charles's cabin and be ushered inside by the waiting Ewan Fletcher, who would then leave her for an hour of delightful privacy, having thoughtfully laid out soap, sponges, and plush towels for her use. Their shared secret forged an intimacy that sprang up quickly between them, the dour, grumbling Irishman finding his kindness rewarded by the undemanding, innocently given friendship of a gentle-hearted young girl.

Yet this intimacy, along with the whispered conversations that took place daily on the polished deck or in the narrow corridor, did not go unnoticed for very long by the *Orient Star*'s ever-watchful captain. Their paths had not crossed at all since their turbulent encounter, but Charles, watching Raven with brooding eyes as she talked and laughed with his men, glossy hair streaming behind her in the warm breeze that had blessed them until now with fair weather, quickly became aware of their many exchanges. His suspicion ripened, for Charles believed that the beautiful Raven Barrancourt was using her charms to extricate from an unsuspecting Ewan Fletcher the evidence she needed to indict the crew and captain of the *Orient Star* as smugglers.

Actually, the sleek clipper ship had carried more legal goods than contraband in its twelve years of service beneath him, and Charles, though Raven would never believe it, had truly intended to sever Josiah Blackburn's throttling hold on the liquor distribution in Cornwall by causing a local market glut. He had also known at the time that charitable compulsions had not governed the greedy Hubert Mudge, but the opportunity to unload the surplus rum and strike a blow against a rapacious aristocrat, whose sort Charles detested, had proven too easy to be ignored.

Who would have suspected that the run would have been witnessed by a proud, manipulative wench who was aboard the *Orient Star* at this very moment and who, because of a mishap that had embarrassed her in a faraway Indian bazaar, was now hell-bent on revenge? Charles was well acquainted with the workings of the minds of spoiled, beautiful young women. No matter what Raven Barrancourt pretended to be in front of his men, he knew that she would never allow him to forget his attempted seduction of her that night on the beach or the fool he and Zergeyev had unwittingly made of her in the Bombay bazaar. All lies, too, that nonsense about her trip to Lahore being important enough to her that she had been willing to overlook the fact that she would be traveling alone, but for the protection of an aging nanny, aboard what she knew was a smuggling ship.

Charles remembered now the glimpse he had caught of North Head through his spyglass while they waited for darkness before reefing the sails and steering the *Orient Star* close to the treacherous shoals beyond the cove, and he had to admit that the age-worn manor, its twin turrets like silent sentinels facing out to sea, had been impressive. But not for a moment did he believe that Raven Barrancourt truly cared enough for her home to brave a journey halfway across the world to save it. Women were the same the world over, and he had known enough of them in his time to learn that they cared for little other than fripperies and baubles, and a wealthy, preferably handsome husband to warm their beds at night. Raven, for all her extraordinary beauty, was as conniving and deceitful as the rest of her ruthless species.

"Kristos, my friend, if your look grows much blacker you'll have the Devil himself quaking in his boots."

Charles did not react at all as he received a back slap from Dmitri Zergeyev that would have felled a lesser man. "What evil," the big Russian continued, taking his place at his captain's side, "are you planning now? I've seen that look before, and it's never boded good for anyone." His black eyes darted quickly to the lower deck where Charles's brooding gaze had been focused, and his bearded face split with a knowing grin as he saw Raven speaking earnestly with Ewan Fletcher in the shadow of a bulkhead, the sun reflecting the glossy blackness of her hair. Without a bonnet the heavy mass gleamed like polished jet, the thick braid pinned in a dangling coil that brushed enticingly against one slender shoulder. She was wearing a heavy-woven muslin gown of forest green, the sleeves and pleated skirts piped with lemon satin, her full breasts rising above a tantalizingly tiny waist. Even from the upper deck the two watching men could see the tawny color of her wide, sloping eyes and the animated flush to her hollow cheeks, her soft lips parted as she laughed in response to the grinning Irishman's comments.

"It's our mysterious beauty that troubles you, tovarich," Dmitri observed shrewdly. "I've seen you watching her before, and when you do, it's the only time in our long years together that I can't guess your thoughts. I think you dislike her, which saddens me deeply, and yet—"

"Spare me, Dmitri," Charles said curtly. "I've never known you to wax analytical, and now is not the time to start."

Dmitri shrugged his massive shoulders, but his tone was stiff. "As you wish, captain."

Although Charles heard the affronted tone of Dmitri's voice, he did not call him back when the big Russian turned and walked away. Inwardly his irritation increased, for he and Zergeyev rarely argued, and Raven Barrancourt had already caused him enough troubles to tolerate adding dissension with his first mate on top of them. Charles's smile was grimly amused as he recalled his first meeting with Dmitri Zergeyev, twelve years ago in the unsavory waterfront haunts of Lisbon. Both he and Dmitri had taken a fancy to a dark-eyed Portuguese beauty whose name Charles could no longer remember, and, neither one inclined to let the other have her, they had come to blows in the dimly lit interior of the crowded tavern.

Dmitri, thirteen years older and an enormous bear of a man, had pommeled the youthful sea captain with his awesome fists, but Charles, taking advantage of the Russian's drunkenness, had fought wisely, moving like a cat, jabbing when he could and ducking always in the nick of time. In the end both of them had wound up lying on the wet cobble streets, Charles with a blackened eye and splitting headache, Dmitri with two loose teeth. The big Russian had propped himself on one elbow, unmindful of the filth in which he lay, and had spit out a mouthful of blood before bellowing with laughter.

"Kristos, the wench isn't worth the trouble! Where did you learn to fight like that, Englishman? You are the first to lay Dmitri Zergeyev to the floor!"

"Doubtless because you've never picked a worthy enough opponent before," Charles had replied scornfully while studying the big man before him, his green eyes assaying his worth, measuring strength and endurance and thinking that he would like to have such a man serve aboard his ship, the *Orient Star*, outfitted and launched from Le Havre less than eight months ago. Still in the process of assembling a worthy crew, Charles St. Germain, the recently renounced Comte de Monteraux, knew the lusty Russian would suit his purposes well indeed, and

Zergeyev, studying the lean young man before him, seeing the arrogance in the emerald eyes and the firmness of the square jaw, knew that here was an equal to be reckoned with.

The friendship that had grown from that first violent encounter had lasted through a great many adventures, the telling of which never failed to bring admiring gasps and disbelieving squeals from the pretty young ladies Dmitri courted, though it both amused and angered him that their soft, imploring eyes gazed more often than not at Charles, whose aggressive masculinity and classically handsome features had every last one of them at his feet. Yet Dmitri had never resented his friend and captain his strange, almost hypnotic effect on the female gender, though it annoyed him at times that Charles, who could certainly have his pick of any eligible lady he wanted between Macao and Mexico, showed little inclination to involve himself in more than an occasional tryst.

The sound of soft, tinkling laughter roused Charles from his thoughts with a start, and he glanced down sharply at the lower deck to see Raven's glossy head close to the steward's grizzled one as the two of them shared a light-hearted moment. His finely molded lips compressed into a thin, angry line, and his emerald eyes narrowed to slits. Raven, laying her small hand on Ewan Fletcher's sleeve, stood on tiptoe to whisper something into his ear, then vanished with a swirl of muslin skirts down the gangway, leaving Charles to ponder what she was plotting.

In the privacy of the captain's spacious quarters, Raven waited while Ewan brought in the last of the steaming kettles of water, longingly eyeing the magnificent brass hip bath that was filled almost to capacity. Restlessly she turned and moved to the stern windows where the gilded cage hung from a hook, the fragile bird inside protected from the light by a dark velvet cover that blocked out the sun. Raven lifted a corner and peered inside while the nightingale, disturbed from its sleep, cocked a quizzical eye at her. In the daylight its sleek black plumage reflected rainbow prisms, and Raven found herself wishing that the captain would grant the lovely bird its freedom. Not since the night of the dinner party had she heard it sing, and she wondered if its captivity might be responsible.

"Someday I'll see that he lets you go," she whispered, her tawny eyes angry. "He has no right to keep you a prisoner here for his own enjoyment."

"Here you are, Miss Raven, the last of 'em."

She turned and lowered the cage cover while Ewan poured the contents of the copper kettle into the tub. Satisfied that he had prepared everything for her, the steward gave her a wink and went out, closing the door behind him, and Raven, calling her thanks after him through the thick wood, slid the bolt into place. Then she sighed happily, knowing that no one would disturb her and that she could bathe for over an hour if she felt so inclined.

Stepping out of her gown and soft undergarments, she slipped into the tub, the warm water lapping about her, and closed her eyes, savoring these few moments of privacy aboard the limited freedom of a sailing ship, the close quarters made unbearably smaller of late by Raven's inability to find escape from the chilly, watchful eyes of Captain St. Germain. She thrust his image from her mind, frowning slightly, and began to lather herself with the scented soap, her ivory body glistening. She had pinned the thick black braid of hair to the top of her head, her long neck rising like a graceful swan's from the water, the fragile collarbones visible beneath the creamy smoothness of her flesh.

Thrusting a long, slender leg out of the water, Raven scrubbed it industriously, the sponge dripping moisture between her slim fingers, and hummed to herself, feeling content with her lot for the first time in many days. Everything had been so hard for her of late, the peace of mind which had slowly begun to restore itself after the untimely death of her father shattered by Squire Blackburn's loathsome marriage offer and further destroyed by the strange, undefinable hold the captain of the *Orient Star* seemed to have over her. If only she were home again, riding Cinnabar in a mad gallop along the cliffs, blissfully unaware of the existence of a man who, with only the power of his fiery touch, had made Raven aware of a part of herself she only vaguely understood and could not control. Much as she hated Charles St. Germain, part of her longed for him, yearned for a fulfillment which she sensed only he could satisfy, and the realization of her need for him angered and terrified her.

"What the devil are you doing here?"

A small shriek escaped Raven's lips, her heart stopping as she jerked about to find the towering object of her tormented fascination standing in the opening between the richly paneled wall and the lacquered screen, long legs straddling the floor as he gazed down with disbelief at the startled, thoroughly naked young woman in his bathtub.

"How did you get in here?" Raven whispered, her voice trembling.

"It is my cabin," Charles reminded her with a mocking smile. "I have a key of my own."

Raven bit her lower lip in consternation, her widened eyes meeting his glittering emerald ones. Beneath the lapping water her flawless body was mercilessly exposed to his gaze, the smooth skin flushed pink, reminding Charles of the softness of a newly opened rose. Droplets of water ran in slow rivulets down the enticing hollow between her full breasts, the slender curves of her hips tapering to long, shapely thighs and calves. Raven, watching every nuance in the handsome visage, saw the beautifully masculine features transforming from incredulity to something else, the emerald eyes growing dark and watchful.

Bending down, Charles wrapped his long fingers about Raven's slender wrist, feeling the wild, frightened pulse there as he pulled her easily upright. When she was standing before him, her small feet between his heavy leather boots, smooth thighs brushing against his worn breeches, he allowed his gaze to travel hungrily over the achingly lovely perfection of the body that had been haunting his waking hours and invading his sleep. Raven could see the pulse beating strongly in his temple, his nostrils flaring, and she shivered in the coolness of the cabin air, prompting a cruel smile to twist Charles's sensual lips.

"Frightened, Raven? How can you be, when the act of lovemaking is not strange to you?"

"Damn you!" Raven cried, lifting her arm to strike him.

Charles, having expected her fierce reaction, easily caught her flailing fist and slid his free hand about her waist, his strong fingers curving over her hipbone, pulling her toward him so that the length of her body was pressed against his hard chest and muscular thighs. "No reason to fear me, sweet, enchanting Raven," he whispered into her fragrant hair. "I intend to love you better than any man ever has."

His handsome visage darkened at the thought of anyone else gazing at the beauty of her slender body, caressing her silken skin and kissing her parted, inviting lips. "You'll want no one again after I've loved you, Raven," he promised in a harsh voice, his breath warm against her fiery cheek, ignoring her frightened protests. "Your passion was meant to be awakened by me, regardless of how many lovers you have taken to your bed in the past."

"No," Raven murmured weakly, frightened by the emotions beginning to smolder in his devil's eyes. She tried to twist away, but Charles tightened his arms about her, making escape impossible.

"You wanted me the first night we met, Raven," Charles reminded her huskily. "God's blood, you can't pretend now that my kisses meant nothing!"

Before she could reply, he had pressed his mouth to hers, attempting to possess her with the searing insistence of his lips alone. Raven, the pliant leather of his tight-fitting breeches riding against her naked thighs, could feel the hardening of his manhood against her. She groaned and tried to pull away, but Charles seized the back of her head, preventing her from turning, and kissed her more deeply, until Raven's senses began to swim.

"Charles, don't, please," she gasped, but her body betrayed her as he caressed her naked breasts boldly, leaning against him as her limbs lost the power to support her.

His hawkish features rigid with the force of his desire, Charles lifted her into his arms and carried her to the roomy bunk, laying her amid the soft blankets, where Raven trembled, her golden eyes wide and fearful as she gazed wordlessly up at him. Her thick braid of hair had worked itself free in the roughness of Charles's embrace and lay in a blue-black cloud about her exquisite face, and Charles feasted on the breathtaking beauty of the young woman who had the power to awaken his desire with her innocence alone.

"You want me to love you, Raven," he whispered hoarsely, removing his muslin shirt and revealing to her widening eyes the rippling muscles that lay beneath the sun-bronzed skin, his broad chest covered with a thick furring of fine golden hair that tapered down across his hard, flat belly.

"No, it isn't true," she whispered, despair overwhelming her when she realized that it was. As she watched, hypnotized, Charles unfastened the leather breeches and let them fall to the cabin floor, revealing to her for the second time in her life the splendor of his male body. Despite her fear Raven could not help thinking that he was beautiful, the raw, sun-browned hardness of him a startling contrast to her own ivory softness. His hips and flanks were lean, tapering to a manhood emboldened with anticipation, his passion further emphasized by the heavy-lidded sensuality in his glittering green eyes.

"I know you want me to love you, Raven," Charles repeated as he stood over her, unable to drink in enough of the silken body awaiting his possession. "I can see it in the fire in your eyes, feel it in your lips when I kiss you."

"Y-you're wrong," Raven insisted doggedly, the tremor in her voice revealing her uncertainty.

Charles's smile was wolfish as he pulled her to him, the mattress sagging beneath his weight. "Am I?" he mocked, running his hands across the silken curve of her hips. "Am I, Raven?" he repeated harshly as she trembled. Lowering his head, he covered her lips with his, his hot tongue plundering the soft interior of her mouth. With firm yet gentle hands Charles roved her flesh, enjoying the feel of her, having completely forgotten that he had been anticipating this moment with burning impatience, his planned seduction an execution of bitter brutality.

Now he found himself a victim of the sleepy lioness eyes, the overpowering allure of a woman whose beauty ignited deep within him the desire to experience a pleasure he sensed would be more intensely poignant than any he had ever known. Pulling her unyielding body against the length of his, Charles let her feel the searing contact of their flesh wherever they touched so that she, too, would know what lay in store for them in the consummation of their mutual need.

"I nearly had you once," Charles whispered, his voice throbbing with emotion, "and it drove me mad to let you go. But now there's no one to stop us, Raven, no one."

"I won't let you d-do this," Raven protested raggedly, trying to arch away from the heat and hardness of his powerful body. She felt drugged with the seductive persuasion of his kisses, the clean masculine smell of him filling her senses, making a mockery of her denials. Yet still she struggled valiantly against it, aware in some little-understood way that if Charles St. Germain were to take her now she would be lost, lost forever.

"How can you continue to resist me, tempting Raven?" Charles demanded, bending his head and trailing feathery kisses along the arch of her throat. "Though you seem as maddeningly elusive as the Faerie Queen, I vow you are in truth a flesh-and-blood woman."

Raven shuddered beneath the tantalizing touch of his lips, and Charles lifted his head to gaze deeply into the passion-darkened depths of her golden eyes. "A flesh-and-blood woman," he repeated wonderingly, trying to convince himself that it was so, "and by God, I mean to have you. Don't turn me away, Raven. I'll not be able to bear it."

In the tension-filled atmosphere of the luxurious quarters there came a tranquil sound, interrupting his hoarse words as it floated soft and serene from beneath the dark velvet cloth that covered the gilded cage containing the rare black nightingale. Both Raven and Charles grew still at the seductive beauty of its song, Charles's hand on Raven's hip, his hard thighs pressed against the softness of her own. In the dark green eyes that met the golden ones there was reflected the startled awareness of what lay beyond the burning need of passion unfulfilled, a dawning realization of where destiny was meant to lead them, the magic of the nightingale's song drawing them irresistibly toward an inevitable awakening.

"Raven," Charles repeated urgently, only to be silenced by the warmth that flowed into the golden depths of the tawny eyes, enveloping him and tempering the intensity of his burning desire with a tenderness that was new to him. Without a word spoken between them, Charles knew he had won her and placed his big hands beneath her small buttocks, rolling her under him, his movements slow and gentle, the frenzied urgency under control. This time Raven responded when his mouth came down on hers, her parted lips clinging eagerly to his, her slender arms sliding possessively about his broad back.

Charles felt the silken thighs parting beneath him, the silent invitation sending a shiver of longing through him, and he knew he could wait no longer. Slipping his arms about her waist, he pulled Raven to him, hungering for this final contact, and as Raven arched against him he moved and became part of her, driving deep inside the most intimate part of her woman's body, his loins on fire. Raven, every sense heightened in anticipation, was unprepared for the shattering pain that accompanied his possession of her, and a whimper escaped her bruised, still yielding lips.

Thinking she had cried out with pleasure, Charles responded with an unleashing of passion unlike any he had ever experienced. Covering the length of her slender body with his, unwilling to break the searing contact for even a moment, he moved against her, driving deeper, wanting to possess Raven Barrancourt as he had never yearned to possess anything in his life. Her sudden stillness became obvious to him after only a moment, but even before he could check his burning desire, he felt her begin to move beneath him, responding slowly at first, then with a passion that soon matched his own. Once the pain abated, Raven, driven wild by the bold, hard touch of this man, found herself riding higher and higher into a realm of sensual awareness she had never dreamed existed. The wiry golden hairs that pressed against her soft breasts, the tautness of his belly, the sinewy hardness of his arms about her magnified these sensations until suddenly the world seemed to burst into fire around her. Charles caught her to him and held her with the fierceness of his great strength as they soared together, Raven rising to meet him, their bodies merging and melding into one. Raven cried out without realizing that she did while Charles's lips clung possessively to hers, his arms tightly about her, gentling her until it was over and all was as it had been before.

Charles, sweat glistening on his wide, sun-bronzed chest, waited until his racing heartbeat had slowed before he glanced down into Raven's face to find her lying beneath him with her eyes closed, her hollow cheeks stained rosy pink, her glossy black hair spilling onto the pillow. Lowering his head, he touched his lips to hers, not in a passionate kiss, but in an attempt to draw her back to him. She started at the gentle touch, and Charles felt his chest constricting oddly as he found himself gazing into the tawny eyes, the still-smoldering fires of her passion giving them a sultry radiance he found indescribably beautiful.

With one long index finger he traced the intriguing arch of her dark brows down to the slim, upturned nose, smiling rather cynically to himself when it occurred to him that in its aquiline perfection lay Raven's undisputable stamp of aristocratic breeding, a characteristic he shared in common with her, had she but known it. He wondered as he continued to gaze down into her exquisite face what she would say if she knew he was the former Comte de Monteraux, half French by birth, a nobleman who had given up his lands and title years ago when the restless lure of the sea proved too strong to be denied.

Better let her go on believing he was a thief and a pirate, Charles decided, his full lips twitching, well aware of how quickly the lingering passion in those remarkable cat's eyes could turn to icy indifference or burning outrage. And it would certainly serve to make the voyage more interesting if Raven continued to amuse and annoy him with her fiery temperament.

"To think you've been down here in my quarters every afternoon making use of my bathtub without so much as a by-your-leave," he remarked, his deep voice hardening slightly as he recalled that he had suspected her of involving Ewan Fletcher in some scheme of betrayal against him.

"Because I didn't think you'd grant me leave if I asked," Raven replied a trifle coolly, having seen the angry darkening of the sea-green eyes and responding in kind.

"You're as prickly as a porcupine, my sweet," Charles said with a laugh, his loins tightening despite himself as his eyes were drawn to her parted lips. Lowering his head, he kissed her lingeringly, the heat beginning to rise in his strong body so that Raven was aware of it, too, and she responded with a boldness that surprised and delighted Charles, offering herself to him with unabashed eagerness. He caressed the rosy nipples of her breasts with his tongue, then ran his lips along the smooth, arching column of her throat, breathing in the wild, exotic scent of her, his senses swimming alarmingly. Raven's small hands traveled down the rippling muscles of his wide back, and Charles shuddered at the soft, caressing touch, his lips finding hers at last and closing about them with burning abandon.

"Miss Raven! Miss Raven?"

The unmistakable Irish brogue of Ewan Fletcher came to them through the thick wood of the cabin door, and Charles lifted his head as Raven's soft body went rigid beneath his.

"Miss Raven, the captain left the helm and I don't know where he's at. Best hurry and finish with your bathin'."

"I will," Raven called back in a breathless voice, choking down her giggles as she responded to the laughter in the sea-green eyes meeting hers. Charles's smile was gentle, and for a moment they shared a look of intimacy, until the silence surrounded them again and Charles's expression changed, the lean, hungry look that entered his eyes a sign of his reawakened passion.

"Raven," he murmured, seeming to derive satisfaction in hearing her name fall from his lips, but as he sought to touch her, she moved away from him and held out a restraining hand. Charles's jaw hardened in response, and Raven shivered at the expression she saw in his handsome face, the smile no longer kind, his green eyes cold and savage.

"So eager to leave my bed, Raven?" he asked, seizing her hand, his fingers closing like a vise about her slender wrist. "Did I not pleasure you well enough?"

To Raven, her oval face only inches from his, he was no longer the gentle, experienced lover of a moment ago, but the cold, ruthless captain of the *Orient Star*, a man to be reckoned with and an enemy to be feared. The tender, impassioned moments they had shared were gone, replaced by the hostility with which they usually confronted each other, the tawny eyes that blazed back into his mirroring the anger and the unyielding pride that were burning within him.

"Nay, I'd be foolish to think you didn't enjoy that round of coupling," Charles said, his words like the lash of a whip, hurting her deeply.

"Is—is that how you saw it?" Raven whispered, the tawny eyes dark with pain at his callous dismissal of their lovemaking.

Charles felt his conscience stirring at the wounded look in the golden eyes, darkened now to the heavy blackness of port wine, the soft lips trembling slightly, and he cursed beneath his breath, enraged at himself for allowing this deceiving wench to affect him this way. After all, she had given herself to him willingly, and doubtless he was only one of many lovers the sultry Raven Barrancourt had taken to her bed.

"Surely you didn't perceive it as something more," he mocked, his tone unaccountably harsh. "A woman of your experience should know that trysts like these are usually as meaningless as the rutting of barnyard animals."

Raven jerked free of his grasp, her strength suprising him, her eyes searing him with her hatred. "Damn your soul, Charles St. Germain!" she cried, her voice unsteady and throbbing with passion. "You make a mockery of everything! Is there no ounce of compassion within you? How can you live with yourself when all that's good and loving within your heart has died? You think yourself all-powerful, the supreme master of your destiny and everything that surrounds you, but what do you call a man who inhabits a shell of stone? What sort of man are you who takes all that is beautiful and destroys it with bitterness?"

She leaped from the bed and drew her discarded gown over her silken body, one shapely calf tantalizing him before she gathered up her undergarments and fled to the door. With her hand on the latch she turned, her oval face stark white, her whispered voice so low that Charles almost didn't hear it.

"There has been no one else but you, Charles, ever."

The cabin door closed behind her like a thunderclap, the spacious quarters chilled with the force of her leaving. In the narrow corridor Raven paused for a moment, leaning her head against the wall, her eyes closed, tears trembling on her lashes.

It was too much, she groaned to herself, too much to bear! The death of her father and her precarious hold on North Head had created within her a yawning emptiness which, for a precious moment in time, Charles St. Germain had managed to fill in a more sweetly satisfying manner than Raven had ever dreamed possible. In showing her the delightful secrets that existed between a man and a woman, Charles had also stilled her yearning for protection, for comfort and love, with a completeness that had stunned her.

A sob tore from Raven's throat and she covered her mouth with her hand, fleeing to her cabin and slamming the door behind her. How could he have so heartlessly destroyed the wonderful intimacy that had sprung up between them and blacken the beauty of the experience they had shared? She felt as though he had taken her newly mended heart and broken it more cruelly than it had ever been broken before.

"I hate him," Raven whispered to herself, the tears flowing unchecked down her pale cheeks. "Judas, how I hate him!"

Chapter Seven

With the slow, ponderous speed that was more characteristic of a lumbering East Indiaman than a rake-masted clipper, the *Orient Star* progressed down the flat, marsh-banked main channel of the Sutlej River, the Indus behind them, Kasur, Ferozepore and the Himalaya Mountains ahead. She had traversed the foothills of India and the plains that flattened into the sweltering Thar Desert, and the end of her journey that had begun thousands of miles ago in distant England was near. The riverbank was stark and lined with mud huts, the native fishing boats that flitted about the sand banks trailing nets were more numerous now than they had been along the long, deserted stretch of river between Chachran and Bahawalnagar where the Indus had left them, following the feet of the mountains, and the *Orient Star* had steered west with the branching Sutlej.

Yesterday, during the afternoon watch, the Himalayas had appeared for the first time, the excited clamor on deck having lured Raven from her cabin, her curiosity piqued. At first she had seen nothing in the empty, hazy sky where the excited deckhands pointed, but suddenly, lifting her eyes higher and higher, she had seen the snow-encrusted peaks shimmering before her and had gasped at their sheer magnificence. Towering above a stretch of endless sky, they seemed to hover above the earth, only to vanish again in the next instant as though they had never existed.

Raven had been astounded by this miracle of nature, agreeing with Geoffrey Lytton, who had hurried to her side to inquire shrewdly if she had seen them, that the sight had, in a sense, changed her forever. Obviously nothing was permanent in this world, she decided now as she came up on deck after sharing a light breakfast with Danny below, seeing the empty sky stretching ahead of the *Orient Star*'s sleek bow, for even the towering, stalwart mountains could become transient if they chose. Though Raven knew that they were still there and might reappear at any time, it was the power of illusion that made her realize nothing was ever as it seemed and that even the strongest and most permanent fixture could vanish in the wink of an eye.

Hadn't her father's life ended like that? One moment flashing his handsome, infectious grin as he guided the long-legged colt over the seemingly easy hurdle of stone and wood, the next lying in a crumpled heap on the springy turf, his body twisted and unmoving? Hadn't her mother abandoned her as well at a time when the beautiful promise of life together as a family had stretched endlessly before them? So, too, would North Head slip from her grasp unless Raven could return in time, and so, too, had the ideals and beliefs of childhood vanished with the opening of her eyes, led across the threshold of womanhood by a man who had not known at the time of the changes he was taking her through.

Raven was in love with Charles St. Germain, and the discovery had brought bittersweet agony, a torture of the heart she had never before experienced, not even when she had been plunged into the depths of despair by the discovery that North Head, the only immovable anchor left in her life, might very well be lost to the grasping ownership of a man whom she despised. Ever since Charles had made love to her, had awakened within her the awareness of the delightful mystery that existed between man and woman, Raven had tried hard to ignore the yearning of her heart, telling herself that he had used her cruelly and that he hadn't experienced the same sweet joys that she had.

But try as she might, Raven could no sooner deny the feelings within her than she could the need to breathe, and as the *Orient Star* began the last leg of her long journey, she found herself tormented by a heart she could no longer control. Even the mere sight of Charles standing at the helm, handsome countenance proud and forbidding, was enough to make her knees grow weak with the longing to feel his lips upon hers again, his strong hands caressing her intimately, and Raven, though she despised herself for that weakness, was unable to fight her emotions. Moreover, she was terrified that Charles would discover how she felt, would use her love against her, and Raven knew that she would be lost if he took her again only for the pleasures of the flesh, to satisfy his own lusts as he had once before.

Coming up onto deck on that cool morning after the Himalayas had been sighted, she wandered morosely to the rail, every fiber of her being taut with awareness of the broad-shouldered man on the deck above, who, his chestnut head bent over Jason Quintrell's ledger book spread before him on the binnacle, was oblivious to her presence. Slender arms propped against the worn wooden beam, Raven stared down into the coffee-colored water, her expression one of unhappiness and self-loathing. She told herself with forced levity that she was naught but a weak-willed, infatuated spinster, but her attempts to cheer herself fell miserably flat.

"Your heart is heavy, little princess."

Raven jumped, not so much at the unexpected appearance of the hulking Dmitri Zergeyev at her elbow as at his uncanny observance of the truth. She turned and smiled at him, but her soft cheeks did not dimple and the glow was gone from her tawny eyes. "I'm just thinking," she told him evasively.

"Of how much you will miss Dmitri when we dock in Kasur?" he asked with a wide, coaxing grin, and had the satisfaction of seeing the dimples appear after all.

"I will miss you horribly," Raven admitted. She was aware that these past few weeks aboard the *Orient Star* had been a precious gift of peace for her soul, the gentle rocking of the ship lulling her into a sleep that had refreshed and soothed her like the dark, velvet nights at North Head with the sound of the sea drifting through her open window. For a time she had even been able to forget what lay ahead of her and the troubles she had left behind, caught up in the lives of the clipper ship's contented crew, learning to tie the intricate knots and stitch the stiff canvas sails from David Cotter, the *Orient Star*'s carpenter-sailmaker, and becoming surprisingly adept at the use of the sextant under the patient tutelage of Geoffrey Lytton.

"Where will you go after Kasur?" she asked, her face strained and anxious, the thought of the *Orient Star* sailing away with her captain to distant places and adventures which she couldn't share suddenly unbearable for her. Judas, how she hated herself for the mealy-mouthed, vacillating creature she had become, pining after Charles St. Germain like some lovesick dolt in a Shakespearean play!

It was the first time she had ever inquired after the *Orient Star*'s plans, having assumed all along that it would return to Bombay after replacing the English goods in its holds with Indian ones, yet never really wondering what would become of the enormous clipper after that. Now it seemed of vital importance to her, and Dmitri, seeing the sadness in her eyes, was moved to make a disclosure he might otherwise have not. Leaning closer, enjoying the nearness of the beautiful young woman whose slim fragility was further enhanced by the velvet morning gown of pale rose she wore, he whispered conspiratorially,

"We're going to Lahore, too, the captain and I."

Raven's heart stopped. "Lahore?" she repeated, trying to sound casual. "Why?"

"To make ourselves rich beyond our wildest dreams," Zergeyev said simply, as though that explained everything. Seeing the bewildered look on Raven's oval face he laughed, displaying his even, white teeth, and wagged a long index finger at her. "It's really supposed to be a secret, so no repeating my words to anyone, eh?"

"I wouldn't dream of it," Raven breathed.

"There was an Indian in London," Zergeyev continued, his black eyes wandering over the slow-moving water of the river, the cool breeze tugging at his bristling beard. "He told us a secret."

"What Indian?" Raven repeated in confusion. "And when was the *Orient Star* in London?"

"After our run to the Indies," Dmitri explained patiently, and Raven forced herself to listen closely, certain now that what he was going to tell her was somehow linked with the odd look he had exchanged with Charles in the captain's quarters the night of the dinner party, a look Raven had not forgotten, although she had dismissed it since then as insignificant. Now she wasn't entirely sure, and the conspirational tone of Dmitri's deep, heavily accented voice informed her that her suspicions had probably been well founded after all.

"You have never been to London, little one, and you can't imagine what the waterfront of the Thames is like, the drunken sailors lying in the gutters, the offal in the streets, the fights and brawls and crimes." The black eyes went swiftly to her face. "Did you know the British Fleet impresses its sailors into service?"

Raven nodded her dark head, well aware of the cruel practice of sending large gangs of cudgel-bearing tars into the streets to beat innocent men senseless before kidnapping them for a lifetime of agony aboard a battered warship. It had even happened in Cornwall on several occasions, though none of the poor unfortunates who had vanished had been anyone Raven knew; yet the harrowing tales the men of St. Ives had told her of disease, filth, poor pay, and floggings had turned her heart against the queen's navy forever.

"It was down near Battersea," Dmitri went on, "that we came across a poor Indian being thrashed by a gang of them, and all the people of the night, whom you never see until it gets dark, were standing about watching. Of course, they were doing nothing to help him."

"I fear the gentry would have done the same had they been abroad at that hour," Raven interjected softly.

Dmitri shrugged his massive shoulders and looked unhappy for a moment. "You are probably right, little one. Ah, well, you cannot weep too much for mankind or you'll end up with nothing but a soggy shirt front to show for your compassion. The Indian was a scrawny little man, ugly to behold and near the point of expiring when the captain and I dispersed the gang."

Raven could well imagine how the group of cutthroats must have fled at the sight of Dmitri, long hair and black beard flowing, and Charles with his imposing size and strength, coming toward them with purposeful steps. Dmitri, seeing her soft lips curve, chuckled reminiscently.

"Aye, it was something to behold, little princess! I picked up two by the collar and bashed their heads together, and Charles tossed another two or three of them into the river. The rest took to their heels like the devil was after them!"

"And the Indian?" Raven asked breathlessly.

"Badly hurt, as I've said, but we bound his wounds and took him to the nearest alehouse. The captain paid well for his room and board, and we left him, because that was his wish, but not before he repaid us for rescuing him."

Raven turned her head to look up at the quarterdeck, where

Captain St. Germain was still discussing the contents of the worn ledger with his supercargo, his broad back turned toward her, the muscles rippling beneath his muslin shirt. She felt her throat constrict, wondering how she could possibly have thought him a heartless criminal. It had been true, after all, as the astonished Geoffrey Lytton had confessed when she asked, that the rum run to North Head had been made for humanitarian purposes, as Charles had stated. Since then she had also learned that Jason Quintrell had been signed aboard the *Orient Star* despite his youth and inexperience because Captain St. Germain had agreed to take a chance on him, knowing that the boy had an invalid sister and a dying mother to support at home. Ruthless, manipulating, and, yes, heartlessly unkind when he wanted to be, Charles St. Germain had shown a side of himself that Raven would never have believed him capable of possessing had the confessions not come from his first mate and boatswain, men Raven had learned to trust completely.

"There is a treasure, little one," Dmitri went on, rousing her from her thoughts, "that men have been seeking these nine years past, since the death of the Sikh emperor Ranjit Singh, a treasure that is worth a thousand fortunes. With it I will be a prince again, and the captain . . ." He shrugged and grinned lopsidedly. "The captain will have whatever he wishes, though I'm not certain even he knows for what he seeks."

"And this Indian whose life you saved, simply gave it to you?" Raven asked doubtfully.

"No, no, little one, he gave us a name, the name of the man into whose hands it has fallen!"

"What is it?" Raven asked curiously, never having seen the big Russian so animated before except when they happened to be discussing his favorite vintage of red wines or reminiscing over past *amorosos*. "Gold? Silver?"

"No, my beauty," Dmitri replied smugly, "it is a diamond, the most bewitching of all, the famed Kohinoor of the Mogul Empire."

Raven had never heard of the diamond before, but the romantic name brought to mind a glittering stone the size of a man's fist, twinkling with hypnotizing beauty, the owning of which would see a man crowned king.

"In the Persian language, *Kohinoor* means 'Mountain of Light,'"

Dmitri went on with a covetous gleam in his black eyes. "Truly one would have the world at his feet with a diamond like that."

"And why did this Indian tell you where it could be found?" Raven asked suspiciously. "Why does he not seek it himself?"

"Many have lost their lives trying to possess it, little one, and still more have lost their lives trying to keep it. One fellow, as legend goes, refused to tell of its whereabouts, and the sultan of Brunei, furious that he couldn't have it, had the pitiful wretch's eyes plucked out. No wonder so many are afraid to own it, for once it is theirs they must fear for their very lives and spend their waking and sleeping hours with an eye over their shoulder."

Raven shivered. "You say it belongs to someone now, Dmitri. Are you going to steal it from him even though it's rightfully his?"

"It belongs rightfully to Emperor Ranjit Singh, ruler of the Punjab," Dmitri told her, oblivious to the censure in Raven's soft voice, "and he has been dead for many years."

"I still don't understand how you plan to make it yours," Raven protested, her smooth brow wrinkling. "Are you going to steal it from this man, or wrest it from him physically?" Her cheeks drained of color and her eyes widened. "Surely you don't intend to kill him for it!"

"Now, now, little one, we're not a band of pirates," Dmitri assured her hastily, seeing that he had distressed his beloved princess. Though he had come to realize some time ago that Raven felt only a friend's fondness for him and that she would never look up into his face with her lioness eyes filled with passion, he could not help feeling fiercely protective over her, the intensity of his feelings startling him at times, making him laugh uneasily at himself. These feelings were new and strange to him, yet not at all unpleasant, and though he did feel regret at times knowing that he would never savor the irresistible softness of Raven's slender body, he was aware that the friendship she offered him was worth far more than any brief moments of intimacy he might be able to coax from her.

"But you mean to get the diamond, and it belongs to someone else," Raven said, her tawny eyes beginning to flash accusingly.

"Every man has his price," Dmitri informed her slyly, but Raven's disapproval was unrelenting. Were they pirates and smugglers at heart after all? she asked herself, unable to resist stealing another glance at Charles St. Germain's towering form, her heart growing cold. Had her love for him rationalized his behavior of late, hiding the truth she had originally been able to see so clearly? Yet why should she condemn anyone for succumbing to the lure of untold wealth? Was she not herself willing to sacrifice everything she had in order to collect her fifty-thousand-pound reward? Dmitri, with his dream of restoring his family's fortune, was really no different, was he?

Only Charles St. Germain, as usual, eluded all efforts to be labeled driven by a just cause. Raven was sure, watching the unrelenting sternness of his expression, that he was seeking the fabulous Kohinoor diamond for personal gain alone, or perhaps even just for the pleasure of the chase. Never had anything other than personal gratification governed his thoughts or movements; shouldn't she have realized that when he seduced her with his experienced touch and irresistible kisses?

"Your heart is filled with anger, little one," Dmitri observed, startling Raven yet again with his surprising powers of insight. What was it about this giant of a man that made her think him a great, affectionate hound dog one moment and an all-seeing soul-friend the next? Were her thoughts always so candidly revealed upon her face or did the bearded Cossack truly have the gift of looking into her heart?

"It is the captain who distresses you," Dmitri went on when Raven said nothing, her delicate profile averted, the breezes from the river caressing a glossy tendril that lay against one smooth temple. She shook her head, her soft lips compressed, knowing that if he looked into her face he would clearly see her heart in her eyes.

"You mustn't dislike him so," Dmitri pleaded, wishing with his entire being that he could make friends out of the two people he cared for most in the world. There was a time, shortly after the voyage had begun, that he had felt his hopes rising, sensing a distinct softening in Raven Barrancourt toward his captain, but somehow everything had gone lamentably wrong since then. For almost a week now Charles St. Germain had been like a stranger to him, his mood savage, temper easily aroused, his thoughts unreadable in his glinting emerald eyes. And Raven, pale and silent, had wandered the decks like a wraith, or retired to her cabin for hours on end, avoiding the quarterdeck and Captain St. Germain himself as though he were beset by the plague.

"After all," Dmitri added with a placating smile, "we are all kindred spirits, you, myself and the captain."

"How so?" Raven inquired stiffly, still refusing to look at him.

"Why, you are fighting to keep your North Head, I've lost my Kybrovo Park, and the captain is no longer master of Monteraux."

Raven's golden eyes were wide with surprise. "What, in God's name is Monteraux, Dmitri? Is it some sort of estate?"

"Kristos, yes!" the Russian responded eagerly, determined to press home his point. "Once he was the rich and respected Comte de Monteraux, and now what does he have to show of his birthright? Pffft!"

"He—he is an earl?" Raven whispered in astonishment.

"Not since he left his inheritance to that effeminate cousin of his, Frédéric de St. Germain," Zergeyev replied, his deep voice filled with contempt for the thin, parchment-white young man he remembered meeting years ago during a visit to Paris with Charles—who had, naturally, taken the glittering city by storm, capturing more hearts with his dark good looks than Dmitri had been able to collect with his gifts of jewels and tales of adventures on the high seas.

"He gave it away?" Raven echoed faintly, and for the first time Dmitri became aware of her utter bewilderment. Propping his elbows against the rail he stared at her earnestly.

"Did the captain never tell you?"

"We—we rarely speak," Raven confessed.

"His mother was an Englishwoman," Dmitri explained obligingly, though he knew he was risking the captain's wrath should Charles catch him discussing his past without consent. "The daughter of the British envoy to Louis XVIII. I saw a portrait of her once," he added reminiscently. "Such a delicate angel; I was not surprised to learn her health was not good and that she did not live long. Her last request was that her little son Charles be educated in England, and so he was sent to Sussex to the home of an aunt."

"All alone?" Raven asked.

"Charles does not speak of her at all. She was already quite old when he arrived and, as I remember, had never married. Not a loving home for a motherless lad, eh?"

Raven shook her head, her heart aching for the lonely little boy Charles St. Germain must have been at one time. How well she could understand the feeling of abandonment he must have experienced arriving motherless and alone in a country that was strange to him! Though she could scarcely remember her own mother, Raven could recall many painful instances throughout her childhood when she had longed for the soft, loving presence of a woman, of a mother, in her life.

Though her father had loved her dearly and had not been one to hide his affection, he had not been able to fill his daughter's need for a confidante of her own sex as she grew older and her body had undergone the changes into womanhood. Raven had never been able to define the odd, scarcely realized emptiness within her until now, when her awakened passions and feelings for Charles left her confused and frightened and longing for the mother who might have explained to her the changes she had just gone through.

Yes, indeed, she could understand well what Charles must have experienced, and her heart constricted with love for him and the overwhelming need to tell him of it.

"What about his father?" she asked, being careful not to reveal her tumultuous feelings in her voice or on her face.

"His father died when he was still in school, and when he was old enough he returned to France, to Château Monteraux, but it was the sea that called to him, little one, and so he went, the invalid Frédéric becoming the new comte."

"And so he gave away his ancestral home?" Raven demanded incredulously. "Just like that? To become a . . . a sailor?"

Dmitri's eyes flickered at her contemptuous tone, but he could see that his disclosure had come as something of a shock to her. "Do not judge him too harshly," he began, but Raven interrupted him, her voice cold, her gaze fixed on the towering figure of Charles St. Germain with resurging hatred.

"I won't judge him at all, Dmitri, for what can one think of a man who throws away his past, his future, his birthright to gallivant about on the high seas, fornicating where he will and looking to steal diamonds from the hands of innocent men?" Her golden eyes were fixed on Dmitri now, and he shifted self-consciously at the accusing fire in their topaz depths. "What can one think of a man like that except that he is nothing? Nothing at all!"

She turned and fled for the companionway, leaving Dmitri open-mouthed with astonishment at her outburst. Women! He'd never comprehend their lightning mood changes if he lived to be a thousand! Oh, he could understand well enough why Raven should be so upset, struggling with all the determination a young orphaned girl was capable of to save the very thing which Captain St. Germain had willingly given away. Kristos, it was a cruel and unjust world, yet one had to do what one considered best. He laughed at himself for his philosophical musings and decided that once the Kohinoor was in his possession, he would, if necessary, buy North Head away from the fat Squire Blackburn and deliver it upon bended knee to the beautiful young woman he had come to adore as the sweet captor of his heart.

On the quarterdeck above, Charles, who had been watching the exchange between Dmitri and Raven Barrancourt with heavy-lidded, expressionless eyes, shut the ledger book with a snap and motioned to Jason Quintrell that their meeting was over. The young officer retreated hastily, relieved to be out of the presence of his captain, whose mounting anger he had felt as tangibly as though it were heat rising from his powerful body. Left alone at the helm, Charles took the wheel in his big hands, long legs planted firmly apart, the breeze tugging at his chestnut hair. The emerald eyes roved the taut rigging overhead, experience telling him that the rudder was set just so and that the *Orient Star* was making the best use of her sails that she could. Though he would have preferred to be on the open seas, the canvas snapping, water dashing over the decks and frothing in the scuppers, he knew that it would be useless to grow impatient and that a great deal still lay ahead of them before the rake-masted clipper would once again feel the surging ocean beneath it.

Automatically his eyes went back to the main deck, but it was empty of the slender figure in the flounced velvet gown that had graced it with beauty and laughter since the *Orient Star*'s departure from Bombay. Charles's big hands tightened viciously on the wheel, his handsome features rigid with suppressed anger. Why, in God's name, he wondered, did he still lust after Raven Barrancourt now that he had satisfied himself with her once?

Because the pleasure of caressing and touching her perfect body had been sweeter than any he had ever known? Aye, he couldn't deny that he wanted her again, despite her lies and deceit, despite the tiny drops of blood he had found on the soft blankets after her stormy departure, telltale evidence that had disturbed him more than he cared to admit to himself. It was inconceivable that she had been a maiden when she gave herself to him, for he had had virgins before and had quickly grown bored with their blushing shyness and clumsy inexperience. Doubtless Raven had been suffering the onset of her womanly troubles and had intended to cause him guilt by claiming he was the first and only man to love her.

Lying wench, what did she hope to gain from such a confession? A vow of his undying love? An offer of marriage because he had compromised a young lady of quality? Charles's sensual lips curled into a sneer. Surely the haughty Miss Barrancourt had set her sights higher than a seafaring captain, even one who was rightfully master of a magnificent manor in southern France!

"Will you be takin' the morning watch as well, cap'n?"

Charles turned and glowered at Geoffrey Lytton, the diminutive Welshman having come on deck to take over the helm. Though it normally took two to four men to handle the enormous wheel and the heavy rudder, the watches had been decreased since the *Orient Star* had left the Arabian Sea, the sleek-hulled clipper needing only a modicum of experienced coaxing to keep it on an even keel during its journey upriver.

"Take her if you will, Mr. Lytton," Charles replied with a growl and made his way below, wordlessly shouldering aside Ewan Fletcher, who passed him in the narrow corridor, leaving the steward blinking in astonishment at his captain's abruptness. Surly fellow! Ewan thought disloyally to himself. What in Christ's name had made him so unapproachable of late?

Charles scowled as he entered his cabin, the emerald eyes narrowing as his gaze swept over the brass hip bath standing behind the ornamental Japanese screen. Despite himself he was reminded of the beauty of Raven's ivory body beneath the lapping water, her wide, golden eyes staring solemnly into his, and he cursed beneath his breath, turning away and pouring himself a brandy from the crystal decanter that stood on his small writing desk. Two more days, he thought to himself, two more days on this slow-moving, God-rotting river with its uncommonly mild breezes, and the *Orient Star* would be in Kasur, and Raven Barrancourt gone from his sight forever. The black nightingale, forgotten in its gilded cage, uttered a single melodious sound, startling Charles from his angry reverie. Without thinking, he reached out and rapped against the cage, startling the delicate bird into silence. Charles's lips tightened grimly. If there was one thing he didn't desire at the moment, it was the annoyingly poignant song of a bewitching, raven-plumed bird.

"Charles—"

He turned quickly at the sound of her voice, having thought for a moment that he had imagined it, but when he saw her standing in the doorway of his cabin, her full breasts rising and falling beneath the rose-colored bodice trimmed with satin rosettes, he set the brandy snifter down and came swiftly toward her.

"What the devil are you doing here?" he began, then, seeing the fear in her large golden eyes, his harsh voice softened immediately and he put his hands on her slender shoulders, staring down into her upturned face. "Raven, what is it?"

"It's Danny," she replied, swallowing the lump of fear that was constricting her throat. "I think she's ill. I just went to look in on her because she'd been feeling poorly at breakfast and I found her in bed with a fever. She says it's nothing, but—"

Charles's hold on the slim shoulders tightened. "Stay here," he ordered. "I'll have a look at her."

"But you can't!" Raven protested. "It—it isn't proper!"

Charles's expression was grimly humorous. "Since when have you known me to exhibit decorum, my dear?"

"Oh, must you always make a mockery of everything I say?" Raven cried, distraught.

The aristocratic brow darkened, Charles's only intent having been to soothe her with levity. "Stay here until I've talked to her," he ordered in a tone that brooked no argument, ruthlessly ignoring the nervous trembling of Raven's lower lip. "You don't want to catch whatever she may have, do you?"

Raven's knees grew weak, for his words only echoed her own fears. She had learned from Nathaniel Rogers the names of the numerous diseases that ravaged India from year to year, names that now struck terror into her heart: smallpox, malaria, black cholera. . . . She pressed her hand to her lips and willed herself to remain calm, telling herself that her first instinct to go to

Captain St. Germain had been the right one. In her anger at Dmitri Zergeyev's disclosure, she had sought out Danny's companionship, knowing that, though she would never tell the older woman of her thoughts, Danny's harmless prattle and reminiscences of home would soothe her as they always did.

She had entered the elderly woman's cabin without knocking, expecting to find her busy with her needlework in the roomy sea chair Captain St. Germain had provided for her, and her eyes had widened with astonishment when she saw Danny, wan and shivering, lying in her narrow bunk.

"Did you decide to start the morning all over again?" she teased, the impish smile on her soft lips changing to a gasp of dismay as she felt the burning fever and saw the exhaustion in the red-rimmed eyes.

"I was feeling a little tired during breakfast," Danny replied weakly in response to Raven's anxious question, "so I thought I'd lie down again after you left. The fever came on so suddenly!" A fit of coughing overwhelmed her, and Raven, greatly afraid, had hurried to the captain's quarters for help. It was only natural that she should turn to Charles, she told herself defensively, for he was captain of the ship, after all, and was, though she didn't like to admit it, the most dependable one to turn to in a crisis.

Now as she nervously paced the spacious quarters, oblivious to the nightingale that preened and fluttered about in its gilded cage, she tried to thrust away the growing fear in her mind. Mrs. Trentham had told her that only the summers were to be feared, that in the heat the fevers grew and raged, and it was November now, the weather cool and pleasant. Judas, what was taking him so long? Raven asked herself, although Charles had been gone less than ten minutes. Resenting the fact that he had forbidden her to accompany him, even if it had been for her own safety, she ran across the polished floor in her soft kid slippers and was about to open the cabin door when it swung in of its own accord and the towering form of Charles St. Germain filled the threshold.

"Danny?" Raven whispered, fearfully.

"A simple fever, Raven, nothing to worry about."

The calm, authoritative tone of his voice washed her fear away, but her expression remained anxious. "Are you certain?"

The full lips twitched into an unrestrained grin. "Trust a woman not to be satisfied with the words she hears. Aye, I'm certain. No doubt the change in climate and the weeks aboard ship have taken their toll. Mrs. Daniels isn't exactly young, Raven, and certainly the rigors of looking after you haven't been easy on her, either."

Raven was so relieved to hear his prognosis that she felt no resentment at his statement, which, because she knew that Charles St. Germain was incapable of teasing, had been genuinely meant. "I'd better go stay with her," she said, but Charles put a restraining hand on her arm.

"Let her sleep. I spoke with her briefly and she said she was tired, so I had Ewan bring her a small dose of laudanum in a cup of hot tea. I've no doubt the fever will be broken by this evening or tomorrow morning."

Raven lifted her head to look up into his eyes, suddenly aware of his nearness, the heat of the strong fingers about her arm making her tremble unexpectedly. He was standing very close, leaning over her almost protectively, and she could feel his warm breath on her cheek, his gaze fastened on her soft, parted lips.

"Raven," he murmured, his hold tightening, his free hand sliding about her curving hip and drawing her closer. "Raven—"

She could feel herself melting against him, her hands pressed against his hard torso. Lifting her face almost unconsciously to his, she closed her eyes in anticipation of a kiss she yearned for with every fiber of her being.

"Here we go, cap'n! Thought I'd bring you an' Miss Raven a pot of tea, seein' as I made some for Mrs. Daniels."

Charles and Raven broke apart as the cabin door swung wide to reveal Ewan Fletcher's grinning face, a tea service on a wooden tray in his hands. Raven, hollow cheeks flaming with color, did not trust her voice enough to refuse the steward's kind offer, and sat down mechanically at Charles's writing desk, her eyes lowered.

"Mrs. Daniels'll be fine," Ewan assured her, misconstruing her strained silence for worry. "Just a wee touch of the flu, nothin' serious." Placing a mug before her, he filled it with the fragrant, steaming tea, then poured a second one for his captain, who remained standing near the door, his handsome face forbiddingly cold. "Will you no have a cup, captain?" Ewan asked brightly, seemingly oblivious to the tension that crackled in the air.

"No," Charles retorted curtly, his savage voice making Raven wince. "I'm needed topside. Drink it yourself."

The cabin door slammed behind him, and Ewan, cocking his grizzled head to one side, studied Raven's averted, achingly lovely profile. For a moment he was silent, pursing his lips in a thoughtful manner; then he shrugged and grinned his Irishman's grin, lifting Charles's mug in a proper toast. "To life, Miss Raven, and to health, for without the latter you'll soon rue the former!"

Raven lifted her bowed head and smiled at him despite herself, her soft cheeks dimpling. "Oh, go on with you, Ewan, it's only tea!"

True to Captain St. Germain's predictions, Danny's fever had abated by nightfall, and when Raven tiptoed into her darkened cabin shortly after dinner, she found the elderly woman sleeping peacefully, her wrinkled face composed, her forehead cool to the touch. Weak with relief, Raven lowered herself into the chair in the darkened corner of the tiny cabin, preparing to wait until Danny awoke. The laudanum would be wearing off at any moment, and she would probably be hungry when she came around. Raven had been peeking in on her at intervals throughout the entire day, still greatly concerned despite the captain's and Ewan's assurances that Danny was suffering a simple bout of influenza.

Thankfully, she had not encountered Captain St. Germain during her fretful ramblings about the main deck, for she was annoyed with herself for the swiftness with which she had succumbed to his amorous advances and was not overeager to lay eyes on him so soon thereafter. What a wanton woman she had become, prepared to throw herself at the handsome captain of the *Orient Star* after only the merest invitation on his part! Spineless wench, Raven thought with utter self-contempt, her soft lips tightening. Did being in love with a man mean such total enslavement? Judas, in that case she might as well be dead!

A low moan from the bunk made Raven straighten in the comfortable chair, her velvet skirts spreading around her like the inverted petals of a rose. In the shadowy darkness she could see Danny's lips move in soundless words, then the faded eyes open. Scrambling to her feet, she bent over the supine figure, a tender smile lighting her delicate features.

"Are you feeling better?" she inquired softly.

Danny's voice was weak but decisive. "Certainly not! How

could you let that man come in here while I was abed, Miss Raven?"

The smile deepened until the bewitching dimples appeared. "Oh, Danny, what a silly thing to worry about!"

"Alone in a woman's cabin without an escort!" Danny continued peevishly, her voice gathering strength. "What got into you to allow such a thing?"

"I had no choice," Raven explained patiently. "First because Captain St. Germain does whatever he pleases and I can't possibly stop him, and second because he's familiar with fevers and insisted on making sure you weren't coming down with something more serious." Her throat constricted as she recalled the fear of the previous hours. She laid her slim hand over Danny's gnarled one, thinking to herself how very dear this old woman was to her and how alone she would have been if she had lost her. "Oh, Danny, I was so worried!"

The former governess smiled at her, the round little face with its numerous lines beginning to lose its terrible paleness. "Now, if Captain St. Germain said I was going to be fine, why didn't you listen to him?"

"I—"

The gnarled hand tightened about hers in a firm grip. "You must trust him, Miss Raven, there be no finer man to be found on the face of this earth! I know you've been troubled since we came aboard and that the two of you can't seem to make peace with each other, though I'll never understand why, but you've got to realize that he's not the sort to utter lies to anyone merely to protect them from the unpleasant."

"Amen," Raven agreed with a heart-felt scowl. "Are you hungry?" she asked in the next breath, not caring to discuss the roguish sea captain's virtues with Danny, who obviously worshiped the very ground upon which he stood. Judas, was it possible, she asked herself, to love a man so deeply and feel nothing but exasperation and annoyance toward him at the very same time?

Danny shook her head in reply to Raven's question, but her young mistress would not be pacified until she had extracted from her a promise to swallow a bit of Ewan Fletcher's bracing barley soup. Negotiating the narrow corridor with the aid of a lantern, Raven found Ewan still hard at work in the small cooking area that had been sectioned off amidships to serve as his galley, a blackened kettle of hot wash water standing on the worn pantry top at his elbow.

"Miss Raven, what's amiss?" he asked, startled at her sudden appearance, her velvet skirts swirling about her, jet-black hair gleaming in the orange glow of the embers in the fireplace.

"Danny's awake and asking for a cup of your wonderful soup," Raven explained with a reassuring smile. "Is any left?"

"A wee bit. I'll heat it up, and you can bring it to her if you like."

She nodded, and he smiled at the happiness radiating softly from her lovely face. "Didn't the cap'n and I tell you 'twas just a harmless fever?"

"I should have believed you," Raven admitted, "but I've heard so much about the terrible diseases here in India that I couldn't help worrying."

"Of course not." Ewan hung a cauldron on the wrought-iron hook and began to stir the coals to coax forth more heat. "Pray to God you'll never have to see the dark side of India, lass. Most Westerners don't, if they stay in Calcutta or Bombay or on the cantonments the way you're going to."

"I've heard some perfectly horrible tales," Raven said, lowering herself onto a stool and resting her slim arms on the tabletop. "Are they true, Mr. Fletcher?"

The Irishman's expression was troubled. "Aye, I'm afraid so. You get hardened to it after a time, but there're memories that never leave you. I spent a week in Agra my first time over, and they had special carts that went round every morning just to collect the dead from the doorsteps and gutters. Corpses are something you get used to seein', and I can't remember how many bloated ones I've seen floatin' in the rivers."

Raven shuddered, thankful that she had not yet witnessed the terrible filth and poverty that went hand in hand with the opulence and pageantry of India. Of course she had the journey to thank for that, for what horrors could she possibly experience firsthand from the polished decks of the mighty clipper ship, with India sliding harmlessly past the *Orient Star*'s sleek hull, separated from its beauty and horrors by a length of swirling black water? In truth she had witnessed nothing but the unexpected delights of life on the river, the sight of the herdsmen who flung their bawling, struggling sheep into the water in a comical copy of an English sheep dip, the magnificent Hindu temples and Moslem mosques that were visible through the cypress and mango groves, the twinkling lights of villages as the clipper slipped soundlessly past in the night. Once or twice she had caught glimpses of mighty elephants laboring in the fields, carrying timber or uprooting trees, dark-skinned little boys beating their tough hides with sticks and shrieking orders, and the air was always alive with the shrill cries of brightly feathered parrots.

Sometimes, when the river narrowed, the *Orient Star* had sailed close enough to shore for Raven to watch the ever-present monkeys with the aid of Dmitri's spyglass, laughing helplessly at their amazing antics as they swung from one towering tree to another. Surely these were not examples of the abject misery of which Nathaniel Rogers and Mrs. Trentham had spoken. Even in the Bombay bazaar, where Raven had been face to face with the natives who toiled through lives so glaringly diverse from her own, she had seen nothing but the sparkle of the jewels in the goldsmith's booth, the dazzling brightness of the silk saris, the very air alive with exotic scents, all exciting and strange. She remembered Edgar Murrow telling her that one could travel throughout the length and breadth of the Indian subcontinent and never lose the feeling of being at home, the British army and the East India Company dominating the land and its people so completely.

"Here you are, Miss Raven. Do you want me to carry it to Mrs. Daniels's cabin for you?"

Startled from her thoughts, Raven looked up quickly at the kindly steward, who held a steaming mug of soup in his leathery hands, his lips twitching as he saw the thoughtful frown on her lovely face. "Don't dwell so much on dire musing, lass," he told her jovially. "Life's too short for serious thinking and, besides, 'twill wrinkle your bonnie brow far too early."

Raven laughed at this and took the mug out of his hands. "I imagine you're right, and thank you, Mr. Fletcher, I'll take it up to her myself."

She found Danny propped against the pillows, her color greatly improved even in her young mistress's short absence. Hanging the lantern back on the heavy beam overhead, she placed the soup in Danny's hands and watched with all the concern of an overbearing mother as the elderly woman began to eat, her slender arms akimbo, expression so serious that Danny was forced to laugh.

"It's the look of your father you've got on your face, Miss Raven, the way he used to glower at me and make me feel as meek as a ten-year-old child."

"Oh, go on with you," Raven retorted, "Father never glowered at you a day in his life!"

"Oh, but he did, and it was always for some scrape or other I'd let you get in to."

Raven tossed her dark head haughtily, secretly pleased to see her former governess returning to normal so rapidly. "No one could keep me out of trouble, Danny, least of all you, and Father never blamed you for anything I did. Now," she added, taking the empty cup from Danny's hands, "don't let's get into an argument about which of us is right, because I know I am, and furthermore, you need to sleep. I'll look in on you later in case you need anything else."

Closing the door softly behind her, she tiptoed across the short space to her own cabin and slid the bolt behind her. Humming to herself, she unpinned her hair, and as the heavy mass fell free beneath her fingers, the candlelight highlighted the dark midnight color with pinpoints of fire. With a sigh she collapsed amid a flouncing of velvet skirts onto her bunk and opened the worn book of poetry Ewan Fletcher had lent her the day before, intending to read for a short while before checking in on Danny and retiring herself. Raven had been surprised at the crusty old steward's possession of a gold-stamped volume of early Italian poems and sonnets, her inquisitive gaze having brought a self-conscious blush to his leathery cheeks.

"Sometimes a man gets a wee bit bored at night, you see," he had explained in a halting voice when he handed her the well-thumbed book. "All the work's been done and there's nothing to do but abide i' your cubicle till bedtime. Why don't you give 'em a try, Miss Raven? Some of 'em aren't too bad."

They were, in fact, delightful, the translations into English having lost none of their meaning or meter, and Raven, deprived of books since Theodore Stanridge had taken his collection with him off the *India Cloud* in Bombay, read voraciously. From time to time she would shake her head, unable to believe that Ewan Fletcher, with his dour, down-to-earth manner, could own such a book as this. Surely a poetry-loving steward, a boatswain who was well versed in the classics, and a righteous-thinking deposed Russian prince were as far removed from low-born, vicious smugglers as one could come! Raven felt a moment of shame at the ungracious comment she'd made when she first came aboard the *Orient Star,* loudly declaring in the officers' presence that she thought the ship and her crew of more than dubious virtue.

How well she could understand now their disapproving murmurs and black looks, having come to realize herself that the *Orient Star* was a ship any man would be proud to serve upon. Only Captain Charles St. Germain—Raven drew a deep sigh—as usual, only Charles St. Germain did not fail to reinforce her first suspicious thoughts. It was true, he was a rogue, an intolerably arrogant, long-legged devil, and she couldn't for the life of her understand how she could love him. Yet love him she did, even now, after learning that he had given up, by choice, the one thing that Raven sought to save for herself, the ancestral home—and that of the St. Germains was doubtless every bit as magnificent as the Barrancourts'.

Wrapped up in her brooding, Raven almost didn't hear the ship's bell strike on the deck above, but when the two solitary chimes echoed away into stillness, she lifted her head in astonishment. Could it really be one o'clock? she asked herself disbelievingly. How long had she been lying here on her bunk reading? Suppose Danny had been calling for her and she had been too absorbed in the book to hear?

She sat up, tossed the book aside, and fumbled for her soft kid slippers. Smoothing her wrinkled skirts, she picked up the sputtering candle that stood on the small table near her bunk and tiptoed across the pitch-black corridor. The door to Danny's cabin creaked alarmingly, and Raven held her breath, afraid that she had awakened her, but in the faint candlelight she saw the elderly governess wrapped snugly in the thick woolen blankets, her breathing deep and regular. Raven withdrew silently, glancing at the end of the narrow corridor, where a pale light still glowed beneath the captain's door. What was he doing? she wondered despite herself with a stab of unexplained longing. Was he reading or prowling restlessly about his spacious cabin?

Suddenly restless herself, she climbed up on deck, savoring

the cool night air that wafted to her from across the river, bringing with it the slightly acrid odor of the marsh. Jackals howled in the darkness and then were still, and pariah dogs answered with piercing barks from the villages. The silence soothed Raven, the deserted decks a haven from her troubled thoughts concerning Charles St. Germain, whose image had stubbornly continued to dwell in her mind no matter how hard she tried to thrust it away.

"Damn him!" Raven whispered to herself. "I hope he finds his cursed diamond quickly and leaves Lahore, and me, in peace!"

Velvet skirts rustling across the smooth wooden planks, Raven wandered to the rail and stood leaning into the wind, her long black hair wafting gently behind her. Try as she might, she could not stop dwelling on the handsome captain of the *Orient Star* and the fears Dmitri Zergeyev had instilled in her heart with his tale of diamonds and long-dead Sikh emperors. So it was the Kohinoor that had brought Charles St. Germain to India, she thought, and her tawny eyes grew hard. How like him to risk so much for the sake of amassing wealth! Or was it, she wondered again, merely the pleasure of the chase, the lust for the kill that drove him relentlessly? Would he have no desire for the fabulous diamond once he held it in his hands, the thrill of pitting his great strength and keen wits against its present owner gone? So, too, had he tired of her, or would have tired of her, had he been able to complete the conquest of her he had begun in his cabin earlier that evening.

Raven bit her lower lip and shook her head at her own morose thoughts. She was, she decided, too bewildered by everything she had experienced that day—Danny's brief illness, the discovery of Charles's true identity, Dmitri's startling disclosure of their reason for traveling to the Punjab—to think clearly anymore. Whether or not Charles St. Germain had tired of her already was immaterial. She would never allow him to touch her again, and as for his quest for the Kohinoor diamond... She blinked and peered out into the darkness, thinking to herself that she was so caught up in the tale of the fabulous gem that she was even beginning to imagine she could see one floating ahead of her.

Like the legendary dagger that appeared before Macbeth in her favorite Shakespearean play, Raven could clearly see the brilliant sparkle of a jewel in the dim starlight as it bobbed in the swirling water directly below her. She caught her breath, aware that hallucinations were not supposed to happen to level-headed young ladies of acceptable intelligence, and leaned over the rail, straining to see through the darkness. A faint, almost inaudible lapping sound came to her, moving in the direction of the ship, and as her eyes grew more accustomed to the night, Raven could make out an inflated skin boat drawing stealthily alongside the *Orient Star*'s hull. In the darkness its occupants were mere shadows, but she counted three of them, tall and muscular, the one kneeling in the bow holding a curved dagger in one hand, its jeweled handle twinkling ominously in the starlight.

It took several seconds for Raven's frozen mind to begin working again, the shock of seeing the tiny boat drawing alongside the enormous clipper in the dead of night having momentarily taken away her powers of reasoning, but then she opened her mouth and screamed, the obvious truth dawning upon her. The *Orient Star* was being boarded by river pirates!

As Raven's cry of alarm echoed over the deserted deck, the men in the boat below sprang into action. Instead of fleeing, as she had expected them to do, they leaped from their crouched positions for the boarding nets, scrambling up with the agility of monkeys, and behind them came another group and then another. Footsteps pounded on the deck behind her, and the voice of Peter Hagen could be heard issuing orders to the rest of the watch, their shouted questions adding to the confusion. Raven, her skirts flying behind her, raced along the deck toward them, her heart thundering in her breast.

"Mr. Hagen! Mr. Hagen, we've been boarded!" she cried, her voice filled with terror.

"Sound the alarm! Spencer, go for the captain!"

"All hands on deck! All hands, action stations!"

Behind her Raven could hear the steady slapping of bare feet on polished wood, and she screamed in fear and pain as her long black hair was caught in a restraining hand and pulled with a sharp tug that almost spun her off her feet. Another scream rose in her throat but died there as a naked arm slid about her waist and jerked her backward, a big hand clamping down painfully over her mouth. Her arms were pinned behind her back, and she was imprisoned against the wide, naked chest of an enormous man whose breath rasped against her ear.

"What's going on, for God's sake? Wasn't that Miss Raven who screamed?"

"Damn it all, it was a woman, that's all I know!"

In the darkness the sound of running footsteps came closer, and Raven, eyes widened with terror, felt a stab of pain as a lantern was thrust close against her face.

"Good God!" It was Peter Hagen with the night watch clustered about him, all carrying assorted weapons and belaying pins, coming to a dead halt as they rounded the far corner of the great cabin to find Raven held fast in a dark-skinned native's grasp, a dozen or more others gathered in a menacing semicircle behind him, naked but for filthy dhotis, each carrying a glinting tulwar, their eyes silent and watchful. The leader, his dark beard streaked with silver, tightened his hold about Raven's slim waist, the point of his jeweled dagger pressed against the soft, hollowed cleavage between her breasts.

"Hagen! What the devil—"

Raven could have wept with relief at the sound of the deep, menacing voice of Charles St. Germain, her knees growing weak as he strode into view, the watch parting soundlessly to let him through. He was wearing nothing but his tight-fitting breeches and sea boots, his chest bare, having ignored the rest of his attire in his dash topside after the first call to arms. Not having heard Raven's screams, he was unprepared for the sight of her on deck, the muscular arm of the bearded Indian wrapped about her tiny waist, her breasts rising and falling as she gasped in sheer terror, the gleaming point of the dagger poised directly above her heart.

His expression went rigid and he halted instantly, arms hanging loosely at his sides, powerful hands clenched into fists, and Raven, despite her fear, saw the emerald eyes begin to glitter with a strange light. The Indian who held her uttered a curt order in an unknown dialect, his harsh voice grating in Raven's ear, his beard scratching her soft cheek, although she was too frightened to notice.

"In God's name, captain!" Peter Hagen whispered in the ensuing silence. "What's he saying? That's not Hindustani!"

"It's Pushtu," Charles rasped, his glowing eyes never leaving the tall Indian leader or the woman he held in his fierce grasp. "They're Afridis."

From the murmurs that rose at this, Raven gathered that the

news was bad. Her arms were being cruelly twisted from behind, and she was so frightened that she couldn't even think. Her wide eyes fastened onto Charles's broad form as though he were a lifeline and she drowning in the sea.

"Charles—"

His name was wrenched from her in a breathless whisper, and she saw him wince and move toward her, but the guttural command from the Afridi leader and the quivering of the dagger in the dark hand made him halt instantly.

"Be still, Raven," he commanded. "It's not you they want." In Pushtu he addressed the bearded leader, his tone as savage and unafraid as the Afridi's, and Raven, numb with terror, listened to a dialogue she could neither understand nor endure. She knew only that the dagger that hovered above her could plunge down at any moment into her heart, and beyond that she could not, she dared not, think.

Charles's broad shoulders and wiry chest gleamed with sweat, his nostrils flaring as he shook his head in response to the Afridi's rough question. The sight of Raven being held so cruelly, her little oval face rigid with terror, was doing away with his sense of reason, and he forced himself with his entire will not to throw himself at the Afridi who imprisoned her, aware that, no matter how swiftly he might pounce, the dagger would be faster. God, he thought in agony, where was Dmitri? Blood lust was rising in him, making his chest feel thick, and he knew that he could not control his feral instincts much longer.

"Charles, don't, please don't."

The nearly inaudible whisper had come from Raven. Her anguished eyes gazed beseechingly into his, and his heart exploded within him, aware that she had been able to read the madness in his eyes and that her fear was for him entirely. With an inhuman cry he leaped forward, no longer capable of controlling himself, but even as he moved, a blood-curdling yell came from behind the assembled group of Afridi warriors, and Dmitri Zergeyev, brandishing a pair of long-barreled pistols, charged into the melee. Black eyes glowing fanatically, he plowed into the group of half-naked men, scattering them and roaring like a maddened bull. The bearded leader turned, taken by surprise, and as an explosion of powder and gunshot reverberated over the decks, Raven felt herself being jerked out of his grasp by a pair of powerful hands.

For a moment she was pulled against a broad, comforting chest, then she was thrust away, forced into the protective recesses of a bulkhead, where she trembled in the darkness. Two more shots rang out into the night air, and the sounds of battle grew fiercer. Through the glinting flash of dancing knife blades and blinding explosions of powder Raven could see Charles, the muscles in his lean back convulsed, locked in deadly combat with the leader of the Afridis. The crew of the *Orient Star* had leaped into the fray after Dmitri's frenzied attack, their knives and pistols wielded with as much enthusiasm as the frantic Afridis' tulwars, and animal growls and curses, shouts and groans filled the darkness, mingling with the deadly clang of bare metal against metal.

Then, quite suddenly, it was over, and with one last blood-curdling yell Dmitri lifted two of his assailants into the air and tossed them bodily overboard. Charles, dispatching the bruised and bloodied leader in a similar manner, stood back with a hideous grin to watch the rest of the band follow him into the swirling black water. Not satisfied with his conquest, Dmitri fired two last shots into the darkness, cursing roundly in Russian, his beard blowing in the wind like a pirate's, his white teeth flashing in the night. Charles, the deadly rage ebbed out of him, moved among his men, examining wounds and issuing curt orders, and only when the needs of his crew had been seen to did he turn to Raven, although her safety had been foremost in his mind.

He found her huddled against the great cabin wall, her face buried in her hands, and as he lifted her gently to her feet she clung to him, her heart beating wildly against his chest, her body trembling. "Are you hurt?" he asked gruffly.

Raven shook her head wordlessly, but he could see the lingering shock in her golden eyes. Taking her firmly by the slim shoulders, he led her belowdecks and into his cabin, where he poured out a brandy and set it before her.

"Drink," he commanded, but Raven shook her head, her face devoid of expression.

"Drink, dammit!"

Automatically she lifted the glass to her lips and swallowed, coughing as the liquid seared her throat. "Damn you, Charles St. Germain!" she sputtered, but Charles, relieved to see the color returning to her hollow cheeks, ignored her angry curse.

Wordlessly he refilled her glass and watched in satisfaction as she swallowed its contents without protest. His powerful arms were crossed before his bare chest as he waited patiently for the brandy to take effect. After a moment Raven raised her head and drew a shaky breath, the tawny eyes no longer vacant as they met the approving emerald ones.

"Who were those men?" she whispered.

"Afridis. From the hills." His voice was unusually curt. "What in God's name were you doing up on deck?"

"I couldn't sleep," Raven confessed, still trembling despite the soothing warmth of the brandy spreading through her. "I went topside and happened to spot their boats coming alongside. By the time I realized what was happening, they . . . they were aboard." She shivered, and Charles's lips tightened grimly at the strained expression on her delicate features. "What did they want?" she asked dazedly.

"Opium," Charles said harshly.

"Opium?" Raven looked bewildered.

"It's the clipper ships that carry the opium to China in exchange for silver bullion, Raven. That pitiful, addicted gang of hill men mistook the *Orient Star* for one of them and decided to commandeer the shipment for themselves. They've got incredible courage, the Afridis, but not much brains, I'm afraid."

"You sound as though you pity them," Raven said accusingly.

A vision of the gleaming dagger poised over the pale rose bodice rose unbidden to Charles's mind, and Raven, seeing the expression that entered his green eyes, recoiled instinctively. "No," he said harshly. "I'm only sorry we didn't kill all of them."

"I hope Danny wasn't frightened by all the commotion," Raven added quietly, and at the thought of the feverish governess she gasped. "Danny! I forgot all about her!"

"Stay here," Charles commanded. "I'll look in on her."

He was back a moment later, his full lips twitching, the last vestiges of the awful tension and savage rage that had been hovering over him finally gone. "Still sleeping, believe it or not. I doubt she heard a thing. We've the laudanum to thank for that."

Raven breathed a sigh of relief. "I'd hate to think of her being as frightened as . . . as I was." Her oval face was pale with the memory, and Charles leaned down quickly to help her to her feet.

"Don't worry about it anymore," he advised. "I've doubled the watch and Dmitri's on guard, so you've nothing more to fear. After a good night's sleep you'll feel much better."

As he guided her to the door, however, Raven suddenly clung to him, her slender arms sliding about his powerful neck. "Don't leave me," she whispered, the golden depths of her eyes wide with lingering fear. "I don't want to be alone. Please, Charles, I can't—"

His handsome visage infinitely tender, though Raven couldn't see it with her face pressed against his bare chest, Charles lifted her into his arms and carried her to the bunk, loosening her stays and removing the rose velvet gown so that she lay amid the blankets in her satin corset and chemise, her arms still clinging to his neck. He could feel her warm breath against his lean cheek, and, disengaging himself long enough to douse the candles and plunge the cabin into darkness, he lay down beside her, cradling her head on his wide chest and covering her slender body protectively with the length of his.

Raven sighed and snuggled closer to him, the comfort she derived from lying in Charles's strong arms unlike any she had experienced since her father had died. The terror of the Afridi raid was beginning to fade as the lingering warmth of the brandy and the heat of Charles's powerful body enveloped her and soothed away her fears. Charles, hearing her sigh, the soft tresses tickling his chin, held her closer, the desire to protect the young girl in his arms a sensation he had never before experienced. One big hand came up to caress the silken curls, stroking them softly, the gentle pressure on his chest as Raven breathed into his ear bringing a warmth of sensation, again, entirely new to him.

The nightingale, coming to life in the velvet darkness of the cabin, began to sing, the tranquil, trilling sound so achingly lovely that Charles found it difficult to understand how Raven could fail to remark upon it. He whispered her name softly, but there was no reply, and from the deep, even rhythm of her breathing he realized that she had drifted off into an exhausted sleep. Gathering her close, he listened to the liquid beauty of the nightingale's song. A strange but deeply satisfying peace descended upon him, and after a while, he, too, slept.

Raven awakened with a small cry of fear, the nightmare that had held her in its suffocating grip having become so terrifying that she awoke, her heart pounding, her breath coming in gasps. Instantly she felt a muscular pair of arms tighten about her, their warmth and strength comforting her, and a deep, reassuring voice whisper in her ear,

"It was only a dream, my sweet."

She opened her eyes to find herself gazing into the emerald-green ones of Charles St. Germain, his normally harsh, forbidding features softened in the pale, golden light of the dawn that crept through the shutters latched across the stern windows. To her innocently wondering gaze it was a beautiful face, the sensual lips curved into a gentle smile, the deeply clefted chin without its usual stern set.

"Was it the attack last night you were dreaming of?" Charles asked gently.

Raven nodded, her lower lip trembling as she attempted a brave smile. "I suppose I'm not very good at dealing with an attempted stabbing by opium addicts."

Charles laughed softly. "Any other female would have dissolved into hysterics or fainted dead away."

"I wish I could have," Raven said with an involuntary shiver.

Charles's hold tightened, and he gazed down into her oval face, thinking to himself that she was more beautiful than any woman he had ever seen with the early-morning sun caressing her dainty features. She reminded him of the breathtaking mystique of the South Seas, her golden eyes the color of a Tahitian sunset, her soft lips as rosy as coral, her dark hair gleaming like rare black jade. She was lying against him, her cheek pressed against his chest, her breasts, taut and firm beneath the satin corset in which she had slept, brushing tantalizingly against him. Where she had fretfully kicked off the covers in the throes of her nightmare he could see the ivory smoothness of one silken thigh, and he felt his loins tighten in response.

Raven could feel the heat rising in his hardening manhood, and she lay still against Charles's side, drawing from his desire until a small flame seemed to leap within her, ignited by the knowledge of how much he wanted her. For a long while neither moved, savoring the intimacy that had sprung up between them and the contact of their bodies, his lean and hard, hers supple and soft, a perfect joining that neither could ignore. Charles slid his hand beneath Raven's head, his strong fingers brushing against her slender neck, turning her so that she was facing him. A thrill shot through him as he lowered his head to kiss her and found the soft lips parted and waiting, and as his mouth closed upon them she sighed in deep contentment.

Though her body was no longer strange to him, Charles left no inch of its silken softness unexplored as he unlaced the heavy corset and impatiently removed the confining chemise. His lips traveled across her bare shoulders, nibbling at the soft hollow at the base of her throat, then moving to the rosy tips of her full breasts, while Raven arched her slim back against him, her hands caressing his chestnut curls. Then his lips found hers again, closing upon them in a demand filled not only with the force of his passion but with a paradoxical tenderness. It was as though he intended to satisfy not only his burning need but also his desire for this one woman who, in a frightening moment of dangerous confrontation, had almost been taken from him.

Raven was his, Charles exulted, gazing down into her glowing golden eyes, his own glittering with passion. Her lips were parted hungrily for his next kiss, her seeking hands making him groan with want, aware that she had the power to enslave him as readily as he had the power to claim her. This sharing of love, new to him who had spent his life in pursuit of the thrill of conquest, made Charles aware of the hold the tempestuously beautiful Raven Barrancourt had over him, and he reveled in it, giving and taking in equal measure until he could wait no longer.

Raven, looking up into the passion-flushed features, Charles's upper lip dotted with sweat, his green eyes like the brilliant depths of cut emeralds, knew that it was time. Rolling onto her back, she spread her slender thighs, the invitation in her own sultry eyes driving him to the breaking point. With a low moan he fell upon her, driving deeply, and Raven, experiencing no quiver of pain as before, rose up to meet him, to take him deep inside that most intimate part of her. Then they were locked together, Charles moving in a rhythm which Raven willingly followed, his hot lips fastened to hers, his powerful arms encircling her narrow waist as he all but crushed her to him. Fever soared, bringing them together until they became one, Charles so much a part of her that Raven could not tell where she ended and he began, and she clung to him wildly. Her joy and love for him threatened to burst her heart, and finally, both approached the ultimate beauty of fulfillment and experienced the sublime.

"Oh, Charles," Raven whispered when their ragged breathing had stilled, her face pressed against his neck. "I—" She drew a shaky breath and fell silent, her confession of love trembling on her lips, her heart so full that she had to speak, and yet she could not. Even in the afterglow of their perfect union, Charles's heart beating against hers, Raven silenced the words, afraid even now to reveal such a vulnerable part of herself, memories of his earlier mockery filling her with pain.

Charles gazed quizzically into the tawny eyes, puzzled by the hardening of their topaz depths which had, only seconds before, been soft and yearning as they looked back into his. "What were you going to say, my sweet?" he asked playfully, and was surprised to see her delicate cheeks stain with rose.

"It was nothing," Raven murmured, attempting to pull away from him.

Charles's brow darkened in response to her unconscious rejection of him. He took her shoulders in a purposeful grip, his strong fingers digging into her flesh. "Nothing?" he repeated, a slight edge to his voice. "Then why do you blush so?"

Dismayed at the shattering of their intimacy, Charles's mood having changed so swiftly, Raven struggled free of his bruising grip and sat up, her long black hair spilling down her sleek back. "I-I better look in on Danny," she said doggedly, and Charles released her instantly.

"So fickle in your devotions, are you, Raven?" he asked as she slipped from the bunk and began to pull on her undergarments, little realizing the effect the sight of her smooth, naked body in the golden glow of dawn was having upon him. "You came to me willingly enough when you wanted me to make love to you, yet when you're sated you're quick to turn an icy shoulder." His voice grew harsher as he watched her lace her satin corset, struggling with trembling fingers to do the difficult task alone. "Cruel, tempting Raven," he mocked. "Does it appeal to your vanity to spurn your lovers this way?"

Raven stared down into his angry face as she smoothed the folds of her wrinkled velvet gown over her hips, her glossy black hair falling in a sinuous cascade below her waist, her soft lips trembling and still moist from his kisses. "I've told you once before, Charles," she whispered raggedly, "that there has never been anyone but you. Though I despise myself for admitting it, by God, I swear it's the truth." The tawny eyes were wide, her soul bared to him so that Charles knew she wasn't lying. With a pained exclamation he rose to his feet to take her into his arms, but she turned and slipped out of the door, the soft clicking of the latch more hauntingly final than her previously stormy exit had been.

Chapter Eight

"Here, now, you young son of Satan, if you try that again I'll box your ears right smartly!"

The vexed words were spoken in Russian, a language the Indian lad could not possibly understand, but as he craned his neck and found himself staring up into Dmitri Zergeyev's bearded face, he uttered a frightened yelp and retrieved his hand from the battered valise through which, with the speed of a ferret, he had been rummaging.

"Oh, Mr. Zergeyev, must these natives handle our luggage so roughly?" Danny cried worriedly. Her small round face was still pale from the vestiges of the fever from which she had suffered two days ago, and dark circles were etched beneath her normally merry brown eyes. She looked down into the swirling water beyond the *Orient Star*'s hull where native crafts of every size and description vied for a place near the boarding nets, voices clamoring for attention. Most of them were shouting offers of taking the trunks and bandboxes ashore; others were hawking wares which they had stuffed into every available inch of space on the boards beside them, holding them aloft for better viewing by the clipper ship's crew that had gathered against the railing to watch.

"Go on, boy, or I'll send you overboard with a flea in your ear," Dmitri threatened the young lad who had been bold enough to venture up the net and onto the ship. Looking down into the pinched little face with its enormous almond eyes, Dmitri relented and, growling beneath his breath, tossed an anna to the boy, who snatched it in midair and vanished over the side with the agility of a monkey.

Raven, who had been standing anxious guard over their belongings which had been brought topside several minutes ago, quickly hid the soft smile forming on her lips when the Russian's coal-black eyes riveted themselves upon her. He was, she knew, daring her to comment on his generosity toward a would-be thief, although both of them knew well enough how soft-hearted the big Cossack could be at times. Instead she turned away and smoothed the skirts of her peach-colored gown and straightened the folds of the long, flowing velvet cape she had spread across her shoulders, while Dmitri assured the worried Danny that their luggage would be taken ashore by the *Orient Star*'s crewmen themselves.

"Then what was that boy doing with my valise?" she demanded uncertainly. It had never dawned on her, as it had upon Raven, that he had boldly clambered aboard to steal.

Dmitri, not wishing to distress the elderly woman, explained hastily that the boy's eagerness to earn a few coins carrying their belongings ashore had caused him to overstep his bounds. "We'll have it loaded into a launch in just a moment," he soothed her, but Danny's expression only grew more concerned.

"Oh dear," she fretted, hurrying toward the companionway, "I'd better make sure we haven't forgotten anything."

Raven uttered a soft laugh as she moved closer to Dmitri's side. "I believe this is the third time she's checked our cabins. Oh, look! The man down there in that tiny boat, he's got a monkey with him!" She watched, enchanted, as the boatsman, aware that he had won the young Englishwoman's attention, urged the chattering little creature to perform an assortment of tricks. The monkey, obviously accustomed to performing, did his work well and was rewarded with a sweetmeat at the conclusion of his act, while his handler shouted something up to the watching Raven.

"What did he say?" she asked, turning curiously to Dmitri.

"For the price of a rupee the monkey is yours," the Russian responded. Seeing the eager look on the beautiful oval face, he smiled. "Doubtless it would bite you and run back to its owner the first chance it got, and you would be without your money and your new pet."

"I couldn't keep him anyway," Raven added with a note of regret in her soft voice. "We're only going to be in Lahore for such a short time." She scanned the village that lay beyond the boat-infested waters of the Sutlej where a handful of men under the guidance of Geoffrey Lytton had vanished a half-hour before.

"How long do you think it will be before they've arranged transportation for us?" she asked a trifle wistfully. Though she had told herself repeatedly that she was glad their journey was over and that soon she would be free of Charles St. Germain forever, she could not rid herself of the sadness that hung over her like a pall.

The *Orient Star* had not, as had been originally scheduled, ended its voyage in Kasur because the autumn rains, which normally swelled the Sutlej with water, had failed to fall in the north that year. The enormous clipper, unable to negotiate the wind-stilled, shallow waterway with its treacherous silt islands, had dropped anchor farther downstream, and Raven and Danny had been informed the previous evening that they would be taken ashore the next day and supplied with overland transportation to Lahore.

Danny, relieved to learn that she would soon be on solid ground again, had not bemoaned the extra days' travel the detour would entail. Dmitri had assured her the dak bungalows in which they would be sleeping at night were as comfortable as any wayside inns in England and that they would not be lacking adequate protection on the road. Raven had accepted the news with similar relief, telling herself that the sooner she bade farewell to Charles St. Germain, the better. They had not exchanged a single word since her tearful exit from his cabin only yesterday morning, and Raven had taken great pains since then to avoid him altogether.

Furious with herself for having succumbed to Charles's fiery touch and impassioned kisses when she had sworn to herself that she would never do so again, Raven had spent a long, sleepless night berating herself for her stupidity. She had tried to convince herself that she had deserved that last painful scene with Charles, for it had proved to her indisputably that he had felt nothing but the basest lust for her, and once that had been satisfied he had quickly turned away, scorning her openly. How glad she was now that she had not told him that she loved him. She winced whenever she thought of the cruel sport he could have made with such knowledge!

Besides, it wasn't true at all. What she had mistaken for love had just been an overblown case of hero worship, for Charles St. Germain had been her first lover, and that had, for some ridiculous reason, made him seem somehow different and special in her eyes. It was merely because she had been lonely and lacking affection since her father's death, Raven had reasoned, and therefore it was understandable that she had transferred her feelings to a man who had, in a brief space of time, been gentle with her. Love! A scornful frown twisted her lips. What did she know of such things? The devilishly handsome captain of the *Orient Star* had merely used her body, driven her to mysterious heights just as he had countless other women in the past, and she, fool that she was, had immediately mistaken her awakening passions for love.

"Damn his soul," she whispered fiercely, her voice trembling oddly.

"Eh?"

Raven whirled about to look into Dmitri's dark, questioning eyes, and flushed deeply as she realized that she had spoken aloud. The golden eyes, which a moment ago had been filled with self-loathing, despair, and an odd, painful longing of which Raven hadn't even been aware, quickly became shuttered and unreadable, and Dmitri, who thought he had come to know her so well, was mystified.

"You are troubled, little one?" he persisted kindly, his heart wrenching as he gazed into her beautiful oval face. The pale silvery rays of the Indian sun glistened like dewdrops on her midnight-black hair, which was drawn softly away from her smooth brow and temples. In her peach gown with its graceful folds and rustling skirts, the same gown in which she had first stepped aboard the *Orient Star* in faraway Bombay, she looked achingly beautiful and oddly defenseless, like a delicate, fragile flower that might not withstand the hardships of the Indian climate. Dmitri chided himself for these thoughts immediately, aware that Raven Barrancourt, for all her delicate beauty, possessed spirit and courage and that it was only the thought of their separation that made him feel so troubled now.

"Look there, Dmitri," she said, ignoring his question and pointing with a slender index finger across the shimmering water. "Here comes the launch."

By the time the longboat, with the oarsmen pulling energetically against the current, had drawn alongside the *Orient Star*, Captain St. Germain had joined the small group clustered about the port entry. With hands clasped behind his broad back, the cool breeze stirring his sun-streaked hair, he waited patiently, his dark green eyes narrowed as he stared off across the water. Raven, while she ignored him completely, was acutely aware of his intimidating presence, and though she had withdrawn to Dmitri's side to escape that disconcerting gaze, she could feel it resting on her from time to time, although the ruggedly handsome visage was grimly forbidding. She prickled resentfully at his refusal to acknowledge her, telling herself she had been correct in assuming he was no longer interested in her now that he had conquered her and satisfied his own urgings. Fool, blind, stupid fool, how could she have fancied herself in love with such a man?

Filled with self-loathing, unable to bear Charles's presence even amid a crowd of jostling sailors, Raven withdrew to her former quarters to await his summons. The sight of the empty cabin, with only the single dresser and the stripped mattress remaining, gave her a moment of stabbing pain, for she realized now how much she had come to love the dark nights on the quiet river, the beams creaking ever so softly, the bullfrogs and crocodiles rumbling in the reed grass, the peacocks shrieking, and the ever-present jackals yapping from the shores. She would miss her life aboard the *Orient Star*, miss the reverberating bells that signaled the end of the watches and the cool, pleasant sun-washed days strolling about deck with at least one smiling deck hand to keep her company.

Such a short journey in comparison to the endless one aboard the *India Cloud*, and yet, Raven realized, it was here aboard the magnificent clipper ship that she had found no small measure of peace, the friendships she had made going deeper than casual acquaintance. She sighed, running her slim fingers idly over the beautiful inlaid ivory that covered the top of the dresser, hating the thought of bidding farewell, doubtless forever, to the officers and hands she had come to know. In the next moment her tawny eyes filled with delight as she recalled that she would see Dmitri again, for he had boasted to her only this morning that he would probably arrive in Lahore before Raven and Danny did and that, his quest for the Kohinoor diamond notwithstanding, he would probably find time to visit her in her cousin's home.

The soft smile died on Raven's lips and her golden eyes clouded. What dangers would Charles and Dmitri face seeking the fabled diamond? She remembered how Dmitri had scoffed at her fears that bloodshed would result from their attempt to steal the coveted jewel, and how sure he had been of his own and Charles's capabilities. Yet surely there was danger in trying to take from another what rightfully belonged to him, especially if countless lives had already been claimed in the past for attempting the very same thing.

Raven told herself firmly that her fears were for Dmitri alone, for she couldn't bear the thought of the fun-loving, life-embracing Cossack prince being killed for the sake of a jewel, even one as fabulous as the Kohinoor diamond. As for Charles St. Germain, he was a blackguard who had thrown away all that was of value in his life, and if he sought now to recompense himself by stealing the wealth of another man, then he deserved to be hanged for it, or at the very least cut into pieces and trampled by elephants, a very fitting punishment which Geoffrey Lytton had described to her only yesterday.

"Miss Raven?"

She jumped at the sound of Ewan Fletcher's unexpected voice although the dour steward had spoken quietly, his grizzled head thrust inside the opened cabin door. Though he found it odd that she was standing motionless in the empty quarters, his expression softened when he saw the wistfulness in her large sloping eyes. Aye, the lassie was feeling the pangs of parting, he decided, and felt unhappiness of his own steal over him. How he would miss her bonnie face and bright eyes; the sight of her breathtaking beauty had always been a welcome escape from the dull existence of life aboard ship.

"Yes, Mr. Fletcher?"

Raven's soft voice roused him from his thoughts and he grinned at her apologetically. "Cap'n wants to see you in his quarters."

Raven hesitated. "Alone?"

"Zergeyev's with him," Ewan answered, thinking nothing odd about her question or the slight nervous catch in her voice.

"Thank you."

She swept into the corridor, her slim shoulders straight, her dark hair piled on her head in a becoming fashion, her long, slender neck rising gracefully from the gathered lace about her collar. Even from behind she was a veritable goddess, Ewan decided woefully, and knew that he would miss her badly.

"You asked for me, captain?" Raven said shortly, striding into the spacious quarters after her knock had been answered with a curt order to enter. She kept her head high, but her heart lurched despite herself at the sight of Charles sitting behind the small desk with the gilded cage hanging above one broad shoulder, the nightingale preening and pecking at the sunflower seeds Dmitri was feeding it. Charles's woven Holland shirt was open at the throat, and Raven could see the golden hairs curling upon his sun-bronzed chest. She recalled with a shiver how comforted she had felt lying against its hardness with Charles's arms about her the night the river pirates had attacked the ship.

Charles, looking up and meeting the guarded golden eyes, responded with a grim tightening of his full lips. Leaning back in his chair in a study of indifference, he said curtly, "Sit down, Miss Barrancourt. We've something of importance to discuss."

Completely bewildered, Raven did as he commanded, her eyes traveling past him to Dmitri, although the big Russian, taking his cue from his captain, regarded her just as solemnly. Raven's gaze returned to Charles, whose countenance had darkened considerably, having seen the questioning appeal in her own when she had glanced up at his first mate. She forced herself to meet the mocking emerald eyes squarely and was dismayed to find her gaze traveling instead to Charles's sensual lips, and as she unwittingly recalled their warmth and taste, she looked away again, her restlessness causing Charles's brows to draw together.

"Your cousin is not expecting you in Lahore?" he asked sharply.

"No, he isn't," Raven replied with tautly stretched nerves, Charles's manner setting her teeth on edge. "I have a letter of introduction from both my great-uncle and John Trentham." Her smooth brow wrinkled, but she refused to ask him why this mattered. He would only mock her typically feminine impertinence, and whatever Charles St. Germain had to say, Raven had learned with despairing exasperation, would be said in due time and on his own terms.

"Then you have no idea what sort of man he is." This time it was not a question.

"Of course not," Raven snapped, beginning to lose patience. "I only know that he is a member in good standing of the East India Company and that my great-uncle, of whom I think very highly, regards him fondly."

"And this Khanapur compound where he lives," Dmitri put in, addressing her from his great height behind Charles's massive shoulder, "it is a regular British cantonment?"

"From what I understand from Mr. Trentham's description, yes, it is." Raven lifted her small face to look up at him. "Why is that so important, Dmitri?"

It was Charles who answered her puzzled question, his voice harsh. "Because Mr. Lytton and Mr. Perry learned when they went ashore just now that the British resident at Multan was recently murdered."

Raven's lovely countenance was filled with bewilderment. "I don't understand."

Charles made an impatient gesture. "Do you happen to know who the Sikhs are, Miss Barrancourt?"

"Why, certainly," she responded sharply, resenting his tone of voice. "Mr. Lytton told me all about them."

"What did he say?"

Eyes flashing with annoyance, Raven said tartly, "That they are followers of Sikhism, which was founded over three hundred years ago by Guru Nanak, who tried to unite the Moslems and Hindus under one religion. *Sikh* means 'discipline,' and Mr. Lytton said that the Sikh men never cut their hair but conceal all of it under their turbans."

To her astonishment Charles merely inclined his head at her tart words, his green eyes watching her intently. "Go on. What else did he say?"

"That they were united into a kingdom here in the Punjab by Govind Singh and later Ranjit Singh, the maharajah, but that since his death they've been ruled by one weak, vacillating hand after another. Four years ago, I think, Lord Ellenborough, who was governor-general at the time, planned to annex the Punjab and had troops brought across the Sutlej, but before they could begin maneuvers, the directors of the East India Company had him recalled to England because they didn't want the Sikhs to make war against them. When Ellenborough's troops were recalled, Mr. Lytton said the Sikhs reacted just the opposite to what had been expected, seeing the withdrawal as a sign of cowardice on the part of the British, and decided the time had come to drive them out of India altogether. Two battles were fought, which the British finally won, and that's how they can to take control of Lahore, which is where Phillip Barrancourt now lives." Raven stopped speaking and regarded him coolly. "Is that all you wish to know?"

"Geoffrey is an admirable teacher," Charles remarked to Dmitri, ignoring Raven's arch question, but before the Russian first officer could reply, he turned back to Raven, his green eyes as hard as emeralds.

"Do you think a people as proud as the Sikhs would take lightly to their defeat, Raven? I'm inclined to think not, and perhaps you might see some significance in the fact that the British resident at Multan was murdered by them."

Raven felt a cold hand of fear wrap about her heart, for she realized immediately what Charles was implying. Obviously this cold-blooded murder was an act of aggression, a sign of the Sikh's continuing hatred for the British. The color drained from her soft cheeks and she looked up at Charles fearfully. "Will there be another war?"

"One wonders if it was merely the act of a handful of mutinous dissidents or if it is a sign of their general opinion toward the British."

His callous reply made Dmitri add hastily, seeing Raven's obvious distress, "That is why you must be sure your cousin is well protected and that the British army resides not far from Khanapur compound."

"But I don't know any of these things," Raven responded helplessly. "I've never met him, and this is my first trip to India. How can I be expected to know?" Her hands clenched into small fists. "I-I came to get my money and then to leave as quickly as possible. I never wanted any trouble. What should I do?"

"Continue with your plans," Charles responded curtly, "but make utmost haste before the British have had an opportunity to plan their reprisal. As for traveling to Lahore, Dmitri and I both agree that you and Mrs. Daniels cannot go alone. We've decided to see you safely there, but after that your welfare becomes your cousin's responsibility."

Raven's brow furrowed. "You're coming with us to Lahore?" she asked faintly, making no attempt to hide her dismay.

Charles's brow darkened, for this was not at all the reaction he had expected. "Indeed I am. I cannot, in good conscience, allow two Englishwomen to travel across the Punjab with only native guides for protection."

Raven's eyes began to flash. "And in doing so you have found a good excuse for being in Lahore while you search—" She broke off, catching sight of Dmitri's warning glance. Rising to her feet she said stiffly, "Very well, captain, I accept your offer of protection, but I won't be fooled for a moment into believing you are accompanying us for humanitarian reasons. I make only one demand, however."

Charles's rugged visage darkened at her haughty words, but she plowed on relentlessly, "Danny is not to learn of the dangers we may be facing or of the threat the Sikhs may pose. I won't have her frightened for any reason, do you understand? Now, if you'll excuse me, I should be seeing to our luggage."

She whirled and left the room, her dainty shoulders stiff, while behind her Dmitri gave a low whistle and grinned broadly. "Kristos, but the little princess can be a lioness when she defends her own! Ah, tovarich, I thank you for the opportunity of letting me remain in her company a little longer."

"You're a soft-hearted, mealy-mouthed fool, Zergeyev," Charles said abruptly. "That woman is a cold, calculating witch, and the sooner you admit it, the safer I will feel."

By the time their luggage had been loaded into one of the longboats, Raven had said good-bye to most of the crew, and they had all wished her Godspeed and a pleasant stay in Lahore, every one of them filled with regret at seeing her go. Unaware that her dimpled smile and delicate beauty had won the hearts of the loyal men of the *Orient Star*, Raven was touched by their fond farewells and felt a moment of stabbing unhappiness as she was handed down into the launch by a miserable-looking Jason Quintrell. She would miss them all, and because she couldn't bear to look up at them as they crowded the railing, knowing she would begin to cry if she did, she looked instead toward the shore, where the thriving village of Hasangei stood against the blue Indian sky.

Yet in doing so Raven's gaze became accidentally locked with that of Charles St. Germain, who, having personally helped Danny into the boat, had turned back to assist her—only to find that it wasn't necessary, for Raven took her seat with admirable balance in the bobbing craft. Charles could clearly see the tears glistening on the thick dark lashes, the golden eyes brighter than usual, her small white teeth clamped firmly on her soft lower lip to keep it from trembling. An odd expression entered the emerald eyes, then was gone, and he leaned over to inquire in a soft, mocking manner,

"So you've come to be fond of the men you once considered cutthroats and smugglers, have you, Raven?"

"All except one," Raven replied in the same soft tone, although there was a biting edge to her voice that left no doubt to whom she referred.

Charles straightened, his handsome face growing rigid, and gave orders for the launch to be cast off in so ominous a tone of voice that Dmitri, sitting in the bow, turned to give him a quizzical glance. Danny, clutching the gunnels with her small, plump hands, seemed unaware of Captain St. Germain's anger, her relief at being put ashore offset by the terrifying certainty that the swaying longboat would overturn at any moment, drowning them all or, at the very least, sending all their belongings to the bottom of the Sutlej.

It turned out to be an uneventful trip, the men at the oars pulling with tireless strength, the flat, shimmering stretch of water easy to traverse. By the time they reached the pier and made fast the lines, some of the color had returned to Danny's cheeks, and she even managed the ascent from the boat without mishap. Raven, lifting her skirts to step onto the pier, suddenly found Charles's strong hand beneath her elbow, and though she felt a curious warmth shoot through her body at his touch, she ignored him as though he wasn't there.

Moving away from his towering form, she turned and looked over one dainty shoulder toward the river where the *Orient Star* lay moored beyond the current, its sails neatly furled, the bare rigging soaring into the sky. Thinking of the journey that lay behind them and the ever-changing panorama she had witnessed unfolding along the wide, swirling stretch of the Indus and Sutlej rivers, Raven felt a moment of deep sadness creep over her. A year ago Raven would have laughed disbelievingly if anyone had told her that she would grow to love the long, cool days sailing across the breadth of India, to be awakened in the middle of the night by the screams of a leopard, to watch for hours on end the diligence of turbaned fishermen casting their nets in the lion-colored reeds. It was true, Raven reflected, she had fallen under the spell of India, despite her unhappy reasons for being there, despite the harrowing, never-to-be-forgotten attack by river pirates, despite her uneasy relationship with Captain Charles St. Germain.

"Miss Raven, will you be coming now?"

Raven turned to find that their luggage had already been loaded into a battered ghari with worn leather seats, a pair of weary-looking dray horses standing with lowered heads in the traces, the turbaned driver already sitting impatiently on the seat. Dmitri was standing like a well-heeled footman before the narrow door, waiting to help the two of them inside, and Danny repeated her question, wondering why her young mistress was staring off across the water with such a wistful expression.

Captain St. Germain, Raven saw, was standing a little way off from the wagon speaking with the longboat crew, obviously issuing last-minute orders to Howard Perry, who would be acting as first mate to Geoffrey Lytton during the captain's absence. Raven wondered how many of the *Orient Star*'s crewmen knew the real reason why Charles St. Germain and Dmitri Zergeyev were accompanying the pair of Englishwomen to Lahore. Probably not many, for Jason Quintrell had innocently mentioned to her this morning that the clipper ship would be taking her consignment aboard here at Hasangei as soon as it could be transported overland from Kasur. The captain and Dmitri, he had explained, would be responsible for seeing that the Indian goods were brought down from the warehouses where they had been stored, and apparently the entire crew wholeheartedly approved of the captain's decision to travel farther north to escort Raven and Danny safely to Lahore. It was obvious to Raven that no one suspected Charles or his first mate of having ulterior motives in mind.

Allowing the grinning Dmitri to help her up into the carriage, Raven told herself tartly that she no longer cared at all what happened to him or his insufferably arrogant captain after this. She was through with the lot of them, the Lord be thanked, and in a few days' time she would be in the custody of her cousin Phillip and the worst would be behind her. Smoothing the rustling folds of her satin skirts about her on the lumpy seat, she glanced out the window to see Dmitri mounting a scruffy but stout-looking bay horse, guiding it toward a towering peepul tree beneath which Charles St. Germain awaited astride a long-legged chestnut.

The Indian driver uttered a sharp command to the horses, which took off at a surprisingly brisk trot down the dusty road, and Raven had only one final glimpse of Charles's broad shoulders and bare head before a cloud of choking dust rose from beneath the carriage wheels and obscured him from view.

"The good Lord have mercy on us!" Danny murmured fervently as the wagon began to jolt through the deep ruts in the road, swaying alarmingly and creaking so loud that it was nearly impossible to be heard above the noise. "Will it be like this the whole way to Lahore?"

"I imagine so," Raven replied, wishing that she were riding in the fresh, cool air beside Dmitri and Charles. The dust cloud had forced her to pull the cracked leather blind down across the window, and it was rapidly growing stuffy within the darkened confines of the wagon. She agreed with Danny that the overland trip would be torturous indeed if the road didn't smooth out soon, but she compressed her lips tightly and swore to herself that she wouldn't complain, certain that Captain St. Germain would mock her for it.

Occasional glimpses through the blind showed Raven that they had left the village behind and were traversing a long valley of dark, fertile earth, the hills surrounding it made green by lush trees and whispering elephant grass, the sky filled with circling kites and purple-plumed birds. Traffic was relatively heavy on the road leading from town, or at least so it appeared to Raven, still accustomed to the solitary life aboard the *Orient Star*. Farmers returning to town from the fields, traders astride camels, and merchants riding sturdy horses joined the throng of colorful bullock carts and chattering pedestrians that moved in a steady stream toward Hasangei.

Very few of them, Raven noticed, paid attention to the swaying wagon in which they traveled, but Charles and the bearded Dmitri, both of them towering above the populace on their horses, were subjected to numerous stares and whispered exchanges. Raven was relieved to see that there was no hostility in the dark eyes that slid quickly over the broad-shouldered pair, for she had been fretting constantly over the reception that all of them as Feringhis—hated foreigners—would receive here in the land of the Sikhs. Perhaps the danger wasn't as grave as Charles had led her to believe, Raven told herself, only to remember in the next moment that both he and Dmitri were heavily armed, each of them carrying a pair of pistols hidden in their belts and Dmitri having added a long-handled knife to the short dagger he always carried tucked in his boot.

"I wish our driver would slow down," Danny complained, the jolting increasing even more when the village and its crowded thoroughfares were left behind and the open countryside lay ahead.

"The sooner we get to Khanapur the better," Raven remarked, thinking of the dangers that might befall them in traveling without proper military escort. There were restless Sikhs and highwaymen, whom Dmitri had told her were called "budmarshes," who could make easy prey of their cumbersome vehicle if they chose. Yet surely the situation wasn't that critical, Raven comforted herself in the next breath, and one single murder didn't necessarily have to be an indication that an entire populace was growing hostile toward the British.

"I know you're eager to get your money and return home," Danny added, misconstruing Raven's impatient words, "but, oh, Miss Raven, couldn't we stay at Master Phillip's a while before leaving again? We've been traveling for so long now, and I'd just like to rest a wee bit before we turn around and start all over again!"

Because Danny was sitting directly across from her on the narrow wagon seat, Raven was able to take a good look at her, and she couldn't help noticing in the filtered light that Danny appeared much thinner and older than when they'd first set out from Southampton so many months ago. The wispy hair protruding from beneath her bonnet was whiter now, she saw, and the lines on her face more sharply defined. It had obviously been a trying voyage for her, Raven realized with a guilty pang, and she wondered in the next moment how much she herself had changed.

Though she had suffered from neither the seasickness nor the fever that had beset Danny so mercilessly, she had nonetheless endured a great deal, most of it on an emotional level. First and foremost, there had been the constant terror of losing North Head to plague her, then the added burden of fear that had gone with the knowledge that she and Danny were traveling at the mercy of a band of English smugglers, a fear that Raven had stoically borne alone. Yet nothing, she knew, had been as difficult to bear as the tormented love she had fancied she felt for Charles St. Germain—a love that, though she knew now it had been misguided, had nevertheless opened her eyes and changed her forever. From the blissful innocence of childhood Charles St. Germain had hurled her into womanhood, awakening within her an awareness of her own sexuality, which she had never before dreamed existed. The heights of pleasure to which both of them had ascended during their last impassioned lovemaking haunted Raven still, and she was unable to deny to herself even in her secret heart of hearts that no man alive but the devilish Charles St. Germain, captain of the *Orient Star* and former Earl of Monteraux, could have taken her there.

"You're not getting ill, Miss Raven?" Danny asked worriedly, her words bringing an embarrassed flush to Raven's soft cheeks. Why on earth did she keep dwelling on that moment? she asked herself irritably, hating the way her breath always caught in her throat and her heart skipped a beat whenever she recalled that final moment of soaring pleasure. Both she and Charles, driven far beyond the sensual satisfaction of their bodies, had ascended to a state of sheer ecstasy in which they had merged and become one, neither in that timeless moment able to exist without the other.

"No," Raven said in a curiously sad little voice, "I'm not getting sick, Danny, I'm just as tired as you are of traveling, and I promise you we won't budge from Lahore until both of us feel up to the voyage home."

Danny found this a very sensible statement, having dreaded that Raven, in her desperation to get back to Cornwall, would insist that they leave immediately. Though she herself missed the comforts of home, and thought longingly of her own sunny bedroom in the east wing of North Head, she knew that Sir Hadrian could cool Squire Blackburn's heels well enough should their return stretch beyond the agreed period of a year.

Both of them fell silent, Danny occupied with plans of what she would do once they returned home, of the mending she would finish, the preserves to be put up for the year, the new gowns she would sew, while Raven sat and brooded dejectedly over the green-eyed devil who was riding out before them. As both of them had expected, it proved to be an endless afternoon, the noisy, rumbling wagon with its narrow seats and darkened windows so uncomfortable that neither of them could close her eyes for even a moment.

By the time the vehicle came to a bone-jarring halt, Raven felt certain that every muscle and limb in her body had been torn asunder. With a groan she rose to her feet, thankfully taking hold of the arm the grinning Dmitri Zergeyev presented to her when he threw the creaking door open. Her knees buckled when she stepped to the hard ground, and Dmitri moved quickly to catch her, his free arm sliding about her slender waist to steady her, the intimacy of the contact bringing a scowl to the handsome features of the watching captain of the *Orient Star*, who had dismounted a short distance away.

"Ho, my little one." Dmitri grinned, releasing Raven with obvious reluctance. "Your legs have gone to sleep, eh?"

"That and every bone in my body," Raven remarked tartly. "How could you lock us into such a contraption of torture, Dmitri?"

The big Russian laughed when he looked into her accusing eyes. "That is all part of what makes India unique, my precious flower, but do not worry. Captain St. Germain has decided on an early stop today."

"I thought Mrs. Daniels might be tired," Charles agreed, coming toward them from the far side of the rambling dak bungalow where he had turned the horses over to a bowing coolie. His green eyes rested briefly on Raven's drawn, exhausted face, his icy glance telling her that his concern had been for Danny alone.

"How kind of you," Danny cried gratefully, and Raven felt a stab of annoyance when she realized that Charles had once again managed to raise his esteem in the elderly woman's eyes. "Is it true we'll be spending the night here, captain?" Danny added doubtfully, surveying the low building of wood and mud, the creeping vines of a rampant bougainvillea obscuring most of the narrow windows.

"You'll find the accommodations acceptable," Charles promised and turned to the hovering coolie to utter a clipped command in flawless Urdu.

Raven and Danny were taken inside by a silent, middle-aged Indian in achkan and trousers, while the wagon was brought round back to be cleaned of the dust that had settled on it from the road, and the weary horses were led away to be fed and watered. True to Charles's word, Raven found the room she and Danny were to share comfortably furnished, and as soon as they stepped inside, no less than half a dozen serving women were there to see to their every need. Dusty clothes were removed and wash water was supplied in stoneware urns, fresh garments were laid out for wearing, and a tray overflowing with chapatis, honeyed sweetmeats, fruits, and tea was set onto the low table beneath the window.

Accustomed to the great number of servants that had tended her in the Trentham house, Raven allowed them to provide for her in the manner they saw fit and responded with a weary smile to their salaaming exit before sinking down hungrily before the heavily laden table.

"Judas, I'm famished," she groaned, helping herself to the flat, unleavened bread that was the mainstay of the Indian diet, and savoring the sweetness of the tea. "Won't you eat a bit, Danny?" she asked, looking up at the elderly woman, who was peering curiously through a slit in the chik blinds toward the quiet, deserted stretch of hard ground that separated their dak bungalow from the road. The afternoon was waning, and bats were beginning to flit through the darkening skies. The yapping of jackals embarking on a scavenger hunt sounded from a distant village.

"I'm too tired to eat," Danny confessed, removing her shoes and collapsing with a look of distaste on the string bed she had chosen for herself, although she was astonished to find that it was far more comfortable than she had anticipated. "I think I'll settle down for the night."

"So early?" Raven asked in surprise, but Danny's eyes were already closed, and she did not answer her young mistress's question.

Raven smiled to herself and finished her meal in silence, the deep, even breathing that came from the charpoy telling her that Danny was already fast asleep. By the time she had sated her hunger, some of her own weariness had vanished, and she tiptoed out of her room and onto the long verandah of the bungalow, her gown of dark Prussian blue blending with the darkness of the evening that fell so swiftly in northern India.

The night was very still save for the distant yapping of the jackals and pi dogs, and Raven wondered what had happened to Dmitri and Charles, whom she hadn't seen since their arrival. No light showed through the slits in the heavy reed chiks that covered the windows lining the bungalow walls, and she had no way of telling how many guests were quartered there for the night. Spreading the yards of rustling blue material about her, she seated herself on the steps and propped her small chin in her hand, her eyes wandering through the darkness.

As she grew accustomed to the sounds of the night, Raven gradually became aware of the muffled sounds of conversation coming to her from one of the rooms located on the far side of the bungalow past the carefully tended gardens. Though she couldn't understand what was being said, there was no mistaking the deep, rumbling laughter that exploded the silence from time to time, and she wondered with whom Dmitri was visiting. Certainly not Charles, for Raven knew very well that the arrogant English sea captain was not given to any form of merrymaking, especially not any as rousing as that which she was overhearing.

Not too long afterward the quiet creaking of the door behind her caused Raven to whirl about, and she felt her heart leap into her throat in dismay when she recognized Charles St. Germain's lean, muscular form loom out of the shadows. In the dim light she could see that he was wearing his nankeen riding breeches and fawn-colored coat with its gold tab collar, his white muslin shirt standing out sharply in the blackness, although she could see the contrasting darkness of his sun-bronzed chest where the garment lay open at the throat.

By the slow walk and quiet tread of his boots on the porch Raven could tell that Charles considered himself alone. She remained silent as he came to a halt by the railing, leaning against a rough wooden beam, his muscular arms propped before his wide chest. Though his stance was casual, Raven could sense the tension within the big body, even though she could not see his face. She was glad now that she hadn't disclosed her presence, for she sensed instinctively that he was waiting for someone, and curiosity was beginning to get the better of her.

"Tovarich?"

Raven's wildly beating heart slowed as soon as she recognized Dmitri's deep voice, and she sat perfectly still on the steps while Charles unfolded himself from the railing and turned around.

"Here, Dmitri. What did you find out?"

The big Russian's footsteps were no louder than a cat's as he joined the tall sea captain on the verandah. Again Raven was aware of the tension in the air, and Dmitri's stealthy appearance confirmed her suspicions that their meeting had been prearranged and was intended to be held away from prying eyes. Charles's blunt question could mean only one thing: that the two of them had already begun making inquiries as to the whereabouts of the coveted Kohinoor diamond, and Raven's nervousness changed abruptly to anger. Above all she did not want to become involved in their mad scheme, and the only way to do so was by refusing to become privy to any information concerning it at all.

Rising swiftly to her feet, she made no attempt to quiet the rustle of satin the movement brought, feeling a moment of grim satisfaction as the two men on the verandah broke apart and tensed themselves. Greedy fools, she thought contemptuously, her disapproval making her feel unkindly disposed toward them. This cloak-and-dagger business was really beginning to grow tiresome!

"Good evening, Miss Barrancourt," Charles said with polite formality, coming forward to greet her, and Raven was forced to admit that she would never have been able to recognize someone else as quickly in the darkness.

"Good evening, captain, Dmitri," she responded innocently enough, climbing daintily up the short flight of steps and pausing before them, thinking to herself that Charles St. Germain must have eyes like a cat's.

"Out for a stroll?" Charles asked casually, sauntering closer.

"I wanted to stretch my muscles after that harrowing drive today," Raven explained glibly, then wondered with a feeling of uneasiness why he and Dmitri were staring down at her so intently. The whites of the big Russian's eyes were clearly visible in the half-light, and Charles's rugged features had taken on an angular harshness that made him seem more arrestingly handsome than ever—yet oddly menacing as well.

"Is that not permitted?" she demanded coolly.

Dmitri and his captain exchanged brief glances, then Charles shook his head by way of reply. "I must caution you, however," he added in that infuriatingly mocking drawl that Raven had come to despise, "that India is not the safe, familiar grounds of North Head, Miss Barrancourt, and that you should avoid going out alone, especially at night."

"I'm not afraid," Raven shot back, annoyed at his tone, tilting back her head to look up into his handsome face with a mocking smile of her own. "You above all should remember that I'm not easily deterred from making midnight sojourns."

Charles knew very well to which long-ago night she was referring, and his full lips tightened grimly, aware that Raven was goading him deliberately. In no mood to humor her, he said with unmistakable warning, "Even armed men have been known to be dragged off into the brush by tigers, Miss Barrancourt, not to mention that the grasses teem with snakes and scorpions. And if the dangers posed by nature are not enough to deter you from traipsing about alone in the darkness, perhaps a brief reference to the river pirates who boarded my ship will remind you that India is rife with criminals?"

"You've made your point, captain," Raven said stiffly, refusing to admit to herself how much his anger and icy formality were hurting her. For all appearances they were once again the haughty, indifferent smuggler sea captain and the irate young woman who had confronted him with the truth upon the darkened deck of the *Orient Star* so long ago. It was as if they had never gone beyond those proud, unyielding facades, Raven thought miserably to herself, never shared anything deeper than antagonism and dislike. No one, not even Dmitri, who was watching them closely, would ever believe that Charles St. Germain had actually held her tenderly in his arms, kissed her yielding lips, and loved her in a rough and gentle manner that had driven her to the wildest heights of ecstasy.

Raven could scarcely believe it herself as she looked up into the stern features, the emerald eyes glittering menacingly in the darkness, the rugged visage filled with nothing save annoyance and hostility. Could this be the same Charles St. Germain who had raggedly whispered her name before taking her, becoming part of her as he drove deep inside her yielding woman's body, his searing kisses branding her burning flesh? No, it was not, she thought dismally, for this was the real Charles St. Germain, not the tender, loving man she had fancied existed and stupidly fallen in love with. No, there was no one at all like that beneath the forbidding, heartless exterior he presented to her now, and there never had been. Whatever had existed between them had been a sham, a clever act improvised by Charles himself so that she would fall at his feet, confess her undying love, and offer to him her innocence as doubtless countless ignorant virgins had before her.

Charles had been watching the beautiful oval face in the darkness, and although he could not clearly see the emotions playing across the delicate features, he could sense the torment within Raven's heart, hear the labored breathing that gave proof to her inner turmoil, and he took a step toward her. "Raven—"

"I've already told you that you've made your point," she repeated in a whisper that vibrated with emotion. "Why don't you leave me alone?"

With a swish of satin skirts she hurried past him across the verandah and disappeared inside, the hinged door slamming shut behind her. For a moment there was silence in the darkness outside until Dmitri shifted uncomfortably and gave Charles a quizzical glance from beneath his bushy brows.

"You shouldn't be so unkind to her, tovarich."

Charles's lean jaw was clenched. "How else could I warn her to keep on her guard without rousing her suspicions?"

Dmitri nodded unhappily. "I suppose you're right." He sighed heavily and refrained from adding that the tension that had always existed between his little princess and his captain seemed to have grown unbearable of late and that he was prepared to do anything at all to help make peace between them. But he said nothing, for when it came to dealing with Raven Barrancourt, Charles was a total stranger to him, and Dmitri did not know the reason why.

"What were you able to find out from the Yorkshireman?" Charles asked, his deep voice breaking into Dmitri's troubled thoughts.

"Oh, him? Pah!" Dmitri replied with heat. "Useless fool! Traveled the entire length of the Grand Trunk Road in the company of over two hundred sepoys being reassigned further south—they were all from Peshawar, no less—and he hadn't even heard of Multan! Unless he's totally deaf and blind, I don't understand how he could have failed to hear their gossip!"

Charles's sensual lips twitched in response to the annoyance in the Cossack's fierce tone. "No matter, my friend," he soothed, "I've news from the Juganar cantonment and the resident commanding officer, who was most happy to supply me with updated reports."

Dmitri spread his big hands helplessly. "I wonder why I even bother undertaking the same missions you do," he complained, "because I am forever coming up with nothing and you, tovarich, end up making me look the fool." Sensing that Charles's mood was grim, he sobered instantly and moved closer to the captain. "What did you learn?"

"That British troops took the field against the Sikhs at Ramnuggar not a week ago."

"Kristos!" Dmitri's voice dropped to a whisper. "It's war, then? What was the outcome? Who won?"

"There was no decisive victory."

"And yet the Sikhs continue to march."

"Aye, and the British continue to mobilize their troops. I'm convinced there'll be another battle soon."

Dmitri was silent a moment and then voiced the question that was foremost in both men's minds, neither having forgotten the terrible massacre of British subjects in Kabul in 1841, the first year either of them had ever set foot on the Indian subcontinent. "The Sikhs are not rising in mutiny against the cantonments?"

"No." Charles sighed and wearily massaged the back of his neck. "Not yet, at any rate."

"So the Punjab is still safe for British citizens," Dmitri finished, idly stroking his beard. "I am glad, tovarich, but I cannot help thinking that the situation may change."

Charles was silent, his handsome face impassive as he stared out into the night, listening to the sounds of the plains that were distinctively India's own. To the quiet rustlings and footfalls Charles listened with only half an ear, for his senses were keen enough to pick out any single one of them amid the multitude, and at the moment it was only man who posed a threat to the inhabitants of the dak bungalow, not the creatures of the night.

"I think you're right, my friend," he said to Dmitri in a grim voice that was far removed from the mocking tone with which he had addressed the furious Raven earlier. "But there's nothing we can do for the time being except watch . . . and listen."

"You are right, as always," Dmitri agreed, and both men again fell silent, for there was nothing else to be said. If Raven had been able to overhear their conversation she would have realized beyond a shadow of a doubt that it was not the whereabouts of the legendary Kohinoor diamond that had been causing Dmitri and Charles so much concern that night.

"Captain," Raven said crisply to the towering gentleman in casual riding attire when they met on the sun-drenched grounds the next morning, "I refuse to travel in that rattling contraption any longer! Danny says she's used to it by now, but I insist on riding."

Charles handed the leather saddlebags he had brought outside to the waiting coolie and turned to Raven with an archly raised brow. "You insist?" he repeated ominously.

Raven retreated a step from the threatening visage but tossed her dark, glossy head in a show of defiance. "I do. If it were you being rattled to the teeth for hours on end, you'd feel the same way."

Charles stared down into the upturned oval face for a moment, seemingly oblivious to Raven's breathtaking beauty. There was a wintry crispness to the air that late November morning, and she had donned her flowing velvet cape, the fur-lined collar brushing lightly against her smooth jaw. Her tawny eyes with their sloping, catlike corners were obstinate, and the soft rosy lips were compressed with what he recognized was a will as unyielding as his own.

"Very well," he said curtly, turning away, "but I don't want to hear a single word of complaint out of you no matter how sore that little derrière of yours gets."

Raven's golden eyes faltered and slid away at the unkindness of his tone, but Charles had already turned away and was shouting in Urdu to the hovering Indian ghari driver and didn't notice.

"I'm afraid, little one," Dmitri Zergeyev's sympathetic voice said in her ear, "that the captain can be curt at times. Do not let him trouble you. He isn't accustomed to dealing with women, only sailors who respond to nothing but barked orders."

"Oh, but you're wrong, Dmitri," Raven disagreed, turning to look up at him with eyes that glittered like cold, cut topaz. "Captain St. Germain has dealt with too many women, and doubtless all of them were mealy-mouthed little nurslings, so I'm not surprised that he's come to think of himself lord and master over my entire sex."

She stalked away with her trim back stiff, and Dmitri couldn't help chuckling to himself, delighted as always by Raven's spirit, yet in the very next moment his heart grew heavy at the sight of Charles's harsh expression, which told the big Russian only too well that his captain had overheard every word Raven had uttered. He sighed and turned away, wondering why the captain seemed to take such pains to be cruel to Raven Barrancourt. Normally Charles treated those he didn't care for with icy contempt or ignored them altogether, but Dmitri had come to realize that he seemed to go out of his way to treat Raven unkindly. Not that she didn't provoke him deliberately, Dmitri admitted honestly, but the clashing of wills and antagonism that existed between the beautiful golden-eyed princess and the green-eyed devil of a sea captain mystified him completely.

By the time the ghari was prepared to embark and Danny was comfortably ensconced within, a suitable mount had been furnished for Raven. Led from the dak bungalow barn by an eagerly grinning proprietor, the thin, rough-coated mare looked as though she would collapse after a half-dozen miles, but Charles, looking her over with a critical eye, bartered for her without hesitation.

"She looks ready to drop," Raven whispered to Dmitri, both of them standing on the verandah while the captain and the dark-skinned Indian haggled in unhurried tones over the price.

Dmitri laughed. "Aye, she does, but you'll not find a stronger creature or one as tireless."

"But she's so—so mangy-looking!" Raven persisted, unconsciously comparing the mare with her own magnificent Cinnabar.

Dmitri's bright black eyes were suddenly as cold as obsidian. "If she were beautiful, little one, she would fall easy prey to the roving eyes of a budmarsh."

Raven felt her heart skip a beat at Dmitri's flat tone. For the first time she noticed that the wagon horses and the pair that Charles and his first mate were riding were sturdy enough but certainly unworthy of attracting attention. Had they been selected for that reason? Was it thieves Dmitri feared or the restless, hostile Sikhs who might be prowling the villages of the Punjab for suitable war mounts?

Surely she was exaggerating, Raven told herself irritably, for if there was any danger at all, Charles would have insisted that she travel in the comparative safety of the enclosed wagon. Still, she didn't care at all for the somber tone of Dmitri's words and was noticeably silent as Charles assisted her in mounting the newly purchased mare. For a moment his big hand lingered over hers as he lifted her into the saddle and handed her the reins, but Raven, preoccupied with her own worrisome thoughts, scarcely noticed.

With a pale yellow sun rising high into the cold, clear sky, the small caravan turned onto the road, Charles and Dmitri flanking Raven on either side although she was unaware that they did so deliberately. Raven had forgotten her fears as soon as they were trotting across the hard-packed ground, the feel of a horse beneath her again after so many months making her realize how deeply she had missed being astride. Her velvet cloak fell in folds across the cantle of her saddle, and her glossy hair gleamed in the sunlight, the fur-trimmed hood thrown back, a look of sheer delight upon her delicate features.

Aye, she was a beauty, Dmitri thought to himself, peering with longing into the lovely face, his muscular gelding moving willingly at the scrawny mare's side. How could anyone, he wondered passionately, gaze into that breathtaking countenance and not be moved by its innocence? Aye, only Charles St. Germain appeared capable thereof, riding a good arm's length away along the narrow ditch that bordered the rutted road, seemingly oblivious to Raven's presence. His strong hands were gripping the reins more tightly than was his custom, a muscle in his lean jaw was twitching, and his green eyes restlessly sought the foothills far ahead that rose like jagged boulders from the flat, dun-colored plains.

The three of them rode in silence, their thoughts their own, and even Dmitri showed little inclination to talk or bellow out in a lusty voice the Russian folksongs that had always fallen from his lips during the deck watches aboard the *Orient Star*. Raven soon found herself wishing that she had remained with Danny after all, for at least the old woman never minded talking when her young mistress felt inclined to. Furthermore, the stiff Indian saddle was nowhere near as comfortable as the fine English leather one her father had commissioned for her in London years ago, but Raven, remembering Charles's taunting words, compressed her lips and did not complain.

"We'll stop here for a rest," Charles announced nearly three hours later, indicating a grove of towering peepuls along the roadside where a spring bubbled forth from beneath the enormous roots. Gathering momentum, the cold, clear water surged along a bed of ivory sand, the small stream swelling toward the

Sutlej, which lay like a glaring ribbon of molten silver beneath the sunlight several miles across the plains.

The ghari driver dismounted quickly at Charles's signal and uncoupled the horses, hobbling them with twisted hemp rope before vanishing across the grass-covered ground with the stealth of a native raised in the desert.

"Where is he going?" Raven asked curiously, drawing rein beneath the trees.

"To eat his noonday meal," Charles replied, dismounting and looping the reins loosely about the flap of his saddle. "He is a Hindu, and his religion forbids him to eat in the presence of those without caste."

"Meaning us?" Raven asked, surprised.

Charles nodded and came to stand at the mare's side, strong arms lifted, palms upturned, to help Raven down. She hesitated, then removed her small boot from the stirrup and dropped to the ground without waiting for his assistance. It was fortunate that Charles was there, however, for no sooner had she touched down than her knees buckled beneath her, and she would have fallen if Charles hadn't slid his hands quickly about her small waist and hauled her up. For a moment Raven found herself held against his hard chest, her firm, round breasts brushing against him, her full skirts pressed along the length of his muscular thighs. Charles's arms seemed to tighten of their own volition about her, drawing her even closer, his breath warm against her brow.

Raven lifted her head to find the glittering emerald eyes upon her, her own on a level with his sensual lips, and she found herself growing still, unable to tear her gaze away. Charles, feeling the tremor that traveled through her soft body and the breathless stillness that followed, could scarcely credit the tremendous surge of heat that flowed through them whenever they touched. A seemingly timeless moment descended upon them as they looked into each other's eyes, the hunger and need in Charles's tempered by the longing and scarcely realized love in Raven's.

"Where are the water bags, tovarich?" came Dmitri's shouted question from the far side of the wagon, where he was solicitously helping Danny to the ground.

Very tenderly Charles set Raven aside, making certain that

her aching legs were strong enough now to carry her weight before letting her go; then the emerald green eyes were once again hard and unreadable as he retrieved the goatskin flagons and turned to fetch water from the nearby spring.

"Are you certain riding isn't too much for you, Miss Raven?" Danny asked worriedly, hurrying toward her young mistress from around the wagon, smoothing her wrinkled bombazine skirts. "The road seems better now, and the carriage doesn't sway or rattle as much as it did yesterday."

Raven, who would have confessed less than a minute ago that she would dearly welcome the chance to continue on after luncheon in the relative comforts of the ghari, shook her head emphatically, her eyes following the tall form of Charles St. Germain as he bent down to fill the water bags from the crystal-clear stream. "Oh no, Danny," she murmured breathlessly, "I'm fine."

After a brief meal of chapatis, honeyed fruits, and water, the small party continued along the dusty road that wended its way relentlessly through the grass-covered plains toward Kasur. Raven found the countryside stark and oppressively dull in its never-changing scenery, landscape that, from the deck of the *Orient Star*, had always looked so colorful and exciting to her. Could it be that her fears of a second Sikh war had taken away the grandeur of India for her? Raven told herself fiercely that such thoughts were nonsense and that she mustn't let Charles's dire warning frighten her.

She cast a surreptitious glance at Charles, who continued to ride at her side although he kept his horse slightly behind and to the right of hers, preventing the possibility of any conversation between them. She sensed a restlessness within his rugged frame and guessed that he felt hampered by the pace set by a weary young girl astride an ancient mare and an elderly woman in a lumbering ghari.

The afternoon proved no less tiresome and endless than yesterday. Grimy with the fine layer of dust that had settled on her traveling cloak and hair, Raven kept her eyes downcast, feeling disinclined to talk, and only Dmitri's occasional bursts of singing broke the utter silence that hung like a pall over the undulating plains. But for the creaking of leather and wagon wheels, and the shrill cries of the birds overhead, Raven could almost imagine that they were again aboard the *Orient Star*, where the nights on the wide, slow-moving Indus had been so very still.

"You are tired, Miss Barrancourt."

Charles's curt voice and rigid formality stung Raven from her reverie, and she glanced up at him quickly, her delicately curved brows arched, a questioning look on her lovely oval face. How could she ever have imagined that any tenderness existed between them, that Charles St. Germain could be anything but the ruthless, lawbreaking smuggler sea captain he was?

"I feel quite well, thank you," Raven responded tartly, well aware that Charles had not been inquiring after her welfare but ascertaining how much farther she could travel that day. "If you believe we can reach Kasur by nightfall, then by all means don't stop because of me."

"I have no intention of doing so," Charles informed her coldly. "There are no more dak bungalows along this road, and unless you want to sleep beneath the stars tonight and fall prey to marauding leopards, I suggest we push on."

Dmitri, riding closer to Raven than Charles, was able to catch her sharp, painful intake of breath, but glancing at her keenly, could not read anything in the averted golden eyes. Shooting a quizzical glance at Charles, he received a grim frown in return and turned away, swearing softly under his breath, too familiar with the warning in that rugged visage to pursue the matter further.

It was twilight when the small group approached the Bridge of Boats leading over the darkened waters of the Sutlej. In the gathering gloom the lights of Kasur twinkled beneath the blue-black sky, and the white sails of countless small ships loomed eerily from below. Charles, who was riding in the lead, signaled a halt as the bridge watchman emerged from his booth to meet them. Raven's eyes were heavy-lidded with exhaustion, and she paid no attention at all to the handsome sea captain's brief exchange with the hook-nosed Indian wrapped in a deep blue dupatta. A creaking bullock cart rumbled across the bridge toward them, and its occupants peered curiously at the three mounted Europeans, eyes widening at the sight of the big bearded Russian and the muscular sea captain whose Urdu was nearly as flawless as their own.

Dmitri, alert as always, was aware of the looks and was relieved to see nothing save a mixture of awe and astonishment on their shadow-obscured faces. Reassuring, too, was the ease with which they were granted permission to cross the bridge, the watchman stepping back to let them pass. Briefly his eyes went to Raven, who was riding behind Charles, her tired little face barely visible beneath the fur-trimmed hood of her traveling cloak, but Raven was oblivious to everything and everyone. Never in her life had she felt so tired, her body aching to the point where she felt like crying, wanting nothing more than to rest for just a little while.

Before Charles could give the order to move up onto the bridge, the ghari driver dismounted unexpectedly and, hurrying through the darkness toward the mounted captain as fast as his thin legs would carry him, began gesticulating wildly, the words flying from his lips. Dmitri moved his horse closer to catch what he was saying while Raven took advantage of the unforeseen delay and rode toward the wagon, trying to peer into its darkened confines.

"Danny?"

"I'm here, Miss Raven," came the surprisingly spirited voice from inside. "I've been sleeping most of the way."

"You're very fortunate," Raven remarked ruefully.

"What's causing the delay?" In the darkness Danny's round face was just a blur of white as she peered out of the wagon window.

"I haven't the faintest idea," Raven replied, glancing at Charles and Dmitri, who were deep in conversation with the ghari driver. Her weariness changed to concern when she saw the harsh expression on Charles's handsome profile.

"Oh, what is it, captain?" Danny asked worriedly when the muscular Englishman and the bearded Russian rejoined them.

"Our venerable driver," Charles explained, casting a brief, piercing glance at the Indian, who was hovering nervously behind the sea captain's stamping horse, "has decided his religion forbids him to cross the Bridge of Boats."

"I don't understand," Danny said, turning to cast a puzzled glance at their driver.

"I think it means we don't have a wagon anymore," Raven replied, giving Dmitri an uncertain look. "That we'll have to ride the rest of the way into Kasur."

"I'm afraid that's correct, Mrs. Daniels," Charles agreed.

"Oh, dear, what will happen to our luggage?" Danny fretted.

"That will have to be strapped aboard Miss Barrancourt's mare," Charles explained obligingly. "She's been schooled as a pack animal."

"But where will I ride?" Raven asked, her eyes widening.

"With me," Charles informed her flatly, his tone indicating that it would not be a pleasant experience for him.

"And you, Mrs. Daniels, will come with me," Dmitri added heartily in the ensuing stillness. His tone grew mischievous. "If you can trust me as your escort, that is."

Danny's warm laugh broke the tension that had settled over all of them. "I'd be delighted, Mr. Zergeyev."

Raven watched, open-mouthed with astonishment, as Danny climbed nimbly out of the carriage, her skirts badly wrinkled but her spirits apparently undamaged. What an unexpected reversal of roles had taken place here! Normally it was Danny who was the first to tire or lose the will to push on, and here she was acting as spry as a young girl, even flirting openly with Dmitri, while Raven found it nearly impossible to force herself onward.

"What an odd thing this Hindu religion is," Danny remarked while the relieved driver and Dmitri hastily transferred the few trunks and valises to the swayed back of Raven's unsaddled mare. "One cannot butcher cows or eat in the presence of people of lower caste or even cross bridges!"

"It isn't the Hindu religion that forbids such behavior," Charles informed her, looming out of the darkness toward them, leading the tireless gelding by the bridle. A brief smile lit his harsh features—Raven could see the flash of his white teeth in the darkness—before he continued lightly, "It's the thought of the home and warm bed awaiting him at the end of the journey. By turning around now instead of taking us all the way into Kasur, he's gained at least a half-day of travel."

"But we paid him to deliver us into the city," Raven pointed out.

Charles shrugged his massive shoulders. "Aye, we did, but we are Feringhis—foreigners to him—and thereby easily fooled. Or so he thinks."

"But obviously he knows you speak Urdu as well as he does," Raven persisted. "Why don't you simply call his bluff?"

"This is India, Raven," Charles informed her quietly, moving closer to her side and unconsciously using her first name, which fell far easier from his lips than the formal "Miss Barrancourt." "Our calculating driver doesn't think the way we do, and I won't expose him as a liar by telling him I know damned well nothing in the Vedas prohibits him from crossing that river."

Raven fell silent, her smooth brow wrinkling with disapproval. Apparently the Indian mind worked far differently from that of an Occidental, and obviously Charles St. Germain had decided to adopt the ways of thinking of the country in which he currently found himself, for how else could she justify his irrational decision to place a lying man's honor before her own and Danny's welfare?

"We're ready, tovarich," came Dmitri's deep voice through the darkness, interrupting the protests that rose unbidden to Raven's lips.

"If you don't mind, then, Mrs. Daniels?" Charles asked, and Raven could not help hearing the roguish tone of his voice despite the fact that she could no longer see his face in the darkness. She felt certain, however, that his handsome features were transformed with the warmth of his most charming smile, and for a moment she felt a stab of pain, aware that Charles would never tease her in a similar manner despite the love they had shared between them.

Why was it, she wondered wretchedly, that Charles St. Germain was so kind to Danny but went out of his way to hurt her with his callous words and treat her with such icy formality? Had he already forgotten the fierce joy he had brought her with his impassioned lessons in lovemaking? Apparently so, for it was painfully obvious to her now that he had trifled with her and had taken that precious gift of maidenhood from her without afterward sparing a single thought for her feelings. God willing, she'd never lay eyes on him again once they were in Lahore.

"Miss Barrancourt?"

The deep voice was curt, and Raven was glad that it was dark now so that Charles wouldn't see the fleeting spasm of pain that she felt certain passed across her face in response. He was standing before her, the gelding's plaited reins in one big hand, his green eyes glittering in the darkness.

"Yes, captain?" she asked stiffly.

"Are you ready to go on?"

She nodded, and Charles placed his hands about her small

waist, his fingers curving over her hips as he lifted her into the saddle. Without giving her time to arrange her rumpled skirts, he placed his boot into the stirrup and vaulted up behind her, his muscular arms sliding about her to pick up the reins. Raven, acutely aware of their rigid strength, deliberately arched away from him and was almost unseated when the chestnut gelding took off at a brisk trot toward the illuminated bridge.

"Sit still," Charles commanded with a growl, "or you'll fall off."

Raven ignored him, sitting upright in a deliberate effort to avoid bumping into him again. Laughter rumbled in Charles's wide chest—she could feel it vibrate through her entire body—but she compressed her lips and kept her face averted, cursing the Hindu ghari driver his laziness and Charles St. Germain his misplaced tolerances.

The gelding's hoofs echoed hollowly on the wooden boards, and Raven turned briefly in the saddle to see if Dmitri and Danny were behind them. The movement turned out to be a mistake, however, for it brought her gaze in line with Charles's sensual lips, outlined in the flickering torchlight, which gave them an almost carnal fullness. She shivered despite herself and raised her eyes higher to find them inadvertently locking with his glittering green ones. Charles was regarding her quizzically, thinking that Raven had turned in order to address him, but his expression changed abruptly when he found himself gazing down into the upturned oval face.

In the flickering light of the torches that lined the long bridge, Raven's beautiful features were softened by shadows that added sensual depths to the lines of her firm jaw and hollow throat, and only the angular cheekbones were made more prominent in the contrasting light. Between the folds of her traveling cloak he could see the outline of her firm, gently rounded breasts straining against the shimmering material of her gown, the smooth skin above it glowing rosy in the torchlight. One soft thigh was pressed against Charles's muscular one, her curving hip riding enticingly against his own, and Charles felt his manhood stirring, the scent of her glossy hair, her warmth and nearness filling his senses with a barrage of stimulation he could not ignore.

The wide, sloping eyes were still locked with his, and Charles could see the dancing flames of the torches reflected in the wine-colored depths, the dark lashes that fringed them dusted lightly with gold. In seating Raven upon the gelding's back, Charles had caused the fur-trimmed hood to fall away from her face, and the exposed raven tresses were glittering with highlights that reminded him of precious gems. He thought to himself that if the Kohinoor was only half as brilliant, it would doubtless be worth a king's ransom.

At that moment the gelding stumbled unexpectedly on the uneven planking, and Charles's arms tightened instinctively about Raven to keep her from falling, encircling her and gathering her close against the protection of his wide chest. Raven's head fell briefly against a hard but undeniably comforting shoulder, and for a moment the ruggedly handsome face with its deeply clefted chin and lean, sun-browned cheek was bending close to hers.

"Are you all right?"

The deep, rough voice and his intimidating nearness sent a shiver fleeing down Raven's spine. In the circle of Charles's muscular arms she could feel the unyielding strength and the sinewy toughness of his chest and shoulders. The beating of his heart was strong and sure, and she was breathtakingly aware of the muscles that ridged the hard thigh pressed against her own, conscious, too, of the unmistakably aggressive maleness about him.

"I'm fine," she assured him in what she hoped was an indifferent tone of voice but was annoyed when her words showed a distinctive tendency to waver. "I'm not afraid of falling."

"Certainly not," Charles mocked, and she could feel his wide chest quiver with silent laughter. Releasing the pressure of his arms, he permitted Raven to sit up again, and she moved away from him thankfully, her slender shoulders stiff with disapproval.

Charles laughed again and reined the horse closer to Dmitri's, smiling down at Danny, who sat dwarfed before the enormous Cossack in the saddle. Her hat was awry, and wispy tendrils of straw-colored hair clung in riotous disarray about her round face, but she assured him firmly, when the handsome sea captain inquired, that she was doing fine and would easily withstand the grueling hour remaining before they reached the evening's lodging.

"We'll be spending the night at the British cantonment,"

Charles informed her. "Colonel Bateman is an old acquaintance of mine, and he'll be expecting us."

"How good it will be to find ourselves among our own kind again!" Danny remarked heartily, causing Dmitri to erupt with great peals of laughter.

"No more rough-cut swabs and cursing Russians for you, eh, madam?" he winked when he could speak.

Danny, aware that he was teasing her, laughed with him. "Oh, I assure you, Mr. Zergeyev, I'll sorely miss you when the time comes for us to part company!"

"And you, little princess?" Dmitri asked, his black eyes meeting Raven's in the flickering torchlight. "Will you miss me, too?"

"Of course I shall. I've grown curiously fond of some of you rough-cut swabs," Raven rejoindered, stressing the word *some* to the obvious preclusion of her tall, handsome escort. She could feel Charles's powerful form stiffen and draw imperceptibly away from her in response to her words, and her soft lips tightened grimly. There, you long-legged, self-centered pirate, she thought smugly to herself, you're not the only one who can be cruel!

With the plodding mare in tow, the two burdened geldings left the bridge behind them and swung right along the riverbank, skirting the main road that led to Kasur. Raven, bone-tired and growing increasingly stiff, paid little attention to the narrow alleyways and crowded dwellings they passed, although she would have seen little enough in the darkness even if she had been interested. Try as she might, she could no longer keep her eyes open, and every uneven step the gelding took threw her lightly against Charles St. Germain's broad chest. Though she stiffened and jerked away from him every time, weariness eventually overcame her, and finally she slept in the protective circle of Charles's strong arms, her smooth cheek resting against the softness of his clean-smelling muslin shirt.

Charles rode grimly, narrowed eyes probing the darkness ahead, guiding the gelding with steady hands and taking pains not to awaken the slender girl who slept against him. Now and then, taking liberties he would not have had she been awake, he rested his lean cheek against the silkiness of her hair where her subtle, familiar fragrance filled his senses, his handsome countenance stark.

Chapter Nine

"It's not goin' in you'll be, Miss Bettina, or 'twill be your father I'm tellin'!"

"Oh, Jamie, honestly!"

"Nay, I'll be standin' firm on this one, I will!"

"Jamie—"

Through a nearly impenetrable wall of sleep the two voices filtered into Raven's consciousness, the firm, lilting Irish brogue and the plaintive piping of a young girl making no sense to her at all.

"I just want to peek at her, Jamie. I promise I won't wake her up!"

The voices were louder now, coming directly from the other side of the louvered door that Raven found before her when she stared about her sleepily. She sat up quickly, eyes widening in confusion when she noticed the canopy above her where yards of gauze mosquito netting were rolled and tied back with gold tassel cords. It was only then that she remembered where she was, thinking absurdly to herself that it was winter and far too cold for mosquitoes even this far north.

"Oh, all right, Jamie, stop your fussing! I'll come back later!"

"'Tis a sensible idea, Miss Bettina," came the soothing Irish accent again, and Raven could hear the sound of shuffling footsteps retreating from the door. In the very next moment the latch clicked and the door creaked open, the heart-shaped face of a young girl appearing on the other side.

Seeing Raven sitting amid the rumpled bedclothes the girl uttered a delighted "Oh!" and opened the door wider, stepping inside with a swish of taffeta skirts. "You're awake!" she exclaimed happily. "How did you sleep?"

"Very well, thank you," Raven replied, rather at a loss. Memories of the night before came to her vaguely, of being lifted off the rangy gelding by a pair of strong arms and delivered into the competent hands of a clucking, matronly woman who had hugged Raven's trembling form to her before whisking her away to a room and putting her to bed.

The kindly voice and ample bosom she remembered from last night did not seem to fit the slender young girl in rustling petticoats before her, light blue eyes studying her with unconcealed curiosity.

"I'm sorry," Raven said after a moment when the silent perusal showed no signs of coming to an end. "I can't seem to remember who you are."

The young girl laughed and sketched a dainty curtsy, golden ringlets falling to her creamy white shoulders. "I'm Bettina Bateman, and you're in Papa's house in the Kasur cantonment. You came so very late last night, and Captain St. Germain told Jamie you should be allowed to sleep as long as you like. I wanted to take a peek at you because girls my age are so vexingly rare here, but"—she shrugged, her blue eyes flashing—"Jamie wouldn't hear of it. And yet you were awake, just as I suspected!"

Raven did not wish to hurt Bettina's feelings by informing her that it had been her argument with the formidable Jamie that had awakened her in the first place. She glanced at the clock in its cherrywood case sitting on an octagonal table near the door and saw that it was nearly eleven. "My goodness! I don't think I've ever slept so late in my life!"

"No one can blame you for that," Bettina assured her, refraining from adding that she rarely arose much earlier herself. "If you hurry, Miss Barrancourt, you'll be just in time for dinner. Papa said we're to have it in the salon today in honor of your visit. May I call you Raven? It's such a pretty name. When I heard it this morning I thought it a trifle odd, but now that I see you I can guess why they named you that. Your parents, I mean."

Raven nodded her head in vague agreement, wishing Bettina would go out and leave her alone. Obviously the girl meant well, but Raven had known enough of her kind in England to recall that it took very little stimulation to get them talking but a considerable amount to make them be still. Bettina was beautiful in the classically angelic sense, with a great cloud of golden curls framing her heart-shaped face and enormous blue eyes. Though she couldn't have been much older than fifteen or sixteen, her waist was tightly cinched so that the bodice of the sky-blue gown lifted her small breasts to give them the illusion of womanly fullness. Her soft pink lips wore a constant pout that Raven strongly suspected had been formed by long years of indulgence by doting parents and later, when Bettina realized how prettily it became her, had been perfected for hours at the looking glass.

"I'll send the servants in to help you dress," Bettina added, much to Raven's relief, and scurried outside.

Accustomed to the number of young Indian maids who had seen to her every need in the Trentham house in Bombay, Raven was not surprised by the half-dozen that entered quietly at Bettina's summons. Two of them began to ready the clothes she was to wear, while a third brought hot wash water and a fourth began to comb through the long black tresses that curled to Raven's waist. Still another began to fold back the bedclothes, while the last one set a lacquered tray before Raven and, smiling shyly, poured tea with downcast eyes.

In the study belonging to Colonel Roger Bateman, meanwhile, the bewhiskered British officer was briefing Charles St. Germain and his loyal companion, Dmitri, on the most recent developments in the Punjab. Colonel Bateman had spent nearly his entire military career as a commissioned officer in India, and his command of the difficult Hindustani and Punjabi languages was impressive. Having gained the respect of his Indian footsoldiers as well as his fellow British officers, Colonel Bateman was privy to more inside information than the C.O.'s of other regional garrisons.

It was for this reason mainly that Charles had decided to spend the night at the Kasur cantonment rather than in the nearest dak bungalow, for reliable information was vital to him at the moment. His first voyage to India had seen him and Dmitri unwittingly caught up in the Afghan War, Afghanistan having been invaded by the British in order to protect India from the creeping threat of Russia, which was expanding its borders beyond the Hindu Kush. The intrigues, bloodshed, and narrow brushes with death that had accompanied Charles's first trip through the Khyber Pass had been enough to convince him that his fortune was destined to be gained on the sea, not among nations that waged relentless war upon each other.

Retreating toward Peshawar and the waiting *Orient Star,* Charles and Dmitri had been ambushed by a roving band of rebel Pathans. Upon being rescued by British troops, Dmitri's nationality had for a time caused them to be slated for imprisonment on espionage charges. But through the timely intervention of one Major Roger Bateman, commander of the 70th Foot stationed in Peshawar, where Charles and Dmitri had been taken, the big, blustering Russian had been spared execution. Impressed by Charles St. Germain's intelligence and character, Major Bateman had befriended the young English captain and had persuaded him to take up arms, albeit temporarily, in the cause of British expansionism.

Not content to become a soldier of fortune in what he saw as a cruel campaign to force British sovereignty upon a free nation, Charles declined the offer to join the service, but his stay in India had gained him precious insight into the minds of the Hindu people and astonishing fluency in most of the northern dialects, including Pushtu, the language of the Afridi warrior. Though he had seen little of Roger Bateman in the ensuing years, Charles had never forgotten his brief association with the British military—or the brutal massacre at Kabul, memories which had come back to haunt him relentlessly ever since he and Dmitri had charged themselves with overseeing Raven safely to Lahore.

There was a disquieting restlessness in his large, powerful frame as he lounged in a padded leather chair before Colonel Bateman's desk, his long, booted legs crossed before him on the fine Persian carpet. The colonel, studying the lean, sun-browned features with their unrelenting harshness, wondered where the disturbance might lie, for Charles St. Germain was obviously a driven man. Yet no one but the keenest of observers might have noticed, for Charles was regarding him with an indolent expression, a wafer-thin cup of tea laced amply with brandy held casually in one long-fingered hand.

Remembering the raw hunger for life that had driven the handsome young English sea captain years before, Colonel Bateman saw that little had changed in the ensuing period. And yet there was a refined control and awesome reserve to his power now, as though Charles had learned through countless tests of character and endurance to dominate his great strength and fierce temper. Regarding the glittering green devil's eyes that met his own with cool appraisal, he felt an unaccountable shiver take hold of him, thinking to himself that Charles St. Germain was not an enemy he would care to meet on the battlefield.

"Lord Gough, commander in chief of our armies, took the field against the Sikhs himself at Ramnuggar on the twenty-second," he said now, his high, precise voice seemingly unsuited for such a large and heavyset man. His features were florid, the muttonchop whiskers concealing fleshy jowls, but Charles knew well enough that the soft, padded-looking officer was like a cat on his feet in hand-to-hand combat, his courage and military prowess as deadly as a striking cobra's.

"The victory wasn't decisive," Colonel Bateman continued, helping himself to a pinch of snuff from the gold-stamped box on the desk before him. "Dash it all, Charles, we've got to fight again and this time set matters straight. Both Lord Dalhousie and John Company are crying to see the rebels struck down, and I'm afraid they weren't too happy with the outcome at Ramnuggar."

"Are troops actively engaged now?" Charles asked, his square chin set and his handsome countenance expressionless, so that the listening Dmitri had no inkling of his thoughts.

Colonel Bateman sneezed violently and returned the snuff box to a drawer. Wiping his nose with a large square of embroidered cloth, he shrugged his beefy shoulders. "Hell, the entire army is marching or out on maneuvers, but I can't tell you precisely at this point where the next one will be fought. I've got my own Tenth and Major Anderson's Seventieth Foot ready to leave for Chillianwallah at the end of the week."

There was a moment of silence in the comfortable study while Charles considered this, and it was Dmitri who leaned forward to ask, "What about the Punjab, colonel? You know as well as we do that it is the stronghold of the Sikhs. Are Westerners free to walk the streets of Lahore in safety?"

"There will always be those who feel uneasy," the heavyset British officer replied slowly, and wondered at the grim tightening of Charles's full lips. "Especially with only the EIC regiment to uphold the resident's authority there. And yet the Sikhs are a proud people not given to butchering innocent women and children. I can't see this as anything other than a military campaign."

"And yet you're not entirely convinced," Charles observed roughly.

Colonel Bateman sighed. "The Sikh army is being aided by Afghan horsemen, many of them Afridis. You know their temperament, Charles."

The glittering green eyes narrowed until they became mere shards of emerald in the rugged face. "Aye, that I do," Charles said softly, thinking of the Pathans who had ambushed him and Dmitri in the howling cold of the Khyber Pass. The Afridis who had attacked the *Orient Star* and nearly cost Raven her life he had dismissed as contemptible river pirates whose addiction to opium had robbed them of the fierce pride and fighting skill that were such integral parts of the Afridi character. No, if Raven had been taken prisoner by true warriors of the hills, unpredictable, dangerous, and willing to die for their freedom, she would not have survived, and the thought brought a sudden savagery to Charles's tone.

"Aye, colonel, I know them well," he repeated ominously, and the green eyes bored into the smartly uniformed officer. "Yet even they would not roam the streets of Lahore seeking out and murdering defenseless British subjects any more than their Sikh counterparts."

"That they would not," the colonel agreed. "I would venture to say that Lahore is safe—for the time being. Only the fact that it was once the capital of the Sikh empire and that we British took it from them by force makes me feel they may try to wrest it back from us some day."

"At least our stay there will not be long," Dmitri muttered to himself, and Charles wondered if he was thinking of Raven's visit to her cousin Phillip or their own search for the Kohinoor diamond. For the first time in many days he found himself wondering how they were to find the priceless jewel with the country at war, but his thoughts, and those of Dmitri and the colonel, were interrupted by a quiet knock on the study door.

"Ah, Penelope," Colonel Bateman said, his dour expression brightening at the sight of his wife standing in the doorway. "Is dinner ready? I must admit I'm eager to meet Miss Barrancourt after Dmitri has told me so much about her."

"She and Bettina are waiting for us in the salon," Mrs. Bateman replied, the long, kohl-darkened lashes fluttering girlishly over her watery blue eyes as she smiled at the towering sea captain reclining in her husband's big leather chair. In the light of day he seemed even more handsome and domineering than in the darkness of night when she and Roger had greeted him at the door. She was certain that even Lieutenant David Tyde, whom she had already selected as the perfect husband for Bettina, couldn't possibly compete with Captain Charles St. Germain in terms of strength, looks, or reported wealth. Furthermore, Roger had told her yesterday that Captain St. Germain was an earl, and the prospect of snaring a title for her darling Bettina brought a flush of excitement to Penelope Bateman's fleshy cheeks.

But for her wide girth and too-ample use of cosmetics, Mrs. Bateman might have been termed a handsome woman. Because she was the wife of an old acquaintance, Charles adhered to strict social etiquette and politely offered her his arm as they left the study. Laying the tips of her fingers against the hard ridge of muscle and glancing furtively up into the harshly chiseled face above hers, Penelope felt a shiver run through her. Perhaps he was a bit too intimidating for Bettina, she thought to herself, a worried frown creasing her brow. Bettina was so dainty and small that a man like Charles St. Germain could easily harm her with his great strength, albeit unintentionally.

An elderly native bowed low as they passed him in the long, carpeted corridor, then opened the double doors to the salon and murmured his respects to the memsahib. Penelope, pausing on the threshold in order to introduce her daughter to Charles, saw his emerald green eyes narrow and grow as hard as flint as he stared unseeingly past the simpering Bettina to Raven Barrancourt, who was leaning against the long French windows looking out into the drab winter garden.

The pale afternoon sun shone on her jet-black hair, which a skillful maid had drawn back from her delicate oval face and secured with a pair of mother-of-pearl combs that looked very old and very valuable to Penelope Bateman's experienced eyes. Against the backdrop of light, Raven Barrancourt's profile was wildly beautiful, the soft red lips slightly parted, the shadows etched beneath her smooth cheekbones adding a breathtaking perfection to her aristocratic features. She was wearing a morning gown of sculpted cinnamon satin that shimmered softly in the light, the petticoats full beneath embroidered skirts. The tightly laced bodice seemed to mold itself to her small waist and firmly rounded breasts, and the ruffled flounce that edged the scooped neckline hinted at what lay beneath with an enticing glimpse of creamy cleavage.

Hearing them enter, Raven turned, and Penelope saw a rosy stain creep across the hollow cheeks and the golden eyes widen at the sight of Charles St. Germain towering above her, attired for once in the role of a dandy. In superbly fitting buff-colored breeches and contrasting waistcoat that flared over his lean hips, a snow-white silk scarf knotted about his powerful neck and secured with a glittering sapphire tie pin, he could easily have stepped out of the gaming rooms of any private London club.

Raven, who had seen him attired thusly only that once aboard the *Orient Star*, was slightly taken aback by this arrestingly handsome, fashionably attired gentleman. A momentary strain appeared in the tawny eyes as they searched the rugged features for a vestige of the roguish sea captain who was far more familiar—and comforting. Penelope clearly saw the slight furrowing in the smooth brow relax when Raven noticed that the sun-lightened curls were still as unruly as ever, curling devilishly below the fastidiously turned collar, and that the strong, sinewy wrists that were edged with fine Bordeaux lace were browned by long hours in the sun—the stamp of a sailing man that no London dandy could claim as his own.

The instant smoothing away of anxiety was that of a woman who, confronted unexpectedly by the man she loves in a form that is new and strangely disquieting, is reassured by some familiar, beloved feature that she sees has not changed. And yet, even as Penelope made this startling discovery, she saw the tawny eyes grow hard, the small chin lift imperiously as Raven's softening expression filled with a dislike which was unmistakably directed at the tall sea captain. Penelope blinked, certain that she had imagined the yearning in Raven Barrancourt's lovely face, then hastily beckoned to Bettina to come forward.

"Captain, may I present to you my daughter?" she asked with a proud smile, although she knew very well that it was Roger's place to introduce their only child. The smile wavered when she saw the lack of interest in Charles's gaze, although he was unreproachably polite as he acknowledged the introduction. Annoyance filled her heart at the titled sea captain's unsatisfactory reaction to Bettina's breathtaking beauty, for this was the first time that a man hadn't grown tongue-tied and awkward in Bettina's presence.

Really, Penelope thought to herself, it was all too vexing! Not only had Captain St. Germain failed to make a single gallant remark concerning Bettina's lovely taffeta gown and carefully tonged hair, but he was turning away already to take Raven Barrancourt's small hand in his big one and guide her toward a smiling Roger, who appeared oblivious to the snub their daughter had just received.

Penelope scarcely heard the introductions being made, her pale eyes fastened unwaveringly to the handsome sea captain and the dark-haired beauty at his side. Both were tall and striking, undeniably well suited, the restless energy that seemed to crackle from Charles St. Germain's muscular body reflected by the spirit glittering in Raven Barrancourt's golden eyes. Penelope could sense the attraction between them like charged tension in the air before a storm, but at the sight of the harsh set of Charles St. Germain's rugged features and Raven's unrelenting profile, she could see that only stiff pride and forced formality existed between them. Perhaps there was still a chance—if Bettina played her hand well.

Making a furtive sign to her daughter, she watched Bettina affix a truly devastating smile to her heart-shaped face, and pride flowed into her heart. No man could resist such a lovely simper, Penelope felt certain, for she had spent countless hours helping Bettina perfect it. Of course, it was a gesture far better suited to a drawing room in the evening, with the curving lips half-hidden by a fluttering fan, but Roger had told her they would not be meeting for supper since Captain St. Germain and his big Russian friend—who made Penelope quite nervous, if the truth must be told—would be tending to business matters in the city.

"Captain, why don't you sit beside me?" Bettina invited with a coquettish tilt to her head when it came time to be seated around the elegantly spread board.

"And Mr. Zergeyev, you simply must tell me how you came to find yourself allied on the British side," Mrs. Bateman added quickly, steering the bearded Cossack to the chair which rightfully should have been reserved for Charles, her unwitting remark causing a frown to appear on her husband's fleshy face.

But Penelope remained blissfully unware of it, intent on watching the handsome sea captain lead Bettina around to the far side of the table. Oh, they were so eminently suited! she told herself exultantly, and there was no doubt in her mind that Captain St. Germain, with his dark good looks, was the perfect foil for Bettina's golden beauty.

In her eagerness to make a prize-winning match for her darling daughter, it never occurred to Penelope that perhaps the ruthless sea captain might never turn his interest toward a porcelain doll like Bettina, who was meant to be cozened and surrounded by the finest silks and satins, an adoring husband standing discreetly in the background. There was too much raw, restless energy in the strong hand that guided the fragile Bettina to her chair, and Colonel Bateman, watching the couple as closely as did his breathless wife, saw as much and guessed the truth.

Though he adored his daughter and found her a pretty though admittedly empty-headed thing, Colonel Bateman found his preferences lying with Raven Barrancourt, who sat at his right. The instant he had laid eyes on her and seen the banking fires in her enormous eyes and the youthful strength that graced her willowy body, he had hoped that it was personal concern for her safety that had spurred Charles to Lahore. Unlike his wife, with her uncanny woman's intuition, he had failed to catch the subtle nuances of expression that had fled across Raven's delicate features at the sight of Charles in his gentleman's attire. Instead the colonel had seen only the aversion in the beautiful eyes when Charles had taken her small hand in his, and had felt regret, thinking it a pity that the young man of whom he had developed a genuine fondness and for whom he felt such unshakable admiration could not call this spirited beauty his own.

It proved to be an unhappy meal for Raven, hungry as she was, for she could not lift her eyes from the plate without catching sight of Bettina Bateman flirting outrageously with Charles. What made matters worse was Charles's apparent enjoyment of her attentions, and Raven could feel hot anger choking her at his repulsive behavior. Never had she known that ruthless barbarian to behave so civilly, listening with apparent interest to Bettina's agonizingly dull accounts of life in the cantonment. Worse still were the devilish smiles he gave Bettina in response to her coy simpers, intimate exchanges that made Raven grit her teeth and long to box both their ears.

The fact that Mrs. Bateman was looking upon the entire affair with almost misty-eyed approval increased Raven's disgust, and she told herself that if Charles St. Germain was interested in a bubbling china doll like Bettina Bateman, then they were heartily welcome to each other. Though the meal served to her was sumptuous in comparison to the scanty rations they had been eating the past few days, Raven scarcely tasted any of it. Though she would dearly have liked to question Colonel Bateman concerning current political developments in the Punjab, Bettina's flirtatious conversation with Charles precluded any attempts, and so she remained silent, eyes downcast, her glossy black head bent so that no one could read the strained expression on her face.

"Would you care for more wine, Miss Barrancourt?" Colonel Bateman asked when the main courses had been finished and the dirty dishes carried out by a small army of bearers.

"Thank you, no," Raven replied, roused from her thoughts with a start. Her darkly fringed eyes went to the opposite side of the table where Bettina was leaning toward Charles to whisper something in his ear, her parted lips close to his lean cheek, and she rose abruptly to her feet, her skirts swirling about her. "Would you think it rude of me if I excused myself before dessert? I'd like to look in on Mrs. Daniels."

"Not at all," Penelope assured her hastily, although Raven had addressed the colonel, for Captain St. Germain's eyes had been straying too often to Raven's bent head for her liking.

Raven vanished with obvious relief through the door, her petticoats rustling, and hurried down the corridor toward Danny's room, where the elderly governess had taken the liberty of indulging in a long afternoon of napping. Bettina was relieved, too, to be rid of the only other person in the room she considered a worthy if inferior rival for Charles St. Germain's attention. Turning back to the handsome sea captain, she resumed their conversation, but found to her annoyance that he no longer appeared interested. Instead he cast a swift, unreadable glance at the open door through which Raven had exited and promptly began a thoroughly dull discourse with her father over the likelihood of another Sikh war.

Pleased to see that Danny was sleeping soundly, Raven retreated to her own room and wandered restlessly to the big double doors that opened to the verandah. She could see little of the cantonment save the carefully planted gardens surrounding Colonel Bateman's dwelling, and several outbuildings standing amid the peepul and sheeshum trees. She felt certain that life in the cantonment was stiflingly dull, with only occasional trips to the Kasur bazaars and visits with embattled, middle-aged officers' wives to occupy one's time. Bettina had said at dinner that she and her mother rarely left the military compound, for the British women shopped from their own verandahs when the tinkers and merchants made their infrequent visits.

Edgar Murrow had been right, after all, Raven thought to herself, remembering the words of the timid gentleman who had befriended her aboard the *India Cloud* so long ago: that life in India could be crashingly dull and no different from being in England if one insisted on traveling from one British settlement to another. She hoped Cousin Phillip would show her more of the grand pomp and ceremony she had envisioned before she and Danny began their long journey home.

The jingle of trappings and the stamping of horses' hoofs brought Raven curiously to the windows lining the front of the bungalow. Looking out, she saw a coolie emerge from the far side of the building with two high-spirited mounts held firmly by their bridles. They were magnificent beasts in comparison to the pitiful creatures they had purchased in Hasangei, their military tack gleaming with polish. As Raven watched, she heard heavy footfalls on the verandah that could only belong to Charles and Dmitri, and her heart skipped a beat when she saw them emerge into the pale, chilly sunshine.

Both had discarded their elegant attire. Dmitri was in his customary sheepskin coat and tall sea boots, Charles in his nankeen small clothes and tightly molded calfskin breeches. Dmitri's white teeth flashed against the darkness of his flowing beard and Charles's emerald eyes glowed with the prospect of riding. Watching them swing up into the saddles, Raven felt a momentary pang of loneliness. Obviously they were on their way to Kasur to make arrangements for the *Orient Star*'s consignments, and Raven found herself wishing that she were going with them. Despite the fact that she detested Charles St. Germain, Raven was nonetheless aware of the lusty thirst for life that seemed such an integral part of him, and longed to share his adventures if only to ease the loneliness of her own existence.

She reminded herself sternly that Charles and Dmitri had embarked on a mission of greed that Raven wanted no part of, and she warned herself that the real Charles St. Germain was a ruthless man willing to kill to make the coveted Kohinoor diamond his, not the tender, affectionate lover she had fallen in love with. Judas, how could she have been so naive as to let him deceive her with his honeyed words and gentle touch? How many other starry-eyed virgins had he coaxed thusly into his well-used bed?

Her expression was stark and lifeless as she watched the handsome sea captain canter out of the cantonment gates, the sun turning his unruly chestnut curls to purest gold.

"Raven?"

She turned reluctantly at the sound of Bettina's voice through the bedroom door. "Yes?"

"Mama says now that we're all alone in the house, we ought to play cards." A giggle floated through the thin wood. "Papa's gone to see Major Pelgram, so he won't even know. Would you like to make it a threesome with us?"

Card playing was the last thing Raven cared to indulge in at the moment, especially when her host obviously disapproved, but she knew that she couldn't be rude to her hostess, who had shown such kindness in taking her in. "I'll be out in a minute," she promised.

The afternoon, which Raven found never-ending, waned at last into a chilly evening, and silent bearers went from room to room to light the lamps. Charles and Dmitri had not returned by eight o'clock when the Batemans sat down at the table, so Danny and Raven were forced to dine with them alone. Fortunately it was Colonel Batemen who dominated the conversation this time, and his discourses on Indian life proved far more interesting than Bettina's mindless anecdotes had been.

As a result of an entire day's inactivity, Raven found herself unprepared to retire at the early hour with which the Batemans excused themselves. Penelope had tried unsuccessfully to cajole her husband into sending round last-minute invitations so that the other army wives might have the chance to meet Raven—and Charles, if he returned in time—but the colonel, to Raven's relief, firmly maintained that rest was what his visitors needed in order to recuperate from the exhausting ghari ride from Hasangei.

Bidding the tired Danny a good night, Raven withdrew to her bedroom and leafed idly through the pages of a book Bettina had lent her which was presumably intended to appeal to any young girl's romantic heart. Quickly bored, Raven tossed it aside and exited restlessly through the French doors onto the verandah, her slippered feet making no sound. The night was very dark, a crescent moon and a sky filled with stars offering little light to illuminate the darkened bungalows and grounds of the sleeping cantonment.

Raven shivered in the cold wind that blew from the mighty Hindu Kush, this first real breath of winter reminding her that it was nearly December. She was still wearing her cinnamon satin gown, and the rustling material felt cold against her skin. Hugging herself with her slender arms, she sank down on the cypress swing and listened to the dry rattling of the creepers that grew along the verandah posts. From somewhere in the cantonment a dog began to bark, and in the distance Raven heard the muted echo of a bugle and the voices of the Gurkha guards as the watch was changed.

A mongoose, made bold by the cover of darkness, scratched industriously amid the shrubs in the garden, and Raven watched it in the dim light, shivering when she remembered having seen one of the furry little creatures unleash its ferocious energy against a menacing cobra in the bazaar in Hasangei to the accompanying encouraging shouts of the watching villagers who had laid down their bets against the slithering reptile.

The snorting of a horse roused Raven from her thoughts, and she looked up quickly to see two men riding toward the compound stables, their faces obscured by darkness. She relaxed when she recognized Dmitri's lusty voice as the big Russian sang beneath his breath, his droning chants interspersed with drunken hiccups. Dismounting, the two men turned their horses over to a coolie who emerged from the stable doors, and vanished into the bungalow, where Raven could hear the study door down the corridor open and close.

Curiosity getting the better of her, she rose to her feet and followed, pausing before the closed study door and knocking discreetly.

"Come in," Charles's deep voice invited, and Raven found him lounging alone in an armchair with a brandy bottle at his elbow, his cravat undone, looking, she thought irritably, quite at home in the colonel's private domain.

"I thought all young ladies were supposed to be abed at this hour," Charles remarked, gazing up at her insolently when she appeared in the doorway, a vision of innocence in cinnamon satin, her sloping eyes glittering in the warm, flickering light.

"Where is Dmitri?" Raven asked, ignoring his comment and wondering to herself if he had been drinking. There was a lazy drawl to his deep voice and an uncharacteristic slouch to his big frame as he stretched his long legs before him, and she didn't care at all for the way his heavy-lidded emerald eyes were raking her figure.

"Gone to bed," Charles replied obligingly. "We've an early start of it tomorrow, and I suggested to him that he might like to sleep off the alcohol before morning."

"Then you have been drinking," Raven observed.

"Indeed we have," Charles admitted and tilted back his handsome face to look into her eyes, his full lips twitching. "And what recriminations are you going to make now, Miss Barrancourt? We're both grown men, and you, thankfully, are not married to either one of us and therefore have no right to play the nagging wife."

"Certainly not!" Raven agreed heartily, her aversion to the idea of being wed to him obvious in the loathing on her delicate face.

Charles's countenance darkened in response, and he seized her skirt in his strong hand, pulling her toward him until she was standing beside his chair. The heavy-lidded green eyes traveled from her rounded breasts and creamy flesh to her face, where her tawny eyes were flashing with annoyance.

"Let me go!" Raven ordered in a fierce whisper, afraid to awaken the Batemans by raising her voice.

In one easy motion Charles rose to his feet and stood towering over her, his full lips twitching. "You should be thankful that you aren't my wife, Raven," he said in a curiously harsh tone that belied the amusement in his rugged visage, ignoring her command entirely. "I abhor disobedience, and I fear I'd beat you constantly."

"Then be thankful we aren't wed," Raven retorted, her breasts rising and falling with agitation, disliking to have him stand so close, his long fingers still holding firmly to a handful of shimmering satin. "I wouldn't care at all how much you beat me because I would never, ever give in to you!"

The emerald eyes seemed to darken as they met her wide-eyed gaze, and Charles's voice was rough when he asked softly, "Wouldn't you? Perhaps there are other ways to prove my superiority over you, Raven, than by the use of brute force."

"What do you mean?" Raven asked tremulously, suddenly unsure of herself. She had seen that look in his eyes before and could feel her knees grow weak, her mouth suddenly dry.

Charles released the swatch of smooth material and placed his hand over the curving hip that lay beneath it, his big thumb resting over a pulse that was beginning to beat in wild rhythm. With his other hand resting in the small of Raven's trim back, he was able to draw her toward him so that she fit between his legs, the length of her slender thighs pressed against his muscular ones through the crushed layers of petticoats.

"I believe you know very well what I mean, Raven," Charles told her, his own breathing ragged. Through the thin muslin of his shirt he could feel the tips of Raven's breasts brushing against him enticingly, their warmth spreading through him and causing a wave of heat to travel like a current through his loins. Raven's lips were parted, her tawny eyes glowing with the inner fire he knew their intimate contact had aroused, and yet she tried to arch away from him, her small hands pressed against the unyielding ridge of muscles across his wide chest in an effort to free herself.

Hungering for more, Charles slid his arms about her small waist, pulling her closer so that she was locked against the length of him, feeling angry with her for trying to break away. "Don't, Raven," he murmured, his breath warm against her fiery cheek, "don't fight me."

"Charles, no—" It was a breathless sob.

"You want me, Raven, don't pretend you don't." There was no mockery or triumph in the ragged voice, only the breathless statement of truth.

Raven could feel desire stir within her. A tide of burning need coursed through her veins and made a mockery of the denials rising to her lips. Through the gauzy layers of petticoats and satin that separated her from Charles's big body she could feel the heat and hardness of his manhood, and another sob tore from her throat. She knew it was true; that she yearned for him with every fiber of her being.

"Let me love you, Raven," Charles whispered hoarsely, his lips stirring the soft black tendrils that brushed against her ear, sending shivers of delicious anticipation fleeing down her spine.

She made no reply, but the slender arms that wrapped themselves about his powerful neck were answer enough. Exultantly Charles pulled her to him. His lips met hers and parted them, and Raven clung to him. Their tongues touched in an almost desperate need for what might be the very last time. Raven had completely forgotten where they were, responding as she was to Charles's kisses with shameless abandon, her fingers caressing his chestnut curls as he bent his head to run his lips across the enticing hollow of her throat and the curve of exposed collarbone.

Then he laid her gently onto the thick carpeting and stepped back, his emerald eyes meeting hers with bold promise, and Raven watched as she had so often before as he shed his clothes above her. The sight of his hard, powerful body excited her, the lamplight flickering over muscles that rippled when he moved, dancing across the smooth expanse of sun-bronzed chest covered with its dense layer of curling golden hairs.

Leaning down, his rugged countenance infinitely tender, Charles unlaced the flounce-edged bodice, drawing the gown back over Raven's shoulders and exposing the firm breasts held captive by the embroidered corset. In a moment they, too, were freed, and Raven shivered when Charles's seeking hands closed over their heavy roundness, his fingers burning trails of fire over her flesh.

Lowering his head, Charles placed his lips upon a rosy nipple, caressing it with his tongue until it rose to his touch, then allowed his seeking mouth to travel the smooth arch of Raven's throat. Her head was thrown back, and he cradled her slender neck in one big hand, freeing her long hair from its confining mother-of-pearl combs so that the mass fell free, spilling into his hands and reflecting mysterious blue-black highlights in the dancing lantern light. Its sweet fragrance filled Charles's senses, and he gathered Raven into his arms, tossing aside the gown and remaining undergarments so that she lay naked before him, her smooth ivory body glinting gold against the plush carpeting.

"My God, you're beautiful," Charles whispered, drinking in the sight of her with eyes that glittered like cut tourmaline. A groan escaped him as he fell upon her, covering her soft body with the length of his hard one. He deliberately willed himself to be patient, wanting this enchanted act of love to last as long as it could, reluctant to end a moment he would even now gladly lay his life down for to savor again.

Raven let her hands travel across the rippling muscles along Charles's broad back, loving the feel of him, her ardent response to his insistent kisses driving both of them to dizzying heights of desire. His bold, insistent manhood probed the soft flesh of her inner thighs, and Raven, giving in to a need she could control no more than Charles, spread her legs in silent invitation. Charles drew back slightly in order to look down into her exquisitely lovely face, the fire in Raven's topaz eyes reflected in his own. For a timeless moment they stared at one another, Raven poignantly aware that the rugged countenance, made roughly tender with the force of Charles's passion, was more dear to her than life itself.

Seeing the wild, scarcely realized love for him in Raven's beautiful eyes, Charles groaned and fell upon her, thrusting deep inside her where her warmth and softness opened up to accept him. Then they were no longer two impassioned lovers but one, united being—ascending with the strength of their mutual need toward a state of unparalleled ecstasy. With the joining of two bodies that were now perfectly enmeshed, Charles and Raven felt their consciences meld as they soared on a rising tide of sensation until the universe seemed to burst into blinding light about them.

For one moment of divine creation that seemed never to end, they rode the crest of ultimate fulfillment, transcending even the ecstasy of their last perfect union. A whimper of sheer joy fell from Raven's lips, which Charles claimed fiercely with his own. Their soaring beings came hurling down to center in a final glorious moment at the origins of their passion where Charles, in his ultimate possession of her, planted his seed again deep amid the fertile fruit of love that Raven was already bearing for him.

In the study, where reality should have painted a scandalized picture in the flickering glow of the lamps, there was only the sound of Charles's harsh breathing and Raven's muffled gasps, the emerald eyes meeting and holding the brightly shining golden ones. As yet the spell had not been broken, the heat of their bodies encircling them like a warm cocoon that excluded all else. Lifting his hand, Charles gently smoothed back a strand of shining black hair that clung to Raven's damp forehead, his big thumb stroking a fiery cheek, then traveling lightly over the soft lips that were bruised and swollen from his insistent kisses.

Neither spoke, for both were content to lie in an afterglow in which words were unnecessary. Looking up into the angular features above her, Charles's upper lip lightly dotted with sweat, Raven realized how truly handsome he was, every rugged feature attesting to his maleness as readily as the powerful body that still covered hers. She closed her eyes and sighed deeply when Charles lowered his head and left feathery kisses across her lips and cheeks that sent shivers of contentment through her.

Absorbed in each other, the world having ceased to exist but for the two of them, neither heard the sharp intake of breath that came through the tiny crack in the study door. Nor did they see the wide, disbelieving eyes of Bettina Bateman peering in at them before the study door closed softly and Bettina hurried soundlessly back to her room.

Shivering with agitation, the young girl climbed back into bed, her mind burning with the image of the hard, sun-browned body covering the length of Raven Barrancourt's smooth white one. Though Bettina had been raised in a virtuous and closeted world as the only child of the fastidiously proper Colonel Roger Bateman, she was intelligent enough to realize that the handsome sea captain and the beautiful dark-haired woman had been coupling. For all her inexperience she had seen the lingering passion in their eyes when they looked at one another, and she sobbed a little, sensing that Charles St. Germain would never look at her in the same manner.

Ever since luncheon Bettina had been infatuated with memories of Charles's handsome face and powerful form, her body tingling in a deliciously uncomfortable manner when she recalled how hard and strong his arm had been when she had teasingly brushed her fingertips across the sleeve of his coat. After retiring, Bettina had lain sleepless in bed waiting for him to return from town, thinking to herself that she must somehow make the long-legged Englishman her own before he left or die of longing for him.

Her thoughts had wandered through delightful fantasies of what it would be like to be Charles's wife, of having him escort her to the Officers' Ball, the military parades, the holiday pageants. She would be the envy of all her friends, her tall, attentive husband at her side, more handsome even then Lieutenant David Tyde, who had certainly caused her heart to flutter often enough whenever he bent over her dainty hand.

Foolish as she might be, Bettina had not been unaware of the unconscious current that ran between Raven Barrancourt and Charles St. Germain during dinner, though both of them had seemed oblivious to the attraction themselves. It would take much more than coy words and arch glances to win Charles's heart, Bettina had decided, especially with a rival like Raven Barrancourt to contend with. Vain as she was, Bettina reluctantly admitted that Raven was more beautiful, if only because her more womanly figure gave her an unconsciously sensual allure. Though Bettina didn't fully understand why she should feel inferior to Raven when she knew herself to be so attractive to the masculine gender, she did know that unless she tried something drastic, Charles St. Germain would ride out of her life tomorrow morning and she'd probably never see him again.

The thought was too painful for Bettina to bear, and as she lay tossing and turning in her satin-covered bed a plan began to form in her mind. Though it was a wild one that made her heart beat faster with fear and anticipation, she was firmly resolved to carry it through. She would wait, she decided, until Charles was undressed and in bed, and then she would creep stealthily into his room.

Not that she would let him make love to her, Bettina decided, shivering with trepidation at the thought of what the handsome sea captain must look like naked and what it would feel like to have a man lie with her. It must be an awful thing, she decided, if half the stories she overheard from Mama and her friends were to be believed, but of course she wouldn't go so far as actually to let Charles touch her. She would merely wait until he became aware of her presence and had leaped out of bed to confront her, and then she would scream and scream until Papa came running. Of course the entire household would be aroused by then, and everyone would stand witness to the terrible truth.

Naturally Papa would insist that, because his daughter's virtue had been compromised, nothing could be done to right the situation except that Captain St. Germain agree to accept Bettina's hand in marriage. Charles, being a gentleman and a friend of Papa's besides, would have no alternative but to do so. Examining the plan backward and forward, Bettina had been unable to find a hidden obstacle. Except for the fact that poor Mama would be horrified, which Bettina regretted but shrugged off as unavoidable, everything should have gone exactly as planned.

And yet nothing had. Charles had not withdrawn to his room as expected but had gone instead to the colonel's study, which was located at the far end of the corridor, past Bettina's bedroom. Bettina had waited in an agony of impatience for him to retire, but had waited in vain. Mustering her courage at last, she had crept into the corridor and stealthily opened the study door, intending to surprise Charles there. And yet it had been she who had received the shock, and the unpleasantness of it still lingered in Bettina's mind. The way Charles had been holding Raven in his arms, cradling her against his muscular body—it made Bettina livid to think of it, and her eyes began to flash spitefully in the darkness.

Did Raven Barrancourt think for one minute she had a better chance of succeeding with Captain St. Germain where Bettina herself had failed? The thought rankled, and Bettina decided that she would simply have to alter her plans a little and think of some way to drive the two lovers apart. Her pouting lips curled into a complacent smile. Yes, that was it. Come morning she would plant the seeds of doubt in Raven Barrancourt's mind and make certain they were carefully nurtured. After all, she soothed herself, rolling over and closing her eyes, if she couldn't have Charles St. Germain for her own, then she was going to make absolutely certain that Raven wouldn't have him either.

When Raven opened her eyes the next morning it was to find shafts of sunlight pouring through a crack in the heavy drapes and falling over the embroidered coverlet of her bed. Throwing back the blankets, she rose and slipped barefooted to the window, her long black hair falling unbound to her waist. Drawing the dark velvet material aside, she looked out into the garden at the coarse blades of grass touched with frost that reflected dancing prisms of sunlight. The panes were frozen as well, and Raven could make out her reflection within them, her eyes bright, her soft cheeks dimpling.

Pressing her slim nose against the cold glass, she peered outside again, but her thoughts were not on the frost-sprinkled garden this time but on Charles and what had happened between them last night. Her body was bruised and sore from the insistent pressure of his roving hands, but Raven, stretching like a contented cat before the window, relished every stiff muscle. After their passion had been sated, Charles had held her in his arms for a long, timeless moment, caressing her and allowing his lips to travel in feathery kisses across her face. His teasing actions had unexpectedly rekindled the fires between them, and he had loved her a second time. Raven felt a spasm of longing flee through her as she recalled how slow and deeply satisfying his lovemaking had been then.

Afterward she had urged him to retire before someone in the Bateman household stumbled upon them, and Charles had agreed, but when she had tried to break free of his hold, he had refused to let her go. Cupping her face with his hands, he had kissed her relentlessly, filling her with a languor that had robbed her of the strength to leave him. Only after they had been startled by the sound of Colonel Bateman's sonorous snoring in the adjoining room did they break apart, Raven giggling helplessly. Gathering up her discarded clothes, she had smiled at him, and Charles, bewitched by her dimples and shining cat's eyes, had reached for her one last time, kissing her passionately until both of them were dangerously breathless.

It had taken Raven a long time to fall asleep that night. Lying alone in the big bed, she found she still ached for Charles, a desire that remained with her even now as she turned away from the window, a tender smile curving her lips and transforming her features with a soft, compelling radiance. Her curving brows drew together when a knock sounded on her bedroom door, for she wanted no one to intrude upon her private thoughts; but she relaxed when she saw that it was only the serving girls who had been so attendant on her yesterday.

Returning her smile with shy ones of their own, the young girls deposited the urn of wash water and the breakfast tray they had brought with them and proceeded to help Raven dress. As one of them combed her long black tresses, openly admiring their healthy sheen, the other laid out the gown Raven had selected from the clothespress. Her heart was brimming with joy at the thought of seeing Charles again, and her impatience mounted as she slipped into her petticoats, quickly sipped her tea, and swallowed a few pieces of honeyed fruit.

As anxious as any young woman hoping to please the man she loves, Raven cast a critical eye at her reflection in the glass before leaving the room. The eldest serving girl had arranged her hair in a becoming fashion, the midnight curls swept gently from her face and caught in the back with Raven's treasured combs. Her gown was of dark green velvet, exactly the color, Raven thought lovingly, of Charles's eyes, and she felt enormously satisfied with her choice, for the gown was truly magnificent with its three-quarters-length sleeves and pleated skirts piped with lemon satin.

Entering the fashionable parlor with its formidable collection of Penelope's bric-a-brac, Raven was immediately pounced upon by Dmitri, who seized her small hands in his big paws and whirled her about until the heavy skirts billowed, revealing her slender, satin-clad feet.

"You are a vision, little princess," he informed her with a broad, leering wink. "A delectable vision of loveliness!"

Realizing that the two of them were alone in the room, Raven returned his wink with a saucy, dimpled smile, her delicate face glowing with happiness. "Oh, go on, Dmitri," she teased, "you'll turn my head with such talk."

The hulking Cossack stared down at her keenly, unable to credit this joyous young thing that seemed to float above the ground before him. Something had happened to change her, he saw, yet couldn't even hazard a guess as to what it might be. Delighted by it, whatever the cause, Dmitri lifted her into his huge arms and gave the astonished Raven a bear hug that all but crushed the breath from her body. Recovering herself, she laughed gaily and returned the hug with equal enthusiasm, her slender arms wrapped about his thick neck.

"Oh, Dmitri," she whispered into his ear, "I'm so very happy and I did so want to share it with somebody!"

Dmitri laughed and set her down gently, savoring the brief moment of enjoyment that holding her slender body in his big hands had given him, though the hug had been one of pure platonic friendship. Opening his mouth to speak, he was interrupted by a discreet cough from the direction of the doorway and looked up to see Bettina Bateman watching them with narrowed eyes. For a moment Dmitri saw something akin to hatred pass fleetingly across the flawless doll-like features, then her expression froze into a mask of smiling mischief.

"My goodness, Miss Barrancourt, Mr. Zergeyev!" she exclaimed, "I never suspected the wind might lie in that direction!"

Raven, though by nature a candid person, was caught off guard. Blushing furiously, she looked away quickly and in doing so missed the brief flash of confirmed suspicion in Bettina's blue eyes. "It isn't what you think," she said weakly, but Dmitri interrupted her smoothly, making a gallant bow in the younger girl's direction.

"My apologies, Miss Bateman. It is the custom of Russians to greet their dear friends after any length of separation with an embrace." His bearded face split with an endearing grin. "Much better than saying 'good morning,' wouldn't you say?"

Bettina shrugged her shoulders stiffly. "I imagine so, but being a young woman of virtue I really can't condone such behavior." Although her smile never wavered, her tone indicated clearly that she considered Raven apart from that ilk.

"Why, Bettina, what on earth are you doing up at this hour?" Colonel Bateman's surprised question brought an end to the unpleasant scene, and Raven turned as he strode into the parlor, whiskers neatly groomed, his regulation trousers and long-sleeved shirt fastidiously pressed.

"I wanted to bid farewell to our guests, Papa," Bettina explained sweetly.

Her father harumphed disbelievingly, although he regarded her with a doting eye. "Good of you, my dear, and I must say it's a far greater effort than your mother chose to make, who," he continued, addressing Raven, "asked me to extend to you her warmest regards and wishes for a safe stay in Lahore. Under the circumstances, your early departure, I mean . . ." He spread his pudgy hands and let the sentence hang.

"I understand, colonel," Raven replied, smiling up at him warmly. "I wouldn't care to get up this early either if I could help it."

Watching the pleasure creep across her father's face in response to Raven's lovely smile, Bettina felt the bile rise in her throat. What an accomplished tease Raven Barrancourt was! Not only had she taken Captain St. Germain to her bed, but she was leading the slobbering Russian on as well and flirting outrageously with Papa while Mama slept innocently down the hall. Bettina's pouting lips tightened. Just you wait, she swore silently to herself, I'll fix you but good, Raven Barrancourt!

A mustachioed bearer entered the parlor at that moment to inform the colonel-sahib that the carriage was ready and that Captain St. Germain-sahib was waiting outside. Stepping out onto the verandah, Raven smiled when she saw Danny standing beside the stamping horses overseeing the loading of their luggage by a group of silent coolies who were totally ignoring her fretful suggestions. Doubtless Danny would live years longer if she would only stop worrying about the welfare of their trunks, Raven thought to herself, but she forgot everything as Charles swung into view from the far side of the carriage.

Wearing a frock coat of impeccable cut, the collar trimmed with silver marten fur, he strode toward the assembled group with long, easy strides, a riding whip in one gloved hand. His chestnut hair curled carelessly below his collar and the angular features were as harshly set as ever, but the emerald eyes that sought out Raven's were warm and alive, sending a delicious shiver through her.

"I can't thank you enough, colonel," Charles said formally when he ascended the steps to the verandah, "for permitting us to use your carriage. I'm convinced Miss Barrancourt and Mrs. Daniels will find the remainder of the journey much more comfortable because of your generosity."

"Oh, come off it, Charles." The colonel beamed. "No need to make pretty speeches; I'm glad to do it. Now, then, are the horses ready?"

"They're being saddled now," Charles replied, his eyes continuing to hold Raven's. She felt slightly breathless at the intimacy in their smoldering depths and longed to go to him but dared not, aware of the others gathered about her.

"Miss Barrancourt?" Charles addressed her with an insolent grin. "Are you ready to depart?"

Holding out his hand to her, he allowed his leather-encased fingers to curl possessively about her slim ones, his grip warm and sure as he led her toward the waiting carriage. Danny had already been helped inside by the attendant bearer, and Charles, all but shouldering the waiting man aside, proceeded to assist Raven inside himself. For a moment his strong hands lingered about her velvet-encased waist, then he lifted her bodily into the carriage, where he did not release her immediately but continued to gaze at her, his lean, handsome face very close, and Raven found it impossible to tear her gaze away from his smiling, sensual mouth.

Then Charles stirred and stepped back, sketching her a mocking bow before slamming the door and turning away. Raven, still tingling from the brief contact of his hands about her waist settled with a happy smile against the plush squabs, spreading her velvet skirts more comfortably about her.

"Miss Barrancourt?"

Amid the shouts and impatient orders as the coolies scrambled to fetch Charles's and Dmitri's horses, Raven did not hear the whispered voice of Bettina Bateman, who was standing on tiptoe peering through the carriage window. At the insistent hiss that followed, she turned her head, and leaned forward to address the young girl below.

"Yes?"

"I hope you have good luck in Lahore," Bettina said.

"How very kind of you to say that," Raven replied, genuinely touched by what she thought was a sincerely uttered sentiment. "I'm certain my cousin will prove as generous a host as your father."

"I didn't mean with your cousin," Bettina retorted with an arch glance that seemed too old and knowing for a girl of her tender years. "I meant in dealing with Charles."

Raven's brows drew together. "Charles? I don't understand. You mean Captain St. Germain?"

"Of course I do," Bettina retorted, annoyed at the unmistakable softening of her voice when Raven mentioned his name.

"What about him, Bettina?"

The young girl moved closer, her voice dropping to a conspiratorial whisper. "I only thought it fair to warn you that he isn't the man he seems."

"Honestly, Bettina," Raven said, unable to keep the impatient edge from her voice, "I don't know what you're trying to tell me!"

Seeing that she was losing the other girl's interest, Bettina said quickly, "Why, I wouldn't want you to be fooled by thinking he cares for you when in truth you're just as fleeting a diversion for him as I was."

Raven's indrawn breath told Bettina that her hurried words had found their mark. For a moment her courage failed her, thinking that she had overstepped all bounds of common decency, but when she looked into Raven Barrancourt's stricken eyes she felt her resolve harden. There could be little doubt that Raven loved Charles St. Germain, for the oval face was filled with naked emotions of a depth Bettina found unnerving, yet a vision of the hard, sun-browned body pressed against the soft ivory one reared its evil head in her mind.

"If only we had more time to talk," she continued in a thoroughly convincing show of torment, "because I know I must speak the truth, if only for your own safety."

"What truth?" Raven whispered, her throat so constricted that she could scarcely breathe. "What truth, damn you?"

"I didn't know any better," Bettina insisted, wide-eyed, while inwardly her poisoned heart reveled in Raven's obvious distress. "Mama never told me much about what happens between a man and a woman, so when . . . when Captain St. Germain came to my room last night I let him in. I never suspected—"

"He came to you last night?" Raven echoed, her words nearly inaudible.

"Yes, right after he finished making love to you." With words that destroyed the beauty that had existed between Raven and Charles the night before, she added with feigned innocence, "He said he hadn't been satisfied enough by you, and would I please—"

"Bettina, come away from there! The carriage is ready to start!"

Bettina instantly obeyed her father's authoritative command, deliberately turning her head away so that Raven could no longer see her face. With a bone-jarring jolt the vehicle took off down the winding cantonment road, the unexpected movement throwing Raven forward so that she struck her head painfully against the window post.

"Sit back, Miss Raven, you'll fall off the seat!" Danny cried worriedly.

Raven obeyed automatically, her small white teeth clamped so tightly to her lower lip that she tasted blood in her mouth.

It couldn't be true, she told herself in anguish. Bettina Bateman was lying; it had been obvious in every word, every movement the young girl had made! Charles would never go to her, never, especially not after the deeply satisfying love they had shared between them!

Raven moaned low in her throat, but the sound was drowned out by the creaking of the carriage wheels and the clopping of hoofs as the team of horses fell into step behind Charles and Dmitri's mounts. Yet suppose it was true? Raven asked herself, agony tearing her heart asunder as she recalled how Charles had responded to Bettina's accomplished flirting at the dinner table yesterday afternoon. Suppose Charles and Bettina really had... no! She clutched her hands to her aching head as the interior of the carriage swayed sickeningly. Judas, it couldn't be! And yet how else could Bettina have known that Charles had made love to her last night? How else could she have known?

"Oh, dear God," Raven whispered, tears misting her vision.

On the steps of the verandah Bettina Bateman watched the carriage turn through the cantonment gates with a satisfied smile tugging at her pouting lips. Casting a last longing glance at the broad-shouldered form of Charles St. Germain riding with a finer military seat than her father's upon his rangy gelding, she turned and disappeared into the house, confident that she had accomplished what she had set out to do. Her intent hadn't been deliberately cruel, she appeased her guilty conscience, which began to nag at her annoyingly as she remembered the stricken look on Raven Barrancourt's lovely face. She had merely wanted to plant the seeds of doubt in the other woman's mind and thereby drive the two of them apart. After all, she reasoned, no real harm had been done.

Yawning widely, Bettina withdrew to her room, little realizing that in her vindictive attempt to keep another from having what she could not, she had effectively destroyed the chance of union between a man and woman who had been destined from birth to belong to one another.

Amid the lush but rockstrewn lands of the northern Punjab stood the ancient city of Lahore, a former crown jewel of the once flourishing Mogul Empire. Though the last of the Mogul rulers had been buried centuries before, vestiges of the empire's former greatness were still evident in the bustling city. Thirteen massive gates formed ornately carved openings in the enormous brick wall that surrounded the thousand-year-old section once exclusively inhabited by the Moguls themselves. Ruins of ancient mosques and soaring Hindu temples battled for room amid the houses and shops that cluttered the narrow, twisting streets. Sikh shrines of magnificent architecture had been erected over long-destroyed palace squares, and above the city itself loomed Fort Ackbar with its miles of underground rooms, now the garrison of resident British troops.

Instead of passing through the old carved gate that led into the crowded city, the Bateman carriage, dusty from long hours of travel on dry, wind-swept roads, turned north toward the fertile farmlands. The settlements here consisted mainly of outlying British residences, for a proper European settlement in Lahore had not yet been established. At a signal from the tall, chestnut-haired Englishman who rode in the lead, the carriage drew to a halt before a pleasantly landscaped European bungalow where a growling dog, bristling with importance, left the rambling porch to meet them.

"Oh dear," Danny remarked, peering out of the window at the animal nipping furiously at the horses' heels, "do you expect us to get out with that ferocious creature, captain?"

"Not at all, Mrs. Daniels," Charles replied, and with a sharply uttered command he sent the dog slinking back to the shadows of the verandah. "This is the home of Major Thomas Wyandotte, an acquaintance of Colonel Bateman's," he explained, dismounting and approaching the carriage. "Phillip Barrancourt resides a small distance further north, but as neither Mr. Trentham nor I knew the exact location of Khanapur compound, Colonel Bateman suggested we stop here and inquire."

"How thoughtful of him," Danny remarked with a relieved sigh.

Charles moved closer to the carriage, his green eyes searching the darkened interior. "And how are you faring, Miss Barrancourt?" he inquired casually, though he was concerned by Raven's refusal to leave the confines of the vehicle during their afternoon stop when they had eaten a quick meal from the contents of the hampers Penelope Bateman had provided.

"She's sleeping now, captain," Danny replied, lowering her

voice to address Charles, who stood directly before the carriage window, hands propped on his lean hips, his flaring frock coat stirring gently in the breeze. "I hope she's not coming down with any illness. She seemed rather pale and subdued when we left Kasur."

Charles's brows drew together, and he was reaching out to open the carriage door to see for himself when the dog began barking sharply on the bungalow verandah. Turning, he saw that Dmitri's bold knock had summoned a lean, iron-haired gentleman of some fifty years to the door, his casual attire and slippers proclaiming that he had been interrupted at his supper.

"Yes?"

There could be no mistaking the authoritative voice of a British army officer, and Charles forced down a mocking grin as he strode forward, pausing at the foot of the steps. "Major Wyandotte?"

"Speaking." The major's keen eyes studied the handsome gentleman before him, not caring overly for the swaggering insolence in his manner, though his tone had been respectful enough. What now? he asked himself irritably. Couldn't a man have a few moments of peace in the evening hours without being disturbed by the general riffraff that swamped the Punjab by the thousands? His unfriendly gaze traveled the length of Charles's long, powerful frame, then switched to Dmitri, eyes narrowing at the sight of the flowing black beard and barrel chest, the aquiline features bespeaking a Cossack inheritance the major instantly recognized.

"I'm Major Wyandotte," he repeated, some of the hostility in his tone dissipating. Whoever these two unlikely gentlemen were, they seemed to command a certain degree of respect. The flinty eyes moved past Charles's broad shoulders to the carriage where Danny's lined face peered out at him, the wispy silver curls framing a ludicrously large bonnet with a sagging, sadly defeathered ostrich plume. "What the devil is this?" he demanded, his gaze snapping back to Charles. "Your name, sir?"

"Captain Charles St. Germain of the clipper ship *Orient Star,*" Charles replied with a bow so brief that it bordered on insult. "Bearing greetings from Colonel Roger Bateman of Her Majesty's Ninth Hussars."

Major Wyandotte relaxed visibly. Obviously this was just another of those self-important captain-owners licensed by John Company whose ship was doubtless at the moment anchored in the Ravi River groaning beneath the weight of British supplies with nowhere to unload them and no one to give him the authority to do so. Who had sent him here this time? the major wondered irritably. Higgins? By God, didn't the man ever learn he hated to be bothered with matters concerning John Company, especially during dinner?

And yet there was a gleam in the mocking emerald eyes that put the major on guard, warning him that this was no common, uneducated seafaring poltroon, but a man with military savvy who considered the two of them equals.

"Bateman, you say?" he asked less gruffly, stroking his bristling gray mustache. "Haven't seen the old yapper for months, now. Well, no sense in keeping you standing in the cold. You've a lady in the carriage, captain?"

"Two of them," Charles responded with an odd softening of his harsh voice that the major didn't miss.

"Well, bring them in, bring them in," he invited and turned to bark orders in flawless Punjabi to a pair of turbaned bearers that came scurrying down the steps, dodging the bristling dog, which snapped with apparent delight at their bare feet as they passed. "Wallaby, you brainless pest!" the major bellowed, much to Charles's amusement. "Here now, step smartly," he ordered his men, who were climbing onto the carriage to take down the trunks.

"No reason for that, major," Charles assured him, striding toward the carriage and opening the door. "Some refreshment for the ladies and a chance to stretch a bit is all we're after. We're looking for Khanapur compound and a Mr. Philip Barrancourt of the British East India Company."

"Barrancourt?" The major's eyes narrowed shrewdly, and he regarded Charles with renewed interest. "What the devil d'ye want with him?"

"He's my cousin, sir," came a clear and startlingly melodious voice from the interior of the carriage.

"Eh?" Major Wyandotte turned and stood stock-still at the sight of the vision that descended to the ground before him, dark green velvet skirts falling over layers of embroidered ocher petticoats. With a waist so tiny that he knew he could span it with his hands if he tried, the young woman before him was breathtakingly slender, the lemon-piped bodice tightly laced to reveal softly rounding breasts and a long, arching column of smooth white throat.

"Mistress?" Major Wyandotte asked stupidly, totally unnerved by the enormous eyes that met his, eyes that were neither green nor brown nor gold but an enchanting mixture of all three and, hang it all, were maddeningly tilted at the corners like the glittering eyes of the tigers he hunted once a year in the south.

"I am Raven Barrancourt of Cornwall," the vision informed him with an imperious lifting of her chin, the hood of her traveling cloak falling back to reveal hair as dark as night that reflected a sheen like the sleek, healthy coat of a panther.

"I'm honored to meet you, Miss Barrancourt," Major Wyandotte responded in precise military accents, snapping together his heels as he bowed low over her hand, belatedly remembering that he was wearing his smoking and naught but dilapidated slippers on his feet. "Your cousin and I are rather . . . er . . . well acquainted."

Charles did not catch the slight hesitation in the British officer's voice, for he was watching Raven with narrowed, probing eyes, pondering her deliberate refusal to take his hand when he had offered to help her from the carriage, shrinking away from him as though repelled by his touch. Taking a step toward her after guiding Danny to the ground, he saw her move deliberately away, and his full lips tightened grimly. What the devil was going on?

Major Wyandotte turned away from Raven long enough to hurl another series of orders at his bearers, then smiled down at her warmly. "Please come inside while my lads summon your cousin," he invited, offering his arm.

Raven smiled up at him gratefully, her soft cheeks dimpling, unaware of the effect the aching beauty of it had on Charles, who was standing behind her all but forgotten. Watching her walk gracefully up the steps and disappear into the house, Danny trailing faithfully behind, he placed his strong hands on his lean hips and regarded Dmitri grimly.

"I sometimes wonder if women were created merely to drive men mad," he said darkly.

"The good major is quite smitten with our little princess," Dmitri agreed, misunderstanding Charles's words.

"Aye, and he'd better not overstep his bounds," Charles added in a voice that sent a current of warning through Dmitri's brain. Turning, he saw the rugged visage grimly set, a light in the narrowed emerald eyes he rarely saw and never failed to fear when he did see it, and enlightenment exploded at last, bringing a round of disbelieving oaths to his lips.

"Kristos!" he breathed to himself, though Charles was for once oblivious to his companion's mood. Could it be that his captain was feeling jealousy toward another man? Because of the way the major had looked at Raven? No, no, it couldn't be, and yet how to explain the look in Charles's eyes of brutal anger and dire warning and, aye, a soft, persuasive longing?

"Dmitri!"

The big Russian turned and found the handsome countenance rigid, the emerald eyes cold, and he suddenly doubted the validity of his discovery. "Aye, tovarich?"

"See that the horses are watered and the carriage cared for. I want it returned to Colonel Bateman in the morning."

"And you, my friend?"

Charles's features were stark. "I'll pay my respects to the good major and we'll be off to Lahore for lodgings. No use waiting for Barrancourt to get here. Major Wyandotte appears capable of looking after Raven until then."

Dmitri's expression was puzzled. "If such are your orders, my friend. Will you tell Raven farewell for me and that I'll visit her soon—Mrs. Daniels, too, of course?"

This time there was no discernible softening to the rugged countenance, only a grim tightening of the sensual lips that indicated there was still some issue left to be faced, an issue Dmitri didn't understand. "Aye, I'll have a talk with her, Dmitri, that I promise."

Striding into the major's house, he found Raven seated on a settee, her velvet skirts spread about her, a teacup balanced in one small hand. Her eyes went swiftly to him as Charles came through the door, but instead of the softening he had expected to see in their golden depths there was a perceptible hardness as she turned away, her slender shoulders stiffening. Charles felt his temper beginning to rise. What game was the chit playing now? he asked himself irritably. If she expected him to cosset her like some besotted paramour because of the lovemaking they had indulged in last night... Charles's handsome features softened despite himself and his heart beat faster, forgetting his mounting anger. My God, last night...

"Why, where is Mr. Zergeyev, captain?" Danny inquired curiously. Seated beside Major Wyandotte on the adjacent sofa, she looked well rested and decidedly chipper now that their long journey was drawing to an end.

Regarding her intently, Charles realized he had grown fond of the spirited old woman, whose unflagging devotion to her young mistress touched him greatly. Moving to stand behind the settee where Raven's trim, velvet-clad back was turned to him, he gave the old woman one of his rare, charming smiles.

"Seeing to the horses, Mrs. Daniels. We'll be leaving for the city as soon as they've been watered."

He could feel Raven stiffen at his words, and instinctively he dropped his hand to her shoulder, the warmth of her skin so comforting beneath his fingers. Idly, almost unconsciously, he stroked a midnight curl that had escaped from the carefully arranged chignon at the nape of her slender neck. Raven jerked away as though his touch had scalded her, leaping from the couch and whirling to face him while her tawny eyes spewed the fire of outrage. Charles grew still, looking down at her as though turned to stone, the emerald eyes heavy-lidded and unreadable. A tension crackled between the two of them that was obvious even to the major and Danny, sitting halfway across the room.

Her breasts heaving, Raven turned and, catching sight of their shocked faces, realized how explosive her leap from the settee had been, especially since neither of them had seen Charles's tender, comforting caress. Glancing back up into Charles's rigid countenance, she shivered and said in a voice that cracked with strain, "I'd like to say good-bye to Dmitri, if you don't mind." Though her back was turned to him, the major surmised that she was addressing him and he cleared his throat to assure her that she was welcome to do so. Before he could speak, however, Charles stepped around the sofa and his long fingers wrapped themselves in an iron grip about Raven's slender wrist.

"I'm sure Dmitri would be honored," Charles grated, pulling

Raven physically from the room. With long strides that forced her to run beside him, he propelled her down the corridor and out onto the porch, where she tried to shake herself free.

"Let me go, damn you!" she cried, and it was the hatred vibrating in her tone that made him release her instantly.

With blazing tiger eyes Raven backed against the railing, her small white teeth clamped to her lower lip. "Don't you dare touch me, captain," she whispered raggedly, "don't you ever, ever touch me again!"

Charles was stunned by the force of her rage, but when he saw the tears glistening in her beautiful eyes and the uncontrollable trembling of her lower lip, his harshly set features softened and he took a step toward her. "Raven—"

She shrank away, the naked loathing on her face piercing him to the heart. "I meant what I said, captain. Don't you ever come n-near me again! I h-hate you!"

Charles's hands fell to his sides, and Raven knew a moment of mortal fear when she saw the deadly menace in the frozen emerald eyes that were as cold and lifeless as the icy North Sea. On the verge of speaking, Charles thought better of it, his lean jaw twitching as he bowed low, his voice so mocking and cruel that Raven felt herself reeling beneath the onslaught of his words as though he had physically struck her.

"Very well, madam, I will honor your request, and without a moment of regret. After all, I finally got what I wanted from you and have discovered in the meantime that it wasn't as rewarding as I expected it to be." His voice grated. "Rather, madam, I've come to realize that your lovemaking is, in all honesty, shatteringly dull."

With a strangled sob Raven pushed past him, his hateful words confirming everything that Bettina had told her earlier, and Charles let her go, his hands clenched into fists at his sides. For a moment he stood motionless, listening to her slippered feet fleeing across the bare wood of the verandah, then he turned and strode across the grounds to Dmitri, who waited near the compound gates with their freshly rested horses.

Charles mounted wordlessly and spurred the gelding mercilessly so that he was well out of the compound and heading down the carriage road to Lahore before the bearded Russian finally caught up with him.

"Well, tovarich?" Dmitri asked eagerly. "Did you give my regards to Raven for me?"

Charles reined in his mount so fiercely that the startled beast neighed in pain and reared, its front hoofs pawing the air. With words that rang with warning Charles said harshly, "Dmitri, if you mention that woman's name to me ever again, I vow before the heavens I'll put a bullet through your heart."

All but staggered by the ruthless threat, which Dmitri knew Charles would carry out without a moment's hesitation, he dropped back behind his captain's mount, his black eyes filled with despairing anger. I understand nothing anymore, he told himself, nothing at all! Since that cat-eyed beauty walked aboard our ship, our captain has been a stranger to me, and a driven one at that!

In strained silence the two men rode back toward the walled city of Lahore, the sun setting unnoticed in a glorious display of primal colors on the hills behind them.

Chapter Ten

Amid the cluster of weathered warehouses and storage buildings dotting Khanapur compound stood a rambling bungalow with a creaking sign on the front porch proclaiming it the residence of Phillip M. Barrancourt of the British East India Company. In the grip of encroaching winter the gardens looked forlornly neglected, the grass withered and weed-choked, the front porch sadly in need of paint. It was difficult to think of this dilapidated dwelling as a residence preferable to the colorful, exotic setting of Bombay, but Raven reasoned as she studied it from the carriage window that it must be attractive enough in the summer, and certainly far cooler than the sweltering plains.

Yet she found it oddly depressing, even though she knew that being here meant her long journey was finally at an end. Somehow she had imagined Cousin Phillip reclining in the lap of luxury at the expense of the company. The lonely-looking bungalow was certainly not in keeping with the mental image she had developed of him over the long months of idle speculation.

"It doesn't look like there's anyone home, Miss Raven," Danny remarked worriedly, peering out of the window as the carriage turned through the gates and approached the front door.

"Nonsense," Raven replied hastily to cover the misgivings Danny's words inexplicably aroused within her. "If he wasn't home, then he couldn't have sent this carriage to Major Wyandotte's, could he?"

"I wonder why he didn't come to fetch us himself?" Danny mused.

Raven shrugged her slender, velvet-clad shoulders. "Doubtless he was busy, or perhaps he couldn't get away so unexpectedly."

The jolting halt of the vehicle precluded further speculation, and Raven stepped down quickly without waiting for assistance. She turned in anticipation when the house door opened, but it was only a servant who beckoned them inside, a tall, dark-skinned individual with intense black eyes, his expression solemn and not at all welcoming.

"Is Mr. Phillip Barrancourt in?" Raven asked, sweeping up the steps. "I'm—"

"The sahib is waiting for you inside," the manservant informed her in precise, heavily accented English. "Please come with me."

It was growing late and, because the lamps had not yet been lit, Raven found the house dark and oddly gloomy, a feeling that was thankfully dispelled as soon as the servant opened a door at the far end of the corridor and stood aside to let her enter. The small study in which Raven found herself was comfortably illuminated, the walls of burnished tigerwood reflecting the dancing candlelight, a reassuring amount of paperwork and clutter proclaiming the room well used and livable. At the far end beneath the shuttered windows stood a secretary too small to accommodate the pamphlets and papers strewn upon its inlaid surface, and in the leather chair before it sat a man in a watered-silk dressing robe and expensive kid house slippers.

Whatever looks Phillip Barrancourt possessed had come from his mother's side, for his coloring was totally unlike the dark Celts who were Raven's ancestors. In his early forties, a tall but stocky individual, Phillip Barrancourt was blond, the curling beard that obscured the lower half of his face reddish-gold. Glittering blue eyes regarded her intently, although he made no move to rise, and Raven matched his probing glance with an equally curious one of her own.

"You are Cousin Phillip?" she asked.

"I am," he acknowledged, rising at last and coming forward to meet her, his eyes never leaving Raven's upturned, questioning face.

He was even larger standing, Raven saw, a powerful man equally as tall as Charles and as wide of girth as the bearlike Dmitri. She was rather put out by his appearance, for he did not resemble the shrunken Sir Hadrian in any respect save that she saw some of the hawkish thinness of her great-uncle's features beneath the bristling red beard. His skin, she noticed, too, was of an almost unhealthy pallor, and she wondered briefly if his extended stay in Lahore might have been caused by some lingering illness.

"You must forgive me for not coming to meet you, Raven," Phillip said, bending down and kissing her on the cheek, enveloping her with the not unpleasant scent of musk. "Under the circumstances"—he stepped back and spread his arms wide, drawing attention to his attire—"it would have taken me quite a while to dress, and I didn't wish to keep you waiting at the good major's."

"Of course we understand, Cousin Phillip," Raven began, "and—"

"We?" Phillip's gaze slid past her to Danny, who hovered in the doorway.

"My companion, Hannah Daniels," Raven explained quickly.

"How do you do, Mrs. Daniels." Phillip Barrancourt inclined his head politely. "I'm sure both of you would like to freshen up before supper. Ahmed will unload your luggage and show you to your rooms."

It was obviously a dismissal, and he turned back to his paperwork before Raven had the opportunity to thank him. Ahmed, his black eyes resting intently upon her, bowed deeply when she turned her attention to him and indicated with a wave of his hand that she was to precede him out of the room. At the far end of the long corridor that led to the back of the house, the Indian paused before a door and bowed again to Raven.

"The missy-sahib will stay here. Your ayah, here, where missy can call her if she is needed."

Raven thanked him politely and stepped into the room Ahmed had indicated was to be hers. She found it spare and totally lacking in the opulence she had come to associate with the decor of homes in India. A punkah, which was doubtless used often during the summer months, hung from the ceiling, the reed blades unmoving. Chik blinds covered the single window, and when Ahmed bent over to light the small lamp Raven saw in the flickering light that the walls were bare, painted in a harsh bone white she found oddly depressing. To her relief she saw that she was not expected to sleep in a charpoy—the traditional

Indian string bed—but had a genuine European model complete with pillows and a clean woven coverlet.

"I imagine it will have to do," she said to Ahmed with a friendly smile, not at all sure how much English the watchful Indian could understand. "Cousin Phillip seems to enjoy living a spartan existence, or is his summer home furnished only with necessities?"

"Missy-sahib?"

"Never mind." Raven felt certain her cousin's bearer would never understand that she was commenting on the obvious lack of amenities in the house and decided that it really didn't matter anyway. Cousin Phillip was a bachelor and a hard-working one at that, if the disarray in his study was any indication of his workload. Naturally he couldn't be expected to fill his summer residence with fripperies that only a woman would want.

"I will bring wash water and new clothes, missy-sahib," Ahmed told her and slipped noiselessly out of the room. Raven frowned to herself. Were there no other servants here, or was Ahmed expected to do all the work? She forgot the Indian as she wandered about the room, drawing off her traveling cloak and laying it neatly across the back of a chair. Pulling back the blind, she tried to peer out, but darkness had fallen swiftly and she could see nothing in the glass save her own reflection, her face pale, the dark eyes wide.

It was a sad face that stared back at her, Raven realized, and she turned away quickly, letting the blind fall back into place. She mustn't think of that, she chided herself fiercely. Her father had told her once, when she was nine and her beloved hound Janus had died, that human hearts came sixpence a dozen and a broken one could easily be replaced with another. Her smile was wistful. Perhaps that had been adequate comfort for a little girl, but she knew that no amount of wealth could heal the spiritual wounds that Charles St. Germain had inflicted upon her.

"I must admit I'd been expecting something a little less austere than this, Miss Raven!"

"Is your room as bare as mine?" Raven asked as Danny swept through the door that Ahmed had left ajar.

"No worse," Danny observed, her lips compressed with disapproval. "I can see Master Phillip's not too keen on housekeeping! I don't think there's another servant in the house besides that mysterious Ahmed except for a sullen little girl who spied on me through the adjoining door. When I spoke to her, she took off like a frightened hare. Must be the cook's help because she had grease stains all down the front of those odd pants they let the women traipse around in over here!"

"It is something of an odd household," Raven agreed, "but you must remember Cousin Phillip lives here only a few months out of the year. He probably doesn't like to bother bringing everything he owns up from Bombay every summer."

Danny snorted rudely. "If you ask me, Miss Raven, I'd rather stay in Bombay than out here in these wild mountains! At least Bombay seemed more civilized." She shook her graying head. "Besides, it be long past the hot months. Why did he stay?"

"I'm sure Cousin Phillip will answer all our questions at supper. Oh, thank you, Ahmed," she added, seeing that the bearer had returned with an enormous clay urn filled with water. "Set it on the table, will you?" she directed.

"Well, then, I'll leave you to your washin' and changin', Miss Raven," Danny added in a tone that indicated that the topic had not been settled for her yet.

Crossing the bare floor, Raven frowned when she dipped her slim fingers into the water to find it little better than tepid. Aware that Ahmed lingered in the doorway, she said nothing, picking up the sliver of lye soap he had brought with him and scrubbing her hands. Danny was right; the watchful servant was mysterious indeed, yet that was probably because neither she nor her elderly companion understood much of the ways of Indians. Cousin Phillip was even harder to define, for his manner toward her at their first meeting had been vague and somewhat disappointing. After all, she and Great-Uncle Hadrian had taken to each other from the start, and Raven had been hoping to find the son as ebullient and warm-hearted as the father.

Unpacking the smaller pieces of luggage that Ahmed had carried in for her, Raven removed Great-Uncle Hadrian's much-creased letter from her valise, intending to give it to Phillip at the table. Unfolding it, she scanned the small, neat lines of Hadrian Barrancourt's handwriting, feeling a deep pang when she recalled how happy and excited both of them had been as he had penned those lines. How could she have known then what lay ahead of her on the long voyage east, the heartache she felt now as unbearable as the pain of losing her father?

"Oh, Charles," she whispered, the name falling almost unconsciously from her soft lips, tears welling in her sloping eyes. Sighing deeply, she put the letter aside and prepared to dress for supper.

Meals in Phillip Barrancourt's dilapidated bungalow were taken in a surprisingly comfortable dining room, a long table with scratched but otherwise plushly upholstered chairs standing upon a colorful Persian carpet. The service was of good English bone china, and Danny cast an approving glance at Raven as they seated themselves, pleased to see that some semblance of elegance existed in Khanapur compound after all.

"I hope the food is to your taste," Cousin Phillip remarked heartily as he joined them. "Hammad does the cooking, and though I've tried to school him in the way of Western cuisine, he prepares almost everything with ghee, which tends to make it greasy, or curries the hell out of it and burns your insides."

"I'm sure we'll enjoy it, Cousin Phillip," Raven said quickly.

"Call me Phillip, my dear," he said, leaning toward her and regarding her with a smile, his red mustache twitching. "'Cousin Phillip' sounds so formal." The blue eyes made a slow, unabashed study of Raven's muslin-clad form. Raven had exchanged the wrinkled green velvet gown for one of pale lavender imprinted with tiny nosegays of violets. Her dark hair was swept back from her lovely face and held with the gleaming mother-of-pearl combs. She looked fresh, sweet and youthfully innocent, the tormented pain within her young girl's heart effectively hidden by the dark lashes that covered her sloping eyes. Phillip, who could not see the suffering there, nonetheless detected a poignancy to her delicate features that softened them, enhancing her vulnerability so that she wore about her an aura of unconscious sensuality.

"I think," Phillip said abruptly, "that we shall hold a party to introduce you to my associates in John Company, Raven. Lahore may not be the social hub of the Indian subcontinent, but there are people here I'd like you to meet." He nodded to himself, pleased with the idea. "Yes, a party. It's been ages since I've had reason to entertain."

"Oh, you mustn't go to such trouble on my behalf!" Raven protested.

"No trouble at all," he assured her, reaching across the table and laying his big hand over her own. "I would like all my friends to see what a full-blooded, legitimate Barrancourt looks like."

Raven could feel a wave of heat rise to her cheeks, but when she gave Sir Hadrian's bastard son an uncomfortable glance she saw that he was smiling at her without a trace of bitterness, the deep-set blue eyes filled with warmth. Something was different about him, she decided, not exactly sure what it might be. In the study he had seemed vague and diffident; now he exuded welcome and familial warmth. Perhaps he was shy, Raven thought to herself. Whatever the cause may be, she did owe him the courtesy of allowing him to introduce her to the people who were important in his life. Legitimately or not, he was a Barrancourt and doubtless wanted to parade a true member of his kind before his acquaintances.

"I think next Thursday would suit me admirably," he added, nodding to Ahmed, who had entered the dining room followed by another servant, both of them bearing covered dishes set on enormous lacquered trays.

"Will we be staying that long, Miss Raven?" Danny asked worriedly.

"I think that will depend on—"

"What's this about not staying?" Phillip Barrancourt interrupted his young cousin quickly. "Don't tell me you sailed all the way from England just to give me one quick glimpse before you rush off again?"

"Actually I came to see you on a personal matter," Raven began hesitantly. She didn't want to approach Phillip on the subject of Sir Hadrian's money like this, over supper with hovering servants present. She had wanted to talk with him privately and give him time to peruse his father's letter.

"Never mind about that." Phillip waved a languid hand. "I make it a point never to discuss business at the table." His blue eyes regarded her lazily. "We'll talk tomorrow, after you've rested from your journey, Raven, or maybe even the day after. Just promise me you'll stay for my party."

Raven lowered her eyes. "I promise."

Phillip settled back, satisfied. "Excellent! Now, I suggest you try some of this," he added, indicating a serving bowl containing pieces of braised mutton wrapped in some kind of cabbage leaf. "It's a delicacy in Hammad's native province."

Later, after Phillip had retired to his study and the servants had withdrawn, Raven joined Danny, who had gone into the parlor to work on her embroidery. It was obvious that Phillip Barrancourt had not intended to use the normally elegant room for its customary function of receiving visitors, for Raven found it extremely unwelcoming. The few lamps standing about on the bow-legged tables illuminated almost a dozen stuffed heads that were mounted in a row along the walls. There were several ferociously snarling tigers, a leopard, a glassy-eyed ibex, and other species of mountain goats Raven did not recognize.

"Judas!" she exclaimed, stopping short in the doorway, her hand flying to her lips, eyes wide as she stared at Danny, who was sitting on a small damask sofa, her embroidery spread out on her lap, the enormous curling tusks of a bull elephant mounted on the wall directly behind her head. In silence she wandered about the room, the flickering lantern light reflected in the glassy eyes of Phillip Barrancourt's hunting trophies, while Danny watched her young mistress surreptitiously from her seat.

"How can you sit there and sew?" Raven asked at last. "Your bedroom seems far more comfortable than this!"

"I vow it ought to," Danny agreed peevishly. "At least I can stitch without feeling I'm being watched all the time!"

"Then why stay in here?" Raven demanded, her smooth brow furrowing.

"Master Phillip suggested I make myself comfortable here." There was a perplexed expression on Danny's round, wizened face. "I declare there's something odd about your cousin, Miss Raven."

"Whatever do you mean, Danny?" Raven asked somewhat uncomfortably, stepping closer to examine the gleaming fangs of the snarling Bengal tiger that hovered over the older woman's right shoulder. "I thought him amiable enough at dinner."

"But so distant," Danny protested with a shake of her head. "Half the time I don't believe he was paying attention to what either of us was saying."

Raven shrugged her slender shoulders. "I'm certain he had a lot of business on his mind. You know how men can be. Why, even Papa—" She broke off, for memories of her father were particularly painful tonight while her heart was so heavy.

"There, there, Miss Raven," Danny said quickly, seeing the glimmer of tears in the golden eyes. "You mustn't grieve anymore. I'm sure Master Phillip will give you your money and we'll be back safe and sound in North Head before you know it."

"I imagine you're right, Danny," Raven agreed distractedly, wandering restlessly about the stark room, her dark hair trailing behind her. Somehow the thought of North Head did not comfort her tonight, the dull ache she felt whenever she thought of Charles making all else seem insignificant by comparison. She still couldn't quite believe that he had left her arms last night for those of a spoiled child like Bettina Bateman. Judas, stop it! she cried to herself, afraid that she would go mad with the pain if she allowed herself to dwell on the horror of it any longer.

"Why don't you sit and read with me a bit, Miss Raven?" Danny asked with a coaxing smile, disturbed by her young mistress's behavior. The abstracted look on Raven's delicate face reminded her too much of the days immediately following Master James's death. Danny recognized this distraught countenance as a sign of bewilderment stemming from pain and shock that went too deep to be borne all at once. What was wrong with her? Danny wondered, fretfully aware that there was little she could do to help her young mistress if she didn't even know what was troubling her.

"I think I'll go to bed, Danny," Raven replied with a half-hearted smile. "I'm very tired." She looked about her at the mounted heads, and the ghost of a smile curved her soft red lips. "Are you certain you won't be nervous in here alone?"

"Alone?" Danny repeated. "How can I be alone with all of them watching me?"

Raven laughed and bent down to kiss her withered cheek. Her expression was bleak, however, as she straightened and left the room. Exhausted as she might be, she dreaded the coming night, well aware that it would pass sleeplessly while she tossed and turned and relived the pain of her final meeting with Charles. Undressing without the aid of a servant, Raven slipped into bed and extinguished the single candle that glowed on the nightstand beside her. With the chiks drawn over the window the room was plunged into utter darkness, the stillness increasing Raven's gnawing loneliness. It was worse than she had anticipated, for she found that she ached for Charles, missed him with every fiber of her being, her body crying out for the bold, exciting touch of his hands and lips.

Squeezing her eyes shut, she tried to drive his image from her mind, but the laughing green eyes came back to taunt her, the weakness in her limbs mocking her efforts to convince herself that she no longer felt anything for him at all. Where was he? Raven wondered forlornly. Would he come to see her before he left Lahore, or had he meant it when he said that he had taken everything from her that he wanted and that she meant nothing to him anymore?

A single tear escaped from her tightly closed lids, trickling down her cheek onto the uncomfortable pillow. "Oh, Charles," Raven choked, the love she felt for him tormenting her. "Why couldn't you love me just a little?"

"In God's name, Dmitri, will you stop your incessant pacing? You remind me of a tethered bull!" Charles, his hawkish features harshly set, strode into the small sitting room where he stood with his long legs planted apart, irritably regarding his first mate, who wandered restlessly upon the silken carpet before him. It was early morning and the terrace doors had been thrown open, the din from the crowded, narrow streets of Lahore drifting up to them. A myriad of smells filled the cool air, the heady scent of jasmine, coconut oil, and spices mingling with the more pungent odor of cheap tobacco, garlic, and the camels and shaggy ponies that were present below.

Dmitri kept his angry retort to himself, aware that Charles needed little goading to erupt in a full-blown temper. Instead he muttered a blunt Russian curse beneath his breath and stalked from the room, coal-black eyes burning with the force of his own anger. Charles watched him go, the atmosphere in the small room less volatile as soon as Dmitri was gone. Cursing savagely, he went out onto the terrace, staring with narrowed green eyes at the twisting maze of streets below, the great wall that enclosed the city running almost directly beneath him.

The narrow townhouse with its vine-covered piazza had once belonged to a powerful nawab who had made a present of it to a favored courtier. After the British occupancy of Lahore and the ousting of all native rulers, the house had ended up in the possession of a British officer, an acquaintance of Colonel Bateman's who had been only too happy to offer its use to Charles and Dmitri during their stay, his regiment currently away on maneuvers.

Many of the original possessions still remained in the numerous rooms, and Charles found the collection of expensive lamps, hangings, inlaid furniture, and priceless silk carpets oppressive. He longed for the *Orient Star* and the uncluttered freedom of the salt-soaked decks, wishing even now as he stared across the rooftops and the sea of jostling humanity below that it was the westerly trades that stirred his chestnut curls, not the stink of offal and overripened fruit from the vendors' stalls. The lure of the Kohinoor—which had brought him originally to Lahore—had paled for him, and though he had examined this phenomenon thoroughly during the past sleepless nights, he was at a loss to explain why it should have done so.

Perhaps it would also explain the tension that existed between himself and Dmitri, who continued to show his boundless enthusiasm for acquiring the gem by making numerous sojourns into the darkened alleys and bazaars of the inner city to learn what gossip he could. Charles, on the other hand, was spending most of his time at Fort Ackbar, ascertaining from General Bostwick's aide-de-camp the validity of the threat of another Sikh confrontation. The two men were barely civil to each other, a deplorable situation that had never existed between them in all their long years together, and one that Charles had neither the means nor the inclination to rectify. Dmitri might prefer to fall in with disreputable bazaar hucksters, camel thieves, or roving Pathans to find the coveted jewel, but Charles had found his taste for secretive nocturnal meetings, the subtle art of bribery, and the battle of wits between Eastern mind and Western unaccountably dulled.

"Maybe you're getting old," he muttered to himself and was startled by the fact that he had spoken aloud, a sure sign of encroaching dotage that annoyed him considerably. With a scowl he left the balcony, slamming the doors shut behind him and frightening the servant who had entered with chota hazri, a light breakfast that Charles and Dmitri usually took together.

"The burra-sahib wishes something else?" he asked uncertainly when Charles ignored the proffered bowl of sugar-sprinkled fruit and the steaming tea, quaking when he saw that the towering Englishman's visage was black and forbidding.

"Thank you, no, Hakim," Charles responded shortly. Pulling on his great coat and gloves, he said tersely, "When Zergeyev returns, tell him I've gone to see General Bostwick. The jung-i-lat sahib," he added when the servant regarded him blankly.

Hakim's face cleared and he nodded quickly, relief spreading across his ferret-sharp features when Charles left the room, slamming the outer door behind him.

The news from Fort Ackbar was not good, and Charles returned from his meeting with the commanding officer several hours later greatly disturbed. A letter of recommendation from Colonel Bateman had gained him initial access to the British resident, who had been impressed enough with the soft-spoken English sea captain to direct the commander of EIC regiment to keep Charles informed of any developments in the current Sikh war during his stay in Lahore. In addition Charles spent almost as much time as Dmitri among the natives who bartered and gossiped in the streets, listening soberly to their talk and asking terse questions. To his relief he soon came to agree with Colonel Bateman's opinion that the war was strictly confined to military confrontations and that a mutiny among the inhabitants of the Punjab seemed unlikely.

Today, however, General Bostwick had given Charles the disturbing news that troops were being mobilized and that Chillianwallah seemed a likely meeting ground for another battle. Would an outcome favorable to the British spur the Sikhs into retaliation and lead to bloodshed in the streets? Charles didn't know, yet his handsome face was grim as he strode up the musty flight of steps leading to his rooms.

"Ah, tovarich, at last you're here!"

Dmitri, having heard the heavy footfall outside, threw the door open and pounced on him, wrapping his big arms about Charles's broad shoulders and pounding him heartily on the back.

A faint smile curved the sensual lips as Charles looked into Dmitri's beaming face. The Cossack's thick black beard was disheveled and clinging wildly to his leathery cheeks, making him look untamed and ferocious. The coal-black eyes were sparkling, however, and his white teeth flashed as he grinned. Charles folded his powerful arms across his wide chest and stood regarding him silently for a moment. "I believe you're happy, Dmitri," he observed at last.

Dmitri gave a great bellow of laughter. "Happy? I am ecstatic, my friend! I feel like a reformed celibate who has stumbled into the zenana of two dozen bored and beautiful prostitutes! Do you know where I was today?"

Charles shook his head, regarding his first mate indulgently. "I can't possibly imagine. The zenana at the maharani's palace?"

Dmitri rubbed his huge hands together. "Not in the zenana, no, but in the palace, yes."

Charles's amusement vanished. "What were you doing there?"

"Sit, my friend, sit and let me tell you." Dmitri deposited his enormous frame on the richly upholstered settee and waited for Charles to do the same. "It seems that the maharani has in her royal household a Russian from Kursk who never left India after the Afghan War and who fought on her highness's side during the Sikh War. When the British marched into Lahore and the maharani was stripped of power, he refused to leave her service though it's said that her native retainers despise and distrust him." Dmitri lowered his voice and gave Charles a conspiratorial wink. "They say the maharani is very beautiful, and you know how we Russians admire beauty. Small wonder that he stayed."

"I hear she's little more than a child," Charles remarked sharply.

Dmitri gave him a wolfish grin. "Even better! You know how quickly these dark-skinned native beauties ripen, my friend."

"And so you gained admittance to the palace ostensibly to make the acquaintance of another Russian," Charles prompted, his curiosity piqued. Leave it to Dmitri to gain admittance where no other white man ever could, he thought to himself.

"But of course," Dmitri agreed. "Georgi was a most cordial man. We talked for hours, and he shared with me his excellent vodka. After we had done that, he could not help letting his tongue rattle freely."

"So where is it, Dmitri?"

"Eh?" The bearded Cossack regarded him blankly, his excited narration interrupted.

"The Kohinoor," Charles said patiently. "I imagine he told you where it was?"

Dmitri's face cleared. "Aye, that he did, my friend—or," he

added quickly, wagging a long index finger, "at least he told me where it can be found."

Charles remained silent, his green eyes watchful, well aware that the flush on Dmitri's cheeks stemmed just as much from greed as from vodka. Leaning forward, Dmitri announced in a conspiratorial whisper, "It is in Oudh."

"In Oudh?" Charles repeated, startled. "The last I'd heard, it was still here in the Punjab."

"And so it was. Until it came into the hands of some warring nawab who gained possession of it through a violent quarrel between himself and a Punjabi zemindar."

Charles leaned back on the settee, his long legs stretched before him. "So I expect you will travel to Oudh now to find it?"

Dmitri shrugged with feigned indifference. "I do not know if the *Orient Star* can wait forever while its captain and first mate journey once again across the breadth of India in search of an elusive diamond. I would like to go, tovarich, but not without you, and I know you will not leave Lahore until our little princess is safely away from here."

Charles grew still, his lean body suddenly tensed like a panther ready to spring. "What do you mean?" he asked quietly.

Dmitri grinned, feigning total indifference while inwardly steeling himself to withstand the onslaught of Charles's unleashed temper. "I know it is for her sake alone that you are staying on in the Punjab when it is clear to me that you've completely lost interest in acquiring the Mountain of Light."

Charles's full lips tightened. "That's utter nonsense, Dmitri."

The black eyes gleamed. "Is it?" Then why are you always so restless? Why must you pace like a caged tiger around your bedroom every night, and why do you play the amiable gentleman for the jung-i-lat sahib and his officers when I know that you cannot abide the military fools? It cannot be because you are afraid of the Sikhs yourself, because you, my friend, have never known the meaning of fear." The black eyes narrowed. "Until now. The Punjab is rife with the makings of a mutiny, and I can feel the fear within you, fear for the safety of one whom I think you care for more than you yourself will admit."

In one swift motion Charles was on his feet, but Dmitri, who had been expecting it, was ahead of him, tensing to counter the blow that he knew was coming. Though he was a vicious and agile fighter who feared no man, every nerve in his body was specially tensed for an attack from Charles St. Germain, an adversary of equal strength and speed whose mounting anger made him far more dangerous.

The air seemed to crackle as the two big men squared off against each other, Charles's body motionless save for the quivering of rage that seemed to emanate from him like heat. Dmitri, his senses somewhat befuddled by Georgi Nostropovitch's fiery vodka, hoped that the fight would be over quickly. Though a confrontation like this might mean the end of their friendship, he was secretly glad that it was being fought over something as worthwhile as the tempestuously beautiful Raven Barrancourt.

"You see, my friend," Dmitri said hoarsely into the heavy silence, "we have come full circle, you and I. Did our friendship not commence over the smiles of a Portuguese beauty? And will it not end because of your unadmitted feelings for our midnight-haired goddess? Ah, if you must hit me, then do so quickly, because I think it will rid you of the anger you have felt since we left her there at Major Wyandotte's." He belched and added thoughtfully, "Besides, I'm getting hungry."

The murderous blood lust in the sea-green eyes was suddenly gone, the black visage relaxing so unexpectedly that Dmitri lowered his awesome fists, confused. Charles, giving his bewildered first mate a wide grin, slapped him heartily on the back.

"You're nothing but a hot-tempered, drunken fool, Dmitri," he remarked, a laugh of sheer amusement rumbling in his wide chest. "You'll not goad me into a brawl this way, so you might as well give up."

Dmitri said nothing, blinking uncertainly, his ham-sized hands still clenched into fists at his sides. Charles laughed again and gave him a mild punch in the ribs that would have felled a lesser man. "Come on, let's have tiffin. You've eaten nothing all day, I warrant, and that devil aquavit has befuddled you as usual."

"Tovarich, wait!" Dmitri grasped Charles's coat sleeve and gazed at him searchingly. "Will you not go see her? Wait, don't get angry! I am asking you for my sake. I promised her I would come, and we have no way of knowing if this cousin of hers is treating her kindly."

Charles's lean jaw tightened almost imperceptibly. "I suppose you're right, Dmitri," he said mockingly. "Since we took all the trouble of bringing her here, we might as well make sure she's being looked after properly."

Abruptly he turned away and roared ill-temperedly for the cowering Hakim to bring their afternoon meal, and in doing so missed the triumphant gleam that lit the depths of Dmitri's coal-black eyes.

For Raven the afternoon seemed never-ending. The day had dawned fair and cool, but with the waning of morning, dark clouds had scuttled over the sky, driven by an icy wind that howled from the peaks of the mighty Hindu Kush, and brought a decidedly wintry frostiness to the air. The bungalow was chilly, Phillip seeing no reason to light the fires until colder weather arrived, and Raven had donned her warmest wool gown, the sleeves and collar edged with stiff lace that fit her throat and wrists snugly.

She had ridden out briefly before lunch, but her mount had shown an unwillingness to obey that was normally attributed to poorly schooled animals and that, coupled with the fierce scowls of Ahmed, who had been ordered to accompany her, had made Raven end the ride quickly. She had wanted to explore the hillsides that lay between the compound and Lahore, intrigued by the wide, far-reaching land, but Phillip had ordered her to stay within the compound walls, ostensibly for her own safety, and Raven had had no choice but to obey.

Not that Phillip was being deliberately unkind, Raven thought to herself as she wandered idly about her room. In truth he had gone out of his way these past four days to make her feel welcome, but he spent a great deal of his time alone in his cluttered study, so she rarely saw him. In addition he had chosen to wait until the party on Thursday before introducing her to his friends and acquaintances, which meant that Raven did not know anyone as yet whom she could ride over to visit. If the truth must be told, Raven was bored, her kind-hearted but vague older cousin obviously unfamiliar with what was required to occupy the time of an energetic young girl.

Raven chided herself for being ungrateful, for Phillip was very attentive whenever he wasn't working, but she couldn't help feeling restless and impatient. Her nerves were badly frayed, too, and it seemed as if she had developed a tendency for snapping at poor Danny about every little thing. She had tried telling herself that she should have every reason to feel happy because Cousin Phillip, after reading Sir Hadrian's letter, had agreed unconditionally to give her the money she sought. Furthermore he had promised to have it within the week, once the proper drafts had been drawn up by someone in John Company who handled his accounts. Surely she had no reason to feel as miserable as she did, and yet the idle days left little else to do than brood about the past and dream of Charles, the memories of his lovemaking haunting her far more than the bitter words Bettina Bateman had said to her.

"Don't think of him!" Raven whispered fiercely to herself as the image of the tall, devilishly handsome captain of the *Orient Star* rose unbidden to her mind. Tears stung her eyes and she bit hard on her lower lip, berating herself for still loving a man who had used her so cruelly.

"Miss Raven!"

She turned thankfully as Danny hurried into the room, the disturbing image of Charles St. Germain retreating for the time being. "What is it, Danny?" she demanded, aware that the elderly woman looked agitated, her brown eyes wide, her ample bosom rising and falling rapidly.

"Mr. Zergeyev's here! I saw him ride up through the gate! Oh, I do believe he's come to pay us a visit!"

Raven's heart leaped. "Is he alone?"

Danny nodded, not seeing the desperate hope in her young mistress's eyes or the shattering disappointment that followed her words. "If you're asking whether Captain St. Germain be with him, no. He's by himself." She regarded Raven's gray wool gown with a critical eye. "You're dressed proper enough to receive him, dear, but why don't you run a comb through that wild hair of yours?" She cocked her graying head. "Ah, there's the front door. Hurry, now, Miss Raven."

When Raven swept into the starkly decorated parlor a few minutes later, she found Dmitri and her cousin standing before the collection of mounted heads, Phillip explaining with enthusiastic gestures how he had bagged the Bengal tiger south of Lucknow two years ago. Danny was sitting primly on the sofa, feigning deep interest, her embroidery spread as usual in her lap. Despite her disappointment that Charles hadn't come, Raven could scarcely credit the joy that flowed into her heart at the sight of Dmitri's familiar bulk, his black beard flowing, his enormous feet encased in the same leather boots he always wore aboard ship.

"Oh, Dmitri, I'm so glad to see you!" she cried.

The bearded Cossack turned and saw her standing in the doorway, her golden eyes glowing, her oval face radiant and beautiful. He started across the room, arms outstretched, and she met him halfway and fell laughing into his embrace. Giving her a bear hug that threatened to crack her ribs, he savored the feel of her slim body against his, her slender arms wrapped about his neck, and cursed Charles for being a fool.

"You look as lovely as always, my little princess," he murmured, releasing her at last and gazing earnestly into her upturned face. She seemed a little thinner to him, if that was possible given the short time of their separation, and there was a marked strain in the sloping eyes that he didn't like. "Are you being cared for properly?" he asked softly enough so that Phillip Barrancourt couldn't hear him.

"Oh, yes," Raven assured him and grasped his enormous hands. "Dmitri, where is—"

"My dear, dear Raven, do you always make it a habit of flinging yourself on visitors with such abandon?"

Raven looked up quickly at her cousin's casual question, unable to ascertain from the solemn expression and penetrating eyes whether he was displeased or not. A rosy stain crept to her hollow cheeks and she released Dmitri's hands. "Not usually," she admitted, gazing up at him apologetically. "But Dmitri is such a good friend. I-I'm just glad to see him, that's all."

Phillip's deep blue eyes went from the Russian's bearded face to his cousin's pleading one and he shrugged, giving her an indulgent smile. "I understand that Mr. Zergeyev is the one who escorted you and Mrs. Daniels to Lahore."

"He was," Raven acknowledged, dimpling as she gazed up into Dmitri's face, unable to take her eyes off him, his familiar presence soothing her pain.

Phillip continued to regard her watchfully, absent-mindedly stroking his beard, then turned away. "I'm relieved to know you traveled in the company of friends," he remarked, and gave a clipped order to Ahmed for refreshments.

"I can't stay long, little one," Dmitri said as Raven led him to the sofa and seated herself beside him. "I just wanted to make sure you were doing well."

"I am," Raven assured him, her expression clouding. "Must you rush right off again? There's so much I'd like to ask you." The strain reappeared in the magnificent golden eyes. "I'd like to know what you've been doing since you left us at Major Wyandotte's." She bent her head and began to play with the fragile lace at her wrist. "You and Captain St. Germain are still in Lahore, I take it?"

"We are. The captain was going to accompany me here but at the last moment received an invitation to take dinner with General Bostwick."

"Ah, then you've met our resident C.O.?" Phillip inquired conversationally, but Raven scarcely heard Dmitri's answer. Was it true that Charles had intended to come, or was Dmitri lying to make her feel better? How, she wondered forlornly, could the invitation of an army officer possibly mean more to Charles than a visit with her? Did General Bostwick also have a comely daughter?

Raven bit her lip and averted her face so that Dmitri wouldn't see the telltale glimmer of tears in her eyes. What a fool she had been to hope that he would come back to her! During the long, idle hours since her arrival in Khanapur compound, she had come to realize that she would gladly forgive Charles anything if only he would say he loved her. But he had told her at their parting that she had been nothing but a dalliance for him, and Dmitri's casual words only confirmed that now.

"Isn't that right, Raven?"

"What?" Raven looked up, startled, to find Phillip regarding her searchingly over the rim of his brandy snifter. He was seated on the cushions that faced the sofa, the great-horned ibex leaning over one shoulder, a faint smile playing on his lips. "I'm sorry," she said distantly, "I didn't hear what you said."

Phillip shrugged. "No matter. How do you like the wine, Mr. Zergeyev? It comes from Arabia and I find it comparable to, if not better than, the Spanish variety." He lifted the snifter. "I prefer brandy myself."

"And I am a whiskey drinker," Dmitri admitted with a wide grin, "but you may thank my captain for teaching me to appreciate fine wines. Yes, I like it, Mr. Barrancourt."

"This captain of yours seems an interesting man," Phillip remarked, settling his bulk more comfortably on the tasseled cushions. "Mrs. Daniels has told me quite a bit about him. I understand he owns a clipper ship."

"The fastest afloat," Dmitri boasted.

"I see." Phillip idly traced the Oriental pattern of one of the cushions with a blunt index finger. "Does he carry commodities on consignment?"

Dmitri's white teeth flashed in his bearded face. "He will carry anything, sir, if the price is right."

I can't bear this, Raven thought. I must talk to Dmitri, to find out how he is! But that proved to be impossible. The conversation centered on business, her cousin showing a great deal of interest in the *Orient Star* and its hold capacity, and by the time Dmitri announced that he had to leave Raven hadn't had a single chance to question him alone.

Even when she accompanied him to the door, the watchful Ahmed hovered in the background, preventing her from uttering anything save the usual amenities. She waited while Dmitri shrugged into his great coat, her expression anxious, and although he waited patiently for her to ask the question he knew distressed her, she said nothing at all.

"I shall be back soon, little one," he promised, feeling disheartened that he could do nothing to comfort her. "Your cousin is interested in the fact that the *Orient Star* is near Kasur, and is thinking of sending a shipment south with her when she leaves."

"He told me his warehouses are empty this time of year," Raven said, puzzled.

"And why would he still be here if they were?" Dmitri countered and smiled at her fondly. "That is a business matter he will have to take up with the captain."

Raven's throat constricted. "Will Charles—will the captain come here?"

Dmitri shrugged. "I imagine so." He pulled on his gloves. "I must go, little one." Bending down, he made as if to kiss her cheek, but turned his head just a little so that he could whisper quietly into her ear, "Are you certain your cousin is treating you well?"

Raven nodded, her curious eyes searching his face. "Of course. Why shouldn't he?"

Dmitri shrugged again. "He seems a friendly enough fellow." Straightening, he added with a grin, "Look after yourself, my little princess, until we meet again."

"I will," Raven promised, and Dmitri found it difficult to walk unconcernedly down the verandah steps knowing her unconsciously pleading eyes were fastened upon him. She waved when he mounted his waiting horse and rode off, and he forced himself to ignore the poignantly sad little face, although it haunted him on the long ride back to the city.

When Raven turned around at last, sighing deeply, she found Ahmed blocking her path. The Indian was watching her closely, the hawkish features unreadable. "The sahib wishes to see you in his study, missy."

"Will you please tell him I'd rather speak to him later?" Raven requested, wanting to be alone.

Ahmed stood his ground. "The sahib wishes to see you," he repeated.

Raven sighed. "Very well."

Phillip's tone was affable when he responded to her knock on the closed study door, and Raven entered to find him sitting before the cluttered secretary, thumbs hooked into the pockets of his embroidered waistcoat. His eyes were filled with amusement when he saw her standing before him, her reluctance to be there evident in her rigid stance although she was doing her best to conceal it.

"If you think I've asked you in here to chastise you, I'm afraid you're right, my dear," he said, the amusement abruptly gone.

Raven's smooth brow furrowed. "What have I done?"

Phillip regarded her intently. "I may only be your cousin, Raven, and not a legitimate one at that, but I feel responsible for you while you're under my roof, and I cannot condone such behavior from a young woman of superior breeding and upbringing."

Raven was totally bewildered by his words. Though he spoke without anger, she could tell that he was greatly disturbed. This was the first time since her arrival here, not counting their grave conversation concerning money, that Phillip had addressed her in anything other than the lazy, indifferent tone of voice he always used. But now there was an undercurrent of anger to his words and a gleam in the blue eyes that told her he was extremely displeased about something. Furthermore, the normal pallor of his skin had given way to an almost feverish glow, confirming Raven's earlier suspicions that her cousin was not in the best of health. This distressed her, for despite his odd habits and idiosyncrasies, Raven liked him and hated the thought of upsetting him.

"I'm sorry," she said sincerely, "I didn't mean to displease you, but I really haven't the faintest idea what I've done."

"You don't?" Phillip's bushy red brows rose in surprise. "Then it's obvious to me that lessons in manners are sorely lacking in a Cornish upbringing. In India, Raven," he added, cutting smoothly across her protests, "a young lady does not publicly embrace a man who is not betrothed, married, or otherwise related to her. As you know, women observe strict purdah in this country, never allowing their faces to be seen by anyone but their husbands and brothers, never leaving the sanctuary of their zenanas, never—"

"But I am not an Indian woman!" Raven protested, stung by his words.

"Granted you aren't," Phillip agreed, "but I expect you to adhere to our Western ideals of decorum while you're here."

Raven's cheeks grew rosy and she lowered her eyes. "I'm sorry, Phillip. I imagine I did overstep my bounds, but Dmitri..." She paused, searching for the proper words that would describe what she felt in her heart for the big deposed Cossack prince.

"Are you in love with him?" Phillip demanded unexpectedly.

Another wave of heat flooded Raven's cheeks. "Certainly not! How absurd!"

Her vehement denial seemed to satisfy him. "Very good. I wouldn't want someone with your beauty and breeding to be wasted on a lowly tar, and a Russian one at that."

Raven bridled at this unfair description but held her angry retort in check, not wanting to quarrel with Phillip or abuse his hospitality. He was right in saying she shouldn't have demonstrated her affection for Dmitri so openly, but how could she ever make anyone understand that she loved Dmitri deeply, not only for himself but because he meant so very much to Charles?

"I can see that you don't agree with me," Phillip drawled, well aware of her flashing eyes and contained anger. Rising to his feet and moving very fluidly across the room for a man of his height and build, he stood gazing down into her flushed face, the golden eyes filled with stormy fire, the sort of eyes a man could easily lose himself in.

"I meant what I said, Raven." Phillip's voice was unexpectedly harsh. "You're much too beautiful to be wasted on just any man." Reaching out, he took hold of a strand of shining black hair, letting the silken curls run through his fingers while Raven kept her face averted, deeply embarrassed.

"I promise I'll not do it again," she whispered and fled from the room while Phillip continued to stand there regarding the open door with a thoughtful expression on his bearded face. After a moment he returned to his desk, where he sat staring down at his hand, rubbing his blunt fingers together as though he could still feel the soft, shining strands of her hair against his skin.

Chapter Eleven

Torches flickered along the winding drive that meandered from the wrought-iron gates into the confines of Khanapur compound. Smartly attired Ghurka guards—provided by Her Majesty's army for the private use of the British East India Company—flanked the compound entrance and saluted smartly as the two-wheeled traps containing uniformed officers and their richly appointed wives bowled past. Those guests who were members of the Civil Service, who comprised the second ruling caste in India, received similar salutes of honor as they were recognized, but the solitary rider who turned his horse toward the gate from the shadows was immediately stopped and questioned.

He was very tall and elegantly attired in a dark burgundy brocade coat, his starched white collar gleaming in the darkness. Leaning over his horse's neck, he startled both Ghurkas by addressing them in their native Nepalese. Recovering themselves, they exchanged brief glances, their dark features taking on looks of respect, and the mounted gentleman was allowed to pass unchallenged, falling in behind the small procession of swaying gigs and carriages that was moving toward Phillip Barrancourt's brightly lit house.

In her bedroom Raven turned away from the window with a sigh, letting the chiks fall back into place so that none of the arriving guests could see her in the glass, the tops of her creamy breasts exposed by the confining corset that had just been laced about her slender form. Lihl, the sullen young girl who had been assigned to serve Danny and Raven during their stay, had made no effort to hide her distaste for the stiff stays and hoops that made up part of an Englishwoman's evening attire. Raven couldn't find it in her heart to berate the girl for her contemptuous looks, envying her the gauzy salvar and kamiz she wore, the traditional wide trousers and loose-fitting, brightly colored shirt clearly more comfortable than her own confining undergarments.

She cast an even more disheartened glance at the magnificent gown which Lihl was holding aloft, waiting to assist her mistress into it. Phillip himself had selected it that afternoon, sorting through the small collection in the clothespress and emerging at last with a ballgown of pure white silk brocade with full, billowing skirts.

"By God!" he had shouted with pleasure. "I know this material!"

"I beg your pardon?" Raven had asked, standing helplessly beside him as he laughed and tossed it onto the bed, his eyes glowing.

"Shantung silk!" he told her excitedly. "I sent a bolt of it to my father a year ago, as a sample, mind you, to see if Booth's might be interested in offering it on the European market. I had a devil of a time during my visit to Hong Kong dealing with the Chinese for it, being as they're such suspicious, tight-fisted barbarians, but I did manage."

"It's very beautiful," Raven said hesitantly, somewhat taken aback by the blazing blue eyes and flushed cheeks. It was obvious to her now that her quiet, retiring cousin was capable of wild emotions, but it disturbed her to learn that greed seemed to be the motive in rousing him like this. "Great-Uncle Hadrian made a present of several gowns to me before I left for India."

"Yes, it's beautiful," Phillip agreed, letting the smooth material trail through his fingers. "And you'll be the only woman wearing anything like it tonight." He regarded her slender form critically. "Most appropriate, too, this pure, maidenly white. I insist you wear it, Raven."

She hadn't wanted to argue with him and looked away quickly before he could see the color rising to her cheeks. If only he knew the absurdity of that statement, that she no longer had the right to be called a maiden. Furthermore, she would gladly shun decorum to lie in Charles's arms again. A sob rose in her throat, but Phillip, hovering almost worshipfully over the white brocade silk, did not notice.

"Miss Raven? I'm ready to help you put on your gown."

Raven turned away from the bed to smile gratefully at Danny, who had come to assist the scowling Lihl in dressing her. Raven had been filled with chagrin to learn that Phillip had not asked Danny to attend the festivities, but the elderly woman had quickly assured her young mistress that she would be far more comfortable in her rooms than mingling among the fashionable acquaintances Phillip had invited.

With both Danny and Lihl to help her, Raven quickly slipped into the beautiful silk gown, the material falling into place, covering only part of her swelling breasts and leaving her smooth shoulders and throat bare. Lihl, grudgingly admitting to herself that the Angrezi woman's hair was dark and beautiful enough without the added sheen of coconut oil, quickly plaited the long strands and wound them away from Raven's small face so that they fell softly against her bare shoulders. Raven had insisted that she wear the beautiful mother-of-pearl combs that she had brought with her from home, and Lihl obligingly wove them among the glossy strands.

"Raven, are you ready to greet your guests?" Phillip's voice sounded impatient through the thin wood, and Raven hastily adjusted the rustling petticoats before hurrying to open the door.

"Yes, I am," she informed him, swinging it wide.

Seeing her standing before him, the white gown enhancing the midnight blackness of her hair, Phillip's expression froze, his heavyset body unmoving as he stared down into her delicate face.

"Don't you like it?" Raven asked doubtfully, bemused by his silence, her curving brows knitting.

Phillip stirred and came forward to take her slender hand in his. "Forgive me, my dear," he murmured. "I'd no idea it would become you so well."

Raven flushed and looked away, unaware that he had allowed his gaze to linger hungrily on her décolletage. Danny, watching from the far side of the room, recognized the gleam in the blue eyes, and a seed of doubt was planted in her mind. Like Raven, she had thought their host a pleasant yet rather dull individual who rarely showed much interest in his surroundings, but Danny knew enough of the world to recognize lust in a man's eyes when she saw it. And yet it was impossible not to be moved by Raven's beauty, even if you were her cousin, Danny comforted herself quickly, bustling forward to give her silent young mistress a fond embrace before Phillip whisked her away on his arm.

Raven was unprepared for the dazzling alteration the enormous dining room had undergone. The French doors that separated it from the smaller sitting room had been removed, incorporating both of them into one large space. Candlelight twinkled from every available table and newly shined wall sconces, and the plank flooring was polished to a soft, welcoming patina. The dining table had been moved into a corner of the room to accommodate the dancing that would take place, and Raven was astonished to see a group of musicians seated discreetly out of the way, their matching black trousers and white shirts adding a distinctive air of elegance to the scene.

Phillip paused dramatically in the doorway, and the guests who were chattering on the dance floor, champagne glasses in hand, all turned, a collective hush falling. "Good evening, everyone!" he called out in a robust voice that carried across the room. "May I present to you my cousin, once removed, from Cornwall, Miss Raven Barrancourt of North Head!"

As he finished speaking, he drew Raven to his side, bringing her out of the shadows where she had been standing. The expectant hush was broken by appreciative murmurs as the guests, male and female alike, reacted to her breathtaking beauty, the rustling of petticoats breaking the stillness as they surged forward to greet her.

Raven smiled and inclined her head as Phillip, with boundless enthusiasm, led her into the midst of the throng. She recognized only one beaming face among the many, that of Major Wyandotte, the brilliant uniform he wore correct to the toes of his polished military boots and fastidiously turned lapels. Bowing over her hand, he murmured how delighted he was to see her again, then reluctantly gave up his place at her side for Sir Julian Craven, a director in the British East India Company's Punjabi division. He was elderly and extremely hard of hearing, but the gleam in his faded eyes was no different from that of his younger counterparts as he gallantly kissed her hand and professed his delight at meeting her.

"I think you've met everyone, my dear," Phillip remarked at last, his hand still gripping her elbow. "Shall we open the dancing?"

"I wonder if Miss Barrancourt would be kind enough to consent to perform the first dance with an old friend?"

Raven turned at the sound of the deep, slightly mocking voice that was so very familiar to her, her heart leaping into her throat as she found the sea-green eyes gazing down at her steadily. Charles was wearing a superbly tailored burgundy coat, far ahead of the fashion worn by the nonmilitary male guests present that evening, the lapels of gold silk, the tight-fitting material flaring over his hips and showing to perfection the broadness of his shoulders. He was clean-shaven, his lean jaw tensed as the green eyes roved over Raven's willowy form, but a slow smile curved the sensual lips, the familiar mockery in it making Raven's heart beat faster.

"I don't believe—" Phillip began, but Charles had already reached out a muscular arm, his big hand clasping Raven's slim wrist, and before any of the startled spectators could react he had led her onto the center of the floor and signaled the waiting musicians to begin.

"Why, the audacity of the man!" a shocked and secretly envious matron declared, fluttering her fan in a scandalized manner before her rouged face, but the rest of her words were drowned out by the first lilting strains of a waltz.

"I hope you know how to waltz, little one," Charles said as he took Raven's hand in his, unconsciously using the same term of endearment that Dmitri had always used. "Being as it hasn't quite been accepted in proper society yet, you may not have been taught how to perform it." His green eyes rested intently on her upturned face.

"And naturally you would," Raven countered, although her words lacked their usual derision.

Charles gave a low laugh and slipped his arm about her small waist, bringing her intimately close against his wide chest. Other couples were flocking onto the floor behind them, caught up by the rhythm of the music, yet Raven remained oblivious to all of them. With Charles's lean, handsome face close to hers, the rigid strength of his arm about her, she could feel a pleasant warmth invading her body and wiping out the gnawing ache she had felt within her heart since their departure from Colonel Bateman's house. Charles, as it turned out, was an accomplished dancer, and Raven seemed to float about the room in his arms, her sloping eyes locked with his, neither of them speaking although the silence that enveloped them was more eloquent than words.

"I say, they make a splendid couple," Major Wyandotte remarked to Lady Craven, with whom he was dancing.

The elderly woman nodded her elegantly coiffed head, thinking Charles St. Germain far too dashing to be a mere captain-owner of a clipper ship. To the wide-eyed wives and daughters present, that information, which their host had imparted to them earlier, was lamentably incomplete, and all of them—Lady Craven included—chafed with impatience to learn more about the tall, handsome stranger who had appeared in their midst.

To their universal disappointment Charles did not deign to dance again. After releasing Raven into the arms of her cousin, who came forward with a stony expression to claim her at the conclusion of the waltz, he retreated to a corner, where he stood sipping wine, his heavy-lidded green eyes following her as she was squired out by one gentleman after another.

Raven was exhausted by the time the musicians took a brief pause in their playing. She couldn't even remember the names of half the men who had partnered her onto the floor, although Phillip hadn't really invited a large crowd that evening. Her thoughts were always on Charles, whose broad-shouldered form remained constantly within her line of vision. What was he doing here, she wondered, and how on earth had he managed to get an invitation from her cousin? Dmitri! she realized all at once. Dmitri must have arranged it during his visit the other day, but if so, where was he? With her eyes she searched among the shadowed corners for his familiar, bearded form, but she could not find him.

"Miss Barrancourt, you must promise me the next dance!"

"I will," Raven assured the admiring young man with the toothy grin who bowed eagerly before her as she left the crowded floor alone. She slipped past him toward the French doors, hoping to escape unnoticed, and gave a sigh of relief when they closed behind her, shutting her off from the noisy talk and laughter within.

The night was chilly and very dark, the torch flames sputtering with the onslaught of the freshening wind. Leaning against the chipped wooden balustrade, Raven lifted her small face, savoring this taste of freedom after the closeness of the dance floor.

A broad form stepped out onto the verandah behind her, momentarily blocking out the light that filtered through the drawn curtains, but without having to turn her head Raven knew that it was Charles. Her heart began a nervous pounding in her breast, and it was with considerable effort that she managed to compose her features before turning around to face him. For a moment they stared at one another in silence, and Raven, for all the intimacy she had shared with him, could not read his thoughts from the composed set of his aristocratic features. The emerald-green eyes held hers, drawing a response from her merely by their compelling intensity, causing an undeniable yearning to flood through her.

Looking down into the shadow-softened perfection of her features, the soft red lips parted, Charles's lean jaw tightened unaccountably and he turned away, addressing her without looking at her. "I must say, you've made quite a conquest tonight, Raven."

"What do you mean?" she asked, his flat, hard voice hurting her.

"Why, you're the belle of the ball," Charles responded mockingly. "I'm pleased to see Dmitri's fears were unfounded."

"Dmitri was worried about me?" Raven asked, puzzled.

Charles nodded, his eyes unreadable as he watched the swaying figures of the dancers beyond the glass panes that separated them from the dining room. "He seemed to feel you were being neglected and that your cousin lives a monkish existence quite unsuitable for a young woman." His full lips twitched. "I must admit, Raven, that Cousin Phillip has quite outlandish tastes."

"He's been very kind to me," Raven said sharply.

The sea-green eyes bored into her, their intensity frightening her and filling her with an odd breathlessness at the same time. How could he have forgotten so quickly how overwhelming Charles's presence was, how every nerve in her body seemed to vibrate in response to him whenever he was near? "Oh, I'm not disputing that," Charles informed her smoothly. "He has gone to great pains to show you off to his friends, who, I must admit, aren't the most savory people I've ever fallen in with."

"Most of them are British officers and the rest are members of the East India Company," Raven informed him tartly, distressed by the fact that they were once again at odds with one another.

Charles shrugged his powerful shoulders indifferently. "They remind me of vultures. Can't you see the covetous greed in their eyes when they look at you, Raven? Or the envy in the faces of their wives?" His gaze roved over her bare shoulders and low décolletage, scorching her with its intensity. "And Phillip has certainly dressed you to advantage."

"I don't have to listen to this!" Raven said stiffly. "They're Phillip's friends and I happen to like them! I'm really sorry now that Dmitri wheedled an invitation for you tonight."

"So am I." Charles's curt words made her pause in midstride, for she had been intending to return to the house and leave him on the verandah. "I thought I'd come see for myself how you were doing, and instead I find myself thrown to dogs like Sir Julian Craven who want one thing from me: my ship and a license to carry the company's tainted goods to England so that every one of them can grow even wealthier."

"And are you so different?" Raven demanded. Petticoats rustling, she strode to the balustrade where Charles stood, her slim body quivering with fury as she stared up into his handsome face. "At least they go about their trade honestly! They've no need to steal diamonds from others to make their fortunes!"

Charles uttered a hoarse oath and seized her shoulders, his hard fingers digging into her bare flesh. "You little fool!" he rasped. "Is that honestly why you think I came here?"

Raven glared up at him bravely, although the force of his anger unnerved her. "What other reason can there be?" she demanded, her sloping eyes blazing like a tigress's in the darkness.

Abruptly the tension in Charles's powerful frame was gone. The bruising grip on her shoulders relaxed, the big hands sliding almost worshipfully over her silken skin. "Can't you guess, Raven?" he asked hoarsely, the imploring look in his eyes one she had never seen before.

Her breath caught in her throat and the tawny eyes widened, a wild pulse beginning to beat beneath the big thumb that had strayed down to stroke the smooth line of her jaw. Charles allowed his hands to travel down to her small waist, tilting her body toward his so that the cascading petticoats and cumbersome hoops were no longer in the way. Raven found herself crushed against his hard chest, but even before she could make a move to break free he had seized her small chin in his hand and lowered his dark head so that his lips found hers. The kiss was gentle at first, the tentative touching of lovers who have been separated not only by time but by conflict, until Charles felt the warmth and yielding of Raven's lips beneath his own.

With a passion that bordered on desperation he pulled her to him, his demanding mouth drawing the breath from her body and the will from her very soul. Raven clung to him, her heart beating wildly, while the heat of Charles's consuming need enveloped them both. His strong arms were about her, drawing her against him in a hold she did not want to break, and she moaned low in her throat with mounting desire as the power of his kiss forced her back against the verandah railing, where she could feel the heat and hardness of his manhood through the crushed layers of her petticoats.

The sound of applause from within as the musicians finished playing a popular reel forced them apart at last. Charles was breathing harshly, his emerald eyes smoldering as he gazed into Raven's upturned face, her hollow cheeks flushed, her soft lips still parted and moist.

"My God, Raven," he whispered raggedly. "I mean to have you. I must have you. In God's name don't turn me away again."

The beautiful golden eyes filled with defensive pain. "Need I remind you that it was you, Charles, who turned away from me?"

Charles's handsome features were stark. "What are you saying?"

Suddenly Raven could look at him no longer. Breaking free of his hold she turned away, biting her lip and twisting her hands together. When Charles came after her, softly uttering her name and laying a gentle hand on her bare shoulder, she whirled about, eyes bright with unshed tears.

"Don't touch me or I'll call my cousin!" she threatened.

Charles regarded her quizzically, displaying none of the anger she had felt certain her harsh words would arouse. "What is it that distresses you, Raven?" he asked, the unexpected gentleness of his tone making her defenses crumble.

"Bettina Bateman told me what happened between you," she confessed tearfully. Her eyes, hauntingly beautiful and filled with pain, were upon him now. "So you see, Charles, that's how I know that I'm not the one guilty of—of turning away."

"What the devil are you talking about?" Charles demanded, her tears affecting him far more than her whispered accusation.

"Don't feign ignorance with me!" Raven choked. "I can't bear it! You know very well you made l-love to Bettina after . . ." She swallowed hard. "After you left me that night. She told me so herself."

She turned away again, her glossy head bowed, shaking silently with suppressed sobs while Charles regarded her in dumbfounded amazement. "Good God!" he exploded at last, comprehending everything. "Is that what—is that why you told me you hated me?" Seizing her roughly by the arms, he turned her around, drawing her against his chest and forcing her to look up into his disbelieving face. "Is that why, Raven?"

"What else should I have done?" she choked. "Blessed you for your endurance at f-fornication?"

To her astonishment Charles threw back his head and laughed, the sound rumbling in his deep chest while his arms tightened about her rigid body, forcing her more tightly against him. "My poor, sweet innocent," he said roughly when he could speak, his eyes tender as he looked down into her ravaged expression. "Can you honestly believe I'd seek satisfaction from another woman after what you and I shared that night?"

"But Bettina said—"

"Bettina is an empty-headed twit with nothing but malicious mischief in her mind." Momentary anger blazed in the emerald eyes. "I don't know how she found out about us, or even if she did, but I swear to you, Raven, on my word of honor, that what she told you is a lie." His strong finger was beneath her chin, an endearing smile on his full lips as he gazed down into her face. "I realize the word of a black-hearted smuggler may not mean much to you, but even you, Raven, must admit that my tastes in women do not run toward flat-chested little girls with viperish dispositions."

"Oh, Charles," Raven whispered, and suddenly it was as if the heartache of their separation had never been. He gathered her into his arms, held her close, and would have kissed her again but for the ominous slamming of the French door behind them.

Raven uttered a small cry when she saw Phillip Barrancourt

standing in the shadows before them, his blue eyes blazing with suppressed anger. Charles, sensing the quivering rage in the other man, set Raven gently aside and moved to stand protectively before her. Though Phillip was heavier than Charles, his hands clenched into fists at his sides, Charles showed no fear as he folded his powerful arms across his wide chest and stood waiting patiently for Phillip to speak.

"It seems you have taken advantage of my hospitality and compromised my cousin, captain," Phillip said at last, his terse voice grating with annoyance.

Charles inclined his head, amusement burning in his green eyes, but there was a wariness in his stance that Raven, pressed against the railing, couldn't miss. "Perhaps I have, and I apologize for distressing you."

"Is that all you have to say?" Phillip demanded sharply. "You apologize for distressing me? This is an outrage, captain, an unforgivable outrage! I asked you here this evening to discuss business and to thank you for delivering Raven safely to Lahore, surely matters that should have set some sort of precedent! Yet what do I receive in payment? A flouting of tradition and a total disregard for manners when you lead Raven onto the floor to open the dancing, a complete lack of respect for my guests when you spirit her out here for—for—" He broke off, sputtering in his rage.

"Phillip, please," Raven began, but he rounded on her, the venom in his voice unlike any she had ever heard before.

"Go inside! This is no concern of yours!"

Charles's brow darkened and he slowly unfolded his arms, taking a deliberate step toward the older man. Before he could speak, however, Raven rushed forward and placed her hand on his arm, where she could feel the tension of suppressed rage in the rigid expanse of muscles. "Charles, please don't," she implored.

He looked down into her pale face, and some of the rage seemed to drain out of him. Perhaps sensing as much, Phillip stepped forward to take advantage of the situation and seized Raven's hand in a fierce grip. "Come along," he said curtly, "it's time for us to go in to dinner."

Without giving Raven a chance to say another word to Charles, he pulled her forcibly inside, and only after the procession of chattering guests had moved to seat themselves at the elaborately set table was she able to search for him. She found him leaning casually against the wall near the French doors, long legs crossed before him, watching the others with expressionless eyes. Only when her anxious gaze met his did he straighten and come forward, settling himself comfortably at the far end of the table between a formidable matron in mauve taffeta and a blushing young girl with a yellow bow in her hair. Lifting his wineglass in one long-fingered hand, he gave her a mocking toast over the rim, his sensual lips curved, and Raven lowered her head, soft cheeks flushing, her heart flooding with a delicious warmth that tingled throughout her body.

Accustomed to the odd assortment of largely tasteless dishes that Hammad had been turning out since her arrival, Raven's eyes widened at the sight of the trays that both turbaned servants carried in at a signal from her cousin. There was barbecued pork and pickled hog's feet with sweet and piquant jelly, stuffed waterfowl that Phillip himself had shot earlier that week on the Ravi River, prawns rolled in flour and coconut and lightly fried over a fire. Fresh fruits and other delicacies prepared with honey and curry accompanied the myriad of meats, each one with a distinctive flavor of its own.

Raven ate heartily, her appetite restored for the first time in days, always conscious of Charles St. Germain's imposing presence at the far end of the table. Try as she might, she could not keep her eyes off his broad-shouldered form, the candlelight reflecting golden highlights in his chestnut hair. Though he spent most of his time flirting with the wide-eyed, worshipful girl beside him, Raven felt no jealousy at his actions, deeply content now that Bettina Bateman had been exposed as a liar. Once, while they waited for dessert to be brought in, Raven allowed her fingers to stray hesitantly, almost wonderingly, to her lips, which were bruised from Charles's impassioned kiss on the porch. Their glances met, became locked, and Charles gave her another salute with his wineglass, this one devoid of mockery and filled with such unmistakable promise that her heart beat faster.

"Miss Barrancourt?"

Raven turned at the quietly uttered words to find Sarah Broomfield, wife of the brigade major, leaning toward her, her plain features softened with a kind smile. "Don't you believe it's time the ladies retired and allowed the men to their rum and cigars?"

Raven nodded and prepared to rise, a signal for the others that dinner was over. Before she could move, however, her cousin had laid his big hand on her arm to stay her, and with a voice that boomed across the table called out, "Just a moment, please, ladies and gentlemen!"

Silence descended and curious eyes turned to Phillip as he rose and adjusted the wrinkled folds of his elegant but somewhat outdated frock coat. With a silver knife he tapped against his half-emptied wineglass although there was no need to do so since he already had the attention of everyone in the room. Save for that surly St. Germain fellow, Phillip thought contemptuously to himself, seeing that the handsome sea captain was leaning negligently in his chair, an uninterested expression on his aquiline features. Well, he intended to take the wind out of that arrogant bilge tar's sails quickly enough!

"I have an announcement to make," Phillip declared into the expectant silence. "You've all had the chance to meet my cousin, Miss Raven Barrancourt, by now."

"But not all of us lucky enough to dance with her!" came the disappointed cry from a dissipated-looking young man at the far end of the table.

Phillip held up his hands to silence the laughter that followed the complaint. "Now, now, Trelling, remember there'll be more dancing after dinner. Doubtless Raven would be pleased to favor you thusly." He glanced indulgently at his cousin, who sat silently at his right, a rosy stain creeping to her hollow cheeks. "As it were, we'll have all the more cause to celebrate after my announcement."

"You're being deuced dramatic, Barrancourt," Major Wyandotte grumbled as Phillip paused and lifted his wineglass.

"I am," his burly, red-bearded host agreed, grinning broadly. Holding the amber liquid aloft he added, "and with very good reason. It's not every day a confirmed old bachelor like myself can have the honor of informing you that Miss Raven Barrancourt and I are to be married!"

Raven's astonished cry was lost in the uproar that followed Phillip's statement, everyone, it seemed, wanting to be the first to congratulate her. She was hauled, protesting, to her feet, and men with wine-flushed, salaciously grinning faces fought over the chance to kiss her while the women gathered around and offered their envious felicitations.

"There's been some mistake!" Raven cried, trying to fight free of them, but her words were lost in a raucous cheer of "well-met fellow, hail!" to which Phillip responded with a deep, obliging bow.

Struggling against the hands that reached out to touch her, Raven tried to peer beyond the crush of bodies for Charles. A feeling of dread began to grow in her heart when she couldn't find him, and she struggled with renewed determination until she broke free at last and was running out of the dining room toward the front door. Her face was deathly pale and her breath came in gasps. Where had he gone? She had to find him, to explain to him that Phillip's announcement had been some sort of bizarre joke! There would be time later to learn why he had done such an unkind, humorless thing. First she had to get to Charles, whose abrupt disappearance could only mean that he had taken Phillip's words to heart.

Throwing open the front door, Raven felt a wave of relief wash over her when she saw his broad, familiar shadow unhitching a waiting horse from the post beyond the bungalow lawn. Lifting up her skirts, she started down the steps after him, only to be seized roughly from behind. Before she could cry out, a big hand clamped itself over her mouth and she was jerked back onto the portico. She looked up, tawny eyes wide, into the sallow, fanatically grinning face of Phillip Barrancourt.

"Ready to leave your guests so soon, Raven?" he asked silkily. "I don't believe you've given everyone a proper chance to wish us happiness."

"What sort of cruel joke is this?" Raven demanded as he pulled her back into the house and slammed the front door shut with his foot.

Phillip smiled. "No joke at all, my dear. I've been thinking quite a bit since you first appeared like a breath of spring on my doorstep. At first I wasn't sure how best to use this beautiful blessing my father had been kind enough to send me, but the answer wasn't long in coming."

"What—what are you saying?" Raven stammered, totally bewildered. Looking up into his bearded face, she saw a stranger, his blond hair disheveled, blue eyes glazed, his lips parted to reveal long, predatory teeth.

"We'll talk later," Phillip promised, pushing her bodily toward the dining room, an easy task given his stoutness and Raven's ineffectual strength.

"I won't go in there!" Raven cried, her voice suddenly shrill, the numbness of shock giving way to full-blown fear. What was going on here? Was Phillip mad? Looking up into the blazing blue eyes, she could almost believe he was. "I'll tell all of them you invented this preposterous tale!"

Seeing the mutiny blazing in her golden eyes and the trembling of her lower lip, which to him indicated near hysteria, Phillip grabbed her roughly in his arms and half-carried, half-dragged her into her bedroom. "You'll stay right here," he ordered, frightening her with his intensity. "Ahmed will guard the door, and if you so much as make a single sound—"

"And what will you tell them?" Raven spat, jerking her glossy head in the direction of the dining room.

Phillip took a menacing step toward her, making her cower protectively against the bed, certain now that he was mad. Spittle had gathered at the corners of his mouth, and his voice quivered with the force of his anger. "I'll tell them the excitement was too much for you. I meant what I said, Raven. Not a sound out of you."

He wheeled abruptly and slammed the door shut behind him, the lock turning from the outside, a sound so final and filled with menace that Raven was overcome with terror. She sat down heavily on the bed, her silk skirts and petticoats bellowing about her, hands pressed to her hot cheeks, her heart hammering wildly in her breast. None of this was real, she told herself, totally bewildered. Phillip had to be drunk; he had to be playing some hideous joke on her! But why? Why? If only Charles hadn't charged off like an enraged bear she might—Charles!

Raven dashed to the window, ripping back the reed blinds, only to find the front grounds of the bungalow deserted. The torches still flickered on the drive, and far down by the gates she could see the dim outlines of the Ghurkas standing at rigid attention. A sob tore from her throat and she let the blinds fall back, pacing the room and wringing her hands in agitation.

"Miss Raven?"

Her head jerked up at the whisper which came from the locked door, and she hurried forward to lean against the thin wood. "Oh, Danny!" Her voice trembled with a mixture of agitation and relief.

"Master Phillip says you aren't feeling well. I thought I'd see how you were."

"Danny, please unlock the door," Raven begged.

"I can't." The old woman's voice sounded greatly concerned. "He's taken away the key. Miss Raven, what be happening here?"

Before she could answer, Raven heard the low voice of Ahmed, curt and disrespectful, followed by an unintelligible but thoroughly angry remark from her former governess. Ahmed's retort was made with equal heat, and then there was nothing but silence beyond the door.

"Danny?" Raven whispered, hands pressed against the wood, but there was no reply. She turned away, sick with fear, biting her lips to keep the tears from springing to her eyes. She felt as though she had been plummeted into an awful nightmare, yet the bolted door, Ahmed's presence in the corridor, and the bruises on her wrists where Phillip had gripped her so tightly were frighteningly real.

For what seemed like hours Raven paced without rest across the bare wooden floor of her room until she became aware that it had grown very still in the house. Music, laughter, and the muted murmur of conversation no longer filtered through her locked door, and she hurried to the window, drawing back the blinds in time to see the last high-wheeled gig vanish through the compound gates. The wind had picked up considerably in the past half-hour, and Raven shivered as a chilly blast rattled the panes, dry leaves scuttling across the ground outside.

A small cry of fear fell from her lips as the lock turned and the door swung wide, revealing Phillip Barrancourt's burly frame on the threshold. In the light of the single candle that burned on the nightstand he looked larger than ever and more ominous, his eyes red-rimmed, blond hair wild.

"I'm pleased that you were wise enough to follow my advice," he remarked, his voice slurred so that Raven knew at once he had been drinking heavily. She retreated around the bed when he came into the room, bringing a smile of pure amusement to his lips. "Are you afraid of me, Raven? How odd. I thought we were getting on splendidly." The smile vanished. "Or were you being pleasant only because you wanted that money from me?"

"Please," Raven begged in a whisper, "won't you tell me what it is you want with me?"

Phillip inclined his head obligingly. "Certainly. The explanation is quite simple. I'm a penniless bastard, Raven, not a single farthing to my name. I'm too destitute even to return home to Bombay."

"But Sir Hadrian—"

Phillip silenced her with a savage gesture. "I'll not have you mention my father's name again, is that understood? It's his fault entirely that I'm rotting away here in India!"

"He set you up in business," Raven countered, too shocked by his disclosure to heed his threat. "He said you were doing extremely well."

"And so I was," Phillip agreed harshly, "until—" He broke off and shook his head. "The reason doesn't matter. What does is that I had no way of working my way back into the good graces of the illustrious John Company." His voice was little better than a contemptuous sneer. "They all refused to extend my credit and give me another chance... until you came along. You, Raven, are the answer to everything."

"I don't understand," she whispered, moving further behind the bed.

Phillip's answering grin was unnervingly evil. "Don't you? They adored you tonight, Raven, and I don't doubt that with you as my wife that tight-fisted Sir Julian Craven will toady right up to me. You will be the ultimate weapon in my war for power, my dear, and by judiciously dangling you before the beds of a few pivotal individuals, I'll have my former authority back before long."

"You're mad!" Raven cried, her breast heaving. "You can't mean it! Sir Hadrian spoke so highly of you. I won't believe you'd be so cruel to me!"

"Father is a mindless dotard," Phillip said harshly, "and you'd better accept the fact that you will marry me, as soon as I can arrange for a minister to come here and perform the ceremony."

"No!" Raven cried. "You can't do this to me! Captain St. Germain will—"

In two swift strides Phillip crossed the area between them and seized Raven by the throat, effectively cutting off her air. "Your good captain won't do a thing to stop me," he said silkily, grinning fiendishly into her wide golden eyes. "The look on his face when I made that announcement tonight was enough to convince me that he's finished with you forever." He chuckled reminiscently. "One could almost pity the man. He looked as though someone had hit him between the eyes with a fighting iron."

Raven, struggling for breath, what with his enormous hands clenched about her windpipe, could make no reply, but the scorching hatred and fear in her eyes enraged Phillip. "St. Germain must mean something to you or you wouldn't have let him kiss you so passionately on my verandah." His tone grew rough. "You had better favor me that way, too, my tempting Raven, because ours will not be a marriage of mere convenience."

As he spoke he released his hold about her throat and jerked her abruptly against his wrinkled coat. Raven panicked when his lips came down on hers, his beard scratching her face, the scent of stale rum and wine overpowering. She fought like a caged tigress, kicking and scratching until Phillip released her, yelping in pain and covering his cheek where Raven's nails had left a ragged furrow.

"You little bitch!" he breathed, his blue eyes blazing. Turning around, he seized the batik wall hanging that hung over Raven's bed, yanking sharply so that it came crashing to the floor. Pulling free the long length of bamboo with which it had been hung, he turned on the cowering girl with demonic vengeance, the cane whistling through the air and landing with a stinging crack on Raven's bare shoulder.

At first Raven tried screaming, but that only appeared to incense him further, and so she bit her lips until she drew blood to keep silent while Phillip rained a half-dozen more blows upon her bowed and huddled form. Abruptly he stopped and stood looking down at her, breathing heavily with exertion. Raven held back her sobs, the smooth flesh along her back and shoulders dotted with blood and covered with ugly red welts.

"Let this be your first lesson in discipline," Phillip grated. "If you continue to misbehave, I swear it won't be your last." He retreated to the door, turned, and added ominously, "And I warn you to say nothing of this to your governess, Raven. You wouldn't want any harm to befall her, would you? I didn't think so," he added as Raven cried out fearfully. "I promise you I won't hurt her, and unless you continue to disobey I don't see why she can't remain ignorant of the entire situation." He cast a last contemptuous glance at her cowering form and laughed before locking the door behind him.

Raven remained in bed for the duration of the following day. She pleaded a lingering headache to the worried Danny, hoping bed rest might cure the painful welts on her back and shoulders before the older woman noticed them. In the sleepless hours of the previous night she had decided that she mustn't in any way jeopardize Danny's safety by refusing to cooperate with her cousin. Moreover, Danny must not learn of the horror that had befallen her, and Raven was grateful that so far Danny remained ignorant of Phillip's intentions to marry her and use her to regain his position of prominence in the East India Company.

Try as she might, she could not come up with a logical reason for the penury that had befallen Phillip. How could he have lost his entire fortune and his authority in the company without his father being aware of it, and what could have happened to turn such a highly thought-of individual into the monster he had been last night? Try as she might, Raven simply didn't understand enough of the situation to come up with a reasonable answer.

During the long day that followed, Lihl brought her meals to her on a tray, eyes downcast, never speaking, and Raven knew it would be useless to ask for help from Phillip's hostile servants. She was thankful when the sullen girl withdrew at last with each of her untouched meals, leaving her alone with her pain and tormented thoughts. Toward evening she was interrupted from her reverie by an insistent rapping on her door and the sound of her cousin's voice inquiring if she was awake. Raven lay still, her heart pounding, and could have wept with relief when he gave up soon enough and went away. Recalling his vicious beating of the night before and the promise he had made to bed her once they were married made the tears start anew in her eyes, and she cried herself at last into an uneasy sleep.

A pale, cold sun was high on the horizon when Raven finally awoke the next morning. Though her back and shoulders felt stiff and sore, she gritted her teeth and dressed, determined to find some way of escaping the prison Phillip Barrancourt had made for her. The numbing shock had faded and Raven felt much better, intending to see that she and Danny got away from

Khanapur compound safely and that Phillip paid for what he had done to her.

"Miss Raven?"

"Oh, please come in, Danny," she called out in as cheerful a tone as she could muster.

"Are you doing better today?" Danny inquired hopefully, bustling inside.

"I am," Raven assured her firmly. Glancing into the mirror, she hoped she sounded convincing, aware that she was very pale and that dark shadows lingered beneath her eyes. "I think the party was too much for me the other night."

"Humph!" Danny sniffed, unconvinced yet secretly pleased to see her young mistress up and about. "I don't know what the world will be comin' to, Miss Raven, if an eighteen-year-old girl finds dancing and dining too strenuous!"

"Oh, go on with you, Danny," Raven said with a laugh that, to her, sounded decidedly hollow. "I'm starving. Have I missed breakfast?"

"And most of tiffin," Danny added disapprovingly. "I declare, Miss Raven, you're growing thinner everyday. What young gentleman will look at you now? There, there, dearie," she added quickly, shocked when Raven reacted to her teasing with what sounded suspiciously like a strangled sob. "You're still feeling under the weather. Why don't you go back to bed and—"

"I can't," Raven said stubbornly, her youthful features stark. "I've things to do today and I've already wasted enough time."

"Missy-sahib will come to the dining room, please?"

Raven's heart constricted at Ahmed's request, the black-eyed Indian watching her keenly from the doorway. "Is my cousin expecting me there?" she asked nervously.

Ahmed appeared not to understand, or pretended not to, and repeated his request a second time. Raven gave him an irritable nod and squared her slender shoulders, ignoring the twinge of pain the movement brought. For all her outward appearances of bravery she felt sick with fear at the thought of laying eyes on her cousin again. What did he want from her now? Her steps faltered as she heard his deep laugh from the dining room, but when it was joined in by the amused voices of females, she quickened her pace and stepped into the enormous room. Her cousin, resplendently attired in a red silk coat with gold tassels, his thick beard neatly groomed, was presiding over tiffin with

Lady Amelia Craven and Sarah Broomfield in attendance. Raven would never have thought that she would feel so deeply relieved to have two gossipy older women at the table, but at the moment anything was better than dining alone with her cousin.

"Ah, there you are, Raven." Phillip rose to his feet at the sight of her, his tone cordial and warm. Raven shivered when he reached out to take her arm and deliberately stepped around him, bringing an answering scowl to his swarthy features.

"How nice to see you again, Miss Barrancourt," Lady Craven said with an expansive gesture of her bejeweled hand. "Your cousin was just telling us that you were indisposed yesterday with a headache."

"I'm feeling much better now," Raven assured her, seating herself as far away from her cousin as possible.

"Oh, wonderful!" Sarah Broomfield twittered. "Then you'll be able to come to Lahore with us this afternoon!"

"I don't think Raven should be about just yet," Phillip said sharply, his blue eyes holding a warning as they rested on Raven's oval face.

"I'd love to go," Raven responded coldly, her own challenging him. "I've never seen the city."

"We wanted to take you to the bazaars and the Badshahi Mosque," Mrs. Broomfield explained, biting into a ripened papaya. "And Shalimar is lovely, even this time of year."

"I don't see any reason why I can't go with you," Raven insisted.

"Perhaps you should," Phillip agreed unexpectedly. "But I think it would be a good idea if Mrs. Daniels remained here. Lady Craven's ekka is extremely small."

"Oh, you're quite right, Mr. Barrancourt," Lady Craven said firmly, adding in a conspiratorial whisper, although Danny was not present in the dining room, "Besides, it simply isn't proper to drag your servants with you everywhere you go."

"Exactly," Phillip agreed, sitting back in his chair, a satisfied smile playing on his lips.

Raven could feel her heart hammering in her breast. It wasn't because the carriage was too small or because Danny was a mere servant that made Phillip suggest she remain behind. It was his way of telling her that she had better not try anything foolish—like escaping or going to someone for help—while Danny remained an unwitting hostage at the compound. Raven could have wept with frustration because that had been exactly what she had had in mind, but how could she hope to accomplish anything with Phillip making it so plain to her that Danny's safety was in jeopardy?

"You'd better eat something before you go," Phillip was saying in a tone that contained nothing but the greatest concern for her. "Lihl told me you ate nothing at all yesterday."

"I'm not hungry," Raven replied with downcast eyes, then told herself that it would be in her best interest to keep up her strength. Danny had mentioned that she was growing thin and it was true, she did feel rather weak. If she was going to lock horns with her strong, burly cousin, she had better do her best to stay healthy. While Lady Craven and Mrs. Broomfield chattered, Raven ate, swallowing the fresh fruits and honeyed confections although she had no appetite for them at all The milky tea which her cousin was so fond of drinking made her feel nauseated but she drank it nonetheless, and when she finished Lady Craven suggested they go.

"Am I properly dressed?" Raven asked with what she hoped was a suitable display of mindless female worry. She didn't want anyone to know how important this outing was to her and that, regardless of Phillip's threats, she intended to find some way to rescue Danny and herself from this terrible predicament.

"Fetching as always," Phillip remarked, his eyes lingering on her rounded bosom encased in heavy white muslin with a forest-green pattern imprinted along the bodice and full skirts.

Raven shivered and turned away, distractedly accepting her fur-trimmed cloak from Ahmed, who had appeared in the doorway. Despite her misery she felt an enormous sense of relief as the ekka bearing herself and her older companions bowled through the compound gates. She was free for a time, and God forbid that someone should try to stop her from seeking help in Lahore. Glancing at Lady Craven and Mrs. Broomfield, who were talking animatedly together, Raven dismissed the possibility of enlisting their aid. Penniless as he might be, Phillip Barrancourt appeared to be enormously popular with his friends, and she sensed that neither of the two ladies would believe a word of what she would tell them about him. In truth Raven found it difficult to believe herself, for she had thought her cousin so kind and personable when she first met him. His mood changes were swift and, as she well knew by now, extremely dangerous.

Yet how could she and Danny have been forewarned when even his closest associates seemed unaware of them? Why, even Sir Hadrian, Phillip's father, had known nothing of the awesome hardships that had befallen his son. Raven swallowed hard. Gone, too, was the chance of obtaining the money she needed to save North Head. Her throat grew tight at the thought and tears misted her vision. Don't, she whispered to herself, don't think about that now. The most important thing at the moment was for them to get away from Khanapur compound, before Phillip beat her again or, worse, before he tried to make love to her.

"Miss Barrancourt, are you certain you're recovered?" Lady Craven inquired worriedly, catching sight of Raven's pale face beneath the brim of her small hat, a pearl-studded expanse of trim green netting obscuring her glittering golden eyes.

"I'm fine," Raven assured her in an unconvincingly shaky voice.

"Perhaps we should take you back," Mrs. Broomfield suggested. "We can always visit Lahore another time."

"No!" Raven herself heard the note of hysteria in her voice and struggled to bring it under control. "I couldn't possibly wait," she said with a weak laugh. "I've been so eager to see it."

Both ladies appeared mollified by her words. Sitting primly with gloved hands in her lap, Mrs. Broomfield remarked slyly that a young bride-to-be should certainly be interested in the many beautiful cloths one could purchase in the city, materials that should prove quite beautiful for a wedding gown.

"I must admit Phillip's announcement took us all by surprise," Lady Craven added, unaware of the effect their words were having on the pale young woman seated at Mrs. Broomfield's side. "He never mentioned to any of us that you were coming from England to marry him, and everyone knows how much Phillip prefers his single existence."

"Of course, now that we've seen you, Miss Barrancourt, we're not in the least surprised that your cousin decided to forgo bachelorhood," Sarah Broomfield added quickly, beaming at her.

"That's very kind of you," Raven murmured, and both older

women took her averted eyes and flaming cheeks for modest embarrassment.

"If you'll take a look over your shoulder, Miss Barrancourt," Lady Craven remarked briskly, changing the subject, "you'll see the walls of Fort Ackbar there on the hill. Is Brigade Major Broomfield there today, Sarah?"

"I imagine so," Mrs. Broomfield remarked irritably. "Drew hasn't been home at all since the Sikhs went to war. I wish they'd forget all this nonsense about autonomy and go about their business as they did before! We left the maharani her palace when we marched in, didn't we?"

"Oh, heavens, yes!" Lady Craven agreed with a sour expression. "You'd think that was quite enough to satisfy the heathens!"

Raven regarded the older women with astonishment. Apparently both of them viewed the Sikh uprising as little more than an annoying inconvenience. Didn't they realize that one battle had already been fought, with numerous British casualties, and that another would probably happen before long? If anything Geoffrey Lytton had ever told her about the proud, warlike Sikhs was to be believed, they were far more dangerous adversaries than Mrs. Broomfield and Lady Craven liked to think.

She forgot her sobering thoughts as the ekka left the crowded wagon road and turned onto a wide city boulevard that was lush and beautiful despite the chill of winter. Palm trees lined the thoroughfares, and buildings with intricate gatework faced one another along the streets. Raven noticed that some of the natives wore attire similar to their counterparts in Bombay but that many of the women wore trousers instead of saris. All of them, however, observed strict purdah, their faces concealed, and some of them even moved through traffic wearing bourkas, heavy, shroudlike capes that covered them from head to toe and left only a slit or webbing for the eyes.

Old men with stained beards and henna-smeared hands offered their wares or worked their trades along the street corner, while beggars sat cross-legged and puffed their hubble-bubbles, the traditional Indian water pipes. Occasionally a pair of Pathans strode past the ekka, tall and burly, some of them with blue eyes and fair skin. Raven was most interested in the Sikhs, however, who wore their beards long, their uncut dark hair concealed under yards of dyed cloth wrapped into turbans. All of them looked fierce and aggressive, and she shivered, recalling Charles's warning to beware of them.

Charles! Raven felt her heart leap with hope. Dmitri and Charles were staying somewhere in this teeming city, and if she could find them she knew for certain they wouldn't hesitate to rescue her and Danny. In fact, Charles was their only hope, for Raven knew there was no sense in appealing to the British officers at Fort Ackbar for help. Phillip had powerful friends among the military and would easily convince them that his future bride was suffering from delusions or simple nervousness stemming from the excitement of the pending wedding. Raven's soft lips tightened. Oh yes, he was clever, but she would rather be dead than married to him, and she had no intention of giving up without a struggle.

"Look, Miss Barrancourt, the Badshahi Mosque!"

Lady Craven's words roused Raven from her reverie, and she forgot Phillip and even Charles as the magnificent sandstone and marble mosque came into view. Huge white domes rose high into the sky, flanked on all sides by towering minarets. The entire structure was connected by graceful fortresslike walls that stretched far off into the distance and encompassed, she saw as the vehicle approached, a courtyard of immense proportions. The mosque's very size was enough to intimidate anyone, and the architectural beauty of its gardens and dome-topped prayer chamber took her breath away. The ekka deposited the three of them before one of the enormous gates, where they stood watching the never-ending procession of Moslems stream inside.

"It's one of the largest mosques in the world," Lady Craven told the wide-eyed Raven. "Only the Taj Mahal impressed me more than this. There's a depository inside that contains relics of Mohammed himself."

"Can we go inside?" Raven asked eagerly.

"We can take a quick walk through the gardens," Mrs. Broomfield suggested.

With the pale December sun upon them, the three Englishwomen joined the throng of natives strolling down the well-tended walkways, while Raven stared about her in wonder. Most of the Moslems who had come to pray ignored them, and she detected no hostility in the few faces that turned their way.

"During the festival of Eid al-Fitr you can't get anywhere near the city," Lady Craven explained as they wandered across the wide courtyard. "Moslems from all over the Punjab and beyond come here to say their prayers. It's always a good idea, isn't it, Sarah, to stay away when so many peasants are abroad."

"Indeed it is," Mrs. Broomfield agreed heartily. "Don't you think we should take Miss Barrancourt to Shalimar Gardens before it gets too late? Seeing as you like to walk," she added, turning to Raven, "I think you'll find them lovely. There are marble pavilions and hundreds of fountains."

"Oh, I'd like that very much," Raven agreed, sensing that the two older women felt decidedly uncomfortable mingling with the religious Moslems in the courtyard of the mosque.

With apparent relief Lady Craven led them back toward the gate where their carriage waited, but there they found their path impeded by a huge crowd that had gathered before the two-story arch, blocking it completely. Above their heads a lone figure in billowing white stood on a parapet, thin arms raised in supplication to the heavens, his voice rising in loud, angry denouncement. Looking up, Raven saw that his beard was dyed bright orange and his mouth was stained scarlet from chewing betel, and although he seemed very old and frail, his ringing words carried easily through the chilly air.

"Oh dear," Lady Craven exclaimed, catching sight of him, "it's another of those subversive fakirs. I don't think we should go any closer."

"What is he doing?" Raven asked, her curiosity aroused by the impassioned monologue and the fervent response of the crowd.

"Preaching against the British," Lady Craven replied nervously, and Raven glanced at her quickly to see that she had grown pale beneath her rouge and that her fingers were wrapped convulsively about her shawl.

"He's a religious mendicant," Mrs. Broomfield explained, seeming far less unnerved than her companion. "He tells the crowd anything they want to hear, and then they toss him a few coins for his trouble."

"But what is he saying?" Raven persisted, intrigued but not

frightened by the palpable tension in the air.

Mrs. Broomfield looked uncomfortable. "Some nonsense about the time having come to drive the British usurpers from the Punjab forever. He's urging every citizen to rise against us and vanquish—"

"Please, I think we better go," Lady Craven insisted. "The native rabble allows itself to be swayed too easily."

The three of them turned away, only to find that a fresh group of observers had closed in from behind, trapping them amid a crush of people who, at a sign from the fakir high above, raised their arms and began shouting wildly. Lady Craven, close to panic, began to push her way free, her anxiety increasing when it became obvious that the press of bodies prevented them from doing so. Raven, following close behind, realized that they were in no immediate danger, for the crowd was not hostile, merely animated, and yet Lady Craven's obvious distress was infectious.

A deafening roar went up as the fakir shouted a resounding promise of victory, and the crowd surged forward to get closer to him. Lady Craven screamed as she was carried along by the crush, while Raven, her heart pounding, pushed her way forward to help. Someone stepped on her ruffled hem, ripping it, and she stumbled and nearly fell, but before she could go down amid hundreds of trampling feet she was grabbed from behind and jerked upright. A muscular arm slid about her waist and she found herself held against a wide, protective chest while Lady Craven and Mrs. Broomfield were pulled along in her rescuer's wake.

"Are you all right, Raven?"

She looked up as they broke free of the crowd to find Charles St. Germain's handsome face above hers, his green eyes roving her pale face beneath the crooked brim of her hat, his expression forbidding. "I-I think so," she murmured.

"Oh, captain, I'm so very grateful to you!" Lady Craven cried, fanning herself vigorously with her gloves. "We could have been trampled to death!"

"You're lucky I came along when I did," Charles agreed harshly, regarding Raven with a look that snuffed out the joy burning in her heart at seeing him. "Where are your servants? Shouldn't they have been protecting you?"

"We didn't come with any," Sarah Broomfield explained. "There was really no need for them."

"No need?" Charles repeated grimly. "Don't you ladies understand anything about the current situation? You shouldn't be in the city at all!"

"Really, Captain St. Germain," Mrs. Broomfield said frostily, trying to regain her composure in the face of Charles's intimidating anger, "you've no right to speak to us in such a tone!"

"I have every right." His voice grated, the look on his handsome face quelling the older woman to silence. "Now I suggest you get back into your carriage and return to your homes immediately."

"Perhaps we should, Sarah," Lady Craven agreed, less inclined to take offense at the handsome sea captain's rudeness. Unlike her companion, she had been in India during the massacre of Kabul and had never forgotten the violence that heathen ranks were capable of. "Come along, Miss Barrancourt."

"I'll be there in a moment," Raven informed them, and such was Lady Craven's haste to return to the safety of her carriage that she willingly left Raven unescorted in the company of a man, a breach of etiquette she would never have permitted otherwise.

Raven had forgotten her companions, the crowds, and the fakir, and nothing mattered to her at the moment except Charles. Though his green eyes were unnervingly cold, his handsome visage forbidding, she smiled up at him, her eyes shining. "Oh, Charles, thank God you found me!"

"I've no time for amenities, Raven," he said sharply. "What is it you wanted to say to me?"

Raven retreated a step, momentarily unnerved by his palpable anger. "If it's the engagement announcement Phillip made the other night," she said at last, her expression clearing, "I can explain why he—"

"Do you think that's bothering me?" Charles demanded contemptuously. "Not at all. I must admit it was rather unexpected, but then I should have remembered what a deceitful little liar you are."

Raven's delicate countenance filled with doubt. She had borne the brunt of Charles's awesome anger before, and yet his behavior today disturbed her, for it was different, a remote and hateful indifference she couldn't understand. "What are you talking about?" she whispered, totally bewildered.

Charles turned away as though he could no longer bear the sight of her small, questioning face behind the lacy netting of her hat, his gaze roving restlessly over the dispersing crowd of chattering Moslems. "You should have told me right away that you were traveling to the Punjab to be married, Raven," he said after a moment, his hard, final voice sending a chill down her spine. "There was nothing to be ashamed of, after all. Thousands of penniless young girls are foisted off onto wealthy older relations abroad every year. You didn't have to evoke my sympathy or that of my crew by telling wild tales of your noble mission of mercy."

"Oh, Charles!" Raven cried, distraught, afraid that Phillip's engagement announcement had hurt him badly.

"Stay where you are!" Charles commanded as she made a move to touch him. His visage was so black that Raven froze instantly, her outstretched hand falling uselessly to her side. "I want nothing more to do with you, Raven Barrancourt," he said, her name sounding like a curse as it fell from his lips. "In the past you've bedeviled me, bewitched my crew, and caused me more hardship than I've ever dreamed possible. I won't be a total imbecile and deny I had feelings for you, because I must have." His eyes were upon her now, their emerald depths colder than the sea. "If so, I can't remember them now, so it doesn't really matter, does it? My congratulations on your pending marriage, Miss Barrancourt. You and your greedy, grasping cousin suit each other admirably."

Raven stood stock-still, the contempt in his words lashing her. Never in her young life had she felt so hated, so abandoned. All the love she felt for Charles had been flung back in her face, the pain of betrayal more cruel than any she had ever known. She opened her mouth to speak but found that she could not; she was all but paralyzed by the force of his rejection.

In the lean, handsome face above hers a muscle twitched wildly, then Charles turned wordlessly and strode off through the crowd. Her numbness abruptly gone, Raven uttered a hoarse cry and started after him. It was no use. Impeded by her torn skirts, her vision blurred by the tears that coursed down her cheeks, she quickly lost him in the massive courtyard. When she saw that it was hopeless she stopped, face buried in her hands as she wept, the despair of having lost him far more painful than the knowledge that she would have to confront her cousin when she returned home.

Chapter Twelve

In the winding streets below the small terrace all was quiet. Hucksters, vendors, and tradesmen had packed up their wares long ago, and in the glimmering twilight the booths stood dark and deserted. The square, which only a few hours ago had been filled with laughing spectators watching a dancing camel perform, was empty as well, and only the beggars on the doorsteps and the pi dogs in the gutters were left to face the coming darkness. The air was frosty, the north wind gusting, but the terrace was sheltered by its low sandstone wall so that its single occupant could sit comfortably and hum to himself as he looked over the sprawling rooftops of Lahore.

Life was good, Dmitri Zergeyev was thinking to himself. Life was lusty, amusing, satisfying, and never tiresome. If he had his own way he'd be aboard the *Orient Star* right now, leaning into the wind while he clung, grinning wildly, to the yards high above the deck, the ocean surging far below. But that wasn't possible with the clipper so far away, so he was content to settle for the next-best thing: sitting on a terrace with a bottle of rum at his elbow, the minarets and rooftops of a darkening Indian city before him, and the fabled Kohinoor diamond awaiting him in Oudh. Tomorrow morning he would be continuing the hunt for it that had begun half a world away in England, but for now he was content to sit and ruminate, wondering how his little princess was faring and deciding on the setting for the emeralds he would buy her when he won his fortune.

Aye, life was grand, but, as always, bittersweet. In gaining something of value one never failed to lose something in return, and Dmitri had to admit to himself that the friendship of Charles St. Germain was a very bitter thing to lose. Not that it had been by choice, Kristos, no! But how could one remain friends with a man who was like a spirit possessed, pacing sleeplessly about his room until dawn and exhibiting a violence of temper that was frightening to behold? Had the captain's vicious behavior been caused by the announcement—which Dmitri himself couldn't accept as true—that Raven Barrancourt was to marry her cousin?

Perhaps, yet when Dmitri had asked, Charles had in no uncertain terms ended their friendship by informing his first mate—former first mate, Dmitri reminded himself—that his services aboard the *Orient Star* were no longer required and that he might as well ship off for Oudh in the morning. Not being one to beg, Dmitri had withdrawn with a curt nod and had cushioned the blow of Charles's dismissal with a generous padding of rum. Now, as he sat in blissful comfort on a richly upholstered pillow with gold tassels, he raised the bottle in flippant farewell to his erstwhile captain and closest friend. Why cling to the past? Dmitri asked himself with good common sense. Ever since they had begun their journey up the Indus, Charles had alienated him, become a stranger, and if he chose to ruin his life now by eschewing that which lay closest to his heart, it was his own God-rotting fault.

"I'll play nursemaid no longer," Dmitri muttered to himself, the hurt he felt carefully hidden by anger and liberally softened by the numbing haze into which he had drunk himself. Aye, he would make his own fortune by finding the Kohinoor, and then he would return, wealthy, untouchable, a true deserver of his birthright, and he would beat Captain St. Germain senseless if by that time the arrogant sod hadn't mended his foolish ways.

Dmitri chuckled, the idea appealing to him immensely. Belching loudly, he wiped his mouth with the back of his hand and stretched his long arms lazily over his head. Aye, life was grand, and far easier to deal with when one finally decided not to worry any longer about problems that had been dogging one relentlessly.

"To life!" Dmitri muttered, and emptied the contents of his bottle before dashing it against the balustrade, where it exploded into thousands of shattered fragments, the sound and violence of it pleasing him.

"Sahib?"

"Aye, what is it?" Dmitri whirled, scowling irritably, the expression on his bearded face causing poor Hakim to cower back into the recesses of the room behind him. "Well?" Dmitri demanded when no answer was forthcoming. "What reason do you have for bothering me now, you worthless, sheet-wearing excuse for a dog?"

"This servant regrets to bother the sahib, but there is an Angrezi lady to see him downstairs."

Dmitri's coal-black eyes widened. "What? A lady? Show her up, Hakim! Why did you leave her standing in the darkness?"

The servant scurried off, and Dmitri cursed beneath his breath, adjusting his rumpled attire and rubbing his drink-reddened eyes with his fists. Hearing voices inside the house, he left the terrace and found Hannah Daniels, wrapped in a warm cloak, staring about her at the opulent room. The tapers were lit, softly reflecting the rich colors of the tapestries and hangings, the brass ornaments gleaming. Dmitri saw at once that the wrinkles on the round face had deepened since he had last seen her, and she seemed to have grown thinner.

"What a pleasant surprise!" he exclaimed heartily, coming forward to take both her hands in his. "How have you been, Mrs. Daniels? Did you bring little Raven with you? No," he answered himself, his eyes sliding past Danny's stooped shoulders, "I can see that you didn't." He regarded her fondly. "Why have you come? It's growing late and—"

"Oh, please, Mr. Zergeyev!" Danny burst out, "I must see Captain St. Germain at once! Is he here?"

"Indeed I am, Danny."

They both turned as the door swung wide and Charles strode into the room, his chestnut curls disheveled, his handsome features grim. Pulling off his gloves and coat, he tossed them aside and motioned to the hovering Hakim to take them away. Coming to a halt directly before the elderly woman, he stood staring down into her pale face, his hands propped on his lean hips. "You wanted to see me?"

"It's about Miss Raven," Danny began, but Charles held up a hand to silence her.

"I saw her this afternoon," he told her harshly, "and doubtless she failed to inform you that I made it quite clear to her that I will no longer concern myself with her welfare."

"Kristos!" Dmitri muttered beneath his breath. He should have known that Charles's volatile mood earlier today had had something to do with their raven-haired beauty.

Charles shot him a sour glance, then turned back to Danny, who was nervously twisting her plump hands together. "If you've come here at her request to mend our differences, I can assure you that—"

"I came on my own," Danny interrupted with more courage than she felt, trembling as she gazed up into the forbidding visage. "I couldn't bear it any longer with the way she was crying and that horrible man beating her like there was no end to it!" She tried to say more, but her words ended on a choked sob and she began to weep silently, the tears coursing down her weathered cheeks, her graying head bowed.

Charles's expression changed abruptly and he shot Dmitri a probing glance from beneath knitted brows before leading Danny gently to a nearby settee. Though his manner was solicitous enough as he towered over her, Dmitri could see the tensing of his lean jaw and knew that he was exerting considerable effort to hold his impatience in check.

"Why was Raven crying, Danny?" Charles demanded. "And who was beating her?"

Danny tried to speak, but the sobs grew more uncontrollable. Striding to the door, Charles pulled it open and roared an order to Hakim, who appeared a moment later, eyes bulging with terror, a liberally filled brandy snifter in his shaking hands. Slamming the door shut in the startled servant's face, Charles returned to the settee and ordered Danny to drink the dark, fragrant liquid.

"Oh no, captain, I couldn't!" Danny protested feebly. "I never touch spirits!"

"You did a fine job on my Madeira the night we all dined together in my quarters aboard the *Orient Star*," Charles reminded her, his full lips twitching. The green eyes were gentle as they met hers, and Danny accepted the offered glass, drinking dutifully and sputtering as the fiery liquid seared her throat. The coughing and tears ceased simultaneously, and Charles, taking the empty snifter from her, repeated softly, "Who beat Raven, Danny? Was it her cousin?"

Danny's lower lip trembled but she managed to control herself this time. "He did it with bamboo, captain. She was locked in her room, but I could hear the blows. She didn't scream, the poor little duck, but the whimpers—" She put her shaking hands to her hot cheeks. "I'll never forget them as long as I live."

"Why?" Dmitri demanded hoarsely, pushing his way forward. "Why was he hitting her?"

Charles was startled by the angry accusation in Danny's eyes as she stared at him from the settee. "Because she saw you in the mosque today, captain. Lady Craven said that you'd saved them from some sort of mob, but Master Phillip seemed to think something else had happened between you and Miss Raven, and he—he punished her for it."

Charles inhaled deeply, battling with his entire great strength to control himself. "Why don't you start from the beginning, Danny?" he asked softly. "Why would Phillip Barrancourt beat his fiancée for accidentally meeting me in a crowded mosque?"

"That's just it, captain!" Danny cried. "She's not his fiancée! At least, she never agreed to marry him! He be forcing her into it!" Lowering her head, she twisted her hands together in her lap, forcing herself to explain the situation calmly. "Master Phillip was very kind to both of us when we first arrived. I thought him a little strange and Raven did, too, but not in a bad way, really."

"In what way, then?" Charles inquired impatiently.

Danny shrugged her rounded shoulders. "Just that he spent all his time locked away in that messy study of his, and when he did come out to talk to us you always had the feeling he was never really there. It's hard to explain," she added, looking up into Charles's handsome face appealingly. "Like his head was in the clouds most of the time."

"I think I understand," he told her slowly. "Was there ever any evidence that he was burning anything in his study?"

Danny nodded. "Oh yes, he burned incense all day long. I thought it smelled terrible, but I couldn't complain, not as a guest in his house."

Charles and Dmitri exchanged brief glances. *Metyeryebets,* Dmitri thought grimly to himself, his alcoholic haze dissipating completely. There is danger indeed for our little princess if her cousin is addicted to opium.

"Go on, Danny," Charles urged in the same deceptively soft tone.

Danny glanced at him helplessly. "There isn't much else to tell, captain. He was kind, he agreed to give Miss Raven the money she needed to save North Head, and then told her he would give her a dinner party in her honor, too. I was thrilled for the little dear and she looked so beautiful in her gown. Oh, but surely you must remember that, Captain St. Germain. You were there."

"I was." Charles's expression softened for a moment before a terrible urgency settled over him. "Please hurry, Danny. What else is there to tell me?"

"I didn't find out until tonight," Danny went on quickly, "but Master Phillip made an announcement during dinner that Miss Raven was to marry him. Right after that he locked her into her room and told everyone she had a headache. I tried to see her, but they told me to leave her alone. I didn't know," she went on, tears of shame welling in her eyes. "I didn't know that he had already beaten her once and threatened to hurt me, too, if she told me anything. That be why he made me stay in the compound when Lady Craven and Mrs. Broomfield took Miss Raven to Lahore today. He was holding me just like a hostage, to make sure Miss Raven wouldn't try to run away."

"So that's what she wanted to tell me," Charles said almost to himself, the naked self-loathing in his green eyes piercing Dmitri to his very soul. "And I never gave her the chance. She seemed so glad to see me, and free of cares. I didn't realize."

"When she came back," Danny continued shakily as Charles fell silent, turning away and wearily massaging the back of his neck, "Master Phillip found out she'd seen you. He was sure she'd asked you for help. That be when he started beating her, captain, and I couldn't speak to her until this evening because her door was locked and guarded. After it got dark I went out on the verandah and whispered to her through the window. The poor thing was still crying and I just couldn't bear it anymore. That be why I came to fetch you."

"How did you get here?" Dmitri asked curiously.

"I took one of the compound horses," Danny explained. "I haven't ridden since I was a young girl, but under the circumstances—"

"You did a brave, brave thing," Dmitri told her gravely, taking her shaking hands in his huge paws and squeezing them reassuringly.

"Will you help her?" Danny whispered, her reddened eyes moving to Charles, who still stood with his broad back to them.

"I be so afraid for her. She told me that Phillip lost all of his money and that he wants to use her once they're married to win it back."

"How?" Dmitri demanded.

"Miss Raven wouldn't tell me," Danny whispered. "I pleaded with her, but she said it was too horrible—"

She broke off in confusion as Charles wheeled abruptly and started for the door. Instantly Dmitri was behind him, but Charles turned on him with the force of a snarling tiger. "Stay here, Dmitri. This is my affair."

The big Russian shrugged his massive shoulders. "It would seem to me that I am a free man now and don't have to take orders from you anymore."

The smoldering green eyes met the unwavering black ones for a tense moment, then Charles relaxed visibly and slapped him on the back. "Let's go."

"Don't you worry, madam," Dmitri added with a roguish grin in Danny's direction. "We'll rescue our little princess for you. If you're hungry, speak to Hakim. He's a worthless beggar, but his English is good."

In the utter darkness of her room Raven sat on the edge of her unmade bed and tried not to wonder what had happened to Danny. Though Phillip thought the elderly woman was sound asleep in her bed, Raven had seen her ride out of the compound gates nearly two hours ago. Visions of an attack by roving budmarshes or a fall from the horse tormented her, and she dashed the tears from her eyes, telling herself she was being ridiculous. Yet she knew that if any harm did befall the loyal old woman it would be her fault, and Raven coudn't bear the thought any more than the haunting fear that Danny wouldn't be able to find Charles and persuade him to come back with her.

Raven rose from the bed and walked stiffly to the window, her body bruised and aching. She had had no choice but to agree to let Danny ride for Charles, the only one she trusted enough to help her out of this dilemma. Phillip's rage after her return from Lahore had convinced Raven he was mad, and the beating he had given her as insurance against future disobedience had made her fear for her life. She shivered and drew her cloak around her with shaking fingers and was thankful that Phillip had retired to his bedroom several hours ago. She had decided as she lay weeping on her bed that she would wait until midnight for Danny to return, and if that failed to happen, she would try to escape herself.

It was fear for the elderly woman's safety that prompted her into action, and she turned from the window, straining her eyes in the darkness to read the shadowed hands of the clock nearby. It was nearly eleven, and Raven knew that she could stand the strain of worry no longer. She had packed a few of her belongings earlier by the light of the moon that cast its pale light onto the compound grounds, but now she decided reluctantly that it would only hinder her progress if she was forced to drag a bulky valise with her.

She caught her breath as the window frame creaked alarmingly in response to her insistent tugging, aware that Ahmed would probably be standing guard outside her door. Thank God Phillip hadn't thought to station Hammad on the verandah or she would never have been able to get word to Danny or try to slip out now!

The window refused to budge. Raven gritted her teeth and tried again, straining with all her might against the wood, her arms aching. When her strength failed, she leaned her hot cheek against the cool pane, trying to catch her breath while she fumbled with the latch. Her trembling fingers encountered a jagged splinter on the frame and she looked up quickly, searching along the length of it and straining her eyes in the darkness. Clouds had gathered over the heavens during the past few hours, obscuring the moon, and Raven could not at first see in the utter darkness what was the matter with the window. When the truth dawned on her at last she turned away, a sob of helplessness and despair choking her throat. Sometime during her absence that afternoon Phillip must have ordered her window nailed shut.

How was she to escape? Raven asked herself, near panic. Even if she managed to break the panes of glass without rousing Phillip from his sleep, she would never be able to squeeze between the narrow wooden mullions. She was furious with herself when the tears began again, running hot down her hollow cheeks, the racking sobs coming unchecked although she bit down hard on her lower lip to control them. She threw herself face down on the bed, oblivious to the pain in her bruised body, crying uncontrollably and aching forlornly for the comforting arms of Charles St. Germain about her.

"Sniveling again, are you? I thought I'd cured you of that."

Raven uttered a small cry of fear and rolled over quickly as the door crashed open, revealing Phillip Barrancourt's burly frame on the threshold, a gutted candle flickering in his hand. She pressed herself against the wall, tawny eyes wide and luminous as he advanced to the corner of the bed and stood looking down at her contemptuously. Seeing the velvet cloak about her slender body, a cruel smile curved his lips.

"Surely you weren't thinking of escaping, my dear?" he asked nastily.

"I was cold," Raven whispered, her heart thundering in terror, certain that he was going to beat her again.

Phillip glanced down at his own loose-fitting trousers, which were made of thin muslin and, as the sputtering candlelight revealed, were none too clean. "Odd. I don't find it cold in the house." The blue eyes bored into her. "Why don't you speak the truth, you worthless wench? You were trying to escape, weren't you?"

"Yes!" Raven blazed at him, goaded into defiance by fear. "I may not succeed tonight, but Judas, I swear one day I shall and you'll pay for what you've done to me!"

"I see I haven't succeeded in breaking your spirit after all," Phillip mused, ignoring her outburst, his attention caught instead by Raven's heaving breasts, encased in the velvet folds of her cloak. Her long black hair was unbound and hung in a wild cascade down her slender shoulders and back, her eyes glittering like a caged tigress's in the flickering light. "Perhaps another lesson might convince you of my superiority," he added. Seeing her cower back into the corner, he smiled wickedly. "Oh, don't worry, my dear, I won't mar that perfect body of yours again with the cane. No, this time I have something else in mind."

Raven nervously licked her dry lips. "Wh-what do you mean?"

"I don't think," Phillip began, setting the candle aside and bending down to remove his worn slippers, "that our acquaintances will object overly to the fact that I won't be marrying a virgin."

Raven buried her face in her hands, sobbing uncontrollably as Phillip unfastened the strings of his trousers. Suddenly he froze, cocking his head as if listening, and Raven, looking up, also heard the sound of heavy footsteps pounding up the verandah steps. Before Phillip could react she had scrambled across the bed, nearly tripping over her skirts, and was running down the corridor screaming. The front door burst open, nearly knocking her down, but Raven saw only the familiar towering form that loomed on the threshold before she fell, sobbing, into Charles's outstretched arms.

"Raven, Raven," he murmured into her hair as she clung to him, his voice hoarse with emotion. "Did the swine hurt you badly?"

She lifted her head from the soft, clean-smelling front of his shirt, and Charles could plainly see the dark bruise beginning to discolor her cheek where Phillip's bamboo cane had missed her shoulder. His lips tightened ominously, and a dull rage began to burn in his eyes. Lights suddenly sprang on in the adjoining dining room, and Raven gasped when she saw Phillip and his servants standing menacingly in the doorway, her cousin carrying a lethal Chinese fighting iron in his big hands.

"Get out of my house, St. Germain," Phillip commanded in a low voice.

Charles gently detached himself from Raven's grasp and put her behind him, motioning curtly to Dmitri, who loomed from the darkness to stand protectively beside her. Neither of them could help noticing how skillfully Phillip Barrancourt wrapped the leather thong of the fighting iron about his wrist. Ahmed and Hammad stood behind their master, their bony features tensed, dark eyes watchful.

"Get out," Phillip repeated icily.

"I will," Charles replied, equally cold, "but not until I thrash you within an inch of your life, you sniveling woman-beater."

"You'll die for that, St. Germain," Phillip growled low in his throat, his hands closing convulsively about his weapon.

"I imagine you're too much of a coward to make good that threat unarmed," Charles remarked casually, his lack of fear infuriating Phillip.

"Not at all," the older man grated, "but since I intend to kill you with this," he held up the fighting iron, "what's the sense in laying it aside? My men can easily handle your Russian friend there, too."

"Can they?" Charles asked arrogantly, eyebrows raised. "Perhaps you may kill me with that weapon, Barrancourt, but you'll not subdue both of us. Dmitri could take on a half-dozen more of you if he chose." The emerald eyes gleamed. "And he's extremely adept at snapping necks in two. Even a thick one like yours."

Ahmed and Hammad, seeing the deadly menace in the glittering devil's eyes, glanced at one another uneasily, and Phillip, sensing their fear, turned his head to berate them fiercely. It was the opening Charles needed. Moving forward with incredible speed, he brought his hand down hard on Phillip's wrist, causing the fighting iron to fly from his grasp and sending it smashing to the floor at Dmitri's feet. Stooping quickly, the big Russian snatched it up and gave Charles a wide grin.

"Well done, tovarich!"

Charles ignored him, his green eyes boring into Phillip's, his handsome visage black and forbidding. "I promised you I'd thrash you soundly," he snarled, spreading his long legs in a fighting stance. "What are you waiting for?"

"Do you expect me to attack you bare-handed?" Phillip demanded contemptuously.

"Are you afraid?" Charles taunted, "or too much of a gentleman to settle the score the way our good English farmers do?" He held up his awesome-looking fists. "With these."

"Done!" Phillip roared. "By God, St. Germain, I'll relish the feel of your bloody flesh beneath my hands!"

"If you'll give me a moment, then," Charles said, sketching a mocking bow. Nonchalantly he removed his vest and dusty boots, stripping down to his shirtsleeves while Phillip doffed his wrinkled nightshirt and stood before him bared to the waist. His muscular chest was covered with thick red hairs, his skin gleaming with sweat, and he rubbed his enormous hands together, grinning wickedly.

"Every man enjoys a little pugilism now and then, St. Germain. By God, I'm going to enjoy disfiguring your goddamned good-looking face!"

"Dmitri, I don't understand any of this," Raven whimpered as the big Russian pushed her protectively into a corner. "Why doesn't Charles just take us away from here? Why does he have to play games?"

"It's not a game, little one," Dmitri assured her grimly, having seen the look in Charles's eyes when Raven had lifted her bruised and tearful face to his in the darkness. "There's a score to be settled, and neither one of them will back down now."

Raven bit her lip as Phillip took the first swing, the breath rushing from his lungs with the force of it, but Charles countered neatly, blocking him with one arm and swinging with the other. The blow caught Phillip full in the face, staggering him, and when he righted himself he was bleeding heavily from the nose, his beard stained an even darker red. Feinting with his right hand, he managed to catch Charles unexpectedly with the left, but the tall sea captain darted nimbly aside so that the force of it landed on his jaw, bringing a howl of pain from Phillip as his hand connected unexpectedly with hard bone.

Both men seemed to realize at the same time that the other would not be defeated as easily as had been expected. More cautiously they squared off again, bodies tensing, each waiting for the other to make the first move. It was Charles who struck unexpectedly, his long leg lashing out and hooking itself around Phillip's calf, sending him crashing to the floor. Instantly the dark-headed Englishman was upon him, wielding two awesome fists as he managed to throw several sharp jabs at Phillip's unprotected face before the older man kicked him off. A well-aimed punch by Phillip brought a trickle of blood from Charles's lower lip and a grin of satisfaction to the older man's face.

"You'll not win this one, St. Germain," he panted, his blue eyes gleaming fanatically. "She's mine, do you hear? I'll bed her yet, and once I'm through with her I'll give anyone in John Company who's interested a chance at her."

A low, guttural growl tore from Charles's throat, the taunting words having set fire to his temper. With terrible violence he threw himself on his burly opponent, seeming not to feel the blows Phillip managed to rain upon him, intent on pummeling him mercilessly. Neither man was taking precautions to protect himself any longer, inflicting damage and ignoring the pain, the quiet of the room broken only by their dull grunts and the muted sounds of fist meeting flesh.

Dmitri, hovering on the outskirts of the small circle where the two big men were locked in mortal combat, kept a watchful eye on the servants, the fighting iron swinging warningly before him. Although he could easily have knocked Phillip unconscious with one blow and just as quickly dispatched the Indians, he made no move to interfere. This had been building inside of

Charles for some time now, he knew, and his captain's terrible rage must be unleashed and vanquished before he could be whole again.

Casting a swift glance at Raven's pale face, her eyes wide with suffering as she watched Charles, he felt regret that she had been forced to witness the fight. But the little one was strong, he reminded himself, and Charles would win, and in the end she would stand to gain far more than if it had never happened and the captain had continued to bury his torment and pain deep within him.

It was over far sooner than Dmitri had expected. Phillip, battered senseless by a man who fought like a demon possessed, swung wildly, blood trickling into his eyes from a cut on his brow, blinding him so that he left himself critically exposed. Charles moved quickly to attack the unprotected face. Lashing out at Phillip's bloodied nose, he shattered it completely, and Phillip collapsed with an animal grunt, his head lolling.

Charles straightened, his lips twisted into a grimace of pain, wiping the blood from his chin with the back of his hand and turning to stare at the servants, who were edging nervously toward the door. Something in his blazing eyes made them freeze, but before Charles could speak to them, the deafening report of a rifle rang through the air. Charles whirled about, instinctively moving to block Raven with his body, until he realized that the shot had come from somewhere outside.

"Dmitri!" he commanded, but the big Russian was already gone, the cold wind rushing through the door, which he had ripped open in his haste. He was back almost immediately, his expression grim.

"The warehouses have been set on fire, tovarich. There are at least a dozen armed and mounted men on the grounds." His words brought a disbelieving gasp from Raven and a babble of questions from the servants.

"Raven, get your things together quickly!" Charles commanded harshly as she hesitated, staring helplessly up into his bruised and bloodied face, her heart in her eyes. She obeyed without protest, swallowing hard to contain her fear, vanishing amid a rustle of petticoats down the corridor.

"Sikhs?" Charles demanded as soon as she was gone, turning to regard Dmitri, who was bending over the prostrate form of Phillip Barrancourt, feeling for a pulse.

"It may be, tovarich." Dmitri's black eyes were filled with urgency. "We must get out of here quickly. Kristos, I did not believe they would mutiny!"

"Excuse me, burra-sahib." It was Ahmed, tugging respectfully at Charles's bloodstained sleeve.

"What is it?" Charles demanded sharply, rounding on him.

"It is not you they want. It is him." Ahmed gazed down at his fallen master with a look of mingled pity and loathing on his hawkish features. "If you go now, quickly, you will be left in peace." His black eyes met Charles's unflinchingly. "They were promised arms by my master to fight the Angrezi rissala. Their money was lost. The guns never came."

"Dmitri, find us some weapons," Charles ordered, pulling on his clothes. "Where the devil is that woman? We haven't much time. Raven!"

"Here I am," she replied breathlessly, emerging from her room with the bulky valise, her traveling cloak wrapped tightly about her. Stepping gingerly over the unmoving form of her cousin, she tried to fight the nausea rising within her at the sight of his ruined face. "What is happening?" she asked fearfully as Charles took her hand and pulled her toward the door. "Is it true the Sikhs have mutinied? I heard Dmitri say—"

"I don't think so," Charles assured her, his eyes narrowed as he peered outside.

Raven gave a small cry of fear as she heard a cannonade of shots thunder through the darkness. "What are they doing?"

"There isn't time to explain." Charles turned his head as Dmitri appeared behind him carrying an ancient muzzle loader and a pair of rusty dueling pistols. "Is that all you could find?" he snapped.

"Aye, my friend, but they're primed and ready to fire."

Charles took the pistols from him, tucked one into his belt, and brandished the other menacingly before him. "Cover me from the rear, Dmitri. I'll circle around and meet you back at the gate. Is that clear?"

Dmitri grinned broadly. "Aye, aye, captain."

"Missy-sahib, wait!" Ahmed was suddenly blocking the doorway, ignoring the pistol that Charles thrust warningly into his face. He was trembling with fright and his forehead glistened with sweat, but he did not waver as he held a small bundle out to Raven and urged her to take it. "The sahib says you are to have it," he told her fervently. "It was payment to him from Sajid Wali Shah, brother of the nawab of Oudh. You are to keep it."

Moving as though in a trance, Raven accepted the muslin-wrapped object, turning her head slowly to look down at Phillip, who had regained consciousness and was struggling slowly with the help of Hammad to rise. "Take it, Raven," he whispered through torn, swollen lips. "T-take it. It's all I h-have left. Get out of here, q-quickly!"

A loud explosion from somewhere on the compound grounds fueled the urgency in his command. "Hurry!"

"Can you make it, love?" Charles inquired, looking tenderly into Raven's pale face, his own bruised and bloodied but dearer than life to her.

She swallowed hard and tried to look brave. "If you're with me."

Charles grinned despite the pain and slipped his arm about her, drawing her protectively against his chest as he stepped out into the darkness, the pistol held before him. Raven gasped when she saw the flames shooting high into the night sky as the main warehouse at the far end of the compound was torched. Nearby trees were ignited by the heat and shooting sparks, creating an inferno that was moving inexorably toward them. Yet it was not the fire that terrified her so or the deafening roar as stored munitions exploded. It was the horsemen that galloped through the melee, brandishing swords and rifles and shrieking triumphantly.

"Are they going to kill us?" Raven whispered, her eyes wide, reflecting the flames that leaped about them.

"They won't be able to catch us," Charles replied gruffly. "And besides, it's not us they want. It's Phillip."

"Phillip?" Raven repeated disbelievingly. "Is that why you didn't take him with us?"

"They would have slaughtered all of us if they'd found us together," Charles said grimly. "This way we still have a chance. Don't look so frightened, love," he added, his harsh expression softening as he gazed down into her pale face. "Just keep your head down and be quiet. We'll be all right."

Wrapping her cloak more securely about her trembling form, Charles pulled her close against him and stepped from the verandah, running toward the sheltering hedgerow across the lawn.

The branches snapped alarmingly as he pulled Raven down behind the tall shrubbery, but the horsemen careening around the corner of the bungalow were too intent upon getting inside to notice them. Leaping from their horses, the turbaned riders burst through the opened door, and Raven could hear the sputtering burst of gunfire that accompanied their blood-curdling yells.

"Come on!" Charles all but shouted, stooping to pull her trembling body upright. When Raven resisted, he lifted her into his arms and carried her a dozen yards or more before depositing her and forcing her along at his side.

"Did they—did they kill him?" Raven cried, gasping for breath in the cold night air.

"Hush," Charles commanded.

No one tried to stop them as they ran through the gates to the road where Charles's horses were tethered. Quickly unlooping the reins, he lifted Raven into the saddle and regarded her intently. "Can you ride alone, Raven, and ride hard?"

She nodded wordlessly, the leather straps wrapped tightly between her fingers, shivering uncontrollably. On the other side of the compound walls she could hear the shouts and explosions continuing, flames leaping high into the chilly night air.

"Thank God we've got three horses," Charles was saying, strapping her valise to the dee ring on the cantle of his horse's saddle. "I couldn't believe my ears when Danny told me she'd ridden that one all the way down to the city by herself." He looked up at her worriedly. "Are you sure you can ride? I wouldn't mind taking you on mine, but we can travel faster when they aren't carrying double."

Raven smiled at him weakly. "A Newmarket jockey couldn't ride faster than I intend to," she promised. "What is it?" she added quickly when Charles laid his hand over hers.

"I should have known you'd be teasing me in a situation like this," he told her roughly. "We'll get out of here unharmed, Raven, I promise. Don't be afraid."

"I'm not," she whispered earnestly, peering into his face. "Not with you."

Charles's hard features softened and he came closer, his eyes compelling. "Raven—"

"Tovarich!" It was Dmitri, his beard and hair wildly disheveled as he appeared through the darkness, breathing heavily.

"Kristos, the mad creatures nearly roasted me alive!" he howled, gathering up the reins that Charles tossed to him. "For a moment there I fancied myself a side of beef on a brazier spit!"

"Dear God!" Raven whispered, horrified. "Did they set fire to Phillip's house?"

"Dmitri, let's go!" Charles commanded, his tone forbidding further conversation. Vaulting up into the saddle, he lifted his hand and brought it down with a stinging blow onto the rump of Raven's mount. Seconds later the three muscular horses were galloping at breakneck speed down the dark, dusty road, the buildings of Khanapur compound aflame behind them.

Chapter Thirteen

Below the teeming trade city of Hyderabad the mighty Indus River flowed swiftly southwest, transversing the wide, arid plains before emptying its numerous branches into the Arabian Sea. Through its swirling brown water the clipper *Orient Star*, running before a freshening wind, was moving swiftly under taut canvas, the lines singing, the throbbing rhythm seeming to infect the entire ship. Water gurgled in its wake, and the ancient dhows and native craft negotiating the crowded waterway scurried to keep clear of her path.

"By God!" Geoffrey Lytton remarked as he ascended the quarterdeck ladder at the start of the watch, "it's like she knows we're heading back to sea!"

"And glad I'll be of it," Ewan Fletcher agreed with a scowl as he handed the diminutive Welshman a mug of steaming coffee. "I've had enough of these silt-infested rivers and stinkin' tributaries floatin' with offal. It's the good, clean sea I'll be havin' below me feet, thank you, sir."

"And home we'll be soon enough, laddie," Geoffrey remarked, tamping his pipe with nimble fingers. His gray eyes glowed. "Be good to get back home again."

"And what've you brought the missus for her troubles this time?" Ewan demanded dourly. "A case of the clap?"

Geoffrey snorted good-naturedly and turned his back to the wind, lighting his pipe. "That's between her and me, my friend."

Ewan grinned and descended to the main deck, whistling tunelessly to himself. All was well with the world and he couldn't, despite his normally pessimistic nature, be happier than he was at the moment.

Both Dmitri and the captain were back aboard safe and sound, Miss Raven was again gracing the decks with her incredible beauty, and the *Orient Star* was putting out to sea, where it rightfully belonged. What did it matter, Ewan asked himself flippantly, if the captain had grown remote and unapproachable since his return to the ship? What did it matter that Miss Raven scarcely smiled anymore and always looked so sad and wistful that even a hardened seaman like himself could weep? They'd endured the burning and looting of Khanapur compound, not to mention the murder of Phillip Barrancourt and his unlikely accomplice, Major Thomas Wyandotte, and were to be excused if they chose to withdraw completely into themselves. Ewan knew that time would mend Miss Raven's wounds and that the sea would heal the captain. It always did.

Similar sentiments were shared by Dmitri, who, as first mate, held the unenviable position of working the closest with Captain St. Germain. Though others shuddered at the thought of having to stand watch with the captain in his present intolerable state of mind, Dmitri welcomed the chance. Sniffing out like a loyal hound dog the reasons behind Charles's black moods, he happily reported them to a bewildered and heartbroken Raven not many days after Hyderabad had vanished behind the clipper's stern.

As had become her custom on their return voyage down the Indus, Raven came topside directly after she and Danny had shared breakfast together in her cabin. Wandering to the starboard rail, she peered with unseeing eyes toward the land, which unfolded, flat and never-changing, beneath the dun-colored sky. Since most of her clothes had been lost in the fire, she wore the same lemon-piped gown in which she had first arrived in Lahore. Her beloved mother-of-pearl combs had escaped the roaring inferno that had swept through Khanapur compound, and Raven was so grateful for this that she could readily overlook the loss of her other gowns.

Besides, she asked herself as she leaned forlornly on the rail, the wind stirring the soft black curls at her temples, what did any of that matter now that Charles no longer loved her? The thought brought a knifing pain to her heart, and she bit down hard on her lower lip to keep from crying, for she did enough of that at night when no one could hear her muffled sobs as she lay sleepless in her cabin. During the harrowing ride down to Lahore to fetch Danny and the endless hours of traversing the plains back to Hasangei, Raven had been too numb with the shock of everything that had happened to pay much attention to anything or anyone around her.

Only later, when she emerged from her protective shell back into the world of the living, she found Charles, the man she needed and loved, a stranger whose treatment of her was little better than callous. He was barely civil whenever they met and seemed to prefer spending his time alone or with Dmitri, shunning her almost entirely. Whenever their eyes happened to meet or he inadvertently touched her, Raven could feel his immediate withdrawal, and it hurt her to the depths of her soul, for she was certain that she must have done something to destroy his love for her.

"Tsk, tsk, what is this?"

Raven whirled about to find Dmitri leaning against the rail beside her, hands propped comfortably against the smooth wood, his black eyes regarding her delicate profile intently. "Weeping again, are you? Fie, little one, what has happened to your courage? We escaped those rascals, didn't we? None of us lost so much as a finger or a toe, and that is a reason for rejoicing, not crying, hmm?"

"Please, Dmitri," Raven whispered, looking away, "I'd like to be alone."

Dmitri threw up his hands in mock defeat. "Bah! I've heard that request so many times that I think I'm going mad! At least you ask politely," he conceded, "not in a shout like our pigheaded captain." He paused, dark head cocked to one side, regarding her expectantly.

Raven dabbed ineffectually at her brimming eyes, then turned to him helplessly. "Oh, Dmitri, what's wrong with him? What have I said or done to make him hate me?"

It was the opening he had been waiting for. Gleefully assuming a grave expression, Dmitri clasped his hands behind his broad back. "Now, now, little one, you mustn't berate yourself for something that hasn't happened. It is not you that Charles despises. It is himself." Ignoring her disbelieving expression, he added confidently, "Oh, I know it to be true, and I don't doubt that the problem can be remedied easily."

"You're talking utter nonsense, Dmitri," Raven informed him tartly, retreating behind a wall of defense.

Dmitri raised his bushy eyebrows heavenward. "Am I? Think

for a moment, little one." His manner grew serious. "Think what it would be like to be a man as proud and in control of his destiny as Charles St. Germain. Think of the self-loathing that would overwhelm you when, through your own foolish blindness, you nearly permitted the woman you loved to be wed to a brute like Phillip Barrancourt. Even worse, when she tried to explain everything to you and begged you for your help, you, in your intolerable pride, would not listen. That in itself caused her to suffer horribly, being badly beaten by her cousin and almost killed at the hands of vengeful Sikhs."

Raven's eyes were wide in her pale face, her hands clenched at her sides, an almost defiant arrogance in her stance as she looked up at the big bearded Russian.

Thinking that perhaps he hadn't convinced her enough, Dmitri hurried to add, "I believe, little one, that the captain, in blaming himself for what happened to you, is certain that you blame him, too. I think, for the first time in his life, he cannot face up to what he has done. After all"—Dmitri shrugged his massive shoulders—"how does one go about saying 'I'm sorry' to someone whose life was nearly lost because of one's own stupid pride?"

"I want so much to believe you, Dmitri," Raven said haltingly after a long moment of pensive silence. Her eyes were dark with pain as she glanced at him briefly and then looked away. "But how can I when everything you say is based on the premise that he l-loves me? He has never told me so, and even if he did, what would it matter?" The delicate features were stark. "Soon I will be back in Cornwall and wed to Squire Blackburn." Her last words were little more than a tearful sob, and Dmitri cursed hopelessly beneath his breath as he watched her flee across deck and vanish down the companionway, her dark green skirts swirling about her.

"A pox on all that is sacred to the British," he muttered. "Honor, duty, pride, what feeble reasons are there for putting them above the heart?"

Alone in her cabin, Raven dissolved into heartbroken tears, her soggy handkerchief pressed to her lips as she tried valiantly to check their flow, hoping no one would hear her sobs through the thin wooden door. At least the crew was occupied topside, she comforted herself, for Jason Quintrell had told her yesterday that the *Orient Star* would be docking in Karachi later that afternoon to take on fresh supplies. Still, she knew that Charles hadn't made an appearance on deck yet, and the thought that he had to walk right past her cabin door in order to reach the companionway brought the sobs to a rapid halt.

Drying her eyes, Raven gulped and hiccuped, then drank some of the water from the pitcher Ewan Fletcher always left filled for her on the small dresser. Mulling over what Dmitri had told her earlier, she found herself wishing with all her heart that the big Russian's words were true. Even if she believed only a small part of them, she knew that she wouldn't hesitate for a moment to go to Charles and tell him how she felt, but she was afraid, terribly afraid to have it all thrown back into her face. Though her love for Charles St. Germain had brought her more happiness than Raven had ever thought possible, it had also brought her too much suffering, and at the moment she did not feel strong enough to be rebuffed again.

Perhaps later, when the horrors of the past few weeks had faded, when she felt her spirit and her battered body healed, she might not harbor the same unbearable fear she did now of being hurt or rejected again. Raven's expression was suddenly hopeless. What did it matter if she ever found the courage to bare her soul to Charles? Perhaps Dmitri was right after all and he did have feelings for her, but to what would they amount? Nothing. As soon as it was outfitted anew, the *Orient Star* would be off on fresh adventures, perhaps to continue seeking the fabled Kohinoor, and there was little room in Charles St. Germain's life as a sea-scouring pirate for a woman who wanted nothing more than to return to her beloved North Head.

"Don't!" Raven whispered to herself, tears brimming in her eyes. Why must she torment herself like this and dream of a life that was utterly futile at best? Charles did not want her, and even if he did love her even a little, he would never forsake the sea for the life Raven longed to lead in Cornwall. Even if either of them did have the fifty thousand pounds needed to save it, Raven told herself bitterly.

"Miss Raven?"

She dabbed quickly at her eyes and cleared her throat before opening the cabin door to find Ewan Fletcher standing without. If the steward noticed that she had been crying, he gave no sign. "What is it?" Raven asked softly.

"I wanted to remind you that the cap'n'll be havin' his dinner party tonight." Ewan grinned widely. "I thought maybe you forgot about it."

"As a matter of fact, I did," Raven admitted and found herself cursing Dmitri inwardly for having suggested it in the first place.

"We'll be docked by then, and I'll be goin' ashore to find the makings for the finest meal you'll ever have the pleasure of eatin', to be sure," the steward added. "In the meantime you can give me the gown that you'll be wearin' and I'll be right proper proud to press it for you."

Raven's soft lips curved, and the bewitching dimples appeared in her cheeks. "I'd be glad to, Mr. Fletcher, but what you see me wearing now is the only gown I have left."

Ewan's eyes widened as he regarded her slender form. The dark green velvet suited her midnight hair and golden eyes beautifully but, in his firm opinion, was not appropriate for a dinner in the captain's quarters. After all, Miss Raven had been wearing it steadily since her return to the ship, and Ewan was determined that tonight would be something special. "Maybe we could come up with something new," he told her thoughtfully. "Miss Raven, would you permit me a look through the rest of your belongings?"

"Why certainly," Raven agreed obligingly, moving aside to let him enter her cabin, "but I'm afraid you won't find anything of use."

"Never underestimate the skills of an Irishman," Ewan warned, wagging an impertinent finger at her. Opening the drawers of the small dresser, he searched through the few belongings that Raven had managed to bring with her in her battered valise. She watched him intently, shaking her head as he made a thorough inspection, hiding her amusement when his cheeks flushed pink as he opened the bottom drawer containing her undergarments.

Having expected him to give up then, she was surprised when he turned toward her clutching a piece of lavender material in his hands. "What's this?" he inquired curiously. Shaking it out, he saw the fine piece of silk become a pair of wide trousers that were gathered at the ankles, and Raven was forced to laugh at the astonished expression on his weatherbeaten face.

"Those are called salvars," she informed him, moving past him and rummaging through the same drawer in which Ewan had found them. Withdrawing a shirt of gay colors that was cinched at the waist, she held it out for his inspection. "You wear them with a kamiz like this. At least Punjabi women do. My cousin made them a present to me before . . . before everything happened. I was expected to wear them in the house, but I was a little bit reluctant, so I hid them in the bottom of my valise. I imagine that's how they came to be here with me."

She moved to take them from Ewan, but the steward warded her off, grinning at her roguishly. "Why don't you wear them tonight?"

Raven's slender jaw dropped. "You must be daft!"

"Am I?" Ewan asked mischievously. The more he looked down at the soft, colorful silk garments in his hands, the more he decided he would like to see them on Raven Barrancourt. "Why not?" he wheedled. "It'd be a fittin' farewell to Mother India, wouldn't it? Besides, a bonnie young woman just can't be seen in the same old dress, can she?"

"It's out of the question," Raven retorted. "I have no intention of making a spectacle of myself."

"A spectacle? You'd be a vision," Ewan assured her gallantly.

"No," Raven said crisply.

Ewan's expectant face crumpled. "Aye, I guess you're right, lass. Besides, the cap'n'd have a fit if he saw a proper young Englishwoman such as yourself dressed up like a native."

Crestfallen, he began to fold the garments away, only to have Raven snatch them from his hand. "Would he, Ewan?" she demanded, her tawny eyes glowing with anticipation.

"Would he what, Miss Raven?"

"Be angry if I wore these?" She held the brightly colored shirt against herself and twirled coquettishly before him.

"I reckon that he would," Ewan replied admiringly. "Not much for fun and games, our captain."

"That, Ewan," Raven said firmly, "is something that ought to be changed, don't you think?"

"Maybe so," the steward agreed somewhat hesitantly, suddenly not caring for the sparkle in Raven's eyes or the color that rushed to her cheeks. Then he shrugged to himself. What did it matter if he'd just unleashed a hurricane? It was the first time he'd seen Miss Raven look this happy since she'd come aboard, so what did it matter if she was planning a little fun at the captain's expense? Besides, he wasn't even sure if that was what she had in mind. By the look of things, she was reminding him exactly of a young lass off to her first ball with the intention of capturing a young man's fancy.

For Raven the reason for wearing the traditional Punjabi costume was far more complex and difficult for her to understand. She knew only that she couldn't possibly meet Charles in the intimate atmosphere of his quarters in the same worn gown she had been wearing since their flight from Lahore. The dinner party Dmitri had slyly arranged would offer her the first opportunity of seeing and speaking to Charles at length, and Raven was desperately afraid of letting the chance slip through her fingers. She must somehow capture Charles's attention, rekindle the magic that had transported them to such wild, ecstatic heights in the past, or it would be lost to them forever.

It had suddenly become clear to Raven after her talk on the deck with Dmitri that she could not let the *Orient Star* sail away without her. Even without the odious Squire Blackburn in attendance, her envisioned life at North Head seemed to stretch into a yawning emptiness without Charles there to fill her days and give them meaning. She would swallow her pride, Raven had decided, and beg him not to abandon her. He didn't even have to say he loved her, Raven told herself as she prepared for the evening with almost feverish determination. She would even be happy to become his mistress if that was what it took to have him keep her by his side.

"It's true," she whispered to herself later that evening in the lantern-lit interior of her cabin. "I'll be anything he wants me to be, if only he lets me stay!"

Unaccountably, tears brimmed in her eyes at her vehement words, but she dashed them away, telling herself that she should be content to settle for that much, which was certainly far better than being the wife of Josiah Blackburn. She would follow Charles around the world if need be because she loved him, and perhaps in time he might revert from his remote, uncommunicative self to the breathlessly exciting, tender lover he had been before. That alone would be worth everything, Raven told herself optimistically, yet she could not understand why her hands shook as she dressed and her throat ached with the effort of holding back her scalding tears.

If Ewan Fletcher had had even an inkling of what he would be unleashing upon the unsuspecting mates gathered in Charles

St. Germain's quarters that night, he would doubtless have flung Raven's clothes to the sharks and thanked God for his insight. As it was, he had spent the afternoon shopping the markets of Karachi, the tiny fishing village on the Arabian Sea where the *Orient Star* had furled its sails sometime after two bells that day. His purchases complete, he had hurried back to the galley to stoke the enormous stove and begin preparations for dinner. There hadn't been time to look in on his young female charge, and Ewan told himself it didn't really matter since he would see Raven when he served the meal. Had he been able to glimpse her before then, he might have realized that Raven's wild, sensuous looks, coupled with an outlandish costume of almost mystical appeal, would wreak dangerous havoc upon the hapless dinner guests.

Raven was not at all convinced that she looked well enough to please Charles, and her heart was pounding uncomfortably as she extinguished the lights in her cabin and slipped soundlessly down the narrow corridor to knock on the captain's door. There was no reply from inside, and Raven swallowed hard before knocking again. After what seemed an interminable wait, she tested the latch and, finding the door unlocked, entered quietly.

The lamps had been lit, casting a soft glow about the room and reflecting the fine stemware that stood in wait upon the elegantly decked table. Though the spacious cabin was empty, Raven did not wonder where the captain or his guests might be, for a tide of memories rushed over her when she stepped inside, memories so overwhelming that they all but took her breath away.

Before the shuttered stern windows the nightingale still fluttered on its perch, and the oft-used brass hip bath still stood behind the beautiful lacquered screen. It was as if Raven could feel the overpowering masculinity of the cabin's owner in every fiber of her being: in the discarded clothes tossed casually across the bunk where Charles had first loved her so roughly; in the sturdy, deeply burnished furniture which stood about; in the familiar, beloved scent of him that assailed and tantalized her senses.

Raven tried to thrust these thoughts from her but found that she could not. The loose-fitting silken length of her costume caressed her body, reminding her of the intimate touch of a lover, of Charles. She bit her lip and wandered toward the table, telling herself that Charles St. Germain was a rogue, a smuggler, an adventurer who would never tolerate a woman underfoot and that she had been a fool to think she could make him believe otherwise with the silly garb she was wearing. It would be better to pretend that Dmitri had never raised her hopes so cruelly by insisting Charles loved her and that—

"God's blood!"

Raven whirled about at the hoarse oath, the long single braid of black hair bobbing, the sight of Charles in the doorway, green eyes wide and disbelieving, rendering her speechless. He was attired completely in dove gray, his soft, tight-fitting breeches molded to his muscular thighs, the hint of lace at his throat and sun-browned, sinewy wrists breaking the severity of his formal attire. He had just come down from the quarterdeck, and his chestnut curls were wind-blown, falling in a devilish fashion over his wide forehead, his cravat slightly crumpled.

A muscle began to twitch in one lean, bronzed cheek and Raven, recognizing it as a sign that he was trying hard to keep his temper in check, felt the dismal pain of failure overwhelm her. She could not know that Charles had first mistaken her for a Hindu beauty that his officers had, in jest, provided for his enjoyment that evening. The first sight of her, glossy black hair pulled back from her achingly lovely, high-boned face and dangling provocatively below the belt of her purple, crimson, and green kamiz, had brought a familiar tightening to his loins, an instant response to her beauty that had shaken him with its intensity. Then she had turned, the silky material clinging diaphanously to her slender body, and he had seen that it was Raven.

In the lamplight he saw that the sheen of her hair was not produced by a skillful rubbing of coconut oil as he had first suspected, but that it shone with a gloss all its own. She had secured the thick braid away from her face with her carved mother-of-pearl combs and threaded a dark purple satin ribbon through the midnight plaits, letting it swing enticingly below her hips. The loose-fitting shirt was cut low at the throat, revealing a creamy expanse of smooth flesh before falling like a whisper over her full, curving breasts. The gathered waist enhanced her slimness, and her slender ankles were exposed below the gripped ends of the trousers, her small feet tucked into shimmering green satin slippers, the only pair she had managed to bring with her from Lahore.

To Charles she looked wildly beautiful, alluring, the mysteries of the Orient mingling enticingly in the seductive form of an Englishwoman he knew as intimately as he knew himself. Her wide, sloping eyes reflected the golden glow of the lamplight, the dark lashes that fringed them giving her a sultry appearance. Yet it was the tears he saw glittering in their tawny depths and the unconcealed trembling of her soft, kissable mouth that brought Charles back to his senses.

"Raven, you're not crying, are you?" he asked disbelievingly.

She shook her head vehemently, wishing that she had never undertaken this madcap scheme, dismally aware that it had succeeded beyond her wildest imaginings. Charles's green eyes were fastened almost hungrily to her silk-clad body, the gleam within them one of easily recognizable desire. He wanted her; it was obvious in the way he looked at her, but the realization did nothing but make Raven feel the hollowness of defeat inside. She had not wanted Charles to look at her like that, as though he desired nothing more than to take her to his bed. She had wanted him to hold her tenderly, to tell her that he loved her and that she meant more to him than as a lover who sated his unquenchable sexual appetites.

And yet what of the woman who had only minutes ago sworn that she would be content to play the role of Charles St. Germain's mistress? Hadn't she told herself that she would be happy to remain at his side even if he kept her there merely because she satisfied the needs of his flesh? Lies, all lies, Raven realized now, deceptions she had practiced upon herself while burying deep down in her heart the fact that she ached for so much more from him.

"Raven, what is it?" Charles asked as she turned her back on him, her glossy head drooping.

The unconscious tenderness in his voice and the strong hand that he laid on her arm betrayed her, the tremor that ran through her body at his touch igniting a flame that leaped tangibly between them. Gently Charles turned her around so that her beautiful oval face was raised to his, the tawny eyes beneath the arching brows still wet with tears but glowing now with all the love and passion Raven was unable to deny him. Looking down at her, Charles felt his loins tighten, and as he realized the depth of his feelings for her he cursed softly to himself and turned away. He could not take her now, for his mounting desire was too strong, too raw still with the memory of how close he had come to losing her. She seemed so fragile, so ethereal beneath her clinging silken garments, and Charles, for the first time in his life, was shaken by the brutal force of the need within him.

With his broad back turned to her he could not see the pain that crept into Raven's eyes, a wounded look of defeat on her delicate features. She had been so breathlessly certain as they stood staring at one another that Charles would take her into his arms and kiss her, mending at last the yawning chasm that had separated them since their return from Lahore. She could feel the scalding tears begin again in her eyes, her throat aching as she tried to quell her sobs.

"Well, tovarich, have you started the meal without us?"

The door to the cabin burst open and Dmitri lumbered inside, the expectant grin on his face fading as he caught sight of Raven standing before him in her slim trousers and shirt, her midnight hair braided and dangling below her hips. "Mother of God!" he burst out, coming to a dead halt and causing Geoffrey Lytton and Jason Quintrell, who were following close on his heels, to barrel one after the other into his broad back.

"Ummpf!" the diminutive Welshman grunted. "Dmitri, what the devil are you doing? Can't you see I—Christ have mercy on us!" he whispered, seeing what had halted the first mate in midstride. "Miss Barrancourt, am I deceived or is it really you?"

Raven drew in a long, shaky breath, then smiled up at all three men, tilting her head coquettishly. "It is. Do I not meet with your approval, gentlemen?"

Their stammering assurances that she did and the bumbling manner in which they fell over themselves to be the first through the door did much to bolster the self-confidence Charles had so effectively, albeit unintentionally, crushed within her seconds before. Raven tilted back her head, the long braid bobbing, and dimpled as she studied the three expectant faces above her. "I was beginning to think you'd forgotten all about me."

"Never, little one!" Dmitri assured her, shouldering his way forward and offering her his arm. "Will you not sit beside me? Kristos, I must confess you are a vision, my princess, a vision of what heaven holds in wait for me!"

"Unbelievable, captain," Geoffrey Lytton remarked quietly,

watching as Dmitri seated Raven beneath the stern windows, an eager Jason Quintrell hovering nearby to offer her a glass of wine. "I had no idea Miss Barrancourt would look so...er...fetching in Indian costume. Was it your idea?"

"No," Charles growled, and the bosun glanced up quickly to see his captain dangerously tight-lipped as he, too, watched Raven laughing and flirting with his officers. "It was hers alone, and I'm beginning to suspect that she did it to annoy me."

Geoffrey raised a questioning eyebrow, but Charles said nothing more, striding toward the table and seating himself opposite Raven, his handsome features stark. Geoffrey, trained for long years as an observer, did not miss the look of yearning and pain that entered Raven's eyes as she looked at him, though she continued to grace Dmitri and Jason with dimpled smiles that made them blush like schoolboys. Something was badly amiss here, the diminutive Welshman decided, yet he had no inkling at all of what it might be.

It became obvious to him soon enough that Raven was thoroughly enjoying herself at Charles's expense. The blacker the captain's expression became, the more she ignored him, lavishing gay smiles and saucy looks upon her other table partners. Even Ewan Fletcher was not spared her charms, and the dumbstruck steward came dangerously close to spilling his painstakingly prepared dishes as he tried to serve and gaze at her at the same time. Though Geoffrey himself thought her charming and incredibly beautiful, he was constantly aware of the smoldering anger that emanated from the grim-visaged captain beside him, a situation that to Geoffrey spelled considerable danger.

The atmosphere in the spacious quarters was rife with charged emotions. Raven, her golden eyes bright, two spots of color burning high in her hollow cheeks, laughed and chattered incessantly, while Dmitri and the worshipful supercargo chimed in, growing more boisterous as the evening wore on and the empty wine bottles began to accumulate on the cabin floor. The more ebullient his officers, the more remote and grim their watchful captain, who said nothing at all throughout the first few courses, silently twirling his wineglass in one long-fingered hand as his heavy-lidded emerald eyes rested thoughtfully on Raven's animated features.

"Do you know, Miss Barrancourt," Geoffrey remarked during

a lull in the conversation, deciding it was time to cool things off before Charles's awesome temper exploded, "no one has ever really told me precisely what happened to you in Lahore. Dmitri mentioned that your cousin had been killed, and I must confess I've been intrigued by the matter ever since. Obviously there was no damage to your person or Mrs. Daniels's, though her absence tonight suggests to me that she's still suffering from fatigue."

Raven sobered instantly, a shadow passing across her lovely face at the bosun's quiet words. In truth she was greatly relieved to find the conversation turning toward more serious matters, for she was exhausted with the effort of maintaining her forced gaiety, her anxiety having been at a feverish pitch ever since it became obvious that Charles continued to remain indifferent to her blatant flirtations with Dmitri and Jason.

"I believe the subject should remain buried," Charles remarked warningly, straightening his large frame in the chair where he had been leaning indolently for the past hour.

"Oh, please," Raven begged, "can't we talk about it now? There's so much I've been meaning to ask you, but there hasn't been much of a chance since . . . since we returned to the ship."

Charles found that he could not ignore the unspoken pleading in the tawny eyes. Since their escape he had deliberatly avoided mentioning the subject to her and had instructed Dmitri to do the same, certain that Raven would recover from the shock more rapidly if no one spoke of the horrors she had endured. Yet she appeared strong enough now to listen to what he had to tell her, and, the devil take it, anything would be better than watching Dmitri and young Quintrell drool over her silk-clad figure while his own temper simmered toward the boiling point.

That she was deliberately trying to provoke him Charles had realized immediately, yet her reasons for doing so had remained a mystery to him throughout the course of the evening. Was she trying to punish him for having abandoned her so cruelly to her half-mad cousin? Charles felt convinced that Raven did not possess a vindictive nature, and yet she had unwittingly succeeded in her efforts, for Charles found it difficult to sit there calmly while she charmed the very souls from his officers with her pouting red lips and sloping tigress eyes. Worse to endure was the response he felt within his own self at Raven's sensuality, contrived or not, and he found the desire to kiss those soft, parted lips was far more overwhelming than the longing to turn her over his knee and liberally spank the seat of her salvars.

"What is it you want to know?" Charles asked indifferently, addressing his boatswain, although he knew how much Raven was yearning to ask him questions of her own.

Geoffrey Lytton's pale, intelligent eyes rested briefly on Raven's hurt, bewildered face before returning to the lean, sunbronzed one of his captain, the aristocratic countenance, usually so familiar to him, that of a stranger's tonight. "The last we'd heard was that Miss Barrancourt and Mrs. Daniels had gone to the Punjab to collect a loan from her cousin," he began lightly. "Not a fortnight later you're all back aboard ship, Dmitri spouting tales of murder and mutiny, and you've got the *Orient Star* running before the wind like the devil himself was at her heels. Begging your pardon, sir," he added respectfully, "the crew did wonder a bit about what had happened. We knew there was war brewing with the Sikhs, but when I went ashore to load our consignments I kept my ears opened and didn't hear much untoward."

Charles nodded. "That's because the Sikhs probably won't regroup before the end of December, perhaps longer. When we left Lahore, troops were being mobilized and Chillianwallah seemed to be the most likely place for the next confrontation."

"But captain, what does that have to do with what happened to Miss Barrancourt at her cousin's?" Jason Quintrell demanded curiously. His speech was slightly slurred and his red hair disheveled, the tip of his nose glowing like a beacon thanks to the princely quantities of Madeira he had consumed.

Charles hid his amusement; he liked the lad despite the anger he felt toward him and Dmitri tonight. If it were up to him he'd lock both panting churls into the brig for the night, to teach them the wisdom of resisting the allure of a pair of sloping golden eyes. "If you will recall, Mr. Quintrell," he remarked lazily, leaning forward to refill his own glass, "the British resident at Multan was murdered late last month, precipitating a confrontation between the British army and dissident Sikhs."

Jason nodded, his brow furrowed in concentration.

"Consider, if you will," Charles continued, "the Sikh army, untrained, undisciplined despite their admirable nature, and, most importantly, poorly armed. Surely certain British individuals, not caring whether the Punjab is annexed or not, would be quick to capitalize on the profits that stood to be gained by supplying the rebels with arms."

"Preposterous!" Jason Quintrell cried. "What British subject would contemplate treachery like that?"

Charles shrugged his wide shoulders. "It turned out to be someone who had plummeted low into the depths of poverty and despair, whose addiction to opium had robbed him of every shred of self-respect, and who viewed the chance of making money as being far more important than the interests of John Company and Great Britain itself."

"My God, Phillip!" Raven whispered, her voice so low that only Charles could hear her.

"Correct, my dear," he said flippantly, but his emerald eyes lingered on her upturned face, his brows drawing together when he saw how pale she had grown.

"So that's what Ahmed was talking about that night," she went on disbelievingly. "It made no sense to me at the time, but it does now. Phillip took payment for guns he had no intention of delivering, using the money to buy more opium for himself, didn't he?"

Charles nodded. "Only Phillip did intend to supply the arms in good faith. Little did he know that he had been double-crossed by Major Thomas Wyandotte, his supplier. Wyandotte used him like a pawn, planning to ambush the Sikhs on the night of the exchange and thereby gain a healthy commission for himself."

"Which means, little one," Dmitri added, "that once the Sikhs discovered they had been betrayed, it was only natural that they came to Khanapur compound to loot it and kill your cousin. We were never in any real danger that night because it was Phillip they wanted, not us."

"But they might have killed us, too." Raven shuddered.

Charles shrugged, feigning indifference, although her pallor was worrying him. "It was entirely possible, which is why we had to make such haste in escaping. I wasn't sure how far-reaching the repercussions would be, but I imagine the entire bloody affair will hasten the next military confrontation."

"How did you know about all of this?" Raven asked, peering up into the handsome face across the board from her. "About the opium and the guns?"

"Ahmed told me enough to rouse my suspicions, and a quick dispatch to Colonel Bateman confirmed them before we weighed anchor in Hasangei." Charles regarded her intently, his voice unconsciously gentle. "You mustn't think of it anymore, Raven. It's behind us and you should be glad we escaped unharmed."

Raven nodded and averted her face, remembering, Charles knew, the beating she had received at her cousin's hands and the cruel fate he had planned for her as his wife. His lean jaw tightened ominously, and he grappled with the overwhelming desire to take her into his arms and comfort her. Aware that Geoffrey Lytton's pale gray eyes were resting pensively upon him, Charles rose abruptly to his feet and strode across the cabin, bending to throw back the lid of his seaman's chest. Lifting out a bulky object, he returned to the table, the eyes of all guests, save one, upon him.

"Do you remember this, Raven?"

At the sound of his deep voice she looked up to see him standing before her, a bundle wrapped in hand-dyed saffron muslin in his hands, his emerald eyes gentle as they gazed down at her. "Yes," she said dully. "Phillip gave it to me before we left. I'd forgotten all about it."

"I've been keeping it for you," Charles went on, speaking to her as though the two of them were alone. "Do you still want it?"

"What is it, Miss Barrancourt?" Jason asked, unable to contain his curiosity.

Raven smiled half-heartedly at the eager expression on his boyish face. "I suppose I should unwrap it and see," she agreed dubiously. As Charles handed it to her, their fingers accidentally touched and she jerked away, hating herself for the responding tremor that tingled through her body. She tried to hide her nervousness as she set the bundle before her on the table, but her fingers trembled and grew clumsy as she fumbled with the jute twine.

"Let me help you," Charles offered. Bending over her shoulder, his lean cheek close to hers, he undid the knots, pulling the wrapping aside to reveal a Chinese ginger jar of wafer-thin china covered with hand-painted figures and intricate designs of burnt sienna, emerald, and indigo.

"It's beautiful!" Jason breathed.

"May I see it, Miss Barrancourt?" Geoffrey inquired politely.

Raven nodded, watching intently as the bosun lifted it into his small hands and examined the bottom carefully. Taking off the lid he peered inside, then set it gently onto the tabletop. "It's old and, by my guess, rather valuable. You'll have to get it properly appraised before you can be certain of its worth," the Oxford-educated sailor added. "My guess is that it won't be a fortune, but you'd be foolish not to leave it locked away somewhere in safety."

"It doesn't matter," Raven said dully, pressure beginning to build behind her eyes, portending a headache. "If it won't bring fifty thousand pounds, I'm afraid it's of little value to me."

"I should imagine it would fetch you considerably less on the market," Geoffrey informed her regretfully. "I'm sorry."

Raven smiled at him sadly. "Thank you all the same."

"Raven, you look exhausted." It was Charles at her elbow, peering down at her with concern. "Why don't you let me take you back to your cabin?"

He half-expected her to make a tart remark in reply to his offer, and his concern increased when she merely nodded, her slender shoulders stooped as though weighed down by an unbearable burden. "Perhaps I should. Thank you, gentlemen, it's been a pleasant evening."

All three of them gallantly rose with her, voicing their regrets and wishing her good night, and it was Charles, standing close beside her, who caught her elbow when she wavered. "Raven, are you all right?"

She shook off his hand and gave him a defiant look. "Of course I am. It's just the wine. I think I've had too much." She turned away from the table, but another wave of dizziness overwhelmed her and this time Charles had to move quickly to catch her before she fell.

"By God, she's fainted dead away!" Jason cried worriedly as Raven's head fell against Charles's broad chest.

"Kristos, what's happened?" Dmitri bellowed, wild with fear.

Charles ignored them as he lifted Raven's limp form gently into his arms and carried her over to his bunk. Geoffrey was there before him, turning back the bedclothes and stepping aside as Charles laid her down, covering her slippered feet and legs with the blanket, his brow furrowing as he saw the ashen cast of her hollow cheeks.

"Is she hurt?" Dmitri demanded, pressing close. "What has happened to the little one?"

"Step back and give her some air!" Charles commanded, rounding ferociously on his first mate.

"I'll get Mrs. Daniels," Jason volunteered, certain that an unconscious woman would benefit most from the ministrations of another female.

"Come on, Dmitri, we'd better go topside, " Geoffrey urged, watching intently as the tall captain of the *Orient Star* leaned over Raven's prostrate form, his aristocratic features stark with concern.

"I will stay until the little one is better," Dmitri said doggedly, his red-rimmed eyes filled with worry.

"She'll be fine," Geoffrey assured him. "It's common for women to have spells like these. I warrant the evening was too much for her." He slapped the big Cossack heartily on the back. "You'd be doing her a favor if you left her alone."

Dmitri cast a quick glance at his captain for confirmation, but Charles seemed unaware of his presence. Reluctantly he allowed the bosun to lead him away, while Charles, his expression infinitely tender, smoothed back the glossy tendrils from Raven's brow with one big hand.

"How did it happen, captain?" Danny's voice was crisp and authoritative as she swept into the spacious cabin, rolling up her sleeves and all but slamming the door in Jason Quintrell's worried face.

"She simply fainted," Charles replied, straightening and allowing Danny to take his place beside the bunk.

"Nonsense," Danny said tartly, placing her hand on Raven's hot forehead. "No one simply faints. It be a complex process and happens for a variety of reasons. Did she complain of pains in the stomach? A headache? Nausea?"

"No."

"Well, then, did she have too much to drink?" Danny persisted, having noticed the abundance of empty wine bottles scattered upon the tabletop and the polished planks of the floor beneath the stern windows.

"Not enough to make her swoon like that," Charles growled. "She did seem pale to me tonight and rather anxious, but Raven isn't the nervous type."

"Certainly not," Danny agreed. "Lord have mercy!" she exclaimed as she drew back the blankets draped over Raven's inert form. "What in heaven's name does she have on?"

Despite his overwhelming worry, Charles was forced to smile at the outraged woman's accusing expression. "Believe me, Danny, I was as shocked as you were to see her in it."

"I can see she's chosen to ignore every rule of convention I've ever tried to teach her," Danny sniffed disparagingly. "My word, what an outfit!"

"She looked very beautiful in it," Charles said softly.

Danny shot him an acid glance. "She looks beautiful no matter what she's wearing, I'll thank you to know, and she doesn't need no indecent, half-transparent pair of pantaloons to charm you, captain, I'm convinced of that!"

"Is that why she wore them?" Charles demanded, startled.

The elderly woman threw him a contemptuous glance. "You ought to know that better than me, captain! Here now, quit hovering over her like that! She isn't going to die! Better yet," she added, rising to her feet and exhibiting more energy than Charles had ever known her to, "why don't you wait outside? There be a few questions I'd like to ask Miss Raven when she comes round, and she doesn't need a man there when she answers them."

The expression on her round face softened. "Go on, captain, I'll take care of her. She'll come to no harm, I promise."

The arrogant countenance relaxed and Charles's sensual lips twitched. "I know, Danny."

Danny sighed as she shut the door softly on the captain's broad, retreating form, well aware that he would be waiting impatiently outside until she summoned him. It was not like Captain St. Germain to give in so readily to such a request, she knew, even if it had been sweetly uttered by a kindly old woman. But perhaps he had sensed some of the urgency she felt within her, and Danny's plump hands twisted nervously in her lap as she seated herself on the bunk beside the prostrate form of her young mistress and waited for her to regain consciousness.

It seemed an interminable wait until Raven stirred at last, her soft lips moving soundlessly as she opened her tawny eyes to find a familiar face hovering mistily over her.

"Charles?" she whispered uncertainly.

"Hush, dear, it be Danny." Plump fingers were squeezing her own reassuringly, and Raven blinked until the round, wrinkled face swam into focus.

"Oh, it's you, Danny," she sighed. "What happened?"

"You fainted, dearie, nothing more," Danny crooned soothingly. "Now lie still until you feel strong enough, and then I'll fetch Captain St. Germain to carry you back to your cabin."

"Charles?" Raven repeated, her tawny eyes searching the darkened cabin. "Where is he?"

"Gone topside," Danny informed her. She rose and disappeared from Raven's line of vision, and returned a moment later with a glass in her hand. "Drink this," she commanded, and Raven gratefully swallowed the contents, feeling the soothing coolness of the water against her parched throat.

Satisfied to see the color returning to her young mistress's cheeks, Danny helped her sit upright and plumped the pillows beneath her slender shoulders, arranging the blankets comfortably before pulling up a heavy sea chair and seating herself beside the bunk. "Captain St. Germain says you simply keeled over."

Raven nodded uncertainly. "Yes, I think that's what happened. I remember talking to Dmitri and Mr. Lytton, and then suddenly everything went black."

Danny reached out tenderly and smoothed back the glossy braid that spilled over Raven's shoulder onto the rough blanket. "You didn't feel sick before it happened, dear?"

"No, just a little dizzy," Raven replied, her brow furrowing as she strove to remember.

"And this be the first time you've felt this way?"

Raven was mystified by Danny's quizzing. "Of course it was. You know me well enough, Danny, I've never fainted in my life! I imagine it was the wine or even the party itself." She stared down at her small hands, which were gripping the blankets almost convulsively. "I wanted so much to . . . Charles and I—" She broke off and bit her lip. "Perhaps I was trying too hard."

"Don't think about it, dear," Danny said gently, patting one of the cold hands lying on the cover. "But I do want you to think about something else." The brown eyes were suddenly regarding her solemnly. "Miss Raven, can you remember when you last had your monthly troubles?"

"Oh, for heaven's sake, Danny!" Raven protested. "What does that matter?"

"Think hard," Danny persisted, ignoring her young mistress's impatient question. "Try to be exact."

"I don't have to try," Raven said, fretfully pushing aside the blankets covering her body. "I remember exactly. It was three days before we docked in Bombay. Don't you remember how sick I felt the day we made landfall?"

Danny's lined face seemed to sag. "And since then, Miss Raven? You've not had them since then?"

"No," Raven replied promptly, then stopped. "That is, I don't think... well, with everything that happened I simply must have forgotten." She peered up into the aged, familiar face before her, and the truth she read in the faded brown eyes made her panic. "Surely I must have!" In her mind she raced back over the events of the past two months, feverishly trying to link the days with a time when she should have been beset with her "female curse," as her young friend Elspeth Killigrew in Falmouth had always termed it. Try as she might she could not remember having suffered through it since the last time aboard the *India Cloud*, before she had embarked with Danny down the Indus on the *Orient Star*, before Charles St. Germain had made love to her.

"Judas!" she whispered, the color draining from her cheeks, leaving them more ashen than before.

"It's his child you're bearing, Miss Raven, I'm certain of it."

Hearing the words fall from Danny's lips, firmly and without censure, Raven clapped her hands over her ears, her eyes wide and disbelieving. "No, no, no! It can't be true!"

"Aye, it must be," Danny insisted.

Raven closed her eyes and felt the hot tears scalding her eyelids. What was she to do now? If Charles found out he would insist on marrying her, for Raven knew that he was too proud not to accept the responsibility fully. She couldn't let that happen, for she'd rather die than accept his pity, to take his name only to make respectable the child she carried within her.

"Don't cry, my darling," Danny murmured, seeing the hot tears that coursed silently down Raven's hollow cheeks. "Why, it be a rare blessing, indeed! I know how much he loves you, and when he finds out that you—"

"He will not find out!" Raven cried, her eyes glowing feverishly in her pale face. "You mustn't tell him, Danny, not ever!"

"But Miss Raven, why not?" Danny demanded, shocked.

"I won't marry him just to save his pride the truth of knowing he has sired a bastard! And why are you so certain he'll marry me? You know how cruel and manipulative he can be! Suppose he arranges for me to l-lose the baby? That would be the most convenient solution for him, wouldn't it?"

"You mustn't speak like that, Miss Raven," Danny pleaded. "I can see how much this has upset you on top of everything else you've been through, but Captain St. Germain be a good man and he'll stand by you. He'll see that you and the babe won't be left wanting."

"That's just it, Danny," Raven said hopelessly, bitterness and despair rising like bile in her throat. "I don't want his charity, his pity, or his name. You say he loves me, but how can you know?" Her tawny eyes were stark. "He's never told me so before, and if he did so now it would only be because of the baby I'm carrying!"

She turned her face to the wall, crying silently while Danny twisted her hands together, knowing there was nothing she could say to comfort her young mistress. Raven, she knew, was too proud to accept the offer Danny felt certain Captain St. Germain would make with a pure and honest conscience.

"Miss Raven, please," she begged as the weeping continued, Raven's slim shoulders shaking with silent sobs. "Captain St. Germain will be back in a few minutes, and if you tell him the truth I think he'll—"

"No!" Raven groaned, turning to look at her former governess, her eyes swollen and filled with wounded pain. "I don't want to see him! Not ever again!" Leaping out of the bunk, she fled from the room, slamming the cabin door shut behind her.

When Charles returned not ten minutes later, his patience worn thin waiting for the summons that never came, he was startled to find Danny sitting helplessly before his empty bunk. "What the devil?" he demanded, stopping short in the doorway. "Danny, where's Raven?"

"Gone back to her cabin."

"Is she feeling better?" Charles asked, regarding the elderly woman keenly. Seeing the nervous trembling of her lower lip and the mistiness of the faded brown eyes, he uttered a hoarse oath beneath his breath and strode to the door.

"Captain, wait!"

Charles turned impatiently while Danny hurried toward him, peering up into his handsome face with a pleading expression. "Leave the child be, captain, please. I think the best thing you can do for her right now is to leave her alone."

"Why?" Charles demanded, unconvinced. "Is she ill?"

"A little overwrought," Danny explained with a smile that was intended to be convincing. "Young women can be so very high-strung at times, if you know what I mean."

"I know exactly what you mean," Charles replied shortly, "and I don't believe a word of it, at least not where Raven is concerned. I'm going to see her myself."

The tone of his deep voice was one that brooked no argument, and Danny watched helplessly as he strode through the doorway and down the darkened corridor, his handsome visage grim. Oh dear, she thought fretfully to herself, with Miss Raven so distraught and Captain St. Germain looking so determined, there was bound to be trouble!

It was not anger that spurred Charles into a confrontation with Raven, but concern that had rankled within him ever since the elderly woman had sent him out of his own cabin. Knowing Raven's constitution and temperament, he was convinced that some serious illness had caused her to faint dead away like that, and he intended to take no chances by following Danny's foolish but well-meaning advice to leave Raven alone. Suppose her condition was such that it required the attentions of a physician? Charles's heart contracted uncomfortably. Karachi was a primitive fishing port with no modern facilities, let alone a citizen with professional medical training.

Urgency quickened his stride and his knock was bold as he rapped his fist against the thin wood separating Raven's tiny cabin from the corridor. "Raven?" he called out sharply. "It's Charles. May I come in?"

There was no reply, and Charles knocked again, more forcibly this time. His patience all but gone, he threw the door open at last, half-expecting to find Raven on the threshold confronting him with flashing tigress eyes and angry protests. To his surprise he found the cabin empty, the covers on the bunk neatly folded.

"Danny!" he roared, thrusting his head out of the door, bringing the elderly woman at a run, her round face pale with fright. "I thought you said Raven had gone to her quarters," he grated, indicating the darkened cabin with a savage sweep of his hand. "Where the devil is she, then?"

"Why, I-I don't know, captain," Danny stammered.

Charles's lips thinned and he stepped past the quaking woman, threw open the door to her own quarters, and made a quick search inside. "God's blood, what's happened to the wench?" he snarled beneath his breath.

"Tovarich, what's all the excitement about?" Dmitri demanded, hurrying down the corridor with a lantern swinging before him. "The entire watch can hear you ranting and raving abovedecks!" His black eyes widened with apprehension. "Kristos! Raven! Is she still not better?"

"She must be," Charles snapped, "otherwise she wouldn't be traipsing about topside."

"Topside?" Dmitri repeated, puzzled.

"Aye, she's not down here," Charles said darkly.

"Then you better look again," Dmitri told him soberly, "because Hagen and I just finished the rounds. The little one is not on deck."

Charles's aristocratic countenance went rigid. "By God, *you'd* better look again, Zergeyev, because if you don't find her I'll have you and the entire watch keelhauled, is that understood?"

Dmitri snapped to stiff attention, worry for Raven overriding his resentment at Charles's harsh treatment. "Aye, aye, captain."

The search had not been under way for more than fifteen minutes before a nervous young sailor was hauled before the captain and roughly prodded until he confessed to having seen a young woman in traditional Punjabi costume leaving the ship in utter darkness less than an hour ago. Further castigation prompted him to add that he had seen her slip across the wharf toward town, stammering fearfully that he had thought her a native girl one of the men had smuggled aboard, which was why he hadn't thought to raise an alarm. Quaking in terror, the sweat pouring down his back, the young recruit found it difficult to look squarely into the face of his captain, the handsome features taking on an almost demonic ruthlessness as he spoke. Expecting to be told he was beached on the spot, he could only stare, open-mouthed, as the captain turned heel without uttering a single word, striding toward the entry port with a grimly silent Dmitri Zergeyev behind him.

Not until a pale dawn spread across the sky did the weary search parties return to the ship. Charles, who had himself spent all night turning the sleeping village upside down, listened tight-lipped to the reports of failure offered by his disheartened crew, the final words of a deeply discouraged Geoffrey Lytton echoing darkly within his heat.

"I can't imagine where Miss Raven's run off to," the exhausted Welshman told him as they met on the main deck, the cold winter sky above them turning from rose to copper to gold. "It's as if she's all but vanished off the face of the earth."

Raven awoke to utter blackness. There was a ringing in her ears and bright flashing lights before her unseeing eyes, and she bent forward, clutching at her stomach until the wave of dizzying nausea passed. Then she lay back, panting, her smooth brow dotted with beads of perspiration. Her head ached abominably and her tongue felt parched and swollen in her mouth. After a moment, when her racing heartbeat slowed, the dizziness faded and she was able to sit up, straining her eyes to see through the darkness.

She had no inkling of where she might be. No sound came to her at all beyond the steady blowing of the wind somewhere outside. Rising up on her knees, she reached out her hand until she came into contact with a wall made of clay and wood, cob-webs and dust clinging to its rough surface. Edging along the length of it, Raven uttered a shrill scream as her seeking hand came in contact with something warm and alive that squealed in response and quickly fled. Shaken, Raven huddled in the corner, her knees drawn up against her chest, her breath coming in gasps. Where in the name of God was she?

"Think, damn you!" she whispered fiercely to herself. What had happened since she left the *Orient Star* last night? Was it last night? How could she be sure when she found herself in a freezing blackness more complete than even that in Cornwall when darkness descended over the seas and the sky was without moon or stars?

Dully, her head aching, she forced herself to think back over the last few events that remained clear in her mind. As if in a dream she remembered the dinner party in Charles's quarters, the silver and crystal gleaming in the candlelight. How hand-some and debonair Charles had looked in his dove-gray coat and breeches, his devil's eyes gleaming whenever he had stared into her flushed, defiant face. She had been flirting with Dmitri and Jason, Raven recalled, desperately hoping to evoke some sort of response in the captain, and then she had fainted, simply slipped unconscious to the floor because...because she was carrying Charles St. Germain's child within her.

A low moan escaped Raven's tightly compressed lips. She had been so upset by the discovery, so certain that Charles would force her to marry him merely to give the babe his name. She had convinced herself that she would rather die than agree to become wife to a man she loved above all others but who did not care for her in return. Hadn't his indifference last night proved once and for all that she meant nothing to him? She bit her lip against the rising tide of pain within her. No, she would not marry Charles when the only claim she had over him was the life he had planted within her during those sweet and passionate hours they had shared in his quarters.

Feeling the hot tears coursing down her cheeks, Raven forced herself to stop thinking of Charles and to concentrate on what had happened to her afterward. She remembered fleeing from his cabin, shouting at Danny that she would never accept Charles's pity, running blindly into the night, the intimate quarters of the *Orient Star* having suddenly closed unbearably about her. She had wandered like a lost wraith about the darkened, twisting streets of Karachi, dodging snarling dogs and beggars who snored in the doorways until, her grogginess fading, she had become aware of the danger she had so foolishly placed herself in.

In trying to return to the ship, she had become hopelessly lost. Above the rooftops she could see the soaring masts of the few ships lying silently at anchor, but the maze of twisting streets did not open on the waterfront no matter how close she came to it. Exhausted and frightened, she had paused to rest near a well in a market square, listening to the silence of the night and the wind sousing in the gnarled trees overhead.

After that, Raven's memory became vague and blurred. She strained to remember how long she had rested before getting up and continuing on her way, then realized after a long moment of introspection that she had never made it beyond her seat by the windlass. The sound of a pebble being dislodged on the narrow wall behind her had caused her to whirl about, but she had seen nothing at all. No, Raven decided, that was wrong. She had seen something, but what? A hand, she remembered vaguely, a hand that seemed to shoot disembodied out of the darkness, clapping itself over her mouth, pulling a dark cloth sack over her head and twisting it tightly so that she choked and gasped for air, trying to scream and clawing at the unseen hands that held her... gasping and growing weaker until velvety blackness had descended.

Raven shuddered and moved away from the dusty corner in which she had been huddling. She had remembered what had happened to her all right, but how did that explain where she was at the moment or who had kidnapped her, if indeed that was her fate? Gathering her courage, Raven began a systematic search of her dark prison, feeling along the filthy clay floor until she had learned that the room was of narrow dimensions and seemed to contain no openings whatsoever.

For a panic-stricken moment she envisioned herself trapped in a tomb, but her imagined terror quickly became real when she heard a sound outside. Flattening herself against the wall, she held her breath and listened, cringing back when a dull rumbling came from the far side of the pitch-black room. It took a second for her to realize that the sound was that of stone grinding against stone, and she gasped when a beam of light sliced through the darkness, revealing that a heavy arched door had been laboriously pushed aside in the opposite wall.

A harsh masculine voice uttered something in a tongue totally foreign to her, and Raven caught her breath when the swaying lantern light revealed the shadow of an enormous man wearing a hood and flowing white robe. Piercing black eyes regarded her with hostility as the lantern held aloft in one clawlike hand shed its light on her huddled form. The harsh voice repeated its unintelligible words, and this time Raven heard the imperiousness of command within it. Rising to her feet, she came hesitantly forward and the towering, white-robed man seized her arm and pulled her bodily outside.

A second man was there to meet them, quickly throwing a stifling bourka over Raven's head, the small eye-slits making it nearly impossible for her to see. She managed to catch a glimpse of her prison as she was herded down a darkened corridor and saw that her earlier fear of being locked into a tomb had not been totally unfounded. Flat stone steps led to a small prayer chamber of age-worn sandstone, the crypt in which Raven had been imprisoned without windows, the walls thick and totally impenetrable. Hurrying down the arched-roof walkway, Raven stumbled over the long flowing length of her bourka and was jerked upright by the hook-nosed man in the white robes who uttered a sharp rebuke before pulling her along even faster behind him.

With an abruptness that took Raven's breath away, they emerged outside, the sky above them of deep indigo blue and filled with countless stars. Disoriented, Raven faltered, but her captor was there to push her ruthlessly onward. Try as she might she could see nothing out of the eye-slits of the concealing, shroudlike bourka save the shadowy outlines of aged, decaying buildings. Beneath her slippered feet the street felt hard and rock-strewn, but after a few minutes Raven heard the dull echo of wood underfoot. She felt her heart skip a beat. Was it possible that they were on the docks? Hearing water lapping softly around her, Raven felt a surge of hope within her. Perhaps the *Orient Star* or another English ship lay at anchor nearby. If she could only scream loud enough to make a scene, someone ought to hear her!

Even as Raven took a deep breath and prepared to let it out in an ear-piercing cry for help, something hard and sharp pricked her painfully between the ribs. She did not have to see to know that the tall, black-eyed man had thrust the tip of a knife warningly into the folds of her bourka, and the air rushed from Raven's lungs in a sob of defeat. Seconds later she felt the planks beneath her become uneven and knew that she was being led up a gangplank. Judas, she moaned to herself, where was she being taken?

Voices came to her on the still night air, but the words were unfamiliar. Through the eye-slits Raven could see a small group of men milling about near the wheelhouse of the small cutter aboard which she had been taken, all of them dressed in the same flowing robes as her captor. She had heard enough Urdu and Punjabi in the past few weeks to recognize them by now, but the tongue in which these men addressed one another was totally foreign. No one gave her a glance as she was whisked past and tossed without ceremony down a hatch, the cover slammed shut and secured above her. Landing on her knees, the bourka twisting so that the rough material scratched her face, Raven lay in a crumpled heap in fetid-smelling straw, tears of pain and fright gathering in her eyes.

Above her, the small ship sprang into life, footsteps pounding across the deck, canvas unfurling, voices shouting unintelligibly to one another. Moments later Raven could feel the deck lean to starboard, the familiar creaking of timber telling her that they had cast the mooring lines and were heading out to sea. Dear God, she groaned to herself, where were they bound, and who in the name of Christ had brought her here?

Crawling through the darkness, she sought shelter against a beam, curling herself into a ball and pulling the thick bourka back so that she could breathe more easily. Laying her forehead against her drawn-up knees, Raven let the hot tears roll down her cheeks. Never in her life had she felt more frightened and alone, and the tears flowed faster as she thought of Charles, wanting the safe, protective circle of his arms about her. Was he worried about her? she wondered. Had anyone even noticed that she was no longer aboard ship? Suppose he had sent out a search party to bring her back? A loud, near-hysterical laugh fell from Raven's lips. Even if Charles himself had gone out in search of her, it would do him no good, what with her stowed away like so much baggage in the black hold of some strange ship, her captors, her whereabouts, her destination all unknown.

A loud shout, muffled by the thick planking about her head, brought the flow of Raven's anguished tears to an abrupt halt. Lifting her wet face in the darkness, she listened and could hear an answering cry farther off. The sails must have been reefed, for Raven could feel the distinctive rocking of a boat adrift and the pull of the tide beneath her. Water splashed against the hull, and footsteps pounded across deck, accompanied by still more unintelligible shouts. Abruptly the hatch was thrown aside, and Raven scrambled to her feet as the same harsh voice she had heard in the prayer chamber called sharply down to her. Reluctantly Raven approached the hatchway, peering up at the dark, unsmiling face framed by the stars above her. Bending down, her captor reached out his hands to her and gave a curt command. When Raven hesitated he repeated it, more menacingly this time, and she lifted her arms resignedly and let him pull her easily to the deck beside him.

Rubbing her wrists, Raven looked quickly about her, glad that she had left the muffling bourka below. Dawn was approaching, the eastern horizon silver against the velvet-blue backdrop of night, and in the dim light Raven could see that they were out at sea, the mainland a mere strip of black behind the cutter's stern. Turning to look over her other shoulder, she gasped as she saw the immense hulk of a sailing ship loom out of the darkness ahead of her. Like the *Orient Star* it carried a full complement of sails, but its hull was square and thick, suggesting that it belonged to the lumbering class of merchantmen rather than the sleek, streamlined clippers.

A signal light flared on the bow of the cutter and grappling hooks were secured so that the tiny ship was bobbing alongside the hull of the mammoth cargo vessel. Boarding nets were lowered, and Raven cried out as the grinning man in the white robe prodded her forward with the tip of his knife. Motioning to the boarding net, he indicated that she was to climb up, but Raven hung back, terrified of the height and the precarious handholds. She was still wearing her salvar and kamiz, but even without cumbersome skirts and petticoats to hinder her, she knew she could not navigate the treacherous nets without falling.

Her captor motioned toward them again, more impatiently this time, but Raven shook her head dumbly, her tawny eyes wide in her pale, grimy face. Uttering a savage oath, the towering man reached out and snatched Raven about the waist, lifting her off her feet and tucking her without ceremony under his arm. With the agility of a monkey he scaled the ropes, never hesitating in his stride, until he had deposited Raven, heart hammering in her throat, into the hands of the grinning crew who had watched his ascent over the gunwales.

"Well done, Kamal!" someone shouted, but Raven, swaying dizzily and close to fainting from fright, hunger, and fatigue, did not even notice that the words had been spoken in English.

Someone seized her by the hair as she stood bewildered by the rail, yanking her unceremoniously across the worn deck and tossing her roughly down a hatchway into a hold as black and foul-smelling as the last one. Hauling herself upright, Raven sensed instantly that she was not alone. In the darkness around her she could hear quiet, rasping pants and feel countless pairs of eyes, as if the entire hold were filled with unseen bodies. The sharp smell of sweat and fear was there, too, and she bit back her scalding tears, afraid to draw attention to herself by crying.

Crouching down in the darkness, too frightened to search out a more comfortable place, Raven listened to the sounds of suffering humanity around her, wondering how many other pitiable wretches shared her prison with her.

Abovedecks the crew shouted lustily as the boarding nets were reeled in and the grappling hooks and lines cast. Slowly the ponderous merchantman gained momentum, the massive rudder turning it into the current that led it in a wide arc around the drifting cutter. The seas were calm, the breaking dawn bringing with it mild, steady winds that filled the patched sails, gentling the big ship as it set a new course that would take it far away from Karachi and the sub-continent of India, which was falling slowly away from its stern.

Chapter Fourteen

In the elegant stern quarters of the *Orient Star*, Captain Charles St. Germain was standing with his long legs planted firmly apart, staring out of the windows at the primitive, untidy houses that dotted the quay beyond the docks where the clipper ship was moored. His emerald eyes narrowed to slits, Charles studied the tiny fishing port as though expecting it to reveal to him where amid its filthy, teeming alleyways it had hidden the object of the most painstaking search ever conducted by the *Orient Star*'s captain and crew. For two nights and a day Charles and his men had been hunting for Raven Barrancourt, who had slipped off his ship in the dark of an evening, never to return.

At first Charles had been consumed with rage to learn Raven was gone, his awesome temper striking terror into the hearts of his loyal crew. Then he had begun to grow afraid, and as the relentless hours ticked by and Raven remained missing, the numbing certainty began to build within him that she would not be found alive. While his men scoured the streets and alleyways, questioned the villagers, and searched through the surrounding countryside, Charles retreated to his cabin to think. It was obvious to him that Raven would have returned long before this unless she had met with foul play, and that likely prospect brought the cold sweat from every pore in his body.

"Captain?"

Charles turned to find Danny standing nervously in the doorway. The sight of her gaunt, haggard face concerned him, and he led her quickly to a sea chair before her wobbling legs gave out from under her. She had aged incredibly since Raven's disappearance, the once merry brown eyes lifeless and reddened from constant crying. Charles poured her a brandy from the nearby decanter, insisting that she drink it.

"I didn't want to bother you," she said after the fit of coughing had subsided and the fiery liquid brought a touch of color to her pale cheeks, "but I just woke up. You haven't found her, have you?" Her voice trailed off as she looked up into Charles's lean visage, the answer written there as plainly as if he had spoken. Her lower lip began to tremble dangerously, and Charles turned away to allow her the chance to compose herself.

"Dmitri has gone to the street bazaar to make inquiries," he said, his broad back turned toward her, the rising sun illuminating the hard, angular planes of his face as he moved restlessly to the stern windows. "Raven didn't just disappear without a trace. Someone must have seen her." His lean jaw clenched. "We'll find out who, Danny, I promise you that."

The elderly woman shivered unconsciously at the veiled threat behind the softly spoken words. She had liked Captain St. Germain from the beginning and had never had cause to fear him before, but she did so now. Since Raven's disappearance he had changed before her eyes, grown unreachable, dangerous, his strong emotions smoldering beneath the surface like a volcano ready to erupt.

"I still don't understand it," Charles added, speaking so softly now that Danny could scarcely hear him. "What made her leave the ship that night?" He turned around, and Danny was shocked by the haunted look on his handsome features. "Did I do something to drive her away? You must know, Danny."

"In faith, I wouldn't, captain," she replied nervously, her fingers shaking as she ran them through her unruly graying curls.

"Dammit, woman, you're lying!" Charles grated, moving forward and pouncing swiftly, seizing her plump fingers between his.

Danny winced as the pressure of his hand tightened like a vise, and Charles, seeing it, released her instantly, the bottled anger he had let escape quickly under control again. "I'm sorry," he said hoarsely, his emerald eyes resting intently upon the old woman's upturned face. "I didn't mean to hurt you, Danny, but you must tell me. There is something, isn't there? In God's name, won't you tell me what it is? Perhaps it may help us find her."

"Do you think so?" Danny inquired hopefully.

"I won't know for sure until you tell me," Charles said quietly.

Danny looked away. "Miss Raven said I shouldn't."

"Raven isn't here," Charles reminded her savagely.

Danny hesitated, and Charles fought the urge to shake her. Fond as he was of the old woman, he held nothing sacred where Raven's safety was concerned, and he'd beat it out of her if he had to, if he thought for one minute that what Danny had to tell him might help return Raven to him again.

"God's blood, woman!" he roared at last, his patience at an end. "Speak!"

"It—it be the babe, sir," Danny whimpered tearfully.

Charles's head snapped up abruptly, his nostrils flaring. "Baby? What baby?"

"The one Miss Raven be carrying," Danny whispered. "That's why she fainted that night. The poor dear was distraught when I told her. I'm sure that's why she ran away."

Charles slumped into a nearby chair, cradling his head in his hands. "In God's name, why didn't she tell me?"

"She didn't want you to know," Danny explained, unnerved by the humbled expression on the once-arrogant features. "She felt sure you'd be wanting to marry her to give the babe a name, and she said she wasn't about to accept your charity."

Charles startled her by giving a low, harsh laugh. "Aye, I can well imagine how she despised the thought of evoking my pity." He straightened, his chestnut curls disheveled. "Well, she was wrong, Danny, wrong in thinking I would marry her for that reason alone. Even if there had been no baby, did she actually believe I was going to permit her to return to Cornwall and keep her word to wed that dissolute swine?"

"How could she have thought otherwise?" Danny flared, numbed by the futility of Charles's confession at this time, when it might prove so dismally late. "You didn't even spare her a civil word after we escaped from Lahore!"

Charles's broad shoulders slumped as he admitted to himself the truth of Danny's impassioned words. "Raven once accused me of having no heart," he said, his voice low and ugly with self-condemnation. "She was right, Danny. I'd survived so long without love, without feeling, that it became easier to bury emotions that proved too difficult to deal with than to face them honestly. It was easier to be unkind to Raven, or to ignore her, than to admit how deeply I cared for her. When my pride nearly cost her her life at the hands of that madcap cousin of hers, I wanted to tell her how deeply sorry I was." His voice grew bitter. "But it was easier to retreat into silence, easier to convince myself that she blamed me for what had happened and that I owed her nothing at all."

A tender look suddenly entered the burning emerald eyes. "Deep down I knew that Raven would never blame me for anything like that. It's simply not in her nature, and yet I chose to believe it was, because that was easier than admitting to myself that my pride and arrogance alone had forced us so far apart."

Danny was silent, and Charles, seeing the compassion and pain mingled on her lined face, laughed harshly. "Oh, I can admit it to you now, Danny, because I've decided not to be a fool anymore. If Raven were here right now, I'd even have the courage to tell her the same thing, but that's a non sequitur, isn't it? Raven is gone and now it's too late."

"Tovarich, look!"

Both of them glanced up quickly as Dmitri burst through the door, the weariness that had dogged him relentlessly for the past two days replaced by elation. Like his captain, he had not slept at all since Raven's disappearance, but there was a jaunty bounce to his step as he strode toward the table where Charles was sitting, a piece of embroidered muslin in his outstretched hand.

"I bought these from a huckster in the bazaar," Dmitri said, laying the square of material in front of his captain. "He is waiting without to speak to you. Treat him gently, my friend. He is very nervous, but I think he has much to tell us."

Charles impatiently unwrapped the objects Dmitri had given him, but the scowl on his handsome face froze into disbelief as he lifted them with fingers that were suddenly unsteady. Danny gasped, her hands flying to her breast, when she recognised the beautiful carved mother-of-pearl combs Raven had been wearing in her hair the night she had fled from the *Orient Star*.

"Where did you say you got these, Dmitri?" Charles asked slowly.

The big Russian spread his beefy hands wide. "In the bazaar. Here, meet Hajid Imam. He will tell you more." Turning, he gestured dramatically toward the opened cabin door, but the threshold remained empty. Grinning unabashedly, he stepped outside and exchanged a few irritable words before returning to the cabin with a thin, aging native, dressed only in baggy muslin trousers, held firmly by the arm. The huckster, taking one look at the glowering, chestnut-haired man seated tensely before him, retreated hastily, but Dmitri's firm grip prevented him from escaping.

Charles, much to the watching Danny's surprise, treated the timid old man kindly, although it was obvious to her that he was brimming with impatience. Leaning forward, he addressed him in several different languages, settling at last on a dialect that Danny did not know, and she watched helplessly as the terse exchange progressed. Gradually the huckster grew more animated in response to the captain's softly uttered questions, gesticulating wildly and rolling his antimony-blackened eyes as he loosened a torrent of information. Charles and Dmitri listened grimly while Danny wrung her hands, anxious to know what was being said.

At last Hajid Imam fell silent, and it was obvious to Danny that Charles was concluding the interview when he pressed a coin into the outstretched, henna-smeared hand. Hajid Imam salaamed gratefully, then withdrew a small leather pouch from his trousers and handed it with great ceremony to Charles. It was, he explained, a gift for the venerable sahib, and contained the dust of rare lizards which, if conscientiously used, would prevent the loss of virility during the sahib's later years.

Charles thanked him graciously although his mind was elsewhere, and it was Dmitri who roared with laughter as he showed Hajid Imam out. "What need do you have of such hocus-pocus, eh?" he demanded, grinning broadly when he returned to Charles's quarters. Studying the powerful muscles that strained the fine Holland cloth of Charles's shirt, he added, "Master Imam should have realized that loss of virility is a disease which will never plague you, my friend."

"Dmitri," Charles said shortly, "send the search parties out again. I want this fellow Kamal tracked down." His handsome visage was suddenly as ruthless as a hawk's circling in for the kill. "When he's found I don't want anyone to touch him, is that understood? Leave him to me."

"Oh, captain, have you found Raven?" Danny cried as soon as Dmitri was gone.

"No, but I think I've learned who kidnapped her." Charles strode to the washbasin that stood in the corner, stripped off his shirt, and began to splash water on his face, the sun-bronzed muscles in his back rippling as he moved. "Mr. Imam purchased Raven's combs from a Turk named Kamal who supposedly haunts this coastline several times a year. Imam doesn't know where he comes from, only that he appears every so often, spends a few days, and is gone. All of Karachi seems to be afraid of him, but I assured Mr. Imam that if this Kamal fellow is indeed responsible for Raven's disappearance, then I'd see to it that he was taken care of... permanently."

Danny shivered at the underlying savagery in Charles's casually spoken words. "Then he didn't know exactly if this person has Miss Raven or not?"

Charles shook his head, reaching for a towel behind him. "He could tell me little more than that the Turk approached his booth with the combs and told him to name a price. Apparently he always has jewelry and other baubles to sell Imam and the other bazaar traders whenever he appears in port." The emerald eyes narrowed thoughtfully as he pulled a clean shirt over his broad shoulders. "Curious. Now, if you'll excuse me, Danny, I'll try my own hand at bringing this fellow in."

In a tiny Indian port village inhabited mostly by small, dark fishing folk, a tall Turk in flowing robes was not difficult to find. Conducting his business openly, the Turk named Kamal moved unafraid amid the bartering men and women of the bazaar, turning his long hooked nose up at the smell of fish rotting in an auction booth nearby. Unlike Karachi's citizenry, he did not stop to barter or gossip, but moved purposefully through the throng, his destination unknown but his description easily fitting that which the huckster Hajid Imam had supplied Captain St. Germain and his crew.

Having reached the end of the square, the Turk turned down a narrow alley, hunching his razor-thin shoulders against the whirling dust that blasted between the dense row of buildings. At the far end of the twisting alley he stopped abruptly, his path blocked by a half-dozen cudgel-bearing sailors who emerged silently and swiftly from a nearby doorway. His contemptuous gaze moved over them swiftly, his black eyes shifting like a ferret's, his instincts urging caution because these were, as Kamal quickly recognized, Englishmen. He had dealt with the British only rarely, for he found them a disorganized, pompous lot less trustworthy than the lowest of camel thieves, whose concern lay mostly in lining their own pockets with gold and in the expansionism of Great Britain in the name of the Angrezi rani, Victoria.

Slow-witted, without honor and exceedingly soft, the British were nonetheless unpredictable, and Kamal regarded the hostile group warily, as yet unafraid. Only one of them caused him some concern, and that was the tall, bearded one with the dark Slavic features, whose grip on the cudgel he carried informed the watchful Turk that he was not a stranger to hand combat. The alley was dusty, the sounds of the bazaar muted, and early-morning shadows still lingered on the littered street. The Turk's thick robes billowed gently in the breeze, but he did not move, his long, thin arms held at his sides while the crew members of the *Orient Star* circled around him as cautiously as if they had cornered a tiger.

"What do we do now, Dmitri?" Geoffrey Lytton asked, his pale gray eyes never leaving their quarry.

"Wait until Mr. Quintrell has summoned the captain," Dmitri responded tersely. "Kristos, I hope this fellow speaks something other than Turkish, for that, I fear, is a tongue beyond the captain's ken."

Although he had understood only a few of the words, the Turk made an abrupt attempt to break free. Instantly the circle tightened about him, the seamen's menacing intent obvious, and Kamal reacted instinctively. Throwing himself back against the wall of the building behind him, he whipped out a curved, evil-looking knife from the folds of his robe. Brandishing it in the air, he grinned, his long, broken teeth flashing in his dark face when he saw the uneasiness that appeared in the eyes of the younger recruits.

"I see you've found him, Dmitri."

The circle of men parted respectfully as Charles stepped into their midst, the relief on the faces of the less experienced men obvious even to the Turk.

"Aye, tovarich, and he's a feisty one," Dmitri declared, his deep bass voice filled with animosity.

Charles turned his head slowly and studied the man who had stolen Raven from him, his emerald eyes heavy-lidded. Kamal returned the appraisal with equal deliberation, but there was a wariness in his spare frame that hadn't been there before. Like a wild animal that senses danger, he sniffed the air, and the filthy hand that curved about the knife handle tightened almost imperceptively. Though he did not know what these men wanted from him, he was still not afraid, and he had learned the lessons of survival well. He would listen and wait and find his opening without forcing it; then he would pounce swiftly, like a tiger leaping in for the kill.

Yes, he thought to himself, the green-eyed one was the potent enemy, and the one he would have to kill, if that was what would be required in getting away from this group of Englishmen whose designs on him were as yet unknown. Kamal had learned to kill in his early youth, to kill swiftly and without mercy, but as yet there was no need for that. He would be patient.

Charles moved forward, pausing just out of knife range, and regarded the cornered Turk intently. His tone was curt as he tried various tongues, exhausting most of them without success until he settled at last on Arabic, a language the Turk understood. Charles's command of the ancient tongue was limited but sufficient to make clear to Kamal what he wished to know. The crewmen of the *Orient Star* listened tensely without comprehending, the dusty alley silent but for their captain's harsh voice. At the far end of the street where the alley spilled onto the bazaar, a few curious spectators gathered, but when they saw the weapons and the dark, hostile faces, they slipped quickly away, not wanting to become involved.

Kamal's watchful black eyes never left the aristocratic face of the grim Englishman. The Englishman was seeking a young woman, English like himself, who had disappeared from his ship two nights ago. Kamal shook his head in annoyance, for he was far too wise to involve himself with the women of the British. Certain now that the green-eyed Englishman would be satisfied with his denial, he moved toward an opening in the circle but froze when Charles's grim expression changed to anger. Kamal tensed as he saw the Englishman reach into his breeches, his piercing black eyes widening when he saw the mother-of-pearl combs displayed in the extended palm.

"I have never seen those in my life," he said in Arabic, but the flickering eyes had given him away.

"You lie!" Charles burst out in English, pouncing so swiftly that he took the Turk unawares. The knife went flying from Kamal's hand, clattering to the stones as the powerful Englishman threw himself forward, his great weight sending his opponent smashing against the wall of the building. Then he was lying face down on the street, the dirt filling his mouth and nose, one of his arms pinned behind his back in so painful a manner that sweat broke out on the Turk's broad forehead.

"She was wearing the garb of a Punjabi woman," Charles grated, the Arabic words rushing with every panted breath from his lungs as he straddled the body of the fallen Turk with his own, his muscular legs pinning him to the ground. "You sold the combs to a bazaar peddler. Tell me what you've done with her or I'll carve your heart from your body."

"I do not know of whom you—" Kamal began, but the words ended on an agonized moan as his arm was wrenched higher, the pain shooting through him like a knife wound, hot and fierce.

"Where is she, damn you?" Charles rasped. To the watching crewmen he seemed like a stranger, his lips drawn back in a feral snarl, his green eyes smoldering with blood lust.

"I have told you," Kamal panted, but got no further. Digging his knee into the Turk's back, Charles jerked roughly on the pinned arm and the Turk shrieked as he felt the bones crack, white-hot pain lashing him. "The c-cutter *Noria,*" he moaned, tears coursing down his dirty face. "I took her there after hiding her all night in the c-catacombs of Siva."

"Where is the ship?" Charles grated as Kamal collapsed, half-delirious with pain.

"On the f-far side of the village."

Charles released him and rose to his feet. "Dmitri, tie his hands and bring—"

No sooner did Kamal feel the weight of the Englishman lift from his back than he rolled over, ignoring the pain as he landed on his broken arm, using his good hand to expertly fling his knife at Charles's unguarded throat. In the next second the alleyway echoed with the deafening thunder of an explosion, white-hot flames of powder releasing acrid smoke into the air. The Turk slumped back, unmoving, the front of his robes stained crimson as blood spurted from his chest, the sternum smashed into fragments by the path of a deadly lead ball.

Dmitri, holding the still-smoking pistol in his hand, glanced quickly at Charles, a weak grin of relief curving his lips when he saw that the knife had merely grazed his captain's cheek. "You are unhurt, tovarich?"

Pressing the handkerchief Jason Quintrell had shakily produced to the side of his face, Charles nodded curtly, intent on stanching the flow of blood. "Thanks to you, I am." His emerald eyes were expressionless as he stared down at the dead Turk. "Mr. Lytton, have your men bring him along."

It was late afternoon before the captain and the crewmen of the *Orient Star* returned to their ship. An overwrought Danny was waiting on the deck by the entry port when they silently came aboard, her tear-streaked face growing pale at the sight of the ragged wound on Charles's lean cheek. Charles brushed past her as though he did not even hear her dazed questions, and Danny, staring after him with wide, frightened eyes, seized Dmitri's sleeve as the big Russian prepared to follow his captain below.

"Oh, Mr. Zergeyev, what is it? Where's Miss Raven? How badly is the captain hurt?"

"There isn't time to explain," Dmitri informed her curtly, then relented when he peered down into her ashen face. Briefly he told her of their bloody encounter with the Turkish slave trader Kamal and how he had directed them to the cutter *Noria*, which he and his cutthroat crew had sailed throughout the breadth of the Asian and African coastlines in search of slaves.

"Not your ordinary African field laborer whose kind is shipped by the thousands to America and the islands to work and die," Dmitri added harshly, "but Indian and Nubian beauties, young women who will bring high prices on the market. Kamal bought most of them himself, paying money for the daughters of Indian families, because here in India daughters are of little value. Some he kidnapped, and I'm afraid that's what happened when he discovered Raven wandering about the streets of Karachi at night, her costume and her looks declaring her a great Hindu beauty."

Danny's lips took on a grayish cast, and Dmitri wondered if it would have been kinder to spare the old woman the truth.

"Where is she now?" Danny demanded, clutching his shirt front with stiff fingers.

Dmitri sighed heavily. "She is gone, Danny."

"Where? Where?" she cried hysterically.

"Two nights ago the cutter *Noria* had a scheduled rendezvous with a slave trader named the *Cormorant*," Dmitri said heavily. "Her crew was quite eager to tell us everything when we carried their dead captain's body aboard, I promise you that."

"And Miss Raven is aboard that slave ship now?" Danny gasped.

Dmitri's dark eyes mirrored her anguish. "Aye, bound for New Orleans to be sold as a fancy at auction, but do not worry," he told her, grasping the old woman by the arms as she swayed. "The *Orient Star* is faster, and we will plot the same course and thereby catch the *Cormorant* before she reaches port, I promise you that, too."

"I believe you," Danny whispered. "I wouldn't have if I hadn't seen the look on Captain St. Germain's face when he came aboard."

"Then you will understand if I abandon you now to bear the burden of what I have told you alone," Dmitri said gently, "for I must help make preparations to cast off. We are leaving India, Mrs. Daniels. Pray that our sails are blessed with a stiff wind."

Within the hour the *Orient Star* slid into the clear azure water of the Arabian Sea, its canvas filled with wind, and some of the terrible urgency was replaced by optimism in the set faces of the crewmen who trimmed the sails high in the rigging. Though the *Cormorant* had a two-day lead over them, it was not built to fly before the wind like a clipper, and every man aboard swore he would not rest until the ponderous slaver was in their sights. Fierce was their determination, yet they could not keep from glancing uncertainly at the quarterdeck, where their captain stood alone by the rail, his lean face ravaged with inner emotions, his cheek still bloodied from the slashing wound made by the dead Turk's knife.

Not until late that night, when the moon had already traveled a great arc across the blackened sky, did Charles St. Germain leave his post, and only Dmitri, who was himself pacing sleeplessly on the deck below, saw him return a short time later. Some inner sixth sense warned him that the captain wanted to be alone, and so he did not call out to announce his presence but stood unmoving behind the base of the mainmast, watching as the tall Englishman ascended the ladder and returned to his customary place by the taffrail. In the dim moonlight Dmitri saw that he was dressed in shirtsleeves, his chestnut hair windblown, and his eyes widened curiously when he saw that Charles was carrying the gilded cage containing the nightingale in his hands.

Setting it down on the polished planking, Charles reached inside, then straightened, his broad-shouldered form standing motionless near the rail. As Dmitri watched he raised his arm and unclenched his fist so that the nightingale was clearly visible sitting unafraid on the big, callused palm. For a moment it lingered there, then, as if just realizing it was free, it spread its glossy black wings and launched itself into the air. Charles raised his handsome face skyward and watched as it circled uncertainly until, with the uncanny accuracy of its kind, it took off at last toward the west, where the mainland of India was still visible on the stern.

After a moment Charles stirred, then bent down and picked up the cage and flung it far into the night. With set features he left the deck, not even sparing a glance at the officer of the watch, who, startled by his captain's unexpected presence, snapped to attention. Down in his cabin Charles poured himself a brandy. His cheek throbbed but he ignored the pain, draining the contents of the snifter and filling it again. A single lamp glowed overhead, and his emerald eyes were narrowed as they roved restlessly over the beautiful furnishings. A low growl rose in his throat when his wandering gaze landed on the brass hip bath, for it was almost as if he could envision Raven reclining inside it as he had first seen her, the startled look in her wide golden eyes reminding him of a wary, untamed deer. How slender and breathtakingly perfect her ivory body had been beneath the warm, lapping water, and how great had been his desire to possess it!

Anger and despair exploded within his heart, and Charles turned away with a savage oath. Unexpectedly his eyes fell on the ginger jar which Phillip Barrancourt had given to Raven that fateful night. It was still standing on the table where Raven had left it after she fainted, a circumstance, Charles reminded himself brutally, that had been precipitated by the fact that she bore his child within her. In one savage motion Charles swept the beautiful jar from the table and dashed it with all his might against the richly paneled cabin wall. The sound it made as it exploded into a thousand shattered fragments of china restored him to his senses and he wearily massaged the back of his neck, recalling that he hadn't slept at all in the past thirty-six hours.

With little spirit, he moved to extinguish the lantern that burned near the shuttered stern windows, but paused in the task as his attention was caught by something that glittered on the floor before him. Bending down, he idly kicked through the broken fragments of the ginger jar with the square toe of his boot. Frowning, he stooped to examine them more closely, the lantern continuing to reflect a twinkling prism of light on the smooth planking amid the colorful shards. Picking it up, he straightened and examined it closely, thinking at first that the odd, misshapen lump was simply a piece of clear glass. Then his full, sensual lips began to twitch, and finally he threw back his head and laughed.

"Have you gone mad, tovarich?"

"Sometimes I think so," Charles responded as Dmitri entered the spacious cabin behind him. "Tell me, my friend, what would you think if I told you that I'd just found the Kohinoor diamond in the false bottom of that ginger jar?"

"I'd think you really were mad," Dmitri replied promptly, shaking his dark head as he saw the shattered fragments that littered the cabin floor.

"Here, then, take a look."

Dmitri deftly caught the insignificant-looking piece of glass and moved closer to the light to examine it. Charles watched him, his hands propped on his lean hips, until the Russian's disbelieving eyes met his across the room.

"Sajid Wali Shah, brother of the nawab of Oudh, was a notorious user of opium," Dmitri remarked thoughtfully. "It's conceivable that the diamond was presented to Phillip Barrancourt to pay for the drug. Silver bullion is the standard method of payment, no? Still, I imagine gemstones are honored as well."

"Given Phillip's state of utter penury I wouldn't be surprised if he knew nothing of the diamond."

"Aye, that could be," Dmitri agreed, "yet how did it get into the ginger jar, and why would Sajid Wali Shah present it to him?"

Charles shrugged his wide shoulders. "That, I'm afraid, is a mystery which will never be explained." He smiled suddenly, a triumphant light burning in his eyes. "God, the irony of it,

Dmitri! Phillip Barrancourt was driven to the verge of bankruptcy by his addiction, suffering the bitter reality of being poor, while a king's ransom sat undetected in the bottom of his ginger jar!"

Some of Dmitri's shock had worn off by now, and he held the stone up to the light, his eyes beginning to gleam. "It's enormous, isn't it, tovarich? Ay, yi, yi, what we couldn't purchase with this, my friend!"

"If the Punjab is annexed, it will belong to the queen," Charles reminded his first mate calmly.

"And you intend to present it to her?" Dmitri exploded disbelievingly. "After all you've been through, after everything Phillip Barrancourt has done?" Waving the diamond excitedly in the air he added, "With this, the ultimate revenge will be yours!"

"I have no wish for it, Dmitri," Charles said quietly.

Sobering instantly, the big Russian laid a hand on the rigid shoulder of his captain and said understandingly, "It is an unjust world at times, Charles. In gaining one fortune you've lost another, and I think the other one was far more precious to you."

Charles's jaw clenched. "I'll find her, Dmitri, on that I'll lay my life."

"And I will pledge my hand to help you," Dmitri said loyally.

The two men looked at each other, silently swearing to gain back what had been stolen from them, and then Dmitri grinned, breaking the tension that had settled over the darkened cabin.

"All right, you worthless sea dog," he growled, "we'll follow the straight and narrow path and bring Queen Vickie her precious diamond—provided the Punjab is annexed."

"Your generosity amazes me, Dmitri," Charles admitted dryly.

"Aye, it does." Dmitri held the big jewel aloft so that the lantern light caught and reflected the shimmering interior. "You're right, tovarich, it is an ugly thing, but it will be beautiful when it's properly cut—and worth a king's ransom." His bearded face split with the width of a complacent grin. "Vickie should be thrilled and," he added with a mischievous wink, "there's no reason to tell her that the Kohinoor she will eventually be presented with will be considerably smaller than it is now, eh?"

"What do you mean?" Charles asked sharply.

Dmitri shrugged his massive shoulders. "Even if it were, say, half the size it is now, it would truly be worthy of the Crown Jewels, wouldn't you say?"

"And the other half?" Charles asked, unable to hide the amusement in his emerald eyes.

"Oh, you have a good imagination, captain," Dmitri answered glibly. "I'm sure you'll think of something."

The longing in Charles's rugged visage was painfully obvious, although his voice never wavered. "Aye, Dmitri, I do have something in mind for it."

He did not elaborate, and Dmitri did not press him, yet inwardly he burned with curiosity. When Charles had a plan up his sleeve, Dmitri knew, the unexpected was bound to happen.

Chapter Fifteen

The long winter months that followed the Dutch slave trader *Cormorant*'s departure from India proved to be the most harrowing in Raven Barrancourt's young life. Crossing the Arabian Sea, the ponderous slaver sailed up the Guinea coast, laying over briefly in Fida to cram even more Africans into its groaning main holds. With the month of January well advanced, it set a new course across the Tropic of Cancer, where winter storms soon howled down from the north to buffet it unmercifully.

Scores of slaves died in those turbulent seas, but they were casualties that Captain Niels Van der Horst had expected, and during calmer days the dead were tossed overboard to lighten the *Cormorant*'s load. Unlike other ships sailing for the Dutch West India Company as human cargo vessels for its lucrative slave trade, the *Cormorant* sailed the high seas during the winter months when the stench of decaying bodies did not hover like a pall over the ship. Captain Van der Horst, preferring the turbulent winter gales to the breathless heat of the summer months, sequestered himself in his quarters and drank rum, the weather little more than an inconvenience for him.

As for the slaves in the main holds and the frightened young woman trapped with her unseen fellow prisoners in the forward compartment, the battering winds and high seas cast them into the throes of hell. Day after day the hapless prisoners were thrown against bulkheads as the *Cormorant* bucked and pitched beneath the onslaught of the towering waves. Seasickness, fear, the agony of bruised ribs and an aching head dogged Raven relentlessly as she grew weaker and weaker on the paltry rations that were tossed down the hatchway now and again. But for Raven the excruciating pain of being flung time and again against a beam was nothing compared with the haunting fear that her child would be harmed. After a few short days she learned to curl herself up in a manner that protected the life within her, but still the constant terror remained.

It was fear for the unborn child alone that kept Raven alive during the long weeks, though the damp cold penetrated her thin clothing so that soon her teeth were chattering and her lungs wracked with coughs. With the hatch completely sealed, she and the rest of her wretched companions lived in total darkness, never knowing when day waned into night or when dawn broke again over uneasy, storm-tossed seas. Sometimes, when the howling winds subsided to a dull roar beyond the battered hull, Raven could hear the frightened whispers and feverish moans of the other women around her. The foreign tongues they spoke and the fact that she could not see them made her feel more wretchedly alone than she had ever been in her life.

The Christmas season must have come and gone weeks before, she thought, passing in a haze of darkness and pain. Memories of another life, of the happy times Raven and her father had shared during the festive holiday season at North Head plagued her constantly, bringing tears to her eyes and overwhelming her with longing for her home and James Barrancourt's loving presence. If it was not Cornwall and her father of whom Raven dreamed, then it was Charles, his rugged visage always floating before her feverish eyes. She found herself hungering for him, daring to dream of what life might have been like for her at his side, their child—a product of their deep and abiding love—safe and happy with them.

It would have been easier, Raven knew, to forget her foolish dreams of the future and give up the battle altogether, sinking into blessed oblivion where pain could no longer touch her. Yet she continued to struggle doggedly against the numbness that crept over her as the days dragged on in a relentless nightmare of darkness.

"I swear to you, Charles," she whispered to herself whenever despair threatened to overwhelm her, "I won't let our son or daughter come to harm!"

The thought of Charles never failed to lend her courage, and often she could clearly envision his sea-green eyes before her glittering with the lusty thirst for life which she now clung to with all of her remaining strength.

"I will survive, Charles," she promised herself stubbornly throughout the countless days, weeks, and months that followed. Often the words lost their meaning and echoed senselessly through her brain, and sometimes it no longer mattered to Raven whether or not she lived. But what continued to remain important to her was the precious gift of Charles's love growing within her that must not be denied the chance to flourish. It was for the child's sake alone that Raven continued to fight.

The few hard biscuits and moldy chapatis she was rationed were hoarded and consumed in a manner that enabled her to stave off total starvation. Unlike the rest of the faceless prisoners who wept and moaned in the impenetrable blackness, Raven refused to permit herself to cry, aware that allowing utter despair to claim her would only poison her resolve to survive. In calmer seas she took to moving about as much as possible, keeping her aching limbs from becoming stiff and useless, forcing herself to remain active despite the increasing desire to give in to lethargy. For the sake of her child she vowed to remain healthy.

What was hardest to endure was the uncertainty of not knowing where she was bound or what her captors intended to do with her once they arrived at their unknown destination. Sometimes Raven was certain she would go mad with fear; at other times she despaired for the life of her baby in the hands of the men who ventured about on the rain-soaked decks above.

During the bleak, lonely hours in her fetid prison she had discovered that the people who surrounded her were all women—although it was impossible to guess how many there were. This obvious lack of men led Raven to wonder what her captors intended to do with all of them. The harrowing possibility dawned on her at last that they had been kidnapped for the very reason that they were women. Still, Raven adamantly refused to believe that intended slavery was the cause of her abduction. No one, she tried telling herself over and over again whenever panic gripped her heart, would dare kidnap an Englishwoman from a sleepy Indian fishing port and sell her into bondage! And even if that was the case, she would certainly be freed once she informed the authorities at their destination who she really was!

Yet despite her determination and vehement promises to free herself, Raven's hope waned as the agonizing days ground on. Had she known that she was bound for a slave auction in New

Orleans to be sold as a mistress, a "fancy girl," to some leering plantation owner, she might not have struggled so valiantly to keep her optimism high. Fortunately the howling winds and buffeting seas carried the moans and wails of the damned and dying in the suffocating main holds away from her, because knowledge of the anguished plight of the suffering Africans would have caused Raven to lose faith altogether.

It was impossible to guess how many days or weeks or even months elapsed in that black and reeking hold. Raven had lost all sense of time long ago, and it was with considerable grogginess and disorientation that she was awakened one day by the sound of the hatch cover being tossed aside to allow shafts of pale sunlight to pour down into the hold. Around her she could hear the others stirring, frightened whispers echoing through the darkness.

"Come on, come on, out with ye!"

The harsh male voice, the first Raven had heard in a great length of time, threw her into such confusion that she didn't realize at first that the words had been spoken in English. Only when they were repeated in the same guttural growl did she comprehend that they were all being ordered to leave their dark prison behind.

Despite her overwhelming desire to go topside into the fresh air, Raven hesitated, afraid to leave the relative safety of the hold for the unknown dangers above. But when a tangy, salt-scented breeze stirred the tendrils of dark hair clinging to her face, she suddenly couldn't stand it any longer. Clutching the uneven rungs of the ladder, she began to climb slowly, only to have someone above grab her by the arms and jerk her upright until she emerged onto a narrow foredeck, the pale daylight making her squint. Dizzily she tottered to the rail, where she clung for support until the light no longer stabbed her eyes. When she opened them at last she found herself looking across the welcoming vastness of the unending ocean.

Lifting her face to the warmth of the few rays of sunshine that filtered through the clouds, Raven felt her weakness being replaced by profound elation. Never would she have thought that the mere touch of the sun or the freshness of a wayward breeze could strengthen her like this. For a moment she remained motionless by the rail, savoring this first taste of freedom before turning her head and looking about her.

The sight that was revealed to her on the foredeck behind her shocked her profoundly, for until that moment Raven had never really been able to envision what her fellow prisoners might look like. Now, as she watched the disheartened, clearly frightened group being ejected from the hold by two roustabouts in rough, homespun sailor's attire, she felt her slim jaw grow slack with dismay. All of them were women as she had already guessed, but their nationalities were a mystery to her. Some with skin as black as night, others with enormous sloe eyes and delicately proportioned features, all of them were dressed in torn, filthy robes that were little more than rags by now. They could have been Moors, Arabs, or Egyptians, any number of things, and yet it was not their ancestry or their origins that affected Raven the most; it was the unhealthy pallor of their sunken cheeks, their stooped frames, the dull, lifeless expressions in their eyes.

Did she look the same way? Raven wondered, horrified and sickened. Glancing down at herself for the first time in months, she noticed that her hands were thin and that they shook slightly, and that her stained and wrinkled salvars seemed baggier than ever. And yet she forgot all of that and the rest of the people on the deck behind her as she saw for the first time the distinctive rounding of her belly beneath the loose-fitting hem of her kamiz.

A moment of breathless joy made her gasp, her feverishly bright eyes burning with the intensity of it, and a single tear trembled on her dark lashes. The child was alive, it was growing within her! Hesitantly, almost reverently, she placed her trembling hands on the gentle curve. Thank God, she thought to herself, thank God she hadn't failed Charles in this!

Behind her the heavyset tars began cursing irritably as they herded the frightened women into a straggling row beneath the massive foremast, and Raven surreptitiously adjusted the folds of the kamiz over her stomach before joining them. She felt more clear-headed now than she had in many weeks, and the fact that the crew spoke English gave her hope to believe that she would somehow be able to extricate herself from the nightmare into which she had been cast.

And yet some overpowering sixth sense warned her to remain still, not to reveal even with the batting of an eyelash the fact that she understood the sailors' words. She must wait and listen,

Raven cautioned herself, and use what she learned to her best advantage.

"Well, have you got them ready for viewing, Rollo? Ah, splendid, splendid!"

Raven turned at the sound of the heavily accented voice and felt her heart skip a beat. An overweight, middle-aged man with blond curls framing his fleshy face was wheezily ascending to the foredeck. The faint morning breeze ruffled the tails of his elegant frock coat, and the hazy sunlight reflected the oily sheen on his high forehead and the bright polish of his brass buttons. Cruel little pig's eyes regarded the row of frightened women with almost greedy intensity while the moist lips sucked methodically in and out. If this was the captain of their ship, Raven realized with a sinking heart, she might find it difficult to convince him of her identity and expect him to show her mercy. There was nothing save avarice in his vapid expression and an obvious enjoyment of the fact that the muted weeping among the women grew more hysterical at the sight of him.

"Which are the ones Kamal brought me?" the captain demanded abruptly, his fat, bejeweled fingers resting on his plump hips.

"These," the ill-kempt sailor named Rollo replied, indicating with a sweep of the belaying pin he carried a small group in which Raven was included.

"Let's have a look at them," the captain suggested. Idly stroking his fleshy chin, he approached a young girl in the middle of the row whose pale, frightened face was averted. She began to sob quietly as the captain roughly jerked her head about and peered for a long time into her terrified eyes, pursing his lips thoughtfully. Raven bit back a horrified gasp as the plump hand strayed down to the small breasts, squeezing them experimentally while the young girl continued her silent weeping. The rest of the women stood as though turned to stone, their unseeing eyes turned toward the horizon, which was visible beyond the heavy railing of the ship.

"She's rather underdeveloped," the captain remarked irritably to Rollo, who stood dutifully behind him. "I shouldn't have accepted her to begin with."

"Mayhap she'll plump out a bit, cap'n," Rollo suggested, leering with spittle-moistened lips at the terrified girl, "if a man be havin' her an' she be ripened to womanhood!"

The captain shuddered delicately. "Please, Rollo, your tawdry comments make me nauseated. Ah well, I expect—"

No sooner had he released his hold of the young girl's breasts than, with a loud, keening wail, she darted away from him. Before anyone could stop her she had flung herself over the railing, disappearing silently into the sullen gray sea below. Raven, her heart thundering in her breast, her stomach churning, closed her eyes against the horror she had just witnessed and willed herself not to faint.

"Rollo, you cursed fool, you're supposed to watch them!" the captain shouted shrilly, but to Raven's ears he sounded more relieved than annoyed.

"I bain't to blame, cap'n!" Rollo whined while the other sailor shifted uneasily behind him. "She be jumped afore I had a chance to stop her!"

"Do cease your pitiable groveling," the captain said with a sigh, continuing, undaunted, the inspection of his property. "This one should bring a good price," he remarked, enthusiastically tweaking the nipples of a slender, dark-skinned girl with enormous brown eyes.

"Yus, cap'n, yus!" Rollo agreed eagerly.

"And this one is rather interesting," the captain added, coming to a halt before Raven. "Rather light-skinned for a Hindu, but then that appeals to some. Her eyes are an unusual color, wouldn't you agree?"

"Yus," Rollo said hastily.

The moist lips curved. "Just see how they blaze with hatred for me, Rollo! How positively amusing! This one, I fear, was raised by permissive parents, but then again a firm-handed owner might do wonders for her." He nodded his gold-curled head as he looked into Raven's flashing eyes. "A pity I've no desire for the female form, Rollo, or I wouldn't mind bedding her myself."

Raven caught her breath as the dark little eyes lingered for a moment on the gentle rounding of her belly that the kamiz hadn't been able to conceal altogether.

"And yet she's a bit scrawny for my tastes," the captain added, dismissing her with a shrug, and Raven could feel the tears of relief start in her eyes. "All of them are positively filthy," Captain Van der Horst continued, removing a scented handkerchief from his vest pocket and pressing it delicately to his nostrils. "I want them bathed and properly attired before we make landfall, Rollo, is that understood?"

"Aye, aye, cap'n!"

"And, Rollo, I want you to feed them a bit more. They were supposed to remain plump throughout the voyage."

"But ye said—"

"I don't care what I said!" Captain Van der Horst barked impatiently, causing Rollo to cower back. "There is a difference, my good sir, between rationing food reserves wisely and total starvation. I can see you haven't looked in on them once since we set out from Fida!"

"The hatches was sealed for crossin'!" Rollo whined fearfully. "I would've looked in on 'em weather permittin', cap'n."

"I expect you would have," the effeminate sea captain agreed at last. "Just make certain you've managed to bring their prices back up before we dock or it'll be the sting of the lash you'll be feeling, do you hear me?"

"Aye, aye, cap'n," Rollo responded sullenly.

"Yus indeed, the cap'n be a bad'n," the other tar muttered when the broad, curly-headed form had descended to the main deck. "I'm almost sorry we jumped our own ship to serve the bleedin' Dutch."

"An' I rather be deaded than playin' nursemaid to these wretches," Rollo grumbled. Irritably he set to work herding the frightened, bewildered women back into the darkness of the forward hold, using the belaying pin indiscriminately and managing to catch a dazed and terrified Raven squarely on the shoulders with it. The blow almost sent her toppling down the ladder, and she fought back the scalding tears as she crawled into her own secluded corner.

Thank God, she thought to herself, thank God she had listened to her instincts and hadn't let them know she was English! She began to shiver uncontrollably and bit her lip as the hot tears continued to roll down her thin cheeks. Suppose the captain had noticed her pregnancy? But for the loose-fitting hem of her kamiz he might have, and she was suddenly certain that the discovery would have prompted him to toss her overboard just like that poor young girl whose suicide he had caused with his cruelty.

The comments he had made to the English sailor named Rollo confirmed Raven's suspicions that she was being held prisoner aboard a slaver and that all of them were intended for eventual sale on the auction block. She shivered again, well aware that she would be useless in the captain's eyes if he discovered that she was with child. Stubbornly she dashed the tears from her eyes and set her small chin at a determined angle. She was not about to wind up at an auction, because by the time the slaver docked she intended to escape.

In response to Captain Van der Horst's orders, the prisoners' rations quickly improved. From that day on the biscuits which had sustained them during the crossing were supplemented with hard tack, dried fruits, and occasionally salted meat. Raven hoarded her share greedily, eating just enough to take the gnawing edge off her hunger and hiding away the rest in the event that Rollo might suddenly decide to abandon his sudden generosity. Because she had no idea how long it would take before they made landfall, Raven refused to indulge herself, although the increase in their meager food supplies was enough to help her regain a little of her strength in the days that followed.

The wash day Captain Van der Horst had spoken of arrived not too long afterward, filling Raven with excitement. Unlike the other women in the hold, she knew that the captain had ordered Rollo to supply all of them with wash water and clean clothes shortly before the voyage ended. She wished there was some way she could make them understand, then realized that the end of this long journey did not mean the freedom for them that it did for her. Perhaps she might be able to help them, Raven thought to herself, yet wondered how she could do so when she didn't even have the first idea where they would be when the slaver docked, or how she herself was going to get off the ship.

Her excitement was replaced by cold, hammering fear when Rollo, descending into the black hold with a lantern in his hand, turned to call up to his companion that it might be wiser if the washtubs were set up on the deck above rather than below.

"Then we can watch them at bathin', by God!" he cackled, and Raven shrank away from his hulking figure, seeking out the dark, protective corners of the hold as the rest of the young women had done as soon as the hatch had opened. Judas, if they were ordered to strip naked on the deck in broad daylight her condition would never escape notice! What was she to do now? she wondered in panic.

"Be thee mad, Rollo?" the voice of the other sailor called down in disgust. "It bain't naked women, it be skeletons they be, an' no feast for thy senses, by God! Cap'n'll be sore if some throwed theyselves overboard like first'n, too, yus indeed!"

Rollo growled a reluctant agreement low in his throat and hung the lantern from a beam so that it cast a narrow circle of light on the musty straw below. As Raven and the others watched from behind the shelter of beams and bulkheads, the two men carried down several large tin tubs and dippers, placing them beneath the beam of swaying light. When they had been filled with water, Rollo reached behind him unexpectedly and seized the arm of the nearest girl, yanking her forward and ignoring her cry of fear. Without ceremony the two men pulled the clothes from her body and lifted the kicking, scratching girl, tossing her into the tub, where Rollo began to scrub her vigorously with a rough piece of cloth.

Raven's heart went out to the girl, aware of her utter humiliation, and the sight of the ribs and collarbones that protruded sharply from beneath her dark skin made her realize exactly how thin all of them had grown. By the time the girl was clean, she had ceased her piteous crying and, dazed and shivering, allowed herself to be lifted from the tub and set down on the floor.

"By God, they be skinnier than pi dogs," Rollo agreed, studying her intently while the other sailor rummaged amid the contents of a large wooden box they had carried down with them. Raven's eyes widened when she saw him lift out a calico frock, badly worn and wrinkled, but nonetheless clean. Thrusting it into the hands of the silent young girl, he motioned gruffly that she was to put it on, and she stumbled off into the darkness to dress herself.

With irritable oaths and pantomime movements of his hands, Rollo indicated that the other girls were to bathe and dress themselves in the new frocks exactly as the first girl had done.

"Bain't thee goan wash them thyself?" the second sailor asked Rollo as he started up the ladder.

"By God, no," Rollo growled. "I be hearty sick already of scratchin' and clawin' by the first'n. We can wait by hatchway," he added, wrinkling his nose in disgust, "an' look 'em over when they beed done. It be too awful to stay here longer!"

Raven waited until the unsavory pair had retreated to the

deck, then came forward boldly to take her turn while the wash water was still relatively clean. Not caring that the others would notice her condition, she stood in the dim circle of light and shed the filthy Punjabi costume she had been wearing for so long now. The air in the hold was hot and close, and yet she found herself shivering as she lowered herself into the icy sea water that filled one of the tin tubs. Gritting her teeth, she began to scrub herself with the coarse rag and the lye soap, aware of the many pairs of eyes turned toward her from the dark recesses of the hold.

Using the dipper she rinsed herself off, then took one of the buckets of water and washed the soap out of her hair, feeling the heavy strands growing clean and soft beneath her fingers. When she was finished she stepped out of the tub and reached for one of the dresses folded in the big wooden box. Shaking out the bodice and wide skirts, she slipped it over her head, her skin still wet but oh so wonderfully clean. When she had finished dressing, she turned toward the darkness and smiled, beckoning with her hand to indicate that bathing was not something to be feared. After a moment she heard the straw rustling, and two young girls came hesitantly forward to follow her example.

For the sake of modesty Raven withdrew to allow them to bathe in privacy, and retreated to the corner which she had long ago claimed as her own. Sitting down in the straw, she smoothed the skirts of the calico frock over her hips, glad that they were full enough to hide all evidence of her pregnancy, and ran her fingers through her tangled hair. By the time it was dry and curled softly down her back, Raven felt immensely better. She was clean again and no longer half-starved, and if the captain's words were to be believed, they should be docking within the week. The fact that all of them had been supplied with frocks delighted her as well, for she had been despairing of her chances of escaping through some unknown city in the grimy attire of a Punjabi woman. Dressed like this, she ought to be able to blend in well enough with the native populace to avoid arousing suspicions.

Not until later that day did Rollo and his henchman return to carry the used tin tubs and buckets back onto the deck. With a lantern in one hand and a belaying pin in the other, Rollo walked the length of the hold to make certain that all of the women had obeyed his orders and had bathed themselves. It amused him to see the wariness and fear in their eyes as they shrank back from the light of his lantern, but he resisted the temptation to torment them or even fondle them a bit now that they were clean and looked half human again. He didn't trust John Sampson at all and felt certain the other sailor would run immediately to Captain Van der Horst if Rollo so much as approached one of the slave women.

Rollo's thick lips curled contemptuously. In God's name, what was he doing shipping out on a stench-enshrouded slaver with a queer for a captain? He deserved better, he did, and someday, by God, he intended to prove to everyone that Rollo Walsham wasn't the failure everyone claimed he was. If it hadn't been for his drunken brawl with the officer of the watch aboard H.M.S. *Persuasion* five years ago, he'd never have been forced to flee and ship out on the only vessel that would have him, Captain Niels Van der Horst's detested slaver *Cormorant*. No matter, what was done was done, and Rollo firmly believed that one of his many schemes would pay off eventually, making him wealthy enough to leave the hated life of a sailor behind him forever.

His inspection nearly complete, Rollo swung the lantern in a desultory fashion over a young woman who sat huddled in a corner opposite the hold ladder, then stopped abruptly and came closer. Unlike the others she stared up at him defiantly, her startlingly beautiful wine-colored eyes meeting his boldly. Rollo paused, intrigued, and carefully studied the hollow cheeks and finely molded features before him. Her long black hair hung unbound to her waist and the lantern's rays caught its blue-black highlights, making it shine softly like a rare black pearl. Rollo caught his breath, never having expected to find such a stunning beauty among the young women Captain Van der Horst had acquired as his fancy girls.

For a long moment the striking eyes met and held Rollo Walsham's, and he found himself searching his memory for her origins. Oh, aye, he remembered at last, she was the Hindu that the reeking Turkish trader Kamal had sold to them. And yet, in a calico print gown, the Indian costume gone, Rollo could swear that this young woman was not a Hindu. Instead her features reminded him more of a European, and the defiance in her sloping eyes and in her rigid body was not that of a woman born and raised in strictest purdah, who had been taught from birth to respect and fear all men.

Rollo's gaze traveled down to the full breasts outlined against the tight bodice of her frock, and he caught his breath as his eyes went lower, to the skirts that were gathered in folds about her slim form. Unlike the captain of the *Cormorant*, Rollo was a keen observer and he had seen too many women in his long career as a slave trader not to realize that this one was breeding. He sucked in his breath and rubbed a hand through his filthy hair. Yus, breeding she was, which proved to him she couldn't be a Hindu. No unmarried Indian girl would dare allow—

"Rollo, stir thyself! I be tired of waitin'!"

Growling beneath his breath, Rollo turned away and followed John Sampson up the ladder, wondering what he should do about his discovery. The captain, he knew, would insist at once on getting rid of the girl when he learned that she was with child, yet, more important, Rollo needed to find out if she was really an Occidental as he suspected. A complacent smile curved his thick lips. If she was, it'd be a secret he'd keep to himself, because he knew enough people in New Orleans who would be willing to pay a high price for prime Caucasian blood.

Hearing the hatch cover bang shut above her head, Raven relaxed and gave a sigh of relief. She hadn't liked the way the sailor Rollo's eyes had raked her body as though he knew every intimate secret about her, and the effort of meeting his gaze undaunted had all but exhausted her. Despite the improved rations, despite the fact that she was clean at last, Raven reluctantly admitted to herself that she was still extremely weak. How would she ever manage to survive even if she did escape the black hold of this ship? She bit her lip and forced herself not to give up hope. She had come too far to accept defeat now. She must think of the baby and of Charles and the love she had for him that had kept her alive throughout the bitter months of imprisonment.

Raven's eyes filled with tears. It had been so terribly long since she had last seen him, and she found that the memory of his handsome, laughing face did not come as easily to her mind as it had before. Would he still want her after all she had been through? she asked herself miserably. Had he ever wanted her at all?

"Stop it!" she whispered fiercely to herself, the sound of her own voice snapping her back to her senses. If she began to doubt her love for Charles or his for her, she would be lost. It didn't matter to her that Charles had never told her he loved her, that he had regarded her with nothing save mounting anger that last night they had been together in his quarters aboard the *Orient Star*. Deep in her heart Raven knew that he loved her—he must, she told herself stubbornly, fighting back the tears. He must, or she was lost.

Awakened from an uneasy sleep not too long afterward, Raven heard the now familiar scraping of the hatch cover as it was thrown back, causing bright sunlight to pour onto the musty straw below. Around her Raven could hear the others stirring as they awoke, their whispered questions audible in the darkness. Heavy footsteps sounded above them, and then John Sampson's florid face was thrust down the hatchway.

"Out, out!" he commanded, motioning with his arm that they were to come topside.

The patch of cloudless blue sky that was visible above them lent all of them courage, and they moved quickly to comply. Coming up onto the forward deck, Raven caught her breath as the others did, her gaze pulled almost hypnotically to the bow of the ship, where a dark strip of land lay between the azure sky and the sparkling green water. The heavy canvas sails crackled in the stiff breeze above Raven's head, and sea gulls whirled and dived around them, their haunting cries filling her with deep excitement. It was warm and slightly humid, but Raven, having suffered through the damp, cold months of the crossing, reveled in it.

She took her place obediently enough when John Sampson prodded them into an uneven line, conscious of the curious eyes of the sailors in the rigging above them. It must indeed be an odd sight, she thought darkly to herself, a dozen thin, black-haired young women with different tones of skin standing at obedient attention, their identical calico skirts billowing in the breeze. She forgot her thoughts as she turned slightly, becoming aware of someone watching her, and her heart lurched when she met the probing eyes of Rollo Walsham across the narrow width of the deck. She shivered slightly, unnerved by the watchfulness in his eyes, and cast a discreet glance at her waistline to see if perhaps he might have noticed.

To her relief she saw that the colorful muslin skirts hid the telltale bulge and told herself that men usually understood very little about the female condition. Besides, some of the other women standing nearby were so pitiably wasted from starvation despite the recent increase in their rations that they, too, had slightly distended stomachs. Raven pitied them the most, seeing that they had weathered their imprisonment badly and that their chances of surviving the brutal hardships of life as a slave were doubtful. Studying the dark faces around her, she completely forgot Rollo Walsham, wondering about the fate of these young women who had lived with her on such intimate terms but with whom she had never exchanged so much as a single word.

"Rollo, watch thyself, it be the cap'n!"

Raven straightened at these words and saw the sulky crewman quickly move away from the railing as the dandily attired form of Captain Van der Horst appeared on the foredeck. She remained very still as he made a brief inspection, his moist lips curved into a smile that grew increasingly broader.

"I must admit that their condition has greatly improved, Rollo," he remarked as he turned to face his expectant hand. "Some of them are hopeless, I'm afraid, but we'll wait and see what price they'll bring. The rest have come along quite nicely."

"Thank ye, sir," Rollo said, casting a triumphant glance at John Sampson.

"We should have the main hold cleared by late tomorrow evening," the captain continued thoughtfully. "Mr. Rawls will oversee their transfer to the pens. After that's finished, I want you to bring this lot over to my private coops. Do you know the ones I mean?"

"Yus, cap'n, over to St. Charles Hotel."

Captain Van der Horst nodded. "Mr. Gibson of Bolton, Dickins and Company will be by the next morning to take a look at them. I expect nothing to go wrong, Rollo."

Even Raven heard the veiled threat behind the innocuously uttered words, and she shivered, wondering what on earth the mentioned coops and pens could be. Was that where the slaves were held before being sold? She shivered again, thinking they were treated little better than cattle if that was indeed the case. Her lips tightened grimly. No matter, she had absolutely no intention of being aboard by the time their hold was unloaded.

Back in the utter darkness of her prison Raven trembled with agitation. If the holds were to be emptied by tomorrow evening as the captain had said, surely that must mean the ship would be docking very shortly. She must come up with a suitable escape plan before then, she knew, and lay sleepless for hour upon hour trying to come up with one. The main problem lay not so much in getting out of the hold, which, now that the winter storms had passed, was rarely sealed, as in getting off the ship itself. It was obvious to Raven that she could not use force, unarmed and outnumbered as she was, and it also made no sense to use stealth, for surely the entry ports would be well guarded. That left nothing at all, she decided forlornly after hours of reflection. Nothing except the fact that she was far more intelligent than most of the illiterate tars who crewed the ship.

Raven sat up, her breath catching in her throat. Judas, why hadn't she thought of that before? Of course she was too weak to fight them, too well watched to sneak away from them, but she shouldn't have any problems at all in outwitting them! Why not? she asked herself excitedly. Why not fool them into believing she was not one of the wretched slaves imprisoned in the hold? If she couldn't possibly get off the ship without a by-your-leave, why not trick the crew into giving her one?

Sometime during the twilight hours of the following day the Dutch slave trader *Cormorant* slid silently into its berth along the enormous docks lining the Mississippi River, its four-month voyage at an end. With the aid of running lights and the lanterns that bobbed along the quay and aboard other ships lying at anchor, it jockeyed itself dexterously into position, its sails furled, the mooring lines laid by. Working silently and quickly to secure it, the deckhands could not hide their elation at the fact that the long, difficult voyage was over and that the holds would soon be cleared. Then, with any luck at all, the captain would order an extra tot of rum for all hands and give them leave to go ashore.

Though the men waited with almost feverish enthusiasm for their shore leave to begin, none of them anticipated the hour with more excitement than young Raven Barrancourt, who sat expectantly in the darkness beside the hold ladder, straining to hear what was going on above. By the subtle movement of the ship and the creaking of the lines, Raven guessed that the ponderous vessel had been made fast at last. She could hear footsteps and occasional muted voices on the deck above, activity that was far too marked to be associated with anything other than a docking. Heavy grinding sounds and dull thuds that made the entire hull shudder began shortly thereafter, and although Raven had no idea what they could mean, she guessed that they had something to do with the unloading of the main holds that the captain had mentioned yesterday.

Raven trembled with nervous excitement, finding the long wait unbearable. If only she could slip out now, with so much activity going on above . . . but she knew that it would be foolish to try, what with the decks teeming with men who would quickly recognize the calico frock she wore. The chance that she might well be thwarted by her telltale attire had caused Raven a great deal of anguish, but she knew that she had no other choice than to take that gamble.

She did not know how long she crouched by the ladder waiting for silence to fall over the ship. Time had lost all meaning for her, and she was cramped and exhausted long before the sounds of activity above her ceased. Perhaps she had even dozed off for a time, Raven couldn't tell, but suddenly she started upright and tilted her head to one side to listen. Around her in the darkness she could hear the deep, even breathing of the others and the occasional murmurs of someone in the throes of a fretful dream. Beyond that there was utter silence save for the lapping of water against the hull and the scratching of rats somewhere in the straw nearby.

With aching limbs, her mouth dry, Raven began to ascend the hold ladder. In total darkness she had no way of knowing when she reached the top until she struck her head painfully against the hatch cover. Biting back a groan, she took another hesitant step, feeling along the seam with trembling fingers and pushing with all her might until the cover began to rise. Taking still another step upward, Raven peered through the small crack, a sob of relief rising in her throat when she saw that it was dark outside, the decks only dimly illuminated by the stars above and the few lanterns that hung from the great cabin wall.

Holding her breath, Raven eased the cover back and waited a few moments before climbing out. When she felt certain enough that no one was standing on the foredeck, she crawled out and, on her hands and knees, turned slowly and lowered the hatch cover back into place. For a moment she crouched beside it, catching her breath and trying to still the fearsome pounding of her heart. Lifting her face to the dark night sky, she felt the faint breeze fan her hot cheeks. The smell of brine and tar was strong, but it was the sweet scent of oranges and spices that claimed Raven's attention. The port cities in India had smelled like that, she recalled, yet there the pungent tang of cloves and curry and the horrible smell of offal had always been present as well. Here there was nothing untoward in the spring night air, and Raven could not even hazard a guess as to where they might be. No matter, she decided, gathering up her courage, she'd find out soon enough.

Rising to her feet, she paused for a moment in the concealing shadows of the massive foremast to peer aft through the darkness. All was quiet, and she began to move slowly toward the entry port. As she had feared, she found it guarded by a hulking tar who leaned in utter boredom against the rail, amusing himself by carving his name into the soft wood with the tip of a small knife. Raven stepped back into the shadows and watched him, her breasts rising and falling in rapid rhythm. How long must she wait before he moved away? she wondered with growing panic. Suppose she was discovered before he did?

Knowing she had no choice but to remain where she was, Raven tried to steady the wild hammering of her heart, telling herself that everything depended on her remaining patient. Glancing over the side of the ship, she saw that the docks were poorly lit and contained a great number of niches where she could readily conceal herself in the event that she was pursued. This piece of good fortune was enough to calm her a bit, and she looked back at the guard just in time to see him lumber from the entry and pause several feet away with his back turned toward her. She saw him fumble with his breeches and heard him humming to himself as he began to urinate into the scuppers, and she swallowed hard, aware that this might be her only chance.

There wasn't enough time to dash down the gangplank without being heard or seen, so Raven drew herself up to her full height and tossed her dark head, trying to appear in total control of herself. Noiselessly she hurried in slippered feet across the smooth planks and managed to reach the entry port just as the sailor turned around and saw her.

"'Ere, what's this!" he demanded incredulously, but Raven permitted him to say nothing more.

"You there!" she said haughtily, stepping back onto the deck as though she had just come aboard and spotted him. Lifting her skirts she marched to within a foot of where he stood regarding her with dumbfounded amazement and stopped, her small chin defiantly lifted.

"What ship is this?" she demanded imperiously.

"The *Cormorant*, miss," he replied, taken aback by her tone.

"Ah, ha." Raven nodded her dark head and glared up at him, hoping she looked sufficiently intimidating, while inwardly she was trembling with fright. Thank God, she thought to herself, that this hulking tar seemed simple enough to be easily manipulated! "Is there a sailor aboard by the name of John Sampson?" she asked sharply.

The tar's jaw dropped. "A-aye, miss, there be."

"Good. I should like to see him."

"I-I'm afraid 'e bain't aboard, miss." Confronted by a young Englishwoman of unparalleled beauty, the helpless sailor was reduced to stammering. Though her attire was rather threadbare from what little he could see in the darkness, his attention was claimed by the midnight hair that fell unbound to her small waist and the enormous sloping eyes that shone with such dark mystery in the hollow oval of her face. From the manner in which she spoke and carried herself, he felt sure she was a lady of some breeding, and her unexpected presence had so befuddled him that he didn't even find cause to wonder what she was doing on the docks alone so late at night.

"Sampson be off duty," he said helplessly.

"I see. And what is your name, sir?" Raven demanded.

His jaw went even slacker. "I—why, it be Barlow, miss."

"Well, Mr. Barlow, you can tell John Sampson when he returns that I've been waiting weeks now for the *Cormorant* to arrive. Tell him I have something to give him which he left here the last time!"

Barlow scratched his head and regarded her in total confusion. "I don't understand, miss."

"No matter, he will," Raven said, giving him an arch glance. "Now, if you'll excuse me, my footman is waiting below." She was just about to step down onto the gangplank when the tar's voice brought her to an abrupt halt.

"'Ey, wait!"

Raven turned slowly, tensing herself to run if she had to, her heart beating so rapidly that she felt herself growing dizzy. "Yes?"

"Who should I tell Sampson be ast for 'im?"

Raven could have wept with relief. "He'll know," she responded shortly, and descended unhurriedly down to the wharf. No sooner did her feet touch the rough wooden planks than she swayed and almost fell, but she forced herself to move on, conscious of the eyes watching her from the deck above. By the time the shadows swallowed her up she was breathing hard and she began to run then, wildly, the blood roaring in her ears, not even aware of where she was going. Stumbling over uneven boards she nearly fell, and she screamed when she almost stepped on a tomcat that was hunting for rats amid the stacked barrels. The cat streaked past her skirts, spitting viciously, and Raven collapsed against a wooden crate, her lungs burning, knowing she could run no farther.

Looking about her, she saw that the harbor was filled with ships, the bare masts soaring into the dark night sky. From a nearby tavern she could hear the muted sounds of talk and laughter, and the thought occurred to her that some of the *Cormorant*'s crewmen might very well be drinking there. Suddenly afraid of confronting one of them who might recognize her telltale attire more easily than the dullard Barlow, Raven rose to her feet and started along the wharf toward the street. There it quickly grew obvious to her that she was walking through a rather unsavory part of town, for the buildings that faced one another along the narrow alley contained nothing but dance halls and cheap drinking establishments from which the sound of tinny music and drunken laughter floated out to her.

Lifting her skirts, Raven began to hurry up the street, anxious to reach a better quarter before her strength ran out. The cobblestones felt damp beneath her slippered feet, and she was shivering despite the humid warmth in the air. The cooling breeze from the riverfront did not extend beyond the tall buildings surrounding her, and Raven was soon panting with exertion. With a sigh of relief she saw the narrow street open onto a wide, tree-lined *allée* of beautiful white houses flanked with delicate wrought-iron gatework. Surely here she could ask for help from someone and not be denied!

Almost all of the stately mansions were dark, but Raven quickly spotted a light burning in a lower story gabled window further down the *allée* and started toward it, ignoring the fearful pounding of her heart. Her mouth was dry and the palms of her hands felt clammy with sweat, but she refused to acknowledge the fact that she was frightened.

Halting uncertainly before the house, she stared up through the broad-leafed magnolias at the illuminated window on the far side of the sweeping verandah. What was she to tell the person who answered the door? That she had been abducted by slave traders in faraway India months before and that she had no inkling of what day it might be or even in what country she now found herself? Her predicament was so absurd, so pitiable, that Raven grappled with the urge to laugh and cry at the same time. If only Charles were here, she thought to herself, but his memory only served to bring a stab of pain to her heart so profound that hot tears scalded her eyes. Nonetheless the thought of Charles gave her enough courage to take a deep breath and open the gate that separated the tidy garden from the street.

"Not so fast, m'darlin'!"

Raven uttered a sharp cry of alarm as the slim hand resting on the brass latch was seized by a large, hairy one, and she whirled about to find herself gazing into the grinning face of Rollo Walsham.

"I-I beg your pardon?" she managed, recovering herself admirably.

"Where be goan?" he asked almost conversationally, refusing to free her.

"I happen to live here," Raven told him sharply, her tawny eyes filled with anger. "Let me go or I'll scream for my father!"

Rollo Walsham cast an amused glance up at the darkened house. "Bain't no relations of yers live there, darlin', but I be likin' yer act. Fooled idiot Barlow, did, but not Rollo Walsham."

"You followed me," Raven said in sudden understanding, staring up at him despairingly. "You saw me leave the ship, didn't you?"

Rollo nodded his head, pleased with her ability to grasp the situation. "I left hatch cover unlatched. I be thinkin' ye'd try to run." His approving gaze roved her slender form. "I be thinkin' when I seed wot ye wore, this'n bain't no Hindu." He grinned widely, revealing long, broken teeth. "An' breedin', too. Bain't wot cap'n wants for fancy girls, but Rollo knows where to sell ye, yus indeed."

"You must be mad!" Raven flared at him. "I am an Englishwoman, and you have no right to detain me! I'm not a bonded servant and certainly not a slave! I insist you turn me loose at once!"

Rollo's smile grew broader. "It be a high price wot ye'll bring."

Raven's delicate face drained of color. After having escaped so easily from the ship, she could not believe that she had been recaptured by this leering madman, who refused to recognize that she was a British subject and a free woman. "Turn me loose!" she commanded furiously, twisting this way and that as she tried to slip her hand from his fierce hold.

Rollo shook his head and Raven opened her mouth to scream, but before she could utter a sound he scooped her up against the scratchy front of his rough jacket and pressed her face into the foul-smelling material so that she could scarcely breathe. Carrying her as though she weighed nothing, he began to run down the dark, deserted street, knowing there was no living soul about who would detain his passage.

Chapter Sixteen

Long before the hot May sun had climbed into the hazy sky, the wharves of New Orleans were alive with activity. On the levees slave longshoremen toiled to haul bales of hemp and sacks of flour from the paddlewheelers that had arrived from upriver, while others unloaded barrels of West Indies rum from the massive holds of newly arrived ships. Beyond the busy wharves the city itself did not stir. The elegant shops were still closed and tightly shuttered, and the second-story galleries of stately townhouses stood empty.

Seafaring ships of every imaginable build and size lined the winding riverfront docks. Clippers, brigs, and enormous East Indiamen lay serenely at anchor, while paddlewheelers and other steamboats chugged in and out of their berths between them. Upriver, flatboats and barges were waiting their turn to unload, their captains and crews cursing the delay and reluctantly resigning themselves to the fact that the cool breezes of early morning would not last much longer.

Moored between a blunt-nosed trading brig and an aged merchantman disgorging silver weathered kegs of molasses, the clipper *Orient Star* floated quietly with bare rigging and deserted decks, the only life visible aboard being the presence of a port sentry standing solemn watch by the gangplank. In the spacious stern quarters near the lapping waterline, Captain Charles St. Germain sat with his long, boot-encased legs stretched before him beneath the windows, a cup of tepid coffee forgotten on the small inlaid table before him. His thick chestnut curls were disheveled, as though he had impatiently raked his fingers through them, and the faintest outline of a beard darkened the sun-bronzed skin of his lean cheeks and jaw.

Charles had slept little that night and had risen long before dawn to stare broodingly out of the stern windows at the dark outline of the sleeping city. It had become his custom to do so every morning for the past week, ever since the *Orient Star* had docked in New Orleans, only to learn that the *Cormorant* had not yet arrived. Abruptly Charles turned away from the window and lifted the coffee cup in one long-fingered hand. Finding the contents cold and unappealing, he set it down with a scowl, the muscles along his broad back and shoulders rippling beneath his muslin shirt. Idly Charles traced the small scar that ran along the side of his cheek, his expression dark and unreadable. Feeling as though the atmosphere in his quarters were closing in on him, he rose suddenly to his feet and, cursing beneath his breath, stalked down the corridor toward the companionway.

"Captain!"

Charles looked up to see Geoffrey Lytton standing above him, the golden glow of dawn surrounding his diminutive frame.

"She's here, captain, the *Cormorant!* Word has it she docked sometime late last night!"

Taking the steps two at a time, Charles shouldered his bosun aside and stepped out into the humid air. "Where?" he demanded curtly, scanning the crowded docks.

Geoffrey indicated the winding stretch of coffee-brown river beyond the port railing. "Up around the bend. Young Quintrell spotted her."

Without speaking, Charles strode across the polished deck, but before he could reach the entry port a half-dozen men had fallen in behind him, Geoffrey Lytton included, their expressions grim. Charles turned slowly and regarded each of them in turn, his sensual lips tightly compressed.

"I thought I'd sent the lot of you ashore for a rest," he said darkly. "I also wasn't aware that I had ordered a boarding party to accompany me."

"Beggin' your pardon, sir." A young hand who had been present at Kamal's questioning months before stepped forward and met his captain's narrowed gaze unflinchingly. "We'd like to come along and make sure Miss Raven is all right."

Charles's probing eyes swept over the other nodding heads and determined faces, and some of the tension eased out of his powerful frame as he relented. Without a word he turned and started down the gangplank, his loyal men falling in behind him.

The *Cormorant*, massive, storm-weathered, and ominously silent, lay moored nearly a half-mile away. Though the slaves had been unloaded from its main holds hour ago, the strong, noxious odor of death and disease lingered, a stench that labeled it a slaver as indelibly as the pennant of the Dutch West India Company that fluttered forlornly from its stern. Charles paused on the wharf below the gangplank, his dark head thrown back, his green eyes narrowed to slits as he studied the ship silently.

"God, she's monstrous!" someone murmured, and it was obvious to Geoffrey that all of them were wondering much as he was if Raven Barrancourt had been able to survive the crossing aboard a ship like that. Casting a glance at his captain, Geoffrey saw the belligerent thrusting of his jaw, as though Charles were unconsciously daring Raven to have done otherwise now that they had found her. For almost a week the *Orient Star* had been lying in wait for the *Cormorant* to arrive, and not a man among her crew hadn't considered the possibility that perhaps she had foundered in a winter gale or altered course and sold her human cargo in another city.

Except the captain, Geoffrey thought to himself. Not once during the long winter months had Charles St. Germain allowed himself to believe anything other than that they would encounter the *Cormorant* in New Orleans and find Raven safely aboard. The cost of forcing himself to go on thinking that way had taken its toll in the gaunt, almost haggard features and the feverishly glowing green eyes. Captain Charles St. Germain was a changed man, and Geoffrey had watched with concern as the forces drove him, tormented him relentlessly during the voyage from India, so that sometimes no single vestige remained of the man he had once been. The scar he carried like a brand on his cheek, the restlessness in his powerfully lean frame, the brooding grimness of his visage made Charles St. Germain seem almost demonic to his worried crew. He had become a man given to bouts of savage, almost uncontrollable rage or deep, unnerving periods of silence, a driven man who no longer knew the meaning of peace.

Well, it was almost over now, Geoffrey thought to himself, thank the Lord God for that. No one should suffer the way the captain had and not deserve to claim his heart's desire in the end.

As though he had completely forgotten the presence of his

men, Charles strode wordlessly on board the deserted slaver, his heavy boots echoing on the rough, unclean planking of the main deck. In growing disbelief he eyed the poorly patched canvas above him and the frayed rigging ropes, the deeply gouged and pitted woodwork, the dull brass fixtures. Neglect, poor workmanship, and a total disregard for the work required in maintaining a seaworthy vessel were evident everywhere he looked, and he wondered with a knot of fear growing in the pit of his stomach if that attitude had also been reflected in the care of Raven while she had spent the voyage locked away in some airless hold.

"What 'ee be wantin', guv?"

The hostile words died quickly on the lips of the scruffy-looking sailor who had hurried from the companionway at the sound of Charles's footsteps on the deck. Looking up into the sun-bronzed features, the thin scar livid against one lean cheek, the crewman came to an abrupt halt, his eyes flickering nervously away from the scorching intensity of the emerald-green ones. Noticing the small band of men flanking the entry port behind this lean, sinew-hard giant of a man, the sailor retreated a step and noisily cleared his throat.

"'Ee be wantin' somethin', sir?"

Charles smiled grimly at the sudden respect in the quavering tone. "Your captain," he said shortly. "Is he aboard?"

"No, sir. He be gone on business."

"The slaves you brought in last night, have they been unloaded yet?"

The crewman relaxed visibly. Apparently the intimidating gentleman was here merely to purchase a few choice workers for himself. "Unloaded last night, sir. Captain Van der Horst be seein' to their sale right now."

"And where is Captain Van der Horst?" Charles demanded, the impatience within him rearing up suddenly to burn like fire in his eyes. When the sailor hesitated, he reached out with blinding speed and seized him by the dirty collar, shaking him as though he weighed nothing at all. "Answer me, damn you!"

"The Fleur Rouge, he be at the F-Fleur Rouge," the crewman croaked, his eyes bulging.

Ten minutes later Charles and three of his officers alighted from a hired carriage before a fashionable building in the Vieux

Carré, the oldest quarter in the city, the fine brass-appointed doors opened to the narrow cobblestoned street. A tall, striking woman in black taffeta with a blood-red rose pinned to her breast met them at the door, her disapproving glance as she took in their seaman's attire changing swiftly to one of quiet watchfulness when she saw the look on Charles's handsome face.

"I am Madame Dussoit," she began in a husky voice. "Does monsieur wish—"

"I am looking for a Captain Niels Van der Horst," Charles interrupted her curtly, glancing over her shoulder into the darkened interior of her establishment. "I was told he is here."

"Wait a moment, monsieur, and I will see."

Before Madame Dussoit could turn away, Charles's hand closed about her wrist, the pressure of his strong fingers making her wince. "If you don't mind, madame," he said, his lips curled into a warning smile, "I will come with you while you check."

Madame Dussoit drew herself up and met his intimidating gaze squarely. "I run a respectable business here, monsieur. I want no trouble."

Charles would have admired her courage at any other time, but his driving need to see Van der Horst consumed him, and his temper was raw. "If you do not take me to him, madame," he said in a low, wrathful whisper, "I shall go looking for him myself, and I promise you," he added meaningfully, "that there will be plenty of trouble."

The color drained from the proprietress's cheeks and she inclined her elegantly coiffed head. "Very well, monsieur, but your men must remain here."

"They will," Charles replied, casting a swift glance containing an unspoken command at Geoffrey Lytton. Wordlessly the Welshman turned heel and retreated to the banquette flanking the street outside, Jason Quintrell and Peter Hagen following solemnly behind him.

With Madame Dussoit in the lead, Charles crossed the polished marble floor, ignoring the elegantly attired patrons that sat in nearby booths sipping drinks they had apparently been nursing all night. Several young girls in revealing satin gowns lounged on nearby stools or reclined like graceful statues on the winding staircase leading to the second floor, their assessing glances following the tall sea captain's progress across the room.

Aware of the covetous gleam in their dark eyes, Charles shook his head, knowing well that an establishment like this never saw the need to close, thereby offering a perfect early-morning meeting place for a man like Niels Van der Horst.

He forgot everything in the next moment as Madame Dussoit led him to a booth in the back of the large room, its occupants hidden by an enormous potted orange tree that blocked them from Charles's view. Stepping in front of her, he came to a halt before the linen-covered table, hands propped on his lean hips, quietly studying the two men who turned startled faces to look up at him. One of them was small and very dark, a pencil-thin mustache curling above thin, bloodless lips. In a dark broadcloth suit and black tie, he reminded Charles of an undertaker but for the enormous diamond twinkling at his throat and on his long, thin fingers.

The other man was short, overweight, and sweating profusely, his curly gold hair clustered damply about his fleshy face. Jowls quivering with indignation, he glanced first at Charles's towering form and then at Madame Dussoit, who hovered anxiously behind his broad back.

"What is the meaning of this?" he queried irritably, his voice nasal and highly accented. "I specifically requested not to be disturbed!"

"You must forgive madame," Charles responded with an insolent smile that brought a flush to the puffy cheeks. "I insisted on seeing you. Captain Niels Van der Horst?"

"Indeed I am, and you—"

The portly captain got no further. With a speed that left all of them gaping, Charles balled his fist and drove it squarely into the center of that fat, dissipated face. Though he would have liked nothing better than to break the fellow's nose completely, Charles checked his great strength and gave him a light punch that nonetheless sent the Dutch captain's head cracking against the back of the carved wooden bench. Madame Dussoit covered her mouth with her hand to hold back her scream of alarm, while the "undertaker" bolted to his feet, eyes bulging in horror.

"Wh-what is the meaning of this?" he squeaked as Captain Van der Horst collapsed dazed and moaning into the corner, blood seeping from his nose. "Madame, you must send for help, quickly!"

"You'll not go anywhere!" Though Charles's voice was too low to be heard by the other patrons, it cracked with authority, and the tall, elegant woman froze at once, her kohl-rimmed eyes resting on his cold, handsome face. "I promised you there'd be no trouble," Charles told her curtly, "and there won't be. That was merely something I've been owing the good captain for quite some time." His lean jaw tightened and the scar on his cheek stood out white against the bronzed darkness of his skin. "That and a great deal more," he added almost to himself.

"What do you want from me?" Captain Van der Horst whimpered, pressing a white linen napkin to his face and fighting back his nausea when he saw it come away stained bright red. "I don't even know you!" Craning his pudgy neck, he turned his reddened little eyes upward till they remained on level with the pulse beating strongly in Charles's throat.

"No, you don't know me," Charles assented, standing over him with his hands still clenched into ominous fists. "But you, captain, have taken something from me, and I've come all the way from India to claim it."

"I don't know what you mean," Captain Van der Horst said querulously. "Oh, Daniel, look, will you? My nose is still bleeding!"

Daniel cast a contemptuous glance at his companion and then looked up into the ruthless features of the chestnut-haired Englishman before him. "I am Daniel Gibson of Bolton, Dickins and Company, New Orleans Branch Office, sir. I want no involvement in the matter you seem to have taken up with Captain Van der Horst. If you'll excuse me, please."

Charles's lips thinned. "Am I correct, Mr. Gibson, in assuming that Bolton, Dickins and Company is a slave-trading outfit?"

Daniel Gibson nodded irritably. He had no desire to have his name involved in a fracas at Madame Dussoit's, especially not if it included someone as contemptible as Niels Van der Horst and this hot-headed Englishman who looked dangerous and angry enough at the moment to try anything. Why in Christ's name had he agreed to meet Van der Horst here, of all places? Suppose his wife discovered he'd spent the entire night upstairs and not in the small room behind his office while he waited for the *Cormorant* to arrive and its supercargo to summon him? Jesus Christ, why hadn't he—

"In that case," the tall Englishman continued smoothly, "my purpose in being here includes you as well, Mr. Gibson. The 'object' which Captain Van der Horst stole from me happens to be a young Englishwoman intended for sale as a fancy girl here in New Orleans."

Both Daniel Gibson and Madame Dussoit gasped, and the effeminate captain, dabbing ineffectually at a trickle of blood that soiled the immaculate whiteness of his shirt front, gaped in astonishment. "That cannot be, sir!" he protested indignantly, recovering himself. "I do not deal in Occidentals!"

"This young woman happened to be kidnapped by a Turkish slave trader named Kamal," Charles grated, his scar throbbing. Leaning forward, he placed his hands on the tabletop and stared darkly into the Dutchman's sweating face. "She was wearing the attire of a Punjabi woman and therefore it's conceivable that she was mistaken for an Indian."

"Preposterous!" Daniel Gibson exclaimed. "The *Cormorant* carried only Africans destined for work in the fields! I watched them being unloaded myself!"

"Did it?" Charles demanded, rounding on him with a vengeance and taking a calculated stab in the dark. "Why don't you admit that you and Captain Van der Horst have been trafficking in fancy girls, earning yourselves thousands of American dollars while the Dutch West India Company and, I warrant, Bolton and Dickins knew nothing about it?"

Daniel Gibson went pale. "Th-that may well be true," he sputtered, "but I've also seen the shipment of fancies, sir, and there was not an Englishwoman among them."

Charles grasped Captain Van der Horst's cravat and pulled him upright so that the sweating face and bulging eyes were inches from his own. "Kamal himself admitted to me she was brought aboard. He died giving me that information, and I swear I'll not hesitate to kill you either if you don't tell me where she is." His voice grew hoarse. "That young woman is going to be my wife, Van der Horst, and she happens to be carrying my child. By God, if—"

Some primitive instinct for survival gave the quaking Dutchman the courage to interrupt the ominous threat. "I swear by all that's holy I had no Englishwoman aboard!" he squeaked, his mouth dry, the taste of blood on his tongue making his stomach churn. "Especially not one that was carrying a child! I inspected all of them myself! I swear to you!" He broke off, gasping for air, the big hands so tight about his fat neck that he could scarcely breathe.

Through the dull, throbbing rage that was consuming him Charles looked into the fear-glazed eyes and knew that the man was speaking the truth. Cold fear washed over him, ebbing his rage and causing him to break out in a sweat. Where was Raven? Where in God's name was she? Jerking the terrified captain toward him, Charles shook him mercilessly. "If you don't know anything about her, then I warrant one of your crewmen has been duping you. Gibson, you're coming with me, too."

"Wh-where?" Captain Van der Horst quavered in complete terror. Never had he known a man to exhibit a towering rage like this one. He could feel the barely perceptible trembling of the big hands that were tightened about his throat, and his heart hammered, aware that they trembled because this enraged giant of a man was using his utmost effort at self-control to keep from strangling the life out of him.

"To your ship," Charles grated. "I'm going to question every damned one of your men, and God help the lot of you if I don't find her."

Aboard the *Orient Star* the hot morning sun had driven Hannah Daniels into the welcoming shade of the awning young Jason Quintrell had erected for her when the winter storms had faded at last into the warmth of spring. Seating herself on the worn wooden bench, Danny busied herself with her embroidery but found that her fingers were trembling too much to keep the stitches straight. With a sigh she gave up and set the sampler aside. Though she had weathered the stormy crossing rather poorly, the warm spring days the *Orient Star* had encountered after she sailed across the Tropic of Cancer had done much to restore the rosy glow to her pallid cheeks. Yet even Danny herself acknowledged that she had lost a great deal of weight and that constant worry over Raven's safety had deepened the wrinkles about her eyes and mouth.

All of them had suffered, Danny admitted, especially the captain, who seemed to have aged before her very eyes since Raven's disappearance. His handsome, arrogant visage lined with weariness, he had rarely left the quarterdeck during the long voyage, forgoing sleep and sustenance, manning the helm himself in the fiercest of howling gales as if to keep the *Orient Star* on course through the sheer strength of his great driving will. No one dared broach the awesome temper that simmered beneath the intimidating surface, and even Dmitri hadn't chosen to argue with him when the captain ordered him aboard the clipper *Bridget Bailey* when they encountered it south of the Cape Verde Islands weeks ago. Sailing east from Tobago, the British ship had struck its colors and hailed them, and Captain St. Germain had invited its commander aboard the *Orient Star*.

Upon learning that the clipper was bound for London via Rabat and Brest, Charles had asked the captain, a man both he and Dmitri seemed to know, if his bearded first mate might obtain passage back to England aboard the *Bridget Bailey*. Actually, Danny remembered, Dmitri hadn't been ordered to go, he had been asked in that quiet, distant tone of voice Captain St. Germain used with everyone nowadays, and Dmitri, much to Danny's astonishment, had agreed. When she had expressed her surprise at this, the big Russian had gravely told her that he was doing it for Raven's sake but only looked mysterious when she questioned him further, refusing altogether to say anything more.

"Besides, I can't do anything for our little princess that the captain can't do himself," he had added, glancing at the chestnut-haired figure that stood silently by the taffrail above them. His black eyes were solemn. "He will find her, Mrs. Daniels, I will lay my life on it."

"Yes," Danny had whispered, feeling a shiver of awe as she followed Dmitri's gaze to Captain St. Germain's unmoving form. "I know he will."

And so it was that Dmitri Zergeyev had parted company with his captain and fellow crewmen, accompanying the *Bridget Bailey* northeast to Morocco while the *Orient Star* trimmed its sails and continued west across the endless Atlantic. Dmitri's willingness to leave the ship before Raven was rescued had puzzled Danny for quite some time, and not one of the *Orient Star* crew members could shed any light on his reasons for going. It was not like the big Russian, who adored Danny's young mistress, to abandon the search for her simply because Captain St. Germain had requested him to, but Danny began to suspect that the reasons must be important indeed for Dmitri to agree to leave without argument.

Sitting beneath the awning aboard the *Orient Star* that warm and humid May afternoon, Danny's thoughts were far removed from the *Bridget Bailey* and its hulking Russian passenger. Coming up on deck after an uneasy night of tossing and turning in her bunk, Danny had learned from one of the crewmen that the slave ship *Cormorant* had finally arrived in New Orleans and that the captain had gone off to find Raven. Now that the four long months of agonized waiting and worry were almost over, Danny found herself in such a state of anxiety that she could scarcely sit still. But for the morning watch the ship was deserted, and she wandered restlessly across the silent decks, paying scant attention to the hum of activity and teeming humanity that passed below her on the crowded wharves.

The shimmering sun was standing high in the sky when a grim Geoffrey Lytton and his men finally returned to the ship. A pale, nervous Danny was at the entry port to meet them, and Geoffrey looked away when he saw the surging hope in her faded brown eyes.

"You've not found her, then, Mr. Lytton?" she asked in a high, strained voice.

Geoffrey wiped his sweating brow with his sleeve. "No, Mrs. Daniels, I'm afraid not."

"But you've been aboard the *Cormorant*, haven't you? And where is Captain St. Germain?"

"Yes, we were aboard." Geoffrey motioned to Peter Hagen to carry their belongings below. "Tell Fletcher to bring up something to drink, grog or beer, it doesn't matter." Glancing back into Danny's expectant face, he explained gently, "Miss Barrancourt wasn't aboard, I'm afraid."

"Not on board?" Danny echoed, tears of despair springing to her eyes. "I-I don't understand, Mr. Lytton!"

Geoffrey wearily massaged the back of his neck. "Neither do we, Mrs. Daniels. The *Cormorant*'s captain claims he had no Englishwoman aboard his ship and, God help the sniveling swine, I believe him."

"Then where is Miss Raven?" Danny cried, distraught.

"I wish to God I knew," Geoffrey responded grimly. "The captain questioned every single one of the men, and all of them swear up and down there was no Englishwoman fitting Miss

Barrancourt's description aboard ship. Even the two tars who cared for the fancy girls during the voyage insist they knew nothing about her."

"Is Captain St. Germain still on the *Cormorant?*" Danny asked, wringing her hands.

Geoffrey shook his head. "I convinced him there was no sense in staying. He's gone to see the harbormaster and to contact the New Orleans authorities. If handbills and the like are distributed, perhaps there's a chance we'll find her."

Danny's eyes widened. "Then you believe she's somewhere here in the city?"

"She has to be," Geoffrey said firmly. "That blackguard Kamal swore just before he died he'd personally delivered her aboard. Except for a stop in Guinea, the *Cormorant* sailed straight to New Orleans."

"And suppose Miss Raven escaped from the ship there?" Danny cried. "How would we find her then?"

The bosun placed a reassuring arm about her shaking shoulders. "Have no fear in that quarter, Mrs. Daniels. Most of the fancy girls came aboard there, and the ship was extremely well watched during the entire layover in Fida. No one, least of all a single young woman, was seen trying to leave the ship."

Danny lifted a tear-stained face toward the skyline of New Orleans, her expression bleak. "I don't understand it, Mr. Lytton! We came so close to finding her! For the love of God, where is she?"

Chapter Seventeen

Flanked by a stately row of huge, gnarled trees, the drive that meandered through the heart of Bellevue Plantation offered a magnificent view of the manor house's front facade. Surrounded by the lush greenery of summer, the soaring white columns graced three stories of the wide, rambling house, creepers with scented blossoms twining themselves through the wrought-iron railings of the upper-story galleries. Inside the house the air of graciousness was enhanced by high-ceilinged rooms and polished woodwork, the flocked wallpaper and elegant carpets as fine as any found in the chateaux of France or the country estates of English gentry.

Despite its deceptive air of genteel charm, Bellevue was a working plantation, and the small army of slaves that labored in the cane fields was never idle. With a full complement of house slaves, the mansion itself showed no trace of neglect, and the task of overseeing the work force had been the primary responsibility of one Tyler Jacobs for the past eighteen months. Short, dark-complexioned, and often brutal, Tyler Jacobs wielded a braided whiplash that could ravage the flesh of a man's back with one expert flick. The Negroes were terrified of him and remained obedient, and in the absence of Bellevue's owner—when Jacobs was in sole charge of the plantation—they were doubly careful to seem respectful and hard-working when his short but dashing form rode into view.

In the two days since her arrival at Bellevue, Raven had learned to fear and loathe Tyler Jacobs as intensely as the Negroes did. Not one single slave, he had explained to her when Rollo Walsham first carried her to his small house on the far side of the plantation grounds, had ever escaped from Bellevue. Well guarded, constantly patrolled, the plantation was flanked on two sides by the winding, strong-currented river, and the scrub lands on the other two sides were infested with snakes, mosquitoes, and treacherous swamps.

"It would be foolish to try to run away," the overseer had told her, his small eyes roving her thinly clad body as Raven stood shivering before him, Rollo Walsham grinning approvingly in the background. "I'd hate to be the one to pull your white, bloated corpse from the swamp when we did find you. It'd be a shame, eh, Rollo?"

"You can't keep me here against my will!" Raven said stubbornly, small chin imperiously lifted, tawny eyes blazing. "I am not a slave! I am a British subject and free to do as I please!"

Tyler Jacobs cast a rueful glance at Rollo. "Fifteen hundred dollars is a little steep for a sassy-mouthed wench like this, friend. I suggest you drop the price to a thousand even."

"Bain't a prettier piece in all Louisiana," Rollo replied defensively, his thick lower lip thrusting.

Tyler Jacobs nodded his head in agreement. "That may be true, but her looks'll suffer some if I have to whip that mean streak out of her."

"You wouldn't dare!" Raven cried, the color draining from her delicate cheeks.

The overseer's lips parted in a cruel smile. "Oh, but I would, and I will. Got to knock all those rebellious thoughts out of your pretty head before Mr. Spright returns. Don't care too much for sassy slaves, Mr. Spright don't." He came closer and leered into her face, his foul breath hot on her cheek. "And I'll just bet you wouldn't want to risk hurtin' that bastard brat you've got in you, eh? I've seen it happen before. A good whippin' and—"

Before he could make a move to protect himself, Raven had thrown herself at him, her fingernails raking a furrow down his stubble-roughened cheek. Howling with pain, the overseer slapped her hard, the impact of his palm spinning her around so that she stumbled over a stool and fell. Fighting back the tears, her head spinning, Raven glared up at him defiantly.

"He's not a bastard brat!"

"Why, you little bitch—!" Striding forward, Tyler seized Raven's arm and jerked her to her feet. Lifting his hand to strike her again, he was intercepted by Rollo Walsham, who feared that her asking price would be lowered if Joshua Spright saw her covered with bruises. After the sale had been made they could do with her as they pleased, but while she remained Rollo Walsham's exclusive property, no one must harm her.

"Leave this'n be, Tyler," he pleaded. "Mayhap ye'll be hurtin' babe wot Master Spright might want."

Tyler Jacobs was breathing hard, the hatred in his pale eyes as he looked into Raven's face frightening her, warning her that she must tread carefully if she was to keep Charles's child from harm. That this was a cruel, conscienceless man capable of cold-blooded murder was obvious to her, and her throat constricted with the knowledge that she had made a bitter enemy of him.

"I'll wait," the overseer agreed, panting still. "I'll wait until Mr. Spright says the bitch stays, and then, my fine girl, I'll make you regret the day you were born!"

"Maybe your Mr. Spright will refuse to buy me," Raven challenged him, although her voice trembled noticeably. "Maybe he'll agree that it's madness to purchase and keep an Englishwoman who has been kidnapped against her will!"

Tyler pulled a soiled handkerchief from his vest pocket and dabbed away the few drops of blood that seeped from the scratches on his face. Fixing Raven with a cold, vengeful stare that made her cringe, he shook his head slowly. "Don't start dreamin' about kind-hearted Joshua Spright settin' you free, girl. One look at you and he'll be slaverin' like a dog to get you in his bed." His contemptuous gaze fastened itself to the gentle rounding of her belly beneath the calico skirts. "Breedin' or not. It's them dark Creole bitches old Spright lusts after, but their menfolk guard them from us Americans like they were all virgin princesses. You'll be much easier to take and"—he laughed cruelly, studying her midnight hair and delicate features—"better lookin' than any simperin', blue-blooded Creole I've seen in these parts."

His hand reached toward her unexpectedly and Raven cried out, thinking that he was going to hit her again. Instead he curled his blunt fingers around the neckline of her calico frock, pulling the bodice downward so that the rounded cleavage of her full breasts was bared to the hot night air.

"I'll be puttin' Bellevue's brand here myself," Tyler told her, touching the smooth, creamy flesh and grinning cruelly when he saw the tears of humiliation spring into Raven's eyes. "Will you still be so full of fire, girl, with the brand of ownership on your breast? I wonder."

"Here, now, Tyler," Rollo said nervously, intervening again. "I be goan back to ship. Leave this'n be until Master Spright returns."

"I suppose I can keep my hands off her until then," the overseer agreed. Licking his lips, he stared with unconcealed desire at Raven's bared breasts, and she turned away, trembling uncontrollably as she covered herself, aware that the rage and hatred in his pale eyes had been replaced with unmistakable lust. Judas, how was she to escape this madman before he tried to touch her?

Rollo Walsham remained at Bellevue long enough to make certain his prize had been safely locked into the wine pantry in the back of the manor house itself. His reluctance to leave demonstrated his doubt that Tyler Jacobs could be trusted not to lay a hand on her until Joshua Spright returned home, but he had stayed away from the *Cormorant* long enough and didn't want Van der Horst to accuse him of deserting ship. Punishment for a crime like desertion was severe, Rollo knew, and not worth at all the thousand dollars or more he stood to earn from this sale.

Though Tyler Jacobs did keep his word in the two days that followed, it did not prevent him from tormenting Raven unmercifully. While she worked alongside the silent house slaves polishing silverware or laundering countless pieces of linen, Tyler forced her to listen to lurid descriptions of what he planned to do to her once his master returned. The coarse language he used and the obvious delight he took in sparing no detail of her pending corporal punishment made Raven's stomach churn and her mouth grow dry with fear.

She fretted especially for the life of her baby, which just that morning had awakened her by kicking lustily, an unmistakable sign of its existence that had filled Raven with both a heavenly glow of love and an overwhelming surge of despair. Everything that Tyler Jacobs threatened to do to her seemed certain to harm the baby, and Raven, after feeling it move within her, knew that she could never let that happen. She would escape, she told herself as she labored doggedly beside the tight-lipped Negroes, and even the unknown terrors of the swamp couldn't be as awful as the degradation she would suffer at the hands of Tyler Jacobs.

Locked into the hot, airless pantry that night with only the hard stone floor to sleep on, Raven spent hours weeping and railing hopelessly against her fate before drifting off into an uneasy slumber. Morning brought the hated face of Tyler Jacobs leering in at her from the unbolted pantry door, his snarling order to rise making Raven scramble to her feet and glare at him defiantly.

"No reason to look at me like that, my proud beauty," he said with a scornful sneer. "Mr. Spright's due back from New Orleans tonight, and he won't tolerate that kind of disrespect any more than I do."

Despite the overseer's dire prediction, Raven experienced a surge of hope at hearing of Joshua Spright's impending return. Surely he couldn't be as cruel and hateful as his overseer! As a landowner and a man of position and wealth, he would never agree to keep a young Englishwoman as a slave, would he? Raven felt convinced that she would be able to reason with him as an equal and that Tyler Jacobs would pay for the abuses he had heaped on her since Rollo Walsham had brought her to Bellevue.

It was with a lighter heart that Raven followed the taunting overseer into the enormous salon where two young Negresses in cotton print skirts and colorful turbans were giving the furniture a fresh beeswax polish. "Hetta, you'll be watchin' this one until Mr. Spright arrives," he told the older of the two, a coffee-colored woman with pale brown eyes. "I don't want anything to happen to her, is that understood?"

"Yes, Mist' Jacobs," Hetta replied, lowering her eyes, the veiled threat in the overseer's words not having gone unnoticed.

"I'll be in the fields, girl," Tyler added to Raven as he started for the door. "It won't take but a minute to ride back to the house if Hetta calls me."

When the door slammed behind him, the two young women resumed their work, neither paying the least bit of attention to Raven until Hetta tossed a rag at her and indicated the carved wooden mantel with a jerk of her turbaned head. "Mist' Jacobs says work. You better do what Mist' Jacobs says."

Wordlessly Raven began to polish the woodwork while the two of them talked in low tones between themselves in a language Raven didn't recognize. She forgot them quickly enough as she tried to decide exactly what she would tell Joshua Spright when they finally met. For the remainder of the morning she followed Hetta from room to room, cleaning and polishing until her arms and back began to ache. It was difficult to ignore the veiled hostility in the eyes of the house slaves, whose whispered comments led Raven to believe that they were discussing what their master intended to do with her when he returned home. She found it difficult to blame them for treating her with the contempt they did, for surely all of them were aware by now that she was intended to be Joshua Spright's new mistress despite the fact that her belly was swollen with child.

Raven's soft lips tightened grimly. They were all mistaken if they expected that to happen, and if Mr. Spright turned out to be of the same mind as his abusive overseer, he was in for a rude awakening. Unlike the delicate Creole women Tyler Jacobs had described to her, Raven intended to fight—with violence, if need be—to protect the life of her unborn child and gain her freedom.

By noon Raven was exhausted. The child felt heavy within her and every muscle in her body ached from overwork. She longed to sit down and rest for just a moment, but Hetta, ruthlessly domineering in her role as housekeeper, showed her no more mercy than she did the house slaves under her rule. When the cleaning was done Raven was sent to the kitchen to help the cook pluck the freshly killed fowl that would be served for dinner that night. The faint smell of blood that still clung to the meat made her stomach churn, and Raven rose abruptly from the table, stumbling outside into the herb garden, where she gratefully gulped down lungfuls of fresh air.

Lifting her head, she stared through the dense cluster of oleanders surrounding the garden and felt her heart skip a beat when she saw a carriage swaying up the drive toward the house. Behind her a young Negro carrying firewood from the woodpile paused as he noticed it, too, and Raven heard him curse softly beneath his breath.

"Is it Mr. Spright?" she asked, rounding on him.

"Lord knows," he replied, "but I sure hopes not! He'll be breathin' fire nobody came to the landin' to meet the riverboat. How was we to know he'd be early?"

Raven did not answer. Running back into the kitchen, she ignored the surprised exclamations of the cook as she began to scrub her hands and face vigorously in the basin of wash water standing on the worn oak table. She intended to look as dignified as possible when she spoke to Joshua Spright, and wasn't about to meet him with chicken blood and feathers clinging to her hands. Drying her face with the apron that covered her colorful calico skirts, Raven smoothed back her disheveled hair and started out of the kitchen, only to find Evangeline, the enormous cook, blocking the doorway with her bulk.

"Let me pass," Raven commanded, staring up into the dark eyes with a bravely lifted chin. "I must see Mr. Spright immediately!"

"Give him time," the big woman told her gently, her tone sympathetic as she looked down into Raven's pale, determined face. "Smokes and drink first, then his mood will be better."

"Do you think so?" Raven asked uncertainly, unable to ignore the kindness on the Negress's round face.

"I been with Michie twenty-nine years," Evangeline said solemnly. "I seed him through Missy Sarah's death when she birthed that sickly baby boy; I seed the fancies come and go in this house." She chuckled, revealing a gap between her strong white teeth. "I knows him, missy, like I knows gentry when I see them." She snorted, her tone suddenly derisive. "You're no fancy girl any sooner than I am! Whatever reason that devil's whelp Tyler Jacobs brung you here for, you ain't no mist'iss to no white man!" Her dark eyes studied Raven's rounded belly. "You some man's lady love, uh-huh."

Embarrassed by the tears that suddenly stung her eyes, Raven turned away and felt the cook's big hand settle on her shoulder. "Smokes and drink first, missy, then you talks with him."

In the darkened study in the rear of Bellevue's manor house Joshua Spright opened the glass-fronted cabinet and took out a bottle of dark Kentucky bourbon. With fingers that shook, he splashed a generous amount into a glass and tossed all of it down his throat. Noticing that the shaking did not subside, he swore softly and poured himself another. Restlessly he paced to the window and parted the heavy drapes, staring out into the sun-drenched gardens. Turning away, he pulled a scented handkerchief from his pocket and mopped his brow, feeling the sweat trickle down his back.

"Goddamn!" he muttered to himself, pulling irritably at his high collar. Why had he insisted on staying in New Orleans so long? Why had he been such a muttonhead and agreed to spend another night at Nicholas Guildford's watching Nick and his wife make fools of themselves parading their horse-faced spinster daughter before him in the hopes that he might be interested? Good God, the girl was forty pounds overweight, if not more, and he was old enough to be her father! Joshua's thin lips tightened. He'd like to see the look on Nick Guildford's face if he confided to him that white women did nothing for Joshua Spright, that only a leggy octaroon with skin the color of caramel could succeed in making him a man. Now and then he'd tried to prove himself with a Creole woman, but by God, they were harder to get at than the mistresses their menfolk kept in stately houses on Rampart Street!

"Goddamn!" he said again, aware that none of that mattered anymore. If only he'd come home two days ago as originally planned! How long did he have to wait now, fear dogging his every waking moment, until he knew for sure whether or not . . .

"Mr. Spright, welcome home!"

Joshua turned and composed his features, his weak chin quivering with ill-concealed dislike as Tyler Jacobs, his officious overseer, came unbidden into the study. It was a hot afternoon and Tyler was sweating as profusely as his master, the faintly acrid scent of unwashed flesh accompanying him inside. Joshua moved away from him and took another sip of bourbon, savoring the covetous gleam in the other man's pale eyes, well aware that Tyler expected to be offered some and feeling pleased that he wasn't going to be.

"I didn't send for you, Jacobs. As a matter of fact I told William I didn't wish to be disturbed by anyone."

The overseer's pale eyes narrowed angrily. Master and hired hand were of roughly the same height, although the overseer was stocky and strong while his employer was thin, his receding hairline edged with gray. A weak and vascillating man, Joshua Spright nonetheless enjoyed the power he held over Tyler Jacobs, power that arose from the fact that the brutal overseer, after whipping to death a perfectly healthy and valuable field hand over at the Hairston plantation two years ago, had been shunned like the plague in his search for new employment until Joshua Spright had agreed to hire him on. The plague . . . God be damned, Joshua swore to himself, thinking it ill luck to use the word so lightly.

"I'm very busy, Jacobs," he added curtly, setting the empty glass down with a bang, tiny droplets of bourbon spraying over the clean ink blotter on his desk. "Busy and tired. The riverboat wasn't fast enough, so I borrowed Guildford's carriage. I—"

"Yes sir," the overseer interrupted confidently. "I'm sorry no one met you at the door, but you weren't expected until tonight."

"I wanted to be here two days ago," Joshua snapped, "but Nicholas Guildford—" He broke off, passing a trembling hand across his eyes. "Get out, Tyler. I want to be alone."

The overseer struggled to maintain a suitably respectful expression. "Yes sir, but first I want you to have a quick look at the fancy girl Rollo Walsham brought over for you. You'll remember him, I trust? He's been sailing with the *Cormorant* ever since she began her Antilles–New Orleans runs."

"I'm not interested in any fancies at the moment, Jacobs," his employer snapped, his uncustomary vehemence surprising the overseer into silence. "I've got other things on my mind and—"

A quiet but firm knock on the cypress door of the study interrupted him, and both he and Tyler Jacobs turned their heads. "What is it?" Joshua barked irritably.

The door opened and Joshua Spright's eyes widened at the sight of the young woman standing on the threshold, her small white teeth clamped on her lower lip as though to keep it from trembling. Raven, having followed Evangeline's kindly advice, had waited nervously in the cavernous kitchen, but when she had seen Tyler Jacobs ride up to the house and vanish through the study door, she had been unable to contain her impatience any longer. No telling what sort of lies the brutal overseer would tell about her before she had the chance to confront Bellevue's owner herself!

Joshua Spright was not at all the man she had envisioned. In a travel-stained, sweat-dampened broadcloth suit, he stood no taller than Hannah Daniels, though he was a good deal thinner. A nervous twitch appeared spasmodically beneath his left eye, and his long, thin hands fidgeted constantly. An unhealthy pallor and sunken cheekbones attested to a life of restricted physical activity, and Raven guessed that he must have been extremely sickly in his youth.

"Excuse me," she began, ignoring Tyler Jacobs, who stood in a darkened corner behind her, "are you Mr. Spright?"

Joshua stirred and blinked disbelievingly. A Creole, he thought to himself, a Creole who spoke with the well-bred accents of an

Englishwoman? It couldn't be! No Creole woman would allow herself to be seen in the calico frock of a slave, nor wear her midnight tresses loosely about her shoulders like this one. She could not be a Creole, for she was staring at him far too boldly, the amazing golden eyes meeting his squarely. Nor would a Creole ever appear alone in the home of an American. Besides, Joshua thought to himself, he knew all of the Creole families between here and Baton Rouge, and this young woman was certainly not one of them. And by God, he swore to himself, taking another look at her, seeing for the first time the obvious rounding of her belly beneath her starched white apron. Pregnant, the golden-eyed bitch was pregnant!

Nonetheless he could not help gaping, for she was beautiful, the simple, threadbare frock somehow enhancing the unnatural delicacy of her features, her looks undeniably those of an aristocrat. Yet there was an unhealthy hollowness about her exquisite cheekbones, a hunted look in the magnificent eyes that belied the aura of pampered good breeding she had about her.

"Mr. Spright!" Tyler Jacobs's eager words roused him from his thoughts. "This is the girl I was telling you about. How do you like her?" Coming forward, he took Raven by the arm and tried to drag her toward the desk so that his employer could have a better look at her.

"Keep your hands off me!" Raven cried, twisting free and glaring into the overseer's dark face, her tawny eyes blazing with hatred. There could be no denying the unconscious air of nobility about her in the arrogant set of her dainty chin and the tone of her voice as she addressed a man she so obviously considered beneath her station. "Mr. Spright," she went on, gathering her courage and addressing the astonished man behind the desk, "your overseer has been keeping me here against my will! I am not a slave to be bought and sold at any man's whim! I am a British subject and I—"

"Good God!" Joshua Spright's dismayed exclamation interrupted Raven's angry tirade and she watched, wide-eyed, as he collapsed into the big leather chair behind his desk.

"I-I beg your pardon?" she asked helplessly, regarding him in astonishment and thinking that he behaved just as though someone had dealt him a physical blow.

"Your name," Joshua Spright said slowly, his watery eyes on her puzzled face, "wouldn't happen to be Raven Barrancourt?"

"Yes, yes, it is!" she said, stunned. "How did you—"

"Tyler!"

Startled by the lashing intensity of his employer's tone, the overseer sprang to the edge of the desk, his swarthy face glistening with nervous perspiration. "Yes sir?"

"Where did you get this . . . this young lady?" Joshua's hand gestured weakly toward Raven.

"Rollo Walsham brought her upriver from New Orleans," Tyler explained somewhat uncertainly. "Says she came from India."

"Where I was kidnapped against my will!" Raven cried, casting a hateful glance at the overseer. "Sir, I've tried to explain to this—this—"

"I understand, Miss Barrancourt." Joshua Spright rose to his feet and stared coldly into Tyler Jacobs's face. "You fool!" he spat with unnerving intensity. "You stupid, greedy fool! Do you know what you've done?"

Dumbfounded, the overseer shook his head.

"New Orleans has been inundated with handbills describing the kidnapping and consequent disappearance of one Raven Barrancourt from the trader *Cormorant* three days ago. Guildford's wife could talk of little else during my stay. Seems the entire city has been besieged by a madman, a pirate, some even say, who doesn't look as if he'll rest until he finds her."

"Charles!" Raven whispered, her heart leaping into her throat. Could it be true that Charles was here?

"That's ridiculous!" Tyler Jacobs snorted, but the uneasiness in his tone was unmistakable.

"Is it?" Joshua demanded, thrusting his face close to the overseer's sweating one. "I've seen the man myself, Jacobs. He's twice the height and build you are and looks capable of tearing you limb from limb. He'd do it, too, I imagine, if he thought you'd mistreated Miss Barrancourt here." Unable to contain his dislike for the overseer, his tone grew ugly. "I imagine the very least he'd do is have you arrested on kidnapping charges."

"The fellow has no case against me!" the overseer protested, licking his lips nervously, his fear increasing.

"No?" Joshua Spright demanded contemptuously. "This 'fellow' also happens to be an earl as well as the respected captain-owner of a clipper ship. According to the handbills, Miss Barrancourt is his intended bride."

"Oh, that unspeakable rogue!" Raven whispered, her eyes shining, though neither of the men seemed to have heard her.

"I didn't know," the overseer added in desperation, never having expected his employer to take such a vehement stand against him. "If anyone's to blame it's Rollo Walsham because I just figured you'd want to purchase the wench, seeing as she's better-looking than all those Creole bitches you've been trying to—"

"Get out of here, Jacobs!" Joshua Spright snarled. "Get off my property and don't ever show your face around here again! I've been looking for an excuse to get rid of you long enough, and this one's as damned good as any. I'm only sorry I hired you to begin with."

A vein in the overseer's temple began to throb. "Why, you lily-livered bastard!"

Raven screamed in alarm as the overseer lunged across the desk, seizing Joshua Spright's vest between his fingers, his hands reaching for his throat. For a moment she stood transfixed as the two men, locked in combat, grappled before the big leather chair before both of them went crashing to the floor. Turning, she raced for the door, flinging it open and calling for help. No one appeared at the end of the cypress-paneled corridor in answer to her horrified cries, and it took only a moment for Raven to realize that the terrified slaves must have hidden themselves away, refusing to get involved.

Acting purely on instinct, she pulled open the heavy front door and fled down the walk toward the carriage house. Inside the cool, dark stable she came across an elderly Negro rubbing down the sweaty horses that had brought Joshua Spright from New Orleans. Seeming not at all startled to see the panting, disheveled young woman appear before him, he raised a snowy eyebrow and regarded her quizzically.

"I've got to get to New Orleans," Raven told him breathlessly. "Please, will you saddle a horse for me?"

"Can't send no horses out less Mist' Joshua gives orders," he told her soberly, regarding her with rheumy eyes.

Raven glanced fearfully over her shoulder, half-expecting to see Tyler Jacobs coming after her. There was no doubt in her mind that Joshua Spright would have willingly taken her to New Orleans himself, but she was afraid of the outcome of their struggle, afraid of the demonic thirst for vengeance she had seen in the overseer's pale eyes just before he had attacked his employer. Recalling his brutal threats to her, shuddering as she remembered the touch of his hand on her breast and his promise to brand her himself, Raven was driven to desperation. Looking frantically about her, she suddenly spotted the newly arrived carriage standing outside the door, its brightly painted sides covered with dust. Lifting her skirts, she ran toward it and threw back the door, hauling herself with considerable difficulty inside.

A gentleman in England, Raven knew, never traveled anywhere in his carriage without his pistols, and she prayed that here in America the custom was also observed. A small whimper of relief passed through her lips when she spotted a leather holster dangling near the window, and with trembling fingers she wrested the handsome ivory-handled pistol from inside. Stepping back down onto the dusty ground, she marched back into the darkened interior of the stable where the old Negro continued to groom the weary carriage horses as though nothing were amiss.

Her father himself had taught her to shoot, and Raven, inspecting the pistol to make sure it was primed and cocked, held it with both hands before her, barrel aimed at the startled groom's narrow chest. Noticing how badly she was trembling, Raven clenched her teeth and tried to sound brave. "You'll saddle me Mr. Spright's fastest horse, is that understood?"

The Negro swallowed hard. "Yes, missy."

She waited, heart pounding, as he fumbled with the saddle and bridle, his arthritis-crippled fingers made even more clumsy by the fact that the pistol trained on his heart barely wavered in its aim. Raven could have screamed in frustration at the delay, casting numerous glances over her shoulder, wondering in an agony of doubt why the big manor house remained so still.

"I'm finished, missy."

Raven watched as the old groom led the big rangy hunter to the mounting block, then motioned that he was to step away. With an uneasy eye upon him, she made a quick inspection of the tack to assure herself that he had done everything properly. She herself would be to blame if he successfully managed to sabotage her escape by failing to buckle the girth. Lifting her skirts with one hand, Raven ignored the scandalized widening of the watching Negro's eyes and slipped into the saddle, her slender ankles and the badly frayed toes of her slippers showing.

"Miss Barrancourt, wait!"

Raven stiffened at the sound of her name and looked up to see Joshua Spright hurrying across the lawn toward her, the sunlight glaring on his balding head and stooped shoulders. His coat and shirt were badly rumpled, but he appeared otherwise unharmed, and the reason for his victory over the more powerful overseer was quickly explained by two muscular house slaves who appeared behind their master, carrying the unconscious man between them.

"Stay where you are!" Raven commanded, her voice quivering almost as much as the pistol she held in one hand.

The big Negroes obeyed instantly, halting on the thick carpet of grass, Tyler Jacobs's lifeless body swinging between them, while Joshua Spright advanced a little further and stood looking up at her intently.

"Is he dead?" Raven asked, her stomach churning. The big hunter, sensing her uneasiness, began to stamp impatiently, and she soothed him with a hand on his muscular neck.

"Unconscious. William's extremely adept at wrestling," the disheveled plantation owner informed her, nodding in the direction of the bigger of the two house slaves. "Won't you come down, Miss Barrancourt?" he added after a moment, eyeing her exposed ankles and the wavering pistol barrel with equal interest.

"I've got to go to New Orleans," Raven said stubbornly. "Charles—the man you say is looking for me—doesn't know where I am."

Something odd passed across Joshua Spright's thin, sallow face, a look that Raven could not fathom, which nonetheless caused her heart to skip a beat. "What is it?" she demanded fearfully, tightening her trembling hold on the handle of her pistol.

"Why, nothing," he assured her, spreading his hands wide. "Come inside. You can't possibly ride to New Orleans alone, not in this heat and certainly not astride. I'll send one of my men down for you and—"

"There is something," Raven insisted, interrupting him sharply. Her soft lips tightened grimly. "Will you please tell me what it is?"

Hearing the faint note of hysteria that had crept into her tone, Joshua Spright said reluctantly, "It's Bronze John, Miss Barrancourt. You'd be a fool to go down there now. I came back as soon as I heard, but you can never tell how or where it will spread."

"Bronze John?" Raven repeated sharply, frightened by the uneasy looks exchanged by the two black men who stood behind their master.

"In England I imagine you call it yellow fever," Joshua Spright explained. "Rumor has it a bark fresh from the West Indies brought it in, or one of the clippers that arrived last week from Rio. It's said several crewmen died aboard both ships from some kind of fever. You just can't tell where—"

"Yellow fever?" Raven repeated. In her mind she saw the crowded wharves along the Mississippi River where native whites, blacks, quadroons, and foreign crews all mingled together. Obviously it would be simple to carry a fever off one of the ships and allow it to spread through the taphouses and boardinghouses along the waterfront as well as into the city and onto the other ships—even onto the *Orient Star*, which had to be berthed somewhere along the river. And what about Charles, who, according to Joshua Spright, was searching the entire city in his efforts to find her? Wouldn't the danger of infection be greatest for him?

"Which way to New Orleans?" Raven demanded, her tawny eyes burning with sudden urgency.

"What?" Joshua asked, bewildered by the sudden change in the young woman, who until now had been sitting pale and shivering on the back of the enormous plantation walker.

"I said which way to New Orleans?" Raven's voice was hard, the pistol now leveled directly at Joshua Spright's heart, the other hand wrapped securely about the horse's reins.

"Down the plantation road to the river," he explained reluctantly. "From there you can follow the banks south to the city. But you can't possibly ride all the way alone, especially not in your condition! And what about—hey!" he shouted after her, but Raven, with a hard grinding of her heels into the horse's sleek sides, was gone, a trail of dust and the thundering of hooves on hard-packed ground the last he saw of her.

"Should we go aft' her, Mist' Joshua?" William asked.

Joshua shuddered at the thought of exposing one of his men to the fever. The fear that he might already have contracted it made his throat tighten, and he shook his head vehemently.

"No need to. I've a feeling she'll turn around when she gets too hot and tired. Damn this rotten luck!" He rubbed a shaking hand through his sparse hair and glanced contemptuously into the pale face of his unconscious overseer. "Put him in irons and leave him till he comes around," he commanded. "I sure hope that St. Germain fellow doesn't come looking for him here! I'd almost rather face the plague than him." He nudged the unmoving body with the toe of his boot. "Damn Tyler Jacobs! Why'd he have to let Walsham bring that girl here to begin with?"

Turning back to the house, he dismissed Raven Barrancourt from his mind, for the threat of yellow fever disturbed him far more than concern for her welfare, and he appeased his guilty conscience by telling himself he would have been risking his own life or that of a valuable house slave by escorting her to New Orleans in the middle of an epidemic. Besides, the girl had threatened him with a pistol and stolen one of his best mounts. As far as Joshua Spright was concerned, he had washed his hands of the matter completely.

For Raven the afternoon proved to be a trying ordeal. As the day progressed the May sun grew hotter and hotter, beating down on her bare head and shoulders with merciless intensity. By the time she reached the uncleared forest tracts through which the road led south, she was miserable, and the big hunter's sides and glossy neck were flecked with foam. Despite the welcoming shade of the moss-hung oak trees, the woods offered no respite, for here the deerflies and mosquitoes swarmed and bit, driving the skittish horse to the point of madness. Fearing that the sweeping gait of a hard gallop might harm her child, Raven had originally slowed him to a canter and from there to a plodding walk, but now she urged him to a run, unable to bear the torment of the clouds of buzzing insects any longer. Leaning low in the saddle, she twined her fingers through his long mane to keep from sliding off, well aware that a fall from the horse would undoubtedly harm the child.

Yet at the moment Raven's thoughts were only for Charles. Yellow fever—the words echoed numbly through her brain, and she tried to still her growing panic, certain that Joshua Spright had been exaggerating the spread of the epidemic in the city. Still, the chance existed that not only Charles but everyone aboard the *Orient Star* might become infected—Dmitri, Danny, Geoffrey Lytton, Ewan—all the people she cared for most in the world, and she would have only herself to blame if anything happened to them, because it was for her sake that they had come to New Orleans.

"Oh, Charles," she whispered, tears rolling down her grimy cheeks. "How on earth will I find you before it's too late?"

Biting her lips, she urged the horse to a faster pace, no longer caring how recklessly she rode, not even aware of the fact that her skirts were hiked precariously above her knees. Two old, bearded men passed her along the riverbank, their mule-drawn cart loaded with sacks of corn flour, but Raven scarcely gave them a glance. Her appearance was so startling that neither of them thought to lift their hats and mumble a proper greeting as she passed.

Not much farther down the road the horse stumbled suddenly, nearly unseating her, and after several limping strides he came to a halt, one forefoot cocked, his head hanging forlornly. Raven slipped from his back and hurriedly examined his hoof, groaning in despair when she saw that he had cast a shoe and that the sensitive frog had been cut by a broken nail. For a moment she closed her eyes and clutched the stirrup leather for support, swaying dizzily. Her mouth was dry and her throat ached with the effort to keep from crying. How was she to continue on when she was utterly spent, the child lying heavy and uncomfortable within her?

Wiping the dust from her eyes, she turned and looked about her. Beyond the scrub and stunted palmettos, the river flowed swiftly along the embankment. On the other side the road was flanked by tangled vegetation and a forest floor made damp by seeping groundwater. As Raven watched, a watersnake slithered along the twisted trunk of an oak tree and vanished into the quagmire, its silent passing marked only by the rippling of rotting leaves on the water's weed-choked surface.

Raven shivered and looked away. Beyond the shimmering bend in the river she could detect no plantation landing, no clearing, no sign of civilization whatsoever. It was as if everything and everyone had ceased to exist but for her and the lame horse and the pair of poor dirt farmers she had passed some time ago. Yet she must go on, Raven told herself stubbornly. The longer Charles remained in New Orleans searching for her, the greater the chance that he could be infected with the yellow fever. The thought frightened her and drove her into action. Tucking the barrel of the pistol into the front of her apron, she pulled the reins over the horse's head and patted his sweating neck apologetically.

"Looks like we'll have to walk the rest of the way," she told him, and with chin defiantly set, she started off down the dusty road, the horse limping painfully behind her.

Chapter Eighteen

In New Orleans most of the inhabitants scoffed at the whispered assurances that a yellow fever epidemic was upon them. The wharves and riverfront establishments were always beset with fevers carried in by unsavory foreign crews, they argued. How many people had already died? others questioned contemptuously. Only eight this week, and all of them from bars and boardinghouses, no one of color, no Creole; not one of them had been an individual who had lived in the warm, humid climate long enough to grow accustomed to it.

Though many people refused to believe that Bronze John was responsible for killing the hapless fever victims, Charles St. Germain, listening to the heated arguments and vehement denials, took no chances. The *Orient Star* was ordered away from the docks by her captain and moored farther upriver, accessible only by a single longboat and that made available only to Charles himself, who had ordered all others confined aboard ship. Though the New Orleans officials who had originally agreed to assist in his search for Raven were now preoccupied with calming the rumors that ran more rampant each day, Charles continued his hunt alone with dogged persistence. And though the handbills that had been distributed throughout every quarter of the city had not provided him with a single clue as to Raven's whereabouts, they had helped convince him that Raven had not slipped off the *Cormorant* alone as he and his officers had originally suspected.

If Raven had indeed managed to escape, Charles knew, she would have turned to someone for help by now, someone who would not have failed to recognize her from the description provided in the meticulously distributed papers. Therefore,

Charles reasoned, her disappearance must have involved a member of the *Cormorant*'s crew. Someone aboard had lied to him, Charles admitted to himself at last, someone cunning or desperate enough to bluff his way through an interrogation that in Charles's eyes had been painstakingly thorough.

Three days after her arrival in New Orleans, the big Dutch trader, her departure delayed by order of the harbormaster himself at Charles's behest, was visited again by the grim captain of the *Orient Star*. The crewman on watch recognized the tall, chestnut-haired man who strode authoritatively up the plank, but he was aghast to see that the demonic glow in the devil's eyes was more intense than ever before and that the ruthless sense of purpose about him had increased to seemingly murderous intentions.

"Where is your captain?" Charles demanded, stepping aboard and glaring fiercely down into the sailor's frightened eyes.

"In quarters, sir," he squeaked, unnerved by the palpable anger that exuded from the broad-shouldered form. The small scar on the lean, unshaven cheek did not help to dispel at all the rumors that had abounded throughout the riverfront establishments that the captain of the *Orient Star* was in truth a black-hearted privateer.

"Go below and tell him that I want his entire crew assembled on the deck within the hour. Every man, is that understood?"

Without waiting for his reply, Charles left the ship and shouldered his way through the throng of roustabouts working on the docks below. An hour later he returned, bringing Geoffrey Lytton and Jason Quintrell with him, and as he stepped on board Captain Van der Horst himself was there to receive him, red-faced and annoyed, thinking to himself that this insolent Englishman had caused him quite enough trouble already.

Yesterday, when he had tried to press charges against Charles St. Germain for handling him so roughly at the Fleur Rouge, the New Orleans authorities had proven vexingly uncooperative and, shockingly, he had found himself threatened in turn with imprisonment if in truth he had kidnapped the missing Englishwoman, Raven Barrancourt, and attempted to sell her into slavery. Then, too, there was the chance that he might lose his license now that the company was sending an investigator to look into his clandestine business deals with Daniel Gibson, who had already been dismissed from Bolton and Dickins. It was really too much to bear, Niels Van der Horst decided, and he especially resented Captain St. Germain for ordering him about as though he himself were a mere tar instead of a ship's commander in his own right!

"Really, captain," he began plaintively as soon as Charles stepped onto the quarterdeck, "I demand an explanation for—" His words died away as he stared up into the handsome, rigid face, for never in his life had he seen such a cruel, inhuman look in a man's eyes before.

"I mean to question your men again, Van der Horst," Charles said coldly, wishing as he always did whenever he laid eyes on the effeminate slave trader that he had twisted his fat head right off his pudgy neck the first time they'd met. "I'm convinced one of them knows something that he didn't tell me before." His lips tightened ominously. "By God, he'll answer to me now."

"I don't see how it will do any good," the Dutchman complained bitterly, but again a murderous look from Charles silenced him. Grudgingly he accompanied the two Englishmen and the solemn Welshman to the main deck, where the entire complement of the *Cormorant*'s crew had been gathered in neat rows to face the wrath of Charles St. Germain.

Because he was a good judge of character and because his senses were keen, honed from long years of delving into the minds of his fellow creatures, Charles was able to dismiss most of them immediately, men who swore they knew nothing of the existence of an Englishwoman aboard ship and who, Charles knew instinctively, were speaking the truth. Unlike the last time, he knew now that one of them had deliberately lied to him, and a half-hour later he had been able, based on that certainty, to narrow the choices down to a mere handful. With a glum, muttering Van der Horst trotting behind him, Charles retreated to the rail, where his officers joined him.

"I want them brought here to me one at a time," Charles told the perspiring Dutch captain, his tone brooking no argument.

The morning sun had risen high in a hazy sky during the inspection of the *Cormorant*'s crew, and now it beat down on the deck with an intensity that was almost suffocating. Even the wharves and the city behind them seemed to be cloaked in lethargy, the heat bringing the usual bustle of activity nearly to a halt. Charles, dressed in buckskin breeches, a shirt of fine Holland opened at the throat, did not seem to be affected by the oppressive warmth, and the wilted Dutchman hated and envied him his composure. Little did he realize that Charles was exercising his utmost will power to remain calm and detached while inwardly he was grappling with a rising sense of panic. Fevers grew and festered in moist heat like this, he knew, and the longer Raven remained in New Orleans, the greater the chances of her coming into contact with it. God's blood, he had to find her and get her out of here!

"I'll start with that man on the end," Charles said, his deep voice ringing with deadly menace as he looked contemptuously into Niels Van der Horst's sweating face. "You can tell him and the others that they had better be thinking hard about what they may have neglected to tell me the last time I questioned them, because I won't hesitate to put a lead ball through every one of them if that's what it takes to jog their memories."

Captain Van der Horst opened his mouth to protest, then shut it again. Looking up into the grim visage with the cruelly twisted lips and throbbing scar, he knew that the Englishman was deadly serious, sensed also that he was growing desperate and thus exceedingly dangerous. Nervously wiping the sweat from his brow with a soggy handkerchief, he turned and motioned for John Sampson to come forward, stopping him briefly to whisper a threat into his ear if the crewman dared try to lie to Charles St. Germain.

John Sampson, as Charles knew by now, had been one of the men assigned to the care of the young African women the *Cormorant* had carried to New Orleans. He had already questioned him once, and the simple-minded sailor had sworn that only Nubians and one or two Hindus had comprised the fancy girls in the forward hold. No, it wasn't possible, he had assured Charles back then, that an Englishwoman had been aboard. After all, wouldn't she have made her presence known when she discovered that she was aboard an English-speaking vessel? Nor had any of the young women been in a family way, he had added firmly, because even though he hadn't looked at them quite that closely, surely after a four-month voyage the condition would have been readily noticeable.

Striking fear in Charles's heart, John Sampson had also mentioned the suicide of one of the girls, but a brief description of her had convinced Charles that it had not been Raven. Still, the news had increased his desperation, wondering as he paced sleeplessly about the *Orient Star*'s darkened decks that night if perhaps she hadn't tried the same thing when no one was watching. Then he had assured himself that Raven would never take her own life, especially not when she carried his child. Her strength and courage would not have failed her, he reasoned, and yet the fear dogged him, gnawed at him until he thought he would go mad with it.

Now, as he looked down into John Sampson's grizzled face, he felt his patience ready to snap. One of these men had lied to him before, and one of them, he felt deadly certain, could lead him to her, if only he could find the means of making them admit the truth. Grinding his teeth together, he fought the urge to lift the man into the air and shake him like a dog until his neck snapped in two.

"Captain."

"Eh?" Feeling a hand settle on his shoulder, Charles wheeled about to find himself looking into the familiar countenance of his bosun, Geoffrey Lytton. The little Welshman was regarding him steadily with intelligent gray eyes, his unruffled demeanor restoring Charles's composure.

"Don't you think we should go about this calmly, sir, to give Mr. Sampson a chance to think?"

The terrible rage ebbed out of him as though it had never been, and Charles's sensual lips twisted into a wry smile. "I imagine you're right, Mr. Lytton." He was glad now that his bosun and supercargo had insisted on accompanying him if only because Geoffrey, with his unperturbable nature, was a great steadying influence on Charles's own unpredictable temper. For the first time in weeks he was actually grateful that he had sent Dmitri back to England, well aware that the big Russian's volatile mood would be the same as his own right now, making it more difficult, if not impossible, to keep his own strong emotions in check.

"Beggin' thy pardon, cap'n," John Sampson said suddenly, and both men turned to look at him as though they had forgotten him entirely. Finding the pale, strangely unnerving gray eyes of the Welshman and the glittering, cold emerald ones of the tall sea captain upon him, John Sampson fell silent, wishing that he hadn't spoken.

"Aye, what is it?" Charles asked, and John's courage returned at the unexpected mildness of his tone.

"I beed thinkin' since last thee came." John hesitated, but when he sensed that the impatience in the tall sea captain was rearing again into a full-blown temper, he held up his hands and said quickly, "Bain't about the lass, cap'n, this be somethin' else."

"What, then?" Charles asked a trifle impatiently, then relented when he saw the wariness in the sailor's eyes. "Go on, Mr. Sampson," he pressed. "It may be important."

John Sampson shrugged. "I beed thinkin' muchly about this'n, sir, but mayhap it doan mean a thing. It was on night we docked in New Orleans. Jim Barlow be on watch. When I got back to ship next mornin' Jim sayed a lady be askin' for me. Sayed she come aboard speakin' my name an' how she beed waitin' for *Cormorant* to return an' that I'd know wot be about."

Abruptly he fell silent and gazed up at Charles expectantly.

"Is that all, Mr. Sampson?" Charles asked irritably.

The sailor blinked in surprise. "Yus, cap'n, but thee doan understand. This'n be my first time wot shipped out on *Cormorant*. I never beed in New Orleans before this. Doan know any woman here."

Charles and Geoffrey exchanged startled glances. While neither of them had any idea how this curious experience could link them to Raven's whereabouts, neither was willing to dismiss it without looking into it thoroughly. "Mr. Quintrell," Charles said quietly.

Instantly the young officer was beside him. "Aye, captain?"

"Tell Captain Van der Horst I should like to see a crewman by the name of Jim Barlow immediately." The emerald eyes grew thoughtful as they met John Sampson's questioning gaze. "I don't know how this may help us, Mr. Sampson. Perhaps it won't, but I'm grateful that you told me."

The sailor gave him a relieved grin. "Thank thee right proper, cap'n." Wiping the sweat out of his eyes, he turned and slipped thankfully away.

Jim Barlow's appearance confirmed again Charles's suspicions that the *Cormorant* was manned mostly by riffraff too surly and poorly educated to be impressed even into the services of the British fleet. An enormous man with great hairy arms and a vacant expression on his bewhiskered face, Jim Barlow was exactly the sort of man best cut out for crewing on a stench-enshrouded slaver. Unparalleled strength, dogged loyalty, and a witling's intelligence, his kind was happiest following orders and earning enough pay to keep them supplied with grog and cheap prostitutes when ashore.

Charles recalled having questioned the man before but only briefly, for it had been obvious to him then that Jim Barlow could scarcely remember his own name, let alone whether or not the *Cormorant* had brought an Englishwoman with them from India. Now he found himself regarding the big sailor with new interest, folding his arms across his vast chest and nodding his head in response to the sailor's terse greeting.

"John Sampson tells me a young Englishwoman asked for him the night the *Cormorant* docked and that she spoke to you while you were on watch."

"Aye, zur."

"Can you tell me what she looked like?"

Jim Barlow's expression softened and his fleshy jowls quivered with the harmless smile of a simpleton. "A reg'lar angel she was, zur, I do remember that! Marched right on board in dead of night an' ast if John be aboard."

"What was she wearing?" Charles prompted.

Jim Barlow scratched his head with a dirty hand and thought hard. After a moment his expression cleared. "Oh, aye, was dark. I couldn't rightly see, but 'er clothes weren't the best what there be, if you know my meanin', zur."

"Did you happen to remember the color of her hair or her eyes?" Charles prompted again, wondering if perhaps he was wasting his time after all.

The hulking tar's expression lit. "Aye, I remember the color well. Was black as night, 'er 'air, an' I remember thinkin' was nothin' I'd ever seen looked prettier. That an' 'er eyes, 'cause they tilted at the corners like a cat, you know what I mean, zur?"

Seeing that Charles had grown still at Jim Barlow's enthusiastic words, Geoffrey Lytton said quickly, "It would be foolish to think it could have been Miss Barrancourt, captain! You know that Creole women are just as dark!"

"But no Creole woman speaks with a British accent," Charles said sharply.

"And why would Miss Barrancourt return to the ship and ask for John Sampson when she had ostensibly just escaped?" Geoffrey argued, worried by the sudden hope he saw in his captain's eyes.

"Barlow, did you actually see the lady come aboard?" Charles demanded. "From what direction did she come?"

The muscular tar scratched his head again and looked blank. For a long moment he remained silent, then said reluctantly, "I don't know, zur. I turned around and there she be by entry port. Said she be lookin' for John Sampson, that 'e left summat with 'er last time 'e'd been 'ere an' that she wanted to give it back."

"It doesn't make sense, captain!" Geoffrey protested. "It's inconceivable that Miss Barrancourt would have done such a thing!"

"Mr. Barlow," Charles said earnestly, ignoring him, "did you see anyone with the lady at all? Anyone waiting on the dock?"

"Said she 'ad a footman be waitin' on 'er," Barlow said at last, "but I didn't see 'im myself."

Charles was silent a moment, then lowered his deep voice and asked sharply, "Did anyone leave the ship to follow her after she left? Did any of your mates go after her?"

Jim Barlow looked up into the handsome face, the green eyes, burning with vitality, on level with his, and searched doggedly through his memory. Three nights past was an eternity for him, all the facts hard to remember.

Geoffrey Lytton and Jason Quintrell had moved closer, their interest quickening despite their belief that the captain was nursing false hopes. The compelling intensity in their gazes unnerved Jim Barlow, and he began to sweat, feeling himself on trial, afraid of earning their censure should he fail to come up with an answer. Then, in a moment of crystal clarity, the pieces suddenly fell into place and he could almost see the beautiful, haunted eyes before him, hear the sweetness of her voice and experience again the awe he had felt at the sight of her.

"It were Rollo Walsham," he said finally, almost unaware that he spoke, seeing in his mind's eye the darkly clothed sailor slipping down the gangplank in the young woman's wake. "Rollo Walsham followed 'er away."

"Captain Van der Horst!" Charles's voice cracked with authority. The Dutchman, who had been watching the small group of Englishmen question Jim Barlow by the railing, felt himself beginning to quake as Charles St. Germain strode toward him, his devil's eyes glowing with purpose.

"Y-yes?" he quavered, retreating toward the handful of men still remaining to be questioned. Unnerved by their captain's obvious fear and the look on the Englishman's handsome face, all of them began to shift uneasily and exchange nervous glances.

"I want to speak to Rollo Walsham," Charles grated, his voice, stinging like the lash of a whip, causing the Dutchman to flinch violently.

Sudden confusion broke out among the waiting men, and Charles leaped forward as an ill-kempt sailor in rough homespun pushed his way free of his companions and dashed toward the entry port. In two short strides Charles had reached him, his hand closing like a vise around the man's throat, and Rollo Walsham felt his heart turn over as he looked up into a pair of green eyes glowing with murderous intent.

"Tell me where she is, Walsham," Charles said, his low, silky voice so deadly that the stink of mortal fear began to rise in Rollo Walsham's nostrils.

Feeling the pressure around his windpipe loosen a fraction of an inch, Rollo coughed and cleared his throat, and in a voice that quavered with fear, he obeyed the English sea captain's ruthless command.

It was late afternoon when Charles and Geoffrey Lytton left the city behind them and galloped their horses over the bumpy road that led north along the lapping banks of the Mississippi River. A Baton Rouge–bound packet would have taken them to Bellevue Plantation in half the time, but with the threat of a fever epidemic, the riverboat lines had been running erratically, and Charles had been too impatient to wait the full two hours for the next one to leave. During the course of the day clouds had rolled in from the delta, a dark, sultry blanket that increased the oppressive heat until it became difficult to breathe. Not a breeze stirred the leaves of the gnarled, moss-hung oaks as the two horses pounded along the levee. Out on the water the current moved sluggishly, the river a sullen mass of gray beneath the overcast skies.

"There'll be rain before long," the Welshman remarked, his experienced eyes on the clouds above. Glancing at Charles, he saw that the handsome profile was grimly set, the small scar on the unshaven, sun-browned cheek throbbing. "We'll find her," he said gravely. "I only wish it were Zergeyev beside you and not a small, useless Welshman."

Charles turned his head to regard his bosun, a faint smile curving his lips, and for the first time some of the terrible urgency that had been dogging him all afternoon fell away. "You'll do, Geoffrey," he said briefly, but the Welshman warmed to the confidence in his captain's tone.

"At least we can be sure Miss Barrancourt is safe from the threat of the fever epidemic," Geoffrey added. "Bellevue seems to lie far enough north of the city to be out of immediate danger."

"She's carrying my child," Charles said bluntly, "and I fear that may make her more susceptible."

It was the first time he had ever mentioned Raven's condition openly to his officers before. During the long voyage from India, Charles St. Germain had retreated into himself, a deeply troubled, driven man whom Geoffrey, for all his wisdom, did not know how to reach. In searching New Orleans, in interviewing countless people, distributing thousands of handbills, Charles had never acknowledged the child as his, never spoken of it as his own—as though he didn't dare claim his right to it until Raven was safely with him again.

Now it was impossible to mistake the rough yearning in his savage voice, to doubt for one moment that what had driven him so relentlessly these long, bitter months had been his undeniable love for Raven Barrancourt and the life he had planted within her.

"Why did you never tell her you loved her?" Geoffrey asked unexpectedly as they slowed their lathering horses to strength-conserving trots.

Charles's lean jaw tightened grimly, and for a moment he struggled with himself as though he had been asking himself the same question countless times in the past and had never had the courage to admit to himself the answer. "I was afraid," he said at last. Glancing swiftly at his bosun to see what Geoffrey's reaction would be to this admitted act of cowardice from his captain, Charles found the intelligent gray eyes regarding him steadily. A short, self-condemning laugh fell from his lips.

"When you spend your entire life building a wall around you, Geoffrey, and an innocent little chit somehow manages to undermine it completely, it's bloody difficult to patch it up again." Charles laughed a second time, derisively, his emerald eyes glittering. "It sounds ridiculous when I put it that way, doesn't it?"

"You certainly fooled everyone with your sullen act," Geoffrey observed, "even Dmitri, for the most part. The poor fellow couldn't understand why you had taken such a strong dislike to his adored 'little princess.'"

"I almost had myself convinced I felt nothing for her," Charles agreed, a warm light beginning to glow in his eyes at the memory of the countless confrontations with Raven that had so angered and delighted him at the same time. "Only Danny was shrewd enough to see through my play-acting. Which is why, I imagine, she wasn't the least bit surprised to learn Raven's child was mine." His deep voice grew rough. "By God, I swear if she's come to harm—"

"That Walsham fellow assured us she was well when he took her to Bellevue," Geoffrey said quickly, thrusting away the disgusting image of the fearful, slobbering sailor whose confession had nearly cost him his life at the hands of Charles St. Germain. It had taken himself, young Quintrell, the burly sailor Barlow, and even one or two others from the *Cormorant*'s crew to pry the weeping, terrified Rollo Walsham from Captain St. Germain's murderous grasp. But for their timely intervention, Geoffrey knew, Charles would have choked the life out of him with his own bare hands.

A rumble of thunder caused him to look up at the sky, forgetting his sobering thoughts. Thunderheads were moving in from the west, great gray and purple clouds that were driven by relentless winds. On the river tiny ripples began to form, the tide lapping with increasing energy against the levee. Dust rose in miniature whirlwinds, clogging the horses' nostrils and stinging both men's eyes.

"We'd better hurry," Charles remarked, his head thrown back as he surveyed the roiling sky. The electric tension in the atmosphere somehow increased his own anxiety, the deep conviction growing within him that somehow Raven was in bad need of his help. Without waiting for his officer's affirmative, he dug his heels into the horse's sides and took off at a flat gallop down the hard-packed road.

The rain began to fall at last, huge, driving drops that roared through the trees, churned the water in the river, and turned the dusty roadway into a quagmire. Farther up the road, some twelve miles below Bellevue Plantation, Raven Barrancourt hunched her frail shoulders as the torrent erupted from the heavens, the rain running down her face and leaving tracks of grime on her hollow, dust-covered cheeks. After a few faltering steps the lame horse, his hoofs caked with mud, came to a halt, hanging his head in abject misery.

"Come on!" Raven urged, tugging at the reins.

The big animal refused to move, and Raven, too weary herself to fight him anymore, let her hands fall to her sides. How much farther, she asked herself dejectedly, before she reached the outskirts of New Orleans? Her slippers were sodden, her gown wringing wet, and she was so tired that she could scarcely remain standing. It would be easiest, she knew, to find shelter somewhere from the driving rain, to rest until the storm passed, but the thought of Charles looking for her in the fever-scoured city galvanized her into action.

With numb fingers Raven unbuckled the girth and slid the saddle from the limping hunter's back. Pulling the bridle from his head, she flicked his hindquarters lightly with the loose leather reins and shouted at him to go on. At first he refused to move, but after Raven had dealt him a second, more stinging blow, he took off at an ungainly trot in the direction he had originally come. Placing the tack on a dry bed of leaves in a cluster of thickets near the roadway, Raven straightened and pushed the sodden strands of hair out of her eyes. He would return to Bellevue unharmed, she hoped, and then she forgot him as the enormity of her own dilemma dawned on her.

She was miles from her destination, clad in a thin muslin gown that clung to her wet skin, her aching feet encased in worn kid slippers that were caked with mud. Exhausted and hungry, Raven wasn't sure that she had enough strength left to go much farther.

"Of course you do," she told herself sternly. She had survived the harrowing voyage from India, hadn't she? Well, then, why should a minor walk of several miles in the driving rain seem so threatening now? Back home in Cornwall she had haunted the moors for hours on end in weather like this and, contrary to Danny's dire warnings, had never contracted so much as a case of the sniffles. Ah, but she had always been healthy and pampered back home at North Head, a strong, vital young girl growing up wild on the Cornish heaths. The months of captivity and advancing pregnancy had taken their toll, Raven realized, but stubbornly refused to acknowledge the fact. Setting her small chin at a determined angle, she began to walk down the road, the mud running in oozing rivulets over her slippers and dragging at the sodden hem of her gown.

A second set of ominous black clouds, driven from the gulf by the rising wind, descended upon her so suddenly that Raven was caught unawares. What had seemed a cloudburst before became an unbelievable deluge as the heavens opened up to drench the soaked ground. Thunder clapped deafeningly overhead and lightning ripped through the sky, a single bolt crashing into the crown of a massive oak nearby, the explosion so close that Raven felt her hair stand on end.

With hammering heart she lowered her head against the blinding sheet of rain that stung her face, and began to run along the soaking roadway, which had turned away from the swollen river into the recesses of impenetrable scrub and thickets. Here the rain roared through the trees, lightning crackling around her, the wind whipping the hem of Raven's skirts so that movement was almost impossible. Dodging branches that came hurling from above, she ran blindly, searching for shelter, a scream tearing from her whenever searing lightning bolts crashed to the earth nearby.

It would be madness to take shelter beneath one of the enormous oaks, Raven knew, but where could she go to escape the lashing force of the rain? She paused for a moment at a bend in the road where a haphazard line of palmettos diminished the gale-force intensity of the wind. Gasping for breath, she tried to peer through the driving deluge, but a flash of lightning blinded her, the accompanying clap of thunder ringing in her ears.

When the sound had rumbled away and the flashing lights before her eyes were gone, Raven looked up and her breath caught in her throat. Through the sheets of driving rain a pair of horses were looming toward her, their riders fighting to keep the frightened beasts from bolting. Great clods of wet mud clung to their hoofs, and their coats were splattered with it, their fine leather trappings thoroughly soaked.

Raven froze, aware that she had not yet been spotted. Since her abduction from Karachi she had learned to distrust all strangers, and now she could feel a sob of pure panic rising in her throat, certain that these two men would recognize from her muddied calico skirts that she was a runaway slave. Turning around, she tried to reach the protective shelter of the trees but slipped in the mud and nearly fell, painfully twisting her ankle. An anguished cry fell from her lips and Raven clapped her hand over her mouth, whirling about to see if she had been noticed. Above the howling wind she heard one of the approaching riders shout to the other, and then the horses were bearing down on her at a dead run. Tears of despair welled in Raven's eyes, aware that it was too late to run even if her throbbing ankle could have supported her weight.

Trembling violently she reached into the front of her apron and drew out the pistol, not at all sure that it would still fire. With both hands clasping the ivory handle, she held the weapon at arm's length, barrel pointed at the taller of the two men, who rode in the lead. Her lips were drawn back in a determined snarl. She could not know that she looked nowhere near as intimidating as she thought she did, her muddied skirts clinging wetly to her body and clearly revealing the rounded outline of her pregnancy. Her midnight hair, hanging in sodden strands down her back, dripped water, and her pale cheeks were grimy and covered with scratches and mosquito bites. Only her eyes remained unchanged, the wild determination to survive glowing in their tawny depths, the long, wet lashes starlike as they framed their sloping corners.

The lead horse came closer but Raven held her ground, and as its rider reined in sharply it floundered and nearly went down in the oozing mud, then pulled itself up and came to a halt.

"God's blood, Raven!"

Her head jerked up at the sound of her name, and through the driving rain she found herself staring up into Charles St. Germain's tormented face, his emerald-green eyes burning, the look within them blinding her to everything but the devastating love and need for her that lay bared in the depths of his soul. Her lips moved soundlessly but she did not stir, the pistol in her small hands still aimed at his vast chest, the rain continuing to lash her unprotected form.

"Raven! My God, Raven!"

She did not even see him leap from his horse and reach for her, nor was she aware of Geoffrey Lytton's beaming face beyond Charles's massive shoulder. All she knew was that suddenly she was in his arms, was being crushed against the great warmth of his body, and he was murmuring against her sodden hair, his voice cracking with emotion.

"Is it really you, Charles?" she whispered, scarcely daring to hope.

"Aye, it is," he assured her hoarsely. "I've found you at last, my own true love."

Aware that she was shivering violently, he gathered her thin body more tightly into his strong arms, shielding her from the relentless onslaught of the rain. When she tried to speak, he silenced her roughly, drawing her to him so that she could feel the wild pulse beating in his throat.

"Hush, my love, don't speak. As soon as the rain lets up I'll take you back to the ship."

Exhausted as she was, Raven could not rest until she had assured herself that he was unharmed, that it was indeed Charles who held her and not some dream dredged from the depths of her feverish imagination. Lifting her head, she looked at him anxiously, noticed how haggard and drawn he appeared, his chestnut curls clinging damply to his forehead. With trembling fingers she reached out and tentatively touched the small scar on his lean cheek, but the question died on her lips when she looked into his eyes and saw the same raw emotions still blazing there.

"Raven, I love you," he said, the rough words torn from him as he gazed down into her enormous tawny eyes, seeing in her thin, hollow cheeks the exquisite perfection of a woman of rarest beauty, the very woman he had thought lost to him forever. Holding her shivering body against his, he could feel how thin she had grown, but the rounding of her belly was firm and ripe, and he groaned and pulled her even tighter against him where his lips devoured hers, clinging with a need so fierce that Raven felt the horrors of the past slipping away until nothing mattered save Charles, who was holding her in a way that told her she need never be afraid again.

Chapter Nineteen

On a warm, sun-drenched morning in late July the clipper ship *Orient Star* sailed past the imposing castle topping St. Michael's Mount while the incoming tide carried her swiftly across Mount's Bay into the snug harbor of Penzance. Reefing her sails and making her mooring lines fast, her loyal crew worked with an urgency that had never been upon them before, while in his spacious stern quarters Captain St. Germain turned restlessly from the windows and looked down with a mixture of concern and infinite tenderness into the strained face of his young wife, Raven.

"Are you sure I can't get you to change your mind?" he asked in a tone that was neither harsh nor commanding, though inwardly he was grappling with the overwhelming urge to shout at her and make her listen to reason.

Raven's lips curved into a soft, loving smile, although her cheeks were pale and her midnight hair clung damply to her forehead. "I'm sure." Something in his eyes made her reach out and grasp his hand, the strength of her grip surprising and gratifying him. "Please, Charles, don't be angry with me."

It was impossible not to relent when Raven looked that way, and some of the tension drained away from Charles's rigid countenance. "How can I be angry with you?" he asked lightly. "If you wish our child to be born in North Head, then so be it. I'm only glad he decided to wait until we arrived in Cornwall."

"And what if he is a she?" Raven teased. Her small face suddenly clouded with doubt. "You wouldn't mind if it was a girl?"

Charles had never thought to see an uncertain look in those magnificent eyes again, and he squeezed her hand reassuringly. "A daughter as beautiful as her mother would delight my heart," he said huskily, and his heart constricted when Raven, smiling up at him, suddenly turned away, a spasm of pain fleeing across her delicate face.

The labor pains had begun some time shortly before dawn, and Charles had awakened to find Raven trembling in his arms, her nightgown soaked, her lips tightly compressed so that not even the barest whimper had escaped to alert him of her distress. He had been angry with her for not awakening him sooner, but as he slipped a clean nightgown over her head and carried her back to the bunk, his anger had changed to the gnawing fear that Raven was not yet strong enough to bear this child. A long, unhurried convalescence in New Orleans would have been best for her, but with the threat of the yellow fever plague upon them, Charles had ordered the *Orient Star* out to sea, and Raven, in her inimitable way, had managed to wheedle from him the reluctant promise to take her back to England so that the baby could be born at North Head.

"Raven?"

Opening her eyes at the gentle utterance of her name, she found Charles's lean face hovering over her own. Gathering her strength, she managed to smile up at him reassuringly, aware that his concern for her was growing. "What is it?" she whispered.

"The carriage has arrived and I've sent for Dr. Tremyn. He'll meet us at home."

Raven felt her heart grow warm at the casual manner in which her husband referred to North Head as his home. She had been fretting silently throughout the voyage that Charles would never be entirely free of the call of the sea and that her love might not be strong enough to hold him there. Now she saw only the depth of his love for her in the burning emerald eyes, and she slipped her arms trustingly about his neck.

"I'll be fine," she assured him as he lifted her against his wide chest. "We Barrancourts are of a hardy mettle."

"Aye," Charles agreed with a long-suffering sigh, his voice sounding gruff in her ear. "But you're a St. Germain now, my dear. I charge you to remember it."

"I doubt you'll ever permit me to forget it," Raven teased, but her words ended on a sharp gasp and tears welled in her eyes as a spasm of pain wracked her. Charles, his handsome features stark, strode quickly up the stairs to the main deck, where Danny stood waiting impatiently to accompany him to shore.

"There you are at last!" she said severely as the tall form of Captain St. Germain emerged into the sunlight with his wife in his arms. "There's no time to be wastin', sir! The babe may not oblige the two of you by waitin' until we get home!"

Charles was forced to grin as he looked down into the round, angry face, Danny's competent air dispelling some of his unspoken fears. A carriage stood waiting for them by the promenade, and the driver, apparently recognizing Raven, doffed his hat and gave her a welcoming smile as Charles lifted her in.

"Look outside, will you, Miss Raven?" Danny invited from the doorway.

With Charles's help Raven raised herself up on one elbow, and through the window of the carriage she could see the crew of the *Orient Star* lined up against the rail, all of them waving down to her and calling out words of encouragement. She waved back, warmed by the sight, until Charles climbed in behind her and put his strong, comforting arms about her. With a contented sigh Raven laid her head against him and closed her eyes, praying that they would get to North Head quickly before the tearing pains began again.

Alerted to their mistress's impending arrival, the staff was well prepared by the time the hired carriage was spotted turning up the cedar-lined drive. The lying-in chamber, as a flustered, acutely embarrassed Parris referred to it, had been made ready, and Dr. Tremyn had been furnished with every item he had requested to facilitate the birth of Raven St. Germain's first child. Sir Hadrian Barrancourt, awakened from sleep by the bustle of activity that had erupted within the great house, had insisted upon being dressed and downstairs by the time his grandniece arrived.

When the carriage drew to a halt before the wide stone steps of North Head's main wing, Raven, lucid and pain-free for the moment, was astonished to see the servants lined up outside to greet her, Sir Hadrian, resplendent in a gold braided waistcoat, heading up the entourage, an ever-watchful Jeffords flanking his elbow.

"Oh, dear, I hope I look all right," Raven said fretfully, smoothing back the wayward strands of midnight hair that spilled over her shoulders. Glancing down at her threadbare gown, the waistline let out by Danny weeks ago to accommodate her young mistress's thickening middle, she gave Charles a helpless look. "I can't possibly face my great-uncle looking like this!"

"In the name of God, Raven!" Charles protested roughly. "This isn't an audience with the queen! Are all women this impossible when their time has come?" he added, giving Danny a disgruntled look.

"I'm afraid so," she responded, smiling at both of them indulgently. It amused and touched her to see Charles St. Germain—normally so arrogant and sure of himself—acting so confused and helpless. Honestly, she thought without a trace of rancor, men were such children when it came to matters pertaining to the nursery! Nonetheless it pleased her to discover that a man as ruthless as the captain was in truth no different from the rest of his sex when the woman he loved was preparing to deliver for him his first son or daughter.

Raven, with that characteristic independence that so annoyed the anxious Charles, insisted upon entering the house without being carried. Relenting with great reluctance, he lifted her gently to the stones and held her to him for a brief moment, his lips against her smooth brow. With an arm about her he helped her up the steps, noticing the warm expression on the faces of the gathered retainers at the sight of their mistress, some of them dabbing at their eyes with soggy hankies. To Charles's surprise that warmth was extended to him as well, and he found himself deeply touched by the words of welcome that were directed toward him.

Raven paused only long enough to greet her great-uncle, and as the glossy black head bent over the leonine one, Charles saw tears of joy springing into the old man's rheumy eyes.

"I told you there was no reason to worry, sir," Jeffords remarked with mock severity as Raven fondly kissed her great-uncle's withered cheek.

"Shows you how much you know, you useless poltroon!" Sir Hadrian retorted. "Money, Raven, money is what I sent you to India for, not hunting for a husband and a babe!"

"I stand chastened, sir," Raven admitted with a soft glow in her tawny eyes as she turned to smile up at Charles, "but I really had little choice in the matter once Charles made up his mind.

Oh!" she added suddenly, her cheeks draining of color, and Charles, hovering anxiously beside her, steadied her with a hand beneath her elbow.

"That's enough chatter, Raven," he told her severely, glowering into her pain-filled eyes. "You've a pressing engagement with the doctor upstairs. Sir Hadrian." He inclined his dark head in the old man's direction. "Pray forgive your grandniece this rude interruption, but I'm afraid she has other commitments at present."

Scooping Raven unceremoniously into his arms, he carried her up the steps, the servants parting respectfully to allow him to pass, the young girls in their frilly mob caps gaping with wide, admiring eyes.

"Insolent whelp, eh, Jeffords?" Sir Hadrian cackled, slapping his thigh with a bony hand. "By Jove, I think she's found herself a wild one, a'right!"

In the enormous bedroom of the master suite located in the east wing of the house, the heavy drapes had been drawn and the big bed remade with fresh linen. With Danny hovering behind him, Charles laid Raven gently onto the smooth bedclothes, his expression stark as he straightened and gazed down into her small, impassive face.

"Captain St. Germain?"

He turned at the sound of his name. "Aye?"

"I am Dr. Tremyn. Your wife requested that I be present at the birth."

Charles studied the small, bewhiskered physician with his small, finely boned hands, liking the steady, appraising gaze that met his own. Despite his thick Cornish accent Dr. Tremyn spoke quietly and purposefully, his manner direct and forthright, and his neatly tied cravat and simple chambray shirt were clean and meticulously pressed.

"I've known Miss Raven since she was a wee girl," he added, hoping to dispel completely the last traces of doubt that still lingered in the broad-shouldered captain's startlingly green eyes. "The first occasion was at the age of five when she took a fall from her new pony." His own eyes twinkled. "I can't remember how many falls, scrapes, cuts, and bruises followed after that."

"I can well imagine," Charles agreed, relaxing. His expression changed subtly as he glanced toward the big bed where Danny and a redheaded serving girl were in the process of removing

Raven's gown. "My wife has not been well," he said gruffly, "and her strength is not what I'd like it to be."

"I don't anticipate problems," Dr. Tremyn remarked confidently. His whiskers twitched. "You must consider, after all, the constitution of the Barrancourts, captain."

"If I ever forget," Charles observed wryly, "I'm sure one of you won't fail to remind me."

Dr. Tremyn beamed. "Now, if you'll excuse us, please, captain, I'd like to examine your wife and see how far along she is."

Charles's expression darkened. "I've no intention of leaving."

"Of course you will," Danny said cheerfully, taking Charles by the elbow and attempting unsuccessfully to guide him toward the door. "This is no place for a father-to-be!"

"Danny..." Charles said warningly.

"She'll be fine," the elderly woman relented, growing serious. "I know a bit about midwifery myself, and Dr. Tremyn be the best in all Cornwall." She indicated the red-haired maid with a nod of her graying head. "I warrant Nan and I could have handled the birth alone, but Miss Raven and I both agreed that under the circumstances it would be wiser to have a surgeon present. Go on, now," she added more forcibly. "You'll only be in the way."

Feeling more helpless than ever before in his life, Charles glanced indecisively at the big four-poster bed. As if sensing his worried gaze upon her, Raven opened her eyes, and he saw the golden depths beginning to glow with love for him. The soft lips curved into a gentle smile, and Charles, reassured, allowed Danny to close the bedroom door behind him.

"Now, now, my boy, you need to relax! When you live to be my age you'll find there's little need to get upset about something like this."

Startled, Charles turned around to find Sir Hadrian Barrancourt regarding him from the end of the sunlit corridor. Though he leaned heavily on a cane, his body frail, his hands deeply lined with blue veins, there was a twinkle in his amber eyes, and the proud carriage of his head reminded Charles all too exasperatingly of his irascible grandniece.

"I hope I never see the day when the birth of a son or daughter will fail to move me, sir," he said sharply.

Sir Hadrian cackled and stroked the silver whiskers that cascaded down the front of his satin-covered chest. "Surly fellow, aren't you? Well, no matter. I forgive you this time, lad, because this whole business of birthing babes can be trying indeed on a new papa, eh? Come along, no sense in prowling before the door like that. You'll only hear things you won't care much for. Better come down to the study with me." He lowered his voice conspiratorially. "If we can elude that muttonheaded valet of mine, I promise to let you sample the finest brandy you've ever tasted."

Charles's full lips twitched and he found himself inexplicably warming to the wizened curmudgeon before him. Aware of it, Sir Hadrian chuckled again and led the way down the spiraling staircase to the main wing where a footman moved quickly to open the carved oak door leading to James Barrancourt's study. Charles was immediately taken with the warm, inviting atmosphere of the room, the walnut paneling lovingly burnished, the Oriental carpet a rare and tasteful work of art to his experienced eyes. It was a masculine room offering a welcome escape from the cares of the world, and Charles's interest quickened as he read a few of the gold-stamped titles of the books lining the carved wooden shelves. Behind the enormous desk the casement windows opened to a breathtaking panorama of the sea, the barren cliffs plunging to a rocky, foam-flecked shore.

Aye, Charles thought to himself, I'll enjoy working here.

With a satisfied smile Sir Hadrian hobbled to the glass-fronted cabinet and removed a pair of balloon-shaped snifters, filling each of them with a healthy splash of fragrant brandy. The smile deepened when he saw Charles settle his large frame comfortably into the big leather chair, his long legs crossed before him, the image of a country gentleman in his leather vest and carelessly knotted cravat. There were hundreds of questions on the old man's mind, but he would not ask them yet despite his great impatience. There would be time later to hear from this man, Raven's husband, what had transpired during the year of his grandniece's absence. First they must await the birth of the child, and Sir Hadrian found he could not get the image from his mind of Raven, thinner, somehow older, but breathtakingly beautiful, leaning on the arm of her tall, handsome husband as he helped her from the carriage, hiding the concern on his handsome face behind a studied show of truly solicitous devotion.

Raven had looked magnificent, her creamy skin turned gold

by long hours in the summer sun, her pregnancy somehow enhancing the graceful fragility of her slender form. And yet she had looked thin and exhausted, the strain in her beautiful eyes too marked to be the result of labor pains alone. St. Germain himself had hovered over her with a kind of ferocious protectiveness, and Sir Hadrian strongly suspected that the bonds that linked the two of them had been forged through deep suffering and tribulation. Somehow that did not bother him exceedingly, for it seemed to him that a love born of pain flourished more strongly and was more everlasting than any other.

Then there was the matter of the fifty thousand pounds owed the obnoxious Squire Blackburn, whom Sir Hadrian heartily detested. He chuckled to himself, imagining the look on his grandniece's face when he told her the wild stories he had spun for the good squire as to her whereabouts, leaving the poor man quite bewildered withall. Yes, indeed, quite a bit to tell Raven, Sir Hadrian decided, and quite a bit she and St. Germain undoubtedly had to tell him, but all of that must wait until young Raven had safely delivered the babe.

Aware that the unnerving eyes of the captain were fastened upon him, Sir Hadrian looked up, and realized all at once that he had laughed aloud at the prospect of telling Squire Josiah Blackburn to go to Hades. "Don't mind me," he said peevishly, "I'm in my dotage and should be tolerated if I talk to myself now and again."

The sea-green eyes warmed a fraction. "At your liberty, sir."

Sir Hadrian took another sip of brandy, smacked his lips appreciatively, and jumped in without preamble. "Well, my boy, all of this belongs to you now. There have been many Barrancourts who've died at the hands of treacherous kinsmen determined to lay their own claim to this land." His unusual amber eyes roved lovingly around the richly appointed study. "Elegance and beauty aside, North Head is a working estate, with arable tillage and tenants to be managed. Not quite the same thing as commandeering a privateer around the world, I'd imagine."

"Probably not," Charles agreed, aware that the shrewd old man was testing him. His lips twitched. "I can assure you, however, that Raven would not have agreed to marry me if she didn't think me capable of assuming the role of gentleman farmer."

"So you intend to settle here, do you?" Sir Hadrian queried, studying the lean, sun-browned face before him. "What about that ship of yours? I wouldn't want to see my grandniece abandoned with an armful of babes when your sailin' blood starts singin' afresh in your veins."

Though Charles would have deeply resented such an impertinent remark from anyone else, he understood that Sir Hadrian's concern was for Raven alone, and where Raven was concerned, he himself couldn't help yielding another man almost any quarter. Imperceptibly his harsh features softened, and his deep voice was without its customary gruffness. "I spent my early manhood on the sea, sir, searching for something that did not have a name or a definition. In truth I wasn't even aware of the extent of the hunger within me until I met Raven and suddenly found it satisfied in a manner I never expected. With the cure," Charles said simply, "I discovered the cause, and there are no longer any ghosts now to haunt me."

Sir Hadrian pretended a deep interest in the contents of his brandy snifter, greatly touched by the English sea captain's honest admission, well aware that the disclosure had not been made lightly. After a moment he shrugged his thin shoulders and regarded Charles with a satisfied grin. "To your health, then, my boy! I've no doubt James's estates are in capable hands."

Charles downed the remains of the excellent brandy and leaned back in the comfortable leather chair, scanning the rows of ledgers on the desktop before him. The prospect of bringing North Head back into prosperous working order did not daunt him, and at the moment he was far more concerned with Raven. How pale and tired she had looked when she had smiled at him so bravely from the big four-poster bed! His lean jaw tightened and the scar on his cheek began to throb.

"Sit down, sit down!" Sir Hadrian said querulously as Charles set the snifter aside and abruptly rose to his full height behind the desk. "You won't be helpin' the lass any bursting down the door! They'll call you when it's time."

"Sir Hadrian!" came an accusing voice from the door, and the elderly man groaned as Jeffords, eyes blazing with righteous indignation, strode into the study and pried the empty snifter from his master's gnarled fingers. "How many times has the doctor told you this stuff is poison to your system?"

"Oh, get on with you," Sir Hadrian grumbled, casting a dour

glance at Charles, who was forced to laugh, his own impatience draining away. Jeffords, a masculine version of the fussing, proprietary Danny, gave the tall sea captain a miffed look, resenting the fact that his authority where Sir Hadrian was concerned seemed to have been undermined. "Mr. Parris sent me in to inform you that luncheon has been laid out in the Conservatory," he said stiffly.

"Oh, all right," Sir Hadrian said peevishly. "We might as well show Captain St. Germain how delicious a true Cornish meal can be."

"Oh, captain, sir!" A disheveled young maid with flushed cheeks burst through the doorway, almost knocking the proper Jeffords down in her haste. "Dr. Tremyn says 'ee maun go up! The babe be arrived, sir!"

"What, so soon?" Sir Hadrian demanded, but Charles was already gone, the serving girl staring worshipfully after his tall, receding frame.

At Raven's whispered request the heavy drapes had been drawn away from the windows so that the afternoon sunshine streamed in unfettered. Propped up with numerous pillows, she could look out over the shimmering sea as she waited with considerable impatience for the moment when Dr. Tremyn would lay her first-born child into her arms. Sarah and Nan, whispering happily in a corner, were bundling up the bloodstained sheets while Danny straightened the lacy collar of Raven's clean new nightgown and smoothed the damp hair back from her young mistress's forehead.

"There, my darlin'," she crooned, her merry brown eyes wet with tears of joy. "All freshened up and pretty as a picture."

Behind her the bedroom doors crashed open, and all of them turned, shocked, to find a disheveled Charles on the threshold, his emerald eyes blazing with wild emotions. Only Raven had not been startled by his entrance, and she smiled and beckoned to him, the gesture bringing a look of profound relief to his rugged features. Crossing the room, he sat down beside her on the bed and touched Raven's pale cheek with stiff fingers, his voice failing him suddenly when he tried to speak.

"Look, Charles," Raven whispered as Dr. Tremyn appeared behind her husband's broad shoulder with a mewling bundle in his grasp. "We have a daughter."

"And a healthy one at that," Dr. Tremyn added, laying the

blanketed infant carefully into Raven's outstretched arms. "The delivery was without difficulty, and our young lady seems to have emerged into the world quite intact."

Staring down into the tiny red face of his daughter, Charles felt an odd tightening in his chest. Her small head was covered with a fine layer of hair as dark and lustrous as Raven's, and when she opened her eyes to look up at him, he saw that they were blue, although the turquoise depths gave promise that one day they would be as green as his own. A smile rich with fulfillment curved Charles's sensual lips, but to his astonishment the baby chose to react to her father's pleasure by opening her rosebud mouth and giving a lusty cry.

Raven laughed at the startled look on Charles's face, but when his eyes met hers, the laughter died on her lips and she blushed deeply when she saw the fierce love for her that blazed within them.

"I love you, Raven," Charles whispered hoarsely. "You cannot begin to fathom how much I love you."

"I can try," she replied breathlessly and raised her face to his as his lips came down hungrily to claim hers.

After Raven had drifted off to sleep and the baby, well fed and content, lay in the cozy bassinet beside her mother's bed, Charles slipped quietly from the room. Feeling the need to stretch his legs a bit, he sent orders to the stables for a horse to be saddled and, adjusting his cravat, stopped in the dining hall long enough to drink a toast to his daughter's health with a blissfully happy Sir Hadrian.

"And what will you name her?" the proud new great-great-uncle asked as he set his empty glass aside.

Charles ran a hand through his unruly chestnut hair. "You know, I'm not even sure. I imagine I'll leave that up to Raven."

"And how is my dear grandniece?" Sir Hadrian asked with an indulgent smile.

Charles's features softened as they always did whenever Raven was mentioned, and Sir Hadrian noted the change with approval. "Doing very well. Dr. Tremyn doesn't anticipate any problems."

"And why should he?" Sir Hadrian snorted. "She's a St. Germain, isn't she? I understand they're extremely tough stock."

The smile still lingered on Charles's sensual lips when he crossed the cobbled courtyard and watched as two young boys attempted to lead an ungovernable bay stallion from the interior of the stables. Prancing sideways, his ears flattened against his noble head, the stallion wheeled and fought the restraining hands, while the young grooms cursed and did their best to keep him in line.

"I imagine this must be Cinnabar," Charles remarked to the grizzled old man who emerged from the small carriage house to watch the fracas.

"Aye, that it be, sir," Sam acknowledged. He had already heard quite a bit about his new master from gossip in the great house, but he was not one to form opinions based on hearsay. And yet he had to admit that the sea captain who had married their beloved Miss Raven was fully as large and intimidating as the general consensus claimed him to be. Being a man himself, Sam couldn't judge whether Charles St. Germain was as devastatingly handsome as the swooning serving girls insisted, but he had to admit that the captain cut a fine figure indeed in his worn calfskin breeches and tall polished boots.

"Would 'ee care to ride him, sir?" Sam asked, indicating the sidestepping Cinnabar. "I had the lads saddle him for 'ee, bein' as no one's ridden him proper since Miss Raven went away, but I'll have 'em ready one of the geldings if he be too much for 'ee."

Charles raised his eyebrows and regarded the head groom speculatively. There was no challenge in the steady gaze that met his, only polite inquiry. "Cinnabar will do just fine," Charles replied lightly. "I imagine he won't be any more difficult to tame than his mistress." Flashing the startled Sam a wide grin, he took the reins from the gaping grooms and swung himself effortlessly into the saddle.

A moment later man and horse were galloping across the wind-blown grass, Cinnabar obediently responding to commands as Charles sat with an impeccable seat in the saddle. Folding his powerful arms across his apron-covered chest, Sam pursed his lips, dawning respect registering on his grizzled face. Not many men could sit a horse like that, he knew, especially if the horse was one like Cinnabar. Aye, he decided, it looked like Miss Raven had made herself a right proper match indeed.

With the salty tang of the sea in his face, Charles turned the muscular stallion away from the house and challenged him to greater speeds so that the two of them were soon racing the wind. The wide, barren moors that led from North Head toward the sea offered boundless open spaces, and Charles let the mighty animal have his head, both of them dispersing their wild, restless energies in an uninhibited gallop.

Where the cliffs met the sea Charles drew rein at last and allowed Cinnabar to blow while he looked out over the rocky, incredibly beautiful coastline, all of it Barrancourt domain that was now his and Raven's to share. But it was St. Germain land now, by God, Charles wanted to shout, and the fact that he now had a home and a family to call his own filled him with profound joy. Years ago he had given up those very things, restlessly hungering for something he had thought to find on the vast, empty stretches of the open sea. What had family meant to him then, a young man without parents or brothers and sisters to fill the gnawing emptiness within him? Raven's deep love for North Head, for the permanence of home and the beloved memories of her own mother and father, had rekindled within Charles the fierce desire of belonging that he had purposely quelled these many years.

And, oh, by God, how well Raven had stilled that pain as soon as it had begun to torment him again! Through her great love for him she had not only filled that aching void, but also presented him with an enchanting daughter and a home more wild and breathtakingly beautiful than the tamed, manicured perfection of Château Monteraux.

Charles's emerald eyes glittered as he looked down at the hidden cove where, months ago, he and his men had unloaded contraband barrels of rum and he had first tasted the passions of a hot-headed, proud young beauty by the name of Raven Barrancourt. Desire for her overwhelmed him suddenly, and the need to gaze into her exquisite face, to touch her soft lips with his, to see the love she felt for him burning in her magnificent eyes, prompted Charles to wheel the unsuspecting stallion and drive him back to the house.

Disheveled, tired, but feeling totally renewed, Charles dismounted and handed the reins to the toothily grinning Sam, who came out of the stables to meet him. In the house a respectful but undeniably happy Parris informed him that Miss Raven was still sleeping and that Sir Hadrian and Mrs. Daniels had also retired to their rooms for a nap. The baby was also well, and Nan would be spending the rest of the afternoon in the adjoining sitting room in the event that either mother or daughter awakened and required anything.

"That's all right, Parris, you can tell Nan I'll sit with Raven," Charles told him and let himself quietly into the master bedroom.

The late-afternoon sun painted the rose-colored walls a bright gold, and a single ray of light fell on the pillows where Raven's glossy black hair spilled over her shoulders. In repose the weariness that had etched itself into her face was gone, and the faint bloom of returning good health tinged her high cheekbones. Charles gazed at her wordlessly for several minutes before she stirred and opened her eyes, the golden depths beginning to glow when she saw his rugged face above hers. Before she could speak the infant in the cradle began to whimper, and Raven watched with great interest as Charles bent down to take his newborn daughter into his arms. Half-expecting him to be clumsy or even timid, Raven was astonished to see him lift her against his wide chest without hesitation and the child, instantly content, drifted off again to sleep.

"I think she's rather taken with you," Raven remarked, her voice trembling oddly.

"And how can I not adore her in return when she is so much like you?" Charles asked, and Raven basked in the warmth of his loving smile.

Not ten minutes later their peaceful intimacy was suddenly interrupted by a commotion on the stairway, and Charles quickly laid his sleeping daughter into Raven's outstretched arms before striding toward the door, where the sound of angry voices and pounding footsteps heralded the approach of what must have been a small army.

"Captain St. Germain, you must come quickly!" It was the usually unruffled Parris knocking urgently on the bedroom door. "Timms is downstairs priming the master's pistols! I tried to keep the fellow out, but he shouldered me aside and—"

"And who would dare refuse me entry into the home of my oldest friend, eh?" boomed a deep, outraged voice from the bottom of the staircase.

"Dmitri!" Charles and Raven exclaimed in unison.

"Aye, Dmitri!" the voice shouted back. "Who else would it be? What is the meaning of this, tovarich, to keep me from your house? All Cornwall speaks of your lovely new daughter, and I am not permitted the chance to see her, eh? Eh?"

"It's all right, Parris," Charles told the agitated manservant as he stepped out into the corridor, a grin on his sensual lips. "Tell Mr. Zergeyev I'll be down directly. Nan," he added to the redheaded young girl who had rushed into the room through the adjoining door, "bring a wrap for Mrs. St. Germain to wear." His expression softened as he looked down at Raven and his daughter. "I'll bring Dmitri up to see you as soon as you're ready."

On the threshold of the Yellow Salon, Charles was stopped short by the sight of Dmitri, who was restlessly pacing the parquet floor within. Gone were the unruly locks of black hair and the great billowing beard that had always given the big Russian his wild appearance. Dmitri Zergeyev was neatly kempt, his whiskers trimmed to a respectable length, his clothing proper from the high points of his starched white collar down to the polished toes of his spangled shoes. A diamond glittered in his silk neckcloth, and when he tossed his head and grinned widely, Charles saw another diamond sparkling in his ear. The sight of it caused him to throw back his head and laugh uproariously, for it was obvious that, despite his dandified appearance, Dmitri was still a pirate at heart.

"Tovarich, I have returned!" Dmitri announced, and the two big men embraced, Dmitri thumping Charles on the back and hugging him in a manner that would have crushed the ribs of a lesser man. Taking a step backward, Charles stood and gazed into Dmitri's eyes, the look they exchanged one of a friendship so deep and abiding that even Charles's decision to leave the sea forever would never affect it. Grinning unabashedly, Dmitri made a mocking bow in Charles's direction and waggled his hips provocatively.

"I don't blame your butler for not letting me inside. I imagine he was rendered speechless by my dazzling appearance."

"You do take one's breath away," Charles admitted with a grin.

"Enough of me, my friend," Dmitri protested, feigning great modesty. "What of my little princess, she is well?"

Charles nodded. "The child was born earlier today, but I imagine you've already heard."

"I came across the *Orient Star* at anchor in Penzance Harbor," Dmitri explained, "and I stayed long enough for Geoffrey to tell me everything that happened. So you married her at last, eh, you rogue?"

Charles's harsh features softened. "In Charleston, when we laid over for supplies. I tried to talk Raven into staying there until the baby was born, but she wouldn't hear of it."

"I can well imagine," Dmitri agreed.

"Besides, the summer heat was intolerable," Charles added quietly. "I wanted Raven to be comfortable and regain her strength without undue stress."

Dmitri's coal-black eyes were grave. "I can only thank God the two of you are back in England unharmed."

Charles nodded, memories of the harrowing months following Raven's abduction bringing a shadow to his handsome face. Dmitri was aware of it instantly and rubbed his ham-sized hands together, smiling endearingly.

"Come, come, we'll talk of it no more on this happy day, eh? You have a daughter, my friend. My blessings to you. I imagine she is as beautiful as her mother?"

Charles's deep voice was gruff and filled with pride. "Aye, she is. Come, I'll take you to see her."

"Please wait one moment, tovarich," Dmitri begged, laying a restraining hand on Charles's arm. "There is a small matter we need to discuss." His voice dropped to a conspiratorial whisper. "It concerns the diamond."

"Don't say a word of it to Raven," Charles warned him. "I haven't told her a thing about it yet. In truth we've talked very little about India or anything that pertained to her journey to New Orleans." His voice grew rough. "I want her to recover completely before we dredge up the past."

Dmitri cleared his throat. "I understand. However, you and I must—"

"Excuse me, sir." A liveried footman stood in the doorway with a silver tray in his hands, and Dmitri's black eyes widened appreciatively at the sight of the unopened bottle of rum.

"Thank you, Timms," Charles said, taking it from him and hiding his amusement as the young footman cast a disbelieving look at Dmitri's outlandish appearance before withdrawing.

Refreshed by the excellent choice of libations, the big Russian seated himself on the yellow upholstered settee, grimacing as the stiff material of his tightly tailored pants refused to yield as much as he would like. Hard put to hide his increasing amusement, Charles turned his broad back on him and strolled to the window, his full lips twitching.

"Apparently you've managed to come away with a good share of the diamond's wealth yourself, judging by the cut of your clothes," he remarked lightly.

"A good share?" Dmitri chuckled. "Tovarich, the gem was priceless, priceless! I had it cut in Paris by an artisan who—"

"Paris?" Charles's expression was stern as he wheeled and looked down at his first officer. "I thought we agreed you'd go directly to London with it."

"Now, now," Dmitri soothed, looking up at Charles placatingly, having forgotten how volatile his captain's temper could be if his orders were disobeyed. "I did bring it there eventually, but the side trip to Paris was necessary."

"Dmitri," Charles said warningly, "I trusted you with the safeguarding of that jewel. I'm sure you've already heard that the Punjab has been annexed. It shouldn't take the governor and his aides long to discover that the Kohinoor was sent to the Punjab by a member of the nawab of Oudh's household. Clearly that makes it the property of Queen Victoria herself, and I've no wish to have her army descend upon Cornwall and demand it back once they've traced it here."

"That will never happen," Dmitri responded confidently, refilling his glass, "because Vickie already has it in her possession."

Charles's rugged countenance went blank with astonishment.

"Aye, it's true," Dmitri assured him, enjoying himself hugely. "Now, if you would curb that tiresome temper of yours, I'll tell my story, eh? Kristos, I can see that being a papa has not changed you at all!"

Seeing the aristocratic brow darken, Dmitri held up his hands and said quickly, "Oh, very well, this is what happened: By the time the *Bridget Bailey* docked in Brest, it had occurred to me that an unkempt, expatriate Russian sailor would never have the chance to gain an audience with Her Majesty, Queen Victoria of Great Britain, to present to her the illustrious Kohinoor diamond. It would have been, I reasoned, a just cause to have me imprisoned in the Tower for its theft. Therefore I resolved to enlist the help of a man who would have more, shall we say, credibility than I?"

"I thought we agreed—"

"A man of title, a well-respected subject, a man," Dmitri continued smoothly, "who would not hesitate to further any cause championed by Charles St. Germain, to whom he owed considerable favors."

"And that was?" Charles asked, resigned to the inevitable.

"Your cousin Frédéric St. Germain, Comte de Monteraux."

Startled, Charles lowered his glass and regarded the grinning Russian keenly. "Frédéric? In the name of God, Dmitri, what—"

"He was more than anxious to do whatever he could for you," Dmitri continued pleasantly. "Apparently your generosity in deeding Monteraux to him gave the whey-faced young boy a new outlook on life. He's not at all as helpless and girlish as I remembered. Perhaps there is something about you St. Germains after all," he added thoughtfully. "Ah well, be that as it may, Frédéric and I had the stone cut by a craftsman in Paris who served as royal gem cutter to the Royal House of Orleans. It was superb, Charles, if I may say so! The diamond was reduced in size by one-third, but the clarity, the brilliance of that small third, ah!" He sighed ecstatically and gave his captain a sly grin, his black eyes twinkling. "Let me tell you about my meeting with the queen."

"Aye, why don't you?" Charles suggested grimly, thinking to himself that his own worry for Raven must have caused him to take leave of his senses for contemplating even for a moment entrusting to a man like Dmitri Zergeyev the welfare of the Kohinoor diamond.

Ignoring the Englishman's tone, Dmitri went on proudly, "Frédéric and I did not have much trouble gaining an audience with Her Majesty. I daresay your cousin possesses a great deal of that famous St. Germain charm, for he had dear Vickie quite enthralled. Naturally she wanted to know how it came about that we had the Kohinoor in our possession, and I told her a very spine-chilling tale indeed."

"You didn't," Charles said with an inward groan.

"I did." Dmitri beamed. "Ah, you would have wept to hear me speak of your valor, my friend! It brought tears to my own eyes to recount how you, unarmed, personally wrested the coveted stone from a half-dozen dissident Sikhs in the name of Victoria herself."

Charles groaned aloud and turned back to the window, wearily massaging his temples. What in the name of God had he done?

Behind him Dmitri chuckled reminiscently. "She was so taken with your exploits that she has requested your presence at Windsor. I imagine the official summons should be arriving any day now. A pity," Dmitri mused, "that she and all of Great Britain will never know that the beautiful jewel you rescued for her is only two-thirds the size of the original. And yet," he reflected, "it is so breathtakingly beautiful now that it has been properly cut that I doubt anyone will notice."

"And the other third?" Charles asked, rounding on him, the green eyes filled with disbelief.

Dmitri indicated his stickpin and diamond earring. "Some of it is here, as you can plainly see, though most of it is being handled in paper by a banker in London who is prepared at your command to draw up the necessary draft to cancel the debts owed by James Barrancourt to a certain Squire Blackburn."

"And the rest?" Charles demanded, refusing to be taken in by the endearing grin on Dmitri's bearded face.

"I've set a bit aside for myself," Dmitri admitted. "After all, I suffered enough throughout this adventure, and it isn't fair that you alone should win a treasure like our little princess. Ah, which reminds me, the last little pieces of the diamond are here."

Fumbling about in his vest pocket, he removed a small cloisonné box, which, upon being opened, revealed the beautiful mother-of-pearl combs that Raven had so treasured.

"Did you take them with you when you left the *Orient Star*?" Charles demanded sharply. "Raven thought she'd lost them after she was abducted, and because neither Danny nor I could locate them once we set sail from New Orleans, I decided not to tell her otherwise." He glared at Dmitri accusingly. "I thought I'd misplaced them somewhere, and I could have kicked myself for it."

"Aye, I took them," Dmitri admitted, unperturbed by his captain's annoyance. "I wanted a gift to give to the little one when I saw her again. Here, pick them up and see what I had the gem cutter do."

Lifting them out of the satin-lined box, Charles saw that a row of exquisite tiny diamonds had been set into the combs, the brilliance of their painstakingly cut facets making them glitter like fire. The artwork was magnificent, and even Charles had to admit the results were breathtaking.

"It was a difficult task to set them without damaging the mother-of-pearl," Dmitri explained, "but as I've said, the man was a true artisan."

Charles returned the combs to the box and handed it back to Dmitri. "I think Raven will be touched," he said gruffly. His emerald eyes met and held the coal black ones. "Thank you."

Dmitri shrugged his shoulders nonchalantly, although he wore a pleased look. "Think nothing of it, my friend. Ah, I almost forgot," he added, rummaging hastily through the oversized pocket of his coat. Withdrawing an oblong box of inlaid wood, he extended it to Charles with a wide grin. "Of all the errands you asked me to carry out, this one proved the most enjoyable. The gem cutter quite agreed with me, and I think you will, too."

Charles undid the delicate brass clasp and pulled back the lid to reveal a rich padding of dark blue velvet upon which lay a stunning diamond necklace. No fewer than a dozen winking gems were strung with precision upon a fragile chain of pure white gold. In the center, capturing the daylight with an inner fire of ice blue, lay a teardrop-shaped diamond larger than the rest, its countless facets breathtaking in their perfection.

"Is it not beautiful?" Dmitri asked as Charles remained silent. "Did you ever suspect that the insignificant lump of glass you found in that ginger jar could yield something this magnificent?"

"No, I didn't," Charles agreed and added softly, "and yet anything less would never have been worthy of her."

Dmitri blinked and cleared his throat self-consciously, the look on Charles's handsome face making him feel awkward suddenly, like an outsider who has stumbled onto a scene where he is not welcome.

For a moment there was silence in the elegant salon, then Charles stirred and clapped his first officer heartily on the back. "Come on, you scoundrel, I want you to meet my daughter."

"And what have you named her?" Dmitri inquired curiously as he followed Charles up the winding staircase that led to the upper story of the rambling east wing.

"Nothing yet," Charles admitted. "Raven claims she can't think of anything special enough. Her mother's name was Gwendolyn, and though I have the greatest respect for the name, Raven and I both agree it isn't quite fitting for a child that entered the world under such dramatic circumstances." His emerald eyes twinkled. "That reminds me, old fellow, I've a perfectly good clipper ship sitting at anchor in Penzance Harbor in dire need of a captain. It seems her owner and his esteemed great-uncle-in-law intend to begin a modest mercantile undertaking with trade to be established between the West Indies and Cornwall. Perhaps you know someone who's interested?"

Dmitri pursed his lips and tried to look casual, but Charles, turning on the staircase, could see the tremendous excitement surging in his black eyes. "I might," the big Russian allowed.

"We'll talk business later," Charles suggested, "and you can tell me whether or not this gentleman has become too much of a luxury-loving dandy to accept my offer. But let me repeat," he added, opening the double doors that led to the master suite, "I would like you to meet my daughter."

Raven, having heard their familiar voices in the corridor, looked up from the big four-poster bed with an expectant smile on her red lips. She wore a satin wrap of pale blue, against which her midnight hair shone darkly, and her tawny eyes glowed with welcome. For a moment Charles forgot the existence of his new daughter, who was snuggled against her mother's breast, Raven's beauty captivating him, as fresh and alluring as the day he had seen her in the crowded marketplace in Bombay.

It was Dmitri who reminded him of the child's existence, bending down to plant a noisy, affectionate kiss on Raven's soft cheek and then turning his head to coo in a startlingly paternal manner at the tiny, rumpled face that was visible amid the folds of the blanket Raven held in her arms.

"She is beautiful," he murmured, his dark eyes bright. "Do you know, little one, she is the color of priceless Russian sable. Look." Reverently he allowed his big hand to stray across the downy hair covering the infant's head. "Like midnight, the color, but when the sun shines upon her one can see the gold sparkling within." He beamed, and Raven's soft lips curved into the special smile she had always reserved for him.

"I'm so glad you came, Dmitri," she said softly, slipping her small hand into his. "You'll stay a while, won't you?"

Dmitri looked offended. "Did you think I would run off and leave you so soon? No, my precious angel, I will stay until the tired shadows are gone from your eyes. And your husband and

I have business to discuss, eh?" Dmitri added, turning and giving Charles a broad wink. A shrewd look appeared in his eyes when he noticed the expression on Charles's handsome face as he watched Raven hold the mewling infant to her breast.

"I think," the bearded Russian added meaningfully, "that I will make myself comfortable downstairs for a time. We never did finish that bottle of rum, tovarich. Madame," he added, making a great show of bowing over Raven's hand, "I will see you this evening perhaps?"

Raven's eyes glowed. "Oh, please, Dmitri, yes. There is so much we have to talk about." A smile still lingered on her lips as she watched him saunter out of the door, thinking to herself that despite his dandified appearance she would always love him for the irresistible rogue he was.

"He should have stayed longer," she remarked wistfully as Charles seated himself beside her, the mattress sagging beneath his weight.

"You're too tired still for lengthy visits," he told her gently. "Besides, the tales Dmitri intends to tell you must wait until you're a little stronger."

"I imagine they're wild indeed if they involve him," Raven agreed. Her golden eyes twinkled mischievously. "Did you see that earring? And those clothes? Judas, the scullery maids will be falling all over him when they see him!"

Charles's lips twitched. "Tomorrow the three of us will talk," he promised, and grew serious. "I think it's time I told you everything I didn't want to discuss with you while you were recovering aboard the *Orient Star*." He took his hand in hers. "Until then, Raven, I want you to rest assured that North Head is free of any claims by our greedy neighbor and that you needn't trouble yourself over finances ever again."

Raven regarded him lovingly, her tawny eyes glowing. "I never had any doubts in my mind that you would find a way to help me, Charles."

He felt his heart warm at the blind trust that radiated from her beautiful oval face. "Raven," he said huskily and bent his head to kiss her.

"Charles, wait," she protested, and he drew back, eyeing her questioningly.

"Tired of my attentions already, my fickle Raven?" he teased.

Rosy color stained her cheeks as she looked up into his handsome, smiling face. "Of course not," she said shyly, "but I've been thinking about what Dmitri said about our daughter."

Both of them glanced down at the tiny face that lay quietly against Raven's breast, one little fist still clutching a strand of shining midnight hair that spilled over Raven's slender shoulder.

"Dmitri said," Raven continued softly, a note of wonder in her voice as she looked down at her sleeping daughter, "that she reminded him of priceless Russian sable. Oh, Charles," she went on breathlessly, "don't you think it's a perfect name for our first-born child?"

"Sable St. Germain," Charles murmured to himself, liking the sound of it on his tongue.

"What do you think?" Raven asked hopefully, turning her face toward him so that her soft, parted lips were almost touching his.

"I think," Charles said huskily, "that it is certainly special enough for a child created from a love like ours." Drawing Raven closer to him, loving the feel of her warm, soft body against his, he lowered his head until his lips found hers in a deep, abiding kiss.